I0523665

WHEN SHADOWS DREAM

SHADOW HOUNDS

REALMS OF MAGIC AND MAYHEM
BOOK ONE

WREN SMYTHE

THORNY BRIAR
PUBLISHING

Ebook ISBN: 978-0-9756210-0-4
Paperback ISBN: 978-0-9756210-1-1
Hardcover ISBN: 78-0-9756210-2-8

First published by Thorny Briar Publishing in 2024

Copyright © Wren Smythe 2024
All Rights Reserved

The moral and intellectual rights of the author have been asserted.

No part of this publication may be reproduced or transmitted in any form or by any electronic or mechanical means, including information storage and retrieval systems, without written permission from the author, except for the use of brief quotations in a book review. Nor may it be otherwise circulated in any form of binding or cover other than that which it is published.

This is a work of fiction. Any resemblance to people both past and present is entirely coincidental and unintentional or within the scope of fictitious use and is not intended to cause harm to reputation or offense.

When Shadows Dream: Realms of Magic and Mayhem Book 1

Cover design & Formatting by Dazed Designs - dazed-designs.com

Edited by Lin Lasky Editing Services

To my amazing family:
*Thank you for putting up with late nights and solo trips to the library.
You are my everything.*

To every unpublished author with a dream:
*You've got this. Whether it takes a month, a year, or a lifetime, never
give up.*

To Lin:
Thanks for believing in me and having my back.

AUTHOR'S NOTE

Dear Reader,

Just a quick note: this novel is intended for those who are 18+. It does contain multiple spicy scenes of a sexual nature, in some cases with multiple people. This book is a Why Choose Paranormal Romance with a HEA ending, although it is the first novel in a series that contains multiple books about the romantic exploits of different characters, they are intertwined and connected. Not every book in the series will be Why Choose. The main characters in this book will show up in other stories as well and this could possibly lead to further developments in their story. This book could also be read as a standalone should you wish it, in my opinion anyway.

I would like to offer the following information up front in the event that you wish to no longer continue reading it thereafter, and let you know that some sensitive topics are covered in this book. I would hate to trigger anyone's personal trauma. I myself tend to not care about trigger warnings, but for the sake of my readers I'll add some below. Feel free to skip it if trigger warnings are not your thing or you don't want spoilers.

This book contains:

- Poly Relationships (MMFM) as well as MF and MM.
- Psychological trauma
- Sexual and physical trauma
- Allusions to child abuse—though these are fuzzy and not very detailed, and is only used so far as it pertains to this book, future books, and as memory sequences
- Elements of torture—both violent and of a sexual nature, but only as a facet of character and story development and not for gratuitous reasons or shock value
- Adult language of a sexual and sweary nature
- Steamy and spicy scenes that are graphically described—no fade to black to be found here
- Violence
- HEA
- Pregnancy
- Family trauma
- Paranormal elements—who am I kidding, it's the whole premise of the book and the series lol
- Monsters
- Gore
- Alcohol consumption
- Witchcraft
- Religious themes
- Intimacy with shifters—though no full shifting in these moments
- And I can't think of anything else at this time . . . If I've missed something please let me know.

Love,

xxv Wren xx

GLOSSARY OF TERMS AND PROPER NOUNS

(the) Almighty (pr. n.) The all powerful creator of realms.

a stór (Uh-Stohr) (n.) (Irish) My treasure.

Agregashi (A-Greg-Ash-Ee) (pr. n.) One half of the Realm of Ghouls. The ghouls of Agregashi deal in nightmares and sinister daydreams. The monster under your bed was actually real and the one who sent it into your dreams was from there.

Anaran'ith (An-A-Ran-Eeth) (pr. n.) The name of the fae realm.

asshat (n.) An imaginary hat worn on one's head when it is so far up one's own ass.

Astral Plane (pr. n.) A plane of existence only accessible when a being is having an out of body experience. Except in the rare and special cases where mates can come together within a dreamscape and be together.

binding ceremony (n.) A wedding ceremony or mating ceremony. It binds soul mates together.

(the) Blessed Reapers (pr. .n) Angels imbued with mist, the light of creation, to protect and carry pure souls or those deemed worthy of another life to the River of Rebirth upon the occasion of their mortal passing.

bookgasm (v.) The feeling one gets when one walks into a room full of books and discovers they are all from their favorite genre. I see you, you horny people lol.

bush (n.) The Australian wilderness, not the standard garden variety shrubbery nor the kind your grandma sported before Brazilian waxes became popular.

cannae (m. aux. v.) (Scottish) Cannot.

cat-head bindi (n.) Epically worse than lego, these three pointed prickles are a menace with or without shoes.

Cathair an óir (pr. n.) (Irish) City of Gold. Name of both the province/kingdom and capital city of one of the five provinces/kingdoms of the dragon realm. A mix of old Irish, Scottish, Welsh, and Saxon earth origin heritage.

(the) Choosing (pr. n.) Long after the Creation when the shadows refused to leave and light and darkness battled for the earth, the Almighty held the Choosing. The first angels stepped forward and were assigned either shadows or mist or something in between. Thus the creation of angel designations became known as the Choosing.

(the) Commander (pr. n.) Leader of the Blessed Reapers. Keeper of Mist.

corazón (Kaw-Rah-Sawn) (adj. or n.) (Spanish) Heart.

(the) Creation (pr. n.) When the first spark of light entered existence the Almighty was born from the ether and through them the creation of all things other than the shadow and the mist was made possible. The creation refers to our existence but not to how it was formed. It encompasses all things. From the air we breathe to the food we eat, but mostly to the time we tell, for time did not exist before Creation entered existence.

Daemoneskra (Day-Mon-Esk-Rah) (pr. n.) Name of the demon realm

demon (n.) From Daemoneskra. not pint-sized but small like a twelve year old human or shorter. These horned beings possess a soul filled with poison. Their red and dark purple skin acts as armor should an enemy get past their three in scalpel-sharp claws. They have a reptilian tongue and large innocent looking eyes, and they cry black tears.

Demon's Den (pr. n.) A british-style pub/bar in its very own pocket of reality. Owned and operated by the charming and mysterious Tzar who employs demons to do his bidding. The place trades alcohol, souls, and information to its many unsavory customers.

(the) Devil's 13 (pr. n.) Lucifer's team of trusted elite Shadow Hounds.

dickwad (n.) A person who displays inept, foolish, sometimes contemptible behavior. Plus, no one wants a wad of dick cheese, let alone to be one.

dinnae (m. aux. v.) (Scottish) Don't.

dragon (n.) Dragon shifters reside primarily, but not exclusively, in the dragon realm, aka Réimse Na Dragan. Nearly all dragons return to the realm to give birth. Dragon shifters originated on the earth realm before their goddess created their realm. They live primarily in humanoid form and shift into their inner dragons regularly. Each shifter has different abilities based on the soul of the dragon they house. One common trait is their love for treasure and precious gems.

dragonfire ale (n.) Brewed only in the dragon realm. Is lethal to humans. The ale has an extremely high and uniquely blended alcohol content designed to intoxicate dragons. Note: Adult dragons are incredibly tolerant to most forms of alcohol and sedatives, so it does not have the same effect on them as it does other species.

Dullahan (n.) (Irish) Refers to a hobgoblin or a wicked unseelie fairy, also depicted as a headless horseman astride a terrifying black horse as it carries its own head and chases down its prey. A story told to terrify children and a secret weapon of the darkest of unseelie fairies.

fae (n.) A realm-locked species of elvish magic wielders from Anaran'ith (the fae realm). They are both good and bad, just like any species, but their Kings and Queens were greedy for power and blamed each other for losses they suffered. A mixture of Celtic and Finnish earth heritage.

fairy (n.) The beings from Underhill (the fairy realm) have long been the subject of fables and lore. And just like their literary counterparts they are both beautiful and terrifying to their core.

Fallen (pr. n.) A title given to an angel who has fallen from grace. One who has committed an act, or acts so egregious that the Praesidium has deemed them unworthy of angel status. Thus the capital F, and the disdain with which they are referred to. They retain their angelic abilities but their soul is corrupted and their inner nature is reflected by their diseased and molting wings, usually a rather unpleasant shade of greenish-yellow. Not to be confused with an angel who takes a sabbatical or permanent sojourn to join humanity on earth.

faun (n.) An immortal half-male or half-female and half-goat-like being native to the fae realm of Anaran'ith.

fero da prora (n.) The counterweight on the top of a gondola's prow, usually made from iron

fething (adv.) A polite, PG version of saying fucking when fucking seems a little too harsh or crass and/or the person saying it is in a group or wants to mix it up.

galhild (n.) A mysterious creature only heard of outside of Anaran'ith in children's tales. A being said to eat all who cross their path, growing larger with every meal. The victims are destined to live out their existence within the belly of the beast with no hope of escape, until the valiant Protector comes to be and rescues them from their plight.

(the) General (pr. n.) Leader of the Shadow Hounds. Keeper of Shadows.

ghoul (n.) Ghouls are beings who create nightmares and dreams. They are terribly beautiful and vaporously elusive. They can be every terrible thing that scares you in your slumber or every joyous dream you have. They are the creators of every monstrous creature in existence and fill Nestradia with the very real manifestations of the stories they feed to your sleeping mind. They are the muses of nations, the creators of empires and artists alike. No being outside of their realm dares enter it for fear of falling victim to them and an eternal sleep.

gorgon (n.) A species of immortal women cursed by the Almighty to live with venomous vipers for hair and to turn all who look into their eyes to stone.

(the) Grand Consortium (pr. n.) Michael's elite team of trusted Blessed Reapers.

Hell (pr. n.) Otherwise known as the Realm of Shadows. Surprisingly the opposite of hellish. This realm is governed by Lucifer, General of the

Shadow Hounds. No lost, wandering, or damned souls suffer their eternal torture here. Just a bunch of Shadow Hounds serving their heavenly purpose under the iridescent glow of their sun.

hellfire blades (n.) Forged by the mighty Hephaestus. These blades are imbued with the red glow of the hellfire which entraps souls within the Well of Souls. The black steel is specific to the Shadow Hounds and they are crafted specifically with each angel in mind. They merge with the shadows of each angel and extract the souls of unworthy humans, carrying them securely to their final destination.

hellhound (n) Originally bred by Lucifer as pets and guard dogs, this wild and unpredictable species evolved millenia ago to the point where they started to shift into people at will and rebel against the constraints placed upon them. Lucifer set them free thinking they were harmless, but once away from the Fields of Elysium they started to lose some aspects of their humanity and sanity. A secondary field was planted in their chosen home and each hellhound wears a locket containing a dried flower from the fields whenever they leave.

Hephaestus (pr. n.) The Almighty's favorite blacksmith. He forges all angel weapons, including hellfire blades, ethereal scythes, shields of justice, the Sword of Vengeance, and on occasion other species. He is the muse for all blacksmiths and metalworkers.

hippocampus (n.) A large creature with the upper body of a horse and the lower body of a fish or whale.

Horde Mines (pr. n.) The Horde Mines are a large mountainous ridge that intersects the borders of the five kingdoms of the dragon realm. Each Kingdom mines its own area and the Treaty of Treasure binds them from committing acts of theft against other kingdoms' mines. The only area of the mountains untouched by dragons is that of its tallest peak and everything beneath it. It is in an area considered sacred and worshiped as the temple of their goddess, Tiamat. No dragon has ever set foot nor claw there.

hybrid (n.) A being born of two different species.

ken (v.) (Scottish) Understand.

mage (n.) Male magic wielders. Generally looked up to throughout the OtherRealm, unlike witches who are struggling to cast off the shackles of human prejudice. Otherwise known as wizards and warlocks. They are generally underhanded and sniveling. Their magic is unnatural and born of jealousy. A gift from a scheming god who seeks his own ends. They despise witches and all women who have power, they primarily came to be after the Inquisition and have insinuated themselves into historical literature through magical means and positive marketing strategies.

manticore (n.) A very rare creature with shapeshifting abilities. They have the head of a man or woman, the body of a lion, and the tail of a scorpion. An ornery species, they are not family oriented but rather exist in a strength and power based society when and if they come together in large groups. Generally solitary creatures, they are known for their bad tempers and quick reflexes, often abandoning their children at the first sign of weakness or disobedience.

merahet (n.) my wife, other half, kindred soul. Feminine.

mi amor (n.) (Spanish) My love.

mi vida (n.) (Spanish) My life.

mist (n.) Born from the spark of Creation. The mist is the glow of eternal light. Paired with angels who seek the souls of the soon to be reborn. They manifest in mist born from eternal light. The opposite of the darkness, of the shadows, yet the same. One end of a spectrum filled with the vast array of every shade of every color imaginable. Long silent, listening and learning, soon they'll make their voices heard.

mo dhuine (n.) (Scottish) My husband.

mo shíorghrá (muh HEER-ggrawh) (n.) (Irish) My eternal love.

modus operandi (n.) A way something is done, usually specific to people. In this case usually a negative trait associated with perceived assholishness.

nargwraith (n.) A vicious, tri-horned beast the size of a pickup truck. Native to Anaran'ith they are rarely found outside of the hunting fields that ring the forbidden forests of Vash'terra.

Nestradia (pr. n.) Also known as the Realm of Nightmares and the Realm of Rot and Ruin.

OtherRealmly (n.) From another realm. This could refer to a being, item, magic, trait, or custom. Basically anything from another realm or anything paranormal or supernatural that isn't human.

outback (n.) The sticks, the ass end of nowhere. Full of dust, dirt, burning hot sun, little to no rain, so many animals that want to kill you, and flies. So. Many. Flies.

Paradise (pr. n.) A bigger on the inside replica of the Garden of Eden, sans Adam and Eve.

portent (n.) A sign that something very good or bad is about to happen.

(the) Praesidium (pr. n.) Angels of Justice. They seek out those within their OtherRealm jurisdiction and police them. They are the cops, and the judges of their own kind and all supernatural beings, with a few exceptions.

prick (n.) Slang for penis. Also an annoying, offensive, worthless asshole. Can be used between friends when they do something annoying or embarrassing. Mostly prick makes me think tiny due to needle pricks being tiny and annoying, which fits the general behavior of pricks, really.

purler (n.) (Australian slang) Outstanding in its class; something exceptionally good, usually in relation to a classic joke or a stellar person.

Réimse Na Dragan (pr. n.) (Irish) Realm of Dragons.

(the) River of Rebirth (pr. n.) Where the souls deemed worthy by the Almighty have a second chance for rebirth after death and collection by the Blessed Reapers. They are released into the flowing waters and await their new lives.

Sáifrai'enna (Ancient Fairy) Help comes when called. A secret phrase once used by the Praesidium's undercover operatives.

Scáth-thiarna (pr. n.) (Irish) Shadow Lord.

shadows (n.) The darkness before the light. Paired with angels who seek the unjust evil of the human world. They manifest in shadows born from eternal night. The opposite of the light, of the mist, yet the same. One end of a spectrum filled with the vast array of every shade of every color imaginable. Long silent, listening and learning, soon they'll make their voices heard.

(the) Shadow Hounds (pr. n.) Angels imbued with shadows, the darkness before creation, to collect and deliver irredeemable souls or those deemed unworthy of another life to the Well of Souls upon the occasion of their mortal passing, sometimes . . . okay, oftentimes with a little help to slip free of their mortal coil.

siren (n.) A being who lures men into intimate acts to sustain their ability to remain one with both land and sea. Traditionally they were known to lure sailors to their deaths but in more modern times they have become more vulnerable and protected by OtherRealm law, having been hunted by humans almost to the point of extinction.

(the) S.R.D. (pr. n.) Search and Rescue Division, a unit within the Shadow Hounds.

succubus (n.) A vampiric being who feeds on the sexual energy of others or through engaging in the intimate act with others and feeding from them, usually resulting in their death.

Thisavros (pr. n. and n.) (Greek) Gold/treasure. The name of one of the five kingdoms/provinces of the dragon realm, aka Réimse Na Dragan, and also its capital. Generally Greek and Mediterranean earth origin heritage.

Tiamat (pr. n.) (Mesopotamian) Goddess of Dragons, Watcher of Réimse Na Dragan, and Bearer of Blessings.

tushies (n.) Plural of tushy. A cute, cushy bottom. Usually in reference to itty bitty bubby bums. Now move your tushy and get reading lol.

Tuo narttu, suolistan hänet kuin vitun galhild kun saan hänet käsiini (Finnish/Fae) That Bitch, I'll gut her like a fucking galhild when I get my hands on her.

vampire (n.) An immortal being who feeds off other beings to sustain their immortal life. This can include blood through bite or other receptacle, through a psychic connection e.g. emotions, memories, gray matter etc . . . or through sexual intimacy, otherwise known a succubus (female) or incubus (male)

Vash'terra (VASH-TE-RAH) (pr. n.) The name of the forbidden forests within the fae realm, Anaran'ith. It separates the borders of both the *Dökkálfar* (Dark Fae) and the *Ljósálfar* (Light Fae). Not much is known of that which lurks within its dark, wooded mass. Though stories have been told to children for as long as it has existed of the horrors which await them should they dare to enter it.

wakizashi (n.) (Japanese) A traditional sword from Japan. Shorter than a *katana*, the length of a *wakizashi* blade is between 30.3cm (11.93in) and 60.6cm (23.86in).

(the) Well of Souls (pr. n.) Where the souls of the eternally corrupted and irredeemable are delivered by the Shadow Hounds to be locked away from the River of Rebirth for eternity.

wendigo (n.) A creature with sunken, glowing eyes, and sharp, yellowed talon-like claws. Its lipless mouth reveals rows of sharp, deadly teeth. Patches of fur cover its otherwise hairless and emaciated body, save for the long, tangled hair on its head. Almost skeletal in appearance, it has pointed ears and antlers, not unlike those of a deer. With exceptional sight, hearing, smell, strength, and speed. They are deadly predators that feast on the flesh and organs of their kills. Be it a person, animal, or fellow wendigo, it matters not. Hearts are a delicacy for their kind and the only ones they won't eat are their own. The smell of rotting flesh permeates from them and is usually the first sign of their impending attack.

witch (n.) A female magic user, usually human with some OtherRealm mixed into her heritage. Most often born to their power, they don't come into it through learned ability. On the rare occasion a witch is gifted their power they are usually cursed, or given eternal life and magic as a reward, or bonded to a powerful being who's immortality becomes their own. There are many types of witches ranging from good to bad and somewhere in between. They each have unique types of magic as well, including but not limited to: nature, each of the elements, superficial, and sacrificial.

THE DEVIL'S 13 + CODE NAMES

Lucifer (Luc) The General
Asmodeus (Deus) The Duke
Malphas (Mal) The Alpha
Marchosias (Marco) The Marquis
Azaroth (Roth) The Wraith
Leviathon (Athon) The Snake
Fenris (Fynn) The Wolf
Andramalech (Malech) The Lich
Agares (Ares) The Hawk
Prosperine (Perri) The Princess
Lilith (Lily) The Flower
Andromalius (Andy) The Earl
Caine The Knight
Dantalion (Dante) The Lion

"In shadows bound we bind the evil of mankind."

MRS BRIARS'S ADVICE

Mrs Briars would like to advise that dreams rarely do come true on their own. Usually, they take hard work, trauma, loss, and an unhealthy dose of getting your ass handed to you first.

CHAPTER 1
DOWNTOWN, NEW YORK

He moved like the night. Stealthy, silent, and ominous. Darkness and danger clung to him like a shroud. His bright blue eyes pierced the eerily quiet alleyway as he prowled toward his prey. His hapless victim was instinctively petrified, yet still completely unaware of the fate which awaited him. The words which were about to slither through the air may clue him in, though. Unless he was particularly dimwitted or had a self-inflated ego the size of a Goodyear blimp, chances were pretty good he was within moments of wishing he'd worn an adult diaper. With ease Roth set the cloaking bubble around himself and his victim. No need to freak the humans out with what was about to go down. They'd just see an abandoned alley and feel the need to keep moving on.

"Oi, dick stain! Care to take a guess how long it's going to take me to gut your pathetic ass?" he growled, toying with the evil asshole as he stalked closer. He was sure he looked like the guy's worst nightmare . . . A really big, broad-shouldered, and muscular one. A portent of death sent to collect the diseased souls of his victims. So yeah, maybe he enjoyed his job a little too much sometimes. Could you really blame him? He was an artist, and his wrath was the ultimate expression of life, well . . . his life anyway.

Pitch black shadows writhed around his ankles, sweeping out to the walls on either side of him. They curled up around his black denim-clad legs, twisted around his torso, and twined about his arms. Wickedly sharp hellfire blades were held firmly within the grip of each calloused palm. The black steel emitted a sinister red glow, casting a devilish menace in its wake; the essence of hellfire forged into its very core. Ready and waiting for each irredeemable soul they'd reap.

Already the stench of fear filled the air between predator and prey, along with a tinge of false bravado and inflated ego. His target's name was Nigel, according to the intel he'd been mind slapped with pre-mission. Nigel, the true monster, rose from his crouched position in the dirty alley, his former excitement no more than a distant memory as he sized up what was headed his way. Nigel's victim was hidden behind the dumpster. His posture showed an ego that was thin and puffed up like a balloon. Before the scumbag could utter even a single word, an invisible hand squeezed tight about his pale throat, cutting off precious oxygen. Life sustaining air a monster the likes of him should never have the privilege of breathing.

Nigel's eyes flared wide, panicked flailing ensued, and soon the tang of fresh urine joined the stench of fear. Yep, there it was. All bravado and ego disappeared.

This one was almost too easy, no fight at all. What did one such as him have to do to get a good fight these days? A challenge even? Someone who wouldn't break at the first parlor trick. Ah! But wasn't that most often the nature of the monsters for which he was sent to hunt? Those preying on the weak, feeding their thirst for power, control, pride, and greed. Their hunger, sated only by the torture and suffering of those they sought to crush, was older than creation itself.

For all his millennia of existence, for all the many and varied ways he had to end these creatures, to rip their souls away and deliver them to the fiery afterlife they deserved, they always succeeded in finding even more terrible acts of evil depravity to unleash upon their fellow earthly inhabitants.

While he loved his job, even he could admit that it was becoming a bit too predictable lately. Where was the fire, the fight, the passion? When had such a level of 'don't give a fuck' taken over this world, this generation of humans, that they were so weak, so willing to give up rather than fight to live? Not that they stood a chance against the likes of him, but still . . . It's the principle of it all, right? Oh, how he longed for the days when the blackened, festering souls he was sent to collect would at least make it a little fun.

Growling low in his throat, frustrated at how easy this was, at the unfulfilled promise of executing his full wrath, Roth unleashed his shadows, sending them forth in a burst of unrestrained, aggressive speed. Red eyes from the deepest pits glowed above a snarling maw filled with sharp and dripping fangs leaped forward at his command. A Shadow Hound, the image of a Wraith of Hell, was the last sight the weak, corrupted soul named Nigel would see before death took him.

Striding forward, his shitkickers making nary a sound, he was completely invisible within his swirling shadows. Even the whites of his eyes had darkened to pitch. A quick and efficient slice to the dangling meatsuit's gullet caused blood to spray and fall in a steady stream to the asphalt below.

By divine grace, or rather, decidedly the opposite, not a drop made contact with him. His lips quirked upwards at the thought of his origins and his boss' tweaks to their powers. Taking one of his blades, he dipped the tip into the gaping wound and gave it a vicious little twist, just for shits and giggles; the Hellfire took over and drew out the diseased and manky soul. Like a moth to a flame, it entrapped the essence securely in the fire-protected reservoir at the core of the lethal steel. Hephaestus's etchings gave it an extra-strong ward so that only the blade's owner could extract it, and then only into the care of one of two wells.

He felt no guilt at what his job entailed. Most of the souls he collected, like this one, were not fit for this world. These were the souls that couldn't be recycled. The ones who couldn't be redeemed. They got no second chances. It was a Hell of a job, but someone needed to do it. And as it was his divine role, he may as well enjoy it and take pride in it, right? And this soul definitely deserved it, judging by what he sensed on the other side of the dumpster.

Pain and agony called out to him, not by sound but by spirit. A hunger for life, a fighting spirit. All he had done just moments before— and it had taken but moments to end that sorry excuse for a life—was forgotten as he was pulled forward toward the essence which called to him.

He knew what he'd find before he saw her, but still, his heart jolted in his chest. She lay there, battered and broken; so much blood. Arms sliced in intricate patterns, and her dress cut away to reveal her ruined torso. Several ribs played peek-a-boo with the night air, shining white amidst a sea of crimson, matching her platinum blonde hair matted in the quickly congealing blood. So many marks littered her body, so much desecration of a human vessel. How she was still alive was a miracle in and of itself.

He looked around, waiting for the flash of light only his kind and the dying could see, a tighty whitey coming to take her soul to Heaven, but it didn't come. His brow furrowed in thought and frustration. It would be just like those pompous pricks to fuck up a soul transfer like this.

Just as he was turning to leave, preparing to pull his shadows into himself and portal back home, a flash of movement had him pivoting back around. His shadows fell still and withdrew into him in his shock. For a moment she seemed frozen, like a macabre statue caught in the darkness of night, her lips parted on a soundless gasp before her posture shifted toward indignant aggression.

Startling soft gray eyes flickered with fire as she glared daggers into him. They seemed to swirl with angry shadows of their own the longer you looked into them. With a deep, gasping breath she leaped to her feet, blood still dripping, her clothing still ruined. Her pale features were almost incandescent with rage and frustration.

"Thanks, asshole," she sneered. "Just when I had him where I wanted him. Argh! And just like that . . ." She lifted her right hand and snapped her fingers sharply. "A perfectly good meal gone to waste. Now I have to start all over again. Which means I have to relax my standards. It's not that easy to find souls *that* evil on such short notice, you know. Whatever." She sighed rather dramatically. "I don't have the luxury of time to nut this shit out with the likes of you, and I get the feeling you won't just hand him over so . . . I'm outtie."

As she strode past him, giving him a middle finger salute on the way, her shoulder brushed against him, sending an electric pulse through his arm. The hellfire in his blade leaped to attention, and his shadows flared around him before settling calmly against his skin.

As he stared after her, the blood and bruises melted away, the torn and bloodstained clothing replaced like new. Her skin was flawless and knit back together with nary a scar. Her hair was now as red as the blood that had been all over her, the blonde of before was nowhere to be seen. Pausing, she threw him one last look over her shoulder and tensed, taking in his eerily still shadows, the pulsing red glow in his blade, and lifted a dainty brow. His heart pounded in his ears as he saw her delicate features clearly for the first time. Not the mask of illusion she'd worn moments before, but what he hoped was actually her true face. A face so beautiful it took his breath and held it hostage. All hint of vulnerability gone, a swirling sense of OtherRealmliness replaced the 'human' he'd sensed earlier. Unless it too was just another illusion or glamour or whatever the fuck she'd done.

"Next time, leave them to me. At least I'd have put him to good use." She smirked, tore her gaze away from his, and raked it down to his booted feet and up again. "Oh, and tell your Boss Man, or whatever he calls himself these days, "We'll meet again". If you could sing it, that'd be a bonus, but it's not essential." With a saucy wink, she strolled away, her hips swaying as she whistled a once familiar tune and slipped around the corner. The echoes of that old Vera Lynn song now stuck in his head. He was left standing there with a look of stunned bewilderment chasing across his chiseled features, even as his cock twitched behind his button fly.

"Just who, and what, the fuck was that?"

ROUNDING the corner onto the street, her spine wilted just a bit, her shoulders slumped. Pain lacerated through her entire being like burning hot hooks pulling at her insides from all directions, tearing through layers of muscle and skin. The agony, made all the more intense by the stampeding of her heart as it tried to escape the confines of her chest, threatened to bring her to her knees. This was her agony; this was her unsated hunger. The bane of her existence. The crux of her curse. This was what forced her to seek out those capable of such depravities as that wretchedly evil scum back in the alley. Even though the Shadow Hound had destroyed the vessel housing it, she could still feel the pull of the festering soul now housed within his blade. So tempting, yet so far out of her desperate reach.

If only he hadn't come, or had arrived a few minutes later. If only she'd fed her hunger for his soul faster, had been able to satisfy her other half at all . . . she'd be free of this torture. Alas, he had come, and even with his shadows she'd seen him, had watched him, even as he'd used the shield that kept human eyes at bay and distorted the reality of what went down in that dark, dank alley. Him, with his piercing blue eyes, his wicked shadows, and his chiseled features. That fine ass cradled in those tight jeans and the promise of some sexy as sin abs beneath his equally tight shirt. The way his midnight hair caressed his jaw and cheekbones . . .

Another wave of agony assaulted her, reminding her of what his interference had cost her. Of what was at stake if she didn't find another soul to take the stolen ones place within the next few hours. Of the choices she would be forced to make and what she would be forced to do in order to survive. Damn it, nope; he definitely wasn't sexy enough to forgive for the torment of her current suffering, no matter how cute his look of shock had been.

She'd felt every lash of pain as that scumbag had sliced and diced her. As he'd run the tip of his knife along her skin, every bone he'd exposed, every flap of flesh he'd folded back thinking he was in control.

Such an easy little puppet to manipulate. So obvious a display of weakness as he sought to show his strength, his perversion of power over the innocent and vulnerable. Tit-for-tat, he'd have been the one found slain behind the dumpster in that dark and dingy place as the light-filled the sky on a brand-new day, not her. One less villain haunting the night. Until that infernal Hound had cut his strings. And damn him for it. That was meant to be her reward. Her service to humanity. Taking out the trash while saving the innocent from the beast now tearing apart her chest—her whole being—as it raged and begged and demanded to be fed. And she would have given him as good as he had given her.

Sure, her pain had been muted as her hunger for his wretchedly evil feelings was being sated, but it still hurt like a mother-fucking Mack truck taking repeated exception to your immortal existence. And it always left the taste of ashes resting at the back of her tongue. A taste that stayed around for at least as long as it took for her to siphon off the much tastier and brighter emotions from innocent beings. Small, barely satisfying amounts that wouldn't be missed. Once upon a time she'd tried for more . . . She threw off the thought as guilt threatened to immobilize her.

And oh, how full she was from the meal Nigel Moreton's maniacal pleasure made, the joy and satisfaction those acts had given him. It's why she'd fed him his perfect fantasy. Basically gift wrapped it and put a big, bright, shiny bow on herself. Her use of illusion really had improved since her early days, so much that she was able to coat herself in the image she'd dragged from his subconscious and hold it so well despite her pain and hunger. He'd seen what he'd wanted to and not realized he was the victim at all. Oh, and when he'd tried to go for gold and disembowel her . . . such euphoria had filled her that the pain had been completely pushed aside. Her illusion had started to fall away, only a moment more, and she would have had him trapped beneath her; her retribution would have taken but a moment, although to Nigel, it would have been a lifetime.

She quickly held out her palms before another searing wave could distract her, and the red shadows she'd managed to hold back earlier surged before her, opening a portal to the one place she was guaranteed to find an end to this torture, one way or another, even if only temporarily.

Damn that son of a bitch straight back to his goddamn home. She didn't care that he was doing his job, the asshole. This pain was his stupid ass fault. Okay, okay, so it was hers too, but it felt so much better to blame him.

She really did need to pick up her game, though, and put the kibosh on her morality versus survival dilemma. Leaving it so long between meals was proving to be a dangerous habit, one that she needed to kick, pronto.

Alas, one day, there would be a reckoning. She could feel it in her bones, in her blood, but she was determined it would only be on her terms. Those bastard Hounds were in for one hell of a rude awakening when the time came. As for those assholes up on high? Well . . . Hell hath no fury like hers.

With each step, it felt like she was being impaled on a railroad spike, her body seeking to explode. As her energy waned, her shadows took control and curled around her, carrying her through the portal to the most dangerous place a human could ever fear to go, a place that not even she wished to go, and she definitely wasn't human. But, desperate measures meant a hybrid like her had to travel into The Demon's Den . . .

As Jezzie hit the deck, she noticed one very painful fact: her shadows, upon entering the portal, had retracted into her body, taking with them any chance of cushioning her landing. If she weren't in so much pain, so close to death, she'd almost think it funny, especially if it'd happened to someone other than her. As it was, every part of her body hurt like a frail old lady. Looking down at her hands, she noted the ashen hue of her skin, a dry, flaky quality spreading over her.

Fearfully, she knew her time was running out. Problem was she had nothing to trade for what she needed. With frantic eyes she scanned the room, her mind spun with possibilities as she took in the myriad of beings, all of questionable and dubious character. What would she be willing to do to continue to exist? And was her existence really worth it?

Elegant loafers leading up to expensive, tailored trousers filled her vision as her eyes shuttered up and down in slow blinks. It hurt to tilt her head up too far, so she saved herself the pain and stopped trying to catch a glimpse of him. He reached down a hand to touch her face, and her shadows made one more feeble attempt to protect her as they snapped at him like whips at the circus lions she'd seen in movies as a child. She pushed herself against the closest wall with the last of her strength. Her eyes didn't make it back up again from their last slow blink down.

CHAPTER 2
DEMON'S DEN

EIGHT YEARS LATER . . .

Fucking fuck nuggets. Those shit stains needed an ass kicking, and she was just the bitch with the balls to do it! If only they'd come within three fucking feet of her. If only she could leave this blasted room. Stupid anti-portal wards. Unfortunately, they could sense how dangerous that would be to their survival, their limited brain cells keeping them back whenever she had the strength to follow through on her thoughts. And yes, okay, so her mother would wash her mouth out with Lysol if she could hear her thoughts right now. And Lord, did she wish she was here to do just that, but even her mother couldn't find her in this rank pit of iniquity. Lord knows she was probably going crazy, turning over every stone earth-side trying to find her. But she wouldn't. The portal had been sealed now except by express invitation. At least she cared enough to try. There wasn't anyone else who would, except Aunt Rai Rai and she'd vowed never to step foot in such a place. She'd probably never even think of it as a possibility anyway.

Eight. EIGHT years she'd been stuck in this place. From the moment she'd fallen out of that blasted portal she'd been stuck here. Her shadows had held fast, thankfully, lashing at every hunched, horned, sometimes horny, always hungry, demon spawn that had sniffed her way, at least for a while. If it had just been her emotions that needed feeding, she would have been fine. Plenty of those here, depravity of all kinds, even some joy and love. Demons had their own unique code of honor and sense of family. That would have been easy to deal with.

But, sucks to be her, she'd gone and fed her need for emotions first and a soul part second. Demons love souls, and Demon's Den had always had a steady supply of corrupt, and sometimes pure, souls going in and out. The demons traded amongst themselves and the darkest of witches. They had a reputation amongst those with the connections to know where and what to look for, and luckily Jez was friends with a couple of witches who skirted the fine line between dark and light, when the need arose.

Except some asshat had raided the place for illegal soul trading just days before her emergency arrival. The angels on both sides detested the trade, and the only souls currently in residence belonged to the owner of the 'portal entry only' dive. One Balthazar Morrigan. The Tzar, as he liked to think of himself. Ballzy, as she preferred to call him. Somehow he always managed to evade them when they came to call. The SOB needed his balls removed with a blunt spoon and shoved so far up his own ass he'd need very invasive surgery to remove them. The damn sexy fucker was a devious little shit that had preyed upon her weakness and caught her unprepared. He'd laid on the charm, claiming to want to help her. Her shadows had lashed at him hard and fast for a while. Protecting her until they too felt the sharp edge of her hunger and lost their will. Succumbing to the promises he'd made, urging her to agree to his offer. She fell for the charm, and into his bed. Realizing too late that she'd have been better served making a deal with the Devil himself. She let her mind wander back to her arrival in this prison of hers . . .

WHEN SHE CAME TO, a handsome devil with a cocky smile was cradling her on his lap as he sat in a red velvet armchair, his face all up in hers. Her head instinctively craned back to create some personal space, and she scrambled as best she could off of him, landing inelegantly in a tangle of her own limbs at his feet, looking up to see his soft smirk and twinkling eyes.

He looked at her with the concern of a parent watching a youngling flounder and fall as they learned to walk. It was kind of nice. She'd never had a male look at her that way before, having been raised by her mother's best friend, a witch. Aunt Rai Rai kept most men at bay. She was kind of prickly about it, but would never say why.

That look of fatherly concern quickly disappeared though as he took in the sight of her cleavage, exposed to him by the disparity of their positions. Her fucked up daddy issues didn't seem to have a problem with the switch. They were just glad that someone seemingly wanted to take care of her.

THINKING BACK ON IT, she felt the urge to vomit slide up her throat and the taste of bile touched her tongue. When she finally met the fucker who'd fathered her, she hoped these shit ass feelings of inadequacy resolved themselves. Otherwise, she'd have to find a shrink who didn't think she was utterly batshit crazy. What with all the supernatural shit that was her life.

Especially considering what those feelings, and Ballzy's asshole behavior had led to . . .

HE MADE her comfortable on a matching velvet covered chaise. She knew he'd spoken, but she wasn't tracking the conversation well enough to make sense of the words or even the sound of his voice. Pain shot white-hot needles through every cell in her body as she lay in that supine position. Soft hands tilted her face toward his, and he held her gaze with a steely determination.

"Listen closely, luv," the pet name rolled off his tongue and somehow added to his allure. "You are close to the end. I can sense it, just as I can sense some vamp tendencies within you. Which makes your presence here even more unexpected, since vamps are pretty clearly on the 'No Entry' list. I don't know what exactly you are, and without knowing, I'm not sure I can fix what ails you. So, you need to *tell me, young one. What exactly is it you need me to do in order to save you?"*

Her eyes flashed to his, judging his intent as though the scales of justice lay in her gaze. She knew better than to trust a stranger, even less so the likes of him. The owner of this place was feared and whispered about in the most hushed of tones, and clearly he was the owner, the way he commanded those in this place and not a single soul had questioned him or made a move toward her.

But she was desperate too. Without a soul to fill the well of her hunger, she would perish, slowly and agonizingly. Like the vampires in the movies she's always loved to watch. Come to think of it, he looked like that one TV vamp she'd crushed on so hard not too long ago. The bleached blond British one who had a streak of asshole a mile wide and an accent that had made her panties wetter with every syllable . . .

"Back on track, luv. Come on, time to focus. Time is something you don't have much of," he reminded her. "Let's start nice and easy. What's your name?"

"J . . . J . . . Jez . . . Jezzie," she stuttered out, hating the weakness of her voice and how hard it was to move her lips and tongue. She wouldn't tell him her whole name. Names were powerful things.

"Okay. Jezzie, luv, tell me, what do you need me to do to stop this madness?" His voice sounded like warm mulled wine on a freezing winter's night.

"S . . . Soul," she uttered between clenched teeth. "Need to . . . eat." His brows swept up toward his hairline with those three little words. She wanted to giggle at the look on his face, but couldn't summon the energy.

"Oh, luv, you came to the right place, but we are fresh out of full ones. We got raided last week and everyone who isn't me got cleaned out." Her heart sank to her toes at his ominous words. His finger lifted her chin back up from where it had dropped onto her chest.

"Not to worry though. I happen to have some coming in soon, but until then I can still offer you a part of one to tide you over. I don't know how you'd eat it though. I've never heard of anyone doing that. Not even a vampire or a demon . . ." His curious tone invited her to share, but her lips remained locked as those secrets were definitely not for his ears.

"I'll just need you to sign a standard indemnity and liability form. It is common practice with the sale of souls, even if I give them away," he said with a flirty wink. "Let me just grab one and something to sign with."

He strode behind the bar, and she suddenly noticed that the place was completely empty, save for a few demons cleaning up the open area. Picking up glasses, wiping down tables, righting tipped chairs and sweeping floors. They paid her no heed. Upon his return, she found a mug placed into her hands as he gently held his over hers, holding her shaking, weak ones steady.

"My finest house beverage, luv. It'll put hairs on your pretty chest, no doubt, but it should give you enough of a boost to get through the legal formalities. Especially since this soul will be a gift, rather than a sale. I do have to cover my ass, especially since no one, to the best of my knowledge, has ever eaten one before." He coaxed it to her lips, but she leaned back a fraction, her reaction stopping him.

"What is it?" she asked, suspicion lacing her words. "What's in it, exactly?" Her words were forced, taking all of her breath and energy to utter.

"This is what I call McGinty's Lost Bet, it's my special moonshine. So named because a lass I once knew, quite well, made a bet with me. Of course, she hadn't stood a chance of winning. A lovely lass, she was. A story for another time perhaps," his chuckle was quite infectious, she almost felt her brittle lips tilt up.

"It's made from mashed maize, luv, corn. Not as common as most moonshine, but this one has a kick that most non-humans can handle. Humans though, not so much. Come, drink up and let's get this done. You're fading faster than I like." A midsize demon approached and placed a small locked chest on the table next to the man, and it occurred to her she didn't know his name. Or maybe she did, but she couldn't for the life of her remember what it was.

"Name?" was all she could get out in a last ditch effort for control of her decisions.

"Balthazar Morrigan, at your service. Please forgive my lack of prior introduction. I'm sure it must have been off-putting. Now, drink up. Time's nearly up."

And drink she did. It burned like the fires of Hell and coiled into *every recess of her body, loosening her tight muscles, and easing the strain in her chest. Her lungs inhaled deeply and her heart thundered in her ears. He was right, she felt no pain, and oh my, did it feel good.*

"It won't last long, luv, so let's get this done and give you what you need, shall we?" His gentle reminder grounded her somewhat. She took another sip at his insistence, she figured it couldn't hurt, she'd already had one after all, right? Mmm, after the burning disappeared it kind of left the taste of popcorn on her tongue, the nice buttered kind you found at the cinema. Her thoughts drifted off slightly on a few different tangents . . .

THE DAMNED MOONSHINE he'd said would take the edge off and help her focus had been laced with a sedative, and something else, some rare drug that'd allowed him to control her to some degree. Something strong enough to have worked on a half-angel hybrid like her. Years later the chatty Cathy, otherwise known as Ballzy, had admitted it was strong enough to work on full-blooded angels, and even some demigods.

It hadn't made her tell the truth, or even offer up her secrets, as much as he'd wanted it to. He'd seemed surprised she hadn't answered any of his questions about what she was. What it had done though, was open her up to his control through the power of his directions. A tether that didn't exactly make her trust him completely, but it did leave her compliant and open to suggestion. Her mind almost pushed to the back as if it, and her body, were no longer hers. If he'd told her to dance naked on the nearest table, she would have had no choice but to comply like a puppet on strings. If he'd told her to admit to some heinous crime? She totally would have.

Because of the sedative, she barely remembered anything until the next day, apart from taking a knife to her palm. The scar still graced her skin and wouldn't fade completely until she was finally free. Not that she remembered ever reading the blasted form. He'd told her to sign and sign she had. Stupid assed idiot that she was.

Even after that shit had worn off, she'd fallen for his charming act and into his bed. Thankfully only once, and even then, the image of the dark stranger from the alley had superimposed himself over Ballzy to get her over the line. Boy, when she'd realized what he'd truly done, she'd hit the fucking roof.

Eight years bound to him. Leaving her stuck in this stupid place. He fed her half souls, or less, once or twice a year. Souls he'd dissected personally, ready for sale, a precious commodity for the practitioners of the darker arts. Ballzy had turned it into a very lucrative business. He'd certainly cornered the market. But that wasn't the only reason he fed her so little, so rarely. He knew better than to allow her to reach her full strength.

The one and only time he'd made the mistake of giving her a full soul, he'd lost two thirds of his little demon minions in less than a minute. If she hadn't already signed that damned piece of leathery hide with her blood, she would've been free and clear soon after. Alas, once she did, she couldn't escape him until the contract that bound her was either voided by him, or had fulfilled its obligations down to the letter. It protected even his soul from her. She could barely sense the thing, let alone sample a small sip, almost like it was locked in a vault inside his chest, hidden from her. A mystery she wanted to unravel. She couldn't take it due to the terms that bound her, so why hide it?

Unfortunately, well fortunately for them, demon souls were filled with poison. Yeah . . . she'd found that out the hard way. One of Ballzy's first fucked up little experiments. Spending four weeks writhing on a hard as rock floor throwing up what felt like all of her internal organs, burning up with an uncontrollable fever, then diving into the freezing depths of hypothermia, before flat lining multiple times. Only to wake up to her body flooded with white-hot, raging inferno of pain and demons licking at her poison tainted, sweat slicked skin. Which honestly, if anything had remained in her stomach, it definitely wouldn't have remained there after that experience.

Ballzy had really kicked into gear with his fun and games after that. Thankfully she'd managed to hide her need to feed on the emotions of others, or that she could sense them around her. There was no way in any realm he'd ever get that information out of her. His obsession with trying to figure out what her fire-like shadows and soul eating ability meant was dangerous enough. Sure, they'd had their moments. Sometimes she won, mostly he did. It was his domain after all, and she wasn't exactly at full strength. Nor did she have as many years of experience behind her as he did, yet. Technically she was still a baby in the supernatural world, she wasn't going to admit that though, not to him, the asshat.

He seemed to delight in her torment. Torturing her with kindness, though, it was something which appeared to be a new concept to him, before he switched to stringing her up and allowing his demons to sniff around her, just so he could see her shadows and watch as they lashed out at his minions as they tried to touch her. Their seemingly insubstantial, oily hands had reached out to caress her, three-inch long, scalpel-sharp claws sliced through her flesh, arms long enough and reflexes far quicker than hers in her disoriented state, as their tongues lengthened and curled toward her from what they assumed was a safe distance. Their grotesque cocks thickened and bobbed in her direction.

Only when they lay slashed and broken against the rough rock walls of his dungeon, and her shadows had subsided, retracted back into her body, would he release her. He'd taken her to his quarters. Quarters he insisted she share. Quarters he'd locked her inside of, like the prisoner she truly was. Her emotional hunger was sated, yet wrath burned in the pit of her stomach.

Thankfully she could hurt him too, so long as she didn't go too far. If she killed him it was game over for both of them, apparently. Not that she was willing to test the validity of his claims. But she'd pissed him off so much that eventually he'd placed her in this fucking cell, with its clear windows. Meaning he could watch her whenever he wanted, so could his little minions. And she couldn't do a damn thing about it. Not in her half starved state.

Speak of the Devil . . . At this point she'd probably welcome that male over the one crossing the threshold of her lavishly decorated prison cell with open arms. His almost black eyes skated to the tray she'd left untouched. Her stomach flipped and growled with urgent hunger, the scent of rich and well-prepared food teased her overly sensitive nose. Too bad her shadows had refused to let her touch it, not to mention she'd felt his excitement as he'd placed it there, letting her know about the drugs he'd tainted it with. His lips quirked up at the corners, his amusement plain to see. His eyes sparkled with a mixture of admiration and rage as she gave him a double middle finger salute from her perch on the bed. Not every meal was drugged, but he'd ramped it up this month with only one in six meals being clean. Pretty sure he realized she'd given up trying to pretend she'd eaten any of it, and he was now just enjoying the show.

He eyed her long legs, taking in her forcibly relaxed pose as she watched him for any sign of what the play of the day would be. If it weren't for his constant ultimate bastard behavior, she'd have considered him classically handsome; he certainly thought he was a hit with the ladies. Smooth and charming was his surface polish, too bad he tarnished so easily. Funnily enough for someone who claimed to love the ladies and that they loved him, they never came back for seconds. One taste of Ballzy was more than any woman could stomach. Thankfully, Jez hadn't even been able to stomach that. Her stomach had revolted the minute he was done. Not that he'd taken the hint, unfortunately.

"What, not hungry, luv?" he taunted.

She was torn between laughing in his face or telling him to 'shove off' in her own parody of his bloody accent. As a teenager, naive and innocent, she'd thought that character the epitome of sexy British sin. Until she'd met Balthazar. He'd crushed that secret fantasy under his soft Italian leather loafers, and he didn't stand a chance of reigniting it. Well, to be fair, none of her old secret fantasies did it for her anymore either, not the sexual ones anyway. Not since her encounter with the Shadow Hound had led her to this ongoing predicament. That wall of muscle, those eyes which screamed hot, hard, unrelenting sex, and barely restrained violence. His shadows had even called to her own. Utter craziness, because that way could only lead to her destruction and pain. She'd never see him again anyway. Especially not any time soon.

Huh, what do you know, Ballzy had used her momentary distraction to crouch beside her and was currently stroking her hair with gentle fingers. A smug look of burning desire lit his features and his lips formed words her ears hadn't caught up with yet.

"That's right, my little bird, sing for me. Moan for me again. I knew you'd come around. We are going to have so much fun." His lips pressed against her ear, his freakishly cold breath caused shivers of disgust through her body. Of course, the dipshit misconstrued them as shivers of desire. Jez closed her eyes and tilted her head closer to him. His body relaxed, his arms moving to gather her closer.

Her shadows warmed beneath her skin in a way only she could feel. They were so in tune with her, some would say an extension of herself, but they were just her, a part of her being that reacted like any other body part her brain sent signals to. Even as they protected her when she couldn't think to do so herself, without conscious thought, they were so ingrained in her psyche that they seemed to have a life of their own. So, when he stroked his palm down over her hip and along her thigh, before trying to slip his fingers beneath her short green skirt, fiery shadows seeped from beneath her in a coiled rope. Reaching down until his semi-hard cock and balls were trapped in a gallows knot. Tighter, tighter, and tighter still . . .

The moment he realized what was happening, he froze, his breath stalling in his inhuman chest. Still, she increased the pressure until his eyes just about bugged out of his overly manscaped face, his jaw popping. Leaning forward, she touched her nose to his, her gaze drilling into him with flames flashing in her eyes, like the biblical fires of Hell.

"I'd rather rut with a gutter rat than with the likes of you, Ballzy. But thanks for reinforcing just how revolting I find you." Her nose wrinkled up as if smelling something foul, emphasizing her disgust.

"As for the moaning . . . If you could see the men I see in my head . . ." Best he believed it was more than one, who knew what he'd do if he suspected her subconscious fixation. "Mmmm . . . boy, your inferiority complex would magnify ten fold. There is just no competition, Baby Ballz."

With that said, she stood and strode to the bathroom discreetly hidden off to one side of the room, her hips swaying with every step.

A taunt? Yes, because she could definitely bring her inner bitch to this little showdown. Just before she closed the door, she risked a glance at his lust glazed face. Dude definitely couldn't take a hint. As the door clicked shut she gave one extra hard tug of her shadow grip on his dick, and his resounding yelp of pure pain was music to her ears. Her smile returned as she leaned back against the too cool metal of the door.

Thank fuck she'd managed to at least bargain him down to fourteen years, six less than he'd intended. She only had six more years before the contract ended. Only six more years of hiding her secret and hoarding her strength little by little, one minuscule soul scrap at a time in the small well hidden within her body, until she was strong enough at the very moment the contract ends, and he comes to renew it. Because he would. His plan had always been to keep her here forever. But she would prevail. She would smite his ass and turn this place to ashes.

This time her grin was full of expectation and excitement. Bring it, bitch boy.

CHAPTER 3
THE SHADOW HOUND FORTRESS, HELL

ROUGHLY THE SAME TIME . . .

He woke in a cold sweat, the images still flickered in front of his eyes, despite his 'eyes wide open' state. He'd dreamed of her, again. And considering his kind didn't dream at all, that was a miracle in and of itself. No way was he going to tell anyone about his nighttime fantasies, though. Not even his brothers and sisters in arms knew he'd been dreaming, and definitely not of some woman from an alley eight years prior. The dreams had started not long after. His shadows continued to swirl and race around him in his agitation. Despite the grief and terror, the anger and hopelessness he'd felt from her and himself in those moments when he dreamed of her, his damn shadows never failed to curl around his cock and wake him to a raging hard-on. Every. Damn. Time.

Where was the she-devil? He'd looked for her every time he'd ventured out of the fortress since that night, whether duty called or otherwise. Hoping to see her, talk to her, figure out the puzzle she'd left him with. She was nowhere. He'd made discrete inquiries. Nada. He'd stopped short at even mentioning her to his fellow comrades—his brothers and sisters—not even Luc had gotten the message she'd wanted him to recite. Every time he'd thought about mentioning it he'd found his lips quirking up at the memory of her sass and beauty, as his brow furrowed in bewilderment at everything else. No way was he going to let his fellow Hounds see him so thoroughly thrown for a loop. He didn't think Luc needed that on top of whatever else was going on with the guy. Not that the General had cared to share. Still, Roth, hell, all of them, had picked up on how the Boss Man hadn't been himself, not since the 1940s. They would've had to be oblivious fucking idiots not to have noticed. Of course, Dante had been the last of them to do so and they hadn't let the little punk live it down.

He hadn't wanted anyone to know about her until he knew who, and what, she was. If she was a threat? Then he would take her out himself, or hand her over to the Praesidium, depending on what the Almighty decreed was best. It was his sacred duty. But if she wasn't? He didn't want to bring trouble to her doorstep and cause her pain. At least, that was his justification for his silence. His shadows warmed under his skin, sending a fluttering feeling through his mind, almost in affirmation that she was special, that he needed her, even if he didn't understand why.

His sheets were too warm, twisted and tangled around his long, muscular legs as they were. Even naked his skin felt too hot, the air too humid. As though the flames in her eyes were still burning him up. His hand made its way down, pulling the damp sheet free from his waist, his back arching, hips thrusting of their own volition, even before the rough skin of his palm grazed his throbbing cock. At the first touch of his hand, his fingers wrapped around his rigid length, his balls drew up tight, and a jolt of sexual electricity shot straight up his spine. Tingles fired in his brain, her image flashed clearly before his eyes. Half naked, her long, dark-red hair caressed her exposed skin as she lent back against a steel door, her eyes sparkled and a grin of pure wickedness curled the corners of her full, luscious lips . . .

His cock pulsed hard, thick hot jets of his seed covered his tanned abdomen, leaving him breathless and gasping. His hand shook as it fell away from his body, even though his erection hadn't lessened. It was always this way. Like she'd cast a spell upon him. He thought only of her, no one else compared. At first, he'd been able to go to the clubs with his friends and hook up. Her image only entered his head toward the end of his encounters. He didn't do relationships. Not anymore. The past had taught him well, and his lessons had been ingrained deeply. As time went on and the dreams got more intense, she slowly took over, and soon he was only attracted to redheads with pale skin, long shapely legs, pert bouncy breasts, and sarcasm streaming from their pores. Not as easy to find as one would think.

Now though, it was getting ridiculous, he hadn't had sex with anything other than his hand and his mattress in over five years. His brothers and sisters had noticed of course, but he'd fobbed them off by pretending to go off with human women every now and then. It seemed with every passing year her hold on him got stronger—it was really starting to piss him off.

As his room finally came back into focus around him, the light from Hell's iridescent golden sun bathed every surface in a fine layer of stardust. Roth snorted at the irony of Hell being covered in a glittery, shimmery light, casting it in a heavenly glow, when all earthly representations were quite the opposite; darkness, monsters, and fiery damnation. He threw off the rest of his sheets and blankets and stormed his way into his completely black bathroom, hoping the cold fall of water would wash away the evidence of how much his mystery woman affected him. His? He didn't even know who she was. Even if he did, she'd never be his. No one would ever be his. Never again.

Thirty minutes later, when the shower idea hadn't worked, he roughly tossed on some workout pants, and slammed his way out of his room, the heavy ebony door defying him as it softly snicked shut, and headed down to the gym to hopefully work off his frustration and irrational anger.

Maybe she was a witch? It would explain how she'd managed to enthrall him. Heck, she'd have to be a pretty powerful one though, since his kind were meant to be immune to the paltry efforts of witchkind. It bore looking into, nonetheless. Or maybe she was a siren of some sort? Possibly even a fae enchantress? That one was a bit far-fetched. The fae were locked out of the earthly realm over a millennium ago, any who'd slipped through the cracks to stay behind would have lost their magic as they lost their connection to others of their kind. Only in large groups could they maintain strong magic for such a long period of time.

When the Almighty got pissed at your entire race or species, they definitely didn't do so by halves, that was for sure. Although some would argue they'd been too lenient in their punishment of the fae, most just felt sorry for the humans unlucky enough to get stuck there with them.

Argh, he needed to stop thinking about her, even contemplating the puzzle she presented was giving him a headache this morning. His hands ran through his dark hair roughly, trying to rub the tension from his scalp. An intense sense of impending doom almost sent him to his knees, his breath trapped in his lungs. Rubbing absently at his right shoulder as a lick of heat flashed under his fingertips he exhaled, fresh air again filled his oxygen starved lungs as he forced one foot before the other.

With limited time before the rest of the fortress' inhabitants ate everything in sight within the dining hall he'd have to hit the gym hard and fast. With that in mind he headed to the shortcut only he and a few others knew about, because heck, they'd designed and built the place after all.

Roth passed Seth and Havoc as he made his way down the corridor toward the haunting painting of a faceless woman, dressed in a velvet green gown from a bygone era. The dark, stormy sky and rocky cliffs fell away beneath her small, slippered feet. One look at his face had the two men nodding quickly in passing before facing forward with military precision and continuing on their way to the dining hall. Smart boys, Roth thought. They weren't in the Devil's 13, and they would never be, but they were damned good at their jobs.

At first only eleven of the original angels were chosen—by none other than the Almighty—to join with the shadows and carry out the sacred duty they'd been assigned. Of the other two, one was created after his mortal death and the other was the first Shadow Hound born to angel parents. They were Luc's most trusted friends. The fact the shadows they'd been born with had caused their once white wings to turn raven black when they'd reached their majority was just another reason why they were so much cooler than Gabe's gang of nitwits.

The Blessed Reapers weren't always so bad. If they could just find

Michael and drag his ass back to heaven he'd have them back to how they used to be. Doing their jobs and staying in their lanes. But Mike had gone missing 357 years ago next Thursday, and the Almighty had 'temporarily' assigned Gabriel to his job. Gabe was still pissed he wasn't permanently in charge yet. A fact the Shadow Hounds never failed to use to their advantage when trying to annoy the shit out of the stuck up prig. What the Almighty saw in the tosser was anyone's guess. Just the thought of him had Roth's lip curling in a snarl and a corresponding growl passing between his clenched teeth.

Still, so much had changed without Michael at the wheel of the other team. The Almighty was playing it closer to their proverbial chest these days. Gabe had ramped up the demands.

And Luc, well, Luc was Hell on wheels when it came to game time. He was a mastermind at his job as General of the Hounds. Hell, he'd been created specifically for it. This was his domain. But even Luc had started acting a little weirder than usual. His intense focus was gone. A new unpredictable side had slowly started creeping in, and they were running out of ideas as to how to help him.

Bringing it to the attention of his sole superior, and especially his counterparts, was not an option any of them wanted to resort to. That jackass Gabriel would do everything in his power to bring down Lucifer, and have someone less powerful and more malleable placed into his role.

What he failed to recognize was that anyone less powerful, and not in the higher ranks, someone who could be corrupted by him, wouldn't last long at all. The men who worked so closely with Luc would chew a lesser angel up and spit him back into Gabe's face within half a day, if that. Luc needed an anchor, something to keep him focused and on track. But they'd run out of ideas as to what that could be.

Just as Roth reached out to stroke the gilt frame of the oil painting he glanced at the plaque attached to the bottom of it. 'An Angel's Fate' by 42. He'd always found it confusing how that faceless female could be any angel's fate, when angels didn't really receive one. Taking a step closer his fingers found the little lever tucked expertly between the painting and the wall, but before he could open the hidden door a strange noise reached his ears.

The haunting notes of a familiar tune floated on the air, seemingly coming from Luc's inner sanctum. Roth's feet froze as if a bolt of lightning had fused him to the floor, his brain screamed that the puzzle of his mystery woman could be just what Luc needed to keep him grounded. A riddle he could help Roth solve.

Suddenly, he found himself running, his feet moving before he could focus on a single one of his suddenly frenetic thoughts. For once in his existence he didn't stop to knock, didn't wait for an answer as decorum dictated, instead he forced himself past the heavy door and into the room unannounced, only to stop dead at the sight before him . . .

Luc was dancing with a phantom woman. The General of Hell softly sang the words to the tune Roth's own mystery woman had put in his head years ago in that dark alley. A wistful dreamy look upon his usually harsh features. His voice, husky and filled with so much emotion. Seemingly oblivious to all else. Roth's entrance caused not even a flicker of an eyelash. Luc's entire being was lost in some invisible woman's arms as the flickering candlelight flung his puppet-like silhouette against the parchment painted walls.

Soft whimpers and whines came from the two domesticated and non-shifting hellhounds who lay on either side of the fireplace. Among the first of their breed Luc had created them to be utterly fearsome and completely loyal. Now they looked up at Roth with big, sad eyes before they returned their massive black and midnight-blue heads to their paws as they watched the King of Hell losing his ever-loving mind, and all they could do was cry.

Roth backed up, closing the door quietly. He didn't think Luc had even noticed him enter; despite how he'd been the complete opposite of stealthy. Nope. Not even going to try to process that mindfuck right now. Best to leave whatever it was for another day.

They had a meeting, sans Luc, in less than two hours to brainstorm ideas about how to help him. Just the Devil's 13. An hour after that was their regular daily briefing, which Luc would oversee. Thankfully, when it came to these, Luc was still on point. The conference call with Gabe and his tighty-whitey little top knots seemed to bring out the old Luc. The bringer of hellfire and ash, vengeance and wrath to all sinners. Possibly why he hated Gabe so much; they all did. Not that they could put a finger on why, but the asshat set their inner radar off, and there was just something about him that didn't add up. Why the Almighty entrusted him with the Blessed Reapers, the so-called Angels of Light, and such a sacred duty was beyond them. It was also beyond their pay grade, to be honest. Not that they really got paid, not in the human sense of the word anyway.

Shaking his head Roth continued through the surprisingly well lit and cobweb free hidden passage to the private elevator that would take him to the gym below. Ready to work his body to the point where the past few hours disappeared into a welcome haze of exhaustion.

CHAPTER 4

Striding into the conference room which overlooked the dense woodlands of the valley their fortress was nestled in, Roth took a deep breath and assessed who was already present. Dammit, every last one of them was already in the room. All but one of them was lounging back on their padded leather seats, ankles crossed on the table made of polished onyx and solidified storm clouds, half empty scotch glasses held out in mock salute. Even Perri and Lily, almost like they'd planned it. The fuckers.

He was never late. He hated being the last to enter a room, as if by not being ready before everyone else meant he'd be ambushed by something, or someone. The fact they'd all noticed, and made a point of acknowledging his tardy entrance, rankled his forced calm. It made his skin crawl and his temper flared. Stopping for breakfast had been a mistake. A big one. No matter how much he loved old Mrs Briars's sweet fae dumplings with rose and honey caramel sauce, they weren't worth this level of anxiety and paranoia.

Locking down his internal demons, Roth cocked his brow at his friends, gave Lily a wink, and headed straight to the bar off to the side of the double doors to grab a glass of Cardhu. He kept his eyes on all of them in the mirrored glass behind the polished black, fully stocked bar.

Three fingers worth should take the edge off; he had a feeling he'd need it. Especially because they only had fifty-five minutes left to get down to the business of discussing their esteemed leader's increasing disconnection from reality.

Looking around at their amused faces, he acknowledged that while they found it amusing, he could truly trust each and every one of them to have his back. They were his family, his lifeline. They'd pulled him back from the brink more times than he cared to admit.

Caine assessed him from a deceptively casual position up against the far wall, his body never fully relaxed, with his blond, shaggy hair he was more reminiscent of a 1990s surfer than an angel created near to the dawn of time. Caine's green gaze bore into Roth, probing. He took note of Roth's reactions, his barely leashed tension and unease. He'd met him in the gym earlier, hell, it was pretty much a part of their daily routine at this point. Both of them pushed their bodies to the limits, punishingly, trying to outrun the demons that plagued them. And they both had more than one. But never in his immortal life would he wish to bear the burden that weighed down on Caine. There was a reason the man was built like a mountain with muscles which rival those of pro wrestlers-turned movie stars, Roth was never good with names like that. Caine castigated himself every day for a past he could not, and would not, have changed, and a future he knew was as unavoidable as the knowledge the Almighty had chosen this fate for him. His 'gift' was his unending punishment and torture.

Looking away from his best friend, his gaze skittered over Athon, Marco, Deus, Malphas, Lily, Perri, Andy, Ares, Fynn, and Malech, before coming to rest on Dante. The class clown. Not one to miss an opportunity to be a smart ass, the cocky little shit began to open his mouth . . . Malphas cleared his throat . . . What do you know, Dante's mouth snapped shut with an audible click. Interesting . . .

"We don't have much time before the others arrive, so we'd best get to it," Malphas stated, drawing everyone's attention back to the reason for their covert meeting. They were becoming increasingly regular the more Luc faded away. If angels suffered from human ailments, one would think Luc was slowly succumbing to Alzheimer's disease. It would be the easy answer, clear-cut and definite. That was not the case.

Mortal diseases, neurological and genetic conditions, simply couldn't survive in the body of one of them. However, they could still get sick. An angel with a cold was one hundred times worse to deal with than a human. Not him, of course, he was as stoic as ever.

"Status report on Luc's current mood and behavior since we last did this shit?" Fynn hated these meetings. He more than most felt that while necessary, they were a betrayal of his brother's trust and position. An angel with a blood sibling was a rare thing in the angel realms, and while Luc already had Michael, he'd also created his own family of brothers and sisters well before the time of the Choosing. In honor of their familial bond the Almighty had chosen them all to house the shadows, and fulfill a destiny their mighty creator refused to share with anyone, not even the most trusted collector of prophecies and fates, the most loyal of the Almighty's counsel, Leraie, knew the exact reason for the bonding of angel to shadow. At least, she hadn't deigned to share if she did, anyway.

"Well, I'm pretty sure he's doing the same as he was last time: sporadic loss of focus when not performing official duties," Perri voiced, hope heavily laced through her words. Her voice was so naturally sultry that if you didn't know any better you'd think she was part siren . . . or a phone sex operator. Thank God she couldn't read minds though, because if she could, that thought in anyone's head could lead to their immediate castration or disembowelment, if they were lucky. Growing back a nut was worse than growing back both legs and a spine, all at once, something he knew from experience. At the memory his balls drew up tight, as if trying to find refuge and protection within his body.

Roth felt like shit as he placed his glass on the table, rolling his shoulders in an effort to loosen the tightly bunched muscles in his neck, the cracks resounding in his ears as he took a seat. He rarely sat, so when he did, they usually knew something bad or mood wrecking was coming. This time it was no different. This time he knew he couldn't bite his tongue.

Athon made it easy for him, as always, paving the way and starting him off. "What's new, Roth? Luc done something strange, my man?" His tanned arms came to rest on the table in front of him, his attention focussed solely on Roth. Voice soft and husky, with an edge to it only

Roth ever seemed to notice. Like the sharp edge of a blade, softened by the satin touch of desire as it stroked him like a lover. It turned the words "my man" into the soft caress of a lover's hand, as if meant for his ears alone. He knew how to help him, he'd always had the knack, that affinity, for pulling Roth out of his thoughts and into confiding almost anything. Almost.

It was probably why the two of them had been so much more, once upon a time. But that was before. Before the Big Bad Bitch had screwed Roth over, and he'd sworn off anything that lasted more than a night or two. She'd screwed over Athon too, to a lesser degree. And yet, he knew he could count on him for anything he needed, to keep any confidence and offer sound advice. Athon was the wise one of their lot, the most empathic, the most understanding and pragmatic.

Then *she* had sashayed her way into his brain, that damn redhead. She became his second greatest secret, and it was starting to scare him even more than opening up to the trusted few in this room. They knew him, what he was at his worst, at his weakest, and also his greatest strengths. Yet, this, he'd kept from them, and he didn't even have a decent excuse for it, not one which held up under any kind of scrutiny.

Athon deserved better than that. He sometimes found himself wishing he could be better for him. The only good thing to come of this situation with the mystery woman was that his shadows and brain were so tied up in knots that random erections when in close proximity to the male across from him became a thing of the past. Focus, Roth. Share and care time was in session.

"Yeah, actually there is. I was heading to the gym via the painting tunnel this morning when I heard something odd coming from Luc's room . . . So I rushed in to check on him. More like I barreled in with the grace of a panicked rhino, but whatever, " he added, aiming for a little levity as he paused to gather his thoughts, but hurried on when he saw the worried gazes of his comrades.

"Luc was listening to an old song and singing as he danced around the room, as if with a woman in his arms, when there was only air. He didn't even seem to know I'd entered, and my entrance was anything but stealthy. I thought for sure he'd blast my ass back out into the hallway and ream me a new one. But he just continued to dance and sing. It was damned unnerving. So, I backed the fuck up and hightailed it out of there."

Shocked faces stared at him with varying degrees of disbelief, horror, and worry. Imagining the King of Hell doing any of that was almost too much for anyone's brain to compute. This was the man they'd served with for millennia upon millennia. To see him so locked inside his own little bubble like this was heartbreaking.

"There has to be something we can do!" lamented Lily, her love for Lucifer as a father figure plain to see. The circles under her lavender eyes attested to her worry. This was hardest on her. Lucifer had picked up the pieces of her shattered soul when her biological parents—tighty whitey assholes of the highest order those two were—had abandoned her after she was chosen to follow Luc and her wings had changed from their original fluffy white cloud color to the pitch black of night, more so when they saw the tips of her feathers had remained pure white. So unlike any of the rest of them. She was special, they just hadn't figured out what it meant yet.

"I have an idea. I'm not sure it'll work though," Roth interjected, his voice unnaturally soft, especially coming from him. "Luc needs something to focus on. A mystery, something he can sink his teeth into, focus all of his efforts on. To break him out of his own head, right?" Heads bobbed in agreement, as they wondered where Roth was going with this, their curiosity clear to see.

"But what mystery do we have that can gain his attention like that? Michael's disappearance hasn't done jack to keep him with us and normal since the goddamn 1940s, and all of our other tasks are fleeting. We collect souls for eternal damnation and police the illegal activities of the darker elements of the supernatural realms before delivering them to the Praesidium for assessment and the Almighty's sentencing. Luc doesn't even directly oversee that part anymore. What the fuck happened back then? He up and disappeared for six months, leaving Caine in charge so he could have a break. Fine, everyone needs one sometimes and he'd been living his work since the creation of time. But then he comes back only to lock himself in his room, ripped the place to shreds and attacked everyone who so much as moved in his presence, before he subsided into whatever the fuck this is." Ares' frustration and fear was clear as his rant came to an end. Lucifer was the glue that held them together as a team. He was, no, is their General. They were doing their best, but they needed him back.

"Well, I have something I think might work. On the other hand, it might just piss him off more. I omitted a few things from an official report regarding a soul collection, oh, about . . . eight years ago," Roth hedged, glancing up somewhat sheepishly.

Heads snapped up, eyes widened, and jaws dropped open. You'd swear they were pelicans catching fish. Or those weird clowns at carnivals that you had to throw balls at. At that thought Roth couldn't contain a chuckle. The image of balls, the reproductive type, not the hard plastic or bouncy kind, in all of their mouths flashed through his brain. And that was it, he lost it. Between gasping, wheezing breaths, and uncontrollable mirth, he managed to convey the imagery to them as they looked at him aghast.

Athon chuckled, Dante lost it too, Lily burst into tears of laughter, and everyone else rolled their eyes and shook their heads as if he'd lost his damn marbles too. And maybe he had, but suddenly he felt lighter than he had in years, and if sharing helped Luc? Well, that was a damn sight more important than his ego and pride.

By the time the ornate double doors swung inwards they'd managed to bring their joviality back under wraps. Well, it was manageable at least.

All heads turned in the direction of the newcomer. Only one person could command the attention of everyone in a room before they'd even laid eyes on him. The power that was barely contained in his aura was beyond belief, and his essence as the King of Hell well lived up to legend. He'd terrified men since time began. He'd seduced more women than even he could recall, and they'd loved every minute of it.

Lips twitched, hands covered mouths. They tried, truly they did, and they possibly would've succeeded if Dante hadn't opened his damn trap.

"Hey, Hades. How's it hangin'?"

This time none of them could contain their mirth and it was less to do with hanging balls and more with the sight before them. Dante even dropped to the floor, rolling around like a pig in mud, tears streaming down his cheeks. There was no doubt who was behind it.

A bewildered Luc gazed at them, his brow furrowed.

"Care to share what you all find so amusing, boys and girls?" Came the honey over steel voice that sent shivers down a lesser being's back but that could send anyone he wished to their knees.

Perri was the first to pull herself together, making her way to Luc's side she placed her arm on his shoulder and indicated the mirror above the bar.

Luc's face was a study of the classic comedy double take as he took in his once midnight black, ear length, hair. Now blue ombre locks shone like a gas flame around his face. His eyes zeroed in without hesitation on Dante, now sitting on the floor looking up at Luc expectantly.

"Come on, Boss, I've got just the stuff to get that shit out back in my room. It'll take just a minute to fetch it and we'll get you back to normal before we chat to the other side. It'll do Gabe good to have to wait for once." Perri tried to usher Luc to the door, but he stood firm.

His eyes hardened and Dante smirked. He liked to push their buttons, and pushing Luc's usually brought back the Luc of old, at least, for a bit. Luc gently pried Perri away and guided her to her seat, before heading back and leaning against the bar. His eyes flashed and sparkles of gold swirled in his dark brown, almost black irises as he locked gazes with Dante.

Lips curling into a sinister smirk, Luc raised his hands and slid them through his hair before bringing them back down with a casual elegance unique to him. He now looked like that Hades character from the *Descendants*, only less rough around the edges. Fucking Dante had made them all binge-watch that shit last week. The fucker had been planning this all along. Admittedly Luc rocked the look and Roth sensed what was coming next.

"Thanks, D, I think I'll keep it." He flashed him a grin full of teeth and a wink before turning to pour himself a drink.

Dante's face went slack, the color in his cheeks leached away. Yeah, he'd fucked with the bull and Luc had him by the balls. Retribution was coming and Dante had gotten what he'd wanted.

Lucifer, at his finest, was in the house.

CHAPTER 5

As he gazed at his reflection in the mirror behind the bar, Luc felt his grip on reality slipping. A steady slide into madness. The amused, yet cautious faces of his friends reflected back at him, but all he saw were pale gray eyes and dark red hair. His favorite colors. The only colors he ever wished to see. Moonlight created a halo around her perfect face. She was here with him now, he could feel her, could almost reach out and touch her silky smooth skin. Why didn't she speak? Why didn't she run to him with open arms and slide her soft curves along the hard planes of his muscled body? He caught a flicker of blue from the corner of his eye and felt her amusement deep in his very soul. Strength filled him, renewed him. She began to fade away, and he was thrust back into the present. More himself than he'd been for a long while. His eyes once again landed on his now blue haired reflection.

Dante was asking for an ass whooping with this latest stunt. Right before a meeting with the head of the 'I have my head so far up my own ass' club, too. It was a good thing he enjoyed a joke. Dante was like the annoying younger brother you couldn't help but love. That didn't mean he was safe from retribution though, and Luc knew just what to do with him. It was a good thing he'd had since the beginning of time to curb his natural inclination toward swift retaliation. This required finesse, and he was in it for the long game. As his face dropped and realization of his fuck up hit him, Dante once again looked like a newbie angel thrust into a role he was not prepared for. Luc almost took pity on him, but the glow from his head was so bright he could still see it in his peripheral vision. Nah, the little fuck could suck it up and deal with the consequences.

Samael waltzed in and the mood in the room immediately shifted into professional mode. Everyone sat or stood a little bit straighter. Dante moved from his position on the floor, taking his seat in a blink and you'll miss it motion. Glasses were placed away from hands and everyone seemed to be watching the door.

Behind Sam came Havoc, Seth, Eli, and Abbie. The latter was so distracted by the screen in her hands that she didn't notice the boys in front of her coming to a halt. And three . . . two . . . one . . . yep, she hit the wall of stone that was Eli and bounced backwards, and would have hit the floor had Eli not reached back with lightning reflexes and wrapped her wrist in his firm grip.

As they passed Luc and the rest of the team they nodded their heads in acknowledgment and respect. Seth and Havoc though, they avoided Roth's gaze and almost bowed in supplication. That told Luc all he needed to about Roth's headspace this fine day.

Yep, this could get ugly. Throw in Gabe, the douchebag, and it could be straight up volatile. With a heavy sigh Luc took his place at the head of the table. His mind wandered as he gazed out of the windows which overlooked the realm he'd created. Soon its beauty would be obscured by the faces of Gabe and his inner circle of idiots.

Luc had tried for centuries to find Michael. Not just Michael, but his Grand Consortium too. Once Gabe took 'temporary' control, what a laugh that was, it hadn't taken long for Michael's inner circle to either be forced out, disappear, or abandon ship to search for Michael themselves.

Not one of the 13 had a shred of respect for Gabriel. They knew what he was truly like. Power hungry and as slimy as a snake oil salesman. Even if his appointment had come from the being who ruled them all, they wanted no part in whatever he had planned.

The third stringers were now Gabe's go-to lackeys. He'd manipulated those weak little shits into believing he was their ticket to the big leagues, and they'd slurped that shit up like tequila off a stripper's toned stomach.

Just then, Gabe's sour, pinch lipped face flashed up on the screen, and for a brief moment an image of Gabe, chest bare except for sequined nipple tassels, spread out on a tabletop with his gang of idiots all over him licking his abs appeared in his mind. An amused huff escaped him, and his lips turned up, which caused Gabe's already severe features to darken with barely leashed rage. The guy had always been such a fucking killjoy.

Time to get to work. There were no niceties, no hello, how are you? Which was totes fine as they would only waste time, and it wouldn't mean a goddamn thing coming from him or his little ass-lickers anyway. Jumping straight into business was always best with this lot. Judging by the look in his eyes, Gabe definitely had an agenda today. His furtive gaze darted to the side more than once, a clear indication of his nervousness.

"Hello, Gabriel," Luc said with a careless grin, deciding to be the bigger man. Which was actually very true in more ways than one.

"Lucifer," came Gabe's clipped response. "Feeling a little Disney today, are we?" he added, sarcasm and disdain slipping into his tone.

"Nothing wrong with a little fun now and again, is there, Gabriel? Or would you not know what that is?" came Luc's swift, yet casual reply. Gabe's lip curled in response, but he held his tongue, even as his eyes flared wide. Time to hurry this shit fest along. "Okay then, let's get this done and dusted, shall we? I don't know about you, but I have a shit ton of things to get to today. I'd rather not waste too much time sitting on my ass, no matter how plush the padding under it may be."

As Gabe went over the stats for his teams soul retrievals and rebirths versus stored souls Luc listened with one ear as he took in every nuance of what he could see on the screen. It was his automatic response, how he processed everything. Always looking for the threat, anything that could be useful information to have. What was the little shit up to? What was he hiding? He was good, he'd give him that, since he'd kept whatever it was under wraps for centuries. The tighty whitey asshole certainly had patience, although lately it seemed much easier to poke the bear.

"Any word on the number of new souls created?" Luc interjected. Gabe had finished his report but had just kept talking. He always did love the sound of his own pompous voice.

"No new souls. We are investigating and have posed the question to the Praesidium and through all major channels. As yet the Almighty has not deigned to answer our queries. Since Michael up and disappeared, not a single new soul has been created, as you very well know." Gabe's left eye started twitching. It was barely noticeable if you weren't looking for it, but Luc was.

Knowing, as he did, exactly why the soul production line had stopped, it always gave him a shiver of joy up his spine to goad Gabe. The souls would continue to only be recycled ones until either Michael returned or the Almighty imbued Gabe with the essence of Michael's magic. That could only happen if Michael died and his magic returned to the Almighty, or it was extracted from Mike and given to Gabe. Gabe being unaware of this information was a testament to the Almighty's lack of faith in him. It yet again begged the question as to why he'd been given such a position in the first place.

It also told Luc two things and gave him hope for Michael's safe return to the fold. The first was that his brother was alive. Secondly, whatever destiny the Almighty had planned, Michael still had an important part to play in it.

Relaxing back into his chair he couldn't help but ask his next question. "What's the status of your search for Michael? How many angels do you have on it? His safe return is paramount."

Like a sulky little toddler Gabe tried to skirt the question and place the focus on someone else. He never truly had anyone's back but his own.

"The search team has come up with nothing new. What have you been doing about it? Surely, with your little consortium being so superior to mine, in your opinion, you've found at least something?" The sarcastic snarl in his tone didn't go unnoticed as someone off camera cleared their throat and Gabe's face paled slightly.

"We have some leads." Luc nonchalantly lied. "We're still following up on them and will include it in our report, should they pan out. I have faith that, even though it has been 357 years since he seemingly vanished, Michael will return, or we will find him and bring him home."

Gabe hated not knowing things. Hated it even more when it was Luc in the know.

"Well, you haven't yet, so let's just see how that works out for you, huh?"

Gabe was losing his cool, and they could all see it. Everyone around the table was trying not to smirk. Gabe had such thin skin. But his friends, his angels, knew better than to offer any input into these discussions until directly asked for it. Because, unlike Gabe, Lucifer always valued the opinions of those under his command.

Caine sat up straighter, his eyes narrowed to laser points at Gabe's last comment. There was something there. Caine was an expert at sniffing out a person's secrets, something which was fairly common knowledge. Gabe avoided being in the same space as him or talking on the screen for any length of time while he was present, which made the fact he seemed to be drawing this out even more strange. Hmm, something was definitely up, he just didn't know what. Might as well help Caine with some extra time to puzzle it out.

"Sounds like you know more than you're letting on, Gabriel. Care to tell us what that may be, and what you think happened to my brother?" His tone was sharper than he'd intended, more of an accusation and less of a taunt laced his words.

"Considering you haven't really given a shit about your brother in the last, what, sixty odd years? And you're now questioning me? Maybe you and your so-called best of the best don't actually measure up to the hype anymore, Lucifer. Better get your house in order. I have it on good authority that representatives of the Praesidium are going to be visiting soon. Wouldn't want to be caught with your pants down now, would we?" Gabe's childish snark was pretty hard not to miss and his pettiness was quite satisfying. The little shit was still such a petulant fool.

"Wouldn't be the first time now, would it? Oh. Are you still pissy that Jeannie got down on her pretty little knees and worshipped at the Temple de Lucifer, rather than sit on your pedestal? She was such a delicious morsel. The French King had damn fine taste when it came to his coveted mistress, the incomparable Madame de Pompadour." Luc feigned a shiver of delight as though remembering the illicit affair, his tone wistful and goading. Around him everyone in the room snickered and coughed into their hands. There was little chance that those on the other end hadn't heard them considering the remarkable hearing angels were gifted with.

Gabe's face turned an entertaining shade of puce . . . maybe slightly more purple than puce, actually. With rage, wordless splutters erupted from his mouth with the occasional 'you' thrown in for good measure. It had been well known back in the day how enamored he'd been of the lovely Jeanne Antoinette Poisson. The fact that she'd preferred Lucifer's darker allure obviously still ate at him, even now.

"Considering you don't seem to have anything of worth to add to this little confab, how about you go and do your job, Gabby, and leave me to do mine." With a grin, a wave, and a nod to the side Luc signed off. Seth cut the magical feed and thrust the wards back up around the room, reinforcing the fortress and portal wards too.

Within moments he found himself surrounded by bodies. Strong hands clapped him on the back and jovial shoulder bumps abounded. It felt good to get Gabriel's goat. Damn, he'd missed these moments with his family.

Knowing they had work to do, Luc sent them back to their seats. Unfortunately, Gabe had been partially right, he'd neglected the situation with his brother for too long, his attention MIA. Also, he'd been totally bullshitting to Gabe about having any leads. Definitely not information that Mr I'm so far up my own ass needed to know. Especially with the suspicion Luc had about why Gabe seemed so nervous.

"I hate to admit this, but we've gotten, no, I've gotten slack after so many years searching for Michael. We need to make this a priority again." Heads snapped up, backs got straighter, and he could see his warrior angels falling into formation, just like old times.

"Perri, I want you to take Sam and supervise the Search and Rescue Division. In saying supervise the SRD, you are one hundred percent correct in assuming that you are leading them in the search for any and all leads that lead to the rescue of Michael. Just try to be your diplomatic best, okay, Princess?" Luc slid Perri a wink.

"Umm, General, what if Michael doesn't want to be found? I mean he could have chosen to leave his duties, right? There have been a few angels who did just that. I mean the Fallen, the banished . . ." Abbie asked somewhat tentatively. She always seemed worried that he'd bite her wings off if she said something out of place. If only he could go back to the hellhole she'd grown up in and royally fuck up those assholes who'd made her so fearful. Luckily she was brilliant at what she did, and while it had taken them a while to get her to where she was, she'd gained a much better family than before.

"It's always a possibility, Abbie. But, I know my brother, and I don't think he'd do something like that without extreme extenuating circumstances. Plus, I'm willing to bet Angel wine to fae dumplings that a certain tighty whitey slimeball has his filthy fucking fingers all up in this mess." Abbie visibly relaxed. Luc felt the impulse to wrap his arms around her in a fatherly hug, an impulse he curbed. It wasn't the time nor place, and she would not benefit from it even if it were. Her pride, her shield, wouldn't allow such a display of weakness in front of the others.

Running through the list of assigned tasks for the week only took a matter of minutes: realm patrols for supernatural crimes, training duties, liaison groups, and supervision for the other teams. The soul collections for the week would come in one by one and were assigned directly by the Almighty into their brain and acted like a transparent viewscreen they could call upon at will until their target was acquired, so thankfully they didn't need to go over any of those. It wasn't long before the meeting came to an official end and the only ones left were Luc and his Devil's 13. At least they thought so until Seth cleared his throat from in front of the viewscreen that maintained all communication in and out of the fortress.

"Sorry, General, I was just about to leave when a top priority, highest clearance only alert came through. Thought I'd let you know and then head out." Came the commanding, succinct tones of the ever efficient angel. He was head of the tech team for a very good reason. The kid had a gift that no other had mastered when it came to angel tech, or any other kind for that matter.

"You can stay, Sthenno. Put it on the view screen, full audio." He'd trusted this kid with his whole fortress. He could certainly trust him with a memo.

'Increasing reports of a being, both top side and in multiple realms, wreaking havoc and mayhem. Previous reports of the creature were less serious, minor memory damage and thought reading, no major actions needed. New intel of increased agitation and assault. Several people left with major damage, mind wipes, brains liquefied etc. All targets seem to be on the darker fringe of society. Several witches and low level demons have been struck down. Suspect's behavior seems to be becoming more erratic and unstable. Visual attached of the only recorded sighting. Be on the lookout for anyone matching the description depicted in the following images.'

A cloaked and hooded figure, obviously female from the way she moved and the way the cloak clung to her profile, stealthily made her way to the city square of the dragon realm. Her walk seemed so familiar, and yet not. The dragon realm was not a place one went without reason, and her determination was clear in the set of her shoulders.

The woman came face to face with a stern, angry looking male. She stopped and held out her hands in supplication, an indication of no ill intent. They spoke. The feed came with no audio, although how they even had the feed was a mystery considering the dragons were so covetous of their privacy and social practices.

Suddenly the man dropped to his knees, fluid leaked from his ears, before he flopped forward. Not a dragon then. A mage perhaps? She turned, and as she did two things happened almost at once. Firstly, she took a step just as a pitch-black portal opened up right where her foot would land. Secondly, she glanced up and the flash of pale skin, brilliant red hair, and hard gray eyes flashed, the curve of her jaw . . .

Luc's heart beat like a drum in his chest, his breath came hard and fast, wood splintered within his grip, breaking the back of his chair. And in the blink of an eye her foot landed in a black abyss of nothing, sucking her in and carrying her away, to a destination unknown. And with her exit, Luc snapped back into himself with a jolt. It wasn't possible. For starters, she'd be dead by now . . . surely. Even if what he'd seen hadn't been real, she'd be at, or very close to, the end of her human lifespan.

The feed ended with another reminder to keep their eyes peeled, but none of them were really paying attention. Roth was making odd sounds in his corner of the room. Very un-Roth-like noises. If he were human one would assume a heart attack of some kind. Watching the usually put together male as he ambled toward the conference table and then seemed to stop, unsure, he definitely knew something big was coming. Had thought himself prepared for anything.

"So, uh, yeah, there's something you should know." Roth cleared his throat. The poor bastard looked nervous as hell, but considering he lived here that shouldn't have been a problem, Luc laughed at his own little joke to break the tension he was feeling.

"Just spit it out, Wraith, surely it can't be that bad."

It couldn't be, right?

CHAPTER 6

Where was she? Why couldn't she track her? Why couldn't she find her? The old witch, her friend, had promised she'd always be able to find her . . . Unless she was shielded in a place she should not be, by someone she should not know?

Hysteria bubbled beneath the surface of her despair. Rage stung her skin like angry wasps at the possibilities running through her head. All the questions left unanswered. The leads that led nowhere. The portal realms were the only answer. This was the last one. The last one she could enter anyway. There were more. One, no one could enter. One only her kind could not enter. And one she dreaded more than any other. She'd find her answers here, or she'd find a way into those other places. No one would stop her.

The mage stood arrogantly in the square, as though he held all the cards, and she'd be the one playing pick up. Little did he know she'd played this particular game for a lot longer than he had.

The dragons were the most secretive creatures, self-isolated as they were. The clans were barely civil with each other. Prior to the heirs of four of the five main clans going missing they'd warred amongst themselves. Their world was governed by demigods and goddesses, as were most of the shifter realms.

She felt the insidious evil attached to the mage. His emotions were so dark, so slimy, like wading through a swamp. He thought to deceive her, trick her. Before he could open his mouth, and lie to her with words his emotions belied, she sent her power out and pulled none too gently at his feelings. Feeding her hunger and gaining his strength, his fear was addictive as he realized what was happening, yet he had no power to stop her, as if his body were encased in ice. She felt the moment he let his thoughts flow into his emotions and the information he'd hidden drifted into her. With a slight 'pop' his brain liquefied, and his knees hit the ground moments before he lay motionless at her feet.

She may not know for sure, but now she had a way to find out, she just needed to find the one person who could help her. If he'd help her after all this time?

Turning she took a step, a single step. One moment there was solid ground beneath her feet the next she was falling, falling into a pitch-black void of nothingness. An abyss as dark as the pitch black of the deepest recesses of space. Falling without landing. Panic flared, she felt her eyes widen, her ribs compressed, and her lungs seized. She sucked in some much-needed air and the panic ebbed with the realization that she had oxygen and wasn't going to suffocate.

The darkness was infinite, yet suddenly she didn't feel like she was falling anymore. At that puzzling thought a heavy wave of fatigue engulfed her. Where was she? What was she doing here? Who was she?

Not yet, the time is not yet here, whispered a disembodied voice.

From one blink of her eyes to another, the deepest sleep claimed her.

PURE RAGE CONTORTED Gabriel's features, his almost too thin lips curled up in a savage snarl. Veins popped out at his temples, and his fingernails bit into his palms hard enough to draw blood. He dismissed everyone with a terse order, until only two remained, unmoving, silent and intent.

The meeting had not gone as he'd thought it would. He'd thought to throw Lucifer off his game, expose his weakening mind by having that little prank planted into that dipshit Dantalion's ear. But instead of being embarrassed by the cartoonish hair, the jackass still seemed to think of himself as the Almighty's personal gift to everyone. His snide remarks about Michael and pointed questions about the recent performance of the Shadow Hounds, all of his attempts to reveal Lucifer's unraveling sanity, had failed. Unfortunately, things had not panned out as he'd wanted.

His taunts and attempts to see Lucifer falter had fallen short, and now two members of the Praesidium were watching him with hard, assessing eyes. His inside man had assured him that the last sixty-nine years had taken their toll on the once wrathful ruler of Hell and that he'd slithered into hiding inside his own mind.

That was the plan after all. So, how did he keep managing to pull his shit together whenever Gabe had his own eyes and ears on him?

He pushed down his rage and blinding frustration and tried to focus on his 'guests'. Not that he'd actually invited them into his place. It was his place, no matter what those assholes kept inferring. Officially, it was Michael's still, but in all the ways that counted he ruled this place, and it was just a matter of time until the Almighty realized Michael was never coming back.

He'd made sure of it.

One prophecy, slightly twisted. They wouldn't believe how fucking easy it was to send Michael into a tailspin. All he'd had to do was whisper in one paranoid little ear and he'd gained so much control, so much power, and yet, it wasn't enough. What he'd wanted was respect. He knew now he'd never get it from those pathetic weasels Lucifer commanded, and it was no longer enough. He wanted them under his rule, kissing his booted feet, subjugated to his whims.

The Almighty seemed to be taking a step back, and he'd fill the vacuum. He had it all planned out. Lucifer would be tossed out, he'd place his own man in charge of the Hounds as a figurehead, in reality he'd command both armies of heaven, and collect *all* souls on earth. He'd decide where they went. Who was reborn. And they would obey him. He'd make it so.

That jackass had to bring up Jeanne though, didn't he? She'd been his, was meant to be his, and that slick bastard had defiled her, literally brought her to her knees, and stolen her affections away. He would have worshipped the ground she walked upon. He had adored the very air she'd breathed . . . Up until the moment he'd spied her betraying his love with his immortal enemy. He'd been content to share her with the human male, the king, until he'd secured her undying affections, but not Lucifer, never Lucifer.

Funny how fleeting Lucifer's interest had been once he'd attained his goal, once he'd stolen that which he, Gabriel, had coveted. No one had even remotely questioned her untimely death. A good thing, too, because if they'd looked too closely they'd have seen his mark. His temper had gotten the best of him that night, and he'd personally delivered her soul to the only well he had access to.

Reining in his wayward thoughts, Gabe straightened to his full height and canted his head toward the waiting interlopers.

"Well, never a dull moment with Lucifer, is there?" He paused for a chuckle, a wry grin, or an acknowledgment. Silence reigned. With a shrug, more to himself than to the humorless twats, he continued on.

"In what way can I assist you both? I'm not sure what purpose you have in visiting with us, but we will all do whatever it is we can, I assure you." He offered with a respectful nod.

Still, they studied him. What was he to make of this unexpected visit? Had he slipped up? What did they know? His brain whirled with possibilities, his thoughts unraveled as he ran through any errors he could have possibly made. All the same, his face remained passive, open, and questioning. He'd gotten good at slipping on a mask to hide his private thoughts. He'd made a deal with someone best not crossed to ensure that no one could read his thoughts or sniff out his intentions. Nor, in the case of those standing before him, dig up his past deeds from his memories alone. He was pretty sure that even the Almighty themself couldn't detect his deeds, neither then, now, or yet to come. And boy, did he have some doozies in the works. It was going to be a fun day in Hell one of these days . . . For him anyway.

"You may or may not be aware that we keep detailed records of all cases that come through our department, including the histories of those involved as they relate to each case?" The shorter, slightly balding of the two Jurors, Shamsiel was his name, said, drawing Gabe's wandering attention back to them.

"We haven't, until now, kept track of any banished angel or other ethereally created beings. Except, of course, for what their punishment, as ordained by the Almighty, entailed. It has been brought to our attention that the time may have come for us to rectify such a lapse in judgment. We have been requested to look into several banished angels and maintain awareness of their locations and general interactions. So far none of those beings have been ones who were sent to the Realm of Nightmares, of rot and ruin, death and decay. I'm sure you are most likely aware that those who enter Nestradia never leave?" he added. Gabe was sure he heard a note of warning in the angel's tone.

The other angel said nothing. Taller than the first, Ramiel was also wider and more intimidating. Menace radiated from his shrewd eyes. He was an angel of many talents. One with even more secrets. The head of the Praesidium always seemed to know things no one else could ever know. A trait he shared with Caine, except there was something more to Ramiel, something no one liked to dwell on long enough to figure out. His gaze bored a hole through Gabriel, at least to him it felt that way.

"And that brings you to our door. Why?" Shaking himself out of his musings, his tone seemed almost hostile, though he'd managed to rein it in by the barest amount as it left his lips, even as his eyes gleamed with a calculated hardness he hoped neither of them noticed.

"We will need to look through all personnel records of those no longer under your command, including those before you took command, as temporary as it currently is. Rest assured, we will be doing the same with the Shadow Hounds," Ramiel rumbled, his voice was gruff and raspy as though he hadn't used it in decades.

"Again, what are you hoping to find? As you said, you already keep track of all information pertaining to their cases. So, what do you hope to find?" Gabe pressed, knowing he had to tread with care. He watched as Ramiel's full lips twitched, and his eyes glowed a light gold.

"There have been . . . reports of suspicious interactions with banished individuals and active angels. A direct violation of protocol, unless explicitly sanctioned." Ramiel paused, for effect Gabe was sure.

"Accordingly, it is our duty to investigate each and every accusation and/or suspicious circumstance. In accordance with that, we will actually need access to all personnel records; past and current. Also, we have complete authority to access all areas of this compound and question any person we deem of interest. All teams, no matter how involved in the day to day they may be." He finished, a full-fledged smirk on his brutal features. His teeth flashed white like the predator he absolutely was.

Gabe felt sweat slide down his spine and coat his palms. Shit. Fuck. How the fuck was this happening? He was always careful. He had no leaks, of that he was sure. It was even more imperative to tread carefully. His contacts would need to lie low, and he'd have to back off his plans for a while. After calling Denario into the room, he turned back to his pesky guests.

"I understand. You will have the full cooperation of all angels under my command and access to any area of the facilities that you need. Denario will be your guide and help you in any way you need while you are here. Although, I do request that should you need to enter the rooms or private facilities of any of the females herein, please notify Denario. We have a policy of no males entering those facilities while they are in use. If a female is to be questioned or their rooms inspected, another angel of her choice is to be present. Such has always been the protocol, but reminders never hurt." With a nod to Denario, he introduced them and instructed his lackey to assist them.

"If you would excuse me, gentlemen, I still have a lot to do today." With a half bow, he turned on his heels and headed to the doors. He only made it two steps before turning his head back to them.

"I would appreciate it if you could share any pertinent information with me once you have finished your investigation here. If any of my Reapers are involved, I need to know. I'm sure you understand steps would need to be taken to ensure it doesn't happen again, yes?" With that he walked with haughty assurance out the door, striding toward his private office, one last phone call to make before it was too late.

THE CALL HAD BEEN EXPECTED. Dreaded more like it. Things had not gone the way Gabe had envisioned. Hadn't gone the way he'd expected them to either. It wasn't his fault Gabe had failed to highlight Lucifer's deterioration. His intel had been good. He had no idea what had happened between then and now. What he did know was that he'd probably get reamed in four . . . three . . . two . . . one.

Drawing in a deep breath he hit the answer button and Gabe's face appeared on the magically enhanced, untraceable human cell phone. Whatever he'd thought would happen . . . He'd been wrong.

Gabe's face was pale. More pale than normal, and that's saying something for someone who gave white chalk a run for its money on a good day. He looked clammy, and his hushed and whispered words passed through barely moving lips on a tidal wave of panic.

"Cease all activities until further notice. Put the word out to all operatives. The Praesidium has eyes and ears everywhere. Soon they will be on your doorstep too. For the time being, all plans are on hold. Cover your asses and hope to the high heavens you all cover mine, or you won't like the consequences."

The line disconnected with a click that sounded loud in the silence of his room and left a sour taste on his tongue. The Praesidium . . . His hand clenched around the device still clasped within it, hard. The dust of what remained drifted to the floor as he relaxed. Luckily the cell phone was the only physical evidence of his involvement. Still, the reality of his situation was filtering through the thrill of the game and the haze that always hung behind his eyes.

CHAPTER 7

The moment Azaroth entered the room lightning sizzled up and down Athon's spine. If he didn't know better he'd think his rainbow mohawk had lit up like a tree at Christmas. It hurt to look at the male across the room from him, feelings flooded him with an intensity he could never deny, but it hurt so much more to look away.

Once upon a time they'd been so much more than what they'd become. They'd loved so hard, so completely, but they both knew they'd been missing something. Some indefinable piece of the puzzle, yet they'd been so determined to make it work. Then, Athon had run across Mara, and she'd seemed like the answer, the piece that might make their puzzle whole. What a royal fuck up that had been. Her name meant female wrath and bitterness, and she'd taken that and ran with it. She'd torn Azaroth apart and stomped on Athon's hopes and love until they'd both crumbled. Neither left with a piece fit for any puzzle for a very long time.

Hundreds of years had passed since then. Athon had rebuilt himself, always holding the love he had for Azaroth within, waiting for him to realize they still had each other . . . And still he waited.

About eight years ago Roth had changed again. No matter what they tried, he'd brushed them off again and again. It felt like history repeating.

The angry outbursts, the withdrawal from the team, the weird behavior . . . only milder, less, yet so similar to how Luc had returned to them all those years ago.

Speaking of Luc. Dante's little prank had helped break the mood and lifted him out of his own head. He was in for some major retribution though. About time too. Dante tended to get away with his pranks and juvenile shit far too often. It was so fucking good to see Luc simply be Luc again. Watching Roth smile, his eyes sparkling, his kissable lips parted on the cusp of a heartfelt laugh . . . Thinking on it, his tongue played with the ring through the right side of his lower lip and his cock hardened. The last time he'd had the pleasure of Azaroth's company his own body had been free of piercings and art. He knew that Roth had some of his own. He didn't know what though as Roth had kept his distance and Athon avoided temptation as much as he could. God, what he'd give for the chance to explore that male's body again. Relearn every hard plane, discover every difference . . .

He'd have to thank the little shit later, his friend had done so well in bringing two of his favorite people such a moment of lighthearted joy.

Throughout the meeting with Gabe, Athon's eyes never wavered from Roth's face. Gabe could go screw himself if he thought he'd show the prejudiced asshole any respect. He was an intolerant prick who'd made it very clear as to what he thought of his and Roth's relationship when he'd found out. Fucking hypocrite. Like he hadn't caught him with his pants down a time or two in a less than hetero scenario. Probably why he glared at Athon with jealous envy and hatred whenever their paths had crossed. Like he gave a shit how Gabe got his dick wet as long as it had nothing to do with him, Roth, or anyone he cared about. He wouldn't want Gabriel near any decent being.

Funny that Luc had brought up Jeannie though, considering Gabe and his proclivities had extended far beyond just the king's mistress, even if he post-justified it as a way to secure the lady in question. Kinda made you feel sorry for the guy, until you realized what an all around asshat he'd always been.

Finally, the farce of a meeting was over, soon they'd be dismissed, and he could watch Roth's ass as he strode from the room. Honestly, some of the best moments of his life in the last few centuries had centered around watching and thinking about that ass and those 'let me fuck you' eyes. Except, a new report flashed up on the screen, and for the first time since the meeting had started Athon's gaze left Roth and focussed on the viewscreen. Roth's gasp and the sound of snapping wood put him on immediate alert. Something major was about to go down.

The screen went black and Luc seemed to calm somewhat. Roth dropped his head into his hands and ran agitated fingers through his hair before looking up and staring blankly over Athon's shoulder. Seriously, what the fuck was up with that anyway? Roth's words looked like they were lodged in his throat and Luc's jovial prodding shocked them all. It also put them all on alert. Because maybe, just maybe, it could be that bad.

Roth inhaled deeply before the words spilled from his mouth, leaving Athon's hanging open. What he said was baffling and yet made so much sense. He informed them about a mysterious pale woman with killer red hair and gray eyes from a random alley eight years ago. The zap he felt as her arm brushed his. Athon's brain tripped over the details. Roth was feeling again, about a woman . . . Not the same as he'd felt for Athon, but equally as intense. Where did that leave him? What did it mean?

"She gave me a message to pass on. One I decided not to, not until I could figure out who or what she is. I didn't want her messing with the head of anyone I consider family." Roth paused, his gaze locked with Luc's. "I'm sorry I didn't deliver it sooner. The whole situation threw me for a loop."

"Better late than not at all," came Luc's breathless response as his body coiled tighter.

"I guess since it took me this long I better do it the way she requested then. She said to tell my 'Boss Man' "We'll meet again"."

With that said, Roth's melodious voice started crooning the most popular song from earth's second world war. Not a single eye remained dry, except Caine's, but that fucker never cried.

Luc had silent tears streaming down his face as he fell to his knees. No one dared to move. Having started talking, Roth couldn't seem to stop until it was all out, apparently there was more.

"I couldn't find her, or any information about her. It's like she just . . . up and disappeared." He took another deep breath, eyeing everyone in the room. He wasn't the only one whose spine seemed to straighten either. Oh shit. What was coming next?

Roth rushed on, and holy fuck! Roth had dreams? Not just in black and white, like the foretelling of the souls they have to take, the ones they all experienced as part of their job. Those are more like daydreams sometimes anyway. Not the full surround sound, full color, cinematic experiences he was describing, even if he only dreamed of this one mystery woman.

From the flush that heated Roth's cheekbones it was plain to Athon that the dreams were way more than PG and that she affected him deeply. It explained so fucking much. His retreat from them all, all those nights at the clubs, his lack of interest in anyone else. He knew Roth still desired him, but even that had seemed to wane the last few years as his distraction and moodiness increased. What did it all mean?

Luc's breath hitched sharply before it quickened to big, deep, aggressive inhales, almost animalistic in quality. Everyone present felt the change, the tension which suddenly filled the room. Everyone except Roth . . . He was so caught up in finally getting it all out that he didn't see what it was doing to Luc until it was too late.

The effect this woman had on Roth was clearly written on his face and in his voice. As his mouth opened to say something else, Luc's shadows burst free, slamming Roth up against the wall roughly, until his feet dangled above the floor. Luc moved faster than he could track, even with his angel sight. Before they knew it he was pulling an in-your-face, to the point they could have been making out. His hand wrapped like steel around Roth's throat, cutting off whatever he'd been about to say.

Wings, larger than any others, sprung from his back to wrap around them. The sharply horned tips which protruded at the upper points pierced the wall on either side of Roth's head. Luc's wings and shadows formed a cocoon-like barrier, a very scary one considering the aggression and barely restrained violence he was exhibiting.

Athon could feel hot breath heating his cheek. No, Roth felt it, but he felt it too, along with the weight of a hand upon his throat. Taking a deep breath he threw off the once familiar bond they'd shared and came back unto himself. He heard Luc snarl, noticed him tighten his grip on Roth's trachea, and saw his shadows act as shackles to Roth's wrists and ankles, spreading them wide. One shadowy tendril slid between his legs and seemed to harden like steel on the underside of Roth's manly attributes, suddenly the threat became so much more real.

Athon didn't know what he'd done or said, he hadn't even realized he'd moved, but from one moment to the next he found both Fynn and Malech were holding him back, barely. Wild noises escaped him, until Fynn shoved a shadow gag in his mouth and hogtied him to the floor.

"MINE!"

The barely recognizable voice of their General snarled in Roth's ear, echoing through the room, probably through the whole fortress. This was the Lucifer the humans feared, this was the mighty warrior who destroyed the evil doers of all realms.

"You don't touch what is mine. Understood? We find her together, but she is mine, and only I dream of her, only I have her. Or you die!" The red glow of primal rage and jealousy from Luc's eyes backlit the room from between them before Roth was abruptly released, his ass hit the floor with a thud.

In the blink of an eye Caine and Deus had Luc hidden behind a wall of muscle, backs to Roth, voices low and strong.

Malech's shadows released Athon, allowing him and Perri to rush to Roth's side, he slid on his knees the last few feet in his haste. His hands touched every inch of his ex-lover that they could reach. Checking for damage, searching for reassurance that nothing was broken, and Roth, in his shock, allowed it, maybe even welcomed it. Perri checked his vitals. While angels couldn't really die by mortal standards, certain angels did possess the power to end an angel's physical existence, Lucifer being one of them, and they could still be gravely injured. Becoming an angelic vegetable was not what any of them wanted to be.

What the fuck just happened? What in Hell's name had just crawled up Lucifer's ass and laid an egg? Never had he been anything other than a friend to them all. The guy could be straight up sadistic when he wanted to be—one crazy assed motherfucker—but never toward them. They were family. Siblings by choice. Sure, they bickered, but holy fuck, never like that.

Roth's forehead dropped onto Athon's chest as he coughed between gasping breaths.

"Maybe that wasn't my brightest idea." Was all that managed to pass between his lips before he slumped forward and passed the fuck out.

***

They'd moved Roth to the private room attached to the meeting room. Nobody but those already present needed to see him in such a vulnerable state, and the fewer questions the better. Caine and Deus had managed to calm down Lucifer. Well, at least he wasn't raging out, so that was a plus.

The others had left Roth to rest while Athon remained to keep an eye on him. For the first time in centuries he was alone with the angel of his dreams, pun intended considering what had just gone down.

Athon watched Roth's relaxed face and lovingly traced the contours of his body under the tight-fitting black shirt and denim jeans, studded leather cuffs on each wrist . . . He refused to think about what lay hidden beneath them, even if the cuffs themselves were sexy as fuck.

Leaning back in the chair against the wall he allowed his eyes to hood as his skin began to heat, his pulse quickened, breath coming faster. He could see Roth was in a similar state but couldn't fathom why. At least Athon had a reason, he thought, as he looked at the object of his abject desire.

Glancing down at Roth's denim covered groin he couldn't help but notice the straining seams, the rigid length trying to break through the thick material . . . He licked his lips to stop the drool escaping. Athon's pulse kicked into overdrive. Needing an excuse to touch him, he hurried over to check Roth's temperature, his hand made gentle contact with warm skin. A feeling unlike any other had him elbows to the mattress before he could think a single, rational thought. Behind his eyelids, that were all but glued shut, he saw what must be Roth's dream, except now it was his dream too.

The naked beauty reclining before them was breathtakingly sensual, from her dark red hair, her piercing and unusual gray eyes, all the way down to her lightly muscled, yet shapely calves. She was laid out on a bed, eyes at half-mast, looking at Roth like he was her last meal before the whole world ended, when she noticed they weren't alone anymore.

"Well, this is new." Her husky voice possessed an almost purr-like quality. "And who might you be, handsome?" After a silent pause she continued with a sigh, "No need to answer, it's okay, the big guy never speaks either. Pretty sure he wants to, though. And by the look in his eyes, you guys are already well acquainted." Her eyes slid over him, like liquid heat caressing every inch of his tall body.

"Love the hair, like my own rainbow to happiness. It's definitely a sight I'd love to see between my thighs. The things I could do to the both of you. The things you two could do to me." Her voice was like honeyed scotch, invading his every breath, every cell in his body.

Positioned as he was, he had a clear view of both Roth and the luscious piece of ass on the bed, and he could see their desire as plain as day. Roth's rock hard cock had made its way free of his button fly. Her glistening pussy was exposed to both of them; the scent of her arousal filled the room. Glancing from Roth's suddenly naked body to his own, he found his own cock standing at attention, out and proud.

Her moans filled his ears, and his head snapped up. Her fingers delved between those slick folds, her eyes moving between the two men before her, the sound of her desire increasing, breathy whimpers falling from her plump pink lips, while her other lips damn near drowned the sheets.

Watching her pleasure herself was a sight he'd not soon forget. Watching Roth stroking his large, thick cock as he watched them both find their own pleasure made his balls draw up, threatening to spill his load sooner than he wanted. His fingers circled the base, above his balls, and squeezed hard in an effort to delay what would soon be inevitable.

Her back arched off the bed, her breasts thrust upwards, hard, pert nipples begged to be licked and sucked. Like puppets, they were pulled forward until each male was beside her. Her mystical eyes flashed heated flames of lust at them, offering herself up to be devoured, an offering they gladly took advantage of.

Athon's tongue flicked out, swirling around the sweet, pink nipple, a stark contrast to her soft, pale skin and their tanned, firm forms. Roth read his mind, and, as one, they licked and nibbled every inch of her bountiful chest, one hand stroking her hair. They caressed their free hands down over her slightly curved stomach and over her hips. Gliding down to her knees and back up behind her thighs, tracing the curve of what promised to be a killer ass. Lifting their heads they glanced at their seductress before locking eyes and twining their fingers together. Her whimpers became mewling prayers for more as Roth and Athon leaned in. Instead of returning to her beautiful body their lips came together in a kiss full of pent-up want and broken restraint as their joined hands descended on her sodden pussy. Two hands, two sets of fingers used as one, they danced over her clit and thrust deep inside her heated core, what would have been two fingers . . . Now four . . . With a shout of ecstasy, her tight heat convulsed around their fingers as their tongues dueled, her ecstasy becoming theirs as they came, long and hard, over her still shuddering torso.

CHAPTER 8

Holy shit! That was one heck of a wet dream and a half. The new guy, with the tatts, piercings, and a gorgeous rainbow mohawk, was a surprise, considering she'd been dreaming of the other one for eight years now, and no one else. But her original dream guy had totally seemed up to it. They both had. The kiss they'd shared, and the combination of their fingers plunging into her wet pussy, had her panties flooded, or would have if she'd been wearing any. Which she apparently wasn't. Peeling her sweat slicked body away from the satin sheets Ballzy insisted on providing, she glanced about and found her clothes tossed willy-nilly on the floor around the bed.

Standing, she felt the cool glide of wetness trickle between her breasts and down her stomach, and she froze. Nope, just sweat from the extremely sexy dream. Absolutely, that had to be it. Despite the sweet scent of cum filling her nose that called her a liar. To believe otherwise just added a whole new level of utter batshit weird to her already fucked up situation.

A glance at the window to her cell revealed Balthazar's lust filled gaze locked on her. One hand fisting his rigid length through his pants. Great, how long had he watched her this time while she'd tossed and turned on the bed dreaming of those two hotties? Glancing back at the completely ruined sheets, she caught a glimpse of her flushed body in the mirror . . .

Fuck! She was still naked! Glaring in his direction again she gave him the middle finger salute and made a dash for the bathroom. His low, rough chuckle followed her walk of shame, even if it was more of a run than a walk.

Closing the door and starting the shower she climbed straight in, allowing the cool water to sluice over her heated skin. Her face tilted up, wetting her from head to toe, her hair plastered to her back, the ends teasing over the rounded curves of her ass. Jezzie slid her hand down over her breasts and stomach. Her other hand froze halfway to the lily scented soap Ballzy gave her no choice but to use.

Shit! The telltale squeaky feel of cum and water on her skin left no doubt. Lifting her fingers, she inhaled the uniquely male scent, her tongue darted out without conscious thought and licked her palm. Just her freaking luck. Super hot dream guys with real life consequences.

Finishing up in the shower she made up her mind to ignore what had just happened and continue her plan for the day. Piss off Ballzy and do as much recon as she could. Over the years she'd gathered bits and pieces of information about the asshat's operation, but there was something he was hiding, and Jezzie was determined to figure it out.

Thankfully her clothing was kept in a closet attached to the bathroom. By the time she was dressed, in the least revealing outfit she could find, thank you, Balthazar, she'd also donned her implacable 'take no shit' bitch face and was ready to face him. It was the best she could do when the need to conserve her shadow energy was paramount, otherwise she'd have walked out of there looking like a completely different person. Fortunately that little trick was something he didn't know she was capable of . . . yet.

Striding out into the fray expectantly she came to a sudden halt as she realized he'd fucking left already. Instead of the defensive fight reflex fading away her anger spiked. She'd been ready to raise hell, and he just walked away? Screw that.

Her 'cell' was always left unlocked, not like she could go anywhere or anything. The demons didn't live here, just worked in the place, so they didn't have to worry about her gutting them in their sleep, no matter how many times she'd fantasized about it, and she wasn't about to let slip her little power storing ability anytime soon either.

As she pushed through the door and took in the hallway, she had to admit the place wasn't what she'd expected when she'd first arrived. The decor was very gothic, but in a beautiful, rich, and plush kind of way. Not that emo goth thing that modern day humans embraced, but the dark timbers and velvets, the finely crafted furnishings, and overall feel of luxury.

Balthazar had mentioned that he'd made all of the furniture by hand himself, apparently he was at least as old as the actual era judging from how he spoke about the comforts of a home he'd once had. It was a rare moment where his mask had slipped, the real Balthazar shone through, and she'd seen the sadness haunting his eyes. It'd been quickly replaced with his usual arrogance though, and she'd been left wondering who Balthazar really was. Until the next round of interrogation had started, that is. Then he'd been firmly entrenched in asshole status once again.

He was so determined to unravel the mystery of what she was. He seemed to think she posed a threat to something, or someone. She had no fucking idea what threat she could pose, really. From the rare occasions her mother had spoken of her father it had all revolved around how they met, why she needed to stay hidden, and who he was. She never really talked about his powers or how they would manifest in her, a hybrid. She felt more power simmering under her skin than what she could currently use, but as yet couldn't access it. And it really was starting to piss her off that she felt so helpless here.

What pissed her off far more was that Ballzy seemed to think it was okay to get off while watching her sleep, and fuck ghostly dream men in said sleep. It wasn't the first time she'd woken to find him observing her. As if he thought she'd spill her secrets while she slept. Like fucking hell she would. First thing her mother and aunt had taught her to do was shield that shit, plus the secret keeper spell the witches had placed on her, until her powers completely came out hadn't hurt, and was still in place until her full manifestation was complete, whenever that would be.

The spell essentially put a mind block on her so no one could read her thoughts or force/coerce information out of her related to her parentage, powers, or species. It also meant she couldn't reveal said info to those not already privy to it. As a child it had made sure she never accidentally slipped up, probably a very good thing too as she'd liked to talk . . . A lot. So, even if she wanted to tell him what he wanted to know, she couldn't, not yet.

Well the fucker had a shock coming his way. She was done with his shit, and there was no way he and his little demons were using her as the star attraction in his little fucked up torture zoo anymore.

Making her way along the hallway to his office at the end, said demons scurried away when they saw her. One even retreated to the room they were leaving and slammed the door in fright. As she came to the solid walnut double doors and paused to collect her fiery temper, lest it get the best of her, she contemplated the best entrance strategy. Did she kick in the door? Shove it open, arms spread wide? Use a touch of power from her shadows? Or go stealthy? Deciding she was pissed off enough that she definitely needed to bring the drama, she lifted her booted foot and slammed it into the hard doors. The hard, locked doors. And promptly found herself flat on her generous ass, with a lovely view of the ceiling.

Looking back at the doors with a glare she found they had been opened, and the current reigning douche bag of her ire lazily leaned against the jamb, ankles crossed and hands in the pockets of his finely tailored trousers. Amusement ran rife over his features, even as he tried to hold it in.

"Next time you're in a snit, luv," he drawled sarcastically, his eyes sparkling. "Try to remember the doors are solid hardwood." He turned to go back to his desk but paused and looked back, nodding toward each of the two doors.

"Also, they open outwards. So kicking them in doesn't do a fucking thing." At the last part he used his powers to close said doors as his full on belly laugh reached her crimson stained ears. With anger, she told herself, never embarrassment, not around him. Never around him.

Jumping to her feet she pulled the doors open and walked in like she owned the place. Hmm, maybe one day she would. See how he liked it when she took everything away from him. Maybe she'd keep him in a gilded cage and make him her pet. Feed from his feelings and his soul, little by little, until there was nothing left but a dried out husk of what he currently was. But, did she really want to be like him? To go down that rabbit hole and possibly lose even more of herself?

He obviously hadn't been expecting her to follow him in. Probably thought she'd tuck tail and run, licking her wounds before coming back for round two. And she would've, before, but something had changed within her in the last twenty-four hours. She was done taking all the shit that was being piled on her. She felt stronger. Not her powers, or her shadows, not even anything to do with feeding, well, maybe she'd dreamed of the feelings Mr tall, dark, and handsome, and his sexy mohawked friend had felt, but that didn't count, right? Shaking her head she got back on track and out of her thoughts. Her inner strength felt more grounded, her walls fortified.

Ballzy was standing at a large bay window which overlooked the purple haze of the meadow outside, his eyes downcast and focussed on the photo frame cradled within his hands. It seemed too delicate and fragile to be in the hands of the monster she knew him to be. Her curiosity piqued, she crept forward on silent feet, thank fuck for plush carpet. She made it ten steps, catching a glimpse of honey blonde hair and baby blue eyes, before he slipped the frame face down onto the desk and turned to face her so fast she nearly landed on her ass again. His face was deliberately blank, no emotion at all, his mask firmly in place.

"Who's that, Balthazar?" Using his name felt so weird, after all this time, but he wouldn't have expected it. She knew she should leave it alone, but she was tired of being careful. She needed leverage to get out of here and away from him before he discovered who and what she was. It was too dangerous for him to have that information. He was a loose cannon who worked for the other side, as far as she could tell. Too many shady people passed through the doors of the club for it to be any other way. Still, he had secrets, and she vowed to herself she'd find out his, before he found out hers.

"No one, luv, not anymore. A long-lost dream best left in the past," was his emotionless reply. Not even a raised brow at the use of his name. Odd, and yet he betrayed that lack of feeling by turning to lock the picture into his desk drawer.

With Ballzy distracted Jezzie took the chance to scan the surface of his desk. Three things jumped out at her, digging their way into her brain to be puzzled out later.

1. A message from G, something about going dark and the Praesidium.
2. A meeting was set up for the following week with someone named R.
3. The meeting had something to do with her. As evidenced by the swirly J in a circle that Ballzy had written next to it. This was the same sign he'd placed on her door to indicate her quarters.

By the time he looked back at her she'd schooled her features and gave away no indication that she'd been looking anywhere other than at him. She watched as his shoulders visibly relaxed and he indicated for her to take a seat on the other side of the large ostentatious desk.

Her mind flashed to the men of her dreams, she wished she had names for them other than Hottie One and Hottie Two, and what they could do both on and over a desk of that size. Not Ballzy's though, that thing probably needed so much disinfectant to make it sanitary that it was probably easier to burn it and get a new one. She must have been staring at the desk for a while, cheeks getting warmer with each naughty thought and scenario that popped into her overactive imagination, because when she looked up, straight into his eyes, he was studying her with a smirk. The fucker even had the audacity to freaking wink at her. Which only made her squirm in her seat and turn a brighter shade of pink.

"Have a good sleep, luv?" His voice was off somehow, not quite as taunting as normal maybe, she couldn't quite place it. Like he didn't really have it in him at the moment to play his usual games with her.

"It was lovely, actually," she sassed back. This different side of Ballzy scared her a little. She wouldn't admit it to him, of course, but like this, she didn't know what to expect from him, and it made her feel even more out of control. And she needed to control these interactions as much as she could.

"It sure as hell looked like fun from where I was standing, luv." He twisted the little knife that was poking at her annoyance already, and she couldn't help but rise to the bait, even as she knew he was deliberately distracting her from what she'd seen. Good thing she had an excellent memory.

"That's another thing. I want fucking curtains for my window. It's getting beyond creepy. Come on, dude, you really have to resort to getting your jollies off watching sleeping women enjoy a good dream fuck?" she bit out at him snarkily, her eyes flashing with ire.

"Ah, but that's the thing, isn't it, luv? We both know there's more to it than just a dream, now isn't there?" came his smooth reply. His gaze scanned her curiously, as though assessing what she knew.

"I don't know what you mean, Balthazar," she was quick to respond, but the flush on her cheeks gave her away.

"Hmm," he drawled. "And I suppose the ropes of jizz I saw coating your torso were just figments of my deviant imagination? Or maybe the sight of your pussy gaping open, as though being plundered by an invisible force, as you undulated with desire and came so hard. I've already got maids changing your puddled sheets. Was that all in my head too, luv?" he sarcastically taunted.

Fuck, she hadn't known about that part. Shit, he'd seen way more than she'd suspected. No wonder he'd been stroking himself behind the glass.

"Whoever it is you are meeting on the Astral Plane, he's a lucky man, luv," Ballzy interrupted her chaotic thoughts.

"They definitely seem to be, whoever they are," she retorted. "What do you mean the Astral Plane?" She hated having to ask Balthazar for information. It was an admission that she didn't know as much as him, and it stung like the dickens to allow him to know that too.

"It's not common, and usually it's a conscious choice to visit the Astral Plane, a meeting usually needs planning, precautions, and to enter a very deep sleep. You've had no opportunities to do those things. Unless you're fucking some of my demons?" At the emphatic shaking of her head he continued, "Hmm, I didn't think so. In that case, I reluctantly concede. Wooing you is no longer a priority, and given your complete and utter disgust with my advances, I've taken the liberty of changing tactics. Unfortunately, luv, as we've already discussed multiple times over the years, you entered my Den under suspicious circumstances and I have certain clandestine activities that I'd rather keep quiet. You, my dear, are too great a mystery to let loose, too great an unknown threat as it were. So tell me what I need to know and you might just walk out of here early. That's not too hard, is it, luv?"

"You've got more luck getting a decent ride on a full blooded demon's dick than getting any info that you could use against me, luv," she tartly snapped out.

"You know, I was kind of hoping you'd say that. It's always more fun to pull the answers out than to be handed them on a silver platter." His smirk didn't quite reach his eyes this time though. Ballzy was looking decidedly tired and something was obviously bothering him.

"As for your previous request, yes, you'll get your 'fucking curtains', as you so eloquently put it. They will be installed as soon as they can be prepared." With that he turned his back on her and once again gazed out over the purple haze of the meadow below.

Jezzie felt like a schoolgirl dismissed by the principal as she stood and huffed her way toward the door, her head spinning with her conflicting thoughts, and her emotions a rollercoaster of anger and confusion. Just as her hand touched the handle of one door his voice froze her to the spot. Turning, she saw he spoke without bothering to look back at her.

"Oh, and get some rest. We have a guest arriving next week. He has some very special talents and he's going to help me get information from a very hard nut I'm having trouble cracking. By any means necessary. And he'll be bringing along a friend for you. Someone to keep you company." His tone was once again cold and hard. Jezzie inhaled sharply.

"I wouldn't expect anything less from you, Ballzy. And here I thought we'd made progress getting out the viper stuck up your ass." She verbally tossed at him before striding out of the room, making sure to keep her stride calm and even until she reached the relative sanctuary of her room.

CHAPTER 9

Luc's head spun as the red haze of rage and jealousy faded from his vision. He watched as Roth's knees buckled, and he fell into Athon's arms. Fynn had come up beside him to help the shell-shocked male lift his former lover, as Perri ran for the door to the side room. He registered it all with the eye of one watching an enemy with suspicion, his teeth still on edge, his body primed for action as adrenaline still pumped through his veins.

Caine and Deus held his biceps in a hold so tight he knew he'd have bruises before nightfall. He shifted, indicating they could release him now, but instead of doing so Andy and Marco stepped right in front of him. Blocking his view of the men carrying his target from the room.

Fuck! What the fuck was wrong with him? Roth wasn't his target. They were brothers and sisters in arms and bonded by their friendship and duty.

Deep down, he knew. He'd known the first time he'd spied her across the room of that dance hall in Chicago. He'd known that without her all hope was lost, all purchase in reality would be clutched to with a desperately tenuous grip. He wasn't the leader he should be. Her love was his greatest victory, her loss his spiral to insanity . . .

His eyes locked on her as if she were the stars on a cloudless night that couldn't be ignored. She seemed so radiant, as if eating up the energy of the room. The servicemen dancing with the pretty ladies decked out in their best dresses, hair rolled and pinned in place to perfection. The worries of tomorrow were lost in the joys of the night before them.

She was absolutely stunning, she outshone them all, and he couldn't look away. As if sensing his interest her gaze snapped to him, her lips parted slightly as she took him in. He wasn't going to lie. He was pretty well put together and had never had trouble attracting—well, anyone he'd wanted really.

The moment her pupils dilated he made his way to her side, the crowd parted as if by magic, he wasn't ashamed to say he'd had a hand in it either, or rather his shadows had sought the outcome of their own volition. Seeing as how they were invisible to humans unless otherwise needed.

They'd had the most amazing week together. Wrapped up in a cocoon of fantastic sex and witty banter. His shadows had rejoiced at her touch, and for the first time he'd felt complete. He hadn't even known there was anything missing in his existence, and yet she'd filled the empty places in his soul.

He'd had to leave, head back to the fortress briefly once that week had ended, with every intention to return in a day or two. He left a note and a single black tulip upon her pillow.

If he'd known it would all turn to shit, he never would have left her there like that. He would have come back sooner, fuck the consequences. Of course, he'd not made it back for another two weeks. It was as if the Fates themselves had meddled with shit just to keep him away. When he'd finally knocked on that unassuming powder blue door, and it had moved inwards at the light touch, his heart had fallen to his toes.

The pretty little human, whose eyes had burrowed into the deepest parts of him, lay in pieces on the living room floor. Glassy eyes so far removed from what they'd been before. For the first time in his existence he'd said hello to his breakfast twice in one day at the sight of such gore and mutilation, he roared his pain and agony to the heavens. He'd forced his way into the Almighty's inner circle and demanded justice, only to be turned away with pitying glances. A crime committed by human hands didn't fall into their purview, especially one they could find no trace of . . .

He'd left in anger, determined to show them his torment. He'd show them traces, he'd bring every part of her, every print, and every speck of blood to them. He'd lay out the image of her death at their feet and ask which human had misstepped so egregiously. He'd demand their name, and he'd take their soul to torture for the rest of his eternal life.

Except, as his booted feet once more crossed the threshold of a place that'd held such wondrous joy, but that now left the taste of ashes on his tongue, he found . . . Nothing. Everything was perfectly in place. Perfectly empty and devoid of life and even death did not linger there. Even the plants she'd so lovingly tended and that he'd glanced at earlier, so green and full of life, were nothing more than dried out husks, quickly turning to dust in the air. With heaving breaths he tried to reconcile the two images now warring in his head as he searched high and low and found nothing, not even a strand of her hair remained.

Her neighbors, whom he'd seen her speak to more than once, claimed the house had been uninhabited for years. All he knew was she was gone, as if she'd never even been real and was just some jack-off fantasy gone wrong.

DEUS COULDN'T HELP WONDERING what in the ever loving fucking love triangle bullshit was up with Luc and Roth? Not to mention the way Athon had stared at Roth with such longing. The poor bastard was still hung up on the stubborn idiot. More so than any of them had probably realized. Anyone with half a brain could see the total love and devotion Athon felt for the guy, and once upon a time Roth had, without reservation, felt the same way.

Noting the others watching him as he held onto Luc's arm as the male snarled and twisted in his fight to be set free, he saw the same sadness and confusion on their faces. The same determination and resolve as well. Whereas anyone else with any sense of self-preservation would be running away with their tails tucked between their legs from what was essentially the Devil himself, they stood as one, ready and willing to fight for their leader, to hold his demons at bay and fight him if need be. Deus didn't have the sense the Almighty gave him as he nodded his head and prepared to take the Devil by the horns, not when it came to his brothers and sisters, his comrades. Not when it came to Luc. The male had saved his ass so many times and pulled his nuts out of the fire. He'd saved them all at some point.

When Ares stepped up to take the arm he was gripping Deus was a little surprised to say the least, normally he was the last to get with the touchy-touchy, and holding tight to Luc was requiring a lot of body contact. It was a sign of how much the guy respected and cared for their General and how far he was willing to go to figure out the cluster-fuck of a situation Luc was in. That they were all in now. He felt like a fucking Musketeer just thinking it. Whatever was going on though clearly revolved around that redhead from the viewscreen. Once this current situation was rectified, they'd really have to focus on finding the bitch who'd brought this shit storm to their doorstep.

With a deep, calming breath Deus released Luc's arm into Ares' capable care and stepped in front of their unraveling leader and prepared to take whatever hits were needed if this didn't work. Which it might not, considering he'd never had to use his voice on such an enraged and primal Lucifer before.

As he came out of his mental wanderings Luc found a set of red ringed white irises playing a game of 'up close and personal' with his. Deus's voice registered as a far off lilt, rushing up like a freight train until he damn well covered his ears and reared back from the incredibly loud motherfucker screaming in his face.

"What the ever loving fuck has crawled up your ass, General? Keep acting like you did with Azaroth, and you'll find that's the only fucking title you'll have. Take your head out of your ass and rein in the fucking shadows."

Luc's jaw dropped, the usually mild-mannered gentleman of the group was up in his grill like a wrestler on fight night. Admittedly the guy hated being ignored and his loyalty bordered on obsession. Nobody ignored Deus, it was almost impossible to do so, he was a very compelling guy, one of his gifted talents was compulsion. Which meant

Luc was more fucked up than he'd thought if he was so far gone that the dude was in his face to this extent.

Luc's shoulders dropped and his eyes reflected the regret he felt deep in his marrow. He felt his shadows riding him, trying to lash out as they sought to protect her, claim her, find her, but he pushed them back into the 'bottle' within himself.

Looking to his left he found his arm still pinned in place, muscles straining. Caine looked bored and was barely breaking a sweat, but with the amount of hours the guy logged in the gym and in combat training that was hardly a surprise. Looking to his right he saw that at some point Ares had taken over from Deus to allow him to sing the song of a very fucked off metal head. Ares looked slightly less comfortable holding onto Luc. The guy hated physically touching others, absolutely detested it. He refused to speak of it, but Luc knew the bare basics, and even those made his toes curl back to his ankles and his spine want to exit his body along with the contents of his stomach. That he was holding tight to Luc like a drowning man to a flotation device told Luc more than anything how much he'd fucked up. His team, his soldiers, but more importantly his truest friends were fucking terrified. Not of him, but for him.

Looking back at Deus he saw the sheer defeat and fear he felt reflected in the male's glistening eyes. Deus leaned his forehead against his, and as he did he found his arms free and his body surrounded by the warmth of Deus's. His clean woodsy scent filled Luc's nose and a sense of calm, a calm only Deus could manage in such a storm of swirling emotions, came over him.

He could have sworn he heard a collective sigh of relief echo through the room before he started slipping away, Deus taking him under with his lilting voice saying it was time to rest.

A muttered, "I'm sorry," left Luc's barely parted lips a split-second before it was lights out.

Luc's EYES fluttered open to the low hum of voices arguing, and quickly closed as light hit his sensitive eyes. Lashes fluttered in an attempt to filter the light slowly, and as he gazed around the room he found he was on the sofa near the door of the meeting room. Everyone from earlier, minus Azaroth and Athon, was huddled around the small computer screen that popped up from the table in front of Luc's chair, muttering and occasionally cursing.

"What the fuck, guys? It's like a fucking wolf mating. But that's freaking impossible for us, so what the fuck is going on? First Luc and now Roth?" one of them exclaimed roughly.

"If the noises coming from the other room are anything to go by, I wouldn't rule out Athon being dragged into this mess either," someone else added almost too softly.

He couldn't tell who the voices belonged to, it was like his brain hadn't fully come back online yet.

"We need to contain this fucking situation before Luc decides to take things too far and does something he'd regret. None of us are a match for him if he truly goes nuclear on anyone."

"It may be time to call in Ramiel, find out if there's any outside influence here?"

"Or one of the Fates?"

"The cryptic bitches might be of some help, but we'd probably end up with more questions than answers." He knew that voice. It belonged to Andromalius . . . Andy. The one before was Fenriz . . . Fynn.

"Guys, the big guy's coming around, so let's table this until we can discuss it as a team. No more secretive bullshit. All the cards on the table, and then we'll form a plan of attack." Dante, of course, was the one to notice he'd come to.

While the little shit was the ultimate prankster, and pain in the ass— and fuck knew he had his reasons—he was a consummate professional when it came to his work and his loyalty to his chosen brothers and sisters. Hell, they all were a little fucked up, and fucked over, by what life had thrown at them, and they all had different ways of coping. Some were better than others.

His gaze zeroed in on Caine and Ares. Those guys had the weight of a thousand worlds reflected in their eyes and strapped to their shoulders. But the one he worried most for was Dante. What would happen the day his laughter died?

Before his thoughts could carry him down that fucking scary road of 'what-ifs' there was a light, yet commanding rap on the door. With only a slight pause the doors were pushed inwards by two of the newest recruits, and Mrs Briars bustled in behind them pushing her motorized cart seemingly loaded with enough food to feed an army of hungry trolls. Truth be told she wasn't wrong in her estimation of what the fourteen of them could inhale, ah, eat, yeah eat, he totally meant eat.

The smells wafting his way had his feet pulling a one foot in front of the other shuffle before he even registered he was upright. Soon Mrs Briars was surrounded by hungry eyes and enthusiastic thank-yous. She went about setting up the table, slapping at the hands of those who tried to help. Mrs Briars was an institution in the compound. Having arrived mysteriously one day—so long ago his memory was foggy as to the year— in the company of Leraie, the Almighty's right hand. She'd helped guide grown angels, raise new ones, and she'd helped mend the broken psyches of more than one of their lot with her kindness, her wisdom, and her magic touch. Oh, and the giant helpings of comfort food, and tough love when needed. No way was she allowing them to set that table though. Not on her watch.

"Where are Azaroth and Leviathon? They never miss a meeting." Her eagle eyes were legendary for taking in everything and her uncanny knack for catching them out on their secrets gave them a sense of motherly love that most of them either hadn't known or couldn't remember. While at the same time making them feel like small children caught stealing the last chocolate chip cookie from the supposedly hidden jar.

As all eyes flickered to Luc, Mrs Briars was quick to follow their lead. With a raised brow she planted her hands on her rounded hips and strode determinedly toward him.

"What have you done, Cifer, my boy?" her head tilted to the left as she looked up into his eyes. For such a short, short woman, she sure as fuck knew how to make him feel an inch taller than pond scum sometimes.

"I . . . I saw her . . . He saw her, he knew her. MY Caria, he knew my Caria. I . . ." She placed her palm on his arm and shushed him, as only she could, at any other time the others would have found it highly amusing, and her gaze hardened

"Make it right, Cifer," was all she said. It was all she had to say. He knew he needed to put his big boy General pants on and apologize, no matter how his shadows rebelled. Roth was his friend, his family, and it didn't sit right that they were at such odds. Especially when nothing was confirmed.

Lily moved to the adjoining door and entered, only to jump back out and slam the door so fast it was amazing luck she hadn't hit herself in the face with it. She spun, her back to the wall and her usually sun kissed golden skin was bright pink, her plump lips parted in shock.

Dante, being Dante, raced to the door like his tail was on fire, well if he had a tail that is. His excitement at catching his fellow Hounds *in flagrante delicto* was palpable. Anything he could use to take his focus away from himself and his crushing self-analysis. They'd mostly decided to humor the bastard. Not that they let him get away with shit completely, not a chance in, well, Hell. Part of the game was payback, just as much as his mischief kept him distracted so too did the anticipation of his comeuppance. He'd just never really pranked Luc before. As Luc ran his fingers through his bright blue hair he couldn't help but chuckle, the sound low, rough, and rumbling; completely unexpected. He felt slightly better as he took in the scene around him. Knowing something was happening behind those doors and that his friends still had his back brought back a calm he couldn't have gained solo.

"Holy fuck!" Dante slammed the door shut so fast it was like he hadn't even opened it. When he turned around, his eyes were just about bugging out of his head.

"They're ghost fucking, sleep fucking. It's fucking weird fucking. I have no fucking words," he croaked out between wheezing breaths.

"Bro, what the hell are you talking about?" Malphas exclaimed.

"Dude, they're asleep, passed out or something. Completely naked and, like, fingering air, and stroking themselves, and making sex noises while they suck face." Lily rubbed her eyes as she spoke as though trying to wipe the image from her mind. "I don't even think they know what they're doing," she added.

Every mouth dropped open and the vacuum of silence which came from the momentary cessation of breath was almost comical. Astral sex.

It was a legend, like a sexy fantasy, but Luc had never known of someone who'd actually done it. It required a deep connection, careful planning, and a complete lack of consciousness that most people never achieved. He'd always wondered if his dreams were like that, but he'd known they hadn't been, even as he'd hoped for it. How could they've been? They'd had no planning. He'd thought her long dead or himself slowly going crazy. But now? Now he had so many questions he had no answers for. The one he dreaded most was who were they dreaming of? His shadows threatened to break free but he pushed them down. He glanced at his arm to see the wrinkled hand of Mrs Briars lightly resting there, a tart held out to him with the other.

"Eat," was all she said to him before she turned back to the others.

"Leave them be, dears," Mrs Briars murmured. "Call for me when they come out, if you've all managed to eat everything by then, and I'll bring more. And you leave them alone about this. No teasing, nothing. Especially you, Dante. No jokes! Or no more dumplings for you. Are we clear? Those boys have been through too much and I'll not see any of you making it any harder for them to sort it all out," she intoned as she glanced around at all of them, they all nodded automatically. Dante copped the glare though, and he swallowed hard. It was a big ask for him not to take it and run with the endless jokes, but her dumplings were one of his weaknesses, and she knew it.

"I'll try my hardest, but it's GHOST FUCKING. Like this is prime material right here for the taking," he wheedled.

"No dumplings and no tarts," came her determined reply. She'd really pulled out the big guns now.

"Yes, ma'am." Dante straightened up like a soldier on parade. The threat of no more of Mrs Briars dumplings or tarts for the rest of eternity took the humor out of the situation with impressive speed.

"Good. Now eat before I take it back to the kitchen and find others who'll appreciate my efforts." She playfully pouted while trying not to grin, before she walked through the doors. Literally *through* the doors. Leaving them to descend on the food like starving hyenas. Momentarily forgetting all of their worries, hopes, and queries.

CHAPTER 10

If Roth kept his eyes sealed closed, maybe he could pretend for a little longer it was actually Athon's warm body pressed up against him, rather than a figment of his imagination. A very vivid manifestation of his deepest desires. He could feel the warmth of his lover's skin seeping into his, Athon's scent enveloped him in a world he never wanted to wake from. The light fuzz of a neatly trimmed beard grazed his shoulder and a low sound of sexual satisfaction reached his ears. Yes, surely it wouldn't be a sin to stay like this forever, to bask in the glow of a love that once was. He knew it wasn't Athon's fault, not really. He'd made his choices too. Yet, the specter of Mara hung like a cloud of doom over him so often. Between them. A reminder of what his blind faith in love could do. What his trust in another could do. Of what he would do for the one he loved, even to his own detriment.

When the phantom hand resting on his muscled chest moved lower and caressed the smattering of hair that led to his suddenly hard again cock, Roth's eyes flashed open and flicked straight to the End Zone. Yep, his cock was as stiff as a goal post and the hand now resting on his hip, after it'd brushed against said cock and thus caused a swift shot of desire to shoot straight to his balls, was definitely real and very familiar.

What the actual fuck? When had he gotten naked? How had he

ended up in this bed? Not that he was complaining, but why was there a very naked, and absolutely sexy Athon seemingly asleep beside him, let alone fondling him while he, himself, slept? The dream, oh yeah, he remembered it now, the mystery woman and Athon. Never had Athon been there until now. He'd often wondered why and how she'd overwhelmed his love and infatuation for the very male he was now resting beside so that he only ever dreamed of her? This time he'd had them both, and damn it, he'd not thought his dreams could get any more orgasmic, but they had. It was just a dream, right?

He turned toward Athon, reached out his free hand, and did something he'd yearned to do for the longest time. Ever since Athon had shaved the sides of his hair short and created his rainbow mohawk Roth's fingers had itched to caress it. The dark hair was clipped short on the sides with the long colorful strands sitting up on top and running down the back. He loved the way it got shorter as it reached the nape of his neck, he felt his lips tingle at the thought of placing light kisses there. This was one of the many post-Roth changes Athon had made to his body and style. Roth approved of them all. Even those he hadn't seen and didn't know about. They were a part of who Athon was now, but they also represented who he'd always been.

It felt so good, softer than he'd ever imagined. He must use magic to hold it up because it didn't have the hard waxy feel that human mohawks so often seemed to have. His gaze roamed where his hands caressed, skimming the piercing in one dark brow . . . and locked with Athon's unique eyes, gold irises rimmed by blue and purple with an almost serpentine black pupil, giving them a predatory edge that usually only came out when on a mission, or in the bedroom. An edge that was definitely present now as he took in the way Roth was touching him, the closeness of their bodies, and as his gaze swept down and back up with light speed quickness, his eyes widened and filled with wonder. Roth knew he'd registered not only their shared naked state, but also the extreme arousal that was prominently pressed between them. Now that he thought about it, he realized his erection wasn't the only one vying for space down there. The fact Athon was equally as aroused as he was had him flushing like a schoolgirl winked at by the high school heartthrob. Athon definitely made something throb that was for sure.

"Azaroth, if you keep stroking my hair like that and rubbing your cock against me you best be prepared to face the consequences," Athon stated. "I'll have you stroking my cock with that precious mouth of yours faster than you can blink, babe."

The soft growl of warning mixed with the raw promise in Athon's voice sent shivers all the way up Roth's spine. His mind flashed back to all the times he'd done just that, and a whimper of longing too long suppressed slipped from between his parted lips.

No sooner had the sound escaped his lips did Athon groan and twine his fingers through Roth's hair, pulled him flush against his body, and took his mouth in a hungry kiss. One soaked in desperation, love, and long denied desire. His teeth nipped at Roth's lips until they parted and allowed his tongue entry. He soothed the sting with his tongue before plunging in and devouring him as if he would disappear and never come back.

Roth understood why Athon would feel that way. What'd happened once could happen again. Even if he had come back, he'd come back broken and not the male he'd once been. As if a bucket of ice-cold water had soaked him he knew they had to stop, at least for now.

Talking was the last thing he wanted to do, but Athon deserved to know what he was dealing with. His time with Mara hadn't been something he'd spoken to Athon about, and the aftermath had seen him lock the male out of anything but a platonic relationship. With all the questions revolving around the mystery woman, the dreams, and everything else, he'd realized Athon was the one person who deserved to know just how fucked up Roth was. Not to mention why he'd hurt the best thing in his life and run away with his proverbial tail between his legs to lick his wounds for over a century and a half.

Removing his hand from Athon's face proved easier said than done. So instead of removing it completely from his body he slid his fingers in a gentle glide over his shoulder, his arms, until he could interlace their fingers. He took a deep shuddering breath and closed his eyes. As he opened them he saw the shutters come down in Athon's, as though he feared the worst and was fortifying himself against the possibility of rejection. And could you blame the guy? After all this time and all that had happened they were so close and yet the divide between them was so wide. So many things they'd never said. So many things he wished he'd left unsaid.

In an attempt to reassure the male before him he raised their joined hands and brought Athon's knuckles to his lips. His lips barely grazed them before he froze, his eyes flaring wide and latching onto Athon's. The other male looked at him in confusion, which quickly turned into a look of 'what the fuck' when Roth's tongue flicked out to lick along his knuckles, followed by the length of one long finger. Unlacing their fingers he bolted upright and pulled Athon with him into a seated position. Grasping the same hand again, this time with both of his, he took the middle finger deep into this mouth and slowly drew it out, his tongue swirling around the digit, sucking gently. The taste, so sweet and musky he didn't think he'd ever get enough. Athon's groans and restless shifting caused him to look up again and focus on the male before him, but not before tasting his other fingers. As he moved his face closer to his own hand he caught the same enticing scent. Dropping Athon's hand he sniffed his own, and felt his brain skip into overdrive as realization struck.

"We need to talk, Ath," he groaned out. "But first, we need to talk."

"Um, okay. We *are* talking and that made zero sense. Why are you acting so weird?" Athon was visibly wary, his brows drawn down, his jaw tense, a slight quiver of worry entering his voice.

Roth knew he wasn't getting his words out right. His brain was on a runaway train because he'd just been dealt a complete mindfuck scenario.

"Although, I'm going to take you calling me Ath again as a good sign, so I won't run screaming from the room for help." The smile on Athon's face was nothing short of preening, he looked like all his dreams had just come true, Roth couldn't help but smile in return. He'd missed this. Moments where he could make the male before him feel as special as he truly was. At his smile Athon's shoulders visibly relaxed.

Giving himself time to process the newest curveball to his reality, and all the implications it carried with it, Roth decided to start with the topic they'd always avoided. Mara. The Mega Bitch, queen of all bitches.

"It's time." That was all he had to say and the tension was back in Athon's entire body.

"You, we, don't have to do this if you aren't ready. I mean, I'm here, not going anywhere and never have, and as much as I want answers and want to help purge you of what that bitch did, I won't push it if you aren't there yet." His voice was shaky, shock resounded clearly through every word. He'd waited too long for this as it was, Roth wasn't going to waste another day. No matter how much the words might cost him. No matter the pity he was so terrified he'd see in his lover's eyes. The disgust he'd feel rising within him with each vocalization of his tormented past with the woman Athon had been so hopeful would complete them.

"Mara." God, just saying that name brought burning bile to the back of his throat. How was he going to be able to get the rest of the twisted mess out into the space between them? But out it must come, before it ate up more of his soul than it already had. "What she did . . . Fuck, I wish this wasn't so hard." His growl filled the air with all of the emotions burning within him, calmed only by the feel of a warm, calloused hand coming to rest over his own.

"We have eternity, so how about I start us off?" Athon, always the facilitator of difficult conversations, chimed in.

All Roth could do was look at their hands and nod.

"She felt like a dream come true, someone who I thought was not only beautiful, but smart and charming, someone who had a spine of steel clothed in fine silk. I liked her, I didn't love her, but I thought it would come to that naturally, later on once we'd formed a bond with her of sorts. If I'd known what she was truly capable of . . . I'd have stabbed the bitch in the heart myself and damn the consequences. While I don't know what she actually did to you, she hurt you, and that is enough to warrant her death by my hand in my opinion. I knew you were wary, less than impressed, when I introduced you to her. I remember you saying you felt like you'd seen her before somewhere, her eyes caught your attention more than anything else. You said she felt young, I responded that compared to us nearly everything and everyone was. I can still hear the echo of your chuckle in my head."

Roth felt Athon's sad smile rather than saw it, for he couldn't find the strength to look up into his face, not yet, anyway. But he nodded his head in agreement. Sometimes her eyes still haunted him, as though begging him for something, begging to be seen, to be remembered. Not from his time with her, but from before he'd ever known her name.

"I didn't understand why you held her at a distance. To me she seemed eager to be with us both. I really wish I'd listened to your instincts, even if you didn't voice them directly to me, and yes, I knew somewhere inside that you just wanted me happy and if that had made me happy you would have gone along with it. I am sorry for that."

Before Athon could continue Roth held a finger to his lips and finally looked the male in the eyes.

"Yes, I would have done anything to make you happy, even sacrificed my own happiness. No, she didn't want us both, not the way you thought. She was at ease with you and seemed to genuinely enjoy your company. With me? She always seemed to have an edge of anger and resentment about her, whether the clenching of her jaw, the air of a predator holding themselves back from attacking at the wrong time, or a barely there tolerance. I knew you didn't see it, but it was there, and there was no way I was going to be the one to point it out to you. That was my first mistake." He took a moment to collect himself and the pad of his thumb caressed Athon's plump bottom lip, causing a shiver to run through them both.

"My second mistake was to assume my happiness meant your misery and your misery meant my happiness. I should have realized sooner that the bond we shared was deeper than that. It is deeper than that. I know now that you would have seen my unhappiness and it would have come back to bite us irregardless of what eventually went down. The solution to our problem, that missing piece, is someone we both want equally. Not someone who could only make one of us happy." A tear slid from the corner of Athon's eye and Roth caught it on the tip of his finger. Bringing it to his lips he licked the tiny droplet away.

"No more tears, my love, or I'll have to lick your face like a golden retriever. You always were an ugly crier." With a tap to his chin Athon chuckled.

"Me? The ugly crier? Oh, really? I'm not the one who got caught watching that sappy chick flick in the media room at midnight on your birthday with a full-on snot face!"

Athon and Roth nudged each other good naturedly before resting their heads on each other's shoulders. Both of them knew they were just about to hit the heartbreaking part of their long overdue therapy session.

"Before we do this, Azaroth, you need to know that none of what you tell me is going to change who you are to me. What happened does not define the male you are. You are not responsible, nor accountable, for the deeds of others. Not even when those deeds are directed at you. I need you to understand that whatever she did, I know that if you'd had the opportunity to end it, to escape or to defeat her, you would have taken it. The sum of you is not defined by your time with that monster. You are so much more. I also know that it will be with you always, and I am here for you, in whatever capacity you wish me to be."

"You are a male worthy of the finest this existence has to offer, Leviathon. I have never been worthy enough, but I never questioned our bond before her. Afterwards, I questioned everything. I questioned my faith in the Almighty, my trust in myself, and in what I could sacrifice to make you happy. What was too much? Had I lost too much already? After what she did . . . I felt used, broken, unlovable and so, so dirty. Dirty in such a way I never thought I'd get clean again. I doubted my judgment as a Shadow Hound."

Athon's shocked gasp surrounded him. His reputation as one of the formidable Devil's 13 had never been questioned, as far as he'd known. He'd never let them see his self-doubt.

"Don't worry, Caine kicked my ass so hard for that one, and does so again every now and then as a reminder, that it was pretty much permanently knocked out of me. Apparently I'd temporarily forgotten that, unlike certain know-it-alls, I can't see the auras and possible intentions of other angels." The rueful tug of his lips as he said this earned him a quick kiss followed by a sweetly masculine whimper of longing. He couldn't help but think this shit needed to be done quickly so he could get back to getting more of those noises out of Athon's pretty mouth.

"Okay, I'm just going to lay it out. It's probably going to be word vomit, but I just want it done. Just let me get it all out, please." It wasn't a question, and he knew Athon wouldn't answer it as one.

Roth took several big deep breaths, trying desperately to calm his racing heart and the tremors that were running through his extremities. Once he felt like he had a semblance of control over his roiling emotions he linked the fingers of both hands with Athon's and tilted his head back to look at the ceiling. Feeling his vision fade and the past take over.

"The night she requested we spend some alone time together, just the two of us, we both assumed it was so that we could form a closer bond, move past whatever awkwardness remained. What happened was not something I expected or thought possible." His voice broke when he uttered the last sentence.

"We ate together, it was pleasant, light conversation abounded. She served wine, red, from Florence, Chianti, which considering more recent movies is quite ironic. As we sipped and chatted she refilled the glass several times and started asking me rather pointed questions. The answers I gave didn't feel like they were truly mine, like my will was being pushed aside. It seemed to make her happy, and she smiled at me in a way she never had before. It was filled with excitement, but also so much malicious intent that my spine tingled in warning and as I went to leap to my feet . . . She spoke only two words: sit down. The command was softly spoken but my body snapped into action without my agreement, and, sit down I did.

"She approached me, gripped my face between her hands and said, "Those who stand idly by are just as guilty as those who wield the whip." She created a portal and took me through to some Hell forsaken place. I had no will of my own.

"Every day a new potion was administered and I'd have to drink it because my body obeyed her, even if my mind rebelled. The bitch would ask me questions, but my answers weren't the right ones, and so she lashed at me with her powers, her fists, blades, whips, basically anything she had at hand. All the while accusing me of heinous things. After a while she seemed to realize that I didn't just have to do what she told me to do, I also had to say what she told me to say. She used this to make me say disgusting things, admit to disgusting things that I would never do. She made me renounce you, our love, even my oath to Lucifer and the Hounds. It broke me down, and the voice in my head that she refused to hear, refused to let me use, started to slowly drive me insane.

"I don't know how long I sat on that bench, the chains on my wrists keeping me upright, stripped naked, caked in dirt and sweat, but mostly blood. My blood. Oh, how I wished it was hers.

"Then one day she entered and seemed to hesitate, she looked almost bored and a little sad. It didn't last, though. She'd apparently decided she was to be done with me. I'd have welcomed death. How sad is that? Death would have been a kindness she obviously didn't think me worthy of, though.

"Instead, she retreated from the room and two people entered, older angels, though I couldn't see their faces, they too seemed familiar. What followed was . . ." He paused to press a hand to his stomach, a valiant attempt to stem the tide of sickness he felt. Slowly, the roiling calmed to a ripple and his breathing evened out.

"They used me. In every way conceivable. Violated every boundary I ever held dear. Took my consent away from me. And all the while I uttered the words they told me to say. I made the noises they told me to make, and I moved where and how they told me to move. Like a lapdog doing their bidding. They beat me and bedded me. Broke me down and left me empty, nothing but a husk filled with shattered slivers of who I thought I'd been." A solitary tear slipped free and Athon reached up to brush it aside with the pad of his thumb.

"Once they left she came back in. Looked me dead in the eye and told me to never forget what it felt like, she hoped it haunted me for the rest of my eternal days, and so far it has. She spit on me, unchained me and shoved me through the portal back to where the whole sordid ordeal began."

No sooner were the last words out Roth leapt from the bed and ran, stumbling on shaky legs to the toilet. The contents of his stomach unable to stay down a moment longer.

Athon's strong, yet gentle hand rubbed soothing circles over his back as he knelt behind him, ready to brace him once he was done. Resting his head on his forearm he felt shame course through him, and he was momentarily terrified of seeing his shame and Athon's pity reflected back at him if he chanced a glance at Athon's beautiful eyes.

"Whatever you are afraid of, *Corazón*, worry not. You are not less to me for all you have endured. You are so much stronger than I ever thought. Ashamed is never how you should feel with me, and I shall never be ashamed of thee." Athon's soft warm breath and loving words brought Roth a sense of calm he'd not felt in centuries, he wanted to latch on and never let go.

Without words Athon rose and started the shower. Spice scented fog filled the air and Roth found himself helped to his feet and guided into the warm water. Thank God the shower was big enough for the two of them, he wasn't sure he'd have been able to hold himself up without Athon's steady strength supporting him. He felt Athon's soap covered hands cleaning his body, it felt amazing, and yet he was still a little detached from it all.

Luckily Athon seemed to understand where his mind was at and that he needed to come back from his nightmarish past slowly. He took his time, making sure Roth was ready before shutting the water off, and guiding him out. They dried off in silence, Athon doing most of it when Roth's hands fumbled with the towel.

They made it back to the bed and Athon tucked Roth into the warmth of his body. Normally he'd have been the big spoon but Roth needed this more than he'd realized. The blankets cocooned them in a layer of protection from the non-existent chill of the room, like armor against the ghosts of the past.

"Sleep, Azaroth. We can discuss that other thing another time. I'm assuming it was about that realistic sex dream that left both our hands covered in her juices and our cocks spent, without any cum to show for it?" he murmured softly.

Roth could only nod his head in stupefaction. How had he figured it out?

"I had time in the shower to think about a lot of things. Especially that dream and how you devoured my fingers. I'm betting it was an astral dream, as unlikely as it is, those are hard to do at the best of times. I've never heard of a situation like ours though."

It made sense, but it was another thing he felt guilty for. Lucifer had staked a claim. He felt stuck. He would never go against his General, but he couldn't control these dreams. Angels weren't even meant to dream. So astral sex made more sense, except for those times he'd seen her, and she hadn't appeared to see him. Those had to be dreams, right? It was so damn confusing.

"Relax, *mi vida*, we can figure it out later. We won't go against our friend, our leader. We will help him find her, and see how it all plays out though. She feels right for us. And I say that on a completely different level to the last time I uttered those words. One thing's for certain though, until we know what is happening with her and Luc, we keep the details of the dreams and anything about her to ourselves. No need for Luc to bring out the devil inside again."

Roth absolutely agreed 100 percent. He drifted off to a dreamless sleep with Athon's warmth curled around him and strong arms holding him close.

CHAPTER 11

She'd stomped out of his office over an hour ago, yet Balthazar's gaze was still locked on the lavender fields that surrounded his own private domain. Sure, beings could come and go, some openly and some by invitation only, but it was his domain. Currently, he only had one being in residence who couldn't leave of their own free will, and she was beginning to become a bigger problem than he'd expected. The question was, and seemed to always be, what to do about the mystery that was Jezzie. He never thought it'd be eight freaking years later and he'd still be no closer to any solid answers. Try as he might the answer eluded him, and the longer he stared at those rolling meadows the more he thought of her . . . Not his reluctant guest, that termagant, Jezzie, but her, his Beth.

Soon enough the scenery disappeared, and her face was all he could see. Sucking him into the past, tumbling him down the rabbit hole, and into memories that battered him like a storm; with its lulls and quiet whispers, and its harsh and brutal beatings.

She'd been so much better than he. The best of humankind. Oh, how he'd loved her, waxed poetic of her beauty and fallen at her feet. Oh, how she'd laughed and batted her lashes, pushed at his shoulders and gently scolded him for his joking. Only, he hadn't been. She'd been the light in the monotony of his existence up to that point. And oh, how brightly she'd flared.

She had been an innocent of the world, like most ladies of her station, but she'd been wild and free when the urge had taken her. Even if the world never truly saw her for who she was, he had. The day he'd met her was the day he'd really started to live.

He'd once mentioned her to Jezzie, the day she'd arrived, but he'd never told her the full story. He wasn't sure she even remembered half of what he'd said that night. His Beth had broken all the rules, but he'd won that bet in the end. So certain she'd been that she wouldn't fall for him, that love for him was something she would never feel, until they'd fallen, both of them. It had surprised the heck out of him to feel that deeply about another, about a human even more so.

He longed to see her staring up at him again, her baby blues twinkling with mischief and cheek. Which brought him back to the present like a slap to the face. He turned from the windows and slumped into his chair, his hand running through his hair, turning it to a rumpled mess, and scrubbing at his face in frustration, in exhaustion, he no longer knew which, just that it all melded together to make him feel weary and old. Granted, he was old, but he damn well didn't look it, and shouldn't feel it, at least not yet.

He needed answers. Jezzie had those answers. He couldn't protect his interests without them. Too much depended on trusting the right people, and something told him that Jezzie was fucking important to his mission statement. Which basically came with the title, 'Don't Fuck This Up!'

So many things to keep straight, so many fingers in so many pies. Some days he thought his head would explode. Jezzie being the catalyst more days than not. So much about her was familiar, and yet so much didn't make sense. She had shadows like a Shadow Hound, but instead of black hers were as red as the blood colored tones of her hair. She needed to feed on souls, he'd never seen the like, at least not in a creature that looked so humanoid. He'd heard tales and seen sketches of creatures in the fae realm, Anaran'ith, who feasted on the souls of children, and lost travelers, in the forbidden forests of Vash'terra, but they were just tales told to keep children in line, at least he'd always thought so.

He knew she was hiding so much more, he felt it in his bones, but he just couldn't place what it was. It was like her power was dulled. There, but not quite. Almost as if some of her power was still dormant, waiting for the right time to come forth.

There was something in the way she walked, when she prowled and fumed, the flash of red in her eyes when she was particularly pissed off. He'd seen eyes do that before, but when he tried to place them it was like a fog descended on his memory, and he couldn't fight his way through to grasp what he felt he should know. Even trying to speak of it tied his tongue in knots. It was like she had a spell on her to protect her identity, her origins.

Fuck! That was it, a fucking spell, and a powerful one at that! He sucked at breaking spells, most angels did, except for Raum. Hellfire, he hated that fucker, even though he knew he had to play the good host to him so very soon.

Raum would arrive a few days early, it was the sadist's *modus operandi*, after all. He'd requested a cell for his current pet, N. Balthazar felt immense pity for any poor soul unfortunate enough to be caught in Raum's clutches. If he could do anything for the poor soul he would try. The fact that Raum had even heard of Jezzie raised Balthazar's hackles. Someone had been telling tales out of school . . .

That was his other problem, damned demons, good help was so hard to find. For the most part they did their jobs, respected his rules, and he was most generous with them and their deviant tastes. Telling tales was not permitted though, and someone was going to find themselves being used as a teaching aid in a 'Don't Fuck With Balthazar' lesson. He just had to figure out which demon spawn had loose lips.

He should probably have warned Jezzie about Raum's particular proclivities. But decided against it. If she let slip he'd said anything it could totally bite him in the ass. He would, however, try to convince her that Raum wasn't someone she wanted to mess with and her new neighbor wasn't someone she should get cozy with. Her cell was actually two cells joined together, she just didn't know about the glass dividing wall currently residing below ground between her room and what would be another cell, or the other hidden bathroom on its far wall. Balthazar controlled everything in his domain. No one knew anything he didn't want them to. Which made the fact that Raum knew about Jezzie that much more problematic.

The fact he was insisting he personally interrogate 'the prisoner' at Gabriel's insistence, made the hairs on Balthazar's nape rise, and his skin crawled with a mixture of fear and revulsion. Raum was known to use whatever means necessary to get the results he wanted. Yeah, not always the truth, mostly what worked in Raum's favor. Gabriel let it all slide because he got things done, and because Raum was one of the few who would do such disgusting, dirty work. Nothing, and no one, was off-limits to Raum, except Gabriel. He disappeared in the wind the moment he was done, and arrived at the most opportune times only for himself. The Praesidium had yet to catch him, he was that good at hiding himself away.

Only one other rogue angel had eluded them to date, Mara. Gabriel had a fair idea where she was, but nothing was going to compel him to spill his intel. Sometimes, when you're so broken, you can't help but break others. Crushed against the jagged rocks of life, your revenge and brutality become the only way you feel anything, the only way you can find to reconcile your reality. And Balthazar had a fair idea what that felt like . . .

Satari rapped on the open door, and at his nod she entered, the deliciously bitter scent of coffee wafted toward him. Reminding him he had so much work to do and so little time. Which was ironic since he literally had all the time in the world. Immortality was both a blessing and a curse.

The matronly demoness, as matronly as a demoness could be anyway, placed her tray on the desk and bowed low as she slowly backed away toward the door. An assortment of pastries surrounded the coffee, and he realized he hadn't eaten in close to twelve hours.

Hmm, normally he loved Satari's coffee. No one made it quite like she did. Knowing he had a traitor in his home though, made his suspicious tendencies slam into place like a reinforced vault door.

"Satari, please wait and take a seat."

The red and almost black but actually purple, server froze. A fine shiver rippled its way across her skin, her hands fisted and fiddled with the hem of her apron as she looked up and stared wide-eyed at her boss.

"Please, Satari, I'd like some company," he reiterated.

"I's can gets you some womens, my lord, to keeps you entertained."

The quiver in her voice showed a fear of him that usually wasn't there. His suspicions skyrocketed, as did his brow, if he wasn't careful they could become a permanent fixture at his hairline. Thankfully he didn't have a mouthful of anything but air, yet even that made him splutter just a little at the thought of little, old Satari organizing his intimate entertainment for him.

"Ah, that won't be necessary. You can assist me with something else instead though. Please, sit." The last was said with a rather commanding tone, at which the demoness shuffled quickly to the seat, and clutched her hands together fretfully in her lap.

Hopefully he could get to the bottom of this mess quickly. Judging by Satari's behavior it wouldn't take much to get her to talk. He sent his special power out to test and scent the coffee, cream, pastries, and sugar for any trace of poison or other substance he should avoid.

The coffee he would avoid and the majority of the pastries. What was interesting was his favorite lacked any sort of tampering. It was his go-to treat of choice, and she goddamn knew he never turned down a caramel custard filled doughnut with strawberry wine icing. Hell, she made them especially for him, he could devour a dozen in one sitting. So, why was it the only one that wasn't laced with something nasty? Something was very, very wrong. He could feel it in his bones and in the way the fine hairs on his spine almost seemed to zap him.

"Satari, luv, tell me, are you happy here? Working for me, that is." As he awaited her response he picked up the doughnut and lifted it to his nose, inhaling the sweet and sugary confection with reverence before taking a bite. The flavors and textures which exploded in his mouth were an experience akin to ecstasy, and yet the bitter aftertaste of his current situation quickly soured his appetite.

Her breath hitched, and if possible her eyes widened even more. Her reptilian tongue shot out to lick at her lips nervously.

"Ye . . . Yesss, sir," she softly hissed. Her answer did nothing to lessen his suspicions as he noted black tears welling in her eyes.

"You know, Satari, I've grown very fond of you over the years. You have always treated me like blooded kin, and if I were of demonkind I would gladly wish that I had spawned from thee." Soft sobs came from the hunched and cowering demoness before him, but he continued on. "I would have thee know, as has always been the case, that you, or any of your kind within these walls, have only to come to me with any matter that may lie heavily upon your shoulders."

At her renewed sobs, and the sight of her black tears as they fell onto her pristine apron he moved to kneel before her. He took her tensed fingers in his and rubbed the back of her hand soothingly.

"Whatever ails thee, I will remedy the situation to thine satisfaction. I just need to know why thou wouldst seek to poison me when it obviously pains thee so?"

Her head shot up, her eyes widened, and her jaw dropped. Unfortunately, it seemed fear regained control again with great speed. Satari trembled even more and shook her head from side to side in sobbing silence.

"It really is okay, Satari, nothing and no one can harm thee here within these walls, and I assure thou, no one can hear what is said in this room."

"N . . . N . . . No, he will know. He will hurt and he will kill . . ." Her clawed hands shot up to cover her mouth and Balthazar's anger rose within him swiftly. Vengeance was needed here, not just for himself as he'd initially thought, but for Satari.

"He cannot harm you, luv. You can stay here until it is dealt with, rest assured you have my protection."

"Not . . . Not me," she squeaked softly.

"If not thee, then whom?" he queried. It was more of a rhetorical question, though. As soon as it passed his lips he had a fair idea. "Your daughter, your grandson, or both? Is it Hadden, Satari?"

Just the idea that someone could harm them made his blood boil, that they could be used and abused in such a manner to gain information about Balthazar's dealings was the icing on the cake of his soon-to-be demise. If it was Hadden, then his existence would end this very night. Balthazar had never liked the demon. Not even the other demons like Hadden. He was considered smarmy and oily even by those in his community. Which was unheard of in demon culture. Hadden had always tried to get Balthazar to hire him, he'd even gone so far as to try to get Satari to further his application. Unfortunately for him, Balthazar was able to see into his heart and ferret out whether his intentions were honorable. They never were. Satari's quiet mumbles drew his attention back to her.

"Y . . . . Yesss. He has Denriah locked in a cage and Thovad as well. He s . . . sayss he will kill them if I speak of it or don't do what he ssssays."

The little demoness threw herself into his arms, her claws catching his cheeks as her arms wrapped around him. He bundled her up and held her as she wept. The poor dear was clearly at the end of her tether and frantic with worry for her family. As he whispered words of comfort and vengeance to Satari, of the impending destruction of Hadden, her sobs started to fade as a plan formed to take the little shite down.

Balthazar made trips to the Daemoneskra Realm every few years. Not something he particularly enjoyed, his price of entry was high indeed. The demon queen ruled her domain with an iron fist. The only beings who could enter at will were the members of the Praesidium. Everyone else had to be approved by the queen directly. Most were rejected immediately, sometimes with a side of death. Balthazar got special privileges, he got to hire demons to work for him, which he compensated them for generously. Still, he only went when he absolutely had to. Sometimes his 'arrangement' with the queen was more than his stomach could handle, or any other part of him . . .

Thankfully, her loyalty to her people would ensure that his entry this time was swift, even if he owed her next time. Demons loved a good bargain, and in this she would get vengeance for her people, and him indebted to her as a bonus. He just had to word it the right way that was all.

As he suited up later that day, not for the first time, Balthazar double-checked his hidden weapons, and thanked his lucky stars the queen had listened to reason. Of course, he'd considered the fact she'd want to go balls to the wall attack mode on the asswipe herself. It'd just taken a lot more effort than he'd predicted in order to calm her down.

Once she'd calmly considered the possible harm to the child from going after Hadden in such a manner, she'd quickly gotten on board with his plan, just with a slight delay to his timeline.

His skin still crawled, his tongue still felt raw and raspy in his mouth, and if he didn't know better he'd have thought he'd extracted his own internal organs when he'd cast up his accounts, along with any bile left in his system. The nature of her juices had left a burning path through his body. Thankfully they were expelled quickly. He was certain that was one of the reasons she used him as she did. Not every being could survive intimate interactions with a demon, much less a full-blooded demon queen. He was a rarity, she must have been so pleased when she'd gotten her claws into him, literally. Not something he enjoyed, but a necessary submission on his part for his own ends.

So, the plan was to go in looking for new hires, extra workers because of the imminent arrival of his 'guests'. As he thought about the plan his lips slipped into an evil smirk of their own volition, and he felt the burning in his palm that came with thoughts of retribution and vengeance. Tonight those present would get a glimpse of what the real Balthazar could do, and who he used to be. Hopefully, putting a stop to any further attempts to sell his secrets at the same time.

HADDEN WAS STANDING at the back of the crowd near the door to the abode he shared with Denriah and their son, as Balthazar seemed to glide down the stone paved road into one of the many demon townships. Balthazar kept him in his peripheral vision and watched as the soon-to-be dead demon's beady eyes shifted back and forth between him and the door he was partially blocking.

What would the greedy little prick do when confronted with his wrath? That was the question. Because try as he might, he wouldn't escape. Not today. Not from him, or the rest of this tight-knit community.

"I need a few new hires to tend to some special guests for a week or two. Conditions and reimbursement is as per my usual terms. Anyone interested please step forward." He didn't need to project his voice too far, it seemed to echo in the silence that had followed his arrival.

Twenty or so demons, women and men, stepped forward. One little girl stepped from behind her mother and made to move closer, but her mother's hand on her shoulder pulled her to a stop.

"Maybe when you're older, poppet," Balthazar told her softly, and her mother smiled at him in thanks.

A demon's smile was more a grimace than a grin, but he understood perfectly. He'd gotten used to their ways after all this time.

He saw Hadden step away from the dwelling, his feet hitting the cobblestones as he came closer. Bloody hell, even the prick's walk was arrogant and full of shit. As he hit the outer ring of those gathered he shoved and elbowed his way past. Some took exception and barely restrained themselves from morphing into another, bigger, meaner form. Other's failed but held themselves back as fighting in town and among themselves was forbidden by royal decree.

As he got closer the more combative and belligerent he became. It was when he came to the mother and child to which Balthazar had just spoken that the whole plan nearly went up in smoke. Hadden dared to lay a hand on the child and shoved her back behind her mother to place himself mere meters from Balthazar's reach. Rage clouded his vision. He could hear the angry mutterings of those around him. They hated Hadden as much as he did. Good, they'd find satisfaction right alongside him this eve.

He looked at the arrogant disgusting prick, the seller of secrets that weren't his to sell or keep, a demon who held nothing but his own gain in his heart, and he smiled. It was a smile that held no sincerity, but it wasn't meant to.

Out of the corner of his eye he saw Satari leading his two most trusted enforcers through the door of her daughter's dwelling to free her family. It wasn't long before the sound of gentle sobbing could be heard coming their way. Hadden's face fell as he swiveled around. Demons looked upon the scene as Satari and his men informed them of Hadden's actions. Angry demons turned as one, but Balthazar held up his hand and called for silence. The crowd stepped back, giving Hadden a wide berth and the unpredictable Balthazar as much space as he wanted.

"This creature, who stands here spluttering like a fool, will stand as a lesson in what not to do, who not to harm, and who not to cross. That last one would be me, by the by. I suggest any children be sent away now so you can all enjoy the show. Ganf, if you would accompany them and make sure they're otherwise entertained, please." He directed the last part to the young mother, who nodded and quickly began rounding up the children and herding them toward the entertainment building a good distance away.

Satari tried to send both her daughter and grandson with them, but Denriah held her ground.

"I need to see hisss ending, to know he isss gone. We desssserves justiccce, and I will sssavour his ssuffering."

She handed Thovad to her mother, and urged her to keep him safe. Satari nodded, knowing her daughter's need to be sure they were truly free from their nightmare.

He understood her need, had witnessed it for millennia, had felt it in his soul and burning through the hearts of countless beings. Vengeance wasn't all hatred and fury, sometimes it was the satisfaction and knowledge of being assured that the monster under your bed truly had been slain, so it couldn't come back again.

Hadden's panic finally unglued his feet as he searched for an escape from the makeshift arena, walled in by the demons he'd pushed his way through. Fuckwit. He moved further away from Balthazar but closer to his own, pissed off kind. True, Balthazar was the bigger threat, but still . . . Not smart.

There was no way out, not unless he went through Balthazar or wanted to fight all of his demon kin, and only an idiot thought they'd stand a chance at that.

"Oh, what do you know? Hello, idiot," Balthazar thought to himself, or had he spoken? Either way the enraged cry of a trapped beast came out of the demon suddenly charging toward him. Not quickly by any means. Balthazar's powers slowed Hadden's movements, and while he appreciated the other demons trying to sink their claws into him, this was his fish to gut. He could feel his anticipation reaching a crescendo in his blood. His smile had Hadden tripping over himself as he stumbled to a halt.

It was showtime, and goddammit, Balthazar had missed this. His divine purpose rushed through his blood. The set up and the fall. As the original Angel of Vengeance released the heat burning through his arm, out of his palm the flaming sword of justice exploded, lighting the darkness of the night that hung over this realm for more hours than not. Balthazar felt freer than he had in hundreds of years. Even though the shackles would be back tomorrow, tonight he could be himself again.

As he strode toward his victim, who was frozen in shock and fear, he thought of his plan to string the bastard up and cut out his tongue, to shred the flesh from his meager bones and leave his dripping carcass to his demon kin. His maniacal laughter echoed in the stagnant air that always seemed to hover in this place, the underlying smell of sulfur enough to warrant nose plugs. None of that even registered as his heart beat in time with Hadden's, tracking his movements, anticipating his need to flee. Fuck, freedom felt damn good. Vengeance too.

Soon he'd get the vengeance he craved most. The vengeance he lived and breathed for. It wouldn't fix what was broken and gone. He knew that on a soul deep level nothing ever would. But, he'd get the bastard responsible. It's why he did what he did, after all.

CHAPTER 12

By the time they'd reentered the main conference room every bite of food had been eaten. Most of the males had undone the top button of their pants and were reclining in various gluttonous poses around the room. Lily and Perri almost looked like they wanted to throw up, and even Luc had an overfed glaze to his eyes that, along with the empty dishes and trays, showed how much they'd all consumed. Roth suspected it'd been a joint effort to purposely make every crumb disappear before he and Athon rejoined the group. For what purpose he wasn't yet sure, but they definitely had one judging by the mirth filled twinkle in Dante's eyes and the upward twitching of his lips.

He and Athon had obviously slept through lunch and dinner, if the fading light outside the full wall of windows was anything to go by. Had they stayed the entire time? Probably. The shitheads were obviously enjoying themselves immensely. What he couldn't figure out was how much they knew of what had gone on behind the closed door where he and Athon had been sequestered. If they knew anything at all, that is. Shaking his head, he dislodged those wayward superfluous questions and focussed on the task at hand.

After they'd awoken he and Athon had discussed the situation somewhat. They knew they were connected to the woman in their shared dream. It was also likely that because Roth had been the one to come into physical contact with her, and Athon had not had that pleasure, he could be a link of some kind between them.

The question they couldn't answer was whether it worked on just anyone, or was it unique to them? Lucifer's reaction suggested otherwise. That he was already connected to her somehow. If this was the case, Lucifer had a previous claim, and they would not, could not begrudge him his happiness. He was their leader, but he was also their friend, their family. They had pledged themselves to not only the service the Almighty required of them, but also to Lucifer himself. They would ultimately sacrifice everything if he asked them to. That Lucifer had reacted to Roth's words in the way he had, felt like a physical blow to Roth, the realms made less sense and the offense he had caused needed to be righted. Athon's hand squeezed his shoulder, knowing what Roth planned next, offering comfort and support.

Lucifer seemed to notice in that moment the serious expression upon Roth's face, and so he rose from his supine position with as much grace as his overindulgence allowed. Yep, Roth noted the unbuckled belt and unbuttoned trousers. His eyes flicked to Athon, and he saw his own inner amusement reflected in his lover's eyes and the tilt of his lips, even as the weight of his unintentional misstep sullied his otherwise good mood.

Warily, Roth approached his General and lowered himself to one knee, head bent in supplication. An act of fealty and loyalty. One they'd each undertaken when they'd first come under his command. One Roth felt the need to renew, even as fear of rejection clogged his throat and brought the burn of unshed tears to his eyes.

"I, Azaroth, child of the Almighty, descendant of no one, offer the renewal of my oath. I pledge allegiance and service to the Almighty, and the destiny set before me. I offer my loyalty, my service, my respect, and my existence to Lucifer, General of the Shadow Hounds. In shadows bound we bind the evil of mankind. In friendship I renew my vow."

As the last words left his lips he felt a tear slip free. The burning pain on his lower back had him arching on a silent scream, the brand of his designation, his preordained path, much as it had when it'd appeared upon his body the first time he'd made his promise to Lucifer and accepted his fate, pulsed with liquid fire. Lucifer's face appeared before his and his arms came to land on his black, muscle T-shirt clad shoulders. Meaning Lucifer was on his knees before him. Something Lucifer rarely did. Fuck, this time hurt more than the first. Or maybe because millennia had passed he'd simply forgotten how bad it'd actually been.

The Almighty loved a good joke though, and being the all-knowing creator of the universe, as far as they knew, had already known what would come to pass, what things would be called and so on. Thus, each Shadow Hound's brand blazed its way into and onto their skin in the exact same location. The slightly raised black tattoo was a bloody tramp stamp of all things. Fucking ass antlers. Right there on their lower backs, just above their ass cracks it sat as proud as punch. Luc assured them every time one of them realized what the placement meant in these modern times the Almighty would be laughing their fucking ass off. He was absolutely certain it was deliberate. But fuck, it was better than what Michael and those tighty whitey Blessed Reapers had ended up with, a freaking welcome mat.

The Hounds may have a sword pointing down to their asses, but at least they didn't have a scythe, a fucking symbol of death, hovering over their privates. Thank fuck humans couldn't see the damn things. Can you imagine the issues with getting laid back in the day if they could? They'd have been burned, or stoned, or some other ass backwards, idiotic shit.

All these thoughts ran through his head until the burning faded, and he fell forward. Only to be held up by Luc's strong arms in a hold that spoke of friendship and felt almost fatherly.

"It is I who should be on my knees apologizing to you, my friend. You did nothing to deserve such a reaction. We will find her and together we'll get to the bottom of whatever's going on," Luc's voice was calm and laced with regret. Something Roth had not been expecting. As he looked up into his friend's face he saw red swirling in the background, felt the tensed muscles as he struggled against his shadows, and was keenly aware of the conflict raging inside of him as only someone who'd waged that kind of war could be.

"You had me pissing my pants, dude. Obviously, since I passed the fuck out and all."

"He had us all pissing our pants, dude," Malech chimed in, causing them all to chuckle, and a rueful smile appeared on Luc's face.

"I feel strangely at peace at the moment compared to earlier, when I wanted to rip your head from your spine. I cannot excuse my behavior, but I also know that in the same position again it would go the same way. My Caria was dead, I saw her lying there, and then she was gone, all traces of her had vanished, and I cannot explain it. The Praesidium said it was not in their purview, as no death had occurred. Yet still I could not find her . . . Until now, for a brief moment, and then she is once again gone. She was human, and if not one then close to it, at least I thought so, but obviously I was wrong."

"Luc, you're wafflin' mate." Andy had spent a fair bit of time on the coast of Australia catching waves and picked up some local phrases and a distinct accent.

"You need to tell us what the fuck has been going on with you the last seventy-odd years. We've tried to figure it out ourselves and come up with bupkis. We've compensated for your erratic, eccentric behavior. It was like you were shut off from reality. You might not have thought we needed to know before, but to figure whatever this is out, we need to know now. Trust us, as we trust you. You too, Roth. You seemed to be following Luc along that path for a bit there, my friend," Marco tried to say it gently, but to anyone who didn't know him well his raspy, gravelly bass would have sounded like an accusation.

"You're right. We are family, you deserve to be in the loop," Luc replied, as he looked at the floor beneath his knees, then stood and offered Roth his hand. Once standing he moved to the conference table again and took his seat indicating for them all to join him.

Mrs Briars entered, almost as if summoned by the rumbling of Roth's stomach, and he saw Athon's eyes widen as he took in the trolley of food she'd brought with her. He could almost see the drool running down his chin, and feel it on his own.

"You boys will eat, now, while the dumb one finally unburdens his soul." The wonderful woman placed tray upon tray in front of two seats side by side and basically shoved him and Athon into them. She'd probably start feeding them too if they didn't tuck in fast enough.

The others in the room covered their mouths to hide their smiles. It was a good thing Luc loved her like the mother he'd never had, because no one else would ever have gotten away with that.

"This lot sure can pack the food away when they want to. You boys pay them no mind, okay? Especially that one," she said, pointing at Dante, who, in turn, looked at her with wide eyes and feigned innocence.

She gave them each a smile and bustled out of the room, but not before striding to Luc, placing her hand on his shoulder, and leaning in to whisper in his ear. Whatever she said had him gaping like a fish before nodding and thanking her.

"Did Mrs Briars dose you?" Lily gasped out, before she covered her mouth and shut her eyes.

What the fuck? Mrs Briars? Their Mrs Briars?

"Yeah, she did," nodded Luc sagely. "Good sense that woman, she probably had it on her hands when she touched me while the boys here were having fun in the other room. Probably around the same time she was threatening Dante with a tartless eternity." Roth swore he saw Luc throw a wink in Lily's direction. The bastard was attempting to deflect the conversation, and damn it, it worked.

All eyes were on Athon and Roth, but the fucker wasn't getting out of this no matter how hard he tried.

"Who's Caria, Luc? What the fucks been your deal all these years? Most importantly, whose ass do you need to kick, and how can we help?"

Praise be to the Almighty, every head swiveled back to Luc. Roth wasn't ready for more talk about himself just yet. Athon's hand on his thigh gave a firm reassuring squeeze. He reached down and laced their fingers together. The small smile that lit Athon's face was like sunshine on a cloudy day. Fuck, what was with the poetic shit, surely he was getting too old for that crap, but apparently not.

Luc took a big deep breath, the room froze for what seemed an eternity, and then he let it all out. He told them everything. How he met her, how he found her, the Praesidium's response, and how it all just disappeared like a dream that never was.

When he was done you could have heard a feather hit the soft carpeted floor. Well fuck, no wonder the guy was acting loopy. Something like that would definitely mess with your head. His mystery woman, their mystery woman, maybe, had only ghosted eight years ago, but he was already starting to slip, and he wasn't even involved with her like Luc had been. To think Luc had been holding it all in for over seventy years; it was almost too painful to think about.

The chick was definitely not human, not from what he'd seen, and he could see by the look in his General's eyes he now knew it too. Luc's previous assumption of her humanity having rapidly dissolved with each revelation throughout the day left questions without answers. Like, what was she, where was she, and how the fuck were they going to find her?

"LIKE FUCKING hell I'm going to sit on my ass while anyone else searches for her! We all saw what happened in the dragon realm. It's her last known location. Nothing short of the Almighty themselves will stop me chasing after her. If you all think you can stop me, then every last one of you is delusional. I want answers. I need them. It's been nearly seventy-three years. I think I fucking deserve answers, don't you?" Luc's voice ground to a ragged halt on the last syllable, but he glared at every set of eyes that dared lock with his own. Reaching for the glass of water before him, he quickly took a few sips to wash away the hoarseness before he devolved into gasping fits of coughing. Not that he could blame his throat or chest for it since he'd spoken without pause and his air intake had been greatly inhibited.

"Not saying you shouldn't go, my brother," Marco calmly intoned. "Just saying we should do this smart and send in some recon first. You do tend to go in like a hammer to an anvil, and, well, dragons don't take too well to that shit on a good day."

"And wait how long? She could be anywhere by now. We wait any longer, I might never find her." He barely recognized the sound of his own voice. It was like all the air was being sucked out of the room and his ears were about to pop. His shadows warmed under his skin, almost writhing in agitation. Murmurs filled his ears, like indecipherable whispers of madness. Control was slipping through his fingers, he was low-key terrified. What the fuck was happening to him? Never had Luc heard of shadows being like this, of having so much power over their host angel.

"We at least need a plan, General. You more than all of us should appreciate a good plan. How many times have you reamed our asses for going off half-cocked, flying by the seat of our pants and nearly ballsing shit up?" Dante smirked at him, completely unaware of the lit powder keg Luc felt was inside of himself.

"Not us," piped up Lily, pointing to Perri and herself, her brow hitched with sass. "We happen to always think things through. Maybe because we don't have said cocks, but more likely because we're just smarter than you lot. Perri and I, that is. Not necessarily women in general. 'Cos I've met some dumb as fuck women over the ages too."

The wet spray of water from Fynn's mouth hit Luc's face and pulled him slightly out of his haze as everyone stared at Lily in wonder before chaotic laughter echoed through the room.

"Remember that time in Athens?"

"The mud wrestling?"

"Or that saloon in the mid-west back in the 1860s?"

"What about that nightclub boss a few years back?"

Luc hadn't seen Lily's face that shade of purple and red in such a long time, he longed to reach out and pull her into his arms, just as he'd done the day they'd found her. He cleared his throat, he knew his eyes flashed red by the scarlet filter over his sight. Thank fuck they heeded his warning and simmered down to silence.

"Yeah, yeah, smart asses. Some other time, I'm going to write a book of all the shit you lot have done over the years. It'd be a bestselling comedy, or maybe a tragedy, depending on how I choose to end it." The stiletto dagger that magically appeared in Lily's hand, she was that fast on the draw, caught their eyes as she twirled it with her fingers like a baton. Every male present shifted in their seats, the sound of mumbled apologies, in such respectful tones, echoed loudly in the quiet room. Luc figured they'd all just been reminded about what had happened to the last guy who'd made fun of her. It hadn't been pretty, but he'd been so fucking proud of her.

Even as these thoughts filtered through his mind, they were lost in the veil forming over his awareness. What the hell? No, this should not be happening. Mrs Briars had double dosed him before she'd left the room. He'd felt it and she'd confirmed it. Without it he was too unstable. Luc began to panic, his eyes darted around the room, he desperately wanted to call for help, but an invisible force held him silent and still.

Whispers invaded his ears, urging him to move, to search, to tear the world asunder to find her. To drag her home to him. Not even the voice inside his head sounded like his own anymore, but he'd gotten used to that a while ago. He'd thought maybe he was going crazy, and maybe he was, but it was better than being lonely. The comfort of another voice sharing in his misery, only speaking it's need to find her too was something he'd come to rely upon. Fuck, his inner psyche was totally messed up

He vaguely saw the faces around him as they shifted from one emotion to another before they all landed on variations of the same; sheer panic. Red filled his vision, his shadows flew about him, knocking everyone backwards out of their chairs. Before he could control it, or even knew it was happening, he was moving through the vast expanse of space that made up the link between realms. The dragons better have his girl, or he'd rip their world apart. Treaty or no treaty.

CHAPTER 13

"Where the hell did Luc just go?"

"What the fuck was up with his shadows?"

"Fuck his shadows. Did you see his eyes?"

"He looked full-blown feral on steroids."

Everyone spoke at once. The shocked faces around the room looked like stunned goldfish, but no one laughed at the comical expressions. Not even Dante.

Luc had been "normal" one moment, then completely deranged the next. Never had he acted more shadow-like than angel before. It was unheard of. The shadows weren't exactly sentient, rather more like an extension of the angel themselves. At least, that's what they'd always believed. Like a superpower that you could wield without really thinking about it. Sure, they manifested in different ways, but that was always unique to the angel. Roth's shadows took the shape of a wraith with red eyes and a gaping maw when he chose to employ it. Thus his code name, Wraith. Athon was called Snake, thus his shadows formed into a very large and deadly serpent or snake, depending on your knowledge of mythology. The others all had their own as well, no two the same. Luc's depicted the devil incarnate, just like those biblical representations he'd always found so freaking amusing.

Roth had felt his shadows still in the alley with the unknown woman. Instinctively he trusted his shadows to steer him right, well, except for Mara. His shadows had hidden in the deepest parts of him, cowering, almost shamefully, definitely fearfully in hindsight. For them to take control of Luc like they had, morphing his features, speaking through him, was next level freaky shit. It definitely hadn't been Luc who'd snarled those words at them before flinging his body through the portal. A portal that looked to be made from the shadows themselves rather than the powers each angel carried within them.

"Fuck outta my way, ants, afore I crush to dust you all," Luc exploded with a barely understandable growl as they were flung backwards out of their seats and onto their asses. Luc was no longer in charge, for the Luc they knew would never speak to them in such a way.

"Mrs Briars, we need you here right now," Lily called, her voice shaking with panic.

"Already here, precious. Felt the vibrations through the whole castle. Not an ounce of energy was left undisturbed."

"How did this happen? You dosed him, he admitted as much. What went wrong?"

At this point everyone but Lily was utterly lost. What the hell was she talking about? Considering they didn't actually know what Mrs Briars was, this could get interesting. All those millennia ago, when Luc had brought her home, they were instructed to just accept her presence, and they had, they'd also eventually given up guessing. Everyone had a story, not everyone needed to know yours. They'd each learned that lesson the hard way. Sometimes, too well.

"Well, cat's outta the bag now, miss blabbermouth. Fine, quick run down boys and girls before we get back on track. I have some magic, this you know, if you don't, then you're a bit slow on the uptake and you may want to get that looked at." She threw a wink at Dante and Fynn.

"I can intensify and/or dampen certain emotional reactions and experiences. Lucifer is aware, always has been, but for the sake of those who needed my particular help on occasion, it was much easier if everyone else remained in the dark. Including you lot. Also, Luc was to take me in, no questions asked, as some of you may remember?"

"What do you mean? How do you mess with our emotions, exactly?" Roth felt his agitation building, like ants crawling over his skin.

"That feeling you have right now, my boy? That's what you feel like most of the time when anything is out of your control." She moved to place her hand on his shoulder and the feeling went away.

"I've not felt it in so long, not since right after—"

"Right after Mara, may she find a particularly hellish spot in Nestradia. Yes, whenever you start to feel that way, I find a way to take it away, to mask it, you could say. Except in that alleyway, I stayed out of that. The lack of control you felt then, the emotions, was nothing like what you are feeling now. They definitely weren't destructive in nature. Over the years I've tried to help you all, where and when I can. Luc has needed quite a bit of my talent lately, but each of you is different."

Not a breath left a single set of lips as they let what she said sink in. Could she read thoughts? Read emotions? Oh shite, of course, every dirty thought Roth had ever had since the arrival of Mrs Briars flashed through his head and his face flamed with the intense heat of his embarrassment. Glancing at Athon, he saw a look of sheer incredulity. Dante's face looked pained with a tinge of anger growing ever deeper. The rest just looked stunned, followed by the dawning of the same thoughts he'd just had. Mrs Briars burst out laughing.

"I cannae read your thoughts, laddie," she sputtered. "And I thank the Almighty for that small boon, to be sure. But I can see things when I need to, yet never when I want, and I know what my charges need and want only so I can help them. Sometimes, even before they do. Now, back to our current, rather urgent, situation."

Mrs Briars looked at them all expectantly. When they still stood there like statues, with about as many brain cells, judging by the look on her face, she huffed, stormed behind Luc's chair, and placed her hands on the high back. She was so short you could barely see her shoulders over the top of it.

"Luc, you idiots," she reminded them. "Pull your heads out of your tushies and focus."

Like soldiers called to arms they raced back to the table, but didn't sit.

"If you dosed him to keep him calm, why'd he go off like that?"

"Love, my dear Dante, is something not even I can fully control. It makes us do crazy things. You all have so much to learn. I'm certain your journeys have only just begun. The Almighty never does anything without a plan, including what the Fates are allowed to set in motion." It was clear from the thread of anger that wove through her voice she had some issues with either the Almighty, the Fates, or all of them.

"That being said, what are you all doing standing around in here still? You have somewhere you all need to be."

"But we don't know—"

She cut Marco off before he could finish. "Where he went? Of course you do! I know none of you are that flipping dense . . . really?"

"Shit, the dragons!" Athon snapped. They all shot into action, each of them manifesting their weapons straight into their palms, considering they were melded with them by divine power as soon as they received them, it was such a natural thing. They were ready to portal immediately.

"Halt!" For some reason, when Mrs Briars spoke in that tone, Roth couldn't move his feet and he noticed he wasn't alone.

"It's going to be one of those days, isn't it?" She took a big deep breath and counted to ten, very slowly.

"Okay, first things first. Roth? Athon? Go get dressed, you both at least need shoes, and your shirt's on inside out, Leviathon."

"Perri, sweet, I believe you have a task you were already assigned, it was entered into the log that only I am privy to, so hop to it. You'll be sitting this one out."

Perri went to argue but Mrs Briars shot her a glare and beckoned her near. After a few seconds of back and forth whispering, Perri exited the room, toying with the blade as she went. Not happy, but resigned to staying behind.

"Dante, Malphas, you know I can feel that too, yes? Go prepare, plan, do your duty. Those souls have proven their lack of worth. Your lack of haste will only incur further losses."

Roth could see them valiantly trying to block out the call. It simply couldn't be done. So, despite their reluctance, they still managed to drag their feet out of the room.

"Marco, you're up. You get to sit this out and watch over the realm and all those in it."

"But, why? Nothing's going to happen. This is a tight ship," Marco protested. He hated staying behind, almost as much as Dante. The thought of missing out on a good fight would drive him crazy.

"Because someone has to be here to meet the two members of the Praesidium that have been detected on the outskirts of our realm. Eastern border. One male, one female. So, can the tantrum and put your big boy pants on." Mrs Briars proceeded to ignore his presence once she'd finished with that little bomb.

"Caine, my boy, my sweet boy." No one but Mrs Briars ever thought Caine was sweet, or if they did, they never dared to tell him so.

"I have it on impeccable authority that the time is drawing near. Very near. The soul will be reborn. Sooner than you think. He grows ever stronger in the womb. I'm afraid you cannot risk taking this journey when your own is about to begin, again." Caine's face turned to stone in an instant, every expression and emotion locked down tight behind layers of hard won control.

Roth knew that expression intimately. Caine had been the one to help him perfect it for himself. Which was why Roth could see behind the mask Caine wore, to the chaos churning away within him. Caine had no choice, even though Roth personally thought Caine should let the soul go. Not that he'd ever tell Caine that. The guy was loyalty and honor personified, all wrapped up with a bow and a tag labeled 'Duty'.

"Gym," was all he said as he marched out, muscles tense, as hard as rock.

"Alright, the rest of you need to get your shit together and get your backsides to wherever in the dragon realm Luc went. Time, she's a-ticking. The longer you take, the more he's going to fuck shit up."

Mrs Briars sank through the floor and disappeared. Roth, Athon, Lily, Fynn, Deus, Andy, Malech, and Ares called forth their traditional amour, made by the Almighty's favorite smith, the ever popular Hephaestus, and ran into the portal Deus had opened in the center of the room, weapons at the ready.

Roth grabbed a hold of Athon's hand at the last second and drew him close. His nearness calmed his inner demons, and sent a sizzle of lust through his veins. He was definitely getting his male naked upon their return. This better not take too long. As imperative as it was that they find this woman, an out of control Lucifer could truly fuck up their chances of doing so. Not to mention the cleanup would be a bitch.

CHAOS MET them as they landed on dragon soil, their arrival was not lost on the shifters gathered in the shadows either. Wide eyes, filled with trepidation and anger, watched them, some eager for a misstep and the chance to fight. Dragons were ever eager to draw blood. At least they used to be. Some still were, but the Clan Wars centuries ago had cured most of them of the character flaw. Still, despite the scene before him, most were holding back, a few injured warriors were strewn about. Then Deus spotted them, the children peeking from behind their mother's legs as they searched for a better view . . . And what a view it was. No one could ever claim Lucifer did things by halves, that was a certainty. For there in the center of the square, crouched over the liquefied remains of the mage, stood the creature of nightmares.

He was still devilishly handsome, just more like the devil than anything else in that moment. His shadows had gathered around him and covered him in the image of biblical evil that he usually found so amusing as a parlor trick. His eyes glowed vivid red and his wings spread wide. The voice, when Deus heard it, sent chills down his spine. Never would Luc allow himself to scare children like this. What the fuck was up with the asshole's shadows? How were they speaking for him? Scratch that. How the fucking shit balls could they speak at all?

"Where is she?!?" the bellowed malevolence demanded. "Tell me. I no kill all gathered here!"

Luc's fist pounded down upon the flagstones and the ground shifted beneath their feet. The Dragon Guard of Thisavrós stood at the ready, eyes flashing with the need to shift. Shit! Could this get any more complicated? Oh, yes, well, of course it could.

Instead of an answer, a young woman strode toward Luc. Was she a fucking idiot? Surely she could see the danger he presented? The moment her eyes flashed completely silver, he knew she was a witch.

She was trying to look directly into Luc's psyche, to puzzle out how to handle him. Problem was, she was going to get it wrong. Luc's brain was an intricate labyrinth of utter complication, it'd taken him centuries of covert prodding to delve in and get even an inkling of an idea as to how to calm him. The tiny little slip of a woman was going to get herself killed if she didn't stop and back the truck up.

Luc saw her coming and rose up to his full height, even taller with the added shadows. The shadows growled and hissed as they eyed her coldly.

Behind her the clan chieftain stood in his full dragon form, twice as tall as the building behind him, ready to pounce. His midnight-blue form had a regal air, predatory, deadly, and yet the man was fully in charge of the beast. When his guards made to move forward, he held them off. Interesting, Deus's brows rose, the chief seemed to trust the foolish wench.

He needed to do something. He needed to bring Luc out of wherever he was right now, and back to himself. The Treaty of the Realms clearly stated that the Shadow Hounds had no dominion over dragon souls and all disputes must be handled by, or with the permission of, the Praesidium. Not only was Luc fucking with the treaty, his shadows were probably going to maim that poor woman. Standing next to Luc she looked so tiny. His shadows had built him up and his wings didn't lessen the contrast in their sizes.

Sword drawn, Deus stepped forward; he felt the others do the same. Always a team, they had each other's backs.

"Step back away from him, woman!" he ordered. His voice cracked through the air like a whip, the command full of compulsion . . . And yet, she did not stop. Instead, she glared at him quickly before she snapped her gaze back to Luc, laid her palm upon his arm, and appeared to take a single, deep breath.

"Shhh, *Scáth-thiarna*. It's time to rein in the rage. To find Decaria, you will need the help of those you now seek to hurt. Big, deep breaths, release your hold." Damn, it wasn't working.

He'd actually grown bigger at the mention of her name. Why couldn't Deca have fallen for a human, or, at the very least, a wolf shifter? A quick tap on the nose and a certain command, and they were putty compared to this one. She'd spoken to the shadows, not the angel. Though they were irrevocably entwined. Scáth-thiarna, Shadow Lord, for that was what he was. The first of his kind, he held dominion over all the rest, if he lost this battle his madness would spread throughout the nest.

From the corner of her eye, she noted the other angels advancing and saw a flash of long black and silver hair falling from under the golden helm of the one who'd spoken up. The strands fell over his broad shoulders as he advanced toward her slowly. She glanced behind him. Yeah, those two were who she really needed to worry about, especially the taller of the two as his hand clenched and unclenched around the hilt of his sword, repeatedly. Guess it was time to bring out the big guns. She leaned further forward, despite Lucifer's agitated growling and the almost certain chance of evisceration, and whispered softly, so only he could hear.

> *"Walk with me on the craggy rocks,*
> *In the moonlight before the dawn.*
> *Lie with me on the hillside, where the shepherds*
> *   tend their flocks,*
> *There to wake within my arms when the sun*
> *   shines in the morn.*
> *When the seas are filled with angry souls,*
> *And the waves come barrelling over,*
> *I'll hold thee safe in my embrace*
> *As the world, it turns to sulfur."*

Beneath her palm she felt his muscles stiffen. In fact, every muscle in his body became so taut with tension she could feel shivers rippling through the air as the whole realm seemed to wait with bated breath for a more likely than not explosion from the legendary Lucifer.

After what felt like eons, but was mere seconds, his entire being, shadows and all, shuddered and curled inwards as he fell to his knees at her feet. She reached down and touched his black hair. Hair that had been bright frickin' blue when he'd first stepped through the portal. It hadn't looked too bad, but seeing his natural hair, now that the magic around it had been nullified by whatever was going on with him, made her heart stutter as she thought of how perfect they'd looked together all those years ago.

In her mind, Sera could still see the smile Decaria had thrown her way as she'd danced with the devil, as she'd later said. It was a smile Sera had never seen from her again. Not after the shit-fest that had found her the moment he'd left.

She'd come looking for her bestie-boo, Deca. When she'd lost the ability to track her through the blood link, she'd almost gone absolutely mental. Knowing her last traceable location, she'd gathered her shit and hot-footed it to the realm of dragon's as fast as she could. Only to find a bigger fucking mess than she'd ever expected. She'd certainly never expected to run into any bloody Shadow Hounds, that's for sure. The meddlesome asshole, the Almighty, certainly liked to fuck with a girl's head. Thankfully her panic had settled somewhat when she'd noted his absence. Nor had she expected to have a crying Lucifer hugging her legs like a devastated man-child. Which it seemed is exactly what he was doing at the moment.

The temptation she'd felt to run when she'd seen them come through the portal was outweighed by the thought of the two most important people in her life. How they seemed to have disappeared completely, despite the tracking bonds she had with them both. While she'd been informed that she was not to look for the first, she would not lose them both, and since no stupid gold-lined envelope had arrived telling her to back up and let it go, she was one bitchin' witch on a mission.

Thank fuck she'd had a full pot of coffee before she'd left, otherwise she'd probably not have recalled the poem Deca had made her memorize all those years ago, just in case she came in contact with the blubbering lump at her feet and needed him to trust her.

"What have you done to him?"

Ah yes, Jackass 2.0 was headed her way now the immediate danger had passed, the anger and concern in his voice both agitated and calmed her. Not that she'd stand for any shit from any of them, but it was nice to see his concern for his boss.

The closer he got, the more aggressive the dragons began to feel. Their energy levels were peaking as they noted the Shadow Hounds still had their weapons drawn. The aggressive tone didn't sit well with them either. The fact it was directed at a female, of the species or not, just added insult to injury. Especially when said female had just informed them the mage they'd long thought a friend had the stench of evil tainting the very essence of his magic. An evil she'd felt before, the same evil Deca had warned her about, one which had pervaded the space the day she'd 'died'.

She tilted Luc's face to look up at her own.

"We will talk more another time. I will help you find Decaria. She is like my sister, and I will not lead you astray in this. I feel the time is coming for you to be reunited. I know she has longed for it." She sighed heavily at the exhausted leader of the Hounds. "But right now? Now I need to go and deal with the idiots about to start a bigger fight than they originally stepped into."

Lucifer went to try and stand, but she halted his feeble attempts and shook her head. "I got this." Her cocky wink had his lips twisting in a tired and grateful smile. There would be time for questions later . . . if he could find her.

"Stand down, boys, I have divine protection. Well, for as long as it suits the Almighty's fucked up purpose. It is what it is."

She shrugged her shoulders, a look of long-suffering boredom on her face to match the rolling of her clover-green eyes. She never got sick of her powers and projecting her voice like this was always so cool. Only in her dreams, her nightmares, did she remember not having them. Remember, not imagine, because she knew after all the lives she'd lived, they were indeed memories and not just horrific fantasies of death and betrayal.

"The time for fighting is not now. Your friend is fine. Your insult to the dragons can be rectified, and the answers you seek here are not as they seem."

The two she'd noted earlier stepped forward, swords down but not sheathed. Swords, sheaths, damn, it had been too long if that was all it took to make her traitorous body tingle.

"We must find her, the one who killed the mage."

Oh, he had such pretty colored eyes, all gold and blue and purple. Sera was mildly jealous of the fact such pretty eyes actually belonged to anyone. Not to say she didn't like her own, she did, but tricolor eyes were just totally awesome.

"And what, pray tell, will you do when you find her?"

"She won't be harmed, I assure you. We just need the mystery of it all to end."

Sera laughed at this so hard she thought she'd wet herself. They thought the mystery would end when they found Deca? Like fuck it would. The Almighty loved long games, and if anyone knew how long the game could go, it was her.

"Surely you know better than that, right? There are always going to be more mysteries. That's the fun of the game of life, even for us non-humans."

Turning to the Chief of Thisavrós, whose name, funnily enough, was Thisavrós, she nodded and gestured for him to call off his guards. Finally, the Chief took flight and sought a private place to shift. Dragons viewed shifting as a sacred, and sometimes intimate experience. Only when absolutely no other option was possible did they shift in public. The guards withdrew to their regular posts, fully aware that she could handle the intruders. It was a good thing dragons could sense the level of magic a witch or mage was capable of, if not the intent with which they would use it.

Weapons disappeared, helms were removed. There were eight of them. She hadn't paid much attention to them earlier, but damn! She could see why Deca had fallen for Luc, he was just her type and drop-dead gorgeous in a very movie star kind of way. The one with the white and red eyes and take-charge attitude was fucking sexy, despite his obvious mental handicap. Seriously, if he thought he could command her like he'd tried to, there must be a few screws loose. Yeah, she'd felt his power threaded through the order he'd given. It didn't do anything to her, except tickle along the arch of her foot, and that was bad enough. What right did they all have to be so fucking hot? If she hadn't already sworn off the capricious nature of men, she'd be all over them like butter melting on a hot corn cob. Was she tempted? Maybe a little. Was it worth it? Lock, stock, and two smoking barrels of 'Fuck, No!' it wasn't. Not even the pretty little dark-haired lass with the lavender eyes could convince her to go near those males for 'sexy time'. Fuck, when had she become such a man-hater? Actually, scrap that, it wasn't really that hard of a leap to make, considering.

"Anyways." She clapped her hands and smiled. "Listen up, stud muffins, and one smokin' hot princess," her voice took on a slightly huskier tone at the last bit, as she threw in a wink aimed at the female, and was rewarded with a faint blush. "When you find them, you'd better be on your best behavior, because if you hurt them, angels or not, I'll rip your wings off and shove them so far up your asses you'll be tasting feathers every time you lick your lips."

Before they had time to pick up their jaws, she made a hasty, slightly ungraceful exit, taking the long route to portal home. Hoping like fuck they chose not to follow.

CHAPTER 14

The fucking bastard! Tears streamed down her face as she clutched at her stomach. Of course, he was the kind of asshole who'd do something so literal. But damn it, every time Jezzie thought she had her laughter under control, she'd catch sight of those fucking curtains again, the ones now hanging along the front of her room, and off she'd go again.

They really were literally what she'd asked for, she couldn't blame him for that. Fucking curtains, and that they were. Couples in every imaginable position and configuration graced the expanse of hanging fabric. Men, women, beings of all realms doing the nasty. Hmm, her laughter petered away as her breath hitched with a flash flood of desire. Oh, but that one looked interesting, the one with the three beefy guys and the ravished woman, cocks everywhere . . .

Wait, were they moving? Jezzie's breath suddenly seized completely, catching her off guard and she was forced to swallow air, which left her wheezing and coughing as she ran for the glass of water she'd left by the remade bed. Surely she'd been seeing things, maybe she'd just been caught up in the sheer eroticism of the scene. She rubbed her eyes, her temples, and rolled her neck and shoulders before she turned back toward them. That sneaky prick! They were actually moving! Ballzy had put up actual 'fucking' curtains, porn curtains. As she crept closer to the image she'd found so intriguing she could see every detail so clearly against the light blue brocade. Sweat glistened on their skin, the contours of their muscles as they flexed, rosy nipples being licked to rigid peaks. Hell, she could even see how wet the woman was as one of the men plunged in and out of her pussy, another buried to the hilt in her ass. Yet the surprises kept coming as her head tilted, her ears honing in on soft sounds. Her body angled closer, her eyes taking in every nuance of the beings fornicating on her curtains. One erotic scene at a time.

Yep, the closer she looked, the louder they got. Her brand new 'fucking' curtains came with surround sound too, no silent movies here. It was just too good. Ballzy probably thought he'd won this round. Too bad for him she had nothing against some sexy pornography, moving or not. Plus, she'd technically gone without for eight years. Dreams didn't count, right? Might as well take some notes; there were a few things on display she'd never seen or tried before.

Just when she thought she was all laughed out and couldn't be any more surprised, the guy right in front of her, whose cock she'd just been eyeing off, winked directly at her, and off she went again. When she made it out of here she knew exactly what she'd send Ballzy as a Christmas gift. Knew just the witch to help her do it too.

When she finally calmed herself down she looked back up, gave the guy a wink right back and watched his smile grow even larger. He turned back to focus on the woman, judging by the point of her ear peeking through her silky auburn hair, she was one of the long-banished fae. Come to think of it, all of the males with her were, except the one with his cock thrusting in and out of her open mouth. He had soft downy looking hair covering his lower body and cloven hooves, a faun then. By gods, his cock was glorious to behold. He pulled out as if sensing her eyes upon him, pre-cum beaded at the tip and as the female flicked her tongue out to lick it up, she locked eyes with Jezzie. Her brow lifted, excitement shone in her forest-green eyes, and then as her tongue traced her lips with the glistening droplet, she winked flirtatiously at a blushing, panting Jezzie.

Fuck. She needed a nice long bath and a decent set of toys.

Thankfully she had access to the former. Unfortunately, there was zero fucking chance she'd ever ask Ballzy for the latter.

———

THIRTY MINUTES and four very nice orgasms later, Jezzie stepped out of the ivory and gold claw foot bathtub filled with tepid water, but which had been steamy and filled with cinnamon and patchouli scented bubbles when she'd first hopped in. Her legs felt weak and all she wanted was to pull on some soft comfy PJ's and fall into bed with a good book. Luckily for her, Ballzy had an extensive library and all she had to do was walk in, think of a title, author, genre, or trope, and a selection would appear for her to choose from. If he wasn't such an asshole she'd consider staying and marrying the guy just so she could keep his library. That was how much she loved to read.

She'd once been asked by a guy she'd dated why she loved reading so much. She'd responded, "Books are like friends. They are there when you need them, can lift you up in moments when you need lifting, they can understand your pain, teach you so many wonderful and helpful things. They can release the stopper when you need to cry, and make you laugh when all you feel is the urge to cry and rage at the world. In some ways, they are better than friends, they don't get angry when you're busy, or need to set them aside on the shelf. But they are always there again when you come back. Never judging you for your absence."

The idiot had looked at her as if she'd had two heads, called her a weirdo, and hailed himself a cab. Leaving her standing on a busy sidewalk on a Friday evening with a bag filled with new books she'd just treated herself to. She'd gone on to have an amazing weekend making new friends, while he probably slithered home to fap one out to the nudie mags he'd thought she hadn't known were hidden beneath his bed. *Moron.*

After toweling herself dry she wrapped the thick, soft, burgundy towel around her torso securely and opened a drawer in the provincial french armoire standing against the far wall intent on sliding her body into a set of soft comfy pajamas as planned. Only, there were none. No soft, fluffy, silky, or even just comfy pajamas lay folded within its drawers. None hung on the hangers. There were no tight leather pants, no boots, no clothing fit for a badass rebel, no slinky lingerie. Nothing but plain cotton shorts, pants, tank tops and one threadbare robe hanging on a hook on the back of the door. What the hell was going on? Sure, she was a prisoner, but Ballzy had never done this before. Was it some new game? A new tactic to throw her off? Well, it wasn't going to work, damn it. So, she pulled on some cotton panties, added a pair of gray drawstring pants, and donned a basic gray tank top which thankfully had a shelf bra built in, because heaven knew her tatas needed the added support. Not the look she originally had in mind, but beggars and all that jazz. Ballzy wasn't going to mess with the rest of her plan though, so she strode out into the other room to grab one of the books on her nightstand and snuggle under the covers. Determined to lose herself in a world far away from here, the kind of romance that would make a girl long for a love that could tear the world asunder but would instead save it, just for her. Holy heck, she was a sucker for a good book.

Her feet froze on the bare floor. No more plush carpet to take away the chill of the cold concrete. Gone too was her large, warm bed, replaced with a prison like cot and some manky looking blankets. The bathroom door chose that very moment to swing shut and hit her in the ass and out of her stupor. It also allowed her to take note of the greatest travesty thus far, the one thing that tripped her over the edge and into the stratosphere of completely pissed off. There was no bedside table. In and of itself not a big deal, but where there was no bedside table there were no books, not even a single sheet of paper.

A low growl started within her chest as her hands clenched into tight fists, her nails biting into her flesh and drawing blood. She might not be one of those typical vampires of legend, but blood still held power. It held ancient magic, and the scent of it, even her own, enhanced her rage, her frustration, and her confusion. Was she hurt he would do this? Yes. Was she kicking herself for letting her guard down even slightly? Absolutely, one hundred percent she was. Not a single luxury was left in the room.

Her body trembled, her agitation pushed her forward, back again, her pacing taking her further into the room with each back and forth, until . . . Smack! What the fuck! She'd barely made it halfway to the opposite wall when she was stopped in her tracks and found herself basically making out with a clear glass wall. A wall that definitely hadn't been there prior to her bath.

A door, exactly like the one to her bathroom stood at the far end of the other room, slightly ajar. Another bathroom? A similar prison style cot sat against the wall, again just like hers, and a metal door like you'd see in a psych ward was firmly shut.

Wait, if all the luxuries she'd been afforded were gone . . . She raced back to the door and breathed a sigh of relief, the bathtub still sat there in all its glory at least.

"Not for long, I'm afraid, luv, and I am sorry for it all too." Ballzy sighed.

"Why? What the fuck kind of game are you playing now, Balthazar?" she sneered, taking in his tense form as he feigned a casual lean against what appeared to be a newly reinforced cell door frame, similar to the one next door. She instinctively sent out her powers to taste his emotions. The guy was so freaking wired, worried, and more than a little pissed. Something had crawled up his ass, and he wasn't a happy camper. But right now he felt trepidation as he stood there waiting for her to explode. She'd always refrained from tasting his feelings. Partly to avoid giving herself away and partly to avoid wading through the quagmire of his sordid and sullied emotions. Well, mostly the former if she were being completely honest with herself.

He should be scared. Right now, as angry and confused as she was, she was liable to unleash her psychic tendencies and devour his mind whole, turning him into a pretty little vegetable. Except, as she delved a little deeper, she felt absolutely no evil in him, she still couldn't sense his soul, but his heart was pure, if a little battered and bruised, and a lot broken. It didn't mean the soul he had hidden from her was pure though, just that his intentions were pure toward whatever goal he had in the moment. A warm gust of fondness washed over her, she looked up to find his eyes trained on her, a wry tilt to his lips.

"You only ever call me Balthazar when you are beyond pissed, and this time I cannot say I blame you."

He stepped into the room and two demons followed, they watched her with interest and fear as they each placed a chair facing the other before they turned and left the room. Yeah, she noticed how their tongues flicked out toward her slightly, their amusement seeped out of them in waves. They found great enjoyment at her change of circumstance.

"Sit. I will explain as much as I can, but not enough to lose it all."

"What's with the cryptic bullshit, Balthazar?" she huffed as she practically flounced onto the chair. She knew she couldn't kill him, else she'd be stuck in the contract forever with no way out.

"Just tell me what's got your jocks in such a twist, that all this"—she gestured around her bare room and to the one on the other side of the partition—"is necessary?"

He took a deep breath and rested his elbows on his knees as he leaned forward toward her.

"It seems I had a little bit of a leak in my house. Thankfully that leak has now been plugged. With extreme prejudice. I had kept your presence here a secret for the most part, for both our sakes. Unfortunately, you haven't revealed yourself as I required, and this 'leak' has now been spread to others. Others I don't want in my affairs, that I don't want near you." Ballzy stood and paced behind his chair.

Her eyes tracked his movements as she tasted the truth of his words. Balthazar was being completely honest with her, as far as he could be. There was no hidden agenda tainting the flavor of his emotions.

"Raum is arriving within the next week. He is not a decent male. He is Fallen, and he is cruelty personified. He will stop at nothing until he has the answers he seeks; the ones either his puppet master wants, or his sick and twisted psyche demands. I don't want to scare you, Jezzie, but you should be scared. The Praesidium has been after him for more than 900 years, with no luck, and now he and his boss know about your presence here." He paused, looking at her for a reaction. Her face felt drawn, almost heavy and blank, even as confusion whirled inside her brain. What was he getting at here?

"And just what's this all supposed to mean to me, Ballzy?"

"Raum is coming to interrogate you, luv. And his means of doing so are endless and more than likely excruciating. He is a male without morals, and he enjoys his job. If he thinks you have any luxuries here, that I show you any extra considerations, he will not hesitate to exploit them. You will have to shore up your defenses, hide your pain, and ignore everything he does to others in an attempt to cause you to break . . . Unless you tell me first what we've been dancing around these past eight years. Which I doubt you will do."

"You could just release me from the contract and let me go, you know."

"Would that I could, but I can't. I am held to the letter of the contract just as you are. I need to know what you are before I can dissolve it, unless the end date of the contract comes into effect first. Which, as we know, is too far away to avoid our current problem."

"I cannot tell you what you want to know, Ballzy, even if I wanted to. I am blood bound not to until such a time as it is evident to all and there is no going back. He can do his worst and I will endure, I assure you."

"Then I fear our path is set." Weary resignation laced his words, aging him far more than his elegant features betrayed.

"What's with the other cell, though?"

"I told you yesterday that our 'guest' would be bringing a friend, did I not?"

Jezzie nodded in response, vaguely recalling their previous interaction.

"Well, let's just say that Raum likes to keep a pet or two at a time. Other beings he likes to force his peculiar attentions upon. He is bringing along his current favorite. The only information I have is an initial, N, and a list of equipment he wants added to both of these rooms."

"Demon's Den is yours though. I don't see why you even have to let him in. Especially since you so clearly don't want to."

"There are things in play here, Jezzie, that you aren't aware of. A much bigger picture than you can see right now. Lives hang by threads. Centuries of machinations and fated actions are in play, not to mention free will. At some point, we all face a crossroads, and usually we have to go through hell to get there. Welcome to my hell."

CHAPTER 15

Fingers wrapped like chains around his upper arm and bit into his flesh. The cold, hard, iron collar burned like ice against his neck. The chain of his leash hung loosely down his spine as he was forced along the narrow path toward the outer edge of the forest he'd called home these past few . . . Fuck, he didn't have a clue how long it had been. The thought registered and filtered through his tired brain, he should be worried, he should be scared, yet all he felt was weary and numb.

They'd been walking for what felt like days but was probably less than one. His bare feet were blistered and bloody. The prick wouldn't even allow him shoes for the journey. Not surprising, since he was kept pretty much naked most of the time anyway. But, come on asshole, shoes would have made this trip a lot faster, if not less painful. It would also be a kindness that his master would never show to anyone.

His other half was silent, not by choice but by design. The plan was simple, they'd said. In and out, they'd said. Well, fuck what they'd said, 'cos apparently they didn't know jack shit about much of anything, and even less about their target.

His master, Raum, was a sadistic fucking monster. Admittedly one of their own making, and still after all these centuries they couldn't catch the prick. Everyone they'd ever sent in had ended up dead, eternally missing, or probably both. Not that he'd been informed of this before he'd taken the job, no, it would have been too much of a courtesy to have given him that info, and they couldn't risk him turning them down.

What they also didn't know was that he'd pretty much had no choice but to take the job. His people had disowned and exiled him. Even his own mother had turned her back to him. It was an image forever branded on his soul. And why? Because he was different, different than the rest of them anyway. The pious bitch he'd loved as a child had turned her back on him when it was she who had lain with his father and conceived him. She hadn't seemed to mind his mixed heritage as he'd grown from a babe to a man, not until the truth had been too hard for her to hide.

Thank fuck she couldn't see him now. Thank fuck none of them could. Still, he had hope. He also had a plan. One of the awesome things about being him was his excellent, above average hearing, even for an OtherRealm being. Raum was headed to Demon's Den. When he'd heard Raum making the arrangements, he'd been well aware this might be his only chance to both escape, and complete his mission. The higher ups had said they had someone in that place, whatever it was, and if things went wrong he was to portal there straight away. Like he'd had a chance to do more than breathe before Raum had him trussed up and stripped down with no way for them to trace his location. Hadn't mattered though, nothing and no one could be traced in Raum's forest.

It was a creepy, forsaken place. The sharp stones along the path lay in wait, red and slippery, as though already coated in the blood of countless others. From the stories he'd heard of the Fallen, it was entirely possible they were. Thorny brambles poked and prodded, scratched and tore through skin, his, not Raum's. Not even the forest dared to harm him.

Gnarled, half dead branches formed a dark canopy overhead, blocking out the light of day. Not that it mattered. Raum seemed to know where they were going, and if a misstep occurred, it was he who stumbled, he who fell, he who flinched in pain as he was propelled forward by the beast at his back. For Raum had learned never to present such a tempting target to anyone. He'd learned firsthand how cunning and brutal the male was after so long trapped in his hell.

Light filtered through the dark up ahead, getting brighter with each step. The fresh scent of daylight and daisies filled his nostrils, pushing away the pungent odor of decaying vegetation and stale air. He could almost feel the wind calling to him, the cloudless sky, the warmth of the sun begging to shine on his constantly cold skin. Just as his filthy foot was about to set down on soft green grass the hand on his arm yanked him back. Like a puppet he snapped back at his puppeteer's command, his back slamming into Raum's thickly muscled chest. The hand on his forearm slithered up over his shoulder until it circled his throat and held him still.

"You will not speak unless I permit it. Understood?"

Raum allowed him only enough room for a small nod.

"You will do as I say, go where I say. Understood?"

Another nod.

"Good. You will be a pet I can be proud of. If you are not . . . Well, you will see first hand how much more fun I can really have."

The maniacal laugh that followed was both chilling and comical. The latter of which he managed to stuff deep down inside himself lest he find out sooner rather than later just how much more of a monster the asshole could be.

Before he knew what was happening, the promise of sunshine disappeared as he was shoved headlong into the disconcerting rush of a portal. His landing wasn't any less abrupt as his knees hit the ground and his torso flopped like a rag doll tossed aside at great speed. He rolled, twisted, and thumped to a stop several feet from where he'd touched down. Thanks be for soft lavender fields and his innate reflexes.

Unfortunately, Raum had been hot on his heels and had landed on his feet. Meaning he found himself in the steely grip of his captor once more. He wouldn't have been able to run though, not with the cuff on his right wrist blocking so much of his magic. Not that he knew where he'd go if he could get away. Who'd want him or tolerate him anyway? He was only useful to the Praesidium as long as he was willing to risk life and limb for their purpose. Something he was coming to realize just wasn't worth it.

Raum once again shoved him forward. This time when he looked up ahead, a pink sun shone over the fields and a large old-fashioned pub loomed in the distance. Not the largest pub he'd ever seen, to be sure, but rather large compared to any outside of his birth realm where they were built to serve fully shifted dragons. At least according to the books he'd seen in the ancient library back in Cathair an óir.

"One last thing, pet," Raum said, as he pushed him along, his body too close, sending panicked signals of danger and fear to his brain. "Be respectful of our host. Obey him, and report everything he says and does when I'm not present. There's a good boy," Raum said at his jerky nod.

Jerky mostly because Raum had forced it, the hand twisted in his long hair making his head move up and down. He felt the shiver of disgust slide up his spine as Raum's wet tongue licked along the curve of his jaw.

"Later, pet. Once we're settled in, we'll have some fun. Now . . . Well, now we have some work to do for my special friend."

His knees almost buckled with dread, but he kept going, one foot in front of the other until they reached the raised drawbridge. Praying his salvation lay beyond the dark stone walls rising up before him.

Jezzie had no idea what was going on with Ballzy, yet she couldn't help but wonder. Had she read him right? What was he really up to? Did he actually care about what happened to her? It seemed so. Apparently he hated this Raum guy, and she had a feeling she was going to hate him just as much. Damn it, she wanted to give Ballzy a hug. He looked like a sad, lost puppy. One you just wanted to bundle up for cuddles and make happy again. But, had she ever actually seen him happy? She didn't think so, not really. Which was kinda sad when she thought about it.

"In order to keep you as safe as I can while our 'guests' are here, I'm going to have to restrict your movements, luv. Basically, you can't leave your room." The bastard did look truly regretful, and Jezzie could see his point, so for once she just nodded.

"I understand, but I hope to hell you have a backup plan if shit turns into Hurricane Hell No! You do, right?" She looked him dead in the eye. He better damn well have a plan.

"I have some contingencies in place, some in this very room should we need them. The less you know the better though, in case you slip up."

For some odd reason, she actually was starting to trust him, despite the room situation and their history. To be fair, her options were pretty fucking slim at this point though. She almost chuckled out loud at her inner dialogue.

"Would it help if I didn't look like myself? Like if afterwards he went away and described someone utterly different?"

"It would. Do you need hair coloring and dyes and things? Do I need to get someone in for a makeover? Honestly, I'm not sure we have time though. The fucker likes to turn up earlier than scheduled, he likes to think he holds the upper hand that way. But we can try." Ballzy sounded anxious and on edge with a hint of 'give me something to do' floating in his voice.

"If he's an angel, Fallen or not, he'd smell that chemical shit a mile away and wonder why I had access to it and what we were up to. No, I have a better way." At her words Ballzy seemed to deflate a little, even as his curiosity was piqued.

She knew that a Shadow Hound's shadows could manifest and surround them changing their appearance into an incorporeal nightmare if they wished. She didn't know what other types of angels could do, but she doubted they had the power to do what she could. So he wouldn't trace it back to angel heritage if she revealed her powers of illusion. If ever there was a time to use them, this seemed to be it. Not only would they give Raum a false sense of what she looked like should she encounter him ever again, but they could shield her from pain, turn it into pleasure when the need arose. Powers that had been itching to be used for so long it would feel so good to set them free. Plus, the look on Ballzy's face might just be priceless.

"Do you have any photographs of women you wouldn't mind seeing tortured and sliced to ribbons, Ballzy?" her tone was sickly sweet and she gave him a wink and a smile.

"Um, not really. Why?"

"Oh well, I guess I can use the same one as last time and just switch out the clothes. Stand back and prepare to be amazed." Jezzie could admit she was a little excited about setting one of her powers free for the first time in eight years, other than her shadows of course, which more often than not seemed to have a mind of their own.

She stood, motioned for him to do the same, and ushered him toward the wall, then stepped back and twirled around like a magician's assistant putting on a show. When she was done with the theatrical flair, she stood stock still with her hands almost touching in prayer. She raised them until they were each pressed to her temples. Her head snapped up, her eyes taking on an iridescent shine as the dark red wisps of her shadows swirled around her. They settled with a flourish, and as she struck a pose she got her first good look at Ballzy's face post illusion. To say he was shocked would have been a massive understatement.

"So, what do you think? Pretty neat, huh?"

Jezzie flipped her platinum blonde hair over her shoulder with one hand, resting the other on her tartan miniskirt-clad hip. The tight white button up blouse hugged her generous curves, the black studded belt riding low on her hips. The thick heeled black platform Mary Janes made her already long legs look even more toned. She knew exactly what she looked like. Ballzy looked like he was about to choke on his own tongue.

"What? How? What the fuck, Jezzie?"

He sounded so incredulous she couldn't contain the peels of laughter that shot out of her. If she'd been drinking at the time . . . Guaranteed, one hundred percent it would have come out her nose.

"A girl's gotta have her secrets, Ballzy. You never know when they'll come in handy. Might I suggest you let your employees know that this particular secret needs to never leave their lips etcetera, etcetera."

He nodded dumbly. "Fuck, luv. What the hell are you? Just when I think I've got you pegged, you throw another curveball."

"Well, you did peg me at one point." She winked saucily. "But seriously? There are so many variables to this whole thing, sometimes I even surprise myself. Wanna know the best part?"

"There's more?" He sounded both eager to know and a little apprehensive.

"My illusions, the forms I can take with them. Well, they dull pain, and in some cases convert it into something much more pleasurable. Allowing me to draw in my victim." The wicked tone of her voice appeared to shock him even more as he started choking on air.

"There's water on the . . . Huh, I guess there isn't anymore. Well, there's water in the bathroom tap if you need it."

Just then a beeping sound came from Ballzy's wrist and a red light flashed repeatedly. He straightened up immediately. Mr All Business was back in control.

"Bloody hell! I knew he'd pull this early arrival shit. I just didn't think it'd be today." He shook his head as he walked toward her, stopping just shy of too close.

His hands came up to cup her face as he looked into her eyes and vowed, "I am so sorry about all of this. If I could let you go, I would. I'll stall him as long as it takes to get the bath removed, which shouldn't take long with demon magic, and to have the curtains boxed up and taken to my room. We wouldn't want to give Raum any ideas. He may not swing your way, but he's proven he'll stop at nothing. In the event something happens to me, place your palm in the center of the third stone under your window, the one with a jagged edge."

Jezzie nodded. It was strange, but it felt like something had shifted between them in the time since their office interaction. Friends. That was it, it felt like they were becoming friends. The protective waves coming off of him were the same as the ones she was feeling herself. Never in her wildest dreams would she have thought it possible . . . She actually liked Ballzy. Not like-liked him, but she definitely didn't want to see him hurt by this Raum guy.

"While I'm gone, prepare yourself. Change the outfit back to the plain stuff. It's more than likely what you'll see, hear, and experience next will be extremely unpleasant."

JEZZIE PACED her now locked cell. She could feel tension building in every muscle. Something was coming, something more than just Raum and this new danger. She was so tempted to touch the stone in the wall

Ballzy had spoken of earlier, but she didn't want to lose an advantage later on if whatever it was was a one shot deal. If it could only be used if something happened to him, it was likely it was his death. In which case it would be an escape route. Her body pulsed, her shadows stayed under her skin, hiding, waiting. Almost like they knew they needed to conserve their energy. Were they sentient on some level? She'd never really thought so before. She'd believed they were just an extension of her own powers, like a limb controlled by her brain, a part of her, but without her they were nothing. But what if they were more than that?

Her brain felt wired. Like a hamster running flat out on its wheel with no way to stop. Whether to avoid reality, or to analyze every possible scenario and outcome, it just kept whirling. The damn thing was making her head hurt. Then all of a sudden . . . It stopped. Everything stopped. Even the dust motes floating in the sun-filtered air froze on their irrelevant journeys. The same went for her heart, the very breath in her lungs . . . Who needed those anyway, right?

Like a deer noticing the presence of a predator, she tilted her head slowly toward the once again bare windows, revealing the empty hallway beyond.

Except it wasn't empty for long. First thing she noticed wasn't Ballzy leading the way, nor was it the intangibly scary dude who came in last. No, it was the one in the middle. He was being forced to move forward by the guy behind him, his feet leaving bloody trails on the marble floor as he shuffled along. The tattered pants barely concealed him from her suddenly ravenous gaze. His bare chest made her mouth water and her mind conjured up all too realistic fantasies.

Suddenly, his head shot up and his eyes pinned her in place, she hadn't realized she'd started moving toward him, until her feet glued themselves to the ground again. Startling amber eyes, shot through with threads of green fire. So pretty, so sad, so broken, and so fucking sexy. Who was he? Was he N? The pet? If that fucker, Raum, hurt him she'd .
. .

Wait, what? Where were those feelings coming from? She had her own ass to save, not his. He looked like he should be able to save his own. So, why hadn't he?

The cell next to hers opened and the mega asshole pushed the sexy one inside so hard he landed in a heap on the concrete with a barely discernible grunt. Just like that, the mega asshole, who absolutely had to be Raum, jumped to the top of her shit list. More so when he waltzed inside after him and whispered roughly in his ear, exposing the male's throat threateningly.

"This the little bitch that won't bark?" Raum smirked at Ballzy as he exited the cell and slammed the door. "Looks like this won't take me long at all."

The smarmy fucker. She felt the fire desperately wanting to flash in her eyes, but she reined it in.

She desperately wanted to retort that her bite was a hell of a lot worse than her bark, and she'd break his little bitch, and his two friends off and shove them down his throat, the overcompensating sadist. But she refrained. Partly because Ballzy, sensing her shift in mood, gave a stern and sneaky shake of his head and quickly diverted Raum's attention. Mostly because for once, her brain was more in charge than her mouth. If it hadn't been, she'd probably be in deep shit and there would have been nothing Ballzy could do to stop it.

As soon as they left the hallway, most likely heading to the security room to see how she and the newcomer interacted, she rushed to the connecting wall. Thankfully she'd been forewarned about the cameras being reactivated, not that she'd known they'd ever been deactivated, thanks Ballzy. Gosh, she was feeling sarcastic today. They only had a few minutes before they'd have to ignore each other.

"Hi. You okay?" she asked.

He looked at her and nodded.

"They'll be watching soon, you know. I'm assuming you're supposed to cozy up to me, right?"

Another nod.

"You know I'm going to have to ignore you. I'm Jezzie. You are?"

"Nithe. I am Nithe. He doesn't know that. I'm not really sure why I'm telling you that either. And yes, definitely ignore me. Ignore what he does to me. For the love of the Almighty, definitely ignore that." His voice was husky, rough around the edges, and it sent shivers of excitement through her to the point her breasts tingled, her suddenly hard nipples pressed firmly against the barely-there fabric of her tank top.

"I feel at ease with you too, and I don't know why, but I trust my instincts right now. Especially since they are screaming at me about that fucker who brought you in. Shit, times up. There's a shower and toilet through the door to your left. I suggest you make use of it quickly. Catch you on the flip side." Jezzie gave him a wink to lighten the mood before she moved to her cot and lay down, closed her eyes, and proceeded to fantasize about all the ways she could fuck Raum up.

If he came close enough, touched her long enough, she could drain him of every emotion and leave him a vegetable as she ate his fetid soul. His brain would leak like coolant from his ears onto the cold hard floor. Pretty sure the world would be a better place if he were to end up a puddle of coagulated goo.

CHAPTER 16

His dragon sight saw through the fuzzy haze of her illusion. The angels obviously didn't, but their sight wasn't like a dragon's. Dragons were designed to seek out treasure, and treasure shone the brightest under the gaze of his kind. Her beauty, though, shone brighter than any treasure he could ever hope to have. The false beauty of her illusion paled in comparison to the radiance of her true appearance.

He felt his dragon huff from deep within as he mentally waxed poetic. Derisive, but not in disagreement, the grumpy bastard. It shocked him though—for so long he'd been without his dragon's company—to feel his dragon pushing to the surface for a look at her as they passed her cell.

He could smell her honeysuckle scent through the small holes drilled into the glass walls. It called to him on a primal level; confused him as his dragon struggled to speak through the shackles binding them both.

Her eyes found his, and by all the heavens he wished she hadn't seen him as he was in that moment, or in any moment which would follow. Another time, another place, a different future, and, most definitely, a different past. Not this version of him. The one who looked tattered and worn, covered in dirt and his own blood. Raum hadn't broken the dragon, but he'd done a hell of a job at whittling away at the man.

Captivating gray eyes traveled over him like flames on a winter's night. He'd not gotten hard since before Raum had trapped him, thank fuck, but apparently one look from her, and he was on the verge of exposing himself through the thin material of his rags. It's what they were. Probably worn by previous pets, to be worn by countless more if Raum didn't destroy them first.

Raum capturing him had been a possibility from the start. More like a probability, but then those sanctimonious prats had thought they'd developed a completely infallible tracking system. They'd assured him they would know his location at all times, he'd only have to send the signal, and they'd swoop in to nab Raum before any harm was done.

If the fucker who'd tasked him with this mission ever crossed his path again, she'd be nothing but a pile of melted goo and ashes.

Raum had him on a short leash as he spun him to the side and unclipped the blasted thing. A hard shove between his shoulders caught him off guard and sent him into the cell and down on his knees. Raum grabbed a fistful of Nithe's long, knotted hair, yanking him backwards. A firm foot against his spine kept him upright but caused his back to arch, his throat exposed and vulnerable. Hot breath tickled his ear . . . Instant limp noodle effect.

"Settle in, N. I'll be back a little later. I think this one might be fun. I think you do too. I notice everything, and I'll use every advantage I can get. Play nice with the bitch," Raum's whispered words were but a breath above silence. No sound carried; he'd shielded his words so only Nithe would hear them. When he was done he thrust Nithe's head away from him, causing him to fall forward once more. If he hadn't managed to get his arms out in front of himself as fast as he had, he would have landed on his face.

Nithe heard the distinct click of the locking mechanism as the cell door shut, and the sound of footfalls as they retreated. After a few moments of silence, bar his own rough breathing and the soft rhythmical ones of the woman in the next cell, he heard a slightly husky voice ask if he was okay.

What could he tell her? No, no, in absolutely no way was he okay.

Forced out of his clan due to the side effects of his mother's indiscretion, said mother turning her back upon him, everything to do with Raum. No! Not okay. The torture, the shame, the utter self-loathing boiling inside him, the injustice of it all, the irony of that very term, injustice, and what it meant deep within his soul. Yet, the sound of her voice soothed his bitterness, calmed the raging fire, and bought with it a moment of blessed peace.

His answer was automatic, he hadn't meant to tell her his name. A name he'd not revealed to Raum. He was simply, N. Which was much better than what Raum had called him to begin with. Worm was just downright offensive, not that Raum had ever given any indication he'd known about Nithe's dragon. Yet, he'd told this woman his name without a second thought. Heck, without any thought at all. So, why? What was it about her that made him break his own rules?

She was trustworthy. He felt it resonate from his dragon, who still could not speak, but who pushed the feeling all the way through him until he knew the truth of it. His dragon was ancient, older than most others, or so he'd said. He'd told Nithe to seek refuge with one of the other clans, but he'd been too angry. Angry at his mother, his prejudicial clan, even at his dragon, and all because he was different.

He'd always known he wasn't the same as other dragons, that his father wasn't a dragon, but he'd never felt unloved. Now he knew that love had been conditional, that they'd been hoping his non-dragon traits would be dormant, then they could fully accept him into the clan of his birth. The problem? He was a perfect blend of dragon and his father's angel heritage. His shifted form was just like any other dragon . . . Well, except that his golden wings looked like large leather feathers instead, and he had a burning pain in his chest whenever he encountered injustice. Or even thought about it.

Shaking his head he focussed on the stunning woman beside him, separated by the thin, unbreakable glass. They'd be watching soon, she'd said. Jezzie, her name was Jezzie, or so she'd said. A simple, yet unusual name, her illusion implied she was going to be full of surprises.

When she lay back on her cot and closed her eyes he raised himself from the floor and looked around the sparse cell.

"There's a shower and toilet through the door to your left. I suggest you make use of it quickly," her words were whispered softly, and he momentarily wished she was saying his name instead of talking about bathrooms. Turning his head and lifting his arm, he took a good solid sniff of himself . . . and almost passed out from the stench of his own pungent, rotten odor.

Pushing himself to his feet, and leaving bloody footprints on the concrete floor, he entered the small bathroom. It was stark white, sterile, functional if not lavish, but better than he'd had access to in a long time. As much as he wanted to step into the shower and stay there under the warmth of the water, until all of his aches disappeared, and he was finally clean again, he knew, deep down inside, he'd always feel dirty, eternally covered in the filth of his time with Raum. The scars on his soul only a miracle could heal. Despite his desire to linger, he knew if he wasn't in the main part of the cell, visibly trying to engage the other prisoner when Raum returned, whatever the asshole had planned would become much worse. So, he relieved himself quickly, kicked off the filthy tattered rags that were supposed to be pants, and stepped into the small shower cubicle only long enough to wash the grime from his body and dull the unwashed odor. He didn't dare use soap or wash his hair. He even avoided getting it wet. Raum had not given him permission for these things, and he knew better than to assume too much. Even though the water stung his cut and bleeding feet, he had to force himself out of the shower; it had felt like a slice of luxury in a nightmare.

Fuck! How had his life become this mess? Where was his strength? He knew the answers though. Hated them, hated all of them. The dragons who'd feared his differences, his own pride and stubbornness. He should have listened to his dragon, he should have ignored the call to deliver justice, and the visit from that bloody angel, Esidriel, who obviously had no clue what she'd actually sent Nithe into. But if he ever got his claws on her . . . the grin on his face, reflected in the small mirror, was filled with slightly deranged anticipation and humor.

When he exited the bathroom he breathed a sigh of relief, Raum wasn't back yet. Then again, from what the mysterious Jezzie had said, Raum was probably watching everything anyway. Adding every infraction and misstep to the tally of his future session with the sadist.

Speaking of the stunning woman in question, she was exactly as he'd left her. On her cot her ankles crossed, her arms up and pillowed under her head, face serene. Well, except for the occasional smirk or inaudible snarl. Happy thoughts, then.

Someone here had a way to contact his handler, a way to get him out. But who? He doubted it was the guy Raum had *not* introduced him to, Balthazar. It looked like they were two fucked up peas in a pod. Why else was Jezzie here, in a cell, no less? She didn't look dangerous, but he supposed looks were often deceiving, he only had to look at his mother to see proof of that. If not the man in charge, then who? Who was brave enough to defy him? Only demons had crossed their path on the way down here, and even they stayed in the shadows. Probably sensing pure evil as it emanated from Raum's fetid soul.

Not only did he need to figure out who it was, and also how to let them know, discreetly, who he was working for, he also had to get closer to Jezzie. Raum would not react well if he didn't, and he would not limit his anger to just Nithe, he'd find a way to hurt the woman too. But it wasn't just Raum's orders making him seek her out, or want to get to know her, find out everything about her. No, it was more than that. It was an imperative need he felt burning in his soul. Almost like his dragon heart was aflame, a wordless plea to get as near to her as he possibly could, in every conceivable way. Especially now he'd washed his own stink away and could clearly inhale the undiluted scent of her through the small holes in the clear cell walls.

Reaching out he found he could just fit his index finger through one of the holes, and out again, fairly easily. Knowing he had to convince Raum he was trying to gain her trust and find out all of her secrets, he let his forehead touch the wall.

"Hey, how long have you been here?" His tongue felt slightly thicker in his mouth than normal.

Only the sound of her measured breathing reached his ears at first . . . And then she started to chuckle, softly one moment and a hearty belly laugh the next.

"Long enough that I know better than to trust just any pretty face, sweetie. Aye, there be snakes in this 'ere garden, don't ya know? Plus," she paused, sat up, and looked directly at him with a tilt of her head as she dropped the playful pirate accent on the last word. "I know I've been out of the dating loop for a while, what with being stuck here and all, but, you can do better." Her wink and the smile that graced her 'real' face almost knocked his socks off. Or it would have if he'd been wearing any.

BALTHAZAR REALLY BLOODY HATED THIS. Hated having his space invaded, having Jezzie put at risk, and he hated having to tolerate Raum most. His skin burned with the need to smite him. Evil pulsed from him in waves that made his skin feel tight and itchy. His palms tingled with the need to release his sword. Plus, he'd come to care for Jezzie, she was as close as he had to a friend, despite their previous intimacy, screwing her over, and some light torture. He felt protective of her. It was a pretty sad testament to his existence, really. His only friend being the woman he had trapped in his cellar. Sure, he'd continued to make passes at her, and he'd have definitely gone for another round if she'd been willing, but he'd had more fun messing with her than he'd had in a very long time prior to her arrival. If Raum went too far he knew without a shadow of a doubt he'd be outing himself, and if he didn't act fast enough, wasn't strong enough, it was all over.

If only the fucking twat would stop touching his things he may have been able to calm the rage within himself. He'd not met Raum before, beyond the reputation he had. A reputation that was justified considering his powers were almost beyond his control. Never before had his powers reacted quite so uncontrollably to an OtherRealm sinner. He was usually quite calm, quite controlled when he carried out his task as executioner to what are mostly considered immortal and paranormal beings. See, it was his job after all, or it had been. He took care of the Evil in the OtherRealm, while the shadows took care of the mortals, and never the twain shall meet. Such a funny saying. Of course they had met. Amazingly, wonderfully so, until it wasn't anymore.

"Step away from my desk, Raum, and do not make me ask twice." His voice snapped out of him like a whip lashing the air between the two men. He hadn't even realized he'd spoken until the last syllable had already left his tongue.

Raum froze, turned slightly, and cocked his brow at Balthazar. His gray tweed three-piece suit was completely at odds with the state of the male he'd brought with him. He looked like he'd stepped straight out of 1920s Yorkshire. The only thing missing was a flat cap. Balthazar was pretty sure he had one to match a similar suit in his own wardrobe. He couldn't fault the guy's sense of fashion, but he'd be damned if he wasn't burning that suit at the very first opportunity.

"Why so touchy, friend? Are we hiding things? Things we don't want our mutual friend to know, maybe?"

Raum looked positively gleeful at the prospect. On the other hand, Balthazar barely restrained himself from saying he saw no friend of his present in the room.

Thankfully everything of a sensitive and personal nature had been securely locked away before he'd left for Daemoneskra. He made it a rule to always be prepared, and it never hurt to have a backup plan.

"No, I just don't like others touching my things. Germs, you know, they're everywhere." He smiled, probably a little too forcefully. "We all have our little quirks, don't we? I mean, it's partly why we find ourselves doing what we're doing, isn't it?"

"Oh, certainly. I can understand an aversion to such things. Not my thing personally, but we all do have them. For me, it's the smell of seawater. Not the out on the ocean kind, more the dirty seaweed kind. Makes me gag every time. It's basically just a giant toilet for sea creatures, blergh."

Balthazar couldn't tell if Raum's shudder was feigned or sincere, and it bothered him. Either he'd just learned something potentially useful, or Raum was toying with him.

Raum moved away from Balthazar's desk slowly, until he was standing beside one of the leather armchairs. Again, he looked at Balthazar, this time with a slightly impatient expectation. Suddenly, Balthazar remembered his manners, even if Raum didn't deserve them, and indicated to the chair.

"Forgive me my lack of manners. Please, be seated." He had long ago been instructed in the manners of London's high society, and found himself falling back into the comfortable ritual of it all as he took the seat behind his desk.

"Not to worry, old chap, I understand. This is your operation, you run a tight ship, and you resent any interference on my part. Rest assured, our friend is merely curious as to why you have kept this morsel a secret for so long, and what it is exactly you think she's hiding." Predatory eyes bored into him, clearly waiting for an answer.

"She and I have history . . . of a personal nature. None of which has anything to do with 'our friend's' plans or affairs. It doesn't even affect my day-to-day business. So I would honestly appreciate it if you would inform our friend and leave me to it."

"And why exactly can you not inform 'our friend' yourself?" Raum parried.

"I'm assuming you haven't been in contact with him since he assigned you this task?" Balthazar inquired.

"Your assumption would be correct."

"And he contacts you directly at all times? No middle man?"

"I trust only him."

"Hmm, well, after I received the memo about your arrival, one of his lackeys contacted my contact, and I was thus informed that our esteemed leader had put out a cease and desist on all activity that could, in any way, be linked to him, and has gone into a communication lockdown until further notice. No contact in or out. I assume this doesn't apply to you, though."

"Why would you assume such a thing?" Raum looked agitated. It was as if thinking of Gabriel, the twazzock, possibly being in trouble was something he couldn't stand even the thought of.

"Why? Because he is the only being you take orders from."

"I don't take orders from anyone." His voice could have frozen the fiery pit itself. "But, I do respect his counsel, and trust his judgment, so I guess you have a point."

Balthazar silently breathed a sigh of relief.

"Alas, for you, I cannot say the same. I will be interrogating the prisoner, as per my orders. One way or another, I will have the answers he seeks, possibly the ones you seek too." Again with the subzero tone. It was like his voice contained literal ice.

"If you harm any part of her, I will take it out of your hide. There is nowhere you could scarper off to that I would not find you. Not now, anyway." Shit, he really needed to keep a lid on the vengeance thing, he really didn't need to let them know he'd never given it up when he'd left his post.

"Don't worry, Balthazar, I won't lay a hand on her at all. I won't need to. There are so many more fun and interesting ways to get answers from others, especially from such unworthy ones."

Well, those words definitely weren't reassuring. Why did Balthazar think it would have been better if he'd left well enough alone and kept his mouth shut? It probably wouldn't have been, but now he had a ball of dread weighing down his insides at the possible implications of Raum's words.

"I need to get back to my pet, see what progress he's made." Raum stood to leave.

"Your presence for that would be disruptive, surely? Why not give him some more time? We can watch from here and have a drink and something to eat before you begin your entertainment."

Balthazar leaned forward and grabbed the small black control screen from atop his desk before once again reclining into his own seat and swiveling around. Suddenly the windows behind the old walnut desk lit up with images of the cells from multiple angles.

"Before I pop the sound on, I'm going to pop an order in for lunch. Any preferences?" Balthazar wanted Raum to get comfortable, and he could see Raum knew it too. It was a game they both must play.

"Surprise me?" Raum's response did indeed sound playful, almost . . . interested? A thought which sent a wave of bile to the back of his throat. No way was he becoming Raum's next pet!

After speaking quickly into the intercom, he jacked up the volume and zoomed in on the two images with the best view of both Jezzie and the new addition. Fuck! He felt sorry for the poor guy. He wasn't much older than Jezzie, at least in looks. Who knew what kind of being he was though. He'd felt like an angel, familiar too, but there was something else. Something that shouldn't be there. That was impossible, but it was so slight he couldn't grab hold of it long enough to unravel the mystery. How he'd ended up with the prick currently invading his home he couldn't imagine.

"Hey, how long have you been here?"

The words from Raum's pet were hoarse and low. Thanks to the awesome surround sound, though, they came through crystal clear.

"Long enough that I know better than to trust just any pretty face, sweetie. Aye, there be snakes in this 'ere garden, don't ya know? Plus," Balthazar prayed she didn't put her delicate little foot in it so soon. *"I know I've been out of the dating loop for a while, what with being stuck here and all, but, you can do better."*

She winked at him. He should have known better than to think she'd rein in her sass, even in a situation as volatile as this one was. Behind him, he heard Raum chuckle.

"You're right, Balthazar. Let's give them some more time. I think it will make what comes after much more effective. Oh, good, the food's here."

As Satari's temporary replacement positioned the tea trolley beside the desk and left in a hurry, Balthazar couldn't help but think his time was running out.

CHAPTER 17

With the others gone, Marco found himself alone in the large, elegantly appointed meeting room. He was almost stunned into stillness. It felt like the last twenty-four hours had been a whirlwind of confusing revelations, emotional explosions, and even more questions. Then it ends up being Mrs Briars who snapped out orders like a drill sergeant setting everyone to their tasks, and when the dust finally settled . . . Silence. An utter cessation of chaos, ringing louder in his ears than the cacophony of what had come before it.

All too soon the silence ended though, as Mrs Briars popped up through the floor directly in front of him.

"Arrggghh!" He jumped a fucking mile and squealed like a scream queen in a B-grade horror flick.

"Calm down, Marco. Big deep breaths. Ramiel is here to see you. He left the other one at the front door . . . Don't worry though, I have Sthenno watching her through the surveillance system, just in case," she chided sweetly, the steel behind her eyes indicated she was not taking any chances with their safety. Honestly, she was the mother figure most of them had never had. The mother some of them could only wish they'd had, instead of the ones they'd been stuck with.

"Thank you, Mrs B. Can you send him in, please?"

"He's outside the doors, honey. I'm pretty sure you have two arms and two legs, and can make your way the five meters there without my assistance, yes? I have more pressing tasks to get to." Her tone was mildly scolding, and her raised brow made him feel the same way he had as a newbie angel when he'd taken an unauthorized trip to the surface of the earth. He'd spent four hours getting reamed out by Luc and the flight commander that day. All he'd wanted was to see the garden, instead he'd landed in the in-between and gotten stuck for fuck knows how long.

Mrs B huffed, and once more disappeared through the floor, but not before poking her finger pointedly at the door and muttering about next time leaving someone else in charge. She was in a snit today it seemed. Thinking about it, she'd been making snarky comments for the last few days. Sure, it had been a wild ride around here, but the unflappable Mrs B certainly had her knickers in a knot, didn't she?

He strolled to the door and opened it just as the hand on the other side came down . . . and knocked him right on the bridge of his nose. With great force. Something warm and wet trickled out and over his lips. The fucker had broken his nose! Not that he'd ever be game enough to call Ramiel a 'fucker' to his face. It would be a very unwise thing to do.

"Shit! Sorry," Ramiel's deep baritone boomed through the room behind him and drilled through the tender flesh around Marco's eyes. "Didn't know you were going to open the door so fast. Let's get you seated, Marco. It is Marco, right? Hard to tell with your hands covering most of your face." He spun Marco around like a spinning top, his big hands maneuvered him with ease, and pushed him into a seat at the large table. Luc's seat.

"Thath's cosh my nosh ith futhing boken," Marco snapped out, or tried to.

"Well, that'll do it. Thank you, Mrs Briars. He'll be fine. I promise I won't break anything else."

Ramiel pulled Marco's hands away and replaced them with an ice pack covered in a dish towel. After a while, sitting in blessed silence, he pulled the cloth covered pack away and assessed the damage. A fair amount of blood coated the cotton material. He lifted his fingers to his face. The cartilage bulged noticeably as he ran his fingers over it, and he winced as he traced the odd angle at which his nose now sat. Ah, fuck it. Reaching up with both hands, he grasped his nose firmly, with a sharp jolt he shifted it back into place, grunting and biting the inside of his cheek at the pain.

"Is it straight?" he asked Ramiel.

"Pretty damn near perfect. Though the small cut at the bridge might leave a nice little scar if you care to salt it and keep it. Otherwise, the perks of being an angel should heal it up like new before the day is done."

"Why would I want to keep the scar, Ram? Why mess with perfection?" He winked and gave Ramiel a crooked smile. Ramiel chuckled softly.

"Sometimes, the scars make the man, my friend," he added softly.

They all knew Ramiel didn't care about scars. He wore them proudly, as if they were trophies or medals. Since angels healed extremely quickly and didn't scar, the only way Ramiel could have scars was to salt them. Not with salt water, though. Actual, pure salt, the coarse ground kind, it'd be tantamount to rubbing pebble-like sand into the wound and leaving it there until the wound had healed underneath it and pushed the invading granules out. Leaving nothing but a silver tinged mark in its place. It was also rumoured to be fucking torturous.

"Well, apart from the broken nose, it's good to see you again, Ram. It's been a while."

"Yes, yes it has," said Ramiel solemnly.

"Ah, so this isn't a social call, I take it?" Marco questioned.

Ramiel's face looked graver than a gravestone as his gaze bore into Marco's hazel eyes. Shit, he was being weighed. Ramiel, as head of the Praesidium, had the ability to see if someone was worthy of being trusted. Something was grinding Ram's gears. Something big was happening, and Marco wasn't sure the Hounds could take any more surprises right now.

"I need your help, Marco. It's very important, and I need you to keep it quiet. This is to be kept between us, and Deus. My intention was to speak to Deus about this directly. But, since he's not here and I trust you almost as much as I trust him . . ."

"Well, thanks . . ." Marco wasn't actually offended by this. To be trusted by Ramiel at all was actually a huge compliment. "But, why not Luc?" Marco couldn't help but ask. "Nothing goes on around here without Luc's knowledge."

"Really? You can truly say that has been accurate these last few decades? What if I told you there was a traitor within these walls? Someone you most likely have never even suspected was capable of such treachery? What would you say to that?"

Marco stared at Ramiel, sure he probably looked like a fish out of water, but never had the thought of any angel within the fortress walls being a traitor even flittered across his thoughts. It was inconceivable.

"A traitor to what? In what way? I don't even see how it's possible. Unless they are Fallen, we've never had traitors before. I mean, angels like Raum and Mara notwithstanding, of course. They betrayed the Almighty, and their designated callings. But, to actively work against a certain group of us? If that is indeed what you are getting at here? I can't comprehend it," Marco's voice trailed off in a whisper as his heart rate sped up to a quick little gallop.

"I know this is difficult to get your head around, my friend. So, take a moment to listen. Hopefully I can shed some light on my suspicions, and the evidence I've pieced together will make sense."

Ramiel dipped his head and took a deep breath. Marco found himself mirroring the action, and when the Angel of Justice looked up he found the light of truth shining from his eyes—his eyes a white and bright as light globes—casting his face in an ethereal glow.

"I've always thought Michael's disappearance was suspicious. So I've had some of my most trusted people, some directly appointed by the Almighty as well, looking into things. The Almighty knows I don't agree with the "it all must play out as it needs to" bullshit, so no info is forthcoming from that sector. What I suspect, but as yet cannot one hundred percent prove, is that Michael going missing was orchestrated by someone looking to gain more power. A dissatisfied asshat, actually. Admittedly, I've never liked Gabriel, always thought he was a bit of a self-righteous prat with an ego problem."

"I mean, I completely agree about Gabriel, but are you suggesting he was directly involved in Michael's disappearance? I know Luc has had his suspicions based on his past behavior and how little Gabriel has invested in trying to find the Commander. How do you know this, though?" Marco was so focussed on Ramiel he could almost feel his ears straining to catch every syllable the male uttered.

Ramiel took a deep, almost weary, breath. "Not just Michael's. There are several other questionable disappearances, deaths, punishments etc . . . throughout the realms that seemingly have little to connect them. In some cases, certain sensitive information was shared with only a select few, and drunkenly shared with a few more. With only one consistent possible source. The info has then been used to start wars, or divide loyalties. In other cases, private rulings and prophecies were leaked, and we have no idea what happened to those put at risk by the sharing of this information.

"What we do know is that Gabriel had opportunities to gain access to this information, either himself or through someone close to him. What we don't know is what he has planned, and how far his network has spread. We suspect he has maintained contact with his old friend, Raum, even now. We also know Gabriel is desperate to discredit Lucifer and bring down the Hounds. We fear he seeks to control the souls within the Well, for what purpose only he knows."

"I still don't understand how you know this? Or is it all just suspicions and suppositions? He's definitely capable of it, don't get me wrong, but so far I haven't heard any actual proof that points directly to him."

"My agents couldn't infiltrate Blessed Reaper headquarters, for obvious reasons—"

"Their wings and mist?"

"Yes, Marco, I thought that was a given?"

"Sorry, continue," Marco murmured sheepishly.

"Anyway," Ramiel continued sternly, "It just so happened, that at around the same time Michael went AWOL, a good friend of mine also lost everything that mattered to him and went off the deep end for a while. Renounced his position and hid himself away. After a while he came to me at the insistence of someone else. We hatched a plan, and he has been my greatest asset to date. Through him, we have built up a case.

We know Gabriel is guilty of many crimes. My friend's contact is sporadic because he's playing the long game. Because Gabriel is certain of his loyalty, he has access to certain information. Unfortunately, until we weed out the traitors in our midst, and learn the extent of his plans we cannot make an outright move against him."

"Why not just use the Hand of Truth?"

"The Almighty has refused to release it to me for this purpose. I have been given some BS line about events still being in play that require free will, it needs to play out as it will, and it will all make sense when the dust lands, or something like that."

They both grunted at his words. The Fates and the Almighty always used the same excuse when they were fucking with the lives of other beings.

"I cannot stay much longer. Currently, Shamsiel and I are staying with the Reapers, and trying to find out what we can. Gabriel is spooked, but we need to do something to shake things up. Things have been stagnant for too long. We will be arriving here next week for the same purpose, though here we will mostly be amongst friends, I hope. Not like the seething viper's nest the Reaper Headquarters has turned into."

As quick as a flash, the High Chancellor of Justice vanished through a portal, taking him out of the Realm of Shadows, aka Hell. Leaving behind one very confused, and unnerved Shadow Hound worrying his bottom lip as his anger increased at the thought of a traitor residing in the only place he'd ever called home.

By the time they made it back home, they were not only exhausted and a little drunk, they were also a seething mass of questions and agitation. Well, Luc was. It was just rubbing off on all of them as they tried to get a handle on everything the dragon chief had discussed with them. Deus felt the steel wool of a migraine scrubbing away behind his eyes.

They'd sat and they'd talked, broken bread and drank a fair amount of Dragonfire Ale. Admittedly the latter probably hadn't been their best decision. But, in the name of diplomatic relations sometimes you needed to get hammered in order to fix your fuck-ups, and an all out war with the dragons would have been an absolute disaster of epic proportions.

What they'd learned in return had been concerning to say the least. The dragons were notoriously private. Kind of a 'what happens in Réimse Na Dragan, stays in Réimse Na Dragan' culture. So, it was somewhat of a surprise they'd been so open, honest, and shared about what had been going on there lately.

A few thousand years ago the Goddess of Time got pissed and took four of the five clan heirs in order to stop the wars from decimating the dragon population. This, they already knew. The Almighty had assigned the last dragon heir to a period of service. Someone, knowing all five dragon heirs were not residing within the realm, had seen it as an opportunity to try to control the Hordes. The God of War himself being the prime suspect. So far, it hadn't worked. But, according to the chief, they'd been so caught up in avoiding War's traps they'd allowed an even more sinister and pervasive enemy to infiltrate their city.

The mage Luc's 'woman' had liquefied, was apparently a fetid, evil spy, according to the witch who'd calmed Luc down. What the fuck was with that anyway? The mage must have been working for someone other than War. War wasn't all that clever; brute strength and ego plays were more his style.

The meeting room was empty as they'd stumbled through the portal. With every step forward, Luc's turbulent feelings pulsed their way through the room. Athon and Roth, subconsciously rolled their shoulders, cracked their necks, and moved into a combative stance. Some of the others backed off, the others froze. As Luc turned around, his eyes flicked frantically around the room. He was a wild animal in a cage that made no sense to him.

Roth growled, and stepped in front of Athon. For a split second Athon's eyes softened as he took in his lover's protective stance. It was quickly replaced by an eye roll as he growled equally as aggressively and stepped to his lover's side with a shoulder bump.

Like a powder keg, the tension in the room exploded and everyone was picking fights. Except him. Deus was the only one not affected by whatever was going on.

Before they could attack each other en masse, Deus saw a fine mist start to settle over them. He quickly closed his eyes and covered his nose and mouth.

"It's okay, Asmodeus, all is safe now. Not an ideal situation, but better than it was going to be."

Looking about, Deus found the rest of his team from the mission, including the General, splayed out in various positions around the room. He raised his brow at a defiant looking Mrs Briars.

"Would you rather they'd turned the room into a WWE arena?" she sassed at him.

"How long will they be out?" he asked, resigned.

"As long as it takes for the residual spell to wear off. Some faint magic was clinging to Lucifer, and with the telepathic connection he has with each of you, he was sending it unknowingly along the link. Even to you, Deus, though not as strongly. They should only be out a day or two at most."

"What do we do with them until then? I need to figure out what's going on and how magic like this is affecting us at all, let alone residual magic."

"It's a good thing I have a big, strong, hulking angel here to help me move them to their rooms then, isn't it?" she huffed. "Marco can help too, he asked to speak to you when you get a moment alone. I figure while you're both getting this lot to bed is as good a time as any."

Deus's head dropped as he contemplated the carpet. Honestly, all he really wanted to do was strip naked and fall into bed for the next week. Unfortunately, he knew his friends couldn't be left on the floor. Not only would they be pissed, but they'd undoubtedly also find a way to pay him back. So, with a deep breath he squared his shoulders just as Marco entered the room. Before he could explain any of what was going on, Mrs Briars gave one last forceful instruction.

"Azaroth and Leviathon stay together, either room is fine. I'll see you in the morning. Goodnight, boys." The smile on her face showed how much she was enjoying herself at their expense. The laughter buried in her voice trailed after her as she waltzed out of the room through the door Marco had left open. Marco looked at the bodies on the ground, then up to Deus, over his shoulder at the already gone Mrs Briars, and back to Deus. The confusion was justified, and so too was the thin veil of fear. Whether he was afraid of his friend's reactions when they woke, or of Mrs Briars, was yet to be determined.

CHAPTER 18

Nithe beckoned her over to the wall separating them with a crook of his finger and a wink. Despite what she'd told him earlier, she'd found him impossible to ignore. He was funny and clever. It didn't hurt he was kind of a hottie too, especially with most of the grime washed away. They'd been chatting on and off for a few hours. Nothing deep and meaningful, nothing personal. A few chuckles here and there. Mostly they'd surreptitiously stared at one another when they'd thought the other wasn't looking. Which had led to more embarrassed chuckles. She felt much the same way as when little Danny McGuire had asked to hold her hand at the county fair when she was nine. All butterflies and bubbles. Except, this time she saw the heat banked behind his stare, and her own horny, dirty thoughts as they flitted through her brain didn't help with the thrum of desire that begged her to go to him. To touch him, to find a way to push him to the ground and claim him. WTF? Okay, so apparently she desperately needed to get laid.

"Seriously?"

"Yeah, why not? It's not like I could do anything to you, what with this wall between us and all."

"Um, for all I know you could be some form of body snatcher who needs a new meat suit, and you've decided I'll do."

"And how exactly would I go about getting a hold of your, uh, 'meat suit'?" his voice rang with unconcealed amusement.

"How would I know? I've never met one before, unless you are one, then yes, I've met one, you. For all I know you wouldn't even have to touch me to do it. Though, touching might be fun." Gosh, it was fun to joke around like this. Their circumstances might not be the best, but they could at least lighten the mood for a little bit, right? "Fuck it, if you are a body snatcher or some shit, I will haunt your ass for eternity."

With that said she flounced up off the completely uncomfortable cot and over to stand before Nithe.

"I'm not a body snatcher, gorgeous, but you definitely have an impressive one. Red hot to be exact." This time it was he who winked. He'd placed subtle emphasis on the word red and Jezzie got the distinct impression he'd seen through her illusion. Which both terrified and excited her.

"It's natural, you know? Except there's no rug to match the drapes."

His breath hitched and he swallowed reflexively. She could've sworn she caught the aftershocks of a soundless groan on the air as his left palm came to rest on the cool glass by his shoulder. Without thought her right hand followed his lead, less than an inch separated their skin. Leaning her cheek against the glass she watched as both hands slowly moved toward the small holes drilled into it. Finally, her palm came to rest over a cluster of them, and she closed her eyes. She could feel the heat of his skin as it radiated toward her, setting fire to her libido and soothing her aching soul.

She gasped, he touched her. His finger to her palm. She giggled and pulled back slightly.

"Was the tickle quite necessary?" She heard the smile in her voice.

"Oh, absolutely. I think making you giggle might just be my new happy place."

How could someone sound so sad, desperate, and happy at the same time? She wanted more than anything in that very moment to fling herself into his arms and tell him it would all be okay. She'd slay the giant fucktard named Raum and all would be well in all the realms.

Instead, she placed four fingers through four individual holes, and touched his. What she didn't expect was the tug of a tether as it got stronger, a bond she felt might now be much harder to break. The zap of electricity that flung her body back onto the hard gray floor hadn't been expected either, in hindsight.

"Well, well, isn't this sweet? So heartwarming to see the two of you getting along so . . . intimately," Raum's disgusted sneer at the last word came across crystal clear.

Was he jealous? Sure sounded like it to her.

"Jealous, sweetie? Such a shame no one wants to be near you willingly. Not really though, I can definitely agree with their aversion." She couldn't stop the words before they slipped out.

Shit! Ballzy looked nervous as fuck standing off to the side and slightly behind Raum. One day she might just learn to keep her mouth shut. But, probably not. At this point she figured it was a genetic failing. Her mum suffered from it too, and she was willing to bet dollars to donuts her dad did too.

"Such a smart mouth you have, young lady. Let's see how smart it is when I'm done with you." The steely glint in his eyes indicated she'd struck a nerve, and going by how he'd just cracked his knuckles, she wasn't going to like what came next.

"You can make it all stop right now, you know. All you have to do is tell me exactly why you're here, and sing like a songbird until you hand over the information my friend Balthazar wants to know," Raum cajoled.

"Seriously?" she said, eyes wide with faux innocence, before she abruptly dropped the act. "I highly doubt you have any actual friends, dipshit."

"I was so hoping you'd decide not to cooperate. I do love it when I get the chance to have a little fun. The harder you make it, the more fun this is going to be. For me, that is."

Raum's smirk may have been a little disconcerting to someone else, but seriously? Considering how many psycho serial killers, and serial killers in the making, she'd soul sucked over the decades, how many blissful moments of delicious torture she'd endured in the pursuit of a decent meal? She was actually looking forward to this as much as he was. Not to mention the added bonus of him entering her cell and his unhindered proximity would place him in the perfect position to become her next yummy banquet. Whatever Ballzy had done to protect his soul, apparently didn't apply to the asshat standing on the other side of the glass with a self-satisfied look on his face. His soul radiated evil, his aura murky, the color of mud and moss mixed together. It called to her, almost begging to be devoured.

Except, he didn't enter her cell. No, he turned and walked to the one next door. Nithe had risen from his shocked position on the hard floor and placed as much distance between himself, Raum, and her as he could without taking his eyes off his captor. Note to self, the fucking glass was electrified, somehow. Nice of Ballzy to give her a heads-up about it . . . not. If they both came out of this unscathed, they would definitely have some words about that little surprise.

"Balthazar, *my friend*," his eyes pierced through her as he uttered them. "Instruct your little minions to bring in the devices. One in each room, please. I'll take care of mine. Strap yours in nice and tight." It was more an order than a request.

Ballzy spoke to the demon huddled behind him, and the odd little creature dashed off to do his master's bidding. What the hell was with his obedience? The more she watched Ballzy, the more anger, frustration, and hatred she felt drifting off him. But it wasn't directed at her, it was focussed on Raum. The emotions he felt for her centered around fear, desperation, and hopelessness.

Demons, two groups of four, entered the wide hallway where Ballzy stood. Each group was pulling and pushing a large metal and wooden X mounted to a base board on wheels. One rolled past and stopped in front of Nithe's cell, the other was brought to a halt in front of hers. Jezzie's gaze darted to Nithe, but he wasn't looking at her. His eyes were fastened to the St. Andrew's Cross being rolled into his cell. It was indeed such a device, seeing the four metal and leather cuffs attached strategically to it triggered her memory.

Sheer terror rolled off Nithe, fine tremors wracked his body, and he shook his head in denial. Clearly, whatever Raum had used these for previously had not been for pleasure . . . At least not for anyone's other than his own. She tried to give Nithe a smile of comfort, but it fell flat, her face too full of tension, his fear too great. His eyes started to dart around the room frantically, as if seeking an escape. She could assure him there wasn't one, at least that she'd been able to find.

The click of her own cell door drew her attention back to her own situation. An identical device to the one in Nithe's cell was wheeled in. The demons stopped a few meters from her and darted back out as soon as they were able.

"You're up, Balthazar!" Raum stated curtly, shocking Ballzy into movement.

Balthazar walked in and shut the cell door firmly. Turning back toward her, he moved himself to stand before her, taking her upper arms in his large, trembling hands. Holding her firmly he spun her around and placed her back to the device, lifting her so her feet rested on the timber slats at the base. Leaning in close he whispered like a soft breeze in her ear, shielding his words as much as he could as he slid his hand down her arm and grasped her wrist, securing one after the other in the tight restraints.

"I'm so sorry, luv. I don't know what is about to happen, but I have his word he won't touch you. 'Twas the best I could do. Rest assured I will do what I can if needs be, but for now I need to strap you in. Please be calm. If what I fear is to come actually comes to pass, your new friend is going to need all of your strength, bravery, and steely determination. Show him how strong you are. How strong he is, too."

"Why'd you make him promise something so stupid, Ballzy? I was so looking forward to some up close and personal time with your little friend." Her wink was sassy, though she felt some trepidation. What was Raum up to? As long as he entered her cell she would be happy. But what if he didn't? Her powers weren't strong enough to cut through the special, magic-proof glass. Trusting Balthazar was something she hadn't expected at all. To have to put so much faith in him so suddenly was testing her nerves.

"Don't forget the waist." The sound of Raum's voice drew her from her introspection, and she realized both of her ankles were already bound firmly. The belt at her waist was pulled so tight she sucked in an involuntary breath.

"Good, wouldn't want the little bitch to be too comfortable. Oh, and just so you know, you worthless little cunt, these bindings are warded against magic from shifters, witches, and even angels." She eyed him defiantly until he turned his attention back to Ballzy.

"You know what that means? I can see you now, isn't that nice?" The fucker sounded way too fucking satisfied. Fuck! Her illusion was gone, and with it her tolerance for the pain to come.

"Move her to face me completely, about two feet away from the glass. I want her to have an unobstructed view of the consequences of keeping secrets, and hiding things from us."

Sure enough, she found herself staring straight into the most entrancing eyes she'd ever seen. Green flecked eyes of gold, like mountains of golden treasure and emeralds. She locked eyes with him and grabbed hold of the tether within her. Though she didn't understand it, she pushed every strong, brave, fierce, and reassuring emotion she had through it. Praying she could infuse him with it, and take away the desolation in his gaze. His lips parted, softening, as his brow creased, he dropped his chin to his chest, and when he raised it . . . What do you know? It'd fucking worked, somehow it'd fucking worked. The man before her even gave her a cheeky little wink.

"Our friend doesn't like unknowns, he also doesn't like the fact you've hidden her away like this, Balthazar. Why would you do such a thing? Unless you keep her for the same reasons I keep my little pet here? No, no I think not. So whatever it is she's hiding must be worth something. Since I cannot sense what she actually is, I assume that has something to do with our little mystery, no? There will be consequences for your failures."

He didn't give Ballzy a chance to answer. Instead, he returned his gaze to her.

"Last chance, or the game is on. Either way I'll find out what it is we want to know. So, will you squeal, or do I sense some fun afoot?"

Jezzie raked her gaze up and down his slim form. She flicked her eyes toward Ballzy's worried expression, then back to Nithe for a little wink of her own, before tilting her head at Raum as if considering his words.

"You want to know my secrets, Raum?" she said in her best cotton candy sweet, slightly vapid voice. "Well, you'll have to earn them, and honestly, I don't think you could ever be worthy."

He looked at her as if she was an idiot not to take his threats seriously. In fact, he looked like someone who hadn't met anyone who wasn't afraid of him in a very long time, and was struggling to comprehend exactly what she'd just said.

"In case you didn't get the memo, dipshit, let me simplify it for you. That was a no to your pathetic little last chance offer. Whatever you think you've got, I can take it and so much more."

His face flamed with barely contained rage. Apparently he didn't like defiance, even as he sought to play whatever game he had in mind. More likely he didn't like a female defying him in such a way. Considering he'd referred to her as a female dog on more than one occasion, she was willing to bet he had major mommy issues. If not mommy issues, he was a major misogynist, him being a sadistic asshole was already a done deal.

Suddenly his face went slack, an ice-cold mask fell, replacing his momentary show of anger. Now this face, with its twisted smile and dead eyes sent a chill down her spine, and had her senses on alert.

"Okay then. Balthazar, leave her cell and lock the door. It's time to play." His voice held the unmistakable slither of pure corrupted evil.

A sound she'd heard so many times before. But, this time it was worse. All those other times they'd come from humans, with human souls, and human weaknesses. This time they belonged to a being of the OtherRealm. A being more like her and less like the humans she preferred to hunt. What she feared the most, though, was not having her powers for what he had planned. Shit! If he was locking her in here, he wasn't coming in either. But without her powers it was probably a good thing actually, especially if she couldn't feed off him while she was strapped onto the cross. Which left the question about what he had planned sitting in the open air like an itch you wanted to scratch, even though it hurt like a motherfucker when you did.

With Ballzy out of the room, Jezzie watched as Raum walked behind Nithe, reached around his waist and grasped the waistband of the tattered rags Nithe wore as trousers. With one swift yank they tore down the center and fell to his ankles.

She tried not to look. Oh, how she tried. She locked her eyes onto his as best she could, refusing to give Raum the satisfaction of a response.

Her nipples hardened at the thought of what was exposed to her sight, she bit her lip hard, drawing a little blood as she did so. She traced his face and took in every line, every whisker, his perfect lips, the arch of his brow, the twist to his smile . . . Was he laughing at her? She swore she could hear the echo of it in her mind. When she looked at his face as a whole again, he gave a small, barely noticeable nod, and her resolve crumbled.

He was absolutely magnificent. His chiseled chest and stomach, the defined V leading to his splayed legs. Finally her eyes landed on the prize of all prizes, and the man was full of surprises. The longer she looked, the harder he got, and what had started as an already impressive sight became more so. Six inches turned into eight, and eight into ten. It wasn't just length, he was thicker than any man she'd ever been with. The man was truly blessed by the Almighty. Her mouth watered as she thought about taking him into her throat, caressing his smooth, hairless balls, and stroking the length of him. Deep inside her a pulse of desire caused her pussy to clench and a trickle of wet promise to dampen her thighs.

Unfortunately her perusal lasted too long, and didn't go unnoticed.

"I'm glad you like what you see. It will make this far easier. He is a fine specimen, an unequaled pet, don't you agree?"

Raum moved around Nithe like a predator stalking their next meal, and it made her sick to her stomach as he ran his hands over Nithe's exposed and vulnerable body. At some point, while she'd been engrossed in checking Nithe out, Raum had palmed a large, curved dagger, a wickedly sharp one undoubtedly. He ran the flat of the blade over Nithe's chest, and their bodies tensed in unison.

"Good, it's working then. But, just to be sure . . ." In a flash of silver he slashed at Nithe's cheek.

Jezzie bit the inside of her cheek as pain seared through her own face, surprising her with its suddenness. What the fuck was that? She watched as blood dripped from the gash on Nithe's cheekbone, scratch that, blood marbled with gold slid down his face. She tried to touch her own as a reflex to the pain, but, bound as she was, she couldn't. Taking a deep breath, she assessed herself. No blood trickled down her face, and the phantom pain faded faster than it should if the wound to her was real.

"Yes, I made a promise to Balthazar, I wouldn't touch you. Not that I would anyway, women are such disgusting creatures. I only touch them when I have to. Thankfully it doesn't happen often, and when it does it's quick and easy, and never for information. Anyway, I'm not touching you, I'm touching him." He pointed the blade at Nithe. "Whatever he feels while on this cross, so will you. The longer you hold out on me, the more you both will suffer."

"You won't kill him. You value him too much. You said it yourself, he's unsurpassed in quality."

"Oh, little girl, don't claim to know what I would do. I'd slit his throat right here, right now, if it got me what I truly wanted."

"You don't truly want my answers though, do you? You want something else. Let's see, can I guess what it is?"

She knew he wasn't bluffing, the truth shone from his eyes. He cared nothing for Nithe. At least now she knew a little more about the playing field. She sent her senses out, through the holes in the glass. Hmm, apparently whatever supposedly stopped a beings magic from working while bound to the cross didn't include her sensing his emotions, or sending emotions to Nithe. Both of those things had been as easy as breathing.

Raum's emotions swirled with twisted desire, jealousy, and rage. All of them were hidden under a veil of sadism and loyalty. When he'd spoken of his and Ballzy's mutual "friend", his voice had changed inflection.

"Does your boss not return your affections, Raum? Is that why you stoop to capturing innocent men and taking out your perverted, twisted desires and rage on them?" she taunted.

She really should learn to shut her mouth, but her tongue had a mind of its own. From the corner of her eye she saw Ballzy shake his head, his mouth slightly ajar. The look on his face reflected his acceptance of her words as probably true.

Raum's hand tightened on the blade. He held it up to the glass.

"You little bitch. You think you're so smart? I will make you scream in pain. The man whose cock you were salivating over is mine. You will never know what his cock will feel like in your mouth, but I will. You've no idea how badly you just fucked up. You think to taunt me? I hold all the power here, you pathetic little cunt, and you will rue this day." She could almost see the flecks of spittle covering the glass between them.

Yep, should've kept her fucking mouth shut. But, oh, had she hit a raw nerve, or what? Jackpot! Turning back to Nithe, Raum ran his free hand along his injured cheek, pressing his fingers into the wound. A pressure Jezzie felt too. His bloodied fingers moved to Nithe's lips, and tinged them red. Moving to stand on the platform with him, Raum made sure Jezzie had a clear view as he placed his own lips over Nithe's and licked away the blood. Nithe stayed rigid, his lips unyielding, his eyes focussed solely on Jezzie.

Anger burned in the pit of her stomach, and from deep within she felt the call of chaos, of destruction, and wrath. It whispered to her softly, like a lover making grand promises. Outwardly she showed no sign of her inner conflict. It wasn't like she could spill the beans anyway, the things he wanted to know were locked within her, as they'd always been, until her full power came to her. Aunt Rai Rai had made sure of it. If those powers even existed. Being the first of her kind, as far as she knew, nothing was certain.

Raum stepped back down off the platform, tracing the blade down the center of Nithe's chest, between his abdominal muscles, stopping just below his navel. A thin line of red welled in the blade's wake, taunting her from the other side of the glass.

Jezzie pulled in a deep breath as the sting echoed on her skin. Mmm, yummy. The taste of psycho was apparently on the menu today, despite Raum's earlier declaration. She inhaled his dark emotions, tinged with the aftertaste of bitterness and self-loathing. They were thick and heavy, it was hard to get a good flow going through the small holes available to her. Like too much oatmeal in one sitting; she knew she'd regret the meal later, but for the time being he was such a perfect target, and he deserved her worst.

If Raum's skin lost some of its color, he didn't notice, too focussed on his so-called "fun". His hand came to rest on Nithe's rigid cock. He gripped it hard, then added a painful twist, causing Nithe to grunt through his clenched teeth, his lips curling in a grimace.

"You see, you little bitch, he belongs to me. I can, and will do whatever I like to him. And you can't do a fucking thing about it."

She vowed to find a way to wipe the smile off his fugly face one way or another. She breathed in deeply and his emotions filled her. His soul beckoned, but she struggled to connect with the pulsing mass of ick.

Another slice, this time to Nithe's thigh, had her leg starting to tremble. Raum grabbed a whip from behind the cross. Shit! He probably had a whole arsenal of twisted torture equipment back there.

The lash to her back caught her off guard and her scream pierced the air before she could stop it. As it faded, so too did Nithe's. The phantom feeling of blood and split skin lingered longer than the cut to the cheek.

"Hmm, yes. Sing, little songbird, sing. You both complement each other so well. What a shame no one cares to save you from the pain." The saccharine sound of his voice made bile rise in her throat as his hand caressed Nithe's perfect balls. Her eyes narrowed on the sight.

"I see you don't like me touching my pet so intimately? And yet, there isn't a thing you can do to stop me, is there? Care to tell me your secrets now?" His hand paused as he awaited her answer.

She looked to Nithe, glanced at Ballzy. Both men shook their heads as stealthily as they could.

"Even if I could, I'd never give someone as pathetic as you the satisfaction."

If he hadn't picked up on her disdain laden tone, surely the way she spat on the ground before her feet showed him how little she thought of his attempts thus far. She'd had worse done by the humans she'd hunted. Although, she'd much rather he was in her cell doing it all to her. Even without the illusion all she had to do was consume his feelings and leech out a bit of his soul and she'd be able to heal herself. Healing Nithe, though? She'd never been able to do things like that.

CHAPTER 19

The bastard moved behind Nithe, grabbed the hair at his scalp, and mercilessly yanked his head back to expose his throat with one hand. With the other he attached a thin barbed length of wire to one of the crossbars.

"Hold very still, pet," he murmured as he released his hold to switch hands and attach the wire to the other side. Nithe's throat grazed the wire and the scent of burning flesh reached her. He pulled back slightly, but every time he swallowed, his Adam's apple bobbed, and a new wave of pain and acrid stench filled her senses.

"Time to step it up a bit, I think." His confidence was truly starting to piss her off.

This time, Raum donned a black leather glove covered in runes and some kind of pattern, writing maybe? Honestly, it just made him look like a Michael Jackson wannabe. A piss poor one, but still it brought humor to an otherwise fucked up situation. Whether it made it more fucked or less, was open to debate.

"You won't be smirking for long, bitch," Raum snarled, his upper lip curled back.

The first glide of the glove across Nithe's chest was agony. Mirrored as it was over her own, Jezzie felt skin melt away in a wash of gravel burn. Her eyes closed of their own volition, teeth clenched so hard they almost cracked. Her shadows rose to just below the surface of her skin, soothing the pain away, turning it to pleasure. When her eyes flashed open, she knew fire flashed in them, and as she locked her gaze onto Nithe, she found his own glowed like golden coins caught in the light of the sun. Another long pull at Raum's emotions had him stumble backwards. He eyed her with suspicion and calculation.

The next time he slid his gloved hand down Nithe's body he slowly ran it down the side of his torso, over his ribs, and up and down his thigh. He paused as he watched her agonized face, and without taking his eyes from hers he slid it over the sensitive skin of his cock. The red and bleeding mass left behind had her screaming on the inside. Her shadows flicked out of her erratically for a few seconds as tears slid down her cheeks. She wished she could tell them her secret, but it was locked deep inside her, and she didn't yet have the key. Aunt Rai Rai would fucking hear about this. She felt no corresponding pain between her legs. Well, she didn't have a dick, so it kind of made sense, right?

Nithe screamed blue murder as sobs wracked his body. He looked at her, pleading. Oh, how she longed to speak the words that would stop it all. But, from the look in Raum's eyes, the maniacal pleasure he felt, the waves of building excitement, she knew even if she were to give her secret away, he wouldn't stop until his own sadistic fun was had.

Nithe looked at Ballzy. "*Sáifrai'enna.*" His voice was hoarse, the sound came out a whispered plea. One he repeated over and over again. She wished she knew what it meant.

Raum knelt at Nithe's feet, his tongue licked along the length of Nithe's mutilated cock as gold tinged blood dripped to the floor. All of which he made her watch. How dare the fucker touch him like that. When he rose and faced her, licking his lips clean, she heard the voice of an angry banshee fill her mind, and while her own thoughts echoed the sentiments, it was like no voice she'd ever heard before.

He will pay with his life. Though they'd been said in a language she'd never heard before, she understood them perfectly.

"You won't find help here with your little codeword. You don't have any 'loyal friends' to come to your rescue. Balthazar, over there, is on the right team, not yours, and everyone here belongs to him. Even your little girlfriend over there can't save you." He pointed to Jezzie with a sneer as he taunted Nithe. He licked the last traces of blood from his fingers, fingers that had held Nithe still for his ministrations.

"Mmm," he moaned, and never had the expression of pleasure sounded so stomach-turning. "Who ever would have thought mixing the blood of an angel with that of a dragon would create a taste so divine, even if you are an abomination."

Nithe's eyes went wide with shock. She tensed. He was a hybrid. Like her, but different. She wasn't alone anymore. Wait. An abomination? Like fuck they were.

"I've known who you are all along, Nithe."

Ballzy gasped from the hallway. She turned her head and caught his stunned expression.

"No one wanted you, boy. Not your clan, not your mother, and most certainly, not your father." Raum grabbed Nithe's face and squeezed his cheeks hard, then released him quickly so his head fell forward, his chin to his chest.

The sudden crack of the whip so close to Nithe's face, made Jezzie recoil. Her heart beat triple time in her chest, as fear and anger pumped through her blood. Balthazar watched her from the side of the room, silently begging her to be strong, even as her shadows pulsed to be set free. To maim. To feed. The pressure building and building, as the voice inside her whispered to tear the world asunder.

"Why do you think he signed off on this little mission of yours? The one that landed you here at my mercy. The great, and just Ramiel, sending his son off to certain slaughter. To me no less, where torture and degradation was guaranteed," he paused, with a snarky smirk of calculation lighting his face. "I mean, you did know Ramiel is your father, right?"

Nithe's head lifted briefly, and in that moment Jezzie watched every imaginable emotion wash over his face like a tide that couldn't be stopped. It was heartbreaking to witness. As his shoulders slumped further down and his head bowed to match them, Jezzie felt how broken and alone he felt. For the first time in her existence, she wished her feeding worked the opposite way. Sure, she could lessen the devastation he felt, but there were no happy emotions inside him to replace the ones she'd eat. Not now. Ultimately, his pain would redouble, and he was already so close to the end of his tether. Her chest started to heat, and the whisper in her mind urged her to push every happy thought she could toward him. Silently she begged him to lift his head, to lock his eyes on hers. And slowly, ever so slowly, he did. It felt unlike anything she'd felt before, not like her happiness was being sucked away, more like a link, where she took some of his pain to eat while giving him light in return for his darkness. When her scalp started to tingle she shut the link on instinct and gasped like a fish. Nithe gave her the smallest of smiles, and it felt like the rays of the sun on a lovely spring day. How was any of it possible?

"Oh, that's just precious. You didn't know, did you?" Raum's laugh was filled with sadistic mirth. "Or did you think he'd be proud of you? Risking your life in the pursuit of justice, just like dear old dad? You never wondered why he didn't come back for you, or your whore of a mother?" Another lash of the whip, this one close enough to split the skin on his shoulder, leaving a trail of blood welling in its place. Nithe still didn't make a sound. The pain of the lash warmed her face and bit her shoulder, but it barely registered through the haze of her anger, and her need to comfort the man laid so bare before her.

"He was ashamed of you, boy. Ashamed of the abomination he'd helped create. While you stayed in the realm of dragons it wasn't an issue. You were a nobody; a nothing. But then you went and got yourself exiled, and instead of going to another clan, which, to be honest, probably would have ended the same way, you left the realm completely. That was a problem. He needed a way to make you, the problem, the mistake, disappear." Raum's lips grazed Nithe's ear. Jezzie could see how his jaw clenched, could feel his disgust at the hot breath and dry lips on his skin. She strained against her shackles without thought.

"I'm very, very good at making problems disappear. I'm the instrument of your demise, pet. The best part? Daddy dearest won't mind if I take my time with you either."

Raum removed the glove and reverently placed it back from where it came. He returned with the knife he'd started this little session with. Digging the tip of the blade into Nithe's left pec, he twisted and turned it.

"Did you think the forest hid the tracking beacon?" Nithe glared at him. "It's what the others before you thought, too. Alas the cold, hard truth is much less comforting. The little tracking beacon sitting in the muscles under the skin right here?" He pressed the blade in deep, bone deep. "It's been working just fine this whole time. Even if the forest had hidden you, didn't you wonder why no one had yet come?"

His cruel laugh echoed through the cells, leaving the hairs on Jezzie's nape standing on end. She'd fucking kill this Ramiel guy herself if this shit turned out to be true. No force in all the realms would stop her.

"The one who holds the receiver to your tracker knows exactly where you are, they just don't care to collect you. Actually, they're just waiting for it to go dead, as soon as you are. Problem solved on their end, pet. Soon, soon enough, it will happen."

Suddenly, he turned his attention back to Jezzie. Catching the fire flaring in her gaze, the light pulsing of the air a few inches from her skin.

"Oh, would you look at that? Hmm, very interesting. What exactly are you? Should I dissect you and find out? With your consent, Balthazar, of course."

"You will not, Raum. In my house your word is as good as a contract, and you will adhere to the terms." Ballzy's hands were shaking as he repeatedly clenched and unclenched them. Inside he was a writhing mass of outrage and anger. He had the look of someone waging an inner battle between action and inaction. Sweat beaded at his temples where veins stood in stark contrast to his skin. She noted it all in the briefest of glances, her gaze drawn back to Nithe and the unstable Raum.

"It seems pain is not a motivator for you, little bitch. But I see the way you watch my pet, the rage you feel when I touch him. So, that's just what I'm going to do. I'm going to touch him . . . all over. I'm going to slice him up into ribbons, until strips of flesh are hanging from his body. But, before I do that I'm going to take his cock in my mouth and suck the shit out of it. Then, I'm going to fuck him nice and deep so there's no doubt who owns his ass, literally, and there's nothing you, or his pathetic dragon, can do about it, not with those cuffs holding him back."

The more he spoke, the more Jezzie felt she was going to explode; the power inside her continued to build and build. She felt like a powder keg near an open flame. When he took Nithe's cock into his disgusting mouth she felt her stomach revolt, but she swallowed it down, refusing to give him the satisfaction of such a visceral reaction.

Nithe's eyes pinned her in place as effectively as the cross which held her up. She sent him every bit of pride she could muster, every bit of strength she didn't need herself. Inside she grabbed hold of the tether and held fast, pulling it to her. In her mind she sent the words, *stay strong* over and over.

Whatever comes next, Jez, don't watch. His response shocked her. He'd heard her and what's more, he'd answered back. Nothing like this had ever happened before, not even with her mother.

Jezzie clamped her teeth shut as Raum stood, licking his lips and smirking at her. Pure insanity lit his features. The pressure in her chest kept growing until it felt like it had nowhere to go. It filled her fingertips, her toes, even the tip of her pert little nose. Okay, so she was rhyming now, maybe a little bit of insanity was rubbing off on her. She did love a good rhyme though. They mostly popped into her head when she was uncomfortable or stressed, and her body was almost tapped out. Exactly like when she'd first stepped through the portal to Demon's Den. Shit! Not again!

Raum stepped behind Nithe and released his wrists from the straps, the metal cuffs remained. Nithe fell forward, his legs spread wide, his ankles still bound to the cross. Grabbing Nithe's wrists he bound them before he had a chance to resist, and stepped between his legs.

Look away now, Jez, please. I beg of you, he whispered to her silently.

Silence met him, her mind too filled with rage. Her power caused her skin to burn.

Raum took out the blade, slid it over Nithe's back, and sliced it down the curve of his bare cheek. Jezzie felt the pain like a dull ache. The power of the cross wasn't as strong without him fully restrained upon it. The sadistic vessel of evil incarnate reached down and forced Nithe's hips up, exposing him further. He reached around with the sharp steel and held it under Nithe's testicles.

Power swelled within her as she watched Raum open his pants and rub his pathetic excuse for a dick while he spat into the crevice of Nithe's ass. She felt the floodgates open as Raum's soul was suddenly exposed to her hunger, and she pulled hard. In the end her shadows stopped her. *Not ours to slaughter, not yet,* they whispered.

As he knelt behind Nithe, ready to take what he had no right to, she felt an explosion of pure agony sear across her shoulders, fire filled her vision, and just before her sight was consumed by flames, she saw a look of awe fill Nithe's partially scaled features. Her body exploded with red shadows and light as pain tore her apart. The sizzle of the scar on her palm fading barely registered through the myriad sensations assaulting her body. A feeling of serenity settled over her after what seemed like only moments had passed. Her eyes opened to a scene full of silent destruction and a calm sort of chaos.

Fuck! No! It couldn't be?

Seriously, it was just his luck, wasn't it? She could have ended up anywhere but here, and yet here she was. An angel hybrid, and not just any angel hybrid, if his guess hit the mark.

His doorstep, and he'd seriously fucked up, but there was no better place for her, he supposed. Except for where he was going to have to send her. The threat to her had become so much greater. Just not from where he'd expected, and with the knowledge of what she was, the contract was broken.

Balthazar rose to his feet from where he'd been thrown by the powerful blast her full manifestation had triggered. She was divine. Her shadows, like fire, filled the space of both cells and the hallway in which he stood. The only clear spots surrounded Nithe and he. Which was a blessing as he watched Raum writhe in agony before going still, burns and mangled flesh littered his body. He doubted the prick would heal from those for a while. Shadow inflicted injuries were rather nasty, if you weren't a Shadow Hound yourself, anyway. If his suspicions were correct, Raum's injuries would be even worse.

Ah, fuck it! If he was right, he was about to find himself on a brand-new shit list. Thankfully he knew he could hold his own if he had to, but he'd rather not fight his old friend if he could help it.

Jezzie's body levitated from the ground, suspended by the divine rite of passage awarded to her. When her shadows settled, their work done, she lowered softly to her feet. Two large, perfect wings bracketed her from behind. They were to fucking die for. Thick black feathers shone in the dull light. Along the lower edge they changed color, like a rainbow in stark relief against the black of the others. Red, orange, yellow, green, blue, purple, and pink, a sight he'd never seen the likes of before in all his countless years.

Shattered remnants of spelled glass littered the ground as he walked forward slowly. He didn't want to scare her, she'd be on edge from the events of the day already, but the manifestation would make it all one hundred times worse. She was in for a rough few days, maybe longer.

Fire still filled her eyes with an eerie glow, and her body twitched, her shadows shifting angrily. He stopped. He heard the sound of movement from behind him and spun. Nithe stood near Raum's twisted body. Free of the cross completely, not a scratch marred his form, his eyes shone bright, like the dragon he was, and dark green, iridescent scales covered parts of his face, chest, legs, and arms. All the places he'd been harmed. Yeah, including the guy's monster dick, which was now covered in the same scales. As he watched, they retracted, and what was revealed, thanks to his partial shift, was a miniature version of what must be his dragon cock. Even in miniature form it was twice the size of some of the most well-endowed males he'd seen. Thank you internet porn.

Raum, who twitched and writhed at his feet, moved to drag himself away. Balthazar moved back toward him, but Jezzie was quicker, her shadows struck and a shimmer filled the air before Raum fell still once more.

Now was not the time for questions, now was the time to get them to safety. The time to bring Raum to justice was here and if it sacrificed his mission, then so be it. The stakes had just been raised. He had a duty to protect the children of his two best friends, and Ramiel could suck it if he didn't appreciate his sacrifice. He'd take out the prick himself if what Raum had said were true. But he didn't believe it to be so.

"Nithe, press Jezzie's hand to the jagged stone beneath the window behind Jezzie. I highly doubt she'll allow it of me right now."

"Come now, Ballzy, I do trust you, not really sure why, and it took some time, but I do." Her voice was huskier than normal, as if her shadows were threaded through it; it added an almost smokey quality to her normal tone.

"But seeing as I can't seem to move right now, Nithe may do the honors."

Nithe moved forward, took Jezzie's hand in his, and led her to the stone he'd indicated. Her palm pressed against the cold wall and they heard a distinct click. A two foot square of concrete flooring dissolved before their eyes, to reveal the two large backpacks he'd hidden there. Thank fuck he'd managed to get rough sizes for Nithe's clothing out of Raum before they got here.

"There are clothes in them for each of you. Get dressed quick, Nithe, you don't have much time. Raum's boss will know he is incapacitated and injured. There is no way he wouldn't be tracking that shit since Raum is his biggest, most loyal asset."

"Why the fuck should I trust you? You work with him!" Nithe's partial change had the rasp of his dragon tongue layered through his voice as he pointed to his tormentor.

"Because, boy, while I work for *them* on the surface, I work for the other side in truth. Now, dress! Unless you don't want to protect the treasure you can't keep your eyes off of?"

Nithe moved so fast he was almost a blur. Leather reinforced paratrooper pants, a black fitted muscle shirt, and sturdy leather boots were donned with precision. But his cock still bobbed out, the button fly undone. He winked at Balthazar.

"Sorry, out it stays. I cannae shift it back until it's healed right." Balthazar looked away and shook his head, of course he couldn't.

"Don't worry. If you shift in them, they won't tear. They'll just melt away and reform when you shift back."

Nithe looked at him with questioning suspicion, "How did you know I could shift?"

"I didn't, but until now I didn't know what Jezzie was either, so I made preparations based on all possibilities. I wish she'd told me, and saved us all this drama, but I would have stayed silent if I were her too. It was the smartest thing to do, though I don't think she actually had much choice in the matter."

Nithe grabbed Jezzie around the waist just as her knees buckled.

"Take both packs, she'll need to change later. I'm going to open a specific portal for you. It is the safest place I can think to send you. Except for the parts that aren't, and for that I am sorry. Oh, and Nithe, don't believe a word that piece of shit said about your father. The male I know would not act with such dishonor. Try to keep an open mind. For your sake, and hers. I fear you will have some competition for her affections."

Nithe nodded, but his eyes flashed with ire at the mention of his father. He grabbed the packs from the ground and scooped Jezzie up into his arms.

"What about him?" Nithe said, pointing to Raum's still body. "What will happen to him? I cannot allow him to go free, not after everything."

"Don't worry, I'm sending a request for the collection of Tartarus' newest inmate as soon as you are safely on the other side of the portal and out of his reach. Jezzie, luv? What exactly did you do to Raum, in case they ask?" Balthazar asked softly.

"Oh, that. I ate his emotions as I sipped his icky black soul. It was truly disgusting, Ballzy Boo."

Ah yes, the deliriously happy drunk stage of the process. Shit, he didn't want to have to send them through right now. He'd rather wait until she was rational and had her wits and strength back. Fuck knows they were going to need it. Wait, she ate his emotions . . . on top of the soul eating thing? Oh brother, her mother wasn't human. There were only a few species who could siphon emotions too. At least it would make her stronger, but the possibilities were endless. How was it even possible? Angels could only breed with humans or other angels, and yet standing before him were two beings who were born of OtherRealmly beings, one of which just happened to be an angel. Suddenly the impossible seemed a reality. The ripple effect of which could change the course of existence.

There was no chance he was going to step into the explanation ring with their fathers if he could avoid it. They'd have to figure it out on their own.

"There's food, med kits, weapons, and other provisions in the packs. Just be careful. Until you get to them, danger lurks in every dark, dank void."

"And just where are you sending us, Ballzy?" came the odd sounding voice of Jezzie again.

"Nestradia, the Realm of Nightmares often referred to as The Nether of the Unjust, or the Realm of Rot and Ruin."

Nithe's growl filled the air, but as he went to speak, Balthazar summoned the portal, and just before he rushed forward and shoved them through, he gave one last instruction.

"Go! Take her to the princes, and the princes will take you to he who is hidden."

"Who is he?" Nithe queried, falling into the opening with Jezzie in his arms, and the packs on his back.

"That, my fellow spy, is his story to tell."

CHAPTER 20

His cock had fucking portal burn from flapping through the void. Being shoved in backwards hadn't helped either. The only saving grace was his ability to cushion Jezzie's fall. Which had been purely coincidental since he was already holding her up. The feel of her body pressed against his sent shock waves to the core of him. His cock got even harder as she shifted, rubbing against him as soft little moans drifted from her lips. The dragon in him roared to be released, demanding their mate bond be completed. Just fucking great. He found his mate in the most fucked up of ways and now can't do anything about it. Jezzie's wings draped over them, blocking his view of their surroundings, and as much as he wanted to stay in the cocoon of them forever, this place was too dangerous; too deadly. Raum was nothing compared to what awaited them here. As much faith as Balthazar seemed to have in the princes, Nithe wasn't sure what lay in store for them there was any better than the cluster-fuck they were about to face, out here in the open.

He shifted his hips in order to gently dislodge her. Bad idea. Very bad idea, or rather, great idea, just not now, not here. Fuck, he was so close to spilling his load it wasn't funny. Before she acquiesced and slid to the ground beside him, she grabbed his shirt and slammed her mouth against his. He shuddered in response, his hands coming up to cup her face as his tongue delved between her delicious lips. His breath froze in his chest as sensation flooded him, his cock pulsed, spurts of cum erupting between them. Yep, he wasn't close anymore. A single kiss from her lips to his, and he'd spent himself like an untried dragonet. Which would be embarrassing if not for the sight of her sliding down his body, and her pretty pink tongue licking the last remnants of semen from his still twitching cock.

Movement from the corner of his eye caused his head to fly up, his eyes widened, and he lunged to his feet, dumping Jezzie unceremoniously on the barren, dust covered ground. He called forth his dragon form, but nothing happened. Try as he might to push out through Nithe's body, a full shift would not overtake him. Talons emerged from his fingertips, long and sharp. His own wings sprung from his back, the shiny gold, metallic feathers lighting the darkness around them.

Holy hell balls, he'd never seen anything like them. They were nightmares brought to life. Worse than any children's boogeyman, or monster under the bed. More like a wendigo on steroids, or if one had procreated with the Dullahan of his childhood nightmares. Part horse, part wendigo, fused together, and covered in thick, black, dripping oil. Its open maw showed rows upon rows of sharp, vicious teeth, its needle like claws dragged upon the ground. It lunged forward suddenly, and on autopilot Nithe opened his mouth and his dragon did the rest. He'd never thought it possible to breathe his fire in human form, and yet here he was. Acid green flames filled the space between him and the monster. What remained of the monster's flesh slid down its body to the ground beneath its slippery black hooves, but the skeletal figure still stood, snarling its angry refrain.

Nithe moved instinctively as he grabbed the packs from the ground, putting the straps over one arm, and a disgruntled Jezzie over his shoulder with the other. His knees bent into a deep crouch before he sprung up toward the sky, his wings beating a steady rhythm through the stagnant, gag inducing air.

Pain slashed down his spine in the darkness. A darkness even he couldn't see through. Neither angel nor dragon sight was able to cut through the thick black gloom which encompassed them. But then, why would it? This was the place where the worst of the OtherRealm beings were sent, where the creatures of nightmares manifested into reality. If they could be seen clearly, what would be the point? Nullifying powers made sense.

He spun in time to drop lower in the air, barely avoiding the razor sharp talons of another monster. The gold of his wings glowed, a lure in the darkness, no doubt. Shit! Not smart. He flew as fast as he could as he breathed his acid fire before them. Downward slightly, of course. It wouldn't hurt him, he didn't think it would hurt Jezzie, still it was a chance he wasn't about to take. On the other hand, it would most definitely incinerate their supplies, and possibly their clothing. Things they may need if they wished to survive in a realm no being had ever returned from. So far, not even the princes sent there in service to the Almighty had been heard from on the outside.

Thoughts raced through Nithe's head as he tried to formulate a plan. He could see vague landmarks below them. Slight outcroppings of rocks and boulders were dismissed, as they offered little to no defensive protection. Spears flew past him as he dodged and ducked, he spun, and shielded Jezzie with his body.

"Let me go, Nithe. I have wings, silly. I can fly all by myself," she pouted.

"That's not quite how it works the first few times, Jez," he gasped out. Another shaft of pain sliced his side. The odor of putrid pus too close for comfort. Unfortunately, his scales were not protection enough.

Jezzie squirmed, pushing against his scale-armored shoulders. His sweat slicked arms couldn't contain her, and she slipped from his grip. He watched as she spiraled, her wings not responding as the wind lashed at them, wrapping them around her body. Below her, the ground rushed to meet her, yet what terrified him more was the creature which rose from the dark swamp; its giant, gaping maw open and ready to feast on Jezzie's flesh. The image of a hippocampus from the fables of old, only twisted, evil, and covered in millenia of whatever fetid vileness filled the swamp and pervaded the soil around it.

Wind burned his face as he dove to catch her. How he longed to shift completely. The scales from the partial shift offered minimal protection, and were mostly for healing wounds and hand-to-hand combat training. Skin grazed skin as he snatched at her leg, the gray material of her pants shredding under his clawed hands. No! Failure was not an option. He wouldn't lose her, not when he'd just found her. She was the light in the darkness he could feel welling in his mind. So many people had let him down, so many had betrayed him, but he knew in his soul she never would.

He shot past her with a burst of speed, the air forcing its way up his nose as it stung his eyes until they closed and wouldn't open. With one last Hail Mary he rolled sideways and offered his stomach to the sky, arms out and in, before he rolled right back out again, beating his wings hard. The hot, rather nasty smell of decomposed flesh wafted up, he looked down into the soulless eyes of a being created to do anything to survive, and nothing else.

His golden eyes scanned the gloom as he moved away from the snapping jaws of certain, if not death, then at the very least a particularly excruciating ordeal.

Harsh drums of thunder boomed from every direction as the creatures converged and renewed their attacks. The wasteland below was covered in a writhing mass of hideous beings, and the sky was filling with more by the minute as they were drawn to the scent of blood, the calls of their fellow monsters, and the light from his wings and fire. He needed to find a safe place to set down, prepare his defenses, and create a shield. More so as he felt one wing dip, agony slicing through him. Jezzie giggled in his arms, her hands roaming his chest as she babbled something about handsome men, fine chests, tattoos, and rainbow hair. Pride swelled in his chest and his dragon was chuffed. Their mate was touching them, complimenting them. Though the rainbow hair bore further exploration, and his dragon seemed a little snarly about it. Dragons typically hated sharing their treasure back in the day. Some still held true to those sentiments, but Nithe liked to think he was more progressive than most of his kind.

Up ahead he spotted a large mountain ridge with a decent sized plateau. The closer he got the more he knew this would have to do, his energy was slipping away by the second. A wall of stone closed off the edge of the ridge from whatever lay beyond.

His breath came hard, his chest heaved in and out between clenched teeth, his arms strained, muscles he'd not used in so long burned and threatened to fail him. Still, onward he flew.

The moment his feet hit the ground, his knees buckled, and he fell forward as he tossed Jezzie and the packs out in front of him. His eyes closed of their own accord as the veil of darkness that hindered his view of the land around him fell over his mind as well and pulled him into the unconscious abyss.

As Nithe went down and she went flying, landing hard on the thankfully soft packed, charred dirt—please let it be dirt, please let it be dirt—the fuzzy haze over her brain started to lift. It wasn't dirt; sludge seeped between her toes and the scent of death became more pronounced. As if the blood of countless beings had been shed here and instead of being washed away or sinking down into the deeper layers of whatever made up this realm, they were kept at the surface to remind those unlucky enough to be sent here exactly what awaited them. Fuck, what was with the morbid, soul-crushing rhetoric her brain kept spouting. Shut the fuck up, brain, you aren't helping.

"Nithe!" she yelled as she rushed toward him. Her knees scraped along the small, sharp rocks. Small fragments, like tiny knives, embedded themselves in the cuts, but she didn't care. Not a single muscle moved for what felt like an eternity. Her breath froze in her lungs as her heart skipped a thousand beats. Was he dead? Had she been so fucking far out of it that her messed up brain had led to his death? This man who'd stood before her, so proud, so strong, despite it all. Even in his vulnerability and torment he was perfection. She may not know him, but she felt his soul, and it was precious. Both to her, and to the shadows she housed within her. Another thing she did not yet understand.

In the blink of an eye, reality returned and joy spread through her to eliminate the growing dread. One gilded wing twitched, a shiver rippled his strange feathers, and a fine gold shimmer disturbed the midnight black that surrounded them. The relief she felt course through her was systemic, it took root and grew to fill her up with purpose. In the next blink, both anger and twisted delight thrust her into action. As Nithe's damaged wing shifted ever so subtly, screeching shrieks filled the ridge, echoing off the rocks behind her. Dark shapes flew in droves to their location from all directions. She spun on her knees mid-slide, thick black debris kicked up as she twisted and jumped to her feet. More cuts, more blood, but she barely felt any of it. Vaguely, she recalled Ballzy's mention of weapons as she lunged and grabbed the bags, dumping the contents unceremoniously at her feet. She had no time for anything but haste.

Ration packs scattered, med kits too, she sifted through the clothing, and came up with two pistols, several boxes of ammunition, something that looked like a small baton, and a futuristic space gun, or a kids toy. Either way it looked awesome, so she picked it up and prepared to fire, hoping like hell it was already loaded.

Above her the sound of scratching reached her ears. Without hesitation, she straightened and raised the weapon at the same time her finger flexed on the trigger. Brilliant orange flames burst forth, reaching higher than two tall men, and incinerated the creature as it prepared to pounce upon her.

A flamethrower! How fucking cool was that! she thought. And Nithe, he got to do this whenever he wanted. It must be so cool. The smile which twisted her lips was a sure sign the party was just getting started.

One after another the charred and crispy remains of the monsters fell. Some into their circle, but most from the sky took the short way off the ridge. She was having so much fun she wanted to cackle like a storybook witch, no offense to her aunt or any other witch she knew, but she couldn't hold the inclination back as it filled the air.

Hoarse groans drew her attention back to Nithe, he didn't look good as he pushed himself up and promptly fell back down again. One wing hung at an odd angle, his strange blood coated the feathers and trickled down. As she watched, the weird, black soil seemed to suck it up, devouring it, even rising toward him in an effort to taste more, and just like that playtime was over.

The flamethrower was tossed aside as the more urgent need for a shield took hold. Her brow creased in concentration, she closed her eyes and held up her palms. Strain showed on her features as she struggled to build the shield she'd practiced as a child, making sure to include a floor to keep out the weird-ass soil, and any ground dwellers who might decide to rise from their burrows. A simple spell her aunt had taught her after the blood bond ceremony had been completed. Magic was more difficult here, even her shadows felt hindered, weighted down. Not bound, but as if they were mired in thick sludge. Finally with a grunt, the dome was complete.

Shrieks of outrage and thuds resounded as creatures flew at them, only to face-plant the invisible barricade. Some extra dim ones pulled back and attacked again. It was futile, really, she'd long ago mastered the art of an impenetrable barrier. Fortunately, the space around them was large and open enough to accommodate it.

Grabbing several of the med kits, she knelt at Nithe's side and placed two fingers on the artery in his neck. Thank fuck, he had a steady pulse. She cupped his grime covered face with soft hands, her skin no less filthy than his. After placing his head gently back down on the clean barrier floor, she grabbed the first bag and checked over their supplies. Bandages, sutures, wipes, needles, syringes, several labeled bottles that did fuck knows what, and scalpels. Another bag held the first thing she knew she'd need. Alcohol. The good stuff too. Grey Goose, the French sure did know how to make fine food, wine, and spirits.

When she touched Nithe's back, he flinched, his eyes flared, and his roar bounced off the barrier walls.

"You'll need to clean it, lass, and stitch the edges back tae'gether," he ground out, but the voice belonged more to the dragon than to the man. It told her more about his level of discomfort than anything else.

"Right." She shoved a leather wrapped metal tube—she'd found it buried under a few bandages—between his teeth, and said, "Here, bite down hard. This won't be very nice."

"Never is, lass," were the last words he spoke as she tipped the entire bottle of vodka over the open wound, along all six inches and between the exposed bones where the upper part of his wing was cleaved from his body.

Orange pus sizzled and the smell of sulfur singed her nose hairs, making bile rise in the back of her throat. But she forced it down, swallowing repeatedly. One lone tendril of shadow reached out and nudged a dark blue bottle closer, the tinkle of rolling glass drew her attention. 'For Poison' read the label. Her brow rose, the shadow nudged it again. Who was she not to trust them? She'd trusted them the moment she'd acquired them, that they were sentient and now spoke to her didn't change that. Did it? No, it didn't. She tore the lid from the bottle and once more went to empty the contents over the gash. Her shadows wrapped around her wrist, forcing the bottle back up and spun it around.

There, under the part about poison, in very fine print were the words, '*One drop to slow it, two drops to heal it, three drops or more? Drop dead on the floor.*' Jezzie felt the color leech from her face. She'd nearly killed him. After all he'd survived, her impulsive reaction had nearly been the end of him.

Big, deep breaths, in and out, she looked out to the landscape beyond their little slice of peace, knowing they didn't have forever. Monsters continued to bombard the barrier, more reckless and desperate than before. Eyes closed she counted to ten. She could do this. Help Nithe, get them to safety, and find a way back home. No biggie. All she had to do was escape the one place no one had ever managed to return from. How hard could it be? As she looked around at the monsters still pummeling the dome, and saw the soil underneath it shake angrily, she felt her confidence fade. Once the dome went down, all bets were off. They had weapons, yes, but their powers were sluggish, they were surrounded on all sides, and she wasn't even sure Nithe could completely shift into his dragon in this Almighty forsaken place. Not to mention she couldn't even make her wings move, let alone fly.

Looking back at Nithe she threaded the needle and took a big, deep breath as she held the edges of his wound as closed as she could. Seemed like it was a day of firsts all around. Hopefully she didn't fuck it up.

CHAPTER 21

Every stitch felt like an eternity as Nithe waited for Jezzie's shaking hands to be done. All he needed was his wing popped back in place and the skin forced back together. Once done, he could retract his wings back in so it could heal much faster. Not to mention it wouldn't hurt like the dickens on an extremely bad day once they were away.

The moment the last stitch was tied off and cut, his wings snapped shut and melded into his back—more slowly than usual due to the injury, but at least they fit back properly—and his claws retracted. His shirt appeared on his body once more, though he hadn't even noticed its absence. While fatigue weighed him down, his 'face flat to the ground' position really sucked, so he flipped himself over to his back, and stared at the fireworks raining down above them. His eyes widened, mouth open ready to let loose his flame. The instinct faded away with a gasp of surprise as the lightning and fire bounced back at the creatures trying so desperately to get to their next meal. Which, unfortunately, might very well be two hybrid angels on the run from the Almighty knows what. He looked over at his mate and knew she'd done this. Well, his Jezzie was just full of surprises now, wasn't she?

He moved to recline against a large stone slab nearby and

summoned his power to his chest. Nithe tried to call forth a portal, and received nothing but a zap of magical electricity for his efforts.

"Jez, lass, can you bring up a portal at all?" he asked.

"Well, fuck. I didn't even think to try." She chuckled self-deprecatingly. "Give me a sec and I'll give it a go. I take it you didn't have any luck?"

Nithe just shook his head as he watched her get to her feet, his blood still coated her hands. Pert nose in the air, shoulders back, thick red hair caressing her taut ass. He was gaining a fine appreciation for yoga pants, that was for sure. She rolled her shoulders, her full, round breasts thrust forward. The wrinkle of her nose became more pronounced, and with a disgusted grunt she placed a hand to her chest, rubbing a small circle over the same place he'd felt his own powers rebound.

"No dice, sweet cheeks. Guess we're stuck here for a while. The barrier should hold up for another forty-two hours, but I'm going to need to recharge before I can put up another, and frankly there doesn't seem to be much around here to help a hybrid like me out with that." Jezzie's features shuttered almost the instant the last word left her lips, before her eyes popped wide, she spun about with her arms out, and let out a squeal of pure delight.

"I'm a hybrid, I'm part angel, part vamp. Oh my gosh, this is so fricking exciting." This time the squeal was almost earsplitting. But she looked so happy, her smile contagious.

"Care to share, lass?" Nithe put on a pout, just in case she thought about saying no. He'd been told, in his youth, he had a damn near irresistible one. Many a lady had fallen victim to his whims. Candy had been the currency of the day, many a time. As he'd gotten older, his penchant for candy had remained, but the women had become much more intimately inclined.

"Never been able to tell anyone what I am, not until now, until my powers fully came in. You're the first. Aren't you a lucky ducky dragon man?" her voice dropped into a husky moan right at the end.

He watched as she shifted, her thighs rubbed together, and her hands ran over her hips and stomach. Until her eyes latched on to the shimmery blood coated skin.

"Umm, Nithe?"

"Yes, Jez?"

"We should clean up a bit, don't you think?"

"Probably a good idea. But we dinnae want to waste too much water either. We'll probably need it." The husk in her voice brought out his own gravelly Scottish undertones.

"Good thing I spotted this in the bag then. Ballzy did put some thought into this. The guy does seem to always have a plan." She chuckled, holding up a couple of clean cloths and two canteens, tossing one of each to Nithe, who caught both deftly in one hand. He read the label on the canteen aloud.

"I thought about a never-ending packet of Tim Tams, but decided on water instead." He looked at Jezzie confused as he poured some on the cloth and cleaned his face of muck.

"Like the Tim Tams ad? Where they wish for a packet that never runs out. Tim Tam's . . . forever! Dude, Ballzy should have done both."

"What the fuck's a Tim Tam?" Nithe felt so out of the loop.

"Right," Jezzie said, shaking her head. "It's an earth thing, probably don't have them in your realm. They are these amazing chocolate biscuits, two of them, with a creamy filling sandwiched in between and covered in a layer of smooth chocolate. Trust me, they are divine, and now I want one, more than one, but one is better than none." She actually wiped at her mouth with her wrist, leaving behind a fresh trail of grime.

"So, are you saying this water isnae gonna run out?"

"That's my theory, yes. Wanna test it?" She didn't wait for his response, but instead lifted the bottle over her face and tipped the contents out. Water sluiced over her, saturated cloth stuck to her skin. The thin gray tank top became transparent, her nipples almost poking through the tight fabric, and yet the water didn't slow its flow even a little. By the time Jezzie stopped, she looked like she'd climbed out of a lake after a rather big dunking. A cold lake, judging by the shivers and goosebumps which pebbled her skin.

"I guess you were right, lass. Come here, Jez. Let's wipe away some grime. I might need a little help since we don't have a mirror."

Jezzie didn't hesitate, her gaze lingered over his body as she sauntered forward, a scent equal parts heaven and sin filled their dome.

Fuck, how was he supposed to resist his mate when she smelled so fucking good. She smiled as she noticed the hardening of his cock, still sticking out of his open fly . . . Well, hell. He hadn't remembered it had been out this whole time, and it looked as if Jezzie had just noticed it too as she licked her plump lips and eyed him lustfully as she stripped off her wet clothes.

Long, warm, toned legs straddled his waist, pressed up against his raging hard on as she rubbed herself against him.

"Jezzie, let's get you cleaned up and in some fresh clothes, shall we?"

"Uh, uh, later." Her lips slammed down on his, nipped and licked at the seam of them, demanding entrance.

Nithe placed his hands on her hips firmly as she ground her bare pussy against him. Oh, how he wanted to flip her over and pound his cock into her. Her, his mate, his one. To forget all he'd been through and allow her all the things he'd so used to enjoy. His dragon certainly was willing, but something in his brain held him back.

He was unworthy, he always had been. Raum had just aired the news, so now he knew it too. A black cloud of melancholy settled over him. Jezzie did not want him for him, he was a warm body after all she'd been through. A way to forget the past, even for a moment. Why would she want a worthless whore like him, used trash, Raum's pet, nothing more, probably less since now he wasn't even that.

Jezzie rocked back as if sensing the turn in his mood, took his face in her palms and forced his gaze to meet hers.

"None of that shit is true, Ni. I don't know how this works, but everything in me—including my shadows—is telling me you are mine. The shadows are very insistent. While it's true I'm super horny, forced celibacy will do that to a person, you are so much more than a warm body to use." Nithe's eyes widened in surprise. How did she know his thoughts? He was certain he hadn't spoken aloud. His lips parted to ask, but she continued.

"You are worth more than you realize, and I will personally help destroy everyone who has ever told you otherwise. I understand we may need to take this slow. So, you're in charge, sexy. I gotta warn you, though, I think the change is still messing with me. Not only can I not control my wings or put them away, but my pussy is so wet I can feel streams of it over my thighs. See?" She rolled her hips and lifted, sliding her liquid heat along the length of his phallus. The sight of her juices coating his cock pulled a deep moan from them both.

He wanted her so badly, wanted to relegate his past to the deepest pits of the Horde Mines, and he knew his mate had the power to help him more than any other. But not here, not like this, on the barren wastelands of a Nestradian ridge, with monsters circling above.

Instead, he would worship the gift the Almighty and Tiamat had given him. He would ease her need as best he could, for he knew how the change could play havoc with one's libido. He just wished it had been Jezzie who had eased his.

He shook his head hard to dispel the unpleasant thought. His large hands pulled Jezzie's hips to his own as he devoured her mouth and savored the taste of her lips. Her arms wrapped tight around his neck as she tried to impale herself on his cock. He wasn't sure she could take it, not yet. She wasn't a dragon, and as she'd said, it had been awhile, so he lifted her up and gently laid her down on the floor.

"Wh . . .what are you doing, Ni?" she stuttered.

"Shh, Jez," he chided as he placed one finger on the lips of her mouth, and one on the lips of her pussy. "You said I'm in charge, yes?" She nodded, her eyes curious.

"Well then, as long as I have your consent, I'm going to eat that pretty little pussy of yours, alright?" Again, she nodded. "Not good enough, sweets, I need to hear you say it. Give me permission, lass, or I stop. Right here, right now."

His finger traced her labia, circled her clit, and slid seductively close to her entrance. He felt every moan, every shiver, and the slick wetness of her coating his finger proved how much she wanted him; how much she needed him as her hips rose from the ground and sought more. But for so long, both of them had been subject to the whims of others, consent was paramount to all his other desires, hers too. Her eyes widened, as if she'd read his mind, and maybe she had, he thought, as her words from earlier bubbled up briefly . . .

"I, Jezzie, give you, Nithe, permission to lick me, kiss me, touch me, fuck me, anywhere, as long as this dome stays strong. Good enough, Ni?"

"Thank you, lass. I am honored." His finger thrust into her hard. He added a second and circled his thumb over her clit. Head thrown back, eyes closed, Jezzie's hips tried desperately to increase the rhythm.

"Not so fast, *a stór*." He removed his fingers from her tight pussy and placed them against her own lips. "Smell that? That's the smell of heaven, of desire and fate, and it smells so fucking good. I'm going to run my tongue through your wet folds, thrusting it into you as deep as I can. And you, my treasure, are going to explode around it, coating it in even more of this delicious nectar of the gods. But before I do, I want to see you lick my fingers clean. I want to taste your pussy on your lips and tongue as I kiss your beautiful mouth. Can you do that for me, Jezzie?"

Her pupils flared wide, her bottom lip trapped between her teeth as he went quiet and waited for her response. Soft lips grazed his fingertips in a light kiss. She tilted her head, her lips at the base of his fingers, and her eyes never left his as her tongue licked up one side of his index finger and down the other. Moving to the crease between his two fingers, she inserted her tongue and licked to the tips. She placed her hands on his and aligned his fingertips to her mouth. The length of them slid into her mouth, her lips resting on his knuckles, before she pulled them out slowly, moaning softly.

If possible, his cock grew even larger, and he could feel droplets of pre-cum leaking out. Her hands reached down to touch him, but he pulled them away, pinning them above her head.

"Uh, uh, *a stór*, not this time," he whispered in her ear moments before his lips claimed hers, and for the first time he experienced the taste of her sweet pussy from her equally sweet mouth.

Jezzie hadn't tasted herself in a long time. Not since she was eighteen and Tommy Higgins, captain of the football team, had eaten her out behind the deserted bleachers with great enthusiasm, if little skill, all the while he'd groaned and praised how she tasted so good.

Curious to know what he'd been going on about, she'd slipped her fingers in next to his tongue to gather some of her juices up and brought them to her lips. Tommy came in his pants within seconds. Later he'd called her disgusting; telling everyone in town there was something wrong with her. It was only after she'd gone home crying to her Aunt that she'd found out boys like Tommy don't like to finish too soon, and in the 1960s men could be major assholes when it came to a woman's sexual independence. Thank fuck they'd left that town. She'd found him, years later, beating the shit out of his wife. The look on his face as she'd pulled every emotion from him, except his fear, and ate his soul, was so worth it. The last word to leave his mouth was her name. So sweet. Not.

Tasting herself now, here with Nithe, was a whole new experience. It was hot as fuck, and as she licked his fingers clean she looked into his lust-filled gaze. Her skin tingled with the need to touch him, her hands begged to run over his hard, lean body, her shadows clamored for her to take his cock in her mouth as she had his fingers. A litany of fate and mate, need and want resounded in her head. So, she gave in and slid them down his shirt covered chest, buttons miraculously coming free as she went. But the sexy fucker stopped her, pinned her arms, and took her lips with an urgent fervor that almost tipped her over the edge. Heat sizzled wherever his skin brushed hers, and she rubbed her hard nipples against his chest seeking friction and satisfaction.

"Do those breathtaking beauties want something, Jez? My hands cupping them? Fingers rolling and twisting, perhaps? A playful little slap or two? Or, do they seek my mouth wrapped around them, nipping and sucking until they're harder than they've ever been before, so you can come around my motionless fingers buried deep inside you?"

Incapable of words, she nodded her head, moans of assent leaving her lips. He lifted himself slightly away from her as he trailed his lips along her collarbone and into the crook of her neck where he inhaled deeply and went still.

Jezzie heard his voice in her head as he argued with who she assumed was his dragon. Something about a bond. Nithe forced the majestic beast back from the surface as he insisted now was not the time, not the place. Hearing him in her head was weird, her shadows talking was weird. She assumed it was something to do with her powers coming in, but as Aunt Rai Rai had always said, with her dad being who he was, there really was no way of knowing what was weird and what was normal.

Small nips replaced the kisses of before and as they descended on one nipple her head flew back, she cried out at the firm grip of his lips, the swirl of his tongue, and three large fingers as they plunged deep into her pussy and curled just right.

As she came down from her first orgasm, Nithe was already on the move, his tongue dipped into her navel, kisses covered her abdomen, and she thought she caught a whispered, "someday," on the non-existent breeze. But considering the power of the orgasm which had just rocked her socks off, she didn't quite trust her ears.

The moment Nithe removed his fingers, with some difficulty, from her still convulsing wetness her body rebelled, urging him back. Thankfully, she didn't have long to wait as his thick, wet tongue slid between her labia. The tip circled her clitoris, and a roughness grazed the sensitive nub, shooting sparks of lust through her. Never had a tongue felt so fucking good, or so thick.

Looking down she caught Nithe's eyes on her as his tongue continued flicking between teasing her clit and sliding along the length of her very wet pussy. Thick at the base and the majority of the length it tapered toward the end, where it came to a point.

Sorry, a stór, but I can't help it. My dragon insists on being part of this. Trust me, he never has before, and I cannot deny him this, he's waited so long. Do you want to see it? Nithe's words were spoken directly into her head.

Jezzie nodded, curious to know what was going on. Nithe's head rose, his mouth opened and out unfurled the sexiest fucking dragon tongue she'd ever seen, albeit smaller than a fully shifted one, which would probably be bigger than her whole body. It wasn't like she'd seen any real ones before, but she'd seen her fair share of history books. Her aunt owned quite a few tomes on nearly every OtherRealm species. Nithe's definitely didn't disappoint. The colors were beautiful, dark blue, purple, and green at the tip to match his flames. She could not stop the moan that fled her lips, or the tightening of her thighs around his torso.

See something you like, my dear? he teased.

"Yes, Ni, I do. Please fuck me! Fuck me now!"

Oh, Jez. I wish I could, but not here in this place, not the first time. When my cock pushes its way into the tight sheath of your pussy for the first time . . .

"Not with your cock, Ni, not this time. Fuck me with that sexy tongue of yours. Impale me on it, as far as it will go. I want you so far inside me you can feel me coming like a waterfall around your tongue as my muscles grip it in place. I want to ride your face the same way I'll one day ride that drool worthy cock of yours." She reached out her hand toward him, and he licked her palm with the rough surface. "We'll get back to the whys and how's another time though. I have a feeling I need to know everything about you, dragon boy." Her voice was full of lust and urgency. "No more talking. Just please, face fuck my starved pussy," she begged.

Holy fuck, the man did not disappoint. The minute she stopped talking he went to work. His fingers spread her wide, and he circled her clit again and dragged his tongue down to her opening. He teased her at first, as he dipped the tip in and out, grazing her walls with each exploration. Her whimpers filled the air as she begged for more. She wasn't embarrassed, just desperate to be filled. By him, and only him, in the moment no one else existed except Nithe.

Just when she thought the torment would send her insane, his tongue thrust forward, deep into her pussy, and stretched her wide, the rough glide along her desire slicked walls sent ripples of pleasure through her overloaded body. She was so close to coming she felt stuck on a precipice. Move and shatter, or hold still and trust him to push her over the edge.

"Holy fuck!" she screamed. "Oh my, oh gosh, oh yes! YES!" Nithe's tongue started to undulate slowly, building up speed and rhythm as it pushed her to completion. The sounds of her orgasm echoed through the dome as waves of exquisite pleasure crashed over her. The feel of Nithe's warm, freshly spilled seed on her thigh as he rose up her body and curled himself against her side brought a smile to her sex slackened features. For the first time in a long time she felt peaceful.

A sound drifted toward her, just monsters again. They were safe in the dome, they could rest for a while. But, it didn't stop, it got louder.

She looked up toward the large rocks on the other side of the barrier, and her mouth fell open as she squealed and jumped over Nithe to hide behind his back. Her wings offered no protection for her nudity, apparently having retracted at some point during her little trip to OrgasmoLand, so much better than a theme park.

It seemed they had an audience, and judging by the hoots, hollers, and applause, they'd certainly enjoyed the Jezzie and Nithe show.

Just her fucking luck.

CHAPTER 22

"What the fuck is it with guys standing around watching me get off? Can't a girl ride out the big O without a fucking audience? I'm so done! Nope, no more. It's definitely ass kicking time!" Exasperation threaded through her words as she hid her heated face against Nithe's back. Why? Why her? At least they seemed to have enjoyed the show, but seriously?

"Who's been watching you? No one should be watching you, except me." The growl in Nithe's voice was more feral dragon than reasonable man as he rolled, wrapped one arm around her, and placed a finger under her chin.

"My treasure, my precious," he spoke in dragon, but she understood him clearly despite never learning the dialect fluently.

Aunt Rai Rai had been determined to teach her as many OtherRealm languages as possible, but only a few of them had really taken root and stuck around for more than a few months. Dragon hadn't been one of them, though. As a child Aunt Rai Rai had made a list of all possible angel traits she might one day inherit, a universal translator built into her brain was one of them, so it wasn't too big of a surprise. But still, what the fuck was up with the possessive alpha shit?

"Um . . . . Excuse me? Think again big guy! I don't belong to anybody! You have two choices. We're either equals, or you belong to me. Your choice. Plus, I'm not even sure how this all works, but from a conversation I had with Ballzy before you arrived, and some pretty realistic dreams, you might not be the only man in my picture frame, sweet cheeks. So cut the asshole alpha bullshit, or be prepared for me to walk away." Her eyes didn't leave his, and she even tapped him on the nose for good measure.

Probably something that'd work more on a wolf than a dragon, but better he learned from the start she wasn't just some jewel to be hoarded. Plus, she was still kinda curious about the whole astral thing, and the two very sexy men she'd been dreaming of. The thought of more than one partner at a time hadn't really entered her mind until recently, and it was definitely an exciting prospect.

Nithe's jaw dropped, his eyes flashed pure gold for about a second, before they snapped shut, and he bit his soft, full bottom lip looking sheepish. What the hell was up with that? Talk about mood swings. The muscles in his arms relaxed, and he stroked her bare back in lazy circles as he skimmed the raised edges of her new tattoo. She couldn't wait to see both the tattoo version of her wings, and the real deal, like properly, in a mirror and shit. Both her mum and Aunt Rai Rai had told her all angels get them, but they weren't sure if she would. Her aunt would be so stoked.

"I'm sorry, Jez. Sometimes the dragon momentarily overrides my better judgment. We can discuss these possible others later. We should probably deal with our voyeuristic guests first, hmm? And get you into some clothes, as well."

Nithe looked over his shoulder with a smile, and in the space of seconds, a large, dark green dragon tail, with purple oil slick colored spikes, dropped a bunch of clothing on them from where it hovered above, along with more cloths and the water bottles they'd previously set aside. Nithe raised his wrist and stared at it intensely. Jezzie watched him as he turned it, studying it from every angle as he pulled at it.

"It's cracked. Not enough to come off but apparently enough to allow my dragon out just a little bit since we've been here. Must have happened either as we landed or when you manifested and blasted the shit out of Raum." His eyes lit up her world and his smile made her wonder what he'd looked like as a child eating candy and playing tag.

Jezzie propped herself up and stuck her head over Nithe's shoulder, her chin in the air, a look of challenge on her face as fire flashed in her eyes.

"Turn around and look away, assholes. Show's over! I catch any of you pervy pricks taking a peek at my curvalicious awesomeness, or checking out my man's yummy bits, I might just be forced to castrate each and every one of you. Capisce?"

All four assholes saluted and spun on their heels, as deep chuckles reverberated through the air. Jezzie wasted no time and hauled ass to wipe Nithe's quickly drying cum from her leg. Fuck, the guy could definitely cover some distance when he shot a load. Her brain couldn't quite compute how it'd ended up where it had with his tongue buried so deeply inside her. Thank you, mind-blowing orgasms. She tossed the cloth to Nithe, only to pause as she saw him pulling off his tight pants completely. Her mouth hung open, the back of her hand came up to wipe at the drool she was certain was about to escape her mouth. Damn! Nithe was one sexy man. He turned and bent to grab something from the ground, but Jezzie couldn't tell what it was. Her gaze was fastened to the firm, perfect curve of his buttocks, and the taut muscles of his back.

What snapped her from the salivating trance she'd been stuck in wasn't the fresh pair of pants he held in his hands, or the rough set of stitches across his back, a stark reminder she'd just been thoroughly eaten out by a man she should have been taking gentle care of. No, it was the smug look of satisfaction radiating from his face because he'd caught her as she ogled him. The cheeky wink he threw her way brought an instant lightness to her often heavy heart. But when he straightened, pulled the dark fabric up his legs, and fastened the button fly, his face was so grave and full of muted vulnerability she just wanted to wrap her arms around him and hold him together as he cracked into a million pieces.

Instead, Jezzie threw out a blinding smile, followed by a wink of her own, and held up her own outfit.

"What the fuck am I supposed to do with this?" she chuckled.

"Wear it?" he returned, "Why? What is it?"

Instead of answering she bent, slid her long legs into the pants, and pulled the loose, butter soft black leather up over her thighs. When she got to her waist, she slipped her arms into the long sleeves of the attached top, and did up the zippered front. They felt like baggy, backless overalls at first, but after a few moments a surge of magic shimmered over her skin and the loose leather shrunk. Molding perfectly to her curves, the built-in bra pushed her breasts up, and the scooped neckline almost put her dusky nipples on display.

The tight leather plunged dangerously low at the back as it caressed her ribs and hips. It hugged her thighs, fuck, it hugged everywhere. A black collar wrapped itself around her neck, the silver clasp clicking shut. The collar was attached across the back, top, and front of her shoulders, and flowed into the sleeves. Sleeves that apparently turned into wicked gauntlets over her forearms and the backs of her hands.

Nithe's groan of approval told her she must look pretty good, and it was certainly comfortable, even if she did look like a gamer boy's wet dream.

"Oh, Ballzy, you're going to pay for this, you pervy, bloody bastard," she muttered half under her breath. Of course Nithe heard her and offered up his own take on it.

"Thank you, Balthazar, you bloody legend. Don't worry, I won't let her hurt you . . . much." He laughed.

"You say that now, Ni. You might just change your mind."

One day she just might figure out which side of the fence Balthazar was on. Or even what the hell was on either side of the fence. But for now, his loyalty was up in the air. So much shit didn't make sense to her. It would though, even if she had to tear this place apart, she'd find out what the fuck was going on. Daddy dearest might even get a little visit too. Lucky him.

Jezzie looked at the ground around them and grabbed two black, steel cylinders with leather grips, and sent up a prayer. They fit in her grasp perfectly, almost as if they'd been made just for her. She twirled them deftly in her hands until she noticed a small black button hidden on the side of each one. Positioning her hands away from her body she activated the devices, and boy she wasn't disappointed. Sinister, black steel blades erupted from both ends of each weapon. Giddiness assailed her. Odd though that her favorite weapons, the ones she was most proficient with, would be in the packs. Ballzy had no idea about her training, or her fighting abilities, so how in the blazes had he picked them?

Out of all the weapons in all the realms, how had these custom-made, enchanted swords made their way to her? Her ones at home, if they were even still there, were nowhere near as finely crafted. As she watched, her shadows rolled like swiftly moving fire over her hands and leapt onto the steel of each blade. That was new. Never had they reacted to a weapon in such a way, almost separating from her completely. Only a small thread along her inner wrist kept them attached. Normally, it was as if they avoided man-made weapons, as though they deemed such things inferior to their own power. Not this time. This time it felt almost like a magnetic pull, her shadows melded with the steel, flickering outward as they searched for prey. Sweet!

Warm leather tingled against her palms, but before she could analyze what it could possibly mean, a movement from the corner of her eye caught her attention. There, by the very edge of the plateau, hidden in shadows, stood a fifth man at the base of one of the large boulders, his eyes trained unwaveringly on them. It was clear he hadn't taken his eyes off Jezzie, or Nithe, the entire time. He was absolutely beautiful, but the hard glare he had leveled on them was filled with no joy, humor, or desire at all, and it cast his features in stone. She realized he looked like a hard-ass guard at a supermax prison. He'd seen some shit, and he was there to do one job. In this case, make sure the strangers didn't pull any stunts while the others weren't looking. No wonder the other's had turned away so easily, with their guard dog hidden off to the side, and away from their antics, they'd still had eyes on her the whole time.

Can I eats thems flesh and spits out the icky bony bits, merahet? Jezzie's shadows whispered earnestly. They would too, if given half a chance. She'd heard the stories of what shadows could do if set loose upon the masses. Occasionally they had been, back in the day. Mindlessly, they'd stripped the flesh and left the bones. She'd always imagined a big pile of fried chicken bones, completely devoid of meat and tossed aside. Yet, she'd never felt the urge from her shadows to test it out. Until now. Unfortunately for her newly sentient shadows, the men outside the bubble, while stained lightly with dark deeds and guilty consciences, were not inherently evil. Nor deserving of such a fate. We all had shit we needed to atone for, after all.

"Turn around, assholes. They're decently dressed. Time to bring them in." Without waiting for the other four, Mr Serious strode forward.

"You might want to ask nicely before you come any closer, Mr Serious," she said sweetly.

Jezzie watched with amusement. This should be fun. Either he didn't know the bubble was there, or he thought himself impervious to its magic. But, instead of the satisfaction of watching him walk face-first into the clear barrier, it was her mouth which hung open momentarily as he stepped straight on through as if it wasn't even there. As he did, the barrier burned away slowly, like the glowing edge of slowly burning paper, its obliteration shimmered above her head. It was only as she stood, face raised to the starless sky, she realized no monsters were attacking, and it seemed as if none still lurked nearby.

"Who are you?" she snapped, as her gaze shot back to him.

"Jez, I don't think we need to find the princes anymore," Nithe whispered in her ear. How he'd snuck up so close she didn't know, but she leaned into his warmth, instinctively breathing him in.

"Why?"

"Because, if I'm right, they just found us."

"Very astute of you, . . . ?" the male closing in on them asked.

"Nitierien Kenacdrath, at your service, but you can call me, Nithe. It is much preferred."

"And the lady? She is?" he asked blandly.

"Able to speak for herself, asshole," Jezzie interjected.

"Of course you can." He inclined his head. "Among my people women hold all the power, sometimes my resentment flares. I apologize. Pray, do tell me your name, lovely lady." Never had she seen a man bow so elegantly let alone with such ease. She felt charmed by the action somehow.

"I'm Jezzie, you don't need my full name yet. Names hold power, and I don't know what you all are yet, or if I can trust you."

"Understandable, I feel the same about you. In fact, that is the exact reason why these measures are necessary. I'm sure you understand."

"What meas—" Jezzie started, but the tight bonds squeezing about her torso cut off her breath and black filled her vision as a bag of some sort was placed over her head. The swords fell from her grip.

She heard a struggle beside her. Nithe! Her panic doubled. No! She prayed he was okay. If they bound him as they did her, after all he'd been through . . . Would he be okay? A red glow filled her vision and the hood started smoking.

A hand took hold of hers. Long, smooth, strong fingers held tight and a feeling of calm pushed away the panic when she realized Nithe was comforting her.

Breathe with us, Jez. We are okay, and so are you. I feel kin nearby. All will be well, I swear to it. Nithe and his dragon spoke as one in her mind, and the red receded slowly.

"Gather their things, boys, so we can get back home in time for the game."

It wasn't long before her upper arm was grasped firmly, and she was maneuvered forward over the once again rocky terrain. What fresh hell was this going to be? Walking for hours to some unknown place through a monster laden wasteland, shrouded in darkness and decay. It seemed fate just felt like doling out more of the same. But she was surprised when she felt a shimmer of dust tickle her nose, her ears popped, and she felt as light as a feather before she heard one last pop and the ground rose to meet her feet. What the fuck was that?

"Sorry about the landing, I'm a little out of practice," the mystery voice tickled her ear as the hood was removed.

"Welcome to our home. It will either be your hell, or your sanctuary. Choose wisely."

Her head turned to the voice, and the delicate beauty of his features fit perfectly with the lightness of his voice. Soft, shimmery, translucent wings fluttered at his back, his feet tip-toeing the ground beneath.

"Yeah, yeah. Fairy, I know. Not very scary for a Prince of Nestradia right?" his sweet smile widened, taking on a menacing kind of joy.

Still not so bad . . . until his eyes darkened and his features morphed. Wickedly sharp, spiked teeth replaced his pearly whites, his slightly pointed ears extended. His skin turned greenish-gray, and his nose took on a goblin-like hook as his tongue flicked out to lick thin lips, leaving blood coated teeth in its wake.

From one breath to the next, from sweet beauty to painful death, and back again. He chuckled as he watched her eyes widen. Not much was known about fairies. Not many who encountered one survived to recount the tales, and those who did usually couldn't pull the words from their muddled minds.

"Never discount the pretty ones." He winked. "They usually have some nasty tricks up their sleeves."

"I like you. Can you come to my next party? Well, it'll actually be my first party. I've never had one with actual guests before, but after the last nine years I think I deserve one. What's your name, pretty fairy?"

"Novarian." He bowed too. She could get used to manners like this. "Though you can call me Rian. We are going to need to know why you're here, by the way. We were not warned of any incoming prisoners, and we very rarely get visitors. Though, I think a nice cup of tea might be in order first, don't you?" he asked, his hand sweeping out toward the large stone castle before them.

On closer inspection, scrap the stone. Blood stained bones and the twisted skeletal remains of countless beings made up the red walls. She'd never seen the like, her inner angel recoiled, her vamp nature liked the bloody sight, the blood imbued power of the place, her shadows queried if they too could make a home like it, oh what fun that would be.

Nithe squeezed her hand gently.

"We must have faith, Jez. He sent us here for a reason. Let's find out what the fuck is going on, and how we are going to stop it. Plus, I don't know about you, but I could eat a decent meal, and a cup of something hot and strong to drink sounds divine. If they give us a clean, soft place to sleep, I just might have found a piece of heaven in this hell. Second only to the taste of your release on my tongue. Oh, a bed. I could do so much more with a bed."

Jezzie's cheeks heated with a blush at Nithe's wink. Desire pooled low in her abdomen, and her thighs quivered as she remembered the feel of his tongue between her slick folds.

"We don't have time for gallantry, Ri. Move your ass, theirs too," a shaggy, dark haired guy said grumpily.

"Oh shush, you grumpy bastard. The game doesn't start for another forty minutes. You really do need to get laid, old man," Rian replied.

"Don't we all," Mr Shaggy mourned, before walking dejectedly through the obsidian gates.

Thank fuck not one of them was looking her way. Except Nithe, and she was totally on board the non-stop train to pound town. Destination: Nithe's magnificent cock.

One final look around, and her feet moved forward over the threshold of the gates. Once more into the lion's den? Fingers crossed they came out again.

CHAPTER 23

The moment they crossed the threshold, the bonds around his arms and chest disappeared and his power surged through him. The cuff around his wrist fell with a clatter to the stones on which they stood. His dragon barreled forward to claim his freedom, too long had it been denied him.

He pushed Jezzie away, knocking her into the arms of the male who smelled like kin, relieved when he caught her as she toppled backwards. His dragon chuffed at her indignant snort, and the way she shrugged off the other male's hold. More so when she turned those beautiful gray eyes of hers his way, awe shining bright as she gazed up at his towering dragon form.

Dark green scales covered his massive body. His eyes shone like gold with black slit pupils, from his large dragon head. A head as large as two men. His feathered, leather wings of pure gold unfurled briefly before tucking in close to his body. A spiked tail cheekily flicked around to gently stroke Jezzie's thigh, dipping between her legs and lifting her slightly from the ground.

Gaining control after so long without a shift took longer than normal. As Nithe struggled he felt a hand touch his snout, and he damn near went cross-eyed trying to get a good look at who it was. He inhaled deeply and the scent of an unbonded male dragon filled his airway. The faintly familiar scent of family grew stronger, and he eyed the stranger shrewdly.

"You smell like I should know you, lad," his dragon voice intoned. Full of bass and the wisdom of the ancient ones.

"I should, cousin, Even if I am a fair few years older than you. I recognize kin when I smell them. Aunt Alentia's boy? Or Aunt Verina, maybe?" the dark haired dragon inquired.

"Close, but I'm afraid we are a little more distant than that, Prince Thaddeus Drakenos, right?"

"Thad is fine, thanks."

"Well, Thad, your uncle, Vasillis, was technically my grandfather. I say it that way because he never actually acknowledged me as such, and immediately sent my mother away for a sudden betrothal in Cathair an óir, when he realized she was pregnant."

"You mean to tell me someone actually ended up sleeping with that creepy fucker and reproduced? No offense." Thad appeared genuinely shocked. "Though, your accent makes sense now."

Nithe didn't really know much about his grandfather, but what he did know really didn't endear the old guy to his grandson.

"Apparently, from what little my mother told me, it wasn't really her choice. In much the same way your tenure here was not yours."

"Well, Nithe, my cousin, my kin, shift back and let us head in. What say you?"

"I think I may be stuck," Nithe uttered beneath his breath. "It's been a while since my last shift." His last word drifted off into silence.

"As your rightful king, I command you, Nitierien Kenacdrath, to shift." Still his body resisted, fought to remain in the form it had long been denied, despite the willingness of his mind, and of his dragon too.

"SHIFT! NOW!"

Every ounce of Thaddeus's alpha power filled the air around them at his roar. Even his friends visibly shuddered, as if they waged some inner battle with their other side.

"Please, Ni. I need you to shift so we can go inside, eat, and snuggle in a nice soft bed. Do you really want me going in there on my own with these assholes?" Her soft voice drifted toward him. He felt his scales shudder with pleasure as his body morphed back into that of a man and the strain from trying to shift turned to relief.

Jezzie sauntered toward him, tapped Thad on the shoulder, and hip bumped him out of the way.

"You boys better have some decent food in there," she said, as she indicated the palatial building beyond the grotesque walls painted in various shades of red with the blood of who knows how many species. But it was palatial none-the-less. "Because, if not, I will seriously kick all your asses."

"Why are women always so cranky when they're hungry?" The one obsessed with some game whispered to Novarian.

He was totally looking for an ass kicking it seemed. Not from him though. Jezzie's back stiffened, her head cocked to the side.

"Nithe, honey, please remind me, if I get desperately hungry, that asshole is the first on my list of fuckers to eat."

She turned and gave him a wicked smile, then looked past him to the male in question and licked her slightly elongated upper cuspids. He still had so much to learn about the woman who already owned his soul, it was a good thing he had an eternity to learn it all. At least, he hoped he did. Stepping through the double front doors his introspection came to a screeching halt, and so too did Jezzie.

From the outside the formidable facade was a terrifying representation of the realm it stood within. Blood, gore, death, and nightmare endings. On the inside though, oh, it got so much worse. The place looked like a bloody high-end 18th century french whorehouse crossed with a strip club. Topless gorgons slithered through the foyer, in and out of rooms, up and down the gilded grand staircase. So many bare breasts, and yet not a single set came close to matching the perfection of Jezzie's. Damn, his woman was blessed with perfect curves. Which reminded him . . .

"So, I'm your man, am I, precious?" The teasing note in his voice thinly veiled the desperation with which his soul craved her affirmation.

"I don't know what you're talking about," she responded saucily with a cheeky wink. Her hand slipped out of his, she quickly slapped his ass before she pushed through the other men, and twirled like a badass warrior princess under the crystal chandelier, with not a single fuck to give.

It took a few moments for the stunned expressions of the others to register. Nithe was completely absorbed in the beauty of his Jez as she danced and sang "I Could Have Danced All Night" from *My Fair Lady* with pure joy. The others were frozen, like deer in headlights, as if they'd never seen a woman behave in such a way. Considering how long they'd been away from their realms it was entirely possible they never had.

Soon enough the scent of roasted meat and vegetables filled the air, making his mouth water and his head turn toward an open door to the right of the central staircase.

"Looks like dinner's up, guys. Let's get these two fed, questioned, and into bed. We have less than twenty-five minutes before the game starts, and I, for one, refuse to miss it for these two uninvited guests."

"You really are an ungracious host, aren't you, Shaggy?" Jez chimed in.

"Who are you calling shaggy, Red?"

"Well, I'd say grumpy, but that's already taken," she replied, pointing at the one who'd walked through her barrier with such ease. He looked mildly amused at the nickname. "Maybe I should change it to dumbass. Would that be better?" Sweetness dripped from Jezzie's voice with saccharine sarcasm.

"The name's Grimm. I won't fucking respond to any of your damn nicknames." He stomped off in the direction of the mouthwatering scents.

"Don't mind him," Novarian bumped Jezzie's shoulder, "He's just got his knickers in a knot 'cos he hasn't been laid in, like, ten years. Not that it's an excuse. Neither have I, and yet, I'm so far removed from assholedom I resemble cotton-frickin-candy."

The fairy burst out laughing, clutching his stomach as though he'd told the best joke ever. The groans from the others indicated they were used to his particular level of weirdness. Jezzie just looped her arm through his, and nodded sagely as she allowed him to escort her to what turned out to be a big-ass formal dining room that could easily seat over a hundred guests. Though, only the first few places closest to them had been set. Enough food to feed an army was laid out before them.

They were escorted to a seat on either side of the table, opposite each other. Nithe felt his skin itch at the distance between them, until he felt a sensation slither over his thigh, and almost choked on his own breath. Looking down he discovered a tendril of red shadows caressing him very close to his groin.

"Food first, questions later. Eat. Quickly," Thad stated like a general to his soldiers.

Nithe looked at the food longingly. Afraid to risk it. Scared of what could be in it, what could be done to him, to Jezzie, if he was wrong about Balthazar, about the princes. He noticed Jezzie looking at the food, her gaze slowly raked over each dish and glass before her eyes met his, and she smiled gently.

"It's okay, Nithe, nothing's tainted. Although, personally I'll be avoiding the gorgon pie, I'm not very fond of eating dead snakes cut from their own heads. But each to their own, I guess."

"We never actually request it. They just keep hoping we'll slip up one day, and they can enslave us that way. Their particular power doesn't work inside the palace walls, and they are bound in service to this place. Their only way out is for us to pardon them. Considering their crimes, we've been strongly advised not to." The quiet, unknown male next to him spoke in such a way that power threaded through each syllable like a death knell.

"Not that I think you are lying, Jez, but how can you know? Raum could hide scents, even from my superior smell," Nithe hurried to explain.

"It's partly something I was born with, some part of my DNA, but I was also blessed to be raised by an amazing witch who helped me hone my ability. Not only do I recognize the scents of drugs and poisons, I can also see them. The faint aura of evil permeates them naturally, no matter the intent with which they will be used."

He needed no further convincing. As he watched her tuck into her food with gusto, he did the same. He, too, avoided the gorgon pie. What a disgusting delicacy, he thought.

"Well, since I'm apparently the impatient one around here." The tall, lean, muscled man beside him chuckled, the one with the long ginger hair, and soft, light green eyes. Nithe was taken aback by the venom that dripped from his voice.

"Ignore Alasdair. As hard as it may be to believe, that's actually his friendly voice. Manticores aren't known for their sweetness, but Dair here is the sweetest little manticore I ever did meet." Seriously, the fairy must have a fucking death wish.

Manticores were rare, like, extremely so. They were also one of the most deadly species in all the realms. The ultimate assassins, the best mercenaries. You didn't fuck over a Manti, if you did, you wouldn't live long enough to reap any kind of reward for it. Except an instant death sentence.

Nithe held his breath and waited for the fairy slaughter, but instead his mouth dropped open as Alasdair blew the fairy a kiss. Novarian saw his response and winked, catching the kiss and bringing his hand to his heart as though slain with a dagger. The theatrics of it all had Jezzie practically giddy. She bounced in her seat and giggled as she clapped her hands at the performance.

"Okay, ask away, boys . . . as long as I get cake and coffee first, I'll answer as best I can."

At Jezzie's words two particularly well-endowed gorgons with shimmering gray skin slithered in holding trays filled with decadent looking chocolate cake covered in thick icing, cream, and strawberries, plus a steaming pot of coffee, milk, and sugar to fill the cups already in front of them. Nithe saw Jezzie wipe drool from the corner of her mouth, not even trying to hide it as her eyes followed the trays with a predatory intensity. In that moment he'd never wished to be a piece of cake more.

Jezzie, for some unknown reason, felt at ease with these men. No, she wasn't attracted to them, they literally did absolutely nothing for her in that regard, despite each of them being exceptionally handsome in their own unique ways. No, it was something else, some indistinguishable trait she couldn't quite put her finger on.

They'd fired off questions one after the other until her head spun and she couldn't keep track. Only her ear-piercing whistle had brought them to silence and allowed her to recount the events of her life in the last eight years. She left a lot out after Nithe started growling at the mention of her interlude with Ballzy. He settled down at her reassurance it'd meant nothing, that Ballzy wasn't of any interest to her in that way. Her shadows stroking over his trouser-clad cock hadn't hurt either. It was odd, they'd never been interested in sex before, never sought to play, plus she'd never been with anyone in the know before, to the best of her knowledge anyway.

At some point one of the snarky gorgon maids slipped a note to the quiet one who'd invaded her shield out on the ledge. He sat at the head of the table watching her face as she spoke.

When she fell quiet, Nithe filled the silence. She could feel his torment, his pain, his anger at his banishment. There was so much he left unsaid. Jezzie's arms longed to comfort him, her shadows squeezed his thigh in response. He spoke about being recruited by some asshole angel named Esidriel, his orders, and his capture by Raum. His voice trailed off into a whimper before he shook his head and skipped over the details of his time in Raum's company to how he met Jezzie, and how Ballzy ultimately sent them to Nestradia.

"As he pushed us through the portal into this place he said, "Go! Take her to the princes, and the princes will take you to he who is hidden." Whoever he is, he didn't elaborate," Nithe finished, and he too fell silent.

The four princes flanking both Nithe and her all looked toward the head of the table, various expressions of skepticism apparent on their faces.

"Theus? What say you? Do they speak truthfully, or do we toss them back through the gates to meet a wretched fate."

Dair really did have a strange voice, like death on an ice-cold day, it curled around your spine as if to rip it from your body, while luring you in so you welcomed death. Only the tether to Nithe and the other two kept her grounded, as she felt them tug her backward from the precipice.

But Theus wasn't looking at any of them as he read from the thick, creamy vellum the gorgon had slipped him. When he was finally done, his gaze rose and landed on Jezzie with unerring accuracy. A slight smile tugged at the corner of his quite lush lips.

"It looks as if Tana's going to gain a friend. Let's hope she's in the mood for a surprise."

Never had she seen a group of men look simultaneously excited and fearful as Theus passed the letter around to each of them. Whoever this Tana person was, Jezzie had a feeling they'd either get on like a house on fire or fight like banshees.

When Jezzie finally got her hands on the letter she saw it was a very brief note from Ballzy explaining he'd sent her and Nithe through, to protect them, get them to the safe point . . . yadda, yadda, yadda, complete with continuing vagueness that told her no more than she already knew and caused her curiosity to raise it's head.

"Um, boys? I'm assuming that's from Ballzy, yes?" Jezzie queried.

"Yes, it is. Why? Also, do I want to know why exactly you call him Ballzy? And does he actually allow it to his face? If so, how are you still here?"

"Because he was an asshole, and it bothered him, like, a lot. Yes, he did. And I guess I'm just that fucking lovable." She winked at Novarian as she answered his questions playfully.

She was careful to keep her feelings attached to Nithe's. Monitoring his reactions. His trauma was semi-dormant right now, too much adrenaline, too many surprises, and a fuck load of danger drowning out the voices in his head. But she felt them there, biding their time as they searched for a moment of weakness. Each time they threatened to break through, she beat them back. Now was not the time nor the place for what was to come.

"As to the why . . . If you only just received this letter, how did you know to come find us?"

Surprisingly, it was Grimm who answered.

"It is our job to monitor those who enter this realm. No one enters without our explicit knowledge. Normally we are informed directly when a prisoner is sentenced and when to expect them. Sometimes that doesn't happen. People slip through the cracks, accidentally portal to the wrong place. Those who don't belong are mind-wiped, and returned to where they came from."

"We personally check each new arrival, just in case. Especially unexpected ones. We made that mistake one too many times before, and we're still trying to rectify it," added Thad.

"You mean we're still paying for it, don't you?" Dair intoned. "And at the rate it's going, we'll forever be on the shit list."

"I'd even settle for less than forgiveness. I just want more than disdain." Grimm pouted.

"Dude, we don't deserve forgiveness. We're fucking lucky we get disdain. It could be much worse," Rian added, weirdly upbeat compared to the tone the others set.

"Disdain is definitely a step up from where we started, remember?" Theus reminded them.

They all shuddered in unison. Looking at each other they nodded their heads in agreement as one.

"Never again."

CHAPTER 24

S haggy pushed his chair back from the table and stood, looked at his bulky black watch, then shook his head in dismay.

"Alright fuckers, times up. I've already missed the first five minutes, I refuse to miss the rest. So anything else can wait until morning." He practically ran from the room, leaving Jezzie bewildered. What sport was so important he had to be such a dick about missing five minutes?

"Why's this game so important to Shaggy?" Jezzie asked, her curiosity piqued.

"Well, as you may have surmised, we don't get out much, and being stuck here with these buffoons, as lovable as they are, can drive even the sanest person stir-crazy. Especially when we can't even really tell the gorgons to fuck off," Theus offered.

"And nobody could ever claim Grimm's completely sane, even before coming here. I mean, have you ever heard of a one hundred percent sane hellhound?"

"He's a hellhound? But they're . . ." Jezzie drifted off.

"Yeah, they're super rare, like manticore. They're also the rightful rulers of all canine shifters, even if they pretty much let the packs manage themselves most of the time."

"Add in the fact his kind is extremely loyal to blood and family, and the fact he's here instead of with them . . . You can't really blame him for being an ass half the time. Every now and then it doesn't hurt to blow off a little steam, ya know? Time moves differently here than in any other realm, so one year for us equals roughly every twelve years everywhere else. Our earth TV reception is actually pretty shitty, and only one OtherRealm species televises their sport, but only once every two decades so you bet your ass we all want to watch it. Some of us are just nicer than others, is all."

"So, what exactly are you guys watching then?" Jezzie asked.

Nithe chuckled behind her.

"Something funny, Ni?" Her raised eyebrow said it all.

"Where'd you grow up, Jez?" he gently asked.

"Earth, fairly remote, and no we didn't often socialize with anyone. I was always told it was best we remained hidden, for as long as we were permitted to hide, and so we did. Still didn't stop Jimmy Tucker, the little fucker, from spying on me while I swam in the lake when I was sixteen." She smiled wickedly. "Aunt Rai Rai hexed him so bad. Sorry, I tend to ramble. Why?"

"Oh, Jezzie, you'll either love it or hate it, there is no in between. Come, let's see which way you go." Novarian hooked his arm through hers and dragged her across the white and gray marble foyer.

She didn't know what she'd expected; football, golf, basketball, but it certainly wasn't almost naked harpies, pretty much mud wrestling in the center of a primitive makeshift arena in the middle of what looked like a jungle. Breasts bounced everywhere, legs were waving. Nothing seemed to be off limits as they bit, scratched, and yanked whatever they could get a grip on. Including nipples, apparently.

One harpy had her thighs wrapped around another's neck, squeezing tight until her opponent's knees buckled. At the last second, before her knees hit the slick ground, she shifted her weight and flipped the thigh strangler over, sending her flying onto her back. Taking full advantage of the switch in positions, she raced forward and leapt into the air, and as her body hit the sprawled out harpy, she landed a vicious blow to her solar plexus. This sent the men into a frenzy of cheering and revelry, their eyes fixated on the large cinematic screen mounted to one wall. Grimm sat front and center. He didn't cheer as loudly as the others, though. He actually looked kind of serious. This guy and fun seemed kind of polar opposites.

As Jezzie looked around, she rolled her eyes, turned away and muttered to herself.

"Of course, I get stuck with a bunch of misogynistic neanderthals." All the while shaking her head.

"You don't like it, Red, you're free to leave the room," Shaggy coldly advised.

Nithe and Rian followed her out the door, but Jezzie couldn't resist one last parting shot.

"Enjoy the circle jerk, boys." She smiled over her shoulder.

Faint muttered words reached her ears as the doors closed behind them.

"Bloody women just don't understand the artistry of war games."

"Told you you'd either love it or hate it. Now, not to be insensitive or offensive at all, but you guys kinda stink. Didn't really notice before, but yeah . . . you could both use a shower, and some sleep. Nithe, sorry dude, but you look almost dead on your feet, my man."

"Why, thanks, Rian. Way to make a girl feel good about being shoved into the Nether, forced to fight off hideously terrifying creatures, and being subjected to Shaggy's stellar personality disorder," Jezzie laughed. "Lead the way, fairy man. I just want a nice hot shower, to wash my hair, and to crawl into bed for snuggles with my own personal hot water bottle." The last was said with a wink at a suddenly alert Nithe.

The fairy signaled to a passing gorgon, who slithered out of the room and returned a few moments later, sans the linens she'd been carrying.

"Vestia, please escort our honored guests to the Black Room, and provide them with whatever they may need for the duration of their stay with us."

The gorgon nodded her head, the snakes, posing as hair, hissed and squirmed, striking at the air around her, even going so far as to sink tiny fangs into her cheeks without care.

"As you wish, Your Highness." Oh, there was definite snark in her tone; it was unmistakable.

Rian leaned in and whispered softly, "Don't worry, they can't turn you to stone if you look upon them. The Almighty took the ability from the ones sent here for their crimes."

Odd, but with everything else going on in her crazy mixed up world right now, the possibility hadn't even crossed her mind.

"Tell me you aren't going back in there to watch it with the rest of them? I mean, yay for female warriors, battle skills, and empowerment and all, but I highly doubt the men watching are doing so for that reason. Especially the naked parts."

Jezzie wasn't sure why she had such a problem with it at the moment. Normally she wouldn't. Maybe, it was a build-up of all the shit she'd had to deal with from men in the last eight or nine years? Maybe, she was simply tired, grumpy, and the rank smell of her own body was pissing her off? Fuck, she'd kill for a nice glass of Moscato and some strawberries right about now as she soaked in a hot bath full of bubbles.

"What time is it?" Nithe asked, changing the subject quickly.

"It's currently one in the afternoon. I'll have a tray sent up. We don't expect to see you until the morning. Portal jag is a real thing in this realm, what with the way time works so differently. Jezzie, get some rest, you obviously need it."

Rian's tone was gentle as far as rebukes go, but Jezzie felt ashamed all the same. Who was she to judge them when she'd been salivating over Nithe's cock all day? She agreed, she was obviously overtired and stressed because even though it was one in the afternoon, it sure felt like well past the witching hour to her bone-tired body.

Nithe placed his arm around her waist, and together they followed the surly gorgon up the lavish staircase. Jezzie couldn't help running her fingers over the gold inlaid, ebony handrail as they ascended to the first floor. Smooth and cool to the touch, it made her feel like a fairy-tale princess. A giggle slipped out as she recalled her earlier reaction to the chandelier. Okay, so, it was possible she'd started to get a little manic. Honestly, she was a little surprised she hadn't gone completely crazy in the last eight years alone, but the last twenty-four hours surely should have tipped her over the precipice and straight into a padded white cell.

When the gorgon opened the door to the dubiously named Black Room and stepped aside, Nithe tugged Jezzie inside, said a quick thanks, and closed the door in the surly cow's face, all while her snakes hissed and tried to strike at them. From the light thump against the ornate wood, Jezzie was pretty certain one of the vicious little things had been hit, fangs first, by the unexpected closure. Jezzie looked at Nithe, Nithe looked at Jezzie. Lips quivered, eyes gleamed, it was enough to send Jezzie into a fit of giggles, Nithe chuckling along beside her.

The feel of his warm, calloused finger under her chin sent tingles through her tired body. She looked up into his eyes of liquid gold, threaded with flashes of green fire. Her breath froze in her lungs, until he turned her face toward the center of the room, at which point it rushed out as she took in the black, red, and gold furnishings.

A four-poster bed, made of what looked like the same wood as the handrail she'd stroked her palm over on the way up, sat on a raised dais against one wall. Gold vines twisted and twined their way up each one before trailing along the edges of the canopy. Jezzie peeled back one of the thick, red curtains to expose sheer black curtains which hung from hidden rails. They were tied back against each post to reveal a turned-down, luxurious, red blanket, black and red silk sheets, and matching pillows. She just wanted to throw her tired, aching body into all that toasty softness and sleep for as long as possible.

Instead, Nithe marched her straight past it, stopping to check a door which led to a gigantic walk-in closet, before finding a bathroom fit for royalty. The bath alone could fit six people and the shower had two large shower heads which hung from the ceiling. The black marble floor sparkled, and the gold fixtures gleamed.

Jezzie caught sight of herself in one of the large double mirrors above the twin vanity, and her nose crinkled up in disgust. The dark circles under her eyes gave her features a sunken, ghostly pallor, and the stains of blood and grime coating her skin taunted her with the reality of what she and Nithe had endured.

Without thought, her hands moved to strip every item from her body until she was bare. She pulled the tie from her messy hair so roughly it snapped, and she tossed it on the counter as she half stumbled, half ran to the shower. Dragging a stunned and still dressed Nithe by the hand behind her.

The shower was a haze of warm, wet bliss. It washed away an

immense amount of dirt and blood from both of them. Jezzie watched it all swirl down the drain, unable to look away. At some point Nithe stripped off his saturated clothes. Jezzie had pulled him into the shower, unaware it would turn on automatically, but he hadn't seemed to care. She was vaguely aware of Nithe's hands roaming over her skin leaving a trail of suds and sweet aromas. Alas, her eyes had already drifted shut, her shoulder against the wall, and for the life of her she couldn't find the will to pry them back open.

<hr>

WHEN JEZZIE's eyes drifted shut in the shower, Nithe just managed to catch her suddenly lax body before it hit the dark tiles and hauled her into his arms, cradling her against his chest. He carried her out of the warm water, which turned off automatically. With one hand he awkwardly grabbed the two fluffy black robes that were folded over the arm of the plush lounge. He strode back into the bedroom, and tossed one aside. The other he lay out as best he could on the bed before he gently placed her clearly exhausted body on top of it, worked her arms into the sleeves, and secured the belt around her waist. After which, he proceeded to grab a towel from the bathroom to dry both of them as much as possible and donned his own robe. Exhausted himself, he climbed in beside her, pulling the covers up as he did so. As his head hit the pillow, Morpheus claimed him, too.

Swirling dreams of blood and pain, of twisted intentions, and forced compliance filled his head with torment. Sounds of screaming filled his head, his mother's whispered words of hate as she turned away from her first-born son. The soft lullaby she'd sung him every night when she'd tucked him into bed. Shackles, knives, and hot, fetid breath . . . Light, the scent of cinnamon and patchouli, lush, red hair, and silver-gray eyes. Whispered words, soft gentle sighs. The stroke of a hand meant to soothe, not to maim.

Nithe's eyes fluttered open as soft fingers brushed his sweat slicked hair from his brow. His ears were still offline, and his body rigid and unresponsive aside from the chills that sent shivers racing through his limbs.

"Shh, it's okay, baby. I've got you. You are safe, and I'll kick anyone's ass who makes you feel otherwise. Shh." Jezzie's soft lilting voice crooned, his head cradled to her chest.

The dream faded faster than it had come upon him, but three things remained with him. Firstly, the heavy thud of his heart as it raced in fear, a fear which slowly turned into desire as he breathed in her scent, his inner beast purring. Secondly, the fact his dream had been full of color. For the dreams of dragons never were. They dreamed in black and white, and shades of glittering gold. Lastly, the sound of an angel bringing him back from despair, and she was literally just that, an angel. Well, half angel.

Face pressed against the creamy, soft skin of her exposed breasts, Nithe nuzzled in closer as he breathed in lungfuls of her unique scent. His tongue flicked out for a taste, and sure enough, it was even better than before. Pure, undiluted Jezzie, and he wanted more.

There was no way she missed the feel of his rigid length as he curled further toward her, his groin pressing against her thigh. From the way she pressed her body closer, the breathy moan that drifted from her lips, and the scent of her desire as it flooded the room, it was a clear indication to him she wouldn't be averse to continuing their earlier intimate activities.

"Ni, you should know, I want you. Like, right here, right now. But I will not take advantage of a vulnerable man, even if I desperately want to suck his glorious cock and caress every inch of him."

If he'd been standing, her words would have brought him to his knees. Shit, how in the hell his life had become, in the darkness that was his every day, had he managed to find her, his perfect mate? Had he been wrong? Did the Fate's not actually hate him, after all?

"Jez, right here, right now," he echoed her words back to her. "I am not vulnerable, for you make me strong. The beast in me desires nothing more than to claim you, and make you ours. The man I am already adores you, and you just tipped him over the ledge into head over heels in love, *a stór*. If you don't take me, I may just shrivel up and die." He pouted playfully, trying to add some levity to his words so she didn't freak out about the whole love thing.

"You love me? Like, really, truly love me? How? You don't even know anything about me. I could be a deranged murderess out on the hunt for my next victim, I'm not, but I could be."

Disbelief quivered through her voice as Jezzie rambled out her questions; her chaotic thoughts. Not even pausing to allow him time to answer.

"No one falls in love this fast, especially with me. No one has ever fallen in love with me, for that matter. Seriously? I mean, I really, really like you too. Okay, I more than like you, and I know it's fast. I've never liked anyone this fast. The guy from the alley years ago, and his dream friend, get my blood pumping and all, same as you, only muted somehow, like they're too far away. And yes, I feel it in my heart that you are mine, and I am yours. Just as I feel they are mine too. I just never really expected anyone to ever feel that way about me. Least of all, someone as drop dead gorgeous and amazing as you are. You are amazing like this all the time, right? I mean, you're not some crazy stalker with a weird penchant for killing women after you sleep with them, right? Or one of those assholes who expect a woman to stay in the kitchen, and pop out babies, while bringing you sandwiches and beer all day? Please tell me you aren't one of those. I will not be in a relationship with someone like that, I think I'd end up committing mariticide. What's with the whole mate thing anyway? I know dragons have them, but I'm not a dragon. I'm half Shadow Hound angel, half psychic vampire. What is it with angels knocking up other OtherRealmly beings, anyway? It's not supposed to be possible from what I've read and been told. Mm, oh, that feels so good."

Jezzie finally paused to suck in a breath then bit her plump lower lip. Her eyes just about rolled back in her pretty head as his hand slid up her thigh, tracing circles on her sensitive skin.

Her head snapped up, her eyes drilled into his, as though she could tell if he lied. Shit! Psychic vampire! She probably could, too. Add in the unpredictable combination when added to her angel side, and who knows what she could actually do.

"Ni, you mean it, don't you." It wasn't a question, but still he sat up and nodded his head. "You know you might not be the only one?"

"What does that mean, Jez? Dragons are notorious hoarders, they value their women, but can be overwhelmingly monogamous, and generally only have one mate. Usually the women are not given any other option, I admit. But I'm unfamiliar with any other way. The angel in me thinks it's bullshit, FYI. Especially knowing how much dragon males and females are sexually diverse prior to finding their mates."

"Did you know angels don't dream?" Jezzie asked.

"Really? Dragons only dream in shades of black and white with hues of gold overlaid. They don't dream at all?" He felt his forehead furrow.

"Nope, no dreams at all. Neither do psychic vampires. Not really, and not in color either. What we dream are the remnants, the emotion infused leftovers of the feelings we siphon from others to feed our own hunger."

"Okay, what does this have to do with other mates?" he queried.

"Well, before I ended up with Ballzy, I met a Shadow Hound in a dark alley. No idea which one, it was a very brief interaction. But, ever since then, I've been dreaming about him. Harmless, sometimes naughty dreams. Until recently. The last time I had one, he had a friend with him, and something extra seemed to tug at another invisible string attached to my heart. It was a really good dream, my brain was obviously working overtime to keep me upbeat, or so I thought. Until I went to shower and realized actual cum covered my torso. Ballzy was watching through the window, clearly not at that stage yet, so it wasn't him. He told me later about meetings on the Astral Plane, how rare it is, and how a strong bond or destiny is usually involved."

"Balthazar was watching you have dream sex?" Nithe growled low in his chest, his fists gripping the silky sheet until his knuckles threatened to break through skin.

"Well, yeah, I was technically a prisoner then. But I feel like we're good now. If not friends, at least not enemies, and it's not like I hadn't slept with him already. Only once, mind you, and never again, eurgh."

He couldn't take the influx of new information right now. The thought of her and Balthazar made his stomach churn. Strangely, the dream scenario actually piqued his curiosity, and caused his cock to twitch, which didn't help his mental state. He focused on her mouth, her still moving mouth.

"No more talking, I can't take anymore right now, please." His last word turned into a gravelly groan.

Reaching forward he pulled her down unexpectedly onto the bed beside him and she squealed in surprise. He angled his large body over hers, slid his muscled thigh between her legs, and laid claim to a mouth straight from the sinful dreams of his misspent youth.

Her tongue pressed to the seam of his lips, demanding entry, a spike of lust shot through him straight to his heavy balls, drawing them up in anticipation. She thrust into his mouth expertly, claiming the space for her own, as she pushed him onto his back and followed him down her mouth didn't once leave his. Soft fingers tangled in his over-long hair, getting caught in the matted knots. It reminded him of how they came to be, snapped him from the moment, and flung him back into a barren place filled with silent terror.

CHAPTER 25

J ezzie pulled back the instant she felt Nithe's muscles tense, his body go rigid, and his breath seize in his lungs. She slid her body off his, curled herself into his side to lay her hand over his heart, and waited.

Eventually his breath escaped, resuming its regular rise and fall. His heartbeat took longer to slow, but when it did, his body relaxed into the bed as tears rolled down his cheeks.

"I'm sorry, so sorry. I'm so fucking sorry, Jez. I don't know what's wrong with me. I mean, I get trauma, and all that shit, but I should be better than this. I should be stronger than this. If not for me, at least for you. With you, the past should just fucking disappear. I want it to disappear, so bad. I want to be more, more than my fucked up past, more than I am, more than half the man I used to be. You deserve so much better than me."

Jezzie held him tight, eyes closed as her tears fell. The more he spoke, the more her heart broke for the man who, whether too soon or not, irrevocably held a major piece of it. She knew she'd never allow anyone to hurt him ever again, including himself. Her body trembled, not with sadness, but with growing rage. Not at Nithe. Never at Nithe. Rather, at the Fates themselves. How dare they do this to him. How dare they allow beings such as Raum to destroy lives. Oh, how she wished she'd ignored the voice that'd stayed her hand when she'd been on the brink of ending the asshole's eternal existence.

She sat bolt upright, and looked him dead in the eyes, not bothering to wipe the tears from her own.

"Don't you ever think for one-fucking-second you are unworthy of me. Do you hear me? You are mine. I am yours. Not by some chemical reaction caused by a mate mark, or some shit. I choose you Nithe, all of you. Your past, present, and future. We don't always get to choose the shit road the Fates lead us down, but we damn well get to choose how we let it affect us. You and me? We have some things in common. Granted, what Raum did to you was way worse than anything I've experienced. What I do know is that you and I will get through this together, and nothing that evil sadistic bastard did to you will ever make me love you less. We can take this as fast, or as slow, as you need." Anger laced her words, softened by her need to comfort him.

Nithe's tears dried up, and he rubbed his red eyes with the back of his hand before offering her a tired smile.

"Do you have any idea how utterly sexy you are when you're angry on my behalf, *a stór?*" he whispered, his voice hoarse.

"I'm glad you think so." She winked. "And you can call me treasure anytime you like, *mo shíorghrá.*"

Apparently, she'd said something right because Nithe sat straight up, pulled her across his lap, and kissed her with such passionate fervor she just about passed out from the heady bliss of his lips on hers.

"I want you, Jez. More than I've ever wanted anything, or anyone, in my entire life. I feel like if I don't have you right now a part of me will wither away, as corny or pathetic as it may sound."

Nithe's hot breath fanned the flames of her desire as it trailed its way down the side of her neck. His teeth nipped a path along nerve endings which led straight to her aching core, where evidence of her desire left her inner thighs damp, her pussy slick, and ready.

"Ni?"

"Yes, Jez?"

"What happened? Before?"

"Nothing. I don't want to talk about it right now, please."

"I understand, I do. I just don't want to inadvertently be the cause of whatever triggered you, again. I need to know what I can't do, please? Was I too forceful? If so, I'm totally okay with you being in control. You can set the pace, promise. I just need you to be okay. Not because I don't want the sex to stop, but because I need you to be okay. And okay, fine, I also don't want the sex to stop. I'm pretty sure it's going to be flipping spectacular, and I definitely want a chance to prove my theory."

"It wasn't you being on top, Jez. Though, I can't guarantee it won't be an issue in the future. I don't really know why, or when my body's going to freak out like it did. This time, it was my hair." He looked down, his hand lifted up to his hair as if to touch it, then lowered to the bed before he could, as if ashamed.

Sure, his hair was matted, longer than he probably liked, almost reaching below his shoulder blades. It could definitely use a good wash, but he'd been through hell and back, and she doubted Raum had allowed him basic hygiene for however long he'd tortured him. The current state of his hair also took nothing away from his allure, despite what he may think.

"What about your hair triggered you, Ni?"

Nithe let out a heavy sigh, and squeezed his eyes shut tight, his fingers clutched the sheets as if he were drowning. Jezzie placed her hands on his shoulders in an effort to rub away the tension from his tight muscles.

"When your fingers got stuck in the knots, Jez. I didn't want it to, but my brain threw me back into the nightmare of what had been my existence for so long. I couldn't find my way out until the memory released me, and your soothing touch helped to bring me home."

She pried his hands, one by one, from the twisted and crumpled sheets, and leapt off the bed, pulling him along with her. Her robe hung open, it almost tripped her up as she tried to stand, so she shrugged it from her shoulders before dragging a nervous Nithe toward the large bathroom.

"When you walk in front of me like this, Jez, it makes me want to scoop you up, bend you over the arm of the sofa, and pound into you until I make you scream my name as you come around my aching cock. I never knew I was an ass man until this very moment." His husky voice tripped her up, her knees almost buckling as a wave of fresh desire swept through her.

"We have a lot to learn together, Ni, and hopefully more than one mortal lifetime to learn it in, thank the stars."

As she walked over the cool tiles she scooped up a metal stool from under the vanity with her free hand. Jezzie placed it down again directly under one of the large overhead lights, and turned to Nithe.

"Um, Jez, What are you doing?" Nithe asked somewhat nervously, as she went to rummage through the vanity drawers looking for a comb and a pair of decent scissors.

Not those silly little nail ones which she tossed aside. Ah, there they were, pretty golden ones with ornate finger rings. She ran her finger along one inner edge. Yep, nice and sharp too. Perfect for what she needed to do. Jezzie turned, held up her finds and gave the scissors a little snip-snip action.

"Do you trust me, Ni?" she asked sincerely, a smile tilting up the corners of her lips. Although, the smile didn't quite reach her eyes, and it made her look just a little bit psychotic.

"As much as I can with you holding a pair of scissors and looking a bit maniacal, Jez." He laughed, half-covered his mouth, and whispered in an aside, "To be honest though . . . it's kinda turning me on."

A wide grin stretched his solemn features and her own lips responded in kind.

"If you want to do this yourself, Ni, I can leave you to it. I want this to be as easy for you as possible, okay? Just say the word, and I'll back away, no offense taken."

At the wash of relief she felt burst out of him she walked up to him slowly, held out the scissors and comb, and turned to walk away.

The firm grip of his hand around her wrist pulled her up short. His soft tug brought her back flush to the solid wall of his chest as his arms wrapped around her, warm breath from his parted lips tickled her ear.

"I need you to do this, *a stór*. I cannot bring myself to look at it, let alone touch it. I need your help. You are the only one I trust."

She felt a shudder run through him, evidence of his vulnerability. Thoughts flew through her head as she imagined what he was like before Raum. Was he the same sweet man, only less tormented? Was there a cockiness she was yet to see? A dominant ego? A feckless womanizer? Would she ever meet the man he used to be? Would she ever want to? Her thoughts ground to a halt, just as quickly as they'd started. This man, no matter who he was before, was her Nithe. How he grew from here? Where he went from here? Was a new path they would tread together. This was their destiny, fate, whatever those bitches wanted to call themselves the mistresses of. But she'd give them some credit . . . Nithe was exactly the man she needed, and it was clear he needed her too.

Sitting him gently on the stool, his back to the mirror, Jezzie set to work. The comb was not going to make it through those knots, not yet. If she tried, she was certain the hard plastic would snap.

"How short did it used to be, Ni?" she queried, softly.

Nithe quickly indicated to his lightly bearded jaw line, about an inch below his ears, before snapping his hand back down to his knee. Where they dug like talons into his bare flesh. His robe barely covered the tops of his thighs, which made her mouth water, and images of him looking down at her as she knelt in front of him, his cock gliding in and out of her mouth, swam in her already lust dazed brain.

Jezzie snapped out of it, and got to work. This was not the time to fantasize. Nithe needed her to put all of that aside and help him attain some semblance of his old self in order to take away a part of the ghost that was Raum and all the damage he'd done.

His hair reached down to mid-shoulder, the knots denser at the ends, thankfully. It was almost as if he hadn't been allowed to lay down his head, as most knots usually form closer to the scalp when people sleep. That fucking bastard! No way was she asking Nithe, but she suspected he'd been tied upright most of the time.

She trimmed as much length off as she could. Her hands were covered in crusty residue, both the rusty hue of dried blood, and other colors she'd rather ignore, and so she did. She said not a word as she placed down the scissors and guided him toward the shower, slipped the robe from his shoulders and placed the stool down inside. Quickly she pressed a red 'STOP' button on the wall, and the automatic water switched off. Gently she urged him to sit before she took hold of a handheld shower head, and got to work rinsing out as much grime as she could. She lathered, rinsed, and repeated a total of five times until she was satisfied his hair was as clean as she could get it. A whole hell of a lot of conditioner was next, she washed most of it out, leaving some in to help untangle the strands. Once all the knots were combed out, she gave it another trim. Not caring as the water washed the lopped off locks down the drain as she washed away the last of the conditioner, her fingers lingered in his hair, massaging his scalp, playing with the soft, wet strands.

His groan was the only warning she had before she found herself pinned to the cool marble wall. His lean body flush against her soft curves, his gaze burned into hers with molten desire as his hands cupped her ass, and lifted her up. She wrapped her legs around his trim waist. Her back arched toward him as the length of his hard cock pressed between her spread thighs, slid against the slick lips of her wet pussy.

She opened further for him, seeking him closer to her core, not just physically, either. The barrier in her that held her psychic powers at bay came crashing down, and they latched hard and fast to him. His desire, his love, but something tickled, like soda bubbles up her nose. A second set of wants and needs. The dragon's emotions mirrored the man's, only more primal, more carnal, more dominant. This should be interesting, she thought.

Resting his forehead against hers he looked into her eyes, his lips a hair's breadth away from hers. She shivered in anticipation. Slowly he pulled away, lowered her to the floor, and hit the green button on the wall. Water cascaded over them, warm and scented like fresh rain.

"Your turn, *a stór*," he whispered as he spun her around . . . and proceeded to wash her flipping hair. She was slightly miffed until she felt the explosion of emotion pour out of him. He truly needed this. To care for her, to show her she mattered more than a tumble. Her knees just about buckled, her heart beat a wild rhythm in her chest, her own emotions thrust themselves outward. Nithe's breath caught in his chest as he felt them. She looked over her shoulder at him with a goofy smile. Like a girl in love, and she realized for the first time in her life that goofily grinning girl was actually her.

"If there's anything else you need to do before we head back to bed, Ni, now's the time. I'll finish up here, you have ten minutes max before I want to be back in your arms, and I don't plan on leaving them for quite a while." She bit her bottom lip, her eyes hooded with carnal intent. Though honestly, if all he wished was to snuggle she'd be totally onboard with that too.

Ten minutes later, he was dried, shaved, minty breathed, and leaning against the door jamb as he watched her rinse and spit, which must've been oh-so sexy a sight to witness.

"Time's up, Jez, and I'm done waiting. I need you close to me, the softness of your skin warming mine." The musky, unique scent of Nithe mixed with the heady fragrance of his desire as he lifted her in his arms. The soft cool sheets caressed her back before she even realized they'd left the bathroom, but it didn't matter as his thigh slid between hers, his cock pressed to her hip.

"Um, can you touch it again, Jez?" came Nithe's almost silent whisper.

"Touch what, Ni? Your cock? As yet I haven't had the pleasure, but I can definitely oblige," she offered saucily.

"My hair, cheeky woman, just to be sure. But I like your idea better, it's next on the list." His wink was soft, a shadow of uncertainty behind his beautiful eyes.

With graceful, languid motions she lifted her hands and buried her fingers in the soft, light-brown strands and gave a light tug to bring his lips close to hers.

"May I kiss you now, my lord?" she breathed, huskily. "You control this, Nithe. All of it. We do this your way, and if it means we don't do it at all I'm just as happy to be wrapped in your warmth for as long as you like. You call the shots."

"Just as happy, huh? We'll see about that, Jez. Prepare to find out just how much happier you can be with more than just my warmth," he growled. The dragon and man both took up a challenge she'd never meant to issue.

Cool air covered her torso as Nithe moved his body down the bed, his hot breath, warmer than normal, left a path of tingles over her skin. Rough palms grazed her full breasts, and teased her hard nipples into even firmer peaks. His tongue swirled around each one before he rained kisses over her abdomen. Little nips lightly stung her skin in a most delicious way as his calloused palms spread her thighs wide, only to hook them over his shoulders. Both palms slid under to cup the cheeks of her ass, lifting her to meet his hungry mouth. His lips, tongue, and teeth devoured every drop of her desire, like a man starved.

Her back arched sharply as two thick fingers thrust into her eager pussy. The wet glide of his tongue joined them, sending her over the edge into a mind-blowing orgasm. Her body trembled and shook as the waves of pleasure slowly subsided.

Jezzie blinked open her eyes, and her heart sped straight back up. Blood pumped through her sensitive body directly to her still aching pussy at the sight of him looking up at her from between her parted thighs. Her juices coated his perfect lips, and a whimper passed through hers. Oh, how she wanted to beg him to take her, to thrust his magnificent cock in and out of her until she broke into a million shattered pieces only he could put back together.

But she didn't say a word, didn't move as she waited for him to be ready. His smile was her reward, and holy hell! Her man had a megawatt grin. Enhanced by the short beard and mustache he now sported. She licked her lips and swallowed hard.

Instead of sliding up her body, he moved further down, ran his warm hands down her right leg, lifting it to place kisses behind her knee, and along the arch of her foot. He nibbled her toes before repeating the same decadent torment with her other leg.

Nithe made his way back to kneel between her spread thighs. Fire flushed her skin as his gaze raked over her nakedness, he flicked her clit with lazy fingers as he spoke, and his words sparked an inferno in her blood.

"Want to touch me, Jez?"

He had such kissable lips, the way they moved, the slight indent in the bottom one. Damn, she wanted to lick it so bad.

"Yes, Ni. More than you can imagine."

"How, *a stór?* Tell me how you want to touch me?" he urged.

"I want to slide my hands over every inch of your skin, do the same with my tongue, along every dip and curve of you. I want, no, I need to run my fingers over the silky hard length of your cock. To explore the way it feels, tastes, looks, and the way it shifts. Such an intriguing talent you have there. One I want to explore, later. Right now though, I want to feel your cock deep in my throat, savor the taste of you as I suck you like my favorite lollipop, and only stop when you make me." Her mouth watered at the thought of it all.

"Do it. Touch me, wrap your sweet lips around my cock, Jez." The switch in positions was sudden, yet smooth, her legs straddled his thighs. "Now, *a stór*! Before I lose control."

Gentle and slow, her fingers glided over the taut skin of his abdomen, up and down over his slightly hairy thighs. Taunting and teasing as she moved ever closer to the prize. Nithe's thick, hard cock stood at attention, easily nine inches long, and all man. No sign of the strange dragon-like cock from earlier. Nithe's natural cock was a thing of mouth-watering beauty.

Blood welled on her bottom lip, from where her teeth bit down to hold her back. Both hands wrapped around his girth softly, up and down, feeling every ridge, every vein. She swirled several drops of pre-cum over the bulbous tip, licking her finger slowly to savor the taste of him. His deep groan morphed into a rumble as she sensed the dragon in him surge forward. Lowering her mouth she flicked her tongue out to taste the tip of him, before she licked the underside of the head and traced a path around the edge.

Suddenly, her back met the bed. Nithe covered her body with his, her legs came up to wrap around his waist, leaving her bare, dripping wet pussy exposed to his thick hard cock. He pressed it against her throbbing core, rubbing firmly over her clit as her wetness coated him, silently begging him to end the torment, to take what she so eagerly offered.

"Are you sure, Jez? You want this?"

"More than anything, Ni."

"You need to say it, *a stór*. I need the words."

"Yes, Nithe. I want you. I want this. I want, I need, your cock to fill my pussy, and make me come just for you."

"I'm not sure I can control my instincts, Jez. My dragon wants this just as much as I do. We need you, and when you talk like that, you shred my control to pieces," with that said, he shifted his hips until the tip of his cock pushed at her entrance.

He entered her slowly until he was seated to the hilt, his cock filling her completely, stretching her, his deep groan warmed the curve of her neck. Impatiently she shifted her hips, seeking friction, movement, something more.

Holy fuck on a hockey stick! His cock seemed to grow larger, the base thickening, spreading her almost painfully wide, he held inhumanly still as he allowed her body to adjust. Her brain glazed over with desire, a fuzzy feeling—almost transcendent—clouded her vision. Without consent from her brain her hips shifted again, eager for more, desperate even. With every motion her pussy soaked his length, and dripped onto the sheets beneath them.

Mouths met, lips, soft and tender. Teeth nipped and tongues clashed. Passion poured from one to the other and back again. With one last barely there kiss to her jawline Nithe finally gave in and pulled away slightly, the tip of his cock almost leaving her, before slamming home. His eyes never left hers as he smirked confidently every time she cried out her pleasure.

Unbearable pressure built in her, but she didn't want it to end, not yet, not without him, not this time. His pace picked up, driving her hard into the mattress. She didn't care. More of him was all she wanted. Her shadows pulsed, on the verge of erupting from her skin. A few rogue tendrils slipped out to caress his balls with each pounding thrust. Her body tensed, his body stilled. Only the sound of their heavy breathing filled the silence around them.

Jezzie tried to lift her hands to cup his face, but couldn't. A look at her wrists revealed they were pinned, one on either side of her head. Trapped between large, sharp claws buried deep into the mattress. Gold eyes shimmered down at her in place of Nithe's usual amber and green, a clear sign his dragon held the reins.

"Mate of mine, your scent drives us to distraction. I cannot be without you. With you, man and beast become one, and you become our everything. Nod, if you agree."

"Yes, whatever it is you both need. I feel it too. You have my consent, both of you."

In an instant his teeth shifted into the sharp pointed ones of his dragon form. His lips caressed her skin softly. Her scream echoed off the walls as he bit down on the soft flesh above her left breast. Pain turned to sizzling pleasure as fire ran through her veins, her back arched off the bed as her pussy convulsed with the most intense orgasm of her entire life. Her shadows escaped, wrapping around Ni's body, binding them together, glittery threads being woven between them as his hot cum shot into her, over and over again.

After what felt like an eternity later, Nithe finally rolled sideways onto the bed beside her. Not far though. Skin still touched skin and ragged breaths filled the room. Sweat slicked bodies began to cool, and yeah, the sheets under her ass started to get cold, and were most likely ruined, probably the mattress too, to be honest. Let's hope they used mattress protectors in this place was her last thought as her mate's arms pulled her close to his warm body just before post-sex, satiated sleep claimed them.

CHAPTER 26

Dreams of naked bodies twisted together in ecstasy. Of Jezzie and him. Of two other men. Strangers, that somehow didn't feel strange. Such images had plagued Nithe's sleeping hours. Yet only Jezzie's voice had filled the silence. No moans of pleasure, save for hers. She'd said his name, but not theirs. So, he'd deduced they must be the men she'd mentioned earlier. She'd given him a small nod, as if she knew what he'd been thinking, and he realized she probably did. The bond was getting stronger, after all, and it was common, even for his kind to form such a link.

So, these were the unknown males. Was he nervous? Heck yes, he was. With no idea what it all meant, for Jezzie, or for himself, how could he not be? His kind took many lovers, sometimes more than one at once, but matings were seen as sacred things between only two. It had never mattered if it were male and female, or any other combination. Their society saw experimentation as the norm, most dragons were bisexual anyway. The belief instilled in their very DNA was that the Fates would ultimately choose your perfect other half. Nithe couldn't deny that in Jez, his faith in them was justified. Even as he cursed them for his past.

With Raum still living in his head, he shied away from their touch. An instinct driven by fear. Not that they tried to touch him, not in the same way they touched his Jez. Mostly they watched him warily, unsure what his presence meant. Yet his skin crawled, nonetheless. He wasn't disgusted by them. No, it was his own weakness. His own fucked up recent past. He liked, and yet he hated. He found pleasure in their presence, even in his discomfort.

Watching the two men was a sight to behold. A beautiful one, which spoke to the him he used to be. Two strong males. So starkly contrasting in looks. With eyes so intense they made Nithe feel exposed, like they could see into his very soul. Eyes that held so many questions. They were curious, a little put off, and in their gaze lay a torrent of, 'what the fuck was happening?'

Strangely, he wasn't jealous as he watched them pleasure his bonded mate. Her honeysuckle scent flooded his senses, the scent of her arousal saturated the very air they breathed. She looked at him, worried, as he stood apart from them. He moved to kiss her lush lips, then gave her a soft smile, his gaze softly resting on hers.

He expected the dragon in him to rise up and demand satisfaction in the form of the interlopers' blood. But, it didn't happen. Instead, warmth spread through his chest and along the bond as he ushered them away gently from Jezzie's naked body. He lifted her up and placed her on his lap, facing the two fit males. His rock-hard cock pressed up against her spine. Her bare ass shifted over his sensitive balls and caused a desperate gasp of need to fill his lungs. The warm, soft skin of her inner thighs, as he spread her wide, made his cock twitch with a jolt of desire at what was to come. Literally, come was exactly what he intended for her to do. Hopefully, more than once.

Stud one and stud two regarded him warily, even as they devoured the sight of Jezzie's pretty pink pussy exposed to them. Nithe ran his fingers over the responsive softness of her inner thighs. Long fingers teased her folds, he slipped two between them, and grazed the little bundle of nerves hidden therein, before he held the slick lips further apart for their viewing pleasure. Her moans were music to his ears.

"That's right, *a stór*, let them hear your pleasure. See your desire spill from your dripping pussy." Huh, apparently he could speak here too.

As he spoke, he unexpectedly thrust one thick digit inside her hot entrance. Her spine arched, her head fell back on his shoulder, and her heat pressed further onto his hands.

Two hard cocks came closer, each gripped in a strong hand. Shock briefly registered on their faces. Though, it disappeared as Nithe removed his finger and brought it to his mouth. The vixen on his lap protested, shifted restlessly, and whimpered sexily.

"Can you two talk yet?" he asked of the two males.

Angels, judging by the tattoos he'd noted earlier, the ones across their shoulders, and the brands above their sculpted asses. He may be dealing with some fucked up issues, but he could still appreciate the finer qualities of all genders.

Heads shook. The darker one had a similar hairstyle to his own, only pitch black, and it caressed his cheekbones as he moved. The other had a slightly brushed back, multicolored mohawk, which barely moved at all.

Okay, just him then. Maybe it was a completed bond thing?

"Totally a question for later, Ni. Please," begged his love, who undulated her hips urgently.

"What do you want, Jez?" he purred so softly only she could hear.

His warm breath fanned the vulnerable skin below her neck. He felt the shivers wrack her body and the warm spill of her desire wet his thighs. He moved his legs further apart, far enough to fit someone between them. Her pert ass felt perfect in his palms as he reclined back on the headboard and offered her up like a feast.

And feast they did.

WHEN SHE AWAKENED, Jezzie found her body covered in a fine sheen of sweat. The air in the room was heavy with the scent of sex. Quickly drying cum cooled beneath Nithe's palms pressed against her stomach, and across her back. Almost gluing them together where she was curled up like the little spoon within his arms.

Nithe started to stir, nuzzling his whiskers into the crook of her neck, which caused her to release a sigh of pure contentment.

Too soon the evidence of her dream started to feel crusty and uncomfortable on her skin, prompting them to seek a shower, and other such amenities. Neither felt the need to speak, content to be in each other's closeness, offering light touches here and there.

When they exited the bathroom Jezzie noticed for the first time, the packs Ballzy had thrust at them during their last moments at Demon's Den sitting beside the closed bedroom door. Everything was there. Clothing, med kits, but most importantly to Jezzie, the weapons. Especially the blades she'd used to defend them in the wastelands. She felt something akin to a kindred connection with the black steel. As if they belonged in her palms, and only hers. She was relieved to see them returned and safe.

As they dressed they made idle conversation. She'd known a little about how he came to be in Raum's sadistic care from their last interaction with the creep. Knowing what she did of the trauma he suffered, she avoided asking Nithe about his time with him. She instead pondered aloud about what would become of Raum, what Ballzy was, and what he'd done after they'd left, whether he in fact was a good guy, or playing for the other team. If he was a double agent, did he even know what team he played for anymore? With everything Raum had thrown at them, all the conflicting information from Ballzy, Nithe expressed he wasn't sure where the lines were drawn anymore. Although, he'd whispered to her softly that if Balthazar was not on their side, he'd still be grateful to him for helping get them out of there, especially her. He was ever so grateful she was away from the fallen monster.

After a while her stomach lost its patience and grumbled so loud Nithe burst into belly laughs.

"Hungry are we, *a stór*?"

Rising from her seated position on the bed, Jezzie waltzed to the thick velvet curtains, and pulled them back. Sunshine didn't wash the room in any sort of golden glow. Instead darkness stretched before her eyes. Vague shadows shifted in the inky black, the occasional set of predatory eyes flashed by quickly, never lingering close by the castle walls. Flashes of eerie lightning lit the cloudless sky.

Jezzie wasn't sure how anyone, including the princes, could tell if it was night or day in this place.

Black skies seemed to forever rule the barren landscape, no matter where the strange colored orb in the sky seemed to flit. Not that it gave off any real light. Not even a trail as it moved could be seen. Though, the beings here were probably used to it after all this time. How long had they actually been here, anyway? She knew next to nothing of this realm, save the scary bedtime stories from her childhood. A shiver of cold revulsion shuddered over her, her hands automatically rubbed her arms as if to chase the chill away.

His body behind hers radiated a soul deep warmth, soothing her sudden fears. He stepped closer, and as his arms slipped around her she knew for the first time just how far she'd go to ensure his happiness and safety. Right at the same time her stomach once again protested loudly.

"I could eat, I suppose," she said, finally responding to his question. " Can we stay here, though?"

"Are you afraid, Jez?"

"And if I was?" she murmured.

"I'll be right by your side, no matter what happens. I just didn't think there was anything you were afraid of."

"Urgh." She groaned, there was nothing worse than having to admit when you'd fucked up. "I really don't want to leave this room. I know we need to, and I definitely should apologize to the guys for being such a bitch. I swear, I'm usually not so judgy."

"I feel a but is coming?" He stroked his hands up and down her arms soothingly until she turned and buried her face into his chest.

"But, I just want to stay here with you while the world melts away and goes and fucks right off. Just us in this bubble, no more drama, no more assholes, no more stress. Just for a little bit longer. I know we can't. I can already feel the tension in this place rising. Something's coming. There's no way the Fates or the Almighty would give us a break just yet. Not when it's just getting to the good part. Ya know?"

"I want that too, Jez. I want it so much. I feel it too, though. Plus, I'm pretty sure you'd rather have some real food instead of the MRE's Balthazar packed us. Trust me, they taste like ass. As for the guys down stairs, it'll be okay. I'm sure once we explain you only just went through your final angel manifestation for your wings and full power, you're still going through it actually, and that your hormones are still out of whack, they'll understand. Not completely sure Grimm will forgive you, but at least Rian probably will."

Jezzie snatched herself free of Nithe's arms, her face incredulous, sparks glittered in her gaze.

"Did you seriously just call me hormonal? I'm not some bitch in heat, you know. I'm actually holding it all together pretty damn well, all things considered. Do you know how fucking insulting it is for a guy to tell a woman she's just being hormonal?" she declared angrily.

Nithe backed up slowly, hands up in surrender.

"Hey, no offense, *a stór*, you're actually doing a hell of a lot better job of holding it together than I did, and I didn't have all these extra stressors either. During my manifestation I had zero control over my inner bitch. Probably why I called my mother and stepfather intolerable worthless assholes. On the other hand, they kind of are, so . . ." he shrugged casually.

Jezzie didn't miss the hurt behind his eyes at the mention of his mother. Her self-righteous misplaced anger deflated like a whoopie cushion as she ran forward and jumped into his arms, her legs and arms wrapped around him tightly. Whereupon she promptly burst into tears.

Fucking hormones.

Nithe was amazing. Truly amazing. He held her in his arms and whispered sweet nothings as she oscillated between tears, anger, hysterical laughter, and even self-pity. She didn't know how long it took, but eventually she settled in his arms. Emotionally wrung out, yet calm in a way she'd not felt in a very long time. There was something still missing but she knew she was on her way home.

His thoughts and feelings spoke to hers. Her shadows had been playing a game of chaotic homicidal thoughts within her and she hadn't even paid them any mind. So absorbed in surviving recent events. Still, in Nithe's arms, even they settled, as if trying to snuggle closer to his warmth.

"Come on, Jez, let's head downstairs and find some food. I'm pretty sure the gorgons in the hallway can hear your stomach growling by now." He chuckled.

"I am starving. Let's go before I lose my nerve . . . Thank you, Ni, for putting up with my crazy, and bringing me back to the now. I . . . I love you."

"I love you, too, Jezzie, and I always will. Have no doubts about that."

"Strangely enough, my love, there is nary a doubt to be found."

JEZZIE WAS ABSOLUTELY ravenous by the time they left the privacy of their room. Another round of intense lovemaking had definitely added to her appetite. Not just for food, either. The bond was stronger.

Voices from the dining hall drew their attention. The sounds of jocular ribbing and camaraderie slowed her steps, her hesitation not unnoticed by Nithe as he rubbed soothing circles on her back.

"You are not a coward, Jez. Yes, you were rude, but you are stronger than your distaste of being wrong. The faster you do this, the faster we eat," Nithe coaxed, warm breath bathing the shell of her ear.

Shoulders back, spine straight, she strode forward into the room beyond the dining doors. Silence. Nothing but light breathing and silence, that's what greeted them. All eyes on her, including the pissy gorgon from earlier.

"Look guys, I'm really sorry for my shitty attitude earlier. I know it's no excuse, but Nithe assures me it's completely to do with some residual energy or something from my final manifestation and stuff. Please know, I'm not normally a judgy bitch."

"The change for any species can do some crazy shit to your hormones, that's for sure. No idea what it's like for an angel but I can only imagine it's the same. Apology accepted," Theus pronounced, his features both soft, yet clinically appraising at the same time.

"You may accept . . ."

"Accepted by everyone, Grimm."

Power pulsed from the statement, not that it really had any effect on anyone but the gorgons, who slithered into the corners of the room.

"Fine, if it means so much to you, Theus. I don't have to like it, but I accept it. If she's a bitch to Tana, though? All bets are off."

"Deal."

Well, that was unanimous. Good to know. Whoever this Tana chick was, she was important to them.

The food smelled amazing. Jezzie's stomach growled so loud Rian actually choked on his food. Spluttering and cursing, as Dair went to slap him on the back.

"Eat, Jezzie. We'd rather not be subjected to a Hishaladap mating call while trying to eat, ever again." Damn, Shaggy actually cracked a smile. Straight, bright white teeth and all.

She should've felt embarrassed as they all started laughing uproariously, but she was too damn hungry to pay them much mind. Bacon and waffles were calling her name.

"Do you think she's actually going to come?"

"Tana should have received the message by now, Dair. Hopefully she comes, but I wouldn't put it past her to toy with us a while, although she could very well end up telling us to fuck off. So, who knows?" responded Thad.

When Jezzie was sure she couldn't swallow another bite she leaned back from the table and heaved a sigh worthy of an overstuffed dad unbuttoning his pants after Thanksgiving dinner.

"Thought you might be hungry, Jezzie," commented Rian. "What with not seeing you and Nithe for the last two days. Plus from what the gossipy gorgons were whispering, you two worked up quite the appetite." His mischievous wink made him look like a kid, though with his youthful fae-like features it would take him forever to look his actual age.

"Lay off it, Ri." Dair shoulder bumped his cheeky friend playfully.

"Come, let's all go to the library. There's so much we need to discuss. So much you probably don't know. Hopefully, we have a little time to fill you in."

Theus led the way to the large wooden doors of the library in silence, even his footsteps made not a sound. Pushing the doors wide open he bade them all enter, shutting them securely, before a gorgon tried to slither in.

The cream painted ceiling was home to an elegant chandelier which cast a bright light around the room. Jezzie took in the floor to ceiling bookcases along every wall, ladders and spiral staircases leading to the upper levels of the three-story room. Books filled each shelf almost to overflowing. She damn near fell to her knees and begged them to let her stay there forever. She was sure if she was alone, without Rian and Thad looking at her knowing, she might damn well have had a bookgasm right then and there. This room was like a dream come true.

A large oak desk sat before a massive bay window. Overlooking what, she couldn't tell, the heavy dark blue of the velvet curtains impeded the view. Though, she doubted it was a very pleasant one anyway.

The wing-back leather chair positioned behind it was facing away, as though whoever had last sat there had swiveled as they stood and left before righting it. As she had the thought the chair swung toward them. She jumped back, Ni's hand steadied her as she landed on his foot. The other men? Well they all but purred.

"Well, well, well, look what the Princes of 'Castle Fuck-a-lot' dragged in. Strays, boys? Surely you have more pressing matters to attend to than your duties? Or are you banging these two as well?" The husky, almost smoke roughened voice of the cloaked woman purred sarcastically.

The stranger sat behind the desk as if she owned it. Owned everything within this realm, including the princes who ran it, and maybe she did.

When she lifted her head, Jezzie gasped. It was like looking into a mirror. Not an exact copy, but those were her cheekbones, nose, and her stubborn chin. The similarities ended there, from what she could tell, anyway.

The woman's vibrant purple hair peaked out from under her hood and framed her face, swirling eyes of blue and amethyst judged them all.

"No offense to the two of you, I'm sure you're stand up . . ." She inhaled deeply. "Hmm, a dragon mixed with an angel? Never heard of that before," she queried, as she gestured at Nithe, who was standing slightly to the side of Jezzie.

"But you," she said, pointing to Jezzie. "You smell more familiar. More like me. Oh, I do love a good mystery . . . Fine, I'll take them to him. Come on."

No one moved, except Tana, who jumped up from her seat and made for the door.

"That is what you wanted me to do, right? The whole reason you dared send for me? I mean, if not, no skin off my nose. Just wasted half my day for nothing. Not like I had anything better to do. I'll just be getting back to Doc for some more fun."

The poor princes all started talking at once, until Jezzie whistled loud enough to burst eardrums, luckily only human ones.

"Hi, Tana, is it?" At her nod Jezzie continued. "We don't really know what's going on, but I'm pretty sure we are supposed to go with you. Right, guys?" More nods, this time from the now silent princes. "Right. So, if you could please escort us, that would be great. We just need to grab our stuff and we are good to go. Also, we'd kinda like to know exactly who this mysterious 'he' is, or at least how he's going to help us. I'd rather not walk into another trap if I can help it. I've definitely met my quota for this century, fuck the Fates very much."

"I won't tell you who he is. He won't hurt you though. Not if you mean no harm. Still want to go?" Tana watched them expectantly.

Jezzie looked at Nithe, he nodded slightly. She looked back at Tana and conveyed their agreement. Tana pushed back the hood, freeing her wavy blue streaked purple hair, nodded, and walked out the door.

Taking hold of Nithe's hand she followed Tana out of the library, only to stop short as a heavy pack slammed into her midriff. Nithe's accompanying grunt told her she wasn't the only one. Good thing they packed them up before they sought out food just in case. The gorgon's cackle of glee as she slithered away set Jezzie's anger on fire. Not fast enough, though, you bitch, Jezzie thought as she trained her magic on the evil cow and slashed at her ass with a crack of whip-like shadows. Flesh and scales, there one moment, and gone the next. The creature's shriek of pain sent satisfaction and happy chuckles through the shadow link. One more thing to add to the growing list of abnormal things happening to her lately. A shadow link she could actually hear.

"Nice. I could totally get to like you. So long as you haven't let these pricks wet their wicks, that is," Tana wheezed between belly clutching laughter.

"Maybe next time give us some warning, Jezzie. So we can crack open some windows. 'Cause that shit stinks. Fried gorgon is definitely not a delicacy I want to try in my non-shifted form, thanks." Grimm grimaced.

"Let's go, kids. I said I'd be back before lunch, so we need to hotfoot it, pronto," Tana stated, skipping her way to the main doors.

"You seem awfully happy all of a sudden, Tana. Jezzie and Nithe will make it to him safely, right?" Thad softly interjected.

"You have no idea, Jezzie, how long I've wanted to do something like that to one of those venomous, hussy, bitches. You know, Thad, I am mostly happy these days, just not around any of you assholes. They'll be fine."

Tana smiled sweetly, and gave each of the five men a middle fingered salute.

"I can take you all there a lot faster if you'd like?" offered Rian.

"Not on your life, Ri-Ri." The bitterness in Tana's voice was hard not to hear.

Either these boys, or life in general had served this girl a hell of a shit hand. Jezzie feared it was not one or the other as she hurried to keep pace with the quickly retreating Tana.

The princes moved to follow them, looking like puppies trailing after a really juicy bone, but Tana wasn't having it as she spun to face them.

"I am not in the mood to deal with you dipshits anymore today. Best you turn around, and walk away."

"Come on, Tana . . ."

"I bet you idiots didn't even check them for weapons, huh?"

"Balthazar sent them, Tana. They checked out, and yes, we did, actually. We just happened to give them back, is all."

"We'll see, I'm sure you'll understand if I don't take you at your word. Let's go. I may have eternity, but I don't want to spend it standing here bickering with them."

"You wound us, love. Your words hurt more than you know."

"Good."

With that they started walking.

The trip was rough, but not as long as Jezzie had assumed. Apparently Tana lived closer to the princes than they knew. Something about always making them take the long way round.

"So who's Doc? And why'd they guys react like that?" Jezzie queried.

"Um, nobody." If Jezzie could have seen her face at that moment she'd swear it'd be bright pink. "Just a brand of pleasure products, not that they guys know that. It's just nice to rile them up sometimes."

"Brace yourselves." Was all the warning they got as Tana placed her hand on a nearby boulder, blood trickling down the rough surface, and the ground fell away beneath their feet.

The pain of a heavy landing never came. Instead, they found themselves walking along a wide corridor, white walls streaked with veins of gold.

"So, who are you? And why do you smell like family?"

Tana's question took Jezzie by surprise. Sure, they looked a little alike, but so did a lot of people. What did surprise her was the fact she couldn't pick up a single emotion from Tana, even when she focussed. Nor could she get a read on the condition of the other woman's soul.

Her thoughts skidded to a halt as a man filled the opening ahead of them. She couldn't think, her brain frozen in fear, recognition, and excitement.

"Because she is, Tana. Say hello to your cousin, if I'm not mistaken? I'd recognize the fire in your eyes anywhere, young lady. Does he know you're here?"

"A better question would be, does he even know I exist? Either way, the answer to both would be no."

"Hmm, this should be an interesting story. Come, give your old uncle a hug."

CHAPTER 27
SHADOW HOUND FORTRESS

ONE WEEK LATER…

Heavy, that's what his body felt like. As if weighed down by an elephant. He struggled even to open his eyes. Athon's thoughts shifted through a foggy haze, bouncing here and there on invisible clouds.

Against his front he felt the cool hard surface of a wall, pressed to his back was the hard warmth of a masculine body, and between his legs pulsed the unmistakable feeling of a raging boner as it moved mindlessly against said wall. What the actual fuck? Was he really sleep fucking a wall? How low could a guy get?

"Hmm, maybe we should put that cock to better use, Ath? What do you think?" Roth asked as he undulated his hips against Athon's ass. His deliciously hard cock pressed hard into the valley between Athon's cheeks and up onto his lower back.

Roth's voice sent tingles up his spine. They hadn't really had much time to talk or be alone together since before they left for the dragon realm, at least not while conscious, and he found himself feeling unsure of where he stood. How long had they been asleep, anyway?

His brain stopped its questions the moment his lover's lips skimmed over his ear and down his neck. The instant he felt the delicious sting of teeth nipping at his shoulder his hips jerked so hard he just about put a hole through the wall. Pre-cum would definitely leave a stain on the purple wall, but he didn't care.

Athon tried to shift his body, to turn over, so he could face his lover . . . and failed. One strong hand gripped his left hip, another wove through his colorful hair and held tightly to his scalp, pinning him in place. Which was totally unfair because his palms itched to caress Roth's perfect body.

"Uh-uh, not this time, Ath. Remember that time in Venice? In the backroom of that merchant's place just before his daughter's grand ball? You were so desperate to have me in your ass you begged, said you'd do anything? I was desperate, too. Maybe even more than you as I watched you unbutton your trousers, put your hands on the wall, and looked back over your shoulder at me. Your eyes were full of lust and love, and so many emotions I can't even begin to put names to them all. Do you remember?"

Every word out of Roth's mouth felt like a touch to his cock as they sent him back in time to a simpler place. A place before Mara, before a wall had gone up between them.

"I remember, Az. You gave me exactly what I wanted. You always did."

"And I always will. I may have been a blind fool for a while there, but I want us back, Ath. I want us back, and whatever the future holds. I'm tired of being afraid, even as I fear what that may mean."

"We'll do this together. I promise you, I love you, Azaroth."

"I know you do, never doubted it, Ath. Right now, though, you're going to give me that tight ass of yours, and I'm going to make you come so hard you see stars. Do you understand?" Roth growled sexily.

"Just like Venice?" asked Athon.

"Just like Venice," Roth confirmed.

"Yes, Az."

A fast sharp pain lashed across Athon's firm buttock, shooting sizzling fire through his blood.

"Sorry, Sir. Won't happen again, Sir."

"Good. Now, get on your knees, Ath, and turn around."

As he moved into position he watched Roth rise to stand next to the bed and face him. The male was absolute perfection. There was not a feature, not a freckle with which fault could be found. The male's lips called to him, oh how he wanted to kiss them, taste the sweetness of them. Like a drowning man needed air, he'd been too long without a consistent supply.

Roth fisted a handful of Athon's hair and dragged him forward. Bending down, Roth claimed his lips in a primal kiss of raw power and passion. With one last nip and lave of his lower lip Athon found himself released, air flooding back into his gasping lungs. Roth guided him off the bed and onto his knees on the rug covered floor.

"Ath?" Roth's voice was commanding.

"Yes, Sir?" Athon meekly replied.

"Your mouth should be around my cock. Now!"

He didn't have to be told twice. Roth's magnificent cock stood tall and proud, jutting out from his body, pre-cum already clung to the tip, glistening deliciously. Athon licked it away and moaned deep in his throat. The taste . . . divine.

He teased Roth with little flicks of his tongue, swirled it around the head, under the mushroom-like rim and traced the veins along his cock's length. Savoring Roth's every groan, and thrusting attempt for more contact. He kept his hands on his thighs, knowing better than to touch without permission. Unless he wanted his punishment, and admittedly he usually did.

"No, not like that," Roth growled, his hand once again found the top of Athon's head, and tilted his face up.

"Suck it like you mean it."

Roth gripped the base, lined up Athon's parted lips, and pushed his head down. His hand slipped from his cock and Athon felt the warmth of his palm caress his throat, he was sure his lover could feel the thick mass thrusting in and out of his stretched throat.

Too long had he been without. Not just without Roth, but without anyone. Without Roth, and the promise of his love and their future he'd avoided all others. Oh, he'd given the illusion of sexual activity, else he'd never have heard the end of it. Still, there was only Roth, and the hope for their future triad.

The hot, hard glide of Roth's cock in his throat was amazing. The thick length stretched his mouth wide. He choked repeatedly, his gag reflex out of practice. Yet, his eyes stayed locked on Roth's as he breathed through his nose, his tongue still swirling around the underside of his tasty meal.

The thrusts started coming faster, harder. The grunting sounds of Roth's desire pulsed within Athon's own untouched cock, and sent him closer to the edge of release.

Too soon Roth withdrew from his mouth, despite his desperate attempt to latch onto the bulbous head with his lips.

"What do you want, Ath? Tell me, beg me, and it's yours," Roth offered.

"I want you, Sir. All of you, all the time, for all time."

"Do you want my cock buried in your ass, or should I bury yours in mine?"

Roth's question sent a shudder of longing through his body. He honestly didn't know which option he found most appealing. Either? Both? Whatever the hell Roth wanted. He was putty in the male's very capable hands.

"Mm, your choice, Sir. I am at your eternal service. I worship at the altar of your supreme cock."

"Oh, you do say the nicest things my little punk rebel. I don't think I ever told you how much I love this look on you. Have I? A grave error on my part, but I'll make it up to you, I promise."

Roth didn't wait for his reply. Instead, he helped Athon to his feet, turned him around, and pressed him down over the edge of the bed, his feet still on the floor.

"Hands above your head, Ath. Don't move them, or I will be forced to spank this sexy ass of yours until it's rosy red and hotter than it already is," Roth instructed.

Rough, warm hands stroked over the taut muscles of his back, his thighs, his ass. Hot lips trailed after, a nip here, a lick there, leaving fire in its wake. Athon pushed his hips back and up, seeking more. He tried to widen his stance and received a swift, sharp slap on his exposed and upturned ass. Then . . . nothing except cold air and anticipation for what his lover would do next.

The heat of Roth's body returned quickly, yet Athon shivered as his legs were nudged apart, and Roth pressed in between his thighs. He felt open, exposed, vulnerable. Fuck! He was so damn ready for this. His cock was so damn hard it hurt, pressed as it was between him and the mattress.

"Up on the bed, on your knees, head down, Ath. Bring your ass to the edge, and lift that bad boy up for me," Roth's voice had gotten huskier, sharper with raw desire.

Athon knew what was coming, his heartbeat triple timed with excitement as he did as he was told.

Two thick fingers teased his entrance, the cool, wet glide of the lube relaxed and excited him at the same time.

He and Roth had never used it together before, it hadn't existed in this form back then. Thank fuck they'd moved on from Ancient Greece and olive oil for lubrication. He kept some for his own use, and for what had seemed a futile hope for Roth's return to his bed. Yay to future planning! He was definitely glad he had because of how long it had been.

Athon moaned, his body tensed slightly as Roth's fingers invaded his body, pressed as deep as they could, and shifted, before retreating. They were thrust back in, this time mercilessly, punishingly, unrepentant in their very welcomed intrusion.

More lube coated fingers breached his anus, they curled to stroke his sensitive prostate, and his balls threatened to empty right then and there.

Removing his fingers completely, Roth pressed something small against his opening. The cool gush of liquid that entered him told him the time was nigh, and Roth was not going to hold back.

The bottle was flung to the floor an instant before Roth took hold of one of Athon's hips and slammed the length of his cock into his well-prepared and waiting ass. He spread his legs wider and seated himself more firmly onto the cock of the male behind him, grinding his hips against him for more contact, more friction, more Roth, more everything.

A firm hand lay between his shoulders, pinned him to the bed, and Roth leaned his body down over Athon's back. His cock slid even deeper into him, unleashing twin grunts of pleasure. Athon felt every word Roth whispered in his ear wrap like fingers around his cock.

"Hold on, Leviathon. It's about to get rough, lover mine."

Athon gasped loudly as Roth pulled mostly out. He moaned as he dipped in and out lightly, teasingly, but it didn't last. Roth rammed his hips forward, holding tight to both of Athon's. He was pulled back onto the hard length of Roth's cock even as Roth himself plunged forward. They met with a passion that bordered on pain, a pain which set Athon's blood on fire. The harder Roth fucked him, the deeper he went, the closer Athon came to his own release.

"Sorry, Ath. Can't stop," Roth gasped out between thrusts.

The body above him stilled. The hips pressed tightly to his trembled and jerked. The cock buried completely inside him pulsed and twitched, emptying a full load of cum deep in his eager ass. His own cock twitched, begging for just a little something more. He pushed his cock into the mattress, almost there. A deep groan filled the air as Roth pulled out, and Athon almost begged him to come back.

Roth gently cleaned him off with a warm damp cloth, and rolled him over carefully onto his back. His legs hung over the edge of the bed, but he didn't mind, his feet on the floor. Such a sweet lover was his Az. Always up for the after care.

"Look at you, Ath, still so hard and ready. I bet you're desperate to come for me, aren't you?"

At his nod Roth slid to his knees. Looking down at the man he'd loved for as long as he wished to remember, the man he knew he'd love for eternity, he felt his heart heal just a little bit more.

"Your turn now, Ath. Don't take your eyes off me as you watch me suck your dick. I bet your cum is going to taste amazing. I'm going to swallow every drop. Any problems?"

Athon nodded. Roth looked curious.

"You haven't started yet," Athon replied, his voice full of sass and desperation.

Roth's lips twitched up in a smile a second before Athon lost the ability to think. His cock disappeared between his male's lips. Fuck! He'd forgotten just how magical Roth's mouth felt. Teeth, tongue, lips, even the muscles in his throat. He used every part to create as much pleasure as possible. Fingers caressed his abdomen, another set fondled his balls. Athon's pleasure rose higher, his hips pumped up and down, thrusting his cock into Roth's welcoming mouth. Soft lips latched on firmly and sucked hard, the fingers on his balls moved faster. Athon reached down and threaded his hands through Roth's hair, holding his head in place as he fucked his male's mouth. Once. Twice. Three times. Ecstasy flushed through his body releasing wave after wave of orgasmic pleasure. His cum filled Roth's mouth, and Athon could feel him swallow every drop, the muscles of Roth's throat contracting around his sensitive flesh.

His arms fell to the bed, his energy depleted, his body sated beyond measure. Roth lifted him onto the bed, curled up beside him, and softly sang him to sleep. The male had the voice of an angel. Funny that he was one. Most angels couldn't sing for shit.

BEING with Athon again was more than he'd ever hoped for. Roth didn't really understand anything that was happening lately, but he knew letting Athon back into his life, into the heart he'd never truly left, was the best decision he'd made in a very long time.

Waking with Athon in his arms felt like coming home. Even if he was more than a little afraid it was just a fantasy, a sick joke by the Fates, just so they could rip them apart again.

Something had changed as they'd slept. He'd dreamed of Athon and the mystery woman again, but this time another male had been present. One who spoke, one who seemed important to her, and he wasn't jealous. It was odd, but as the dream progressed he felt a tether form, a bond, like family, wash over him at the thought of the mystery male. Ni, she'd called him. Athon felt it too. He felt frustration bubble up inside him at not knowing where they were, what they were doing.

"You think she's going to let the other guy go, Az?" Athon asked hesitantly.

They'd never thought beyond their little future of three. The possibility of adding another male to the mix wasn't exactly comforting.

"No, Ath, I don't think she will. If she is destined to be ours we'll need to accept it. If she's destined for Luc . . . heads might just roll."

"Well, that's comforting, isn't it?" Athon muttered sarcastically, joy still lit his eyes though. Nothing dimmed Athon's happy when he was on a post sex high, and after his orgasm with Roth and the dream sex, it was a double whammy of balls empty, baby. On the flip side he always seemed to get a little dopey, according to Ath, anyway.

According to Mrs Briars they'd been out for a little over a week, nine days to be exact. She'd met them in the hallway with two cups of tea and some honey biscuits, and bluntly informed them she wasn't the least bit sorry she'd knocked their asses out. Not just theirs, but the rest of the team who'd gone to the dragon realm as well, all except for Deus. Lucky bastard.

The longer they were awake, the worse they felt, it was worse than the worst damn hangover he'd ever had, and he'd had plenty. Which was why Mrs Briars sat the lot of them in the private sitting room next to the cafeteria and practically force fed them cups of sour assed tea and too sweet biscuits. She watched them like a hawk, ready to swoop in at a moment's notice.

They had nothing to do except ponder the information they'd gathered from the dragons and the strange witch.

"Deus and Marco are acting weird. Anyone else noticed that?" Fynn interrupted Roth's thoughts.

"Nope, what do you mean?" grunted Andy, his head down on the cool wood of the table.

"Well, neither of them have come to see us. In fact, they look like they are actively avoiding this particular room. They are spending an inordinate amount of time with the recruits and general pop, though. Not a bad thing, in my opinion we should be more active in that regard, but why the sudden interest? Not to mention when Luc left a few minutes ago they hightailed it out of his path so fast I thought they both had a serious case of gastric distress. Could you imagine those two running to a bathroom before they shit themselves? It looked kinda like that. Sheer panic, boys and girls. Looks like someone added high-tech security, too," Fynn shared.

"Now that you mention it, and since my headache is finally starting to fuck off, what the fuck is up with that?"

Malech's brow furrowed deeply, as if thinking and talking still hurt, and it most likely did. Fuck, it did for him. At least he could sit upright now, but woe betide the person who even thought of opening the thick brocade curtains. Light was not welcome here.

"So, what do you think happened while we were out? What are they up to? Do you think Mrs Briars knows?" Dante sounded annoyingly cheery as he sat forward in his seat.

Damn mystery loving goofball. Could nothing keep that fucker down? Well, yeah, but better he was up than down. At least this way the world wouldn't burn. He'd come to sit with them in the dark as soon as he'd woken. His trip to the well had taken a lot out of him. The taking and disposing of corrupted souls was never a 'done and dusted in a few hours' kind of job.

"Of course she does. Mrs Briars knows fucking everything. Whether she'd tell us what she knows is a whole other question. From their reactions to Luc, though, I'm betting The General is out of the loop, and if she hasn't told him? There's not a fairy's chance in the Chimerian Chasm she'd tell us," Ares snapped. "Now shut the fuck up. I swear, another noise and I'll knock us all back into deep sleep til this shit wears off. Fucking Dragon Ale. Never again."

About twenty minutes later they were summoned to the conference room. Luc was waiting, his eyes tired, but a smile on his face.

Deus, Marco, Perri, and Malphas joined them not long after. Deus and Marco looked tired. Faces gaunt, as if they hadn't slept a wink all week.

Luc watched them closely. Roth could tell he knew something was up and was mulling it all over.

"Right, lads and ladies," Luc winked. "I've just had some very good news, and as I'm big on the whole sharing is caring thing I thought you'd all like to know the latest."

"Luc, not to be a downer or anything . . . But is there a chance you can spit it out? I'd like to crawl back into a hole and die for the rest of the day, if you don't mind." Lily groaned.

Luc laughed, the happy sound bringing a soft smile to Lily's lips.

She in particular felt the weight of Luc's mental decline, as if slowly losing her father, and in a way she was. Luc was the closest she'd ever had to a loving dad. It always broke her to see him so lost. His smile meant the world to her, it shone from her eyes.

"That's dragon ale for you, Lil. Next time don't drink quite so much of it," came Luc's retort. "Well, Ramiel has just informed me the number one most wanted fallen has finally been captured, and is currently in custody awaiting interrogation."

"You don't mean . . ." Malphas's words drifted off in disbelief.

"Yes, Raum has been found, caught, and was apparently presented to them like a trussed up fattened hog, sans the silver platter. We all know of Raum, his reputation has been legendarily bad. So far he's not talking. Ramiel has not disclosed any other details surrounding the Fallen's capture. All other reports are sketchy at best."

The room filled with a sense that something else was going on. Some hidden agenda, and they were out of the loop. Not their monkey, not their zoo, so it made sense in a way.

"Ramiel will be overseeing his interrogation, and it seems personal. With a motherfucker this far fallen, for this long, in some way, it has to be. Am I happy someone entered our realm without asking, not to mention while I wasn't here? No, but since it was Ramiel, and that last part wasn't anyone else's fault but mine, I'll let it slide. Ramiel's return visit has been postponed indefinitely." His eyes locked on Marco and Deus.

"Everyone else can leave. Marco, Deus, we need to have a little chat."

CHAPTER 28

NESTRADIA

FIVE MONTHS LATER (FIVE YEARS EVERYWHERE ELSE)

"Aaahhhhh!"

Tana's excited squeal still echoed in Jezzie's ears five months later. Uncle Micah did eventually get his hug, like, three hours after his grand introduction. He had to slip in and take his chance when Tana finally let go and went to use the bathroom, but still, he got one, and Jezzie couldn't help but soak up the familial affection like a deprived booze hound.

Her cousin. Gosh! It still felt weird to even think it, the girl who'd grown up with only her aunt, and the rare visit from her mom, actually had a cousin. Not just a cousin, but an uncle too! How cool, and odd, was that?

Anyway, her cousin, Tana, was super excited to meet her, to actually have another "friendly" female around. She'd latched on instantly, and basically turned into a loveable, psycho, bouncy bunny for the next two weeks. She'd settled a bit since, and the two of them got along like a house on fire. Especially since they both liked to set evil things literally on fire.

Five months on, and she still hadn't said much about her mom, nor had Uncle Micah; it was obviously a difficult topic for them. What she did know was the Princes were on Tana's shit list for a very good reason, and as repentant as they were, not even Uncle Micah had fully forgiven them, yet. The death of her uncle's wife, his daughter's mother, well, he cast the blame partly at their feet.

She'd learned to leave that particular topic alone, considering she and Nithe both got along well with the princes, and spent time hanging out with them at their castle every few weeks. Tana sometimes even tagged along. She insisted it was to piss them off, and she definitely succeeded in her task, but every now and then Jezzie caught a wistful look of longing cross her cousin's face. A look of "what if/he's so sexy/he's so funny/I wanna lick him real good" which was quickly followed by a hard glint in her eye, and a sharp jab at the lot of them. As if she could fill her words with enough venom to burn away the pain of what they'd done. Thankfully, and annoyingly, the gorgon maids were always underfoot to help divert Tana's bad mood. Pissing them off never failed to put a grin back on her cousin's face.

Nithe was doing great. Each day he seemed lighter. The bond grew stronger. They were ever by each other's side. Even though his memories of Raum, his nightmares, still plagued him, they came less often than they used to. They still dreamed of their other two bondmates, as Nithe called them, but strangely enough only when they stayed the night away from her uncle's home. Though she did dream with Nithe, and not just about sex. Sometimes she was able to pull him from his nightmares, redirect the course of his dreams. Other times she was the one pulled in as she siphoned off his darker, more heartbreaking emotions and replaced them with as much peace as she could muster.

According to her uncle, five months here was equal to roughly five years in every other realm. Her uncle had been trapped in this place for just over thirty years, Tana for twenty-nine, but beyond Nestradia 362 years had slipped away from them.

Also, they'd had to come clean to her uncle and Tana the first day they'd arrived when two rooms were prepared instead of one. It was a bit awkward introducing your unofficial mate to your newly discovered uncle. Thank fuck Uncle Micah was remarkably chill about it. In fact, he'd been a font of information about the dreams, the Astral Plane, the bond, with its tether-like pull, having experienced it all with Tana's mother. While he didn't have shadows or a dragon, the Blessed Reapers were gifted with the golden mists of light.

"The night we first made love—"

"Ew, Dad. Can you at least wait 'til I leave the room. Sorry, guys, I love that they loved each other, but I much prefer the PG version of my youth, so I'm gonna go and take a shower while you all chat about this," Tana explained, walking away making exaggerated retching sounds and holding a hand to her mouth.

Jezzie and Nithe chuckled at her antics. Her uncle just watched her leave, his face awash with a look of adoration and awe.

"Every time she calls me that I can't quite believe how lucky I am," his voice drifted off a little at the end before he gathered himself and refocused.

"Anyway, as I was saying, when we, you know, I felt my mist, and my soul, connect not just with her soul, but with the soul of her phoenix as well. Like ribbons of glittering gold tethered us together and wrapped around us. Binding us. I didn't know what it was, what it meant, nothing. It was unheard of. Impossible. Yet, there it was. In the same moment I heard my mist speak to her, and then to me. I was in awe. It was yet another surprise. My mist longed for her, I longed for her, still do. Not long after Tana was found, my mist grew quieter, eventually, it stopped speaking to me. While I feel the crushing weight of her absence every day, I refuse to think the worst, though I know I am most likely a fool."

He took a deep breath before he continued on, his right hand rubbing circles on his chest, above his heart. As though it ached still for the love he had lost.

"Like the good soldier I was, I went straight to Leraie, the Almighty's right hand, and was sworn to secrecy. I spent every spare second I could with Idalia. A phoenix having an unauthorized relationship with someone outside their species was almost criminal, but we didn't care. She was so strong, so brave. Two weeks later the Almighty found us in our hideaway, and held a ceremony to declare us wed, our bond officially recognized. Just not publically. Not yet, or so the Almighty insisted. It

was the happiest moment of my life, and the one which fills me with the utmost regret." His gaze drifted away like clouds on a breezy, sun-filled day.

"I don't understand," Nithe gently prodded. "How could you regret such a bond?"

"I could never regret the bond, nor the marriage. What I regret is not sweeping her in my arms and carrying her away with me to some place far from her people the moment the Almighty left our presence. If I had I would have known of our child. I would have spared her the betrayal of her people, her queen, her friend. I would have allowed no one to harm her." Silent tears slid down his cheeks as he spoke, barely a whisper on a breath.

"Instead we indulged our wedded bliss and parted ways for what should have been only a few days or weeks. Someone else had other plans, and I found myself stuck here against my will. Seeing as I was already locked in this space and couldn't leave, some shit about a prophecy. I swear I'll gut those bitches of Fate myself one day. The Almighty gifted me with this place. Including access to news from Earth so I could keep up to date. Apparently the plan doesn't allow me to leave just yet, but when I do I'll find the bastard who sent me here and gut him like a tri-horned nargwraith. I suspect he's also responsible for Tana and her mother being tossed in here too. Especially since the Almighty is staying silent on the topic."

"I'm so sorry, Uncle. I wish I could have met her," Jezzie whispered as she moved to give him a hug, dragging Nithe with her because she refused to let him go.

"I'm so glad you are here, my girl. I can't wait to see the look on your old man's face when he sees you for the first time. At least I hope I'm there for it." The grin on her uncle's face was positively mischievous.

"Oh, and when he meets you Nithe, you better be prepared for the wrath of the father. It's going to be one hell of a show."

As Nithe's face blanched Micah laughed even harder, the sadness of earlier dimming in the light of new joy. Ever present and not forgotten, just hidden for the now.

"Now, I know you probably have a thousand more questions, yes? Alas, I don't have all the answers. When the Almighty sent Leraie here

not long after my arrival her messenger said some vague shit prophecy shit about changes coming for all angel kind, the dutiful would be rewarded after all this time. Shit like that. Then she told me I needed to stay here and await my time. As well as imposing a geas which means anyone who knows of my presence here cannot speak of it with those who don't, not until the Almighty personally allows them to do so. Which means, my dear niece and nephew-in-law, you are now included in some very rare company and unfortunately bound by those same terms. My only advice is to just roll with it. The Almighty is a capricious being who will only reveal things when they wish them to be revealed."

"Jezzie! There you are!" Tana's excited voice called from behind her.

"Hey, Tan, what's up?" Jezzie couldn't help but grin as the pocket rocket barreled toward her.

Tana was all of five foot four inches tall, with long, gorgeous purple hair in a braid down to her butt, swaying all Jan Brady-like as she ran. Her flawless light brown skin always seemed to glow with an ethereal golden radiance when she was happy, and this seemed to be one of those times. She slammed to a stop, her cheeks flushed, and reached up to grab Jezzie's shoulders for support.

Tana was extremely fit. The woman could run a 10k marathon in record time, so it didn't really make sense. Unless . . .

"Tana, shit, it's happening, isn't it?" Jezzie felt herself start to panic. "Did you take the potion Leraie left behind?"

"What? I'm fine. It's not time for that shitfest yet. You're late for your last flying lesson with Dad and your Nithey-poo though, so you better hurry your ass up, cousin mine."

She must have seen the disbelief plainly written on Jezzie's face. Sweat had started to bead at her temples, and her skin was more radiant than usual. In fact, the closer Jezzie looked at her cousin the more her aura shifted. Using her gift she delved into Tana's emotions, saw the utter chaos swirling deep within, and felt the violent tremors of the needing headed her way. Pulling back she focused on Tana's body, lavender-blue flames and golden mist mixed together as they shimmered around her. She had to look hard, but they were there.

"Seriously, Coz, I have another day or two, I swear. I'm perfectly fine. "

And just like that Tana crumpled to the floor in a heap of tight fitted green leather and cream cotton fabric. Thankfully Jezzie caught her head before it hit the flagstones by her bed, called to Nithe along the link they shared for an assist, and told him to bring Uncle Micah with him knowing they were probably waiting for her in 'Paradise'.

<hr>

YOU WANT THEM, Tana. You can have them, all of them.

The voice whispered in her head. She did, she did want them, it was true.

Let them in. Go to them. You can quench the hunger that twists your body into knots of icy pain. They want you too. They long to hold you, touch you, to lick every inch of your body and take you with their impressive cocks.

She could. They would. They all definitely did have impressive cocks. Large and thick, each one unlike the other. They scared her the one time she'd seen them all those years ago, when she'd been naught but a naive virgin. Fine, she was still technically a virgin in the literal sense, but she sure as shit was no longer naive.

Call for them, beg for them. We want them, need them to fill us. To soothe the burn, to ease the need. You can trust them. We can have them now.

Wait. Hold up. WTF? Trust them? The assholes who left us to fight or die? Sometimes both? Who'd hosted massive orgies with the gorgon sluts and any passably pretty bitch sent to this pit? Instead of doing their duty and observing every entry to this realm on the off chance innocents ever made it through the portals? Oh, would you look at that, two did. Her mother had died, forced to leave her alone, with no protection save her wits. With no way back to protect her daughter. All because they couldn't resist getting their dicks wet at every opportunity. Assholes.

Her eyes flew open, but all she saw was white. Pain lashed her body, her limbs felt like they were twisted in agony, the muscles moving in ways they never should. In reality she knew they were dead weights, immovable until the lull before the storm. It would only get worse. Why now?

Of fucking course. She should have paid closer attention. She never spent any time around bonded mates before. The books Leraie had given her had warned her about her kind's cycle being more susceptible to the pheromones of bonded mates. The fact her cousin and Nithe had been taking full advantage of their alone time meant her damn hormones were soaking that shit up, and kicking her ass for not finding her mate. Well . . . No, nope, she hadn't found him. Wouldn't even contemplate those asswipes being hers, destiny be damned. Nope, if so, the Fates were out of their ever loving minds.

Her body burned like dry ice. As the pain spiked higher, black spots filled her vision and her eyelids slammed shut as oblivion pulled her under once more.

"Where is it? It should be here. It's always left in the top drawer of her nightstand."

Jezzie watched her uncle tear apart his daughter's room in a frantic search for the elixir used to stave off the painful effects of the female phoenix needing cycle. She slid a cool, damp cloth over Tana's forehead and cheeks as she lay on the feather soft mattress in her room. They'd brought her here as soon as her uncle had seen Tana's still form and realized what was happening.

Tana's eyes flashed open suddenly, startling a gasp out of her. Her cousin's eyes were completely white, her face expressionless, as if carved from stone. Just as suddenly they snapped closed and her rigid limbs went completely lax.

Turning her head she looked at her uncle. He'd paused his search at her sharp inhalation and regarded his daughter with the look of a tortured, helpless father. Which in this moment was exactly what he was.

"This is just the first wave. The next will be worse, the one after, worse still. Female's of her species, well, her mother's species, have a breeding cycle which lasts thirteen days. The only way, other than the elixir, to negate the negative effects, is to bed one's chosen or fated mate, or at least reaffirm the bond with a ritual. Alas, having been born in this place, and her inability to leave, she hasn't had the opportunity to find that special someone. Stuck here as she is, how the hell does the Almighty expect her to find that someone?"

A silent tear slid down Uncle Micah's cheek as he brushed a stray strand of purple hair from Tana's cheek and tucked it behind her ear. His head dropped forward, his chin dipped toward his chest.

Jezzie opened her mouth to voice her suspicions about the princes, but Nithe's gentle touch, and the small shake of his head, helped her keep her words to herself. He's right, it's not her place to speculate, plus, Tana wouldn't thank her for the interference in her affairs, or lack thereof.

"Leraie!"

Jezzie's head whipped back to her uncle as he threw back his head and yelled at the ceiling.

"Leraie, get your ass down here. Or I swear I'll find a way out of here just to find you."

"Now, now, Michael, my boy, such language. No need to yell."

The soft lilting voice startled her and Nithe, but Michael just spun on his heel and glared at the newcomer. Her long black and white hair, mostly black with white interspersed here and there, hung loosely about her porcelain shoulders, pulled back away from her face in a half up style with long white bangs parted on the side. Her oval face was so pale she was almost truly white, bar the barely visible light flush to her cheekbones. Softly arched black eyebrows lay above sultry acorn brown eyes framed by expertly applied black and gray eyeshadow and long thick matching eyelashes. Black lined, dark red lipstick coated her lips, the lower lip plumper than the upper with its well-defined cupid's bow. She smiled sadly at them from the open doorway.

Damn, this woman either had mad makeup skills, or had her own makeup artist on call. Jezzie had never seen someone whose face held such perfect symmetry. But, she'd definitely heard that voice before. If only she could remember where and when.

Looking past them, the woman focused her gaze on Tana, who still lay unresponsive on her bed.

"Ah, I see it is time," she murmured to no one in particular.

"Where is the elixir, Leraie? I cannot find it. Did you not deliver it? Did you bring it with you?" Uncle Micah fired off his questions to the mysterious Leraie in rapid succession, giving her no time to answer until he was done. Not that she looked overly bothered by his urgency. In fact, her response was delivered with such calm detachment one would think her made of marble, save for the faint glimmer of unshed tears Jezzie could see in her eyes and the barely there tendril of sadness and regret which made its way into Jezzie's pores.

"There isn't one. Not this time."

"What do you fucking mean, 'not this time'?" her uncle growled. His muscles tensed and his body readied itself as if to go to war. Jezzie had no doubt he would do exactly that if he thought it would help.

"The Almighty has decreed it so. The time has come, enough leeway has been given, and destiny will wait for no one. Your daughter needs a shove out of her rut, she cannot keep dragging her feet, Michael. So there will be no more elixir until she figures out her destiny."

"What the fuck? That's bullshit, and you know it, Leraie. She's stuck here just as much as I am, and yet you expect her to find her destiny? In this place? Full of monsters and supernatural convicts who barely survive a year? Tell the Almighty where to shove that proclamation and get me the damn elixir."

Never had she seen her uncle so enraged. His pure white wings made larger shadows fall around the room, and his golden mist rushed toward Leraie. Only to stop short of their target and snap back into his body almost violently.

"Stop the parlor tricks, Michael. It wasn't my call. I'm just the messenger, my boy." She looked sad as she shook her head and made to turn away.

"Cut the shit, Leraie. You could help if you so wished. Instead you choose to be a whipped bitch, servicing a destiny designed by the Almighty, watching as we suffer loss and despair, as my daughter endures pain beyond compare. You choose to do nothing." Came the verbal offensive of one helpless and angry father. "It's like you don't even care!"

It happened so fast Jezzie jumped and glued herself to Nithe's side. His strong arms snapped around her, his warmth soothed her racing heart.

Where once the picture perfect, classically gothic face of the beautiful Leraie had been, dirty skin the color of gray stone now looked back at them, cracked and broken. Her previously golden brown eyes were completely white, except for the black of her pupils. The makeup around her eyes was smeared and smudged, spreading like veins through the cracks in her skin. Her lips disappeared, morphing into a scary black grin which reached from one ear to the other, black tendrils of shadow-like ink licked out above, below, and along its length. She could have stepped straight out of a horror film and scared the shit out of most humans.

What had even Jezzie jumping back though was when she opened her mouth rows of viciously sharp teeth lined the top and bottom all the way along the wide slit, and a red, thick, forked tongue flicked out as she spoke. Her eyes glued to the object of her anger. Her voice, the stuff of nightmares and sin.

"Remember yourself, Michael. Remember your place," she hissed, angrily. "It is not for you to question and it never was. Don't you ever doubt my care for that child! I would die a thousand deaths for any of the righteous. Destiny must be fulfilled, it is the only way. I have seen the sands of time and spoken with the Fates. The Almighty has both blessed and cursed me. I do what I can, when I can."

Turning she locked her creepy gaze on Jezzie.

"Remember, Jezebeth, see past the fear. Remember me."

And then she was gone. Vanished, as if she were never there.

Her uncle's roar shook the cavern, a light layer of dust settled over the room. His anguish plain to see.

It was bullshit, utter bullshit, all of it. Nope. Fuck this shit. There was no way she was going to sit on her ass while Tana endured this pain. No one, not even the Almighty, was going to force her cousin to do something she didn't want, or wasn't ready for. But, what the fuck could she do?

A glimmer of silver caught her eye in the doorway. A mark on the frame no bigger than a quarter, but it drew her closer as she shrugged off Nithe's hold and moved toward it. Her fingers reached out to touch it of their own volition, as if in a trance. The moment her skin brushed against it, she felt a rush of cool liquid spread up her arm and over her temples and a release of pressure she never even realized had been there.

Several memories flooded her brain. Long-lost snippets, moments of her childhood, and in each one Leraie was there. Speaking with her aunt behind a half closed door, smiling at her when she scraped her knee as she ran up the rough path to meet her. Every birthday when she'd handed Jezzie her gift with a smile and hug, reading her a bedtime story the first time she'd cried and questioned why her mom had to leave her behind. Her first heartbreak and the minor hex she'd suggested to Aunt Rai Rai. Most importantly though, was the time she told her aunt to include a young Jezzie in the preparation of potions and spells.

A feeling of familial love spread through her, filling the gap Leraie had left with the block on her memories.

It was a good thing she had a damn near eidetic memory when it came to books, and that her uncle kept a fully stocked herbal garden in 'Paradise'.

She silently thanked her aunt for all the studying she'd made her do, and for training her as she would a born witch. Leraie had obviously planted the seed a long time ago.

One Anti-Needing potion coming right up. Well, as soon as she could make it. She just hoped it worked, considering it was actually for wolf shifters and all. On the bright side it had worked on an eagle shifter once, and since her cousin was also in the avian family, Jezzie was pretty hopeful of a positive outcome.

"Uncle, I can fix this, maybe," she blurted out in excitement when she opened eyes she hadn't realized she'd closed. "There's a potion I know which may work. Though it will take me at least a few hours to prepare it, that's if you have the ingredients I need. Apparently I've known Leraie much longer than just today."

"If Leraie somehow led you to this knowledge, then you will find what you need in the garden. She designed it, planted it, and tends to it personally." A small sigh of relief seemed to deflate her uncle's previous anger, and hope lit like a spark in his eyes.

Jezzie turned excitedly to Nithe.

"Ready to take a trip to 'Paradise,' babe?"

"As soon as possible, *a stór*." He winked, causing Jezzie to feel a rush of heat fan her cheeks as she realized what she'd said. "But right now we have a garden to raid."

CHAPTER 29

As they sprinted away from Tana's room down the polished stone corridors Nithe held Jezzie's hand tightly in his own. His mind was still racing. Sure, he wanted to get his mate naked as soon as possible and ravage her to the point she was barely conscious from multiple intense orgasms, but . . .what the fuck had just happened? All levity aside, internally he was freaking the fuck out.

He'd learned a lot about Jezzie in the last five months. She'd been raised mostly by her aunt because her mother was afraid the mystery man who thought he'd killed her would come back again. Her aunt was a witch, one of the best. Together he and Jezzie had faced, and fought creatures which should only exist within the minds of frightened children, or on the pages of some terrifying horror novel, so he'd seen first hand how tough his Jezzie was.

He was one of the few who knew who her father was, and the thought of meeting him, as daunting as meeting your mate's father after the deed was done already, was, in and of itself, struck icy terror into his heart. If her father dared reject her, he just might attempt to kill the bastard himself. Attempt, because he knew he wouldn't stand any chance of actually succeeding.

All the things he'd learned, big and small, and still she managed to surprise him. She knew Leraie. A being steeped in mystery, someone most never even caught a glimpse of, and she knew his Jezzie. Even fewer had seen her second face, he was sure he'd be impressed if he wasn't also shitting his pants a little at the thought of what she was capable of. The first angel. The very first vessel created by the Almighty to house both dark and light. Rumored to have gone mad for millions of years from the agony of warring forces inside her as they battled for supremacy. Messenger of the Almighty, and Commander of The Unseen.

How did he know all of this? Because, as isolated as his birth realm now was, they hadn't always been so. Leraie was as old as the first stars ever to light the sky of the first realm. Despite popular opinion, that realm wasn't the one named Earth. She was a being of legend, even to dragons. Nobody crossed Leraie, ever. So then, why was Michael still standing with nary a scratch? Why had disappointment and hurt flashed across her face the instant before her second nature took over?

It was that side of Leraie which terrified Nithe. The unknown danger of her dark side which held a slight menace and caused shivers of apprehensive goosebumps to cover his skin. All too reminiscent of the darkness which haunted his nightmares.

His arm bounced up and down, his shoulder jarred as he stumbled over progressively rougher stones in the floor, and he was jolted out of his ruminations. Jezzie's excitement bubbled out of her and filled the air with childlike exuberance. So unlike the somber Jezzie just moments ago. No, now she had a purpose. Some way in which she could ease her cousin's suffering.

The closer they got to Paradise, as Tana had named it, the more rough-hewn the corridor became. The walls, floors, and ceiling became nothing more than a tunnel, dug out with pickaxes and shovels. It was purposely done, unlit and filled with the smell of wet, musty earth.

The Almighty had created this space for Michael back when he'd first arrived. While he was kept captive here with the excuse of some destined fate, it was never intended to be a punishment. Michael, however, saw it differently.

As they rounded the last corner and faced the stone wall of a seemingly dead end, Jezzie reached out her hand to touch the smoothest part of it. The slight hitch in her breath and the sharp scent of blood came seconds before the wall moved, parting like curtains to reveal the splendor of the land within.

It always had the power to inspire both awe and peace in him. The grass was lush grass, the mountains peaked high in the clouds, and the sun shone down on them with a comfortable warmth. Never too hot or too cold, always just right. How such a large expanse of land, complete with its own sky and climate managed to fit in the tiny cutout deep in Michael's lair was a miracle. It rained when the plants needed rain, the seasons shifting on a whim, even as the sun stayed the same until the moon rose to usher in the night. Small woodland animals roamed free, and the waterfall and lochs were a divine experience in and of themselves.

"Come on, Ni. We need to hurry. Thank fuck the gardens aren't far from the door, otherwise we could have been hiking for hours."

Jezzie gave him a wink as she licked at a rivulet of bright red blood as it trickled down her palm toward her wrist. Her pretty pink tongue swirled expertly to catch every drop before it could leave her flesh. Blood held power, he knew that. Dragons were taught the truth of this from the cradle. Many a dragon had been brought undone by blood magic, even at inexperienced hands.

Watching Jezzie lick it up and run her tongue along her pearly white teeth had the instant effect of making him as hard as the stones beneath his feet. So much so the teeth of his zipper were probably leaving permanent indents along his shaft. By her wink she knew the effect her actions had on him, cheeky minx.

Her giggle echoed in the air as she bolted seconds before his hands would have grabbed her waist to haul her up against the monster she'd roused. Nithe sprinted after her, lifting her in his arms as they slid to a stop in front of the garden gate.

Giggles turned to howls and pleas for mercy as he tickled her senseless. She loved tickles in that she loved to be the one tickling, on the other hand being tickled was pure torture for her. Something of which he was reminded moments later as her foot flew back and kicked him right in the balls. Finding herself unceremoniously dumped on her ass on the pebble path, Jezzie let out an indignant grunt. Her grumpy look faded as she noticed him keeled over and hunched on the ground.

"Shit, Ni. I'm so sorry, sweetie. I'll kiss it all better later, I promise. I didn't mean it. Are you okay? Ni, say something. You're scaring me," Jezzie begged, her voice full of contrition and concern as she dropped to her knees to cup his cheek in her palm.

"I'm fine," he managed to wince out before he took a deep breath and pushed to his feet, her soft skin still pressed to his face.

She looked so forlorn he couldn't resist placing a light kiss upon her downturned lips, and found himself wrapped in the tight embrace of her arms in a flash. Another soft kiss on the top of her head as he inhaled the scent of her hair had her looking up with a small smile, her eyes soft and doe-like in the spring sunlight of another day in Paradise.

"Let's get this done, Jez. The longer we take the longer Tana suffers."

Those words set a fire under his woman's ass as she bolted for the baskets kept by the gate. She hurried through it, weaving through the myriad of maze-like garden beds and paths as she shouted instructions over her shoulder, listing ingredients he needed to collect. As if he knew what even half of them were.

She stopped and looked back when she realized he hadn't moved and finally yelled, "Cherries." At last, something he could identify easily. Nithe grabbed a basket and raced to the fruit tree section of the garden.

Once he'd completed the task, he raced back to the gate to await his next instruction. Except, Jezzie was already waiting with three baskets on the ground at her feet filled with a myriad of different ingredients. She watched him approach, and her impatient frown turned into a smile, then a chuckle, and though she tried to hold it back, snorts escaped until she devolved into fits of laughter.

"You, you . . . Sorry, give me a moment."

He stood there utterly perplexed and waited for her to calm herself, unsure as to what he'd done. Did he have twigs in his hair? Cherry juice on his face? Sure, he'd snuck a few in, but cherries were his favorite fruit, what did she expect?

"You told me to get cherries, so I got cherries. Did I do something wrong?" he asked, his brow furrowed in confusion.

"Yes, I did, didn't I? Some cherries, not the whole tree, sweetie."

Nithe felt his shoulders droop, he felt a little silly for having picked so many.

"Ni? Sweetie? I actually love that you picked so many. They're my favorite, too. Also, it means whatever we don't use we can eat later, and I can lick the juice from your sexy as sin naked body."

By the time she finished speaking her voice had turned to a sultry husk and a shiver of anticipation heated his blood. Oh, how he looked forward to coating her smooth, wet lips and licking the mixed juices from between her spread thighs.

"Let's focus then, *a stór*. I know how much Tana means to you. How long will it take to prepare everything?"

Jezzie was silent until they reached the doors to the corridor and stepped through, leaving the beauty of Paradise behind to face reality once more. Her brow was furrowed in thought as she nibbled at the right side of her lower lip.

"Well, it's hard to say exactly. Depending on how long it takes to prep all the ingredients properly. If it's just me, then probably around four hours. If I have help it could be as little as three. Once all the ingredients are combined it has to simmer for about two hours, give or take."

"I'm at your full disposal, my lady. Whatever you need, I will do." He would have offered a gallant bow had they not been in such a hurry.

Reaching the doorway to Tana's room, Jezzie looked at her tired uncle, worry lines etched into his still youthful face.

"Uncle Micah, is there a sacred space around here that has a fire, cauldron, and other supplies? I know it's a long shot but . . ."

He saw Jezzie's shoulders slump slightly as she spoke. What if they didn't have these things?

"I don't, unfortunately, but I think Leraie might have set up what you need. She has a room here, hidden away down a tunnel I'm forbidden to enter. Never been in there myself, but she always referred to it as her sacred space and only the gifted and their familiars would be allowed entry. I'll take you there. I just hope it has what you need."

Michael took one of Jezzie's baskets and led the way down twisted paths to a corridor which seemed to shift with restless energy. On one wall was a gold gilded frame six foot tall and about three foot wide. Within it was a rather odd carving of a wrinkled woman coming out of a tree, or maybe she was the tree. A willow as far as he could see. Either way, it seemed the woman was reaching right out toward them, her lips pulled back revealing rotted, blackened teeth with sharp points, her eyes locked on Michael.

"Yeah, yeah, you crazy old bat, I'm not going to try and enter. I learned my lesson the last fifteen times I tried. I'm just hoping they can," Michael said, pointing toward him and Jezzie sheepishly.

Her gaze flew from Michael's smiling face to lock onto Jezzie's intrigued, and slightly shocked one.

"I've seen you before, I know I have, but I cannot for the life of me place when, nor where," Jezzie whispered breathlessly.

As I have you, child. I have been waiting. She said you would come. You and your familiar may enter herein, the wizened figure croaked out telepathically.

"I'm not a witch and I don't have a familiar," protested Jezzie, sounding rather confused.

Sure you are, child. Your aunt has been training you from the cradle. You may not be a born witch, but you became one nonetheless. Just because he's also your mate does not make him any less your familiar. No other blood-bound witchling has been blessed with a dragon, young one. 'Tis an honor, indeed. You can thank me later.

Nithe swore he saw her wink as a sparkle lit her wooden gaze. Honestly, he wasn't offended to be referred to as her familiar, in fact, it was an honor, one which had the dragon inside him purring with delight. One more thing he could be to her, for her, and would bind them closer than before.

"I'm going to go and keep an eye on Tana. Please send Nithe to get me if you need anything," Michael said as he went to walk back by them and stopped to face Jezzie. "Hurry, dear one. I absolutely don't want to be stuck in that room when the curse of her needing reaches the next stage."

Nithe caught the visible shudder as it moved over Michael's body.

Honestly, he couldn't blame the guy for his reaction. Tana was his daughter, and no parent wanted to even think of their child, even fully grown, going through what Tana was going to endure simply because of her biology. The females of the phoenix species were cursed to suffer greatly through the needing. The next stage would see her body emit pheromones which would induce sexual desire in any male within range. Thankfully blood relations were spared, so Michael was in the clear. Still, her body would writhe and experience the desire she was projecting, and no father wanted to witness that. Nithe wasn't related to her which would have posed a problem had he and Jezzie not completed their bonding with a blood transfer and mutual marking. Unfortunately, he would still be affected by it, except his desire would be directed at Jezzie. Normally a very good thing, but he was worried it would distract her from their quest to help Tana.

Fuck, the girl had become like a kid sister to him. In no way would he hurt her if he had the choice. Not like his bio siblings though, not anymore. Those assholes had turned on him long ago. His brothers, as soon as they'd realized he had a different father, and his sister, when she'd seen just how different he was from the rest of them. The lot of them could go suck a sour, shriveled old wiener for all he cared.

The carving slid to the side, closer to Michael, revealing a sconce lit, yet still darkened entrance passage. Michael nodded to the carving and stepped away from them with a small smile. At some point Jezzie must have responded during his introspective thoughts and her uncle handed her back the basket he'd been carrying. Before Michael could take but a few steps away down the corridor a thin branch flicked out to lightly slap him on the ass.

"I knew you liked me, witch," Michael said with a smug wink.

The carved woman didn't look Michael's way in response. Though, Nithe heard an amused cackle echo in his mind. He doubted he'd have heard her if not for his connection to Jezzie. Dragons could only speak telepathically with their own clan mates, and only when in dragon form. Well, except with their bonded mates. The sound of Michael's amusement trailed behind him as he made his way back to Tana.

Stepping through the oval doorway into the short entrance, Nithe wasn't sure what to expect, but as soon as Jezzie stopped on the first step into the circular room she sighed with what could only be described as contentment. She slipped off her shoes, and he did the same before they stepped down into the hallowed place before them.

Dark wooden shelves filled with books, jars and all manner of strange and mundane objects lined the wall from one side of the door to the other. Three steps led down to the sunken, soft grass and rich soil covered the floor. Except for a stone lined circle filled with sand within which a fire pit sat, a medium-sized black cauldron suspended above it. A large stone table stood off to one side, a gas cooktop with a separate oven at one end, cloth covered items on the other, an electric blender in the middle, and two dark wooden stools sat ensconced beneath it.

"Well, that should cut down on some of the prep time," Jezzie pointed out as she gestured to the blender with a smile.

Light flared from an unseen source, bathing the room in a mystical glow. Nithe looked up in search of its source and gasped, he reached out to tug on Jezzie's hand in order to draw her gaze to the view above. Thick wooden beams traveled up the sloped ceiling from the top of the wall where they were attached to a large circle of thick cast iron about seven feet in diameter. Within the circle a perfect pentagram had been crafted, all five points touching both iron and wood. It was what lay beyond the outline of the sacred shape that caused their wonder, though. For beyond the pentagram lay a perfectly full moon, craters and all, as if it had been hung to fit perfectly within the casing of the circle above. The light it created was magical, as though glittering stardust shimmered through the air and danced like sprites on every surface.

The smell of dried herbs and flowers and old books filled his senses and pulled him away from a sight that werewolves would give their left testicle to see just once. Jezzie made her way to the bench, and he followed, placing his basket down alongside hers. Despite the sand on the ground and cloth covered items not a speck of dust graced the pristine surfaces.

A delicate hand reached out and lifted the silvery cloth to reveal what had been hidden. Two trays of rustic, hammered copper held several mortars and pestles, an array of knives and other implements and vials of all sizes, a decanter filled with dark red liquid, as well as a folded card with Jezzie's name scrawled artfully on one side. She looked at

Nithe in hesitation, his slight nod seemed to be all she needed as she reached out and lifted the card from where it rested. After a deep breath she braced herself and started to read it out loud.

Jezzie,

Dear child, so much time has passed, and yet I know you will remember what to do as if it were yesterday. Your Aunt Sarai taught you well, you were always a quick study, and the blood bond she gifted you with passed the same magic to you that will one day flow through the veins of her children.

I built this place for you so long ago, knowing you would need it, even before your birth. Use it wisely. You will find all you need in this place, whenever you need it.

Your mate shall ground you when you need grounding, and keep you from falling when you need to let the magic in you fly free.

On the seventh shelf of the seventh cupboard to the right of the door as you face it, you will find a collection of sacred items. You will need to choose one for the final step, as I'm sure you remember. Personally, I'd choose the phoenix stone one. Quite apt, don't you think? Though the choice is entirely yours, just remember to follow the call of the magic in your blood, my dear.

May the power of the earth beneath your feet, the moon above you, and the goodness of your heart guide you.

Someday we'll once again sit and laugh over the chipmunks as they play by the lake. Be safe.

Leraie

HE SAW the slow fall of a tear slide down Jezzie's cheek, and he moved to cup her face gently in his hands, wiping the moisture away with his thumb. A small smile trembled on her lips as he placed a soft kiss atop her head and drew her into his arms. He wanted to keep her there forever, but after one shuddering sigh she pulled herself together, and they got to work.

His task was to pit as many cherries as would fit into the bowl she placed before him, probably about a third of what he'd picked. Jezzie prepped the oven and took one of the many trays from a shelf and laid out a few handfuls of chestnuts for roasting before she popped it in to do its thing. The cloves were placed into a heated pan on one of the burners, tossed gently for a few minutes then removed from the heat to cool. Their fragrance filled the room.

Many a summer he'd spent sneaking cherries from his stepfather's orchard. His fingers flew from one cherry to the next as he watched his love grab a board and knife to finely chop the herbs, before placing each one into a mortar and pestle, then wiping everything down to start again. Mint, dandelion, horehound, licorice root, and cowslip flowers.

In a small pot she placed some dogwood berries and water from a tap near the door he hadn't even noticed before, and set it to boil. As she waited for them to be done, she started to work the pestle in the first mortar, then moved onto the next.

Nithe finished the cherries and set them aside. He washed his hands, then started to grind the horehound. Jezzie told him the properties of each of the items as they worked.

Cherries for muscle relaxation and taste. Chestnuts and cinnamon for strength of mind and endurance. Cloves and dandelions for contentment and comfort. Cowslip for privacy. Dogwood berries for sleep. Horehound for healing. Licorice root to slow the libido, and mint for happiness.

Once the cherries were blended and the berries were crushed and strained Jezzie mixed them together. The chestnuts had been removed and allowed to cool slightly before being crushed in the blender as well. Once everything was prepared to Jezzie's liking Nithe started the fire under the cauldron with one burst of green flame. Jezzie was surprised the acid didn't melt everything, but he explained he'd always been able to control the ratio of acid to fire in his flames.

Into the cauldron Jezzie poured the dark red liquid. Wine by the smell of it as it hit the base of the cast iron. One by one the other ingredients were added. With every addition Jezzie repeated a lilting chant.

"Spirits, we thank you."

The last thing she placed into the now bubbling brew was a length of plain white, soft cotton fabric she'd had him cut from a spool, which had appeared on the bench without warning. They banked the fire allowing the brew to simmer. All they could do next was sit back, watch, and wait.

CHAPTER 30

J ezzie paced in circles around the room, checking the cauldron every so often, waiting for the spark of mystical flame to burst free. She'd already grabbed a bag and filled it with the black candles she would need for the ritual, along with a jar of equal parts sand and salt, and two strips of black fabric. There was only one more thing to gather, but still she hesitated. Every now and then she'd investigate the contents of a shelf or flip through the pages of some heavy tome as she wandered, all the while knowing she'd have to slip a sacred athame into her pocket for when it was needed. Thank the heavens for deep pockets, and that she'd chosen to wear this particular knee-length dress and leggings set this morning. She wasn't sure how Nithe would react to what needed to be done, but she couldn't risk him going all overbearing dragon mate on her ass until after the fact.

"Jez, love, stop. You're making me dizzy over here. You've been walking in circles for the past forty minutes. I swear, if you open the same damn book again, for the sixth time in a row, I'm going to have to drag you over here and put those hands of yours to work elsewhere, and that pretty, pouty mouth of yours too. Just go ahead and get whatever it is Leraie said you were going to need. I trust you to do what you need to do, and to keep yourself safe while doing it, okay?"

"The link?" she asked, looking sheepish.

Nithe made his way over to her, cupped her face in his palms, inched her chin up until she looked into his eyes, his head tilted to the side, and placed a soft kiss close to her ear. The warmth of his breath sent sparks of desire through her blood as his whispered words began.

"Even without the link, *a stór*, I'd know something was up. I know you now, remember? You are a part of my soul. Plus, you read Leraie's letter out loud. You've also been a jittery bundle of nerves ever since you suddenly gasped, jumped up, and tried to look busy about an hour ago. How could I not know something was up?" Nithe's amused chuckle made her heart flutter in her chest and the lead ball in her stomach dissolved.

"I just don't want you to worry, I guess. It's stupid really, considering everything we've both been through, and the fact I hunt monsters in order to survive. But, you're right, I wasn't thinking straight. I'd end up doing more harm to you if it were a surprise."

Nithe's thumbs rubbed gentle circles on the sensitive skin beneath her ears, and she felt the tense adrenaline leave her body in a rush. Damn, that felt good.

"Share with me, *a stór*," he whispered. His tongue traveled languidly around the outer edge of her ear before his lips suckled on her earlobe. She gasped wordlessly as his teeth grazed the malleable flesh an instant before he released her and stepped back, his own breathing labored.

"Hop to it, you seductress, you. Else I'll just have to ravish you in the here and now."

His wink was playful and Jezzie couldn't stop the giggle which bubbled up and out of her mouth. Both at his over the top expression and the release of the mental tension she'd been carrying within.

"Well, as tempting as that is, Ni, you're right. I better 'hop to it'. Any release of sexual tension needs to be kept far away from this potion until it can take effect on Tana. Otherwise, it will have the opposite effect to what we want."

She turned and made her way to the seventh bookcase whereupon she pressed a small, hidden button she'd noted earlier. A row of fake books dissipated into nothing but air revealing a rather large, flat, decorative inlaid box. Cherry wood, mahogany, and black walnut if she guessed right. All those decades of studying the different types of plants and their uses under her aunt's strict and watchful eye meant she was pretty confident she was correct. Those damn herbology lessons had been tedious as fuck, but surprisingly useful it would seem.

Lifting the heavy case out she carried it carefully to the seat she'd earlier abandoned and laid it down with reverent care. A quick look at Nithe showed him watching her with curiosity and love. Her fingers shook slightly as she unhooked the latch and raised the lid to reveal the powerful objects that awaited within.

She felt Nithe shift to stand behind her, his warmth seeped into her as his scent calmed her nerves, but she couldn't take her eyes off the powerful blades before her.

There were twelve in total resting on the rich red velvet lining inside the box, all with a matching scabbard placed beside them. Each blade was completely different from the others. Black with blood-red rubies, gold with emeralds, silver and topaz, a jade blade with a handle wrapped in twisted gold, and more. Some straight, some curved, some like the ripples in a stream. They were all beautiful, powerful, and wickedly sharp. Her hand hovered over them one by one as the power they each held hummed against her palm. Though only one called to her, whispered to her soul with Tana's name as it pulled her closer. Only one held the promise of power to fulfill the spell and carry their pleas to spirits that be.

The green and blue splattered white surface of the phoenix crystal blade glowed in the low light of the moon above. The handle was simple, more crystal wrapped in rustic silver in a knotted Celtic style. Jezzie held her breath as her fingers closed around it and lifted it free. She slid it into the waiting scabbard, and placed it carefully into her right pocket. Her shuddering sigh filled the room as she exhaled her pent-up breath and set about returning the box to its hiding spot.

Returning she seated herself back down next to Nithe, who sat and watched her with his legs stretched out before him, his booted feet crossed at the ankles, the same curious expression softening his features as before. Jezzie decided to just jump right in and get it over with.

"So, basically the final ingredient needs to be added only moments before we administer it to Tana. In order for it to work the blood of the witch casting the spell must be added. By doing so it will pull most of the sexual energy away from Tana and channel it through my connection with the earth. Don't worry, it won't affect me the same way it does Tana. In this instance, it will filter the energy through the light of pure white magic and return it to the earth beneath my feet. This will lessen the load Tana must carry. At least, I hope so, considering I never even thought I had any witchy magic in me until today." She looked at Nithe and hesitated as his shoulders relaxed.

Inside she was a twisted coil of nerves and second thoughts. She pushed them away, watching his expression closely.

"Okay, so you slice your hand and add the blood, right? No biggie."

She hated having to wipe the smile from his face.

"Well, not exactly. The blood must come from close to the source of the magic. The hand, even the wrist, is too far away." Taking a deep breath she decided to blurt it out in one go. "Aunt Rai Rai taught me that a witch's power comes from the same place all bonds are made. The place the soul thrives and loves blossoms. I have to slice deep into my chest, over my heart, Ni, and fill the cup til it runneth over."

She saw his brow furrow, his eyes get stormy, and panic start to filter in, so she rushed to reassure him.

"I won't die, not even if I were only a witch, and not part angel and vampire too. The blade is not made of wood thankfully, not because it could kill me but because the splinters are fething annoying to pull out, or worse, to heal over. I'll be fine. In fact, since I fed only a few days ago on that asshole with the siren fetish, I'll be brand-new in less than an hour. On the downside, it'll hurt like a bitch and look even worse."

He was off his stool and hauling her into his arms before the last words left her lips. His mouth devoured hers, his hands tangled in her hair. Her desperate need to soothe his panic seeped into the bond as her mind whispered gently to both the man and the beast who were united in their fear. It was not in a dragon's nature to watch their mate suffer, and the bond vibrated with the protective urges of his dual natures screaming to stop her. She slowed her responses, deepened the kiss, poured her calm into his soul and waited, breathlessly, as he stepped back, his golden eyes aglow.

"So it must be. I trust you and I will serve your needs in this," came the gravelly voice of the dragon mixed with Nithe's own. "We will collect your punishment for trying to keep this from us at a more . . .pleasurable time." The desire roughened edge to his voice had her thighs pressing together firmly. A throb of answering heat flushed outward from her core to encompass every inch of her being.

She shook herself free from his heady spell. Now was not the time. Tana needed her. Uncle Micah was relying on her. What if her memory wasn't as good as she thought? What if she got it wrong and it didn't work? Or worse, what if she caused more harm to her precious cousin than good? Would the spirits smite her? Would the Almighty rain down wrath upon her head? Would Uncle Micah hate her? Tana too? Would she lose this family she'd found? Her chance to ever be looked on as a daughter by her absent father?

The thoughts whirled like a tornado in her head as she watched the swirling liquid bubble and waited for the spark. Instead, she found herself sucked further into the murky mire of her troubled thoughts. He should have found them. He should have tried harder than he did. He's an angel for fuck's sake. One of the best. One of the worst. Guess it depended on who you asked. But he didn't. He barely tried at all. Sure, Aunt Rai Rai's magic was very powerful, and if Leraie helped with the wards he probably wouldn't have stood a chance, and to be fair, they probably had done it together. Didn't make any of it easier on the little girl who'd wanted nothing more than to be held in the arms of her father and told she was loved, she was wanted, she was enough, she was worth searching every realm to find.

Her Aunt did those things in her mother's absence. Her mother did them, when she thought it safe enough. It wasn't the same, and she didn't know what she'd do when she came face to face with him one day. Her uncle told her stories from their younger years. Some funny, some sad. Some downright inappropriate. She soaked them all in, desperate to understand, to know the man behind the name she'd been given. Would she punch him, scream, and kick? Cry? Or would she run to him and not let go? Would she . . .

"Come back, Jez. Out of that pretty head of yours. What will be, will be, and if anyone hurts you? I'll hurt them right back, and spend the rest of eternity making up for their sins against you." His hand stroked up and down her arms, his kisses searing the skin at her temple.

Nithe always knew what to say and do to bring her out of her own head. Just as her eyes began to flutter shut the red and orange spark she'd been waiting for flew into the air. She leapt out of Nithe's embrace and reached out her bare hands to catch the glowing ember, but as it collided with her skin the heat retreated, replaced by the cold polished surface of the gemstone she'd been waiting for. With one hand she reached into the cauldron, it too instantly cooled once the spark left it, and pulled out the potion stained cloth.

"Ni, sweetie, can you half fill that goblet over there with the potion and pop the cover on top, please? I need to get this thing wrapped up and ready to go."

"On it, Jez. Just use the ladle over there, or does it have to be something special?"

"The ladle's fine. Just be careful, Ni. Don't let the liquid touch you. I'm not sure what it could do."

She worried her lip between her teeth as she concentrated on tearing the cloth into equal strips before her fingers braided and knotted it around the stone to form a bracelet for Tana's wrist.

Twenty minutes later they reached Tana's room, supplies in hand and sans shoes. She slipped off her cousin's leggings as she yelled at Uncle Micah to grab Tana and follow them. The man didn't need to be told twice. He was up and running behind them moments later, Tana's body cradled carefully in his arms.

They made it to the doors of Paradise in record time. Jezzie instinctively knew the perfect spot for what was about to happen as soon as she stepped over the threshold. Sure enough, the always locked gates in the far left corner sat open, ready and waiting. The sacred circle of rich soil was surrounded by a ring of purple peonies of varied shades. Jezzie rushed to place the candles into the soil at the points of a ceremonial pentagram as she called out to her uncle over her shoulder.

"Place her flat on her back in the middle of the circle. Her head needs to be pointed at the candle directly in front of you, feet together."

Once she was in position and the last candle ready, Jezzie got Nithe to stand before Tana's feet, her uncle behind her head. She handed them each a piece of thick black cloth and huffed a sigh when all they did was look at her askance.

"This is a witch's spell involving needing and mating rituals . . ." She waited for the penny to drop, it didn't. For Tana's sake she took pity on them. "She needs to be completely naked. Uncle Micah, I'm pretty sure you don't want to be seeing every square inch of your daughter's naked body. Am I right?"

He nodded emphatically as Jezzie poured a thick circle of sand and salt around each of them.

"So . . . put the cloth over your eyes, tie it behind your head, and stand perfectly still. You too, Ni. The both of you will help ground Tana to the earth. When I call, 'So shall it be,' repeat after me, understood?"

Nodding their heads they did as they were told, standing like stone statues.

"The sand and salt will keep you safe from the needing magic as it enters the earth and dissipates," she explained as she set the bottle aside.

Jezzie quickly undid the buttons on Tana's nightgown and slipped it out from under her flushed body. Soon the frenzied fever of desire would fill her cousin with an unrelenting need to be mated and sated. Calm, she must keep calm. Jezzie centered herself as she removed her cousin's underwear and moved her prone body into position, ensuring Tana's palms were facing up, and her legs stayed together. As her naked body sunk into the earth the five unlit candles ignited with purple flames. Jezzie placed the goblet in front of her as she knelt in the soil by Tana's side, her dress allowing the soil to welcome her with its cool softness.

The bracelet Jezzie tied securely around Tana's wrist fit perfectly. She placed the dagger next to the goblet and bowed her head. Melodic words floated from her lips in reverent prayer.

"Spirits, hear us. Spirits, we thank you for past gifts and future boons. Please help this being, our friend, in her time of needing. Temper her discomfort and allow her a reprieve from this burden, 'til she be ready. Spirits, we thank you for your guidance and your grace."

Inside the goblet the potion shifted, the dark liquid lighting up with a swirl that resembled a galaxy, before it settled to match the purple flowers around them.

"So shall it be. Praise be."

"So shall it be. Praise be," the men chorused.

Twice more she repeated the words and as the last sounds faded away she slipped her gown from her shoulders and lifted the dagger in her right hand. She placed the cold stone against her skin, and sliced deep. Thick red blood welled to the surface, it wasn't enough. Deeper, the blood bubbled and spilled down her breast, the goblet in her left hand catching every drop. Faster it flowed until it could fill no more and ran over the rim and coated her hand, seeping into the soil below.

It was meant to hurt. This was her price for the boon to be granted. Still, it stung like a motherfucker. Taking a breath Jezzie tried to rein in her pain and refocus her mind. Her limbs were heavy. Shit! She may have nicked an artery. Oh well, not like it'd kill her. The bleeding was already starting to slow, just not as fast as she'd hoped.

Jezzie put the knife down, dipped her fingers into the now red mixture and anointed Tana's palms, the soles of her feet, her forehead, and her abdomen. After a deep breath she raised Tana's head and brought the goblet to her cousin's lips, which parted on a sigh. Jezzie tipped the liquid in slowly and repeated her prayer.

"So shall it be. Praise be."

"So shall it be. Praise be."

Tana's eyes opened on a gasp, she smiled at Jezzie before slipping into a gentle sleep, complete with snuffly snoring.

CHAPTER 31

Five years of searching for answers and all they'd found were more questions. They were no closer to helping Luc, and no closer to resolving the mysterious erotic encounters that were their dreams. To add to it all, they'd learned there was a traitor in their midst. The revelation had hit them all like a freight train, the anger that had pulsed through the room was so immense it was a wonder their combined shadows hadn't reduced the fortress to rubble.

Thank fuck for Mrs Briars! Somehow she'd managed to contain it all. The kicker was, of course, that they still hadn't figured out who the fuck the weasel was. It was as if the asshole was a ghost. No, scratch that. If they were a ghost they would have been able to track their ass down already, whoever this was, was sneakier than any phantom they'd ever come across.

Luc had been trying to stay on top of it all, but he'd been distracted by the search for the redheaded vixen as much as Roth and Athon were. Still, the General and Caine had made their way through the ranks, searching the myriad minds of those who resided within the fortress walls for answers.

Whoever it was, they were damn good at hiding from them. Something which should have been impossible, and up 'til now, it had been. Luc had unlimited access to the thoughts and feelings of those under his command. Once you made your pledge, he owned your ass, though he never took advantage of it, unless needed. Not even a trace of a blockade glimmered within any of their minds to indicate a shield behind which traitorous hidden knowledge could be found.

Gabriel, for his part, had kept more to himself than usual. No jabs or snide remarks. No fishing for intel he wasn't going to get. Maybe he realized he was on thin ice and suspicions were roused? Maybe he was so far up his own ass he'd gotten bored and went looking for the tiny scrap of self-preservation he possibly had left? Either way, he'd stayed away from any interactions with the Hounds, outside of monthly meetings, that is. He continued to cite an uptick in soul collections and recycling delays. As if anyone believed that bullshit excuse.

Ramiel was still trying to get answers from Raum, with zero success. The fallen was a fortress when it came to the information they all wanted to know, and Ramiel had started to get impatient. Which was saying something, considering he'd once spent ninety-seven years interrogating an Egyptian 'God' about the disappearance of a fae princess whom he'd failed to seduce.

Yet still, they searched for the traitor, for the answers to the threats surrounding them . . . and continued to find nothing but dead end leads and more twisted mysteries.

Not even the witch from the dragon realm had shown her face again. Save for some rather descriptive missives that promised bloody slaughter should they fuck this up. Fuck what up exactly? And how? They had no idea, but they still didn't want to mess with her. Especially when Luc seemed to have decided she was an ally, and not a threat. Those damn letters sounded pretty fucking threatening to the rest of them, though. The hairs rose on the back of his nape just thinking of them. Power laced the blood-red ink that lined those pages. Something he hadn't encountered in a very long time. So long ago he couldn't remember the where, when, or who of it.

Roth was becoming more desperate the longer it took to find her. His shadows roiled beneath his skin, twisted his insides, and drove his libido wild. He was starting to lose focus, becoming more despondent with each passing week. So reminiscent of Luc it caused panic to flood the chambers of his heart.

The only thing which kept him tethered to reality was Athon. He held on for him, for them. For the promises whispered in their dreams, and in the dark as they held each other close. One day, they would find her. One day, they would be complete.

But, what if she was Luc's? What if Luc hurt Ni?

Then we shall takes her. We shall takes them both.

The insidious answer intruded unpleasantly into his brain. The feeling it brought with it was not unlike that of a chill slithering up his spine on a freezing cold day at the same time a swarm of ants tickled and bit their way all over his body at once. From where it came, he didn't know. He didn't like it. Neither the thought of betraying his General, his friend, nor of the redhead belonging to the man he considered a brother, a father, the only real parental figure he'd ever known.

Alas, it was a bridge to cross at a later time. When, and if, they managed to find the vexatious wench! Oh, the spankings she'd get for the trouble she'd already caused. The front on his pants got noticeably tighter with the images that swarmed his mind, mixing with the panicked spiral of his wayward thoughts.

"Az, babe, look at me. We will find her, I promise. Right here and now, though, it's time for us to have some fun. You with me?"

Shit! Athon was pouting. Which meant he'd been stuck in his own head long enough for his male to notice. His male. Damn straight . . . or not, in their case.

"Right! Date night, or is it date day?" he smiled warmly into his lover's tricolor eyes as desire mixed with the adrenaline in his blood, and he locked down his other chaotic emotions.

Athon's serpentine pupils dilated with a flare of awareness, his body leaning in closer to Roth's in such a natural way he was sure his male didn't even realize he was doing it.

How anyone could look as downright sexy as Athon did in a simple pair of jeans, a tight white v-neck undershirt that pressed against the well-defined contours of his generous abs, and an open, worn, black leather jacket was crazy. His pouty bottom lip just begged for Roth to lean slightly forward and nip the supple flesh between his teeth.

Athon's pupils dilated even further, his shallow breaths quickened, those sexy ass pecs heaved a little harder, making Roth's cock grow thicker behind the thick fabric of his pants. But alas, they had a job to do . . . the sex would come later, and the waiting would make it all the sweeter, make the hurt feel so damn good.

Reaching down he pressed his palm against his hard length and adjusted it with a silent rebuke to behave, with the promise of satisfaction later if it did. The thought of never finding their mystery woman flashed across his mind before he could stop it, but even if they didn't, he and Athon would be fine. Surely, they'd be fine with just each other. Or maybe there was another woman out there for them if this one ended up being Luc's . . .

Pain gripped him in its throes, and he buckled to his knees on the cold, hard asphalt. What the fuck was happening? When he looked down at his groin his shadows covered the front of his cargo pants, curling and writhing in what felt like an attempt to twist his fucking dick off. His balls were probably turning purple by now, not even they were safe. Shit! What the hell? Reining them back in took all of his not inconsiderable effort as Athon fussed and freaked on the ground next to him, but they quickly stopped as his hard-on deflated and attempted to shrivel back up, and into his body.

"Az, babe, you okay? Tell me what's wrong."

He felt Athon's rough hands cup his cheeks, and stroke along his sweat covered brow. As he looked up, he saw the concern which dominated his lover's gaze, fear laced the beat of his heart as it pressed up against Roth's own chest.

"My shadows just tried to rip off my cock and balls!?" Roth gasped out, his breaths short and sharp, confusion laced his words, as well as shock.

Never had an angel's shadows caused harm to them before, never had they acted independently, outside of keeping them safe from harm. An instinctive reaction thought to be the angel's own subconscious doing.

Athon helped him gingerly to his feet as the few people walking by stopped to stare. He guided them toward the quaint coffee shop across the street. The smell of fresh bagels and apple and cinnamon pie flooded his senses, taking some of the sting away the closer they got. They sat in a quiet corner, ordered their favorite brews—an iced caramel frappé with extra cream for Ath and a triple shot espresso with two sugars for himself. As they sipped their drinks they questioned this newest disturbing mystery, and came up blank before they decided to bring it up to Luc and Deus later . . . after their date was complete, and after Athon got the chance to kiss it all better. Roth's eyes strayed to Athon's mouth and watched his pink tongue flick out to lap up the cream from his lips. The sight of his black silicone piercing sent his thoughts further south in the direction of his pants. It gave him comfort to feel his cock responding to his x-rated thoughts. Thank fuck, it still worked!

Catching a movie was next on their agenda, there was an 1980s sci-fi classic movie marathon Athon had been bugging him to go see for the past few weeks. He'd made a show of putting up some resistance, but truth be told he loved sci-fi as much as Athon did, more so when he got to see Ath's excitement and joy. Yeah, they had a theater at the fortress and all, but sometimes you just had to get out of the house. Away from the chaos of your normal day to day.

Outside the window a flash of something caught Roth's eye. Their ride had arrived.

<hr>

THE MOVIES WERE FANTASTIC. He'd seen them all before of course, but never with Roth. He'd actually been pretty engrossed in them, even as he'd watched Roth from the corner of his eye. Noted the way he placed the popcorn in his mouth, the way he licked the salty butter from his fingers, wrapped his lips around the thin straw and sucked the fizzy liquid down his throat. His heart raced as he recalled it now, just as it did every time he watched Roth do mundane, everyday things like eating and walking.

The sexy bastard had pulled off such an epic surprise, if he hadn't been so excited to be headed to the most epic movie marathon ever, to him anyway, in none other than a decked out, movie accurate, pristine, and drool worthy DeLorean, he'd have dragged Roth back home in a heartbeat and allowed Mr 'Full of Surprises' to have his wicked way with him in an "anything goes" haze of blinding lust.

He hadn't expected it. Honestly, he'd almost forgotten how romantic and generous his Az could be. This newest reminder of the male he used to be, the knowledge he was still in there just waiting for opportunities to bust out, made Athon's heart skip a few more beats.

Dinner had been delicious. None of that 5-star bullshit. Mrs Briars fed them better than any Michelin restaurant ever could. No, sometimes what you needed most was a greasy triple cheeseburger with extra bacon, and topped french fries and aioli from a little diner, the gem of downtown, over on Locust Street.

Thankfully, it was close to the nightclub they were making their way to. Seriously, he was stuffed full of beefy deliciousness and ready for it to soak up some alcohol. Not the human stuff, which didn't do all that much for his kind. There was only one place in Philly that served ambrosia at its finest.

Epiphany looked like a regular bar from the outside. Stone and dark wood paneling. Elegant, yet unpretentious. The neighbors didn't hear a sound from the place thanks to magical soundproofing. The noise hit them as the door closed shut behind them. Music and voices shouting to be heard over it. Bodies writhed to the music.

Athon knew the nightclub's main floor held no allure to Roth, it didn't really capture his attention either. The humans grinding away on one another to the ceaseless repetitive beat of the music, colored lights strobing over them as the smell of sweat and spilled liquor filled the air were a nuisance their OtherRealm senses could have done without.

As they approached the cordoned off stairs they flashed their exposed wrists, baring the stamp no human eyes could see to the burly bouncer, the wolf in human skin stepped back, taking the thick red rope with him.

The first shot slid down his throat like icy fire, electrifying every cell in his body. The second, like smooth nectar, warmed the blood in his veins. The third took the tension out of every tight muscle and left him relaxed and at ease.

The human chaos had ceased the moment they hit the top of the stairs. The music still sunk its beat into their bones, but the sounds of the humans below had dimmed to a mere hum thanks to a magical filter. The booth-like seats offered them privacy, but still with a view out over the flock below. All sorts of beings were present. Wolves and bears, a vamp or two. A ghoul sat on the other side of the room and gave a quick nod of acknowledgment of his perusal.

Below, a nymph danced in a cage on the stage, enticing the humans to frivolity and fornication. It seemed to be working as more and more couples made their way to bathrooms and booths. One or two passed bills over to the bartender and found their way to private rooms out back.

His eyes latched on to long red hair and creamy porcelain skin. She ground her ass back into some random guy's groin, rolling her hips to the beat of the music, her hands stroked over her curves and cupped her assets. Her face hidden as she looked away. He knew it wasn't her, but his desire rose anyway. Not for the woman he was watching, but for who she reminded him of. Roth's hand slid up his thigh and over his hard cock, giving it a gentle squeeze. Lips and teeth grazed the column of his throat, hot breath took his desire higher.

"Want me to take care of that for you, Ath?" Roth all but groaned.

"Not here. Come with me?" Athon asked.

"Anywhere you lead, I'll gladly follow."

Athon shoved him from the booth and all but dragged him to the stairs. Shoved his way through the crowded dance floor and out the exit door to the alley. As soon as it slammed shut he found himself pressed against the far wall across from the dumpster. His shoulders pinned by the fists gripping his jacket. Soft firm lips crashed against his as Roth's tongue demanded entry. One thick thigh pressed between his legs, and he ground the evidence of his desire in the hard muscles hidden by his lover's pants, the seam of his jeans taunting him with an edge of discomfort that had nothing to do with his lust.

He couldn't help the giggle that escaped him at the realization he was basically humping Roth's leg like a horny dog.

"Come on, horndog, tell me what you want from me," came Roth's raspy, desire filled voice.

Shit, he'd said that out loud?

"Either that or I'm reading your thoughts now? Maybe we're both going crazy? Right now though, I don't really care. What do you want me to do with this thick, hard cock of yours, Ath?" Roth's palm rubbed up and down his jean covered length.

His hips thrust forward, pushing it further into his hold as Athon struggled to find the breath to voice his needs.

"On your knees. I want you on your knees with your lips stretched wide around my cock as I thrust deep into your throat and you take everything I have to give," he gasped out.

"Your wish is my command."

The glint in Roth's eye as he dropped to his knees on the grimy stones promised the same level of obedience would be expected when they got home.

Buttons popped and zips unzipped, good thing he wore no underwear as Roth's warm flesh touched his freed length. It bobbed gently under Roth's hungry gaze, a twinkle of pre-cum glistened at the tip. His lover's slick tongue quick to savor its sweet taste.

Just as Roth's head lowered to take him in, his hands wrapped around the base, the exit door slammed open and shut, and Roth leapt to his feet, shielding him as he fumbled to restrain his cock within its denim prison once more.

Fucking cock blocking assholes, whoever they were. Damn it.

Voices and moans filtered over Roth's shoulder. The sounds of a hot and heavy make out session, not unlike the one they themselves had just been involved in. He tapped Roth's back and pulled him over to the side and further into the shadows to keep them hidden.

Yep, the redhead from the club was wrapped up in the dude's arms like an octopus over a treasure chest, when she unexpectedly thrust him away from her and stepped back, mumbling out her hesitation and reluctance. She stood with her back to them, facing the guy. He had a greasy, sleazy look to him. Desire and desperation gleamed in his eyes. A "bad news" vibe radiated off of him. He was slimy, his soul still had a chance at redemption, maybe not in this lifetime, but possibly the next. It all depended on his choices. Free will and all that jazz. Hmm, there was a thought, their next date night could be a jazz bar. He loved some good jazz. Or maybe a rock concert.

His eyes focused back to the scene in front of him. The woman took a tentative step back, then seemed to brace herself and hold her ground. The creep's voice slithered through the alley.

"No? Oh, baby, you know you want it. You've been begging for this, you little slut, all night long. You can't deny it. You are going to give me exactly what you've been promising me, one way or another."

He felt Roth stiffen beside him. His protective instincts, and frankly common decency, kicked into hyperdrive. They both nodded at each other, prepared to intervene until he caught a scent and reached out to hold Roth back, his arm straight out across his chest. Roth's confusion shifted to recognition as he too breathed deeply. Her head turned and the distinctive pink eyes of a succubus looked straight at them as she placed a finger over her lips.

The situation had gone from benign to cancerous to fair in the space of minutes. It was now a predator meet predator situation, and it was obvious to them who was going to win.

They watched her attack the disgusting human, sucking his desire from him. She built it up and mixed it with anger as she turned him down again, which in turn made his sadistic desire stronger, and drained him further. Content to let nature take its course. It was the way of succubi, and incubi alike, and they couldn't take his soul themselves as he wasn't evil enough yet to have any other chances. This way he could harm no more innocents in this lifetime.

The problem presented itself when an innocent human stepped into the alley and the succubus didn't notice, or didn't care enough to hide her actions from the newest bystander. The small, squeaky shriek alerted them, and should have alerted her, too. Athon threw out a shield, hiding them all completely and the woman shook herself as though she must've been seeing things that weren't there and kept walking.

As the last of the male's energy left him, he was nothing but a zombie waiting on her will. She whispered into his ear, and he reached into his boot and took out a knife. One last scrap of self-preservation and horror flashed across his face as he plunged the sharp steel into his heart and fell forward in a pool of his own blood.

"Well, nice meeting you, boys. But I must needs be off now. Toodle-oo," came her too sweet voice as she waved her fingers at them.

"Not too fast, succubus. I'm afraid we can't let you go just yet," Athon replied.

"Oh, yeah, why's that? You two seemed to be doing just fine without me, or do you think I'd want in on the action?"

"Not in a million years," came Roth's harsh reply.

"No, we can't let you go because you broke a major rule just now."

"Oh, come on. He was scum and fair game to boot."

"Not him. Don't give a fuck about him. If it was, we'd have stopped you, and you know it. No, you let a human witness what you were doing and either didn't notice or didn't care. You can thank us later for being here to cover your ass after you've dealt with whatever the Praesidium has to say about it. Since we took care of it you shouldn't get in too much trouble, but it still needs to be dealt with. We like single malt scotch, for future reference," he winked at her as fear and horror flushed over her face.

"Thanks for holding her here. Roth, Athon."

The newcomer stood directly behind the shocked succubus, whose body had frozen when the Praesidium angel's hands had come to rest on her shoulders.

"Ah, here she is now. Hi, Bezaliel, nice to see you again." Roth nodded.

"Nice to see you both too. Even better seeing you together again. Congratulations, it's been too long." She smiled at them with sincerity. At his raised brow she added, "News gets around pretty fast."

"Yes it has, Zali. Thank you." He smiled back.

"We'll be off now. Enjoy what remains of your night."

And then they were alone once more.

CHAPTER 32

Jezzie had gotten Tana dressed before she'd allowed them to remove the blindfolds, but the dragon in him was already going crazy in his head from the scent of his mate's blood. Too much blood. He'd held it together only because of his faith in her. Then all of a sudden his sight had been set free and his bonded mate instincts had kicked in completely. His roar filled the sky and shook the birds from the trees for miles around.

The sight of Jezzie's blood soaked dress and open wound, with a steady flow of blood still trickling over the already slick curve of her breast, had his beast both raging and rampantly protective. What worried him most, though, was the discomfort of his growing cock pressing against the inside of his trousers. It froze him to the spot.

He didn't want to be a monster. Didn't want to find pleasure in her pain. He didn't want to be the same as the monster who still lived in his past and in the darkest recesses inside his head. He wished the bastard could be forever exorcised from his brain.

Soft, firm hands pried his fingers from his hair and pulled them to his sides, loose tawny strands falling to the ground beneath his buckled knees. Huh, when had that happened?

"Ni, *mo shíorghrá*, look at me!"

Jezzie's strident voice pierced the white noise muffling in his ears, but the guttural scream from his own mouth was much worse than no sound at all.

"It's okay. I'm okay," she crooned in his ear, but all he could smell was the sweet scent of her blood, and he didn't know why. His brain seemed to have been sucked into the beast's inferno of feelings.

"No, you don't understand, Jezzie. Rage burns us. We demand your safety. But, what scares me is my reaction to the sight and scent of your blood as it lingers on your perfect breast, the wound so fresh it has yet to heal. You hurt, and yet my cock grows thick and throbs with the need to take you. Yet, even in my self-disgust this desire urges me to action. To lap at your wound and claim you, regardless of your pain. I don't ever want to be like him," his voice cracked on the final word as tears slid down his face and onto her hands.

Such soft hands, which held him steady as she kissed first one eyelid, then the other, before placing whispered words against his lips.

"And this, right here, *mo shíorghrá*, is why you will never be like him. Not even in your worst moments, not even in the darkest of your days."

She dragged him down to the ground and wrapped him tightly in the warmth of her embrace. Soothed him with the stroke of her fingers through his tawny hair as she whispered words of love and reassurance until he slowly relaxed into her embrace. The occasional vow to eat the decrepit soul of the monster who plagued him thrown in here and there, elicited wry chuckles from him. His Jezzie was going to make Raum beg for death if she ever had the chance, and Nithe would stand beside her when she did.

They stayed that way for who knows how long, laid out on the soil within the circle, though the cold had started to seep into his once too often broken bones. Michael had taken Tana and the supplies back to her room once he'd been assured she was improving, giving them the space they'd needed. He didn't know what Nithe had been through, not exactly, but he knew Raum. Had heard of his misdeeds, and the guy was far from an idiot. His rage had receded, but self-loathing still lingered like a dark cloud threatening the happiness in his heart.

"Ni?"

"Yeah, Jez?"

"I want you to lick me," her voice held a breathy quality, one reserved for intimate moments.

"Now?"

"Yeah, now. Not my pussy, though. I want you to lick the blood from my breast."

"Why would you want that, Jez? After what just happened." Panic started to creep into his brain.

"I think we both weren't thinking clearly. Blood holds power, remember?"

"Yeah, that's kinda OtherRealm 101."

Where was she going with this?

"What was our bond sealed with, Ni?"

"The marking bite?"

"Which involves?"

Oh, shit!

"Blood! I can heal your wound and your blood will reaffirm the bond and calm the panic and rage in both the dragon and in me! How the fuck could I forget that. You are so fucking clever, *a stór*."

He rolled her in his arms until her body was pinned beneath his as he kissed the fuck out of her, leaving them both breathless. He tore his lips from hers with a ragged groan and dipped his head to her breast, only to have her halt his attempt to lick her blood-covered nipple.

"Not yet, not like this. There's something I've wanted to try for a while now, but I'm not sure it's possible?"

"Whatever it is, I'll make it happen for you, Jez. Tell me, what is it?"

She looked at him with an impish grin, and he knew he was in for a treat.

"I wanna give a whole new meaning to the mile high club, Ni. Will you fuck me as we fly? If your wings are out in a glide position and I'm on top riding you, would that work? Or I could be under you, at your mercy, as you fly and fuck me? We could always do it upright, too, I suppose? What do you think?"

Her wide-eyed excitement made him grin back at her and chuckle.

"I think my little Shadow has put a lot more thought into this than I'd cottoned on to. Want to experiment and see which one works best?"

"You mean, you don't know?" She seemed shocked.

The little crease between her brows utterly charmed him, taking away the sting of the memories her question evoked.

"Well, I've heard stories but never done it myself. I was exiled not long after my wings came in and I first shifted into my dragon form, and never got the chance to test them out until we came here through the portal."

"Oh, crap, I'd forgotten about that. I'm sorry, Ni."

"Don't be, Jez. I want you to forget. Hell, I want to forget it all, too."

He shook his head, his shaggy hair falling in front of his face exactly how she liked. His "sex hair" as she often called it. She bit her lip and played with the ends of a few strands against his cheekbones.

"Let's go, precious."

He jumped up, pulling her to her feet with him. In no time they were both naked, wings out, and unable to keep their hands off each other. They made quick work of removing their clothes. Lips trailed over the sensitive skin, his hands found the soft, firm curves of her ass to lift her up. She wrapped her legs around his waist tightly, her core pressed against his cock and spread her dampness along the length of him.

Nithe's teeth nipped a path along the exposed curve of her neck and along her jaw before he kissed the living daylights out of the one person in his existence who shone light into his dark world and took to the sky. His wings beat at the air, and they soared over mountain tops as Jezzie tucked in her wings and giggled, though she didn't put them away completely. She shifted her body, reaching down with one hand to stroke his rock hard length and line them up, before she slid herself down over the tip and took him into his own personal paradise.

Her wings snapped open to help guide their path, beating in time to the rise and fall of her hips as they rolled against his own. The motion languid and teasing. She kissed her way along his neck, nipping and licking at his pulse, which kicked into overdrive as her pussy tightened around him.

"Could your wings keep us up if you were on your back, Ni?" Jez asked breathlessly.

"Yeah, they can, Jez. Why?" his voice as breathless as hers.

"Prepare for the ride of your life, sexy," she whispered in his ear, nipped the soft flesh of his earlobe, put her hand on his shoulders and shoved him backwards.

He had a moment of panic before he straightened his wings out to stabilize them. She sat and impaled herself on him, straddled his hips, and leaned forward to kiss along his jaw. Her heels dug into the muscles of his ass as her wings rose and fell above them. Not enough to take them higher, just enough to help keep them up. Her hands on his shoulders gave her leverage as she moved her hips faster. Her inner walls fluttered, his cock thickened, and shared pleasure took them higher.

He ran his hands over the soft curves of her hips and beneath her hair as he caressed the satin skin of her back. His fingers traced the shape of her breasts, barely making contact. The whimper that left her lips as his hands roamed her body set fire to his desire. His rough palms skimmed across her thighs to grip her knees and pulled them wider, seating himself deeper inside her heavenly heat. He cupped her ass as he felt her legs tremble, her inner walls clenched and quivered. He thrust up harder, faster to match her frantic pace. The pleasure built to a blinding pinnacle as he felt the wetness of her release slide down over his cock and onto his thighs as she let loose the sounds of her ecstasy, leaving them to echo through the valley below. His own shout joined hers as his cum filled her still shuddering sheath.

Heavy breathing filled the air as he held her close. Her breasts pressed to his chest, his nose nuzzled in the crook of her neck surrounded by the pure scent of her. Still, her hips shifted against his. Seeking not to disengage, more like a subconscious need to prolong the moment. Not that he minded. His cock certainly didn't, as hard as it still was. The darn thing actually got even harder. Seemed like they were in for another round much sooner than expected.

Damn, dragon! Should have known he'd want a piece of the action. Nithe chuckled, but it came out with the rough, guttural edge of the dragon within. He felt his cock change shape within her. The base swelled, locking him inside her. At the same time he got longer, the veins thickened, bulging out, and rubbing against her slick walls. She moaned as she tried to slide herself up his length but found nowhere to go, his partially shifted cock locked deep inside her. His breathing quickened, sweat beaded on his forehead as his hips undulated with his own renewed desire. A frenzy of his dual desire.

"Again," Jezzie gasped.

"Yes. Again!" he demanded, the gravel and velvet in his voice demanded satisfaction.

A keening sound escaped her as the length of his dragon-altered cock undulated inside her. She whimpered, stretched her to her limits. His balls tightened, he was so close again, already, and so was she.

She rode him faster, shifted against him harder. He groaned deep in his throat. The land around them echoed the sounds of their passion, driving them both closer to completion. The bond tugged at him; he opened himself to her pleasure and shuddered in ecstasy as the connection slammed into place and his balls threatened to empty into her, again. He held it back, determined to prolong her pleasure as much as he could.

Jezzie sat up, her eyes locked on him. Fresh, crisp air rushed around them as they glided on the breeze, higher than any of the mountains nearby. He wasn't flying fast, and didn't go far but the cool bite of the wind pebbled Jezzie's skin, her already sensitized nipple hardened even further as he rolled it between his warm fingers. His hand at her waist reached up to tangle in the ends of her long red locks and gave a firm tug, forcing her back to arch and thrust her breasts further forward. The triad of sensations rang an almost feral moan from her parted lips. The sudden urge to take a memo brought a smug smile to Nithe's lips.

Note to self: What Jezzie wants, Jezzie should always get. Especially when her ideas are this darn good!

One of her hands rose to cup the breast he was neglecting, the other slipped down to rub at her engorged clit, her fingers dipped down to stroke the spot where they were joined. God, she was so damn beautiful, and she felt amazing. How'd he get so lucky? He watched as she stroked her nipple before pinching hard, her hips moving erratically. He wasn't sure he could last much longer. His fingers pressed hard into her hips as he forced her up, the swollen base stretched her entrance, she made it half an inch before she couldn't take anymore. Seeing her slightly pained expression he slammed her back down and as she cried out her pleasure. Once more, twice, as her orgasm shuddered through her. Her ecstasy echoing through Paradise. He pulled her down to him and locked his lips over the gash at her breast, his tongue swirled as it cleaned away the blood, leaving her skin like new. He flipped her over in an instant as he thrust into her as his cock erupted deep inside her with what felt like an endless amount of cum.

And suddenly, they were falling, spiraling in the uncontrollable rush of their very own paradise.

A QUICK SHOWER LATER, during which they made love again—slowly this time—they were getting dressed and ready for dinner with Uncle Micah as they talked about the bond. Her shadows and his dragon holding their own personal confab. The unanimous consensus regarding mid-flight sex was a resounding yes! Ten out of ten, would highly recommend.

Nithe sat behind her on the bed and brushed her hair. The simple act felt so amazingly intimate and special. He was always so careful with knots and tangles. He felt the missing pieces within the bond, the empty spaces. Maybe not the same way she did, but it was still there. Jezzie knew though, if it came down to it and the other two were duds, Nithe would be enough for her and her eternal happiness. You couldn't miss what you never had, right? At least that was the theory she set on operating under.

When they reached the dining room an hour later, Jezzie was a little surprised to see Tana seated at her usual spot, only a slightly strained smile graced her beautiful face. She raced over and gave her a gentle hug where she sat, insisting she not stand, and quickly moved to sit opposite her cousin. Nithe held her chair out for her, and tucked her in, ever the gallant gentleman she'd come to love. He made her feel like a goddamn princess, and she'd quickly realized she damn well liked it.

"I must admit I'm surprised you're up and about already, Cousin. Seriously, you should still be resting," Jezzie said, concern threaded through her voice.

"Chill, Coz. I'm fine. Whatever you guys did, I feel better than I ever did with the stuff Leraie gave me. Thanks for that, by the way. I mean, it still hurts a bit, and I'm horny as fuck, but it's so much better. Sorry, Dad."

Uncle Micah put his hands over his ears and lalala'ed as theatrically as he could in response, causing Tana and Jezzie to giggle like schoolgirls, and Nithe to snort at their antics. Yes, actually snort. She wouldn't have been surprised if actual smoke rings had come out of his nostrils. The thought made her giggle even more.

Jezzie was relieved to see her cousin really did look good. Small creases still furrowed her brow and the strain of discomfort still covered her features, but she was up and about, and happy, so Jezzie wasn't going to send her back to bed before she had to.

The mood was thankfully lighter after the events of the day as they ate and joked. The large dining room felt cozy and warm with the love of family filling it. Questions flew about how Jezzie knew Leraie, how she was a witch on top of everything else, and what the hell was up with the damn sentient tree carving and how it'd slapped Uncle Micah's ass like that? A question said uncle seemed intent on avoiding, even as his cheeks reddened with his attempts to change the subject.

The food had been amazing, as always, and if she'd been wearing pants, buttons would have popped and zippers would have busted. She gave a proud pat to the little bump of her stomach which contained her most recently devoured food baby, and took another sip of her special dark red wine, and sighed contentedly into the crook of Nithe's shoulder. There was no better remedy for blood loss in angelkind than this particular beverage.

They'd moved into Uncle Micah's sitting room about an hour ago, and were just chilling on the sofa finishing their drinks, conversation lightly flowing.

"Jezzie Bear?"

"Yeah, Tana Cub?"

"Think we can have a girl's night, tomorrow? I mean, if it's okay for me to borrow your lady for a bit, Ni?"

Tana looked Nithe right in the eyes with that puppy dog look all five-year olds can pull off perfectly. Since Nithe viewed her as a little sister, it brought him to his knees. With a big sigh he shook his head ruefully.

"I suppose I could go spend one night with the princes. Thad's been practically begging for a rematch since the last time I wiped him off the face of his Dungeons and Dragons chess board. So, if you wanna have some Tana time, Jez, it's A-OK with me. Not that the choice is ever mine, mind. You are free to make those yourself, as you always have been."

He nuzzled the top of Jezzie's hair. The strong scent which belonged to only him surrounded her in a cloud of comfort. God, it felt good. She breathed deep, taking him into her lungs and smiled up at him.

"Girl's night it is."

Tana squealed but lacked the energy to jump around like she usually would, but the happy glint was still visible in her eyes. Until the light shifted and a curious look filled her eyes. Curiosity mixed with the tiredness she'd been fighting for the last ten minutes.

"Switching subjects. How are the dream guys going? Still hanging around?"

"Yep," Jezzie and Nithe answered in unison.

"I know you guys have discussed what might happen if or when you meet them. But what if only one of you is there the first time it happens?"

"Highly unlikely, especially here, but we trust each other, right, Jez? We've done so much in those dreams already. There is no jealousy on my end when it comes to those two males. But, if they hurt her? My dragon will eat them whole, extra crispy, with no regrets. I'll even break out the marinade."

Jezzie chuckled against his chest.

"You'd have to get in line, Ni. I'd get first dibs," Jezzie added.

"On that note, it's time for bed, kids. The Elders need to talk."

Leraie's sudden appearance in the small room startled them all, including her uncle.

"SERIOUSLY? That punk assed bitch of a motherfucker—"

"Language, Michael. The Almighty does everything for a reason.

Just because you don't know what it is, does not give you leave to act like an ungrateful heathen."

As he stood in his study staring incredulously at Leraie, Michael couldn't keep the anger and pent-up resentment from his expletive laden response. He wanted to rage, to tear the room apart. To storm the heavenly gates and demand the justice long denied him. Long denied to Tana, and to his wife.

"Are you fucking kidding me right now, Leraie? My brother is to arrive here, to find the place I've been hidden away all these years, and you won't even let me walk out there to say hi?"

"Tisn't in the plan, Micah. I am sorry, for what it's worth. You two boys have always been special to me. Part of my DNA makes up who you are, and while I didn't birth you, in some ways I've always thought of you as my sons. It pains me to see the road you have had to tread in recent times. But, I know the end game must come to be. The Fates always have their way," Leraie uttered compassionately.

But Michael wasn't having it.

Fuck compassion.

And fuck fate, and the emotionless bitches who ruled over it!

CHAPTER 33

Almost two weeks after sharing with the others about his shadows trying to castrate him and the clusterfuck that'd followed, Roth was ready to burst, and no, not a nut . . . at least not yet. He was so sexually frustrated by the constant interruptions to his alone time with Athon that all he wanted was to get him naked ASAP. It wasn't like he hadn't gone years without sex before, it was just that now he had Athon back his body believed it should never happen again, apparently.

As they reached the door to their shared room Roth spun Athon around and kissed his lover's lips with gentle passion. He reached behind Athon's back and fumbled for the handle before it swung inward. Roth stepped in closer to Athon's body and herded him into the room, with a hard shove the heavy door slammed shut behind them. He grabbed ahold of Athon's hips and pushed him up against the wall without turning on the light. Falling to his knees on the thick carpet he made quick work of unfastening his lover's pants and pushed them down to his ankles.

Athon's fingers wove through his dark hair and rubbed at his scalp, as his cock thickened and rose before him. His face moved closer, and he allowed his warm breath to fan over Athon's sensitive flesh. His tongue flicked out to wet his parched lips before he licked at the sensitive skin on the underside where the head met the shaft, causing his length to bob in response.

Roth slipped his lips over Athon's cock, opened his mouth wide and took him to the back of his throat. The groan his love released almost undid him, his own cock throbbed with the need to thrust and seek its own release.

Athon thrust in and out, his breathy groans came faster and harder, filling the space and bouncing off the walls as Roth sucked in his cheeks, swirled his tongue, and cupped Athon's balls in one hand. His other hand firmly wrapped around his own cock in a desperate attempt to stave off his own orgasm.

Just when he thought they'd both lose control, Athon gently shoved him back and shakily helped him to his feet.

"Why—"

Instead of answering his unfinished question Athon advanced until they were chest to chest. Heaving muscled pecs against heaving muscled pecs, their tattoos melding together almost as if designed to perfectly complement each other. Sexual tension sizzled in the air as Athon's teeth were bared, a low growling noise coming from deep in his chest, as if it were caught up in the maelstrom of a storm. An answering growl echoed through the room and Roth was stunned to realize it had come from him. Yet while his eyes widened he stepped forward, pushing impossibly further into Athon's space.

Lips locked and hands traveled desperately over hard muscles. They grabbed at hair and scratched at every inch of skin as they exposed it. Their need became more desperate, more carnal, more primal than it had ever been before.

Suddenly, Athon grabbed a fistful of Roth's hair and wrenched his head to the side, exposing the side of his neck. Athon lunged forward and bit down hard, breaking skin and sending fire raging through his blood. Without thought Roth dropped to his knees and bit down hard on the taut flesh just above Athon's cock and to the right. Athon's shout as he cums, hard, sends Roth over the edge, his cock erupting with his own orgasm onto the carpet between them.

Mated! Two victorious and foreign voices echoed through his head. What the fuck?

Before his brain fired up enough to do anything but flounder in ecstasy and confusion Athon hauled him back to his feet. A feeling of rightness settled over his soul and he had the feeling something irreversible had just occurred. They were bound together tighter than they ever were before.

As they leaned into each other, depleted and satisfied, the perfection of the moment washed all other intrusive thoughts away. The moment eventually ruined by the sharp rap of knuckles on the thick wood of their bedroom door.

"Fuck off," Roth grunted, annoyed at the intrusion.

"Come on, my brothers, get your asses dressed and moving. Meeting in five," came Malphas's amused voice.

"I agree! Fuck off, Malphas. We just left a fucking meeting, bro," Athon piped up as he gave the still closed door the finger, his forehead still resting against Roth's shoulder.

"Dudes, don't shoot the messenger. She who will not be ignored is, as of right now, waiting for all our asses in the meeting room. Fuck, even Caine's been called back in, so you know it's gotta be something big. I suggest if you don't want to be bitch slapped back into last century, or worse, erased from existence, you get moving."

The guys were each one leg into their pants by the time Malphas stopped talking. They pulled on shirts as they bolted out the door and raced down the hallway, boots on, but laces flapping with each hurried step.

Leraie held court from Luc's seat as they entered. The throne suited her as much as it suited Lucifer. Regal and dark, the black, studded leather with its elegantly carved, matte black timber frame, flared wide behind her shoulders. She was an impressive woman. Tall and strong. Unique in her power, which oozed into the room and made many wary of what she could do. Leraie was one being, male or female, angel or not, that Athon would never even think to fucking cross. He liked his balls where they were and preferred his molecules in their current configuration, thanks.

"Hi, boys, glad you could join us," she smirked, her nose twitching as though sniffing the air.

Fuck, they smelled like dried cum. Of course she knows what it is. Fuck my life.

"So glad you boys have moved beyond your misguided squabble and made up. Sorry to intrude on such short notice."

She looked tired. Like, bone tired, exhausted and in need of a holiday kind of tired. Since the moment of creation, their entire existence, she'd never truly looked this worn out. As if something heavy weighed on her soul. Not that anyone truly knew Leraie or her soul, outside of the Almighty, and possibly Luc and Michael.

As Dante strolled through the door they all looked around. Caine was the only one missing. Luc sat at the other end of the long table, so they took it as their cue and seated themselves side-by-side. Under the table they laced their fingers together and braced for whatever storm was coming their way. Judging by the look on the General's face, it was bound to be a doozy. Leraie smiled gently, a shimmer in her eyes, like tears, but not. Silver threaded with a storm of emotions too intense and complex to fit such a mundane label.

The doors burst open and Caine came stomping into the room. Anger and frustration rolled off him in waves.

"That fucking rookie at the gates wouldn't let me the fuck in without a password. What fucking password? Since when have we needed a password? Mrs Briars had to chew him a new one in order to get me in. Also, why the fuck did I need to get buzzed in? Why couldn't I portal into the damn forecourt directly?" Caine ranted.

"Uh, um, shit. I forgot to send you the info. Sorry, big guy. My bad," Deus said, sheepishly.

"As for the why, have you forgotten the traitor and all that jazz? Precautions needed to be taken," Mrs Briars added, as she appeared at Leraie's side, drawing Caine's eyes her way.

Athon chuckled, Dante snorted, and Luc even smirked as Caine's face turned ashen and his expression turned to fear and mortification at the sight of Leraie. She'd played a part in his creation as an angel and helped him keep his sanity after his human years were over. While the rest of them didn't know everything that went down in its entirety, they knew Caine both respected and feared her with good reason.

"Sorry, Leraie, for my outburst. If I had been informed you were already present I would have controlled myself better," he uttered as he bowed low.

"Relax, Caine. It's not like I haven't heard the word fuck a time or two in my existence. Hell, I've even engaged in the act a few times. Oh, the shock and horror, I know," she laughed at his discomfort and waved him up from his courtly bow.

"Right, since we're all here, what say you we get started, Leraie?" Luc ground out grumpily.

Someone was in a bad mood and hadn't taken his chill pills today. But that wasn't anything new lately. The added strain of the last five years had taken a further toll on their fearless leader.

"Right you are, Lucifer. Take your seats everyone and we'll get this show on the road. Lace up your boots boys and girls, you're going to need them." Leraie sat back, seeming content to wait until they did as she asked.

It was then Athon realized his boots were undone, confirmed by Leraie's wink as he looked under the table and back up. He squeezed Roth's hand and pushed his chair out to quickly secure his boots, as Roth caught on and did the same.

"Everyone ready? Good. Because even if you're not, the ride's about to start, and you'll be on it whether you want to be or not. The Almighty got word from the fickle bitches of Fate that now is the time. Since other things are in motion elsewhere it was up to either me or them to bring you the news and be your guide."

At Dante's derisive snort, Leraie nodded sagely. His face was pale, his eyes haunted.

"Yeah, no way was the Almighty going to allow them entry here. No matter their protestations that it's their job. Not with their history with you, Dante. They know they are banned from having any further direct interactions with you, or your future."

"Good, 'cos I couldn't have guaranteed my restraint if they ever entered these walls. Even without my own ax to grind, I'd never allow those bitches the opportunity to hurt Dante any more than they already have. Or any of you for that matter," Mrs Briars snarled.

Her snarl was a thing of feral beauty, and it warmed Athon's heart to know this wonderful lady was on their side.

"It's time for what, exactly, Leraie? I'd rather not spend all day trying to figure out your cryptic riddles. Just spit it out," Luc bit out roughly. His tone bordered on derisive.

"Sit up, shut up, and listen, Luc. Cut the attitude with me or I'll put you on your ass. Speaking of his ass, anyone tried to dislodge whatever's been stuck up there lately? No? Shame, he used to be much more fun," Leraie chastised him. Under her breath she muttered, "Damn stubborn jackasses, smart mouths obviously run in the family."

Still, Athon managed to catch the soft-spoken words, and the chuckle that followed.

"Hold onto your britches, boys and girls, we're going on a field trip. One of the things you've been searching for is about to be found. The others not so much, but this one's a game changer."

Questions like where, what, who, and when, flew through the room until Mrs Briars's loud, piercing whistle snapped every mouth shut. Even Leraie flinched back from the noise as it rang out so close to her ear. She shook it off with ease and kept talking.

"As you know, all things come to be in their own time. The when, where, how, and who are controlled by the Fates. Generally, with a few unfortunate exceptions, those bitches are controlled by our one and only Almighty. So, as angry as this may make you all, you need to try to understand that it is only in the now that this information can be passed on to you. All parties needed to be ready, all players in place for the creation of the future the Almighty has planned for all of you. So take a big breath and bite your tongues 'til I'm done." Steel threaded through her voice toward the end.

Athon found his mouth sealed shut as Leraie smiled benignly at them, still, the apology in her eyes was clear to see. Luc, though, looked ready to throttle her, but as he stared at her, he seemed to calm, bit by bit, until he huffed through his nose and leaned back into his—much less majestic—chair. Leraie focused on Luc, locking her eyes on his.

"The woman you seek, the one who'll mean the world to you, your greatest gift and treasure, who will change who you thought you were, can be found in the one place you have never set foot. The one place even angels fear to tread." Leraie's eyes roamed the table and stalled, bouncing between him and Roth before she continued on.

"The red-haired woman is the first key to a future you all deserve. Though the how, may just surprise you. You've all got twenty minutes, then we leave."

The invisible seal lifted from their lips instantly.

"Nestradia? Why the fuck would she be there?" Fynn burst out. "How did she even get there?"

"Because that is where she needed to be, Fenris," came Leraie's tart reply.

"Of course, the one place we can't just portal into on a whim. How has she survived there for, what I'm assuming, is years now?" Malech pried.

"She is so much more than you expect her to be." Leraie reveled in cryptic shit like this.

Athon felt his heart twist. She'd spoken directly to Luc about her and her importance. His very soul ached, how could Luc have survived it all these years? It felt like being ripped apart by his own shadows. The loss he felt, and he hadn't even really met her, hadn't had the chance to get to know her. He knew he had to give her up. But his very being rebelled at the barest thought of it. To know he'd find out her favorite ice-cream, what kind of movies she liked, what songs made her dance. But, he'd never get to hold her close and be a part of her everything.

The one time he and Roth had drunkenly bought up the idea of sharing her with Luc . . . it had not gone well. Mrs Briars had been forced to sedate Luc for six months and then wiped the whole incident from his short term memory. She'd proceeded to cuss them out for three hours straight while saying some cryptic shit about different paths that all start from the same point, and some intertwining stuff they couldn't understand because . . . well, they were still half drunk.

"Oh, the witch sent another gift. I left it on the bar. We'll be back after I get our honored guest some food and a nice cup of tea. Not a word to anyone. We still have a traitor, as I'm sure you all recall."

With that said, Mrs Briars led Leraie out of the room with her head held high.

Malech was the one who gathered himself together first and approached the bar before returning to place the "gift" in front of Luc, who went to open it with a smile on his face. Deus watched with hooded lids from the seat next to him, a scowl plastered across his features.

"Who is this witch, anyway?" Caine asked with confusion. "And what's with the gift? Has she sent more than one?"

Caine hadn't spent much time at home the last few years, his charge had been born five years ago, and he'd been obsessed with his duties, at the expense of all else. He still collected souls when he was meant to, but it was his divine duty to see his curse through until the end. And it seemed it would never truly end. Athon often forgot that Caine hadn't seen the witch, nor her gifts and messages.

"I'm sure you'll get to meet her at some point, Caine. She's my girl's bestie, after all," Luc said gleefully.

The smell hit them first as Luc peeled back the tape on top of the box. A combination of rotten meat and acrid smoke mixed with bitter herbs.

"Urgh, what the fuck is that?" Caine asked, hopping up to peer over Luc's shoulder.

As he got a good look, his face turned green and he covered his mouth with both hands as he raced to the waste paper bin and hurled up the contents of his stomach.

"Looks like char-grilled testes to me," Luc laughed. "Still attached to the base I see. Oh, there's a note."

Damn, the male looked positively delighted at this newest development. Lily and Perri laughed as the rest of them checked and covered their own testicles, as if they feared they'd magically been removed and were now sitting in the box before them.

"With every message and gift my girl crush grows," Perri chortled. "Seriously, if she keeps this up I'm going to fall in love with this badass witch . . . or join her quest . . . or both. Either way, I think she's awesome for gifting Lily and me with the priceless looks on your faces right now. Except the boss, he looks as chuffed as I am."

Luc opened the note and cleared his throat.

Dear boys and girls,

Taking out one evil mage at a time. Careful boys, hurt one of mine and you might just be next on my 'Soon to be nutless' list.

Sincerely,
Your worst nightmare if you're not careful xx

THEY CLEARED AWAY the mess and were ready to go by the time the females returned. Leraie gave them the run down quickly and explained they were headed to a hidden place only she could create a portal directly to and from.

As they all lined up behind Leraie, Luc moved to stand beside her, but Mrs Briars stopped him and whispered loud enough that Athon could hear them, Roth too, judging by how he leaned slightly forward, so the words wouldn't slip away.

"Don't fuck this up, my boy," she sighed heavily. "I know you will, but an old lady can only hope. In the end it will be what it will be, I suppose. Gook luck, laddie." She gave him a pat on the back as Leraie opened the portal and stepped through, Luc close on her heels.

As he and Roth made to pass by their self-designated warden, Mrs Briars' soft hand grabbed one of Roth and Athon's arms, her grip surprisingly firm as she tugged them out of line, and forced them to bend down. She stretched up on her toes as high as she could, and captured them each by an earlobe, pulling them further down, so she could whisper resoundingly in their ears. The rest of the team entered the portal one by one until they were the only ones left.

"The same goes for you two, as well. Don't fuck this up. I can guarantee you'll regret it if you do. And not just because the witch will kick your asses. I, personally, really don't want to go to war with her just because you two act like idiots. Now, give me a kiss on the cheek, and get you asses through that portal before Leraie decides to lock you out and leave you behind."

They barely managed to straighten up just before she gave them a mighty shove through the slowly closing portal, almost as if Leraie had heard her warning.

CHAPTER 34

Nithe had left early the next morning. In his dragon form he'd taken flight and quickly arrived at the palace. The link they shared blessed her with the ability to always be in communication with him, so long as he was open to it at the time, and conscious, of course. Before he'd gone they'd made love with so much passion she'd pretty much passed out for an hour as orgasm induced exhaustion had taken over her body. He'd woken her with soft kisses and a hot cup of delicious coffee. Then he'd left, so she'd headed to breakfast to meet up with Tana and start their girl's night. Which, in typical Tana fashion, actually meant girl's day and night.

Normally they'd train in combat and flight after breakfast, maybe a little monster hunting thrown in for extra fun depending on how much pent-up frustration her cousin was feeling. Unfortunately for Tana, Jezzie was enforcing a strict no strenuous activity order due to her cousin's current situation and the events of the previous day. To offset her cousin's guaranteed annoyance Jezzie had decided they'd do some light swimming after breakfast, followed by Tana's favorite fantasy board game, which usually took a few hours to finish. Especially if she decided to kill off the princes as slowly and painfully as possible, which was more common than not. She'd invented the game for the sole purpose of plotting their demise as a teenager, perfecting it over the years into something pretty awesome and complicated; it could give mainstream games a run for their money.

As she entered the dining room her cousin's face lit up with genuine delight.

"Eep! Girl time!!"

Tana's high-pitched squeal had the potential to shatter eardrums Jezzie thought as she visibly recoiled. Her cousin's excitement was infectious as she jumped up from her seat and bounced around the dining room.

"Calm down, girl. Anyone would think we hadn't done this a time or two already, damn. Plus, you need to rest, remember?" Jezzie paused to look around the room. "Has Uncle Micah eaten already?" she added.

"I think so. That or he ate in his room. Leraie left this morning. Apparently they had something super important to discuss and Dad's going to be locked up in his rooms for a few days working on whatever it is. Leraie said we need to leave him be. She's set the barrier up around his wing so we don't bother him with our fun. How boring is that?"

"Hey, look at it this way, Ta, we can watch all the sexy men movies we want to on the big screen without his complaining . . . that's gotta be a bonus, right?" she gave Tana a cheeky over-exaggerated wink as she watched the cogs turn behind her cousin's eyes at the possibilities of unsupervised girl time.

Sure they were adults, but this was Uncle Micah's house, so you had to follow Uncle Micah's rules . . . most of the time, anyway.

They finished breakfast in silence. Well, Jezzie did. She ate so fast Tana joked she was either starving, going through a growth spurt, or Nithe must have really gone to town last night. Jezzie almost choked on her eggs at her final accurate guess and Tana crowed her victory and cheered that at least someone in this mildly wretched place was getting some.

As per usual Tana trounced Jezzie in her three-hour-long game, crushing her defenses to keep the princes safe from her retribution. So what if Jezzie didn't try too hard? It wasn't about winning. Jezzie had learned a while ago it was more about giving Tana's frustration, anger, and complicated love/hate emotions an outlet.

Going for a swim had been lovely and relaxing, followed by lunch, facials, a mani-pedi, and making some caramel fudge to go with their popcorn and movies later that night.

Relaxing in the hot tub with a glass or two of wine was a perfect way to ease some aches and pains. Tana's expression had become drawn and pinched as the day had worn on. Jezzie added some healing herbs and oils to the water to ease her discomfort before they'd hopped in. She was thankful she had as she watched her cousin's features relax and her limbs sink further into the warm water. Jezzie herself felt renewed in ways she hadn't thought she'd needed until the magic of the herbs and oils started to take effect.

"Gosh, J Bear, this feels sooo good. Whatever you did to the water, it's amazing," Tana all but moaned.

"I know, right? Thank the heavens for Aunt Rai Rai. Every time I even scraped my knee as a kid she'd stick me in a warm bath of this. It was her cure for all kinds of aches and pains. I hope she's okay. I know she will be, because she's Aunt Rai Rai, but she's also not going to just give up on trying to find me. Neither will Mom."

"Enough of the maudlin retrospection and downers. The night is young, we are beautiful, and before we get to dinner and snacks we need to pick our guilty pleasures of the evening while we sip this divine wine and bask in the warmth of this witchy brew. I was thinking either a *Resident Evil* marathon or as many episodes of *The Witcher* as we can fit in. I'd toss a coin to my witcher, alright. Just to see it bounce off his perky backside and have Henry turn and raise his eyebrow at me. Woo." Tana fanned herself as they both devolved into giggles.

Jezzie had to agree with Tana. There was something about the man that could get a damn nun's heart racing.

"I don't want to say no to Henry, but I kinda want to escape reality for a while, and we can pretty much find those kinds of monsters on our doorstep anytime we want. Maybe not Henry," she winked at Tana. "But I have Nithe and my mystery men, and there are five very handsome, very available, and very eager princes up for the taking. Even if only for a spin or two."

Jezzie watched Tana's face closely. The heated blush that swept up her neck and across her cheeks as her pupils dilated, the guilt that pinched her previously parted lips. The emotions rolled off her in waves, one after another. She was so conflicted it felt like torture, and Jezzie regretted poking the bear.

"How about we watch an episode or two of grimed-up-good Henry, followed by two girl's night classics?" Jezzie said, bringing them back on task.

"*Thelma and Louise* and *Grease*?" Tana asked.

"Well, yeah . . . but if you want something else I'm totally on board. We can see what we feel like after those and go from there."

"Why would I want to pick anything else? I mean, Brad Pitt and Danny Z? Seriously?" Tana bounced around and sent water and wine sloshing over the rim of the tub.

"You've got problems, Coz. You seriously need to get laid, for one," Jezzie laughed.

"Tell me about it . . . J Bear."

Tana exaggerated a wink and tossed back her wine so fast she choked a bit, sending them into another round of carefree hilarity.

FOUR HOURS, three bowls of popcorn, a plate of fudge and an undisclosed number of bottles of wine later, they were dancing around the home theater room singing at the top of their lungs and busting out all the moves when a shrill wail filled the air.

"Someone's here. Someone who shouldn't be," Tana gasped, instantly serious as she dove for the remote and turned everything off.

Jezzie reached out immediately to Nithe. Not that the alarm had ever gone off on him before. Leraie was also here, she could sense her, but the same went for her. No alarms rang out for the five of them. So who, or what else, was here?

Babe? All good with you?

Yeah, just gaming with the guys and having a few drinks. You okay? Need me to come back? Worry threaded through his response and slithered into her system.

Nope, all good. We seem to have some visitors. I can sense Leraie's here, though, so I'll keep you updated. Love you, Jezzie rushed to reassure him.

Love you too, a stór.

The warmth of his love settled the raised hairs on her nape and kick-started her brain.

"Weapons?" she asked Tana who usually had a stash hidden in every room.

"Duh, I've got some. Not as fine as those blades of yours, though. Just remember what Dad said. Call them forth and they shall come. They are a gift, infused with your blood, your essence, and linked to the shadows you house. It's even possible they're infused with them as well. Who knows? All I know is Hephaestus is one talented forger, and you are one lucky daughter of a bastard. No offense to my uncle."

Tana gathered her weapons and headed to the door as silence descended. Jezzie followed as they made their way along the corridor outside the theater. Only the first alarm had been triggered, which meant they were in the entrance hall. The further they went along the labyrinth-like passageways the more prepared for a fight they became. Voices filtered down the hallway, indistinct and muffled. Behind a bubble maybe? But why? Were they that bad at being sneaky?

They stopped at the corner of the hidden hallway and Tana poked her head around quickly before she snapped back and slammed a hand over Jezzie's mouth.

"He's here. You can't say anything about my dad, not that you could if you wanted to. I'm sorry, Jezzie, this is either going to go really well, or really badly. Leraie wouldn't be here otherwise," Tana whispered softly into the shell of her ear.

"Who?" Jezzie tried to ask, but Tana just held her hand and dragged her around the corner.

Whereupon, she had her very own 'Sandra Dee caught in the headlights' moment, and froze.

COLD, hard stone surrounded them as they stood in the cavernous room, the portal at their backs. The others looked just as baffled as he felt. Nestradia was a place of monsters and nightmares, so why were they in what looked to be a rudimentary cave system? A large one, but still. Several paths led off from the circular space and Roth found his feet itching to move down one as if a magnetic pull was tugging at his body.

"Are we meant to stand here all day, Leraie?" Luc asked, practically bouncing out of his rubber soled boots.

"Patience, Cifer. She'll be here soon." Leraie gave him an encouraging, but slightly stiff smile.

"Should we try to go further into the cave system? Is it even safe for her down here?" Athon asked with concern.

"It's perfectly safe, I built it after all," she reassured him as she hastily inspected her nails. "Stay where you are. Talk amongst yourselves, and, I don't know . . . try not to be assholes when she does show up?"

Luc started pacing back and forth. Tension filled the space until it was so thick his shadows seemed to clog the very air. Roth moved back and Deus stepped between him and the General. He glanced over and saw Malphas and Caine bracketing Athon as they herded him further away.

"If things go south and you two can't control yourselves, or worse, she shows interest in you two, we need you separated and protected from his reaction. Understood?" Deus whispered directly in his ear, the hand on his shoulder squeezed firmly. "So, whatever you do, keep it in your pants, or I'll chop it off myself."

Judging by the look on his face Deus had attained 'critical injury' levels of seriousness.

He opened his mouth to say something back, to assure the male he knew his place, but words failed him as *she* came into view. More like was dragged into view by someone else. Another woman, though he couldn't describe her if he tried, his eyes were solely focused on the redhead who haunted his and Athon's dreams, his very thoughts. Here she was, so close, yet so far away.

A look of shock was plastered on her face as she elbowed the woman beside her, her gaze locked on Lucifer. In that moment, as his resentment flared he couldn't bring himself to call him Luc, to call him friend, brother, or General. And he hated the tornado of chaos it caused in his brain.

"I don't know who the fuck that is . . . but that's not my Caria!" Lucifer suddenly snarled, whirling away in an explosion of black shadows, disappearing before anyone could react, and as only he could, through the still open portal behind them. The lack of flames an indication of his mood.

Her eyes dropped to the floor as she flinched back as if struck by an invisible blow, her hand held a death grip on the fingers of the woman beside her. And then she looked up and over to Leraie, her chest heaved, whether in anger or some other emotion he wasn't sure. Her eyes, the color of rain clouds.

"It'll be okay, Jezzie, I promise," Leraie's voice interrupted the shocked silence Luc's departure had instilled.

Jezzie's eyes . . . Her name, he finally knew her name, or at least part of it. She wasn't Luc's, whoever, whatever Luc thought she'd be. As that knowledge trickled into his stunned frontal lobe, the force of his loyalty and friendship, the command of his superior—which had held him immobile in his belief she'd never be his, be theirs—shattered. Luc had no claim on her, his warnings were no longer a blockade to Roth's lustful intentions. To his and Athon's plans.

He'd once thought to fuck her out of his system, drive her from his dreams, eradicate her strange hold on him. Facing her now, he doubted any of his previous aspirations would be achievable. Oh, he'd fuck her every which way he could devise, but somehow, he knew she was irrevocably tied to his heart, his soul. The question remained though . . . could he really trust her with either?

Her gaze roamed over them, one by one, before zeroing in on him and Athon. She ignored the others, her eyes flicked back and forth between them as though she didn't quite believe they were there. Or maybe she was worried about what they might do, say, or think. She inched backward until her back hit the wall, and jolted. She seemed surprised to have ended up there, and yet she took a breath and pushed away from it, straightened her back and steeled herself for whatever came her way. Still, she managed to look small and lost, in need of strong arms to help support her. Their woman was full of courage, but he'd known that when she'd stood up to him beside a filthy dumpster in a dark alley all those years ago. Thankfully, whatever had happened to her since hadn't diminished her spirit.

His eyes flashed to Athon, the only one who knew how broken he truly was, but Athon was completely focussed on the woman who could be theirs for eternity, his eyes slightly glazed over, his mouth so lax he was surprised he didn't see any drool hanging out.

Minutes passed in the blink of an eye as Roth moved toward her slowly . . . But Athon got there first. As usual his more empathic side shone through as he wrapped his arms around her, and gathered her close. Suddenly the strong woman from earlier seemed like a child crushed by the weight of the world. Dejected and betrayed. Athon's gaze snapped up and locked with his, heat flared in his eyes, his spine stiffened as lust and magic seemed to wrap itself around him, his head inclined toward her once more. Inhaling deeply, Athon nodded, inviting him to come closer. He watched as Roth reached out, his fingers reverently caressed a lock of her magnificent hair, afraid to do anything more lest he startle her.

Just that slight contact, not even with her bare skin, was enough to send sparks shooting down his spine. A strange magic flared out and encompassed the three of them, swirling and penetrating his very soul. His desire ignited as it licked over his balls, his cock rock hard in an instant. And all the while his eyes never left Athon's face and look of wonder which perfectly portrayed his own awestruck emotions.

Having been unceremoniously dragged around the corner by her cousin, Jezzie couldn't help but stare at the one being she hadn't been even remotely prepared to see. For staring back at her was an almost carbon copy of her uncle. The only discernible difference that she could see was in their hair and the color of their eyes. Where Uncle Micah had forest-green eyes, Lucifer's were the color of lapis in sunlight. Her uncle kept his naturally golden-brown hair cut short but longer on top, and very dapper. Lucifer's hair on the other hand was as black as pitch and reached just below his chin with layers that slightly curled at the ends.

He stared at her for a lifetime, or for what could have been a split second, a micro moment. The passage of time itself seemed suspended, passing without recognition. Emotions flitted through his eyes, across his brow, his features morphing with each one. First with shock, then confusion, and finally with anger and some other indefinable emotion which hovered somewhere between hatred and despair. And she felt them all, tasted the bitterness of his rejection to her core.

Lucifer's angry proclamation shocked her into silence, even as a silent tear slid down her cheek. And then he was just . . . gone. Departing the same way he'd arrived, only, she surmised, much more dramatically, and Jezzie stared down at the floor to hide the raw hurt which filled the little girl she used to be. The one who'd longed for a father, her father, to hold her and love her, to read her stories and all those silly things little girls with fathers took for granted. All those things she had from her aunt and her mother, when she could, just not from her father. A father who hadn't known she'd existed.

She shook herself internally. How could you lose what you'd never had. She wasn't that little girl anymore. She was stronger, strong enough to face the crowd before her. He'd come with others, and Leraie. She must have brought them with her, no way they'd have gotten there otherwise. When she looked over at her questioningly, Leraie shook her head with a sad smile, but her eyes held a fire and brimstone kind of anger she knew wasn't directed at her.

"It'll be okay, Jezzie, I promise," Leraie said trying to soothe her frayed emotions, but it came out through gritted teeth and mutterings about asshole brothers.

"Don't worry about it, Jez. I have it on good authority that he can be a bit of a dumbass sometimes." Tana winked. "He'll figure it out eventually. And then he's going to have to kick his own ass, if someone doesn't kick it for him first."

But Jezzie wasn't listening. She barely noticed Tana walking toward Leraie, and while what Lucifer had done and said had registered like a whip to the chest—her body recoiling and flinching away from the barb-like sting of his words and blatant disregard, even though she knew at some later point in time his words and actions would have a visceral, and overwhelmingly hurtful impact upon her—she found her awareness solely and completely focused on two of the men who stood before her.

The others faded into the background. The men from her dreams had her rooted to the spot. All she could think was that they were both real and standing before her. What should she do? What should she say? Should she call Nithe home, or was it too much, too soon? Of course, she'd known one of them was real, she'd cursed and lamented her encounter with him as many times as she'd fantasized and dreamed of him naked and aroused. The guy from the alley, the Shadow Hound of Hell. But the other one, she thought maybe she'd conjured him from her dreams, that he was little more than a figment of her overactive imagination. Maybe they both were, and they weren't really there at all. Nithe had seen them too, but what if he'd just shared her dreams all along and none of it had been real?

Her back collided with the stone wall. She'd moved without conscious thought, the cold, rough mineral abrading her mostly bare shoulders as her body seemed to seek a way to disappear into it. Was she really this weak? This pathetic? Oh, how Balthazar would laugh if he saw her now. Pulling herself up slightly she squared her shoulders and took a tentative step forward.

The guy from the alley glanced away from her and over to her rainbow man, but Mr Mohawk didn't take his eyes off her, and she felt her mixed emotions bubble toward the surface, threatening to bring her to her knees.

In the space of a heart beat she was wrapped in warm strong arms, the spiced scent of male enveloping her senses and his heartbeat close to her ear. Her breathing settled and the tears which had threatened to spill receded, replaced with an awareness that they were really here.

Mr dark and broody slowly joined them, touching her hair as if it were some precious thing, this chest rising and falling as they all breathed each other in.

Jezzie, a stór? All okay? I can feel your turmoil. Please tell me you aren't watching that movie again. I thought I'd deleted it thoroughly this time. I don't get why you'd wanna put yourself through that again.

Her heart stuttered.

I'm okay. Lucifer was here, but I don't think he knows who I am yet.

Are you sure you're okay? Was he as much of a prick as your tone suggests?

Yeah, he was kind of a dick, but that's not the biggest surprise.

Shit! There's more?

Yeah, our dream guys were with him, and I don't know what to do.

Need me to come home early? I'll be there in five minutes if you say the word. On the flip side, I'll stay away for an extra day if you want a chance to feel them out and get to know them.

You'd do that? Stay away a little longer, and be okay with me and them, and what will probably happen if they don't turn out to be major assholes?

My love, we already know how this will play out. All three of us are yours. I've accepted it, they may have too, and while I know the shock hasn't yet worn off, you want this too. Get to know them, be with them, bond them if it feels right. I'm only a thought away, and I'll be back as soon as you are ready, or I can't take it anymore and need to see you, whichever happens first.

Jezzie chuckled, *I love you, mo shíorghrá.*

I love you too, a stór. Though, I do have a small request . . . block me out if you don't want me to come rushing back too early. I'm not sure I could take all the desire and not want to come back and ravish you or watch them ravish you. But if those boys fuck up I'll snack on their nut sacks, and not in a nice way.

Jezzie's breath hitched in her chest and desire pooled between her legs. A horny and protective Nithe was a whole 'nother level of sexy.

Eventually, she gently stepped forward and noticed they were all but alone. Only Leraie remained.

"I sent Tana to bed, she needs more rest. The others I forcibly returned home. You have three days, Jezzie, before I return. The oath still stands. You will always be welcome here and in the future can come back should you and Nithe choose to leave when I return, though it may be awhile. Roth, Athon, I suggest you make the best of your time here. Not only will the dragon destroy you should you hurt her, but I'll help him." Leraie's smile as she replied bordered on psychotic.

And then, she too, was gone, leaving them standing alone together in the empty stone room.

CHAPTER 35

Sometime later Jezzie had taken the guys to the sitting room and went to the kitchen for drinks, only to be bailed up by Tana with a mountain of questions, which had rained down so suddenly and so fast she'd almost fallen on her ass. She'd answered as many as she could, looked at Tana with a raised brow at the ones she couldn't, and waited for the interrogation to slow to a halt. Meaning, Tana's throat had gone dry, and she'd needed to gulp down some water, giving Jezzie a small opportunity to ask some questions herself.

Questions like, did Uncle Micah know they were here? Could she introduce her as her cousin, or would that be breaking the oath because of connecting dots? What should she do? And, did Tana need a chill pill? The last one had her giggling at Tana's affronted look.

"Leraie took me to see Dad. He's not allowed to see them, and they can't know he's here. And let me tell you, J Bear, he's pissed beyond pissed. A level of pissed I haven't seen since the princes found me. It was a little scary. I'm pretty sure he could give Lucifer a run for his money right now. As for introducing me as your cousin, let's go find out," Tana offered, tossing a wink full of sass over her shoulder as she'd grabbed the drinks tray and sashayed away to meet Jezzie's new special 'friends'.

The answer had been no. As soon as Jezzie had opened her mouth to call Tana her cousin her throat had seized up. She'd looked at Tana who shook her head with a wry smile. So much for dropping hints for later on.

A day had passed since Leraie had left with the promise of returning in three days, and she'd learned a lot. Not everything, but it was a start. Plus, did anyone ever really know everything about anyone else?

Being with them felt nice. It felt right. The guys sat side by side on the plush couch in the den, Jezzie awkwardly seated on both of their laps. Well, one ass cheek on Roth's muscled thigh, and the other on Athon's. Not the most comfortable position, but absolutely worth it. Fortunately for her, she had a little extra natural padding in the booty area which came in very handy in such situations.

Roth lightly stroked her hair, playing with the strands the same way he did that first day, as if he couldn't will himself to stop. His other hand held hers, almost like he was afraid to let her go. Athon, on the other hand, had her head tucked under his cheek, his head tilted to the side, breathing deeply—as if he could will her essence to become a part of him. One arm was slung behind her as he rubbed gentle circles on Roth's neck, or so she assumed judging by the way the muscles shifted in his forearm. His other hand rubbed similar circles on her thigh. He'd started at her knee, but every so often his fingers roamed a little higher. Testing the waters, seeing how far she'd let him go. So far, she hadn't put a halt to it. Still, she wasn't sure she wanted to rush things. She felt strange being so close to them in person rather than in her dreams. Especially without Nithe there to help her. She needed to get to know them, feel them and their intentions out. It all came down to two things: Firstly, if they were as awesome as they appeared to be. Secondly, if they accepted and got along with Nithe. If Nithe wasn't a part of their equation . . . then they wouldn't, couldn't, be a part of hers.

Her heart fluttered as her brain said his name, her thoughts racing out to connect with his, needing his familiar comfort.

Nithe, mo shíorghrá?

Fuck I love the sound of your voice, Jez, even if it's only inside my head right now. How may I be of assistance, my lady? Nithe's brogue felt almost as good to her ears as his dragon's rough tongue sliding along her sensitive flesh.

A stór, talk to me, before I race back home and kick their asses, whether they deserve it or not. The dragon came out in the harsh rumble of Nithe's voice.

All's good, Ni. Just miss you, is all.

What? Two hunky guys keeping you company isn't enough? he joked.

You know I love you, right? I feel so awkward and unsure with them, because I don't want any of you to feel left out, jealous, or weird or anything. She all but whimpered.

I'll be home first thing in the morning, a stór, sooner if you truly need me. I suggest you just be your awesome self. Get to know them more, have fun, let loose. I love you, you know that. Being intimate with them, loving them, won't change how I feel about you. In fact, knowing you are loved by them, not just in our dreams, but in reality, is an amazing feeling. This is meant to be, Jez. And seriously, everything we've done with them in our dreams, we have actually done with them, if Balthazar is to be believed about the Astral Plane. Which, come on, considering the amount of cum everywhere when we were done, we can't deny he told the truth.

Juice came shooting out of Jezzie's nose as she snorted. Fuck. It burned. Stupid citric acid. Her eyes started watering, and still she laughed. Poor Athon's shirt was wrecked, and the guys were eyeing her like she'd grown two heads. Tana, on the other hand, was smirking.

"Nithe whispering sweet nothings to you again, C—J Bear? Maybe filling your head with something naughty?" she winked and cackled.

Damn, she'd make a better witch than Jezzie any day if the contest was based on cackling alone.

Sorry, Jez. You okay?

Just dandy, thanks. Orange juice out of your nose is super sexy, dontcha know? Jezzie said sarcastically.

Well, on that note, I'm going to go rub one out. He chuckled. *Tell me how much you want my lips on you, how much you want my cock in your mouth, in your pussy, then go have fun with my bondmates before I come back just to spank that sexy ass of yours.*

I want you naked under my hands, my lips trailing over you warm skin, my nails raking over your hard muscles as I work my way lower to cup your balls and wrap my lips around your hot, hard cock, and suck you into the back of my throats while Roth and Athon watch, both buried deep inside of me. . . Bye, Ni, sweetest of wanks.

With that said she shut the link with a click and looked up to apologize to the two men still holding an obviously crazy woman close to them.

"Nithe? Is this the mind link thing you told us about, babe?" Athon queried.

"Yep," she popped.

"So?" Roth prompted.

"So, what?" Jezzie teased.

"What did he say to you that had you squirting juice out of your nose?" Roth chuckled.

"He told me to go for it. Take the leap and stop holding back with you both." They both perked up at that bit of news. "He also brought up how it's not like I haven't been covered in cum from all three of you before, reminding me that our intimacy is far from new. Though, I must admit how nice it is to hear your voice after all this time, Athon. And yours again, Roth."

Roth's voice held sexy Spanish undertones, while Athon's was like smooth black velvet covered bass. Both of which slid into her ear and under her skin to pucker her nipples and tease her hussy of a vagina.

"And are you going to take his advice, babe? Fast or slow, we'll do it your way," Athon asked and assured her at the same time.

Instead of answering, Jezzie twisted her upper body to face him, speared her fingers through the rainbow wonderland of his Mohawk, and pulled his mouth down over hers. Lips parted, tongues tangled and explored. The kiss was pure magical bliss. He tasted of cinnamon and spice. Okay, so they'd just finished off a tray of gingerbread biscuits, which accounted for the added flavor, but what lay beneath was passionate desire mixed with reverence and care, and what she could only hope was an emotion that would one day lead to love.

The sound of a deep rumbling growl came from beside them and one of Roth's hands up her back, gently tugging on the ends of her loose hair. His other hand slipped between her body and Athon's, his palm pressed against her thigh, her stomach, until he cupped one generous breast, squeezing it lightly.

The kiss ended as they came up for air, breathing heavily, but before she could recover, or utter a word, she was being turned and dragged onto Roth's lap. Her legs straddled his, and she could feel the long, hard length of him pressed firmly at the apex of her thighs. Her body moved of its own volition, urging for them to come together completely. Roth's large palms cupped her cheeks and slid into her hair, his lips slamming into hers. Unlike Athon's gentle exploration, Roth's was filled with savage fire and unbridled lust. Punishing almost in its intensity.

She felt a body pressed up against her back, Athon's warm heat and sexy scent behind her, Roth's in front, two sets of arms wrapped around her.

Athon's thighs pushed more firmly against hers, straddling Roth's legs like hers. His hard cock rubbed against her ass and back as he pressed it into her.

"Um, guys? I'm still here . . ." came Tana's amused voice. "You guys might be okay with an audience, but I really don't want to see my C— Jezzie doing . . . well, that," she added, flapping her hands at them when they pulled apart and looked at her, her nose crinkled in disgust.

But Jezzie saw the envy and sadness hidden in her gaze, caught the whirling emotions as they swept through the air between them, and instantly felt terrible. She knew Tana didn't begrudge Jezzie her happiness with Nithe, or what may happen with Roth and Athon, but knowing her current situation and the display they'd just made so quickly brought a flush of embarrassment to Jezzie's cheeks. Jezzie shifted and Athon stood and moved to sit beside Roth as she moved from his lap to a free space on the couch. Only for the guys to pull her back into her previous position on their laps.

"Don't you dare feel bad, J Bear. If it was someone other than you getting it on in front of me, I'd probably be totally down for the show . . . but, ick, you know?" Tana scrunched up her whole face like she'd smelled dog shit on the carpet.

Realization dawned as an image of having to watch Tana dry hump any of the princes implanted itself in her head and she started to gag. Yep, ick just about covered it. Tana busted out laughing as Roth and Athon looked confused by their cryptic conversation.

"You could have just left the room, you know," Roth sulked, grumpily.

"You could have moved to an empty room, you know. I'm on bed rest, well, couch rest, right now, and I'm pretty comfy right where I am .. . in my own home," Tana retorted. "Plus, it's not even nighttime yet, I'm sure you can wait a bit longer to get Jezzie alone in her room."

"Tana?" Athon gently asked.

"Yeah, Athon?"

"You know sex can be had at any time of the day or night, right? Lights on or off? Under the covers or on the kitchen counter? Even outside? Maybe not here, cos' monsters, but in safer settings, yeah?"

He wasn't trying to be cruel or sarcastic, Jezzie could tell, he just wanted to feel her out and help her. Luckily, Tana was easy-going with those she liked, and she'd instantly decided Athon was her new big brother, Roth not so much, not yet, so no offense was taken, and while her face flushed with the innocence of an inexperienced maiden, she laughed and gave him the finger.

"Oh, my gosh!" Tana exclaimed. "You know what we should do?"

"What? Find the nearest bedroom and leave you slobbing on the couch alone for a few hours? I agree. Let's go guys." Athon laughed at Tana's faux pout.

"No, silly. We should go hunting! Wouldn't that be fun, Jezzie? I think so. I really need to get out of here, and you could use a top up since you used so much extra energy helping me with that spell."

"So, you're a witch?" Roth asked Tana, suspicion creeping into his voice and causing Jezzie to stiffen.

"Fuck," Athon muttered under his breath as he squeezed her thigh.

"And what if I were?" Tana said, a protective kind of aggression cut like a knife through her tone.

"Well then—"

Jezzie mentally turtled into herself ready for the blow, knowing she'd have to turn and fight if the wrong words escaped his lips. Athon shifted and Roth groaned as his head moved suddenly forward.

"Then nothing. I think it's actually pretty cool," Athon filled the void as Roth rubbed the back of his head with his free hand.

"Good answer, Athon. A prime example of why you're my current favorite. But as you have already deduced, and thickie over there has yet to realize, no I am not a witch. In addition to being all kinds of badass awesome, Jezzie is part witch. A first generation, learned witch. Very rare, or so I'm told," Tana added proudly.

Roth stiffened behind her. What would he say? What would he do? Would he renounce her? Witches more often than not had been dealt a bum rap throughout history, thanks to a few bad eggs and the machinations and superstitions of others. Not just on Earth, but everywhere, it would seem. Witches, for the most part, were actually pretty awesome.

As with every species you had the good, the bad, and the in between. Mages, on the other hand, tended mostly to the self-serving, aggrandizing stereotype of greed and toxic masculinity. Witches stayed away from them for the most part, mainly due to them holding higher social standing within the OtherRealm hierarchy. The original negative narrative about witches was started by a long since dead mage, who upon realizing witches—the females of the species—were much more powerful, and altruistic than mages. Not to mention rather less inclined to kowtow to the bullshit expectation placed on them by the self-described superior gender the mages liked to think they were.

"Did you hear me, Jez?" Roth asked, pulling her from her off-topic ruminations.

"Huh?" was all she could think to respond, knowing she'd drifted off into her own thoughts.

"What kind of witch are you, Jezzie?" he repeated.

"The good kind, of course, you giant dumbass. Plus, it's a very recent discovery, so don't be a dick," Tana jumped in and answered for her, making her chuckle.

"Well, I've not met one of those in a long time. I'm sorry I reacted so poorly. The last witch we encountered has been sending us rather threatening missives and gifts, so to speak. We encountered her while looking for you, or someone we thought was you. It's all a bit confusing now, though, since we found you, and you're clearly not her," Roth rambled.

"Don't mind Azaroth, he's a bit out of practice with women," Athon said cheekily as he winked.

"Bad experiences tend to have that effect," Roth added snarkily, looking sharply at Athon before adding, "Sorry, I have trust issues, big ones. I just hope that the you we get to know here, is the you you really are."

"Oh, it makes sense now," Jezzie thought out loud.

"What makes sense?" Athon asked.

"The emotions pulsing out of him, the contradicting tastes and colors of his feelings. They all make sense now." She turned further toward Roth. "You want me. You don't know if you can trust me, but you desperately want to, almost as much as you want to bend me over the edge of this couch and spank me till my ass is perfectly pink and warm. Yeah, I can see the dominance which flows through you, just as I can see how much it turns Athon on when you are. I definitely don't need to feel the two hard cocks against my legs to know it either, but they are a very nice bonus."

She didn't feed from their feelings, per se, just as she didn't feed from Tana's or Uncle Micah's, or the princes. No, she used them to gauge moods and take the edge off, if she needed, and to help them when she could. Like she could reach out and touch them, see them, smell them, but choose not to feed on them. It was handy to get a sense of situations, or track people if you were close enough, too. Nithe mainly fed her his in a mutually beneficial way that didn't damage his mind, thanks to the bond. The gorgon bitches, and monsters of Nestradia, though, they were fair game. And while she wasn't allowed to kill the gorgons like she killed the monsters, she could still torment the living shit out of them if they overstepped their boundaries in her presence.

"How is that possible," Athon gasped. "No witch can do that."

"Well, since I wasn't born a witch—I am seventy-four years old, by the way—and as Tana said, I only just discovered my aunt's teaching had taken such an effect . . . It makes sense, right?"

She looked at her hands until they both nudged her sides gently.

"Just tell us, Jezzie. I promise if Roth says something stupid I won't have sex with him for a month," Athon cajoled.

"Fine, but don't freak out. I inherited my mother's powers. She was, is, hell I don't know, a psychic vampire," she rushed out, almost blending the words together.

"Like a succubus?" Roth asked, a little tension seeping into his muscles.

"No, no, nothing like that. I can't feed your desire by making you feel artificial sexual feelings that aren't really your own. Sex or desire isn't needed for me to feed off of the emotions of others. Any emotion will do, although some taste better than others. My hunger can only be fully sated by strong emotions, and while desire, love, and pure joy are some of the strongest emotions to feed from, and taste particularly sweet, I've seen first hand what damage can be done to mortal minds should I choose to take them and forget myself. So, instead I incite the depraved emotions and desires of the most evil creatures' humanity has on offer and once they are ripe enough to fill my tank for a good long while I suck them dry, not literally, cos' yuck. Fortunately, my bond with Nithe has allowed me to feed off of him in a mutually beneficial way without fear of taking too much since the monsters in this realm taste like ass, evil prisoners don't usually last long, and I refuse to feed from my friends," she paused, thinking.

"Is there something else?" Roth prompted.

"Ah, yep. My bond with Nithe allows me to feed him comfort if he is in need, usually his own from past feelings and memories, or some from my own. We can also send each other feelings of desire from a distance. And while I learned my lesson at a young age about taking too much from innocent sources, it took me a while to master how to mask my actions and send them some comforting emotions back to them. Not till the bond was fully formed did it all seem to click, and now it's just like breathing between Nithe and I. I suppose, if we choose to bond, it's something you'll need to consider," Jezzie finished, unsure if she'd scared them away.

"Definitely worth thinking about, isn't it, Roth?" Athon said with a smile. "Especially the thoughts of desire and mutual benefits part." His wink was a little wicked.

Thoughts of sharing sensations and passion through the bond with him flooded her mind. Add in Nithe and Roth, and she might just pass out before they could get to the best parts. Her cheeks flushed with heated desire, her clit throbbed and her thighs clenched. The asshat chuckled, knowing just what he'd done to her.

"Right, time to go hunting," Tana declared.

At some point her cousin had left and come back fully dressed in her monster hunting best, her weapons strapped in and all.

"Um, Tana. You're staying here, sweetie," Jezzie said carefully. "Leraie would have my ass if I let you out there right now, and you know it! No fighting for you."

"Fine! It was worth a try anyway," Tana huffed, picking up a bundle from the couch beside her and tossing it at Jezzie. "Here's your body armor. Have fun and think of me here, all alone." She sighed dramatically.

"We can stay, if you need," Athon offered, falling for her theatrics.

"Nope, get your asses out there and whoop some monster butt. I'm good. I'll be watching some sexy guys take their clothes off on the big screen while I eat a gallon of mint choc chip frozen dairy goodness while you guys are getting covered in monster blood and guts. Damn, stupid hormones."

Jezzie got up and gave her a hug, she'd started off strong, but the last part came out like a muttered angry curse, letting Jezzie know Tana definitely had a lot to work through, and she wasn't ready to be out and about.

She donned her supple black and green torso armor that fit like a glove and allowed all of the movement she needed in the heat of a fight. She tightened the buckles before adding the matching pauldrons, bracers, and lastly the greaves which perfectly fit over her boots. Thankfully she'd dressed in her finest black suede leather pants and a cream-colored peasant blouse, so she didn't need to go get changed. Thinking about it, Tana had been the one to pick them from her closet that morning, the devious little wench.

When she turned around, she could practically see the drool form at the corners of their open mouths. Tana just winked at her and skipped away down the hall singing, "All hail Tana, Mistress of Awesomeness." It would appear she'd caught them staring at her backside . . . again. Something Jezzie had caught herself doing to them every chance she got, so she couldn't really blame them.

"Let's go, boys. It seems I'm suddenly ravenous."

CHAPTER 36

Stagnant air hit them in the face like a blast of rotten eggs, mixed with decaying flesh and swamp sludge. It burned the back of Athon's throat as they emerged from a narrow tunnel and through the concealed exit into the dark and barren nightmare that was Nestradia, in all its fetid glory.

The pale glow of the purple moon barely lit the sky, giving little relief from the black abyss. Well, if he wasn't an angel, that would be a problem. Thankfully he and Roth were able to see better than most beings, even OtherRealmers, though Jezzie seemed to be having no such issues seeing through the darkness.

Maybe the vamp in her could see the beasts, or she had cast a spell to help her see? But Tana had mentioned Jezzie had only recently found out about her witchy powers . . . Maybe Leraie had helped her, after all she'd been hunting in this place the whole time she'd been here. The question was why? She was safe in the caverns with ample food, or so they said. So why hunt? For the fun of it?

Suddenly his brain stuttered to a halt and he heard Roth's breath catch in his throat. Or was it his own? Jezzie was picking her way over the rocks and boulders in front of them, her tight pants cupped her rounded curves lovingly. Displaying her rounded cheeks and thighs to perfection. He was pretty sure his drool took a stroll from the corner of his mouth down to his chin, but when he went to wipe it away he couldn't feel any wetness lingering there. Gray eyes seemed to pierce the dark as Jezzie turned her head to look back at them, a smirk tilting up one corner of her lips, a blush heating the pale softness of her cheeks. The ones on her face, not the ones he'd been so preoccupied by only moments before.

"Guys, stop staring at my ass unless you want yours to be grass. If you don't pay attention, you won't last long out here. Right now we are in a protected space. There's a barrier around the caves to keep everyone, including the monsters, away, from outside the barrier you can't even tell they're here. But once we leave this space, you can bet your sexy asses monsters are going to come out to play, and they don't fight fair. We need to work together, but you also need to let me do what I need to do, understood?" Jezzie said, a familiar tone in her voice he couldn't place. An air of command that was almost impossible not to obey.

"As you wish, milady." Roth bowed, and Athon caught a hint of respect mixed with annoyance in his lover's words as they both started the climb.

Jezzie pulled herself up to stand at the top of the ridge, hands on her hips, feet braced apart as she watched them make their way to the top, before she stepped aside to allow them up beside her.

"Two more steps away from the edge our protection ends, I suggest you call forth your weapons and prepare. Whatever happens, I have your backs. Whatever shadowy villain or beast moves, kill it." Jezzie smiled, a smile full of eager anticipation, excitement, and ruthless cunning.

"We are forbidden from taking unauthorized evil souls, if we use our blades they will sense the evil and draw it out. Do we need to go back for other weapons? Where are you hiding yours, anyway?" he queried.

"You have a far greater weapon at your disposal than your Hellborne blades. Your shadows will help you, if you ask. Plus, none of the monsters here have souls for you to take, so The Well won't call to them. The soulless creatures who roam this place have no logic, reasoning, or finer emotions, they are simply fuelled by pure instinct and primal urges. Except for the prisoners, who in my mind are the real monsters. Those are the ones I usually go after. You guys can stick to whatever beastie tries to make us their breakfast, or dinner, I've lost track of which it is . . . not an uncommon occurrence," Jezzie trailed off.

"What about our shadows can help out here? And how do you know so much about our blades? For a vampire witch you sure do know a lot about our kind," Roth tersely asked, his tone ripe with barely veiled suspicion.

"Yeah, okay, so, apart from being raised by a pretty badass witch there is one other component to my biology I haven't mentioned yet. I mean, I figured it might be better to just show you? You know?" Jezzie hedged, looking nervous.

"Whatever it is, Jezzie, we want to know all of you, and I'm sure it'll be fine," Athon tried to assure her as he glanced at Roth, noticing the hardening look in his gaze.

"Right, well, let's start with the weapons then, shall we?" She took a deep breath and closed her eyes. Her features settled into a look of focus, similar to a novice Hound-in-training, before one thin black cylinder appeared in each of her hands.

Shit! Neither he nor Roth were prepared for the appearance of the wakizashi-like, and probably razor sharp, black blades which suddenly exited each end of the grips she held, nor the hint of Hephaestus's magic that surrounded them ever so briefly. What surprised Athon more though, Roth seemingly less so, was the red swirling shadows that erupted from her and danced down her arms to curl around and seep into the sharp steel, licking at the pointed tip as if testing how deadly it would be.

"How did you get those?" The hint of an accusation entered Roth's tone.

"They were given to me upon my full manifestation of being. Or so I've been told."

Her manifestation, into what? What exactly was Jezzie? Angels couldn't reproduce with anyone other than humans—which was hugely frowned upon—and other angels—which was very rare as well. There were other beings whose powers manifested later in their life cycles, or had gradual releases of power before reaching adulthood. But neither vampires nor witches underwent a manifestation as such. Not to mention a hybrid of the two was utterly unheard of, let alone adding anything else to the mix which could go through such a thing. He was starting to get a taste of the confusion and frustration Roth had been enduring for years.

"Roth, Athon, don't panic, okay? And get that untrusting glare off your face, mister. I'm not going to eat the last piece of pie, or murder you in your sleep." Jezzie stuck out her tongue at Roth then chuckled nervously. "I suppose I should just get this over with."

Without warning Jezzie was surrounded in a cloud of shadows as she rose a few feet off the ground. The shadows settled and shrunk back into her body revealing two large, beautiful wings protruding from her back. The black feathers looked so soft and luxurious as they unfurled around her and the small horned tips on top, similar to Luc's but smaller, arched up and in toward her. But what caged his breath inside his chest wasn't that she had wings, no, it was the colored feathers along the bottom of them. The rainbow of colors was perfectly matched to the ones in his own hair. Hair that fell forward from a casual slicked-back, lazy faux-hawk, rather than its usual soft but spiked style, to frame his eyes and catch his gaze as if to declare to all that he and Jezzie were a matched set.

With no small amount of effort he lifted his jaw from where it had hit the floor and tore his gaze away from her wings, his eyes darting back and forth between Jezzie and Roth. Huh! Roth's eyes matched the blue hues of her wings as perfectly as it did the color he'd maybe . . . might have . . . okay, definitely did purposely choose for the blue in his own hair.

Before either of them found the wherewithal to utter a single word, Jezzie spun and took off running. "Keep up, boys." Her words floated back to them on the non-existent breeze.

Athon's blades flashed into his hands and his wings erupted free in one swift, graceful motion as he took off running after the crazy woman he was ready to claim as theirs. Roth was hot on his heels, muttered curses springing from his lips. By the time they caught up with her, she was almost nose to nose with a being so nightmarish it could only have been created by the Ghouls of Agregashi.

Tar-like slick rolled off its skeletal body, sharp claws and even sharper teeth snapped at the fetid air, too close to Jezzie for his comfort. He moved to rush into the fight, but Roth's firm grip on the back of his shirt pulled him up short, and he slid to a halt in the thick soil. Just then Jezzie ducked and slipped behind the creature, the edge of her blade slicing through its midsection as if it were soft butter. Puke-yellow ooze fell at its feet before the creature deflated, its carcass sizzled as it hit the soil. The thick loam sucking up the liquefied remains greedily amid a series of crackles, pops, and slimy slurps.

"She's fucking amazing," Athon uttered in awe.

"If she can handle herself like this, let's see what else our sexy hybrid warrior princess can really do and have some fun ourselves, yeah?" Roth asked, excitement for the hunt filling the space around them as Jezzie sauntered their way.

"I know you probably both have some pretty big questions, but can we have a little fun first? I promise I'll answer anything you want to the best of my ability as soon as we are done here and soaking in the hot tub with a glass of wine and no clothes. Sound good?" she concluded with a wink full of fire.

"Promise?" Roth's voice was stern, unlike his expression which held a soft vulnerability.

"Cross my vampiric-angelic-witchy little heart. Though, just so you know, I can't tell you who my father is . . ."

Roth's emotions went into lockdown as Jezzie paused, but she quickly hurried on.

"At least not yet. You see there's this suppression spell—say thank you to Leraie for that one—that means I can't say certain things which pertain to information that could reveal other certain things until it's time for those certain things to come to light, yada, yada, yada, the Fates, yada, yada, the Almighty's freaking master plan, yada, yada, all that bullshit. Otherwise, I'd straight up tell you right now, so we could all prepare for the inevitable clusterfuck in my future, our future, if you decide I'm what you both want? Me and Nithe, that is?"

"Leraie? You really can't say it? Can Tana? Nithe?" Roth probed.

"Nope. No one who knows the 'big certain something', anyway. Apparently, the mysteries will all start unraveling soon, at least according to both Leraie and the mysterious willow woman who guards my haven," she assured them.

Athon jumped as he felt something slide against his leg and he was suddenly flat on his face in the foul loam. Thick tentacles slid up his thighs as they pulled him along the ground. He twisted his upper body, his wings disappearing into his back, sitting up as much as he could as he hacked at the limbs with one deadly sharp blade, quickly severing them from the creature's largely hidden bulk. The detached pieces searched for their host and slithered away as he scrambled back and to his feet.

Jezzie and Roth grabbed his arms and pulled him further back as they searched for injuries, sighing with relief when they found none.

"You're lucky, they usually inject their victims with a paralytic venom at first touch that lasts just long enough to drag them under the soil to be buried alive before being eaten. But you seem fine, so yay!" Jezzie finished cheerfully.

"How do you—" Roth started to ask something but Jezzie cut him off.

"Nope, no more questions. Too dangerous, and I need to eat."

"Wha—" Athon stammered.

Jezzie just lowered her brow sternly, and shook her head, so he shut his mouth and followed where she led.

———

Two hours later, countless monstrous creatures defeated, and a few cuts and bruises, the guys were leaning against a large boulder taking a break as she searched for the energy of a soul nearby. There, the faint trace of a shiver. Evil personified, poison and rot. But it was so small she couldn't tell how far, or close it could be. Her eyes searched the flat land stretching out in the direction she could sense it. Nothing moved, the air undisturbed by even the smallest of creatures.

Jezzie turned to look back toward Athon and Roth, and caught a glimpse of oil slicked black fur and red eyes climbing up behind them, preparing to pounce. Just as she was about to shout a warning, she was tackled from the side, her body crashed to the ground hard, and went rolling in a tangle of limbs, fur, snapping jaws, and long claws. One wing stuck in the thick mud and slowed her down, flipping her up and over onto her feet and leaving the creature to slide a few extra feet away from her.

A quick look over her shoulder showed the guys battling against the other creature, who looked remarkably similar to the one before her, only smaller. Her attention focused back on her own problem pretty quickly as her opponent, having regained its footing, rushed at her with a burst of unnatural speed—even for monsters of this realm.

The fight was long and brutal. She spun and ducked and took every opportunity to run it through with her blades, until finally it fell to its knees, heaving as it clutched at its eviscerated torso. Behind her, she heard a whimper and the thumping sound of the other creature retreating.

Jezzie lowered her weapons, not all the way, she wasn't stupid, at least not today, but low enough to maneuver herself close behind the fallen beast.

Something was different. Something was wrong. She sniffed the air, leaning in closer to the creature. She could hear Roth's warnings but blocked him out. What was it? No! Surely not. How could it be? A soul inside the beast? Had it eaten one? If so, how was it still there? But it filled the creature's entire body, it wasn't contained within the stomach or bowels, even as faint and fetid as it was, as it would be if it had recently eaten a prisoner.

Bringing her blades up she tucked them under the creature's chin, crossing them as she circled back to stand before it, careful not to take off its head. A little extra pressure tipped up its chin, so she could stare into the gaze of an evil the likes of which she'd never seen. So dark and twisted and utterly devoid of goodness she felt her stomach revolt. It sucked her in, pulled her under and into a world she couldn't escape.

Images filled her head, horrific, unforgettable images ran behind her eyes like old home movies:

A CHILD, so small, so helpless. So lost and alone. A child whose innocence was stripped away, who was beaten and used. Tortured and starved, subjected to every unspeakable thing. Broken. The hands of a man, the hands of the fucked up piece of shit whose outside finally matched their insides.

THE CREATURE GROANED on the ground at her feet.

A WOMAN SLIPPED into her nightmare. But not to save the child, just another monster who deserved eternal pain. Light died in the child's eyes. She got older, older than what they wanted, though still a child to the world. They needed fresh prey, but they couldn't just let her go. She'd ruin everything. Death was their plan. And then . . . she was gone. Until she wasn't. Until she sent them here to fester and rot, the Fallen they should have always been.

JEZZIE'S BODY shook as she came back into herself. What the fuck was that? Nothing that immersive had happened to her before. She'd always chosen what to access, she'd never been forced to see into a person's past. Her hands moved of their own volition, the blades sliding against each other. The monster with a soul's throat opened up, thick red blood leaked out with the consistency of tar down its front. Her blades dematerialized, and she grabbed his face before his imminent corpse could hit the ground. She drew his soul into her, feasting on the last bitter remnants of its soul. A soul that should never, ever be allowed to live again. As she finished up she dropped him to the ground and wiped her blood stained fingers on her pants. It was then she realized she had an answer to the age-old question, well, her question anyway . . .

The question?

What could permanently kill a full-grown angel?

The answer?

Apparently, she could.

SHE WAS DIVINE. So fucking beautiful. Roth watched her from the corner of his eye whenever he could as she fought the beast attacking her and when she brought it to its knees, he almost crowed aloud at her victory. She circled her foe with an agility and grace few warriors could master after such a brutal fight. The creature he and Ath had been battling ran off as soon as Jezzie's bowed in defeat, but he barely noticed as he watched Jezzie size up her fallen opponent.

What happened next was like nothing he'd seen before, and he'd seen a lot. Jezzie swayed on her feet, though her blades held steady as she leaned in real close to the monster's face—too close for his liking— her nose almost touching the cavernous opening that may have once been its own sniffer. Her eyes glowed a vibrant red, and Roth started to worry, his pulse spiked and adrenaline pumped through his veins. This time it wasn't from the fight, but fear.

Beside him, Athon called her name. Nothing. He called again, louder this time. Still she didn't step back or acknowledge him. Roth was two steps into a sprint to her side when she finally moved back, and in the space of a heartbeat three things happened simultaneously. The creature no longer had a head, Jezzie was sucking the last whispers of its impossible soul from its shuddering carcass, and a thousand new questions skipped with the elegance of a wrecking ball into his overloaded brain.

The one thing, though, which shoved him over the edge and had him pulling her tight into his embrace with the intent to never let her go, were the dual rivers of tears pouring from her eyes as her chest heaved with the silent sobs she held inside.

CHAPTER 37

Roth carried her in his arms as she pointed the way back to her home and the safety it offered. He refused to put her down until Tana gently reprimanded him with the reminder of her current state. Not just her emotional one, but her physical one too. She was covered in all manner of unknown substances and in dire need of a shower. So were they, for that matter.

"Roth, babe, we need to get cleaned up. Come on, we'll be back before she's out if we hurry," Athon coaxed gently.

Roth hadn't moved from the spot he'd planted himself, having watched Jezzie disappear behind the bathroom door.

"No, you go. That way you can be with her while I shower after she's out. I don't want to leave her alone, just in case we aren't back yet."

"I understand, Az, but she wouldn't be alone. Tana will be here if we aren't."

"It's not the same," he almost snapped.

"I know, *Corazón*. I feel it too. I'll bring you back some clean clothes. I won't be long," he whispered, before he walked out of the room, his feet making nary a sound on the thickly padded carpet.

It was the fastest shower he'd ever taken. The urgency to get back to her, to both of them, pounded through his heart and flooded his body with a spike of adrenaline he'd pay the price for later when exhaustion came to call. He was thorough and made sure not a trace of the outside realm marred his skin. He had no idea what had happened out there to Jezzie, but he didn't want to risk making it worse by leaving any trace of it on his being.

Once he was dry and dressed he grabbed some clothes from the other side of the dresser and headed for the door. Thank fuck for Leraie and her ability to conjure, plan ahead, or whatever she did that allowed her to provide for situations like their current one. It may not be their usual style, but it would do.

When he entered Jezzie's room he found Roth exactly where he'd left him, down to the restless clenching of his fingers and staring at the door as if trying to will it open.

Athon placed Roth's change of clothes on the end of Jezzie's bed, and took a seat in the corner next to a bookcase overflowing with romance and fantasy novels where he still had a good view of Roth's face and the bathroom door. His eyebrows rose at some of the titles, and some of the covers. Not that he'd ever read much in the way of romance before, he'd studied the *Kama Sutra* back when it was first written, yet he was fairly certain he could still learn a thing or two from the tomes on Jezzie's bookshelves.

The minute Tana opened the door, Roth stepped forward, but she put up her hand and waved her fingers under her nose as if to say he stank. And then she actually said it.

"No touchy. You stinky. She's nice and clean and you need a shower before you can get your greedy, big hands on my girl, yeah?" Tana half joked. "You, on the other hand, can give me a hand getting her settled in bed, while the big lug gets himself sorted," she said, gesturing at him impatiently.

Athon may have snorted a little at the offended look on Roth's face, but he rose from his seat and rushed forward, until Tana stopped him with a hand on his chest, and whispered softly to them.

"Be gentle. I've never seen her have such a visceral emotional reaction to a feeding before, from either a soul or anyone's emotions. I don't know what happened out there, or what went wrong, but if you hurt her? I'll hunt you both down and make you squeal like little piggy's when face to face with the big, bad wolf. And don't let Azaroth touch her until he's cleaned up."

She turned back to the bathroom and ushered a fluffy robed and clearly exhausted Jezzie into the room. He carefully wrapped his arm around her waist and guided her over to her bed, tucking her in once Tana pulled back the sheets. He quickly picked up Roth's clothes and placed them on the bathroom counter, shoved the sexy lug through the door with a quick kiss on the lips, and closed the door, before climbing in under the covers beside Jezzie and playing big spoon, little spoon.

She shivered slightly in his arms, as if her body were warming from a chill, so he hugged her tighter. She squirmed around until she faced him, and buried her face in his chest, her hand searching out his heartbeat. The moment Roth slid into the bed behind her and pressed up close, her breathing settled into the gentle rhythm of an exhausted slumber.

NITHE WAS GOING CRAZY. Her despair had filled his head, her pain a knife to his heart. He couldn't get through to Jezzie. The mental wall had slammed down a few hours ago, and the only reason he hadn't rushed back home to her was because Tana had been in contact to say she was safe, and the guys were taking care of her. So he waited. Albeit with little to no patience.

The guys had tried to distract him, but he wasn't much fun. Thus, Rian and Dair had been bickering for the last half hour over whether to knock him out, or get him high. So high there was no way he could keep stomping through the place slamming doors and insulting everyone. So far he'd avoided both options simply because they couldn't agree on whose idea was better.

It had halted his pacing though, and he'd found himself propped up against the door jamb, slightly amused by the creative insults they tossed back and forth at each other as the debate raged on. He wouldn't be surprised at all if they started swatting at each other like little kids soon.

Which is why he'd ushered over Grimm earlier and asked him if he could secretly record it all for later amusement. Grimm had just chuckled, propped himself on the other side of the doorway, and ordered some popcorn. Which he promptly started tossing at the verbally dueling idiots before them.

The familiar sting he always felt when away from Jezzie slashed across his heart again. A reminder of her pain. The dragon in him grumbled its discontent, and mentally he agreed. Thanks to Jezzie's love his dragon side had come rushing back with more ease than he'd expected. Eager to be with her and to forget the years spent locked up tight in the buried depths of Nithe's mind. Seeing and hearing everything, but held silent and still. He hated being away from their mate too. Possibly even more so than the male himself, however impossible it seemed. For Nithe ached for her nearness the moment he stepped away from her. Sometimes, he worried it was an unhealthy obsession, but Jezzie assured him she felt the pull as well, and that it was perfectly normal among mates.

He rubbed his hand subconsciously over his heart as he promised himself he'd be back by her side soon.

As one Rian and Dair turned to look at him, mischief on their faces, but at that very moment Nithe felt Jezzie reach out to him. A soft touch to soothe his ragged pulse. Her mind waking from a dreamless slumber. And suddenly his calm returned, as if by magic, and the tension in the palace noticeably dissipated.

"Anyone else need a big stiff drink?" he asked his companions cheerily.

"I'm pretty sure I need a big stiff something," muttered Rian under his breath, causing Dair to stiffen and flush beside him.

Grimm laughed and clapped him on the back heartily. "One step ahead of you there, my friend. Let's go to the den, shall we?"

He tossed a look back over his shoulder and winked at Rian before he said with a chuckle, "Sorry, my dude, that's not my jam. Maybe D can sort that out for you later."

An hour and fifteen Phoenix Fire Breathers later, Nithe felt quite the buzz forming as he looked around the room. Grimm didn't look affected by the potent brew one iota. *The sumnabitch.*

"Yeah, I've built up a tolerance to the stuff over the years. We figured we'd learn as much about Tana's culture as we could. I also may have switched to juice about ten drinks back. You're the one who needed to get plastered, not me. And it's son of a bitch to you, asshole," Grimm said gruffly, a smug look of superiority gracing his chiseled features.

Shit! He'd said it out loud. The grumpy hellhound could have taken offense, and he was in no shape to take him on. Thank fuck he found it amusing.

"You are one lucky dragon, dude. What can I say, I'm in a benevolent mood today." Grimm laughed.

Nithe was about to reply when heat coursed through his veins, desire filled his senses, and his cock hardened in an instant. Not his desire, but hers. Jezzie's shields crumpled like rice paper in rain and swept over him, consuming him. He didn't stand a chance as the dragon took over, he raced out of the palace and leapt into the sky. His wings sprung free and took him home. Home would forever be wherever Jezzie was.

Jezzie woke, surrounded by the warmth of hard muscles and masculine scents. Really, really yummy ones that made her thighs squeeze together to quell the tingle of desire, but instead made it stronger.

Hot breath fanned over her neck as Athon snored softly, his face close to her ear. Roth's hand rested on her stomach as she lay on her back, while his nose sang the song of his species. A repetitive pattern of snorts and whistles she found both endearing and amusing at the same time. So much so she could barely hold in her giggles. Her chest shook from the effort.

"I know, right? He'll deny it till he's apoplectic if you say he snores, though. Some nights he's lucky I love him, or I'd have smothered him in his sleep eons ago," Athon whispered in her ear.

Jezzie looked into his gorgeous eyes and watched as the serpentine-like pupils dilated with desire the longer he held her gaze. Without thought, she leaned forward and kissed his soft lips quickly, before leaning back, she reached forward to tousle his multi-colored hair and smiled, her emotions still tumbling through a dryer of mixed memories and mismatched identities. She'd never experienced a soul like it before, and prayed to the Almighty she never would again. It hadn't been a creature of nightmares though. No, the soul had once belonged to a being of light. One tasked with the protection of life. One who had used their power for more evil than she'd ever witnessed before.

Enough. No more of that, she thought. Food was needed. Preferably pancakes with bananas, strawberries and lots of butter and maple syrup, and washed down with a big glass of pulpy orange juice.

"Come on, the big guy can sleep some more while we go get breakfast. What do you say? Wanna play house with me?" Jezzie winked at Athon as Roth rolled over and his snoring got louder.

"Lead the way, milady," he responded gallantly, rolling out of bed and proffering his hand like a gentleman.

Spending time alone with Athon was amazing. He was such a sweetie. Funny, yet sincere, and open about who he was and what he wanted.

"Hey, Jez?" he asked, as they sliced up the fresh fruit.

"What's up, honey buns?" Jezzie returned.

"Is it weird for you? You know, having the three of us in your life . . . romantically? Or would it be if you choose to keep us?"

The hint of vulnerability in his voice sucked the air from her lungs and kicked her in the chest.

"I wasn't expecting all of . . . this." She waved her hand around between them. "You know? Not at the beginning. But, Nithe and I talked and we are on the same page and want whatever love fate throws our way. Especially if it's you guys. He just wants me to be happy. The only big problems are the secrets. The things we don't, or can't, talk about. Plus, I really don't think Roth trusts me yet." When Athon went to interrupt she cut him off, holding up her hand. "I mean, I get it. This whole situation is so out of left field, and we all have our pasts, our traumas, and our demons, so it shouldn't be a case of insta love, even if it feels that way. We've only just met, yet we've known each other for months, years for you, and in Roth's case, decades. But I want this, and if you guys want this as much as me, then maybe we can make this work. It'll just take all of us choosing to be all in."

Athon rounded the kitchen island and pulled her into his arms, looping them above her butt as he leaned down and placed small, soft, coaxing kisses on her slightly parted lips, his tongue playing games with the soft flesh lovingly.

"I'm all in, baby. And Roth will be, too. Though we may need a little extra patience and understanding," Athon whispered.

"What happened to make him so . . . untrusting of women? I'm assuming it's just women, but is it everyone other than you?" Jezzie asked, curiously.

"It's his story, so it's his to tell. Even if it's mine as well."

Wrapped in Athon's warm embrace she let it go, and soon they were laughing, cooking, and eating their fill. Too hungry to wait, they decided to eat first and take Roth back a tray laden with a pancake feast fit for a king, or one very hungry angel.

Which had worked out great. Roth had woken as they'd re-entered the room and after dragging Jezzie down onto the bed beside him and tucking her into his side, he'd dug into the fluffy delights with gusto, and downed the coffee and OJ like a dying man.

Until Jezzie—forgetting she was naked under the robe and having decided she was too hot for the extra layer of warmth with Roth's nearness lighting a fire in her blood—slipped out of bed and slipped it off. She held her breath as she walked over to the wardrobe, in her best impersonation of supermodel glide, and placed it on a hanger before she turned to view their reactions.

Roth was choking on a mouthful of his breakfast, Athon slapped him on the back repeatedly. Two sets of eyes devoured every curve and hollow of her body, and tingles spread over her skin. Her cheeks flushed with desire, lips parted on a breathy whimper, a sound of surrender and need.

Roth's eyes took on the predatory gaze of a hunter stalking his next meal as he set aside the tray and climbed out of bed. Athon closed in from the other side, less alpha but just as intense.

Desire pooled between her thighs and curled in her belly. Her nipples tightened into hard pebbles, so sensitive the air itself shot pleasure through them.

Athon pressed himself against her side, his hand cupping the back of her neck, his fingers stroking her soft skin as his lips trailed over her neck, nipping at her pulse as it raced. His hard cock rocked back and forth against her, as little groans left him.

Roth grabbed her left hip in one large, capable hand and stepped forward. His other hand roughly tangled in her hair and pulled her closer, causing his hard body to collide with hers. His cock pressed into her body and her knees almost gave way. Whimpers escaped her without thought as he stared down at her. His eyes searched her face.

"Do you want this, *mi amor?* Yes, or no?"

His voice was like black satin sheets over hard steel, and she could tell her answer meant everything. It would determine their forever.

"Yes, Azi," she moaned, breathlessly. "Both of you, now and always."

"Hmm, then both of us you shall have, my sweet, little tease," he growled deep in his chest.

She felt his words deep inside and a flood of desire soaked her already wet pussy. He leaned in and took her mouth in a rough kiss. Not the gentle kiss of a lover, but the kiss of a man filled with the raw passion of a mate desperate to stake his claim. He pushed her back against the closed wardrobe door and lifted her off her feet. His arms slid under her thighs and spread her wide, but he didn't step forward to fill the void.

"Ath, be a good boy and get down on your knees. Lick that pretty little cunt so I can see," Roth ordered.

"Yes, Sir," was all Athon said before he fell to his knees and slid between them, the back of his head pressed against Roth's very obvious erection.

He ran his nose along her slick slit, inhaling deeply and a sound of satisfaction echoed from him. Soft kisses landed on the smooth skin of her mound, her hips tried to press closer. A futile attempt to beg for more as Roth expertly held her in place, scolding her softly for her impatience.

The first glide of his warm, wet tongue had her eyes almost rolling back in her head as exquisite pleasure shot through her. She'd dreamed of this so many times, and yet her dreams paled in the light of reality. Athon's tongue delved between her lips and found the tight nub of ecstasy waiting for him. He gave it a quick, unsatisfactory flick before moving down. Jezzie groaned a sound of frustration that quickly morphed into a moan as he thrust his tongue deep into her wet sheath, his eyes locked to her flushed face.

She noted the way Athon's head bobbed forward from where a cock pushed into the back of his head gently as he went to town on her with his tongue and lips, Roth's excitement evident. A quick glance up at Roth, who quickly shifted his gaze from watching her pussy be devoured, was enough for him to smile with a wicked glint in his eye and look back down at Athon.

"Undo my pants, Ath. Now."

And just like that Athon's tongue left her as he shifted around and pulled the string on Roth's pants, letting them fall to his feet. Jezzie sucked in a breath way too fast and almost choked on it, coughing slightly as she took in the sight of his perfect cock.

Athon wasted no time as he slipped one hand around the base and licked the pre-cum gathered at the tip. He slid two fingers over her mound, before pressing them into her heat, the muscles clenched hard in a futile attempt to keep him there as he set a perfect rhythm, thrusting in and out in sync with his mouth on Roth's cock.

Just as she reached the precipice of her orgasm Roth ordered Athon to stop. Annoyingly, he did as commanded and allowed Roth to fill the space he left behind. Unfortunately, not the one inside her, much to her dismay.

"So impatient, little love. Don't worry, soon both your sweet cunt and tight ass will be full of cock. And once we meet Nithe I'm sure your mouth will be too. You'll be so full of our cocks, and our cum there'll never be any question of who you belong to."

His teeth grazed her ear and nipped hard, soothed only by the tender stroking of his tongue.

"Take me. Take my pussy, my ass, my sassy smart mouth. Take my heart, my future, and my very soul. I want it all. It's no more, or less, than I'll demand of you both when you are ready to give it," Jezzie declared, honest truth scorching through her words.

He carried her to the bed and placed her down on the silken sheets before he knelt between her spread legs and tasted of her sweetness. Athon's cock bobbed beside her face and she eagerly raised herself up and opened her mouth, her lips stretched around him. The taste of pre-cum and something unique to him filled her senses and she took as much as she could.

Before she knew what was happening Roth abandoned her pussy and Athon withdrew from her mouth, leaving her empty. Roth lay beside her, pulled her over his body and kissed her softly, his hands guided her legs to straddle his hips. The firm, silky tip of his cock nudged at her opening and she eagerly shifted her hips for more contact. Reaching down she fisted his hard length and ran her palm up and down, eliciting groans of masculine pleasure from him. She lined herself up and slid down with tormenting slowness, until he bottomed out, her muscles gripping him in place.

From behind Athon leaned in and kissed her spine over and over. The shock of the cold liquid that slid over her anus was a surprise she hadn't expected, having not told him where the lube was kept, and he chuckled at her reaction.

First one finger, then another. Once three fingers stretched her open and slid in and out with ease he took them out, wiping them on his discarded clothing, and replaced them with the head of his cock. Her ass burned with sweet, painful pleasure as he slid deeper, stretching her open. He went slowly until he was halfway in, and then he paused completely. Roth lifted her hips, taking her weight and suspending her above him slightly, his cock sliding halfway out just as Athon thrust forward, seating himself to the hilt. Again and again, they moved together, drawing out her pleasure and building it higher and higher.

Fire lit her veins, every wall crumbled, every star exploded, and nothing else existed but the beating of her heart, the shudders wracking her body, and the sounds of completion ringing in her ears.

They stayed that way for what seemed forever, but was probably more like moments, a tangle of satisfied limbs and half erect cocks slipping out of her holes, cum coating them all. The silence was broken only by the sound of the door as it hit the wall , the open space quickly filled by Nithe's large frame. His body casting dark shadows through the room. His cock—twice its regular angel size—thrust out from the tattered remnants of his jeans.

"Ours!" came the roar of the dragon within, and desire flooded her veins once more.

CHAPTER 38

The door hit the wall with a loud thud and Athon froze. Beside him Roth did the same. Jezzie was locked between them as Nithe stood tall and . . . well, not angry . . . No, the male was smiling darkly. Desire heated his eyes and Athon felt the flush of it burn his skin.

"Ours," came Nithe's loud roar as it echoed around the small room in the voice of the dragon, not the one they'd heard so often in their slumber.

His wings snapped back in as they retracted, though the patches of scales across his chest and shoulder remained. The gold leathery feathers stretched out over the wings of a dragon were a surprise which normally would have had questions spilling from his lips instead only caused his brow to raise as he mentally filed it away for later.

He looked over to Roth and noted his gaze shifting between Jezzie and Nithe's impressive length. The large, oddly shaped appendage jutted proudly out from his hips in his half-shifted state and bobbed up and down as if approving of the attention.

Jezzie jumped to her knees and squealed excitedly as she moved closer to the bottom of the bed. Nithe moved further into the room until he propped himself against the wall nearest the bathroom door. They all followed his movements and Jezzie shifted to face him, her breasts bouncing softly.

"Come here!" Nithe commanded, still more dragon than man. His eyes locked on his treasure.

Jezzie looked over at them and blew him and Roth a kiss each, followed by a sassy wink as she slid from the bed and crawled slowly toward her other lover.

"*Mo shíorghrá*, how I missed you so. I see you've missed me too," she purred, her voice husky and seductive. "Would you like me to take care of you?" She nodded, her eyes looked at his engorged cock as she licked her pink lips before she craned her neck up to meet Nithe's eyes.

"I'm fairly certain the guys won't mind. Roth? Athon?" she queried as she looked over at them with big exaggerated puppy dog eyes.

"Not at all, babe. We wouldn't miss this show for all the realms in existence," Athon replied. Roth nodded his head eagerly from his place beside him.

Athon understood that Nithe's dragon nature was in control right now. His need to stake his claim on his female, show them he wasn't to be forgotten, and show his dominance. It was dragon nature, after all.

They watched as Jezzie moved farther away from them. The evidence of their previous lovemaking dripped from her body and down her thighs, a beautiful show which had their cocks standing tall once again.

"Athon, Roth, please come and sit over here, so you can see our Jezzie as she takes me into her pretty little mouth." He gestured to the two armchairs by the bed that would offer them a perfect view of what was to come.

They moved instantly. Roth stopped to check the nightstand briefly, grabbing something before he sat next to him. A package of what turned out to be wet wipes was handed to him with a look down at his cock. Athon quickly wiped himself down, the cool sensation making his breath catch.

Jezzie knelt at Nithe's feet, her back straight, her breasts proudly on display, and her hands behind her hips.

"Good, *a stór*. Now you can suck me however you wish," Nithe stated, his praise making her smile wider.

Wetting her lips she clasped her hand around the base of his cock, her tongue darted out to taste the tip, and it got smaller. Not like, small-small, just not dragon-huge anymore. He was still a well hung male but now at least Jezzie stood a chance of getting some of his length in her mouth.

She licked and nipped, sucked and caressed. Both of her hands moved over him. One cupped his balls, the other ran up and down his shaft. Her tongue flicked out at the base of the head and Nithe gave a deep groan, and she swirled her tongue around the rim, her lips latching over him. She rose higher on her knees and took him deep in her throat, as far as she could. And all the while Athon's eyes were riveted on them as his hand stroked Roth's cock, and Roth stroked his.

The moment Nithe roared out his climax so too did he and Roth. Cum spilled over their hands as Jezzie swallowed as much of Nithe's load as she could, the rest spilling out of her lips until she pulled away, spurt after spurt covering her beautiful face and dripping down onto her breasts.

As they slumped in their seats, Nithe bent down and helped Jezzie to her feet, lifted her chin to place a loving kiss on her cum covered lips, and pulled her into a tight embrace.

Athon realized something within that very moment. The elusive something he'd always felt was missing? The woman they'd been searching for to fill the empty space? This was it. It was Jezzie, but not just her. It was Nithe too. Because if Jezzie didn't feel complete then how could they ever be truly complete themselves?

AFTER THEY WERE all cleaned up—Nithe had told the guys to use whatever they needed from his wardrobe—and Athon and Roth had gone to grab some snacks, they'd all fallen asleep for a much-needed nap.

Upon waking they all sat up cuddled together on the bed, comfortable and content. The feelings of contentment which radiated out of the males soothed her unresolved worries. A balm to her nerves. Nithe and Roth were on either side of Jezzie, and Athon with his head resting on her lap. Nithe refused to let her go, and she understood the need to be close to her completely. Since mating they'd never been apart as long as the past couple of days. Jezzie had never felt so much at peace, or so full of contentment and love. It was so wonderful she almost wanted to break out in song like a princess from the movies she'd watched as a little girl.

Proper introductions had seemed redundant, but they'd done them anyway. They talked about how she and Nithe were hybrids and how it was possible; something none of them knew the answers to. Angel births were rare enough as it was.

Nithe gave half answers about his heritage. Her muttered curses about his mother made him squeeze her tight and kiss the top of her head. She'd skirted any talk of her own childhood and past by feigning yawns and snuggling deeper into her warm cocoon of masculine awesomeness. She wasn't ready to talk about Lucifer, not with the sting of his reaction to her still smarting her inner child's heart.

Athon and Roth had spoken about how they'd realized their sexuality and how it was frowned upon for so long in angel culture. Some angels, just like humans, sadly still held those views. Athon brushed over their time apart, giving her a look to which she gave a small nod and didn't press.

"Actually, it was you, Jezzie, who brought us back together, in a way. Roth's dreams of you and your message—which the big lug forgot to give for way too long—were what led to us reconnecting." Athon chuckled.

"Laugh it up, chuckles. You weren't the one on the receiving end of a Lucifer Special," Roth playfully glared.

"What's that?" Jezzie asked warily.

"He went full Satan on Roth's ass for the shared dreams. We thought it was because he knew you . . . but from his reaction when we got here he thought you were going to be someone else. While Roth was passed out I stayed with him, and when I touched him I got pulled into that dream with you too. From there we finally talked things out and got our shit together," Athon explained.

Well, damn. Seems Lucifer was expecting someone else. In hindsight it was to be expected. Hell, they looked enough alike to be twins most of the time. Jezzie actually felt a bit stupid for not realizing it, and a little better about his reaction. Thinking back she remembered he'd said Caria. But it hadn't registered to her ears past the riotous cascade of his emotions, and the tumultuous expressions on his face.

"You okay, babe?" Athon asked, concern clear in his gaze.

"Absolutely," she said, shaking off her errant thoughts. Now was the time to learn about her mates, not dwell on shit she couldn't change.

"I must admit, if I hadn't been so worried about Az, it would have been kinda sexy to watch."

"Eww!" Jezzie couldn't stop her internal ick factor from manifesting into actual sound.

"What? You don't think Lucifer is sexy?" Athon asked.

"Yeah, nope. Never. Ever. Not for anything would I ever think he was sexy." Jezzie felt the sick burn the back of her throat.

Athon and Roth busted out in laughter, looks of relief flashed across their faces, but also questions. Probably due to her rather strong reaction. Before they could ask them though, Nithe cleared his throat and redirected their attention.

"I want to apologize for barging in earlier. I promised I'd come back only when you were ready, Jezzie, I tried, but the bond was too strong. I felt your pleasure and couldn't resist, the dragon in me simply took over. If my intrusion was unwelcome, I do apologize." Sincerity shone from his eyes. Relief flooded his face as they all rushed to reassure him his arrival had been most welcome.

"The sight of Jezzie on her knees in front of you will invade my thoughts forevermore." Athon winked.

"I'm not used to sitting back and losing control. It's an odd feeling, but kind of natural too," Roth said curiously.

"Well, I must admit the sight of Jezzie naked between the two of you was utterly delicious. It's something I could get used to seeing much more often," Nithe added.

Jezzie wholeheartedly agreed. They had so much still to work out, but they'd make it work. It just felt worth the risk to at least try.

"So, neither of you have really spent any time around angels, huh?" Roth asked.

Jezzie looked at Nithe and blinked slowly. They couldn't really discuss Uncle Micah or Tana. Balthazar might be a secret too. Jezzie decided to vaguely answer with a murmured, "Not really." And left it at that.

"Then let me be the first to welcome you both to the weird and wacky larger angel family. It's confusing, filled with politics, and sometimes utterly batshit pissing contests between all the factions. But somehow it all works." Roth faux bowed with a smile, until he saw the look on Jezzie's face.

She'd frozen, her eyes wide and mouth hanging open as she started to sputter. Nithe belly laughed uncontrollably as he grabbed her close. She elbowed him hard in the stomach.

"Shush, you. You don't know the answer either," Jezzie croaked, sounding sick.

"What is it, Jez?" Athon probed.

"I really should have thought of this earlier, dammit. Oh well, here goes." She took a deep breath and carried on, "So . . . Ummm . . . Are all pureblood angels related? Like brothers and sisters, or clones made from the same DNA and manipulated just to appear different or something? And if they are, are half-angels like half-siblings, or whatever?" she asked hesitantly, her nose scrunched up slightly as she felt her face pale.

If the answer was yes, then she wasn't sure she wouldn't vomit right there on all of them. Because, ewww, incest was totally not up her alley. It shouldn't be up anyone's alley.

"No, no, not at all." Athon rushed to assure her. "The Almighty created angels much the same way they created men . . . and women."

"So, inbreeding to increase the population?" Yep . . . Okay . . . She could taste the sick in the back of her throat now, how could she still be attracted to them? Argh, ick.

"That's another popular misconception actually. The Almighty did create Adam and Eve, but not just one set. Quite a few of them were placed in grouped areas around the globe, all genetically different, and with different names. All within their own personal paradise, their own Garden of Eden. They were all told not to eat from the apple tree." Athon paused and Roth continued on.

"Despite what people think though, Lucifer had nothing to do with enticing them to partake of the forbidden fruit. That was totally on

Adam. Although, Leviathon here, was tasked with watching the fabled couple and the Almighty did temporarily turn him into a snake, but he couldn't talk. Many of us were sent to do the same in other gardens. And each garden was full of wondrous foods. Unfortunately, Adam viewed himself the king of his little paradise, and as such thought himself above the rules. That he had a right to try everything within his domain. Of course, he also thought it was Eve's job to serve him. She was made from him, after all, and thus she should pick the fruit and taste of it first . . . It could be poisonous after all, and as the Almighty had used his rib to create Eve, he could do so again should something go wrong." Roth rolled his eyes, showcasing just how stupid he found that antiquated logic.

"He thought himself special as the original—or so he thought—creation, and thus irreplaceable." Athon snorted.

"They certainly gave every male of every species a bad rap that day. Yeah . . . It was pretty much all of them, all on the same day too, thrust out as one from the paradise they were offered. Sent out to find their own way. One set obeyed the rules though, and got their slice of heaven on earth, for all the good that did . . ." Athon drifted momentarily before adding, "The others went out and populated the planet with humankind."

"Anyway, back on track. The original angels were each created for a different purpose, each designed from scratch. After the originals some were born, some converted from other beings, and some are still created from scratch again when needed. All are different. All are unique. Except those angels born to other angels, they of course share common DNA, though angel birth is not at all common. A child born to two angels usually never has any blood siblings. Lucifer and Michael are rare exceptions. The Almighty created two leaders, twins, opposites with a special bond to lead two specific groups of angels. They share almost identical DNA despite their contrasting features," Roth concluded, watching her expectantly.

"Roth and I are not related in any way, shape, or form," Athon tacked on hurriedly, a slight panicked reassurance to his tone.

That had been the least of Jezzie's concerns. Still, in retrospect, a concern, but definitely not in the top spot. Finally she felt the last trace of skin crawling and nausea dissipate, the vomit feeling, thankfully, a thing of the past.

"I know we haven't talked much since our little hunting trip, but what happened out there, Jezzie?" Roth's question broke the comfortable silence a short time later.

Jezzie shrugged her shoulders, not really sure herself.

"You guys are going to have to fill me in. Jezzie kept me updated on stuff through our link, but then she spiraled and blocked me out. All I could sense was pain and anger," Nithe piped in.

"The link? Is that what Tana was talking about earlier?" Athon asked curiously.

"Yeah, when we mated and sealed the bond with our bites, the connection we had before solidified, and we can use telepathy. It was there before, but we were told it was probably due to me reading his emotions and our unique circumstances. I haven't really tried to read you guys since this is a bit different to the situation we were in, and I didn't want to breach your privacy at all," Jezzie answered softly.

"Oh, oh, do me, do me," Athon begged.

"Calm down, Ath. Not until we know what happened out there. Jez?" Roth said pointedly.

"Fine. Okay, so you guys know I'm part psychic vampire and I need to feed off of emotions, yeah?" she started.

They both nodded, Nithe relaxed and just waited, listening.

"And you've seen my wings are primarily black, and I have shadows, red ones, but still shadows? Obviously my dear old pops is an angel. On top of the emotional eating—like actual emotions, not just 'cos I'm sad or moody—" She stuck her tongue out at Nithe. "Which lately has been mostly sated through the bond with Nithe, I must also take souls," she paused.

"But you didn't use your blades to take its soul, thus you can't deliver them to the well." Uh huh, she could tell Athon was confused.

"Yeah, I don't capture them, babe. I consume them. They are, so I've found, essential to my survival. I need to consume souls to live, ever since I reached my first transition. I've always taken the souls of those I've instinctively felt were irredeemable. Except the first time . . . We didn't know what to expect, and I couldn't control it. Leraie came the next day and talked me through it." At the shocked faces before her, she went quiet.

"Is that what happened out there? You ate the monster's soul?" Roth asked incredulously.

"Yes. Which shouldn't be possible, because the monsters here don't have souls. The ghouls make sure of it. And these weren't just any monsters, at least not the one I fed from. No, he was worse. He was a male of standing, trusted by many. He was a torturer of children and an evil piece of shit. If I could kill him again, I'd take more time, and I'd make him relive the moments of abject terror as he slipped through the portal to this place. He delighted in the torment and agony he'd created. The other may have been his wife, and if so, she deserves the same fate." Jezzie shuddered, glimpses of what she'd seen and felt slipped back into her brain and made her skin crawl.

"They were prisoners? How did they change into those things?" Nithe softly coaxed.

"No, they weren't. Not in the traditional sense. The Praesidium had no part in their banishment here. Nonetheless, justice was served, even if it felt more like vengeance. Sometimes, I guess, they can be one in the same. As to the how, I'd guess their true nature took over and they became what they always truly were. The monsters of their victims nightmares." Kind of fitting in Jezzie's opinion for the outside to finally match the monster within.

"But what were they before, if not prisoners? And how did they portal in if not the Praesidium, assuming Leraie didn't send them here?" Roth looked serious, like he was pondering the ramifications it could cause. "And how long have they been here for this to happen and still have gone undetected by the Guardians of Nestradia, or have the princes gone soft after all these years?"

"Seriously? The Guardians of Nestradia? That's what they're known as?" Jezzie grinned.

"That, or the Forsaken Spares," added Athon.

"Damn, so many lost opportunities. Tana needs to know this. *Hooked on a Feeling* by Blue Swede just became their theme song for the rest of time!" Jezzie said as she devolved into giggles. "Or she can just add it to the playlist she already has. Anyway, back on topic, the worst part is he wasn't just some human who slipped through the cracks, or some random OtherRealmer either. No, this fucker was an angel, his wife too. Somehow they were never suspected, never caught, never sentenced or punished, and were able to hide the evidence of their true nature without becoming openly . . . Fallen. All while remaining well regarded in your society."

"Yours too now, babe." When she glared over at Athon he swallowed hard and hurried on, "Not the point, right. So, how the fuck is that even possible? Holding off the degeneration that taints a fallen? Not to mention hiding their true self? Surely Leraie and the Almighty would have known and put a stop to it. Right?"

"Yeah, I wouldn't count on it. Not lately, or for a long time, I think. From what I can tell, the Almighty is playing the long game, and either their control is slipping, or we're all just dominoes waiting to fall into whatever grand pattern was laid out eons ago." Nithe shook his head and Jezzie felt his annoyance at the possibility of being at the mercy of the Almighty or those feckless bitches known as the Fates.

She snuggled in closer, rubbing her nose into the bare skin peeking through his open collar.

"Ni? I love you. We'll be okay," she murmured softly.

"I know we will, Jez. I'm okay. Doesn't mean I don't want to rip out their black hearts, but I'll refrain from doing so stupid a thing for your sake." His smile was a thing of wonder, and it transformed his whole face. Damn, his eyes even twinkled.

Jezzie looked up, her eyes widened as a gasp escaped her, and she bolted upright as she caught sight of the clock on the wall. Time was flying by and Leraie would be back in less than seven hours. She wanted to spend more time with Tana, unsure when she'd get to see her again, what with how time worked between Nestradia and everywhere else. Nithe smiled and nodded at her next thought, and she realized she'd sent it through the link. Paradise. She still hadn't shown Roth and Athon the wonders of Paradise. And with Nithe now back they could take them there together.

CHAPTER 39

Jezzie was clearly super excited. Roth watched her butt as she bounced and skipped her way down the long corridor, her hair flying out around her as she held onto Athon's hand. She'd left it loose, and he had to admit he liked it that way. The glow from the lanterns danced with the shades of red in her hair and gave her the appearance of a fire nymph. He could, if he didn't hold himself back, just reach out and run his fingers through it, or wrap the luxurious strands around his hand and pull her close enough for him to take her luscious lips with his.

He'd push her up against the wall and press his thigh between her legs. He'd watch her body submit to him and the heat of her lust, even as fire sparked in her eyes. The battle between her fighting spirit and the power of the passion they shared would be explosive.

Damn it, he needed to stop thinking such things, his cock needed to calm the fuck down for five fucking minutes so he could get his head on straight, without imagining her other lips and what could be parting them instead.

She was such a surprise. He knew she was gorgeous, but she was also funny, kind, and intelligent, yet lethal and fierce when needed. Full of energy, and an endless wit so sharp he had no doubt it could cut to the quick when she wished. She was so open with her feelings, and yet he still felt uneasy. She'd said there were things she couldn't reveal, and sure, he understood it. No one wanted to cross the Almighty, or Leraie—mostly Leraie. Hellfire, knowing those two she probably literally couldn't tell them despite wanting to. But damned if he didn't despise being kept in the dark. How the fuck was he supposed to overcome his past trauma and trust her if things, important things, were being kept from him?

Jezzie reached back and grabbed his hand with a big beaming smile. Pulling him along, she swung their arms as she skipped and twirled herself around.

Nithe poked him in the side with his elbow and winked. Though his green and gold eyes remained serious.

"Don't think too hard right now, just enjoy it. Jez on a happy high isn't an everyday thing, so don't take it away from her." The 'or I'll punch your face in' was left unsaid, but the message came through regardless.

Jezzie had said Nithe was the quiet one. Maybe he was, but he damn well got his opinions across loud and clear. Roth sensed a kindred spirit in the male. One with his own demons rattling their cages in a past that hung around to torment him long after the tormentors slithered away.

Roth refocused on his surroundings, tearing his eyes from Nithe's intense gaze, and was surprised to find the corridor had closed in. The walls were no longer stone blocks, but rather the rough look of a tunnel dug from the earth with little finesse or skill. The ground beneath his feet was uneven dirt and crumbled rocks, and the lanterns appeared further and further apart as they went, dimly lighting the way forward.

"Where are we going, Jez?" Athon queried as he hunched his shoulders and pressed up against her side.

"You'll see," she said. "It's so beautiful. Leraie made it to provide all we need here. The princes don't know about it and aren't allowed entrance . . . at least not yet. Maybe once Tana puts the past behind her, but not before then. Leraie sends them all they need, so they're not starving or anything. We're almost there," she finished excitedly.

She picked up the pace and raced forward, dragging Athon along behind her. Nithe laughed, the sound was rich and warm, but with a roughness that implied he didn't do so very often, or it was something he'd only recently started doing. The thought shocked him, until he remembered the passage of time worked differently here. While he and Athon had been dreaming of them all together for years, mere months had passed since Jezzie and Nithe had found each other.

Suddenly, just as he thought he wouldn't fit through the tunnel if they went much further, they rounded a corner and came face to face with a dead end. But Jezzie just reached out her palm to touch a smooth section of stone on the wall in front of her and smiled back at him. What was she doing? he thought to himself. Before he could even part his lips to ask, the wall slid open, parting like curtains, and allowing them to enter.

The moment he stepped through the opening his eyes widened and a gasp left his mouth at the view which lay before him. Unbidden tears welled in his eyes suddenly, and he fought a silent battle to hold them at bay. He hadn't seen it in so long he'd forgotten the splendor and perfection that was the Garden of Eden, or as Jezzie called it, Paradise.

"Isn't it glorious?" Jezzie looked at them expectantly.

"It's perfect. But how is it here? We thought they were all destroyed," Athon asked breathlessly, his eyes wide as they roamed over all they could see.

"What do you mean? Leraie made it, remember? She's amazing. When I was little she told me I could call her Grandma Raie, which made me giggle because I already had an Aunt Rai Rai . . . Funny, how I only just remembered that, but I suppose it's to be expected after she buried my memories of our interactions for so long. A story for another time. So, you guys have been here before?" She looked a tad disappointed.

"Not here, per se, and some things might be different, but it looks like an exact copy of The Garden of Eden. The very first paradise on earth. Not surprising really, since Leraie was in charge of planning and creating them for the Almighty in the first place. It's just as wondrous as I remember. Thank you, Jezzie." Athon swung her around as she smiled radiantly down at him, his hands on her trim waist.

Roth picked his jaw up from the floor, and the moment Athon placed her on the ground he swept forward and crushed her to his chest, a tear slipping from his eye as emotions filled him. Eden was the place he'd first caught Athon staring at his ass, the first place they'd kissed, and the first place they'd ever made love. Not all in the same version of Eden, but it was still a place filled with such special memories. And now he'd get to make new memories here with Jezzie, and Nithe as well.

When he released her reluctantly and stepped back, he found Nithe watching him intently, as if contemplating something. He turned his head and looked at Jezzie, and Roth could tell they were talking in their heads. Fuck, what he wouldn't give to be able to do that. He wasn't pissed they could, he was more envious, and a little annoyed at not knowing what was being said. Still, he respected their right to talk privately, and waited to see what would happen next as Jezzie smiled and gave Nithe a hug before she stepped over to his side and took hold of his hand.

The feel of her satin soft skin in his rough palm shot sparks into his bloodstream, and a low hum of sexual awareness settled over him . . . again. What shocked him though, wasn't the desire he felt, but rather the pure joy which flooded his system and left a smile on his face. One so goofy Athon and Nithe gave each other a high five and a fist bump.

"Jez, Roth. I'm going show Athon around, get to know one of the males I'm sharing my mate with. Why don't you two go exploring together? Get to know each other, and spend some one-on-one time." Nithe's naughty wink set Jezzie to giggles as he beckoned at Athon to follow him.

Roth and Jezzie watched them as they walked away to an open area and unleashed their wings. Athon's soft black feathers in stark contrast to Nithe's leathery gold feathers as they took to the air, and flew off toward the mountains in the distance.

"So, what now, my sweet guide? What are your wicked plans for me now that we find ourselves all alone in this veritable utopia of pleasure?"

"Why, Azaroth, how utterly charming of you to ask." She fluttered her eyelashes demurely before she added sassily, "Catch me if you can."

She took off running, her hair swayed wildly with each stride, and it took his brain a few moments to kick in. Once it did, he sped off after her. He caught her easily. He wrapped his arms around her and swung her up and off her feet, spinning her around as she giggled with unadulterated glee. He eventually slowed to a stop and slid her down his body until her toes barely touched the soft green grass. His eyes locked with hers as their breathing slowed, catching on the heated looks they were sharing.

Shaking himself, he gazed around. They were standing in an apple orchard, dark red and green apples hung ripe on the branches of the surrounding trees. He looked at them all, noting the absence of the golden apple tree which had once stood in the center of a place just like this one. The tree of knowledge, the tree which was the downfall of mankind so very long ago. Probably for the best, he thought.

He breathed deep of the fresh air, the scent of honeysuckle and raspberries drifted from Jezzie, right before she pressed a juicy berry to his lips with hers. Their tongues shared the burst of flavor as it filled their mouths. When the kiss ended, she licked her lips clean of the sweet residue left behind by the fruit. For him the fruit paled in comparison to the delectable taste of her lips.

"Want to see my favorite place?" she asked, looking up at him from beneath her lashes.

"Where you go, so shall I follow, my lady," he responded with a bow.

And so he took hold of her proffered hand, and let her lead him deeper into Paradise.

It'd been a very long time since he'd wooed a female. Well, anyone really. He and Athon had fallen back into place like two perfect puzzle pieces, so all of this was like relearning to ride a wobbly, not quite safe bicycle. For all that he'd learned about Jezzie, he still didn't feel like he knew her, no matter how right the four of them together felt. Only time, and trust could lead to that.

He couldn't contain his smile when she came to a halt. Opening her arms wide she presented him with the waterfall and the serene pool of water beneath it. Smooth rocks added a perfect place to sun oneself, and partake in other far more pleasurable pursuits. The green and blue leaves of the overhanging trees offered enough shade without hiding the warmth of the sun. The crystal clear blue water was just as he remembered it, so many years later.

"Been here before too, huh?" she sighed with cheeky exaggeration.

"We've been everywhere this place has to offer, unless they added something new this time?" he admitted.

Jezzie peeled herself out of her clothes and dove into the water. Hurriedly he followed suit, the warmth of the pool soon taking away a chill he hadn't realized was even there.

They swam, stopping to rest and talk, enjoying each other's company. He told her more about the origins of the Eden and what it meant to him and Athon.

"So, even angels were bigoted assholes then?" She didn't sound surprised.

"Heck, some still are, Jezzie. Unfortunately, every race and species has its bad apples no matter how much we wish otherwise."

Jezzie shook her head sadly. "It's not a surprise really. I've seen the worst of humankind and the best. Same goes for my limited interactions with other beings. But the level of hate that can fill a single body still amazes me sometimes, especially for things that don't even really affect them."

Roth cradled her in his arms, her head resting over his immortal heart as the sun and water warmed their flesh. She shivered as his hands slid along the lines of her body, dipping beneath the water to cup the ass he'd been so fascinated by earlier.

As he looked down into her eyes he saw a forever he hadn't dared to dream of, not really, not completely. Her lips parted in a sigh as her eyes filled with desire, flashes of red streaking through her gaze. Soft hands found the hard muscles of his shoulders and pushed down, so she could wrap her legs around his waist. The move brought her bare folds into contact with his hardened length. Fuck it, he'd been hard the moment her clothes had started coming off, but like a gentleman he'd ignored it, desperately wanting the time to get her know her.

Jezzie gasped, her teeth biting into the tender flesh of her bottom lip as she shifted her hips closer and drew a groan from him. Her breasts pressed to his chest. As hard as he was already his cock surged, thickening to the point of exquisite pain. A torture he hoped he could prolong.

Roth walked toward the waterfall, careful to shield her face as he stepped through the moving wet curtain, and sat on a small ledge beneath the surface. Their hips and waists remained under the water, but from his position her perfectly rounded breasts barely touched the surface as she arched her back.

Her hips rose and fell over his in a slow and gentle motion. Her entrance sliding against the length of him and teasing the head ruthlessly. She ran her hands over his shoulders, along the muscles of his arms, his chest, and his thighs. Her nails left a trail of taunting anticipation in their wake as they wandered, coming back to flick at the hard nubs she'd made of his nipples. Delicate fingers explored the line of his jaw, his cheeks, the shape of his nose and brow, as if learning him and committing every contour to memory.

A deep look into his eyes was all the warning he got before, on the next undulation, she sank down onto him. Encasing the hard length of his cock inside her velvet heat. The further in she took him, the harder the press of her hips, the more ragged her breathless moans came. And still her eyes stayed locked on his. The more he fought to hold still. To allow her to take from him what she needed. His hands roamed her back, squeezed the sweet globes of her ass, and tugged at the long wet strands of her silky hair.

Once she was fully seated, her hips flush with his he couldn't stop his hips from rising, seeking more of her. His cock twitched deep inside her and her corresponding sounds of pleasure sent a thrill through his being. Make it fantastic, that's all he had to do. Easy, right? Nothing but sounds of pleasure left their lips, the need for words long gone. Words, such irrelevant things when one was drowning in pure, carnal sensation

The faster she moved, the tighter she gripped him, and the harder he fought for control. The sounds of her pleasure filled his ears as they echoed in the hidden chamber of stone and water. He pressed a kiss to Nithe's mate mark on the soft skin of her left breast, and he gasped as her inner muscles tightened almost painfully, her moan was music to his ears. And then she kissed him, long and hard, slow and tender, nipping at his lips and soothing the sweet sting until with a shout they both exploded. The release rocked him to his core as her body shook and shuddered in the aftermath.

He felt like an open book, a canvas laid bare. He knew as she looked down into his face what she could see. His lust, his love, his vulnerability. The hard edges, the soft ones, and buried in the heart of him, guarded by the black cage of tortured memory, hid his pain. The memory was locked down so tightly he didn't think even she, with her unique powers, could reach them. He hoped she wasn't the type to try.

JEZZIE WAS happy to stay wrapped in the warmth of Roth's embrace for as long as he wanted to hold her. He smelled divine, whatever it was it made her want to lick at his skin and devour every inch of him, even after the amazing sex they'd had. And yet it calmed her, making her feel like a cat who wanted nothing more than to rub up against him and purr her contentment.

Roth looked shaken as he gazed up at her. His feelings tumbled through her like rapid fire. His pain sang to her of trauma and self loathing, similar to Nithe's, and yet she detected something not right with it. Like a taste which didn't quite fit. She wouldn't force her way in, not now, not ever. She could think of no greater betrayal to one she loved than to pry something like that open and tear it away from them.

Through the darkness of the pain that surrounded his emotions, she caught a flash, brief and bright, and it made her smile. She took his face in her hands and let her feelings sink into him, offering him the love and desire she felt for him.

The light of hope and trust still shone in Roth's heart. And you could bet your ass she'd be the one to set it free. When he was ready, of course.

Large shadows blocked the entrance to the waterfall moments before Nithe and Athon's voices sounded just outside.

"What do you mean we should give them a moment? Like we don't know what they were doing." Athon laughed, followed by a grunt. "Hey! What was that for?"

"For being a dumbass, obviously."

But Nithe didn't sound annoyed. He sounded happy and relaxed, which just added to the feeling inside her that insisted everything was perfect now. Well, almost perfect.

She slid off of Roth's lap and his cock left her greedy little bitch of a pussy, her inner muscles proclaimed their desire to have him back inside her, where he belonged. Stupid body parts. Roth stood beside her and kissed her deeply before they shared a cunning look and splashed through the curtain of water with as much gusto as they could manage. Dousing the cheeky duo on the other side as they hit and kicked at the water's surface.

The guys took one look at Roth, then turned their attention to her before they pounced. Nithe leaped at Roth, taking him under, as Athon dived, his shoulder brushed her knees. He stood and hauled her out of the water, smacked her bare ass and then tossed her back in like a lousy fish.

When she came up sputtering, she saw them laughing their asses off. All except Nithe, he looked wary. Good boy, he knew Athon was going to be in trouble.

"Okay. Right. Athon, my dear?" she simpered.

"Ah, yes, babe?" The laughter was replaced with uneasiness.

"Just remember something, will you? I have a long memory, and an even longer eternity to get you back for this. I'm willing to bet you wouldn't want your cock bedazzled? That shit really hurts to peel off."

The look of utter horror which fell over his previously smug face set Jezzie off in a fit of laughter so intense she had to hold her stomach. Though, she was serious. She'd thought of doing it to Ballzy once. Just for shits and giggles, and because he'd deserved it. But the opportunity never arose and the thought of touching his ding-a-ling again made her feel all icky.

Athon begged for forgiveness and she played along. Pretending to be the evil queen and begrudgingly agreeing to do so, all with a smile on her face that Athon returned.

Soon after, they found themselves lying in a heap on the soft, warm grass. The guys had put their pants back on, despite her pouting, and she'd donned Nithe's black button down shirt and her underwear. Her legs were still too wet and sticky for the torture that was required to pull them back on and the weather was such she was happy to go without them.

"What happened after you left the alley, Jez? I mean, I now know I interrupted your feeding and all, but I couldn't find you. How'd you end up here? Please tell us as much as you can," Roth asked softly as he stroked her hair.

She lifted her head from his lap and sighed, looking over to Nithe who nodded with a wry smile.

"Better get it over with, *a stór*. Then we just have to fill in the gaps later, not the whole thing." His voice hitched a little, so she shifted over and wrapped her arms about his waist and squeezed extra tight.

"If you remember, I may have been a little pissed off as I stormed away?" she questioned slowly.

"Uh, yeah. A little?" Roth stared at her incredulously.

"Yeah, yeah. Anyway, I'd left it too long since my last meal, and with panic setting in at the next to zero chance of finding a replacement as my energy was draining away, my shadows took over." Athon went to interrupt, but she held up a single finger and shook her head. "They took me to the one place anyone who needed a soul was guaranteed to find one."

"No." The faint sound came from Roth's parted lips as his face turned the color of cold ashes.

The place did have a reputation, after all, and Balthazar wasn't known for his kindness.

"Yeah, Demon's Den. Ballzy did help me out, but since I hadn't actually manifested my wings yet, and wasn't able to talk about what species I was and all that, he didn't trust me. So, I ended up stuck there until my contract either came to an end, or he found out what I was and chose to release me. After Nithe showed up, things kind of snowballed and the whole manifestation thing happened. Ballzy had his answers, and it turned out he wasn't as much a dick as I'd thought. He let me go and sent us here through a special portal. I don't know how. 'Cos we can't open one out. Anyway, he told us to find the princes, we did. Then came the stuff we can't talk about yet. Sorry guys. Any questions?" she finished.

Before they could ask, Nithe spoke with a chuckle. "Way to give the Cliffs Notes, Jez."

"How did you end up there, Nithe?" Athon asked.

"You don't have to, Ni," interjected Jezzie softly.

He gave her a small squeeze.

It's okay, a stór. They need to know. It'll come out anyway, and if Raum is still free they need to be prepared.

Okay. But if you need to stop, stop. Or I can tell them for you, if you need? she offered.

I got this. He kissed the top of her head lightly.

"Back when my asshole family banished me, I didn't know what to do, or where to go. My wings had only just manifested, and my dragon had just made himself known to me, so I wasn't in complete control yet. I ended up in some dive bar in a Realm I'd never been, when all of a sudden some prissy little wisp of an angel approached me. Claimed I was one of them and spun me a tale about how much they needed me, how valuable I was to their cause. They needed someone unknown to help with a special case. To get close to their target and help them apprehend the devious, evil Fallen."

"Who?" Roth murmured, but Nithe ignored him.

"Being the desperate and optimistic idiot I was, I jumped at the chance. I mean, I might even get to meet my dear old dad, right? Wrong. What I did get, after stupidly allowing myself to be captured, was nothing short of utter degradation and despair. My dragon side was locked away to protect me, or that was the plan anyway, and I never gave up any information about myself. At least I thought my identity was hidden. Apparently not, since everything was known well before they even sent me in. More than even I knew myself, truth be told. It was a double-cross from the start. And when the slip up finally happened in an effort to do the 'master's' bidding—by taking me along to Demon's Den—well, as Jezzie said, everything snowballed from there," Nithe finished breathlessly, and Jezzie felt more than heard the heavy breath he released at her back.

"Who?" came Roth's question again, more insistent than before. The sound of rough gravel entering his tone in a growl.

"Azaroth, calm down," Athon said with worry laced words.

"Who?" he all but roared, his chest heaving with the effort to hold himself still. Jezzie felt his need to rage and leave a trail of destruction in his wake. But why?

"Raum," Nithe bit out. The name burnt the air like acid, sliced across Jezzie's brain, and opened up the wound of her own anger as she sucked in Nithe's turmoil, and fed soothing calm back to him.

Focussing on Roth, she attempted the same, shocked when it worked and the little tingle of a link formed between them like a silver cord. He jolted, so she sent a little more, until his shoulders slumped and Athon gathered him close.

"I'm sorry, Nithe," Roth mumbled.

"S'okay, man. I get it. We all have our own shit to shovel, and bastards we want to rip apart with our bare hands. Or in my case shred with my teeth and claws, before melting his skin from his body, and pissing on his still writhing corpse. Whatever's left of it. Of course, Jezzie wants to eat his soul for good measure. And I'm not going to be the one to tell her she can't." Nithe's fierce gaze reflected the truth of his words perfectly.

Roth looked down at Jezzie as she huddled in Nithe's embrace, his gaze softening.

"What was the jolt, Jez? And why am I so calm?" His brows rose indicating he had a fair idea of what she'd done.

"I couldn't have you going all rogue alpha angel on us now, could I? Especially not here in Paradise." She searched the space between them, found the faint glow of the link and gave it a little tug. Just enough his breathing hitched and his shoulders twitched forward.

"What the fuck was that then?" he almost coughed out.

"That, Azi, is the start of a tether, our bond, through which our link shall form as soon as we are mated. Athon has one too, though I haven't pushed anything through it yet to test it." She felt a little sheepish at not having used her natural senses more often. The need just hadn't been there of late, and maybe she'd become less reliant on them.

"But angels don't have mates. We figure you and Nithe were because of your other halves. Dragon's have mates, and vamps have beloveds, so it kinda made sense." Confusion and hope laced Athon's words.

"We have it on excellent authority that they can, and more and more angels will get them. It's been in the works apparently. Lots of planning, yadda, yadda. Though nobody really knows about it yet. But we aren't the first." Jezzie watched their stunned faces as her words sank in. Surprise, hope, and finally excitement.

"Do we have to bite you, Jez?"

"Yeah, Roth, you do. Would you like that? Would you let me bite you, too? What about you, Athon?" she asked them both.

"Do we have to be in you when we do?" Athon wriggled his brows in an attempt at goofiness she found amusing and endearing. "Not that I'd complain, but since time is running out, and I assume you want to spend some time with Tana, I have to ask."

"I don't think so. Nithe has obviously marked me already. I'm not sure how it all works really. I suppose you could both try at once, or one at a time, whatever you want. Though I suggest you kiss me first, just to be polite." She winked at them, inwardly unsure of how it would work.

Roth slid closer, and shifted her from Nithe's embrace. They both lay on either side of her, tracing her curves with one hand, while their heads were propped up by the other. Slowly the button of her shirt slipped free and the soft fabric fell open, exposing a swathe of skin from her neck to her already damp underwear.

Athon massaged her feet gently, then moved his way up her body. If massage was meant to relieve tension, he was failing miserably. The fire that flared to life in her veins set her muscles to quivering.

Nithe traced his mark at her breast reverently as he watched Roth kiss his way up her neck. He smiled down at her and whispered in her ear.

"Enjoy this, *a stór*. I am here, but this moment is for the three of you. I love you."

Relief and joy filled her heart, alongside the love she felt for Nithe and the expanding space in her heart for Roth and Athon.

A sudden gasp was wrenched from her as Athon's lips found the soft fold of her labia through the thin fabric. He teased them with licks and nips before he tore the fragile barricade apart, slipped between the wet and eagerly parting flesh to zero in on her sensitive nub. Stars shot across her vision and she squeezed her thighs tight around his head.

Roth's playful nips at her skin got sharper and gooseflesh covered her skin. Athon trailed his lips down to her inner thigh, laving at the extra soft flesh.

As one they bit down and groaned deeply. Her orgasm rocked through her with all the subtlety of a freight train, surprising the shit out of her. Thankfully, not literally.

Both males licked at her flesh gently before they each took her lips in a kiss that spoke volumes about the claim they had on her heart, and she on theirs. The metallic tang of blood lingered on her tongue.

Shit, I'm gonna need fresh pants, before we meet with her friend. The thought came from Roth.

No shit, Sherlock. Same goes for me, too. Athon's response drew giggles from Jezzie.

"Did we say that out loud?" Athon looked at them with a confused expression.

"No, the link works superfast but you won't have proper control over it for a while. Thankfully, only I can hear you both. Wait, Nithe, could you hear them?" Jezzie looked over at Nithe hopefully.

"Sorry, Jez. Maybe it's because they are mates too, even if they haven't sealed the bond yet? Or it could be because they bit you at the same time? We can experiment later, when everyone is more in control, and we spend more time together. Right now we should take a quick swim, get a change of clothes, and go find Tana. We've got less than three hours. Time enough for whatever you girls want to do, and for us to get some dinner."

Jezzie moved as if lightning had zapped her on the ass and grabbed her pants as she ran to the exit. In reality, she knew her cousin was likely to tear her a new asshole if she failed to spend her last few hours here with her.

"Come find me and Tana when you're done," she yelled over her shoulder. She didn't have time to look back.

If she had, she would have seen three sets of eyes devouring the sight of her bare ass bouncing in the breeze.

CHAPTER 40

Her last few hours with Tana had flown by way too fast. Jezzie clung tightly to Tana, soaking up her company as much as possible. They ate dinner, then watched a movie and threw popcorn at the guys as they complained about the chick flick she and Tana forced them to watch. She was a little worried about what would happen next so the laughter and carefree moment was much needed, and had her smiling still as they rounded the bend and entered the den.

Her forward motion was cut short as her group abruptly came to a halt. She didn't want to leave Tana, or her uncle, but her time was up, and the woman standing in the middle of the room surrounded by five fidgety princes was there to make it happen. There were so many unknowns. She needed to contact her aunt and mom. She was looking forward to seeing, or at least speaking to them.

Hell, they were soon to come face to face with Lucifer himself, and she'd have to deal with the fallout. For all she knew he might not even let her cross the threshold into wherever it was they lived, and then all her angst would be a moot point.

"What the fuck are they doing here?" Tana spit out venomously.

Oh, someone was pissed. Rian looked like he wanted to cry. Damn. What the hell had happened?

"Tana, mind your mouth and remember your manners, young one," Leraie snapped, the sharp bite of her tone like a slap to the face.

Considering Tana's instant recoil she'd felt the full force of Leraie's rebuke, but she still glared shards of disdain at the males before us.

"They're here to say goodbye to Jezzie and Nithe, Tana. It's not going to cost you anything to allow them this moment."

"You're right. I'm sorry, Leraie. I'll behave." Tana straightened her shoulders and looked Leraie in the eyes.

The next thing Jezzie knew she and Nithe were pulled forward into a giant group hug. The princes were all slapping Nithe on the back and joking around as they gave her quick bear hugs and promised to kick the asses of anyone who hurts them.

"We're family, Jezzie. At least, we will be once we convince your stubborn cousin of our good intentions and sincerity. Or you marry my boy, Nithe," Thad whispered in her ear, followed by a wink as he pulled back.

"Fucking gorgons," snarled Rian off to her left.

She'd never heard such venom in his voice before, and when she looked over at him a shadowy mask rippled over his features. His ears and nose became more pointed and long, his eyes narrowed, and lines creased his brow. He looked like an evil pixie or goblin from a fairy tale told to children, one without a happy ending. He shook his head and the overlay disappeared, leaving Jezzie to ponder what the fuck was going on, and just what those bitches had gone and done this time.

"It'll be alright. We've got it handled," said Dair cheerfully. "Those cows are going to get what they deserve. You don't need to worry, Jezzie. Just have fun with those hunks of yours, okay? And keep us in the loop."

"Hey," Rian huffed indignantly, and poked Dair in the ribs with his elbow. "They're not as hunky as me though, right?"

Was he seriously pouting? Jezzie couldn't help but laugh as Dair backpedaled and smoothed his ruffled feathers.

"Speaking of your men, are you going to introduce us to the newbies or are we all gonna stand here awkwardly as they continue to glare at us?" Theus piped up.

"They're not glaring. They aren't, are they?" Jezzie asked spinning around to look at Roth and Athon, only to find dark shadows creeping out of them and clenched fists already clutching black blades.

"Seriously, guys? Chill. These are my friends. I'm allowed to have those, right? Or do we have a problem?" Jezzie said, making it clear in her tone just how little she'd entertain their jealousy when it came to the princes. She'd explain later about the whole Tana situation, but now was not the time, she could see how much remaining polite was already taxing her cousin's limited goodwill and restraint.

"Yeah, guys, friends," said Rian, placing a cheeky kiss on her cheek. Seriously? Was the dude looking to die? Or at the very least lose vital parts of himself he may want to keep on the increasingly dubious off chance they do manage to nab her cousin's affections?

Roth's blue irises filled with the black of his shadows as the swirling mass seeped out of him and morphed into a semi-solid form with eyes of ruby-red and leapt forward. Before it could reach Rian, Jezzie stepped forward and flicked it on the nose, twice, and shook her head as she pointed at Roth.

"No," she declared, quite firmly.

The shadow beast pulled to a stop immediately and shook its head, perplexed. She couldn't hold back a soft smile as she reached out her hands and caressed its face gently. Athon gasped, his sound of shock mirrored Roth's own. Although, the more she stroked the beast the more she noticed Roth's gasps turned into moans.

Interesting, she thought, definitely something to tuck away for later.

"Allow me, Jezzie." Winked Dair. "Azaroth, Leviathon, allow me to introduce you to my kindred cursed brothers, my fellow unwanted princes: Novarian, Thaddeus, Prometheus, Grimm, and of course my wonderful self, Alasdair O'Dempsey. You guys saved my prepubescent Manticorian ass after my so-called parents left me to drown in the tunnels under Westminster Palace when it flooded back in 1236. Thanks, by the way." He stepped forward and held out his hand. Athon tilted his head to the side and studied him.

"Dair?" he questioned.

"The one and only." He chuckled.

"Well, fuck. Though, honestly, I can't say I'm surprised they picked you for this, knowing what utter assholes they are," Roth chimed in.

Instead of the handshake they were all expecting, Athon pulled Dair in for a bro hug, and Roth gave him a slap on the back. "Good to see you're still alive, scamp."

They made small talk for a while, the rest of the guys joining in as Jezzie stepped back and sidled up to her cousin and Leraie.

"Men are so weird and confusing," she pondered quietly.

"Without a doubt the most puzzling gender in all the realms," agreed Leraie.

"Which is why I try to stay away from them when I can. Yours are okay, Jezzie. Mostly cos' they're yours and not mine." Tana laughed.

"The day is coming, young one," Leraie murmured softly, "Both time and fate are set on their path, but you still have choices. Don't make the wrong ones, for your sake, and theirs."

"Leraie?" Jezzie asked.

"Yes, little one?"

"Will I be able to come back? Soon? At all? Will Tana and you-know-who be able to leave? I'm going to miss them terribly, you know." The full impact of what it meant to leave hit her like a sledgehammer to the chest as rogue tears slipped past her defenses.

"Of course you can," Leraie reassured her, pulling her in for a hug. "There is a door, the same door, in your apartment at the fortress ready for your use. She will only wake when you wish her to, and you can enter your sacred space whenever you or Nithe have need. From there you can enter here to see them both, and the princes too if you want."

"Did I hear my name?" Nithe piped in as he joined their little huddle, his hand stroking her back in a soothing way.

Of course he'd sensed the shift in her emotions. She looked up to find the gazes of her other mates watching her solemnly. A small smile and a shake of her head had them relaxing back into their conversations.

"I was explaining to Jezzie how you both will be able to visit here if you wish. Unfortunately, the sacred space only accepts Jezzie and her familiar, in this case, you. Roth and Athon will be locked out. They will have to wait until fate and other forces conspire to free Tana, and anyone else who may need freeing before they can visit too. I mean, it won't be long before they know more, but still . . . the stupid, dramatic plan must play out as it must," Leraie said the last part mockingly.

"Ouch!" she exclaimed, jumping as though someone had zapped her on the ass. "Yeah, yeah, sorry for insulting your grand design, oh mighty one," she sassed to the empty space over her shoulder.

"What about our stuff?" Jezzie suddenly remembered they hadn't packed.

"Already taken care of. You both have an identical set of all your belongings both here and in your new quarters. I hope the arrangements are to your liking. You will be sharing a four-bedroom suite with your mates. This way should you wish to sleep alone you may, should any of you wish for privacy in any configuration, you can have it. It also contains a kitchenette, living area, a reading nook, and a central bedroom with a super king-sized bed guaranteed to fit all four of you, decked out with whatever you may need. Now, it's time to go. But before you do, come with me."

Leraie took Jezzie's hand and led her further away from everyone else. When they came to a stop, she held out a small compact mirror which Jezzie tentatively took with a curious look on her face.

"It's very pretty," she said, confused as she looked at the hand painted enamel.

"Open it, silly girl. Seriously, you're not normally this daft, but I'll let it slide considering the circumstances," Leraie joked.

Jezzie snorted, but did as she was told. Inside the mirror swirled before coming into sharp focus.

"Uncle!" Jezzie gasped.

She expected Leraie to shush her and scold her, but instead she received a chuckle.

"Soundproof bubble, little one. You aren't the only one who can do so, remember?" Leraie reminded her.

"Jezzie, my dear girl. I wish I was coming with you. Oh, to see them all again. Since I cannot go, and I can't even give you a hug, I'll settle for some gentle words of encouragement and advice. Keep an open heart and mind. I'm sure it's all going to be a bit of a shock. But I'll be here if you need me. Finding out you're a dad with a teenager is hard enough, when they're all grown up and mated to two of your best friends, well, shit could get ugly before it gets golden. I love you, my niece. I'm glad you have three great males on your side. I'll see you soon." Uncle

Micah's face went blurry before disappearing completely, leaving behind the reflective surface of the mirror.

"Took him fifteen tries to record that message, by the way. Stubborn man kept trying to slip in code words for Roth and Athon, innocuous ones you may have inadvertently let slip. I also had to remind him they wouldn't hear or see him either. Then he kept getting teary and saying it wasn't right he couldn't hug you goodbye and finding the right words was impossible," Leraie sighed softly.

"Tell him it was perfect, and I love him too, please?" Jezzie asked.

"Of course, my dear. Keep the mirror. You can send him and Tana messages, but they will not be able to reply until the time comes. Understood?"

"Yes, Leraie. Thank you," she said, throwing her arms around the older, regal woman.

"And, Jezzie . . . Be brave. He's not as scary as he looked. It's not in your nature to back down from a fight, so give it all you've got. He needs a bit of a bitch slap back to reality. Tell him I said 'hi' and 'you're welcome'."

Striding back toward the portal Leraie clapped her hands, and they all fell silent.

"Time to go, ladies and gents. Slap each other's asses, buss each other's cheeks, whatever it is that's the done thing these days, and get your booties through my portal. I need my beauty sleep and I have a date with some ice cream, some wine, and the most humble, sexy man on earth. Yes, Keanu Reeves does have a new movie out, and I am not going to miss it to watch you guys cry in a circle for another five minutes. So, in you go," Leraie winked at Jezzie and Tana with a teasing glint in her eye.

Jezzie couldn't blame her, they had to leave, it had to be now, and Keanu was one special human male.

With one last goodbye and a kiss on Tana's cheek, Jezzie stepped forward toward the portal. Nithe grabbed her right hand, Athon her left, and Roth stepped up close behind her to wrap his arms around her waist.

And together, as one unit, they stepped into whatever future awaited them on the other side.

Apparently traveling by Leraie's portals was a hell of a lot more enjoyable than her own, Jezzie reflected as she landed softly on her feet in a large living area. It was like landing on a cotton cloud rather than the ankle jarring thud she was used to. She'd have to remember to ask Leraie for some tips the next time they saw each other. It was almost as good as flying.

"Where are we?" she asked no one in particular. It was Roth who answered her.

"Home. We are home."

"Well, our home," Athon clarified. "Welcome to Hell and the Shadow Hound Fortress."

"And I'm pretty sure this is the suite Leraie was telling us about while the guys were talking to Dair and the guys," Nithe noted.

"What suite?" Roth asked.

"Leraie created it for us here. We each have our own rooms for whenever we need them, and apparently one large central bed to snuggle in," Jezzie replied with a wink.

"Yep," confirmed Nithe. "Snuggles, sure, that's totally where all our minds went." He chuckled.

The living space was large and well lit, despite having no windows. She tilted her head to look at the ornate white ceiling and noted the lack of lights turned on, or lights period. Must be magic. The large circular couch looked super comfy and the dark red material popped against the light cream walls, and the dark wooden coffee table. Tall bookcases lined one wall with a rolling ladder at one end. Walking over, Jezzie ran her fingers lightly over a few of the spines, her eyes taking in as many titles as they could as she moved from one end to the other. All of her favorites were there. From classics to Sci-fi, Horror to children's books she'd loved as a little girl, and romance novels of every kind. The names of her most beloved authors popped out to say hello like long-lost friends and her heart gave a jolt as she realized all the characters she'd met before were welcoming her home. Along with a myriad of new ones for her to discover.

When she came to a halt at the ladder she smiled and jumped

lightly onto the lowest rung. With one foot she pushed off and rolled slowly sideways.

"Never is as good as the movies make it out to be, I suppose." She sighed in disappointment. "Definitely not the fairytale zooming I was expecting."

"It's a good thing you have your Prince Charmings to make up the deficit caused by such a lack of zoomability, don't you think?" Athon joked.

"Charming, are you? And here I thought you were the damsels in distress." Jezzie winked and ran for the closest door, Athon and the others hot on her heels.

She quickly came to a halt and felt her eyes just about bug out of her head and her jaw hit the floor. The guys piled into the room behind her and silence reigned. Until Jezzie burst out laughing. The guys all looked her way and lust infused their glazed expressions. Sex toys were displayed in glass cabinets along the circular wall, interspersed by doors. Dildos of every shape, size, and color. Whips and paddles, ropes, and industrial-sized bottles of lube. Ropes, restraints, and harnesses were displayed artistically from what looked like a modified coat stand. A shape against one wall was draped with a length of heavy material, but she had a feeling she knew what lay beneath it, and she was thankful Leraie had been kind enough to be cautious and cover it up for now.

Her gaze settled on the monster of a bed in the very center of the room. Three stairs led up to a raised dais on which the black four-poster with its plush pillows and blankets sat. She took note of the metal O-rings on the posts and the hook which hung from the ceiling, before catching sight of a copy of the *Kama Sutra* propped up on one of the bedside tables.

Subtle, Leraie. Very subtle. Jezzie chuckled even as she got a little breathless and anticipation filled every atom of her being. Her underwear became wet as she clenched her thighs against the onslaught of desire. Oh, what she could do to them, or they to her. Her desire slipped her control and her emotions and thoughts flooded through the links she had with her mates. A quick glance at each of their crotches revealed the outlines of three very impressive erections straining the tight material.

"I guess that's a conversation we all need to have at some point," she said with a giggle.

"Probably a good idea. Roth's going to need to know your limits at some point. But right now we need to clean up and get ready," Athon agreed.

"Ready for what?" Jezzie asked, confused.

"They'll know we're back soon, if they don't already, and we'll be summoned within the hour," he replied.

"Who's 'they'? And we'll be summoned where, and for what?" Nithe demanded as he straightened his shoulders and the dragon alpha in him leaked out, looking for a threat.

"Lucifer and the rest of our team, The Devil's 13, will want an update and to officially meet you both. No one enters the fortress without being vetted, well, not normally, but shit's been weird for a while now. Don't worry, Jez, I'm sure whatever bug was up Luc's ass must have wriggled the fuck out by now. He's been a little off for a fair while now," Roth explained. He shook his head, rubbing one hand along the back of his neck. "I should probably let Deus know we need a little time before we face General Sourpuss, and I just need to check on a few things. Why don't you all grab a shower? It won't take me long, and when I get back I'll join you. Assuming there's a shower in this place big enough to fit the four of us. Find it and have fun." He winked before slapping Nithe on the back, kissing Jezzie on top of her head, and pulling Athon in for a quick, sultry kiss. He headed out the door into the living area. The soft click as the front door to their apartment closed behind him broke Jezzie from her grinning stupor.

She looked at Athon and Nithe furtively then ran as fast as she could to the door closest to her and threw it open.

"Not mine," she shouted after checking out the dark blue interior with its masculine furnishings. "Must be Roth's."

Athon ran in the opposite direction in the circular room. When she looked at Nithe he was watching them with amusement and joy. The emotions wafted from him as if on a gentle, contented breeze and filled her with a pleasant warmth. Athon's child-like excitement felt like soda bubbles and tickled her insides leaving the taste of grape bubblegum on her tongue.

"Nope, this one's too dragon-y. Must be yours, Nithe," he chortled.

"I definitely found yours, Athon," Jezzie shouted as she looked into the room next to Roth's. Sci-fi posters and bass guitars lined the walls like a rock geek's wet dream. If her room wasn't as cool as this one, she might just have to move in with Athon permanently.

"Looks like you're next to Nithe, Jezzie," Athon said as he pointed to the open door.

"Ooo, lemme see," she shrieked excitedly as she ran over and stuck her head through the doorway.

Her inner little princess went weak at the knees. The walls were a lovely pale green, soft pink roses and tulips sat in crystal vases on every available surface, gold gilt framed mirrors and pretty paintings hung on the walls, and a reading nook with a cuddle couch filled one corner. It was perfectly romantic and exactly the way she'd always envisioned her bedroom in her very own forever home. A dream she'd given up on decades ago. The realization she might actually have found a home here with these three men, one she could always call her own and would not ever have to leave behind, had tears well up in her eyes. She managed to hold them in check, barely.

"Hey, goobers," Nithe said. They looked his way, affronted at the name. "It would have been a lot faster if you'd just read the names above the doors." He burst out laughing.

Well, damn. He wasn't wrong, Jezzie acknowledged as she peered up at the gold plate affixed to the doorjamb, and literally facepalmed herself as Athon swept her off her feet and spun her around.

"It's okay, Jezzie. We can be goobers together, forever." Athon grinned and kissed the tip of her nose.

"So, what's the door between your room and Jezzie's lead to?" Nithe asked, pointing to the unlabeled door.

"Storage?" pondered Athon.

"Not storage. It's the communal bathroom Roth was so hopeful for," Jezzie shouted, already inside the beautifully tiled and acoustically perfect room. "You guys need to check out how big the spa and shower is. I suggest you get naked, cos I already am," she teased as she hurriedly shed her clothes, eager to stand beneath the warm waterfall of water sure to rain down on her still sore muscles in the absolutely massive shower.

"Liar, liar, pants on fire," Athon's sing-song voice startled her from behind.

His hands gripped her sides, catching her as she tipped forward. Damn shoes. Yep, pants second, shoes first. In her haste she'd forgotten to take them off and nearly face-planted the glossy black tiles.

Athon dropped to his knees behind her and pulled her back to rest her ass on his shoulder, as if he was her personal stool. He reached around her and unlaced one shoe and then the other, and slipped them from her feet. Her frustratingly blameless pants quickly followed before he helped her to her feet, slipping her underwear from her hips and down her long, shapely legs, her backside bared to his hungry gaze. She knew it without looking over her shoulder, his lust hit her full-on and his thoughts broke away from him. The words traveled straight to her throbbing clit and each one pushed her excitement higher.

Must taste her. Must take her. Goddamn, she's the most beautiful woman I've ever seen. How the fuck did I get this lucky. She'll scream my name oh, so pretty.

Before he rose to stand behind her, his teeth grazed a path over her cheeks which were level with his face. His teeth nipped and bit at the sensitive flesh, drawing breathy moans from her throat as his fingers delved between her slightly parted thighs, and up into her tight core. He took them out far too soon for her liking, after only a single thrust, but when he stood and spun her around in his arms to face him she saw they were coated in her slick wet juices. He held her gaze as he lifted them to his lips and licked them clean. She damn near came on the spot at the sight. Watching his tongue swirl around the two glistening digits made her knees go all weak and rubbery, so she gripped his shoulders. Her nails dug in hard enough to leave little crescents in their wake.

The sound of the shower running intruded into her awareness and she frowned in confusion. Athon chuckled huskily.

"Soon, Jez. Soon I'll have you all to myself for a little while, and I'm going to spend hours eating that perfect, plump, pussy of yours, giving you as many orgasms as you can take. And just when you think you can't take any more, my cock will fill you up and make you scream my name as you climax harder than you ever have before."

"Pretty sure of yourself, huh, Athon?" she tried to sass back. Striving for unaffected aloofness, and failing woefully.

"Are you guys coming in here anytime soon? Or would you rather stand out there naked, in the cold until Roth gets back." Nithe's voice echoed off the tiled walls with amusement.

CHAPTER 41

Nithe's fingers fumbled with the buttons on his shirt for the umpteenth time. Why the fuck wouldn't they just go in the damn holes, for fuck's sake? The tension in his shoulders was threatening one hell of a headache, but he knew it wasn't all his. Jezzie was next door, getting ready for the inevitable meeting, and her anxiety was thrumming along the bond straight into his already tense body.

Before they'd all split up to get ready—an idea he hadn't been very fond of—Roth had returned, but he hadn't joined them in the shower like he'd promised. His still damp hair indicated he'd done so elsewhere, but the almost palpable energy of a caged wildcat which radiated off of him had put everyone off-kilter. Jezzie's hurt expression lingered in his mind even now. Some of her hurt and confusion wove through the anxious feelings she was subconsciously sending out. He wondered if the others also felt it, and if they knew the emotions belonged to Jezzie.

A button yet again slipped from his fingers, this time popping free of its thread and pinging against the mirror in front of him. Fuck this shit. Why was he even dressing up for this anyway? If the assholes didn't like him as he was then fuck them. He ripped the cloth from his body as though the fine material had personally offended him and tossed it to the floor.

His hand went to the bond-mark on the right side of his neck, his fingers tracing the imprint of her teeth which marked him as hers. Nithe's breath left his lungs all at once as he felt the echo of Jezzie's pleasurable shudder ripple through his body, and the gasp that left her lips like a caress against his skin, despite the solid wall between them.

Grabbing his favorite shirt from the end of what was apparently his bed, he threw it on and moved swiftly to Jezzie's door. He hesitated before knocking, the soft murmur of her words drifting to him through the stupid barrier.

"Pull yourself together, Jezebeth. You knew this day would come. You can do this. We'll figure out what crawled up Roth's ass later and put together an extraction plan. But right now you've got bigger fish to fry, and there's no way in, well, this place, you're going to fall to pieces. You've faced scarier shit than this before. Yeah, so what if they hate you? Not like they aren't best friends with two of your . . . Lovers? Mates? Husbands? No, not husbands. How human of me. But wouldn't that be nice? Jesus, Jezzie. Now you're just rambling to yourself like a nut job. Fucking hell."

Nithe silently chuckled as he practically felt her facepalm.

I know you're there, Nithe. Come join my pathetic misery, Jezzie said through their link. Her soft chuckle bordered on manic. His female's mind was going in circles. Something had to be done. A grin lit his features, taking away the worry lines on his brow.

Without warning he raced into the room and picked Jezzie up. He spun her around, her feet flying through the air as she giggled like a carefree lass on a sunny spring day. His lips nibbled at the side of her neck, but it must have tickled as she shrieked and cackled, struggling to shift away. His perfect little witch . . . vampitch? . . . vampitchel? Hmm, maybe he should trademark it.

"Seriously, Ni? Vampitchel?" Jezzie snorted amid a fresh round of giggles. "Gosh, I love you."

"Anything for my lady. Tell me what's wrong, a stór."

His warm breath fluttered over the shell of her ear, and he was rewarded with a breathless moan. All at once he realized she was only wearing a bra and panties. It was his turn to groan. He loved it when she didn't wear matching sets. She did sometimes, but when she didn't, he knew she was comfortable, happy with her body, and she wasn't trying to impress him. She was just Jezzie. His Jezzie.

"Where to start, Ni? I'm going to meet daddy dearest, we have to explain everything that's happened, including our relationship and the whole mate thing. Roth's been acting weird ever since he came back from whatever the hell he went to do. What if they kick us out? What if he rejects me? What if the guys choose to stay rather than come with us? Or worse, they hate us, me, for not telling them the truth sooner?"

"Jez, my love, it's been three days. Nobody can expect to know another being's secrets in three days. Those days were about getting to know if you could trust them. Plus, the whole you couldn't tell them thing Leraie put in place kinda stopped you anyway. As to what's going to happen when we get to this meeting . . . I can't see the future, but if he doesn't fall at your feet and love you for the amazing person you are, then the male's a fool. Angel or not. I'll gladly follow wherever you go, and I'm pretty sure I'm not the only one." His lips found hers in a kiss filled with every ounce of love, passion, and trust he felt for her. Each feeling held equal weight, as trust wasn't something he gave lightly.

"Thank you, mo shíorghrá. You always know what to say." She winked, then bit her bottom lip. "Should I wear a dress, do you think?" She looked so unsure. This whole situation meant more to her than he could comprehend, given his own feelings for his supposed sire being what they were.

"Just be you, Jez. If you want to wear a dress, wear one. Just be comfortable in whatever makes you feel most like you."

He turned her to face the wardrobe and gave her a gentle shove toward it. After a particularly deep breath and a large sigh, Jezzie donned her nicest pair of supple, dark-brown leather training pants—which hugged her ass in just the right way. A fitted cream peasant shirt with bell sleeves, matching leather boots, and braces for her forearms followed.

"Just in case," she whispered, as if to herself.

From the jewelry box on her dresser she pulled a small silver locket, and as she faced him, holding it reverently, he saw tears well in her eyes.

"Thank you, Leraie." Her gaze on the ceiling.

Nithe swore he heard Leraie reply with a softly spoken, "You're welcome."

He helped fasten the chain at the back of her neck, and together they made their way out to the common area. Roth barely glanced up as they entered the room, and Jezzie stumbled to an awkward stop, unsure of his emotions.

"Jezzie, what is he feeling? Can you read him?" His concern and curiosity needled at him.

"Not clearly. So many emotions are swirling around and the taste is bitter and acrid, like buried pain and tortured choices. He's blocking me. He learned fast. I just want to hold him and take it all away, but he's put up a shield, so I can't even siphon some of it off, nor can I feed him any positive replacements or reassurances. What happened, Ni?"

"I wish I knew, a stór. We'll figure it out like you said, after the meeting. It'll all work out, I'm sure."

Athon joined them soon after. A forced joviality to his persona.

"Ready to go guys? It's all going to be fine, Jez. I promise, they're not that bad. Luc's actually a big teddy bear, really he is." Roth snorted from his perch on the sofa. "Well, unless you piss him off like Roth did. But I don't think anyone can piss him off like Roth can." Athon's laugh filled the air and Nithe felt Jezzie relax beside him.

"Um, guys? Before we go, there's something you both really should know." Her gaze was zeroed in on Roth, and then Athon. Only one of them was paying attention to what their girl was saying. "You see, my dad, well, he's—"

"We don't have time for chit-chat. We need to go and get this over with," Roth's words came out in an almost snarl as he shot to his feet and strode to the door. He flung it open with a thud against the wall and stepped to the side to reveal the empty hall beyond.

"Fuck, Roth. What crawled up your ass while you were gone earlier? It certainly wasn't me, that's for sure. Shame. Stop being a dick, *Corazón*." Athon looked at Roth sternly, but Nithe could almost feel the concern which radiated off of him, even as the dragon beneath Nithe's skin writhed and hissed his displeasure.

Nithe took hold of Jezzie's hand and tugged her toward the seething mass of whatever the fuck was going on inside the brain of the meat-slab who resembled Roth. But as they went to pass him, Jezzie paused. She reached up one hand and caressed the hard edge of Roth's tense jaw and the lines creasing the outer edges of his eyes. Before Nithe could react Roth had pulled her in hard against his chest for a punishing kiss. Almost brutal in its intensity and filled with so much heat. Through Jezzie, he felt Roth's tortured pain, his heated desire and his desperation so intense it was as if he wished to crawl inside her and never leave. Then came the anger, the disgust, the conflict which warred within his head, and he abruptly pulled away, thrusting her from him and back into Nithe's arms.

Nithe glanced at Athon who looked as confused as he felt, then back at Roth who shook his head and strode out of the room, leaving them to follow with a curt, "Let's go."

A sense of foreboding filled his chest with lead as they hurried after him.

THEY FOLLOWED ROTH THROUGH LONG, well-lit hallways and staircases, their footsteps silent on the flagstones. Elegant paintings adorned gray stone walls of, from what she assumed, was a very large, very old castle, and curved around every sweeping bend. The matching floor was well-worn and smooth beneath her booted feet. It was like something out of a fairy tale. An image skipped through Jezzie's turbulent thoughts, and she was tempted to stop and look out of one of the tall, thin windows just to see if knights in shining armor were jousting down below. Or if maidens in medieval gowns strolled through a picture-perfect courtyard fluttering their handkerchiefs at potential suitors to show their favor. A silly, fanciful thought, but what the hell, right? Anything to divert her from mentally falling down the dual rabbit holes of Roth's sudden strange mood and the impending confrontation that was all but guaranteed once they reached their destination.

The corner of her mouth twitched at the irony. Hell, the Devil's home, was exactly where she was. Thinking of Roth, his behavior was definitely sudden and odd. It was confirmed by Athon's uncensored thoughts as they raced one after the other along the link, the bond, they shared. She pushed a feeling of calm love and reassurance back to him, his confusion added to hers, but hopefully he felt a little better.

All of a sudden her face was plastered against Roth's shirt-covered back, and she realized they'd apparently come to a halt. Athon laughed softly. Nithe steadied her as she bounced backwards a step. Even Roth turned his head and gazed down at her, concern and love shone briefly in his eyes and vibrated along the link like an arrow leaving the bow. In a flash it was gone, the sharp quiver of pain as the arrow landed its blow stung deep in her heart, and she knew a dread she'd hoped never to feel again . . .

"There you are, my dears. Right on time. Come here, child."

A very short, rather stout, matronly old woman stepped right in front of her. She reminded Jezzie of the fairy godmother from the children's films, only older and with more wrinkles. As the woman's arms wrapped tight around her in a bone crushing hug, she felt both comfort and confusion. There was more here than met the eye. Bright eyes looked up at her with compassion and a shrewdness which belied her sweet little old lady appearance.

"It'll be alright, my dear. He needs this as much as you do," she whispered, before stepping back and releasing her.

"Mrs Briars, this is Jezzie." Athon was the one to introduce them. Roth just stood there looking moody and impatient. "And this is her other mate, Nithe."

"A pleasure to meet you, Nithe." Mrs Briars held out her hand, which Nithe readily accepted.

"The pleasure is mine. What is such a charming woman as yourself doing in a place like this?" Nithe winked at Mrs Briars and threw a cheeky smile to Jezzie.

"I like this one, Jezzie. Keep him around. Head on in. I'll be around if you need me." Mrs Briars made her way down the hallway and away from the imposing black double doors Jezzie only just noticed were at Roth's back. Mrs Briars looked back over her shoulder to check out Nithe's ass, she tossed a double thumbs at Jezzie in approval, causing a snort of laughter to erupt from Jezzie at the old woman's unabashed cheekiness.

Shaking her head she looked at each of the guys, but before she could speak Roth grabbed her wrist and pulled her forward. Nithe gently took her other hand, for which she smiled thankfully up at him. Always a gentleman. Athon stepped up to cover her back, and after a quick hug from behind, placed his palm on her left shoulder, his fingers fiddled with a few errant strands of her hair which had slipped free of her braid.

"We will discuss this later, Roth," Nithe growled low in his throat, a hint of his dragon having seeped into his words.

Roth just raised one arrogant brow and pushed open one of the doors, leaving Nithe to open the other, and strode forward. Dragging her with him into the Devil's lair.

If she'd been expecting open hostility and an angry Lucifer to come charging at her, throwing her immediately out on her ass, she was thankfully mistaken. And yes, it had been high on her list of probable outcomes to be honest. Instead everyone in the room froze as every set of eyes spun their way, smiles were thrown at Athon and Roth, while Jezzie and Nithe received a multitude of reactions. Like the green-eyed guy in the corner who watched her as if awaiting a viper strike, or the brown-eyed guy slouched on the couch who had an almost wicked glint of mischief in his gaze as his lips twisted in an amused smirk. Each one held something different. Confusion, mistrust, worry, cautious welcome, and for each of them the emotions she felt matched what was written on their faces. Each one open, but why wouldn't they be? It's not like they knew what she could do. She didn't pry beyond the surface level, skim reading the room only. But as her power brushed over the tall male with strange white irises rimmed in red, his shoulders shifted as if shaking off a chill, and he straightened from his lean against the wall. Wariness entered his gaze as he searched for the cause of his uneasiness and Jezzie quickly drew her power back into herself to avoid detection. Something which had not happened in a very long time, and definitely not from such a small taste.

"Roth, Athon, welcome home." The one who reminded her of a sad, but excitable puppy with big brown eyes came bounding over and gave them a bro hug. "Introduce us to the pretty lady and her bodyguard, please? I'm in the mood to make new friends." He winked, and in the split second it took for his eye to shut and open again Jezzie felt the twisted pain he held locked inside and the chains of a fate he had lost hope of ever escaping. It hit her in the chest with a force which took her breath and left her gasping as if air could no longer sustain her.

"Dante," Roth warned. "Play nice." His hand slipped down her wrist and his fingers seemed to curl around hers of their own volition. Either that or he was staking his claim. A thought which brought her comfort and hope, despite his earlier behavior.

"Always, Roth. Especially with such a pretty one."

The one named Dante seemed to delight in teasing Roth, his true intentions were as platonic as a brotherly hug. Jezzie liked him immensely. She'd always wanted a brother. A sister too. Or either. A sibling, that's what she'd longed for, but her mother only had one true love and never the two had bumped uglies again since her conception, so her childish wish had remained unfulfilled.

"I'm Jezzie, and this is my mate, Nithe. You already know the other two, obviously." Jezzie laughed lightly, then looked at him seriously. "Want to be my big brother? Or is that too weird? Like, I always wanted one, and you seem like you'd be a great one to have. You can say no, I won't be offended. Sometimes I have impulse control issues. Just ask the guys. I'm usually right though. So . . . I'll just shut up now, shall I?" Jezzie felt her face turn pink, heat warmed her cheeks and she bit her lips together. What the fuck was up with her lately? Word vomit, that's what. Stupid fucking brain.

"You want me as your brother?" he asked, stunned.

"Well, only if you want. And you may change your mind before the day is done. Won't blame you," Jezzie muttered.

Dante leapt forward before she could take another breath and gave her a big bear hug. His arms held on tight as he twirled her around.

"I'd love to be your brother. See that, guys? I'm her brother." He smirked at Roth and Athon as if he'd just ripped the rug from underneath them as he shook Nithe's hand. "Nice to meet my brother-in-law."

"Looks like you've now gained three of those, not just one," Nithe laughed. "Nice to meet you too, Dante."

"What? Three? How? Who?" he stammered.

Nithe looked over at Roth and Athon with a beaming smile. Athon cackled with glee.

"She may be your sister now, D, but mates trump brothers." Athon stuck out his tongue and put his thumbs in his ears as he wiggled his fingers about.

Gasps and murmurs filled the room. Someone went to speak but stopped abruptly as the doors opened behind them. The shift of power filling the room had both butterflies swirling in her stomach and liquid lead trying to drown them. You'd think when the Devil himself walked into a room it'd get hotter than hell, but no. Instead, Jezzie felt pure ice slide down her spine as chills covered her flesh. Probably not caused by him in actuality, and more to do with how this might all play out. If she were honest, his reaction back at her Uncle's place had pissed her off more than anything, but now? If he kicked her out she'd either lose Roth and Athon, or the guys would lose their family, their home, possibly their purpose?

Could that be the reason for Roth's weird attitude? Had someone told him this might all go pear shaped? Was he preparing to say goodbye to her and Nithe already?

She glanced at his face but could detect no real emotion and when she probed along the link and felt the air around him, she found nothing but a solid barrier bouncing her own feelings back at her. How had he learned to do that? And so fast? What even was it?

It appeared, as she shifted her gaze around to watch Lucifer waltz into the room, he hadn't yet noticed her presence. Perhaps due to the fact both Roth and Athon's broad backs shielded her from his view. Nithe sensed her thoughts and moved between her and Athon, trying not to draw attention to them and give her a little more time to breathe.

Feet stopped moving on the carpet as Lucifer reached the table, and the air really did shift, finally filling with a fiery ire. As an angry buzzing filled her ears, he rounded on them, his eyes locking in on her, scanning her, noting her company, and her presence. She could almost see the steam come out his ears.

"Luc, take a breath, mate. Don't go feral." The green-eyed, shaggy-haired blond guy built like a linebacker shook his head with a sigh.

She'd have to thank him for trying later, if she wasn't incinerated within the next ten seconds. Not much could kill her, but someone as powerful as Lucifer stood a better chance than anything else. She inhaled deeply and let it out slowly. It was now or never.

"Hi, I'm Jezzie. I—"

"I don't give a flying fuck who you are, missy. You need to get your ass out of my fortress, away from my realm, and never cross my path again. Show the lady out, Deus," Lucifer snarled, his lip curled up angrily.

"But you don't know me. What the fuck have I ever done to you, Luci?" Jezzie felt rage take over her mouth as the reins on her mixed up emotions slipped her hold.

Lucifer seemed to grow bigger, his shoulders broader, and his skin darkened as he stalked closer, barely leashed menace in every step.

"You stand here, in my home, the very image of the woman I lost, and yet you are not her. Can never be her. Your very presence is a reminder of what I can never have again, and I should let you stay? And it's Lucifer to you. Or sir. Hades, if you wanna die. My friends call me Luc. My enemies don't call me. Ever. Only one person ever called me Luci, and she died, then disappeared without a trace," he said the last part almost breathlessly. Despair filled the narrow space between them. Jezzie felt tears well in her eyes as Nithe and Athon closed ranks beside her, until he snarled his next words and the flames in his eyes snuffed the urge out. "Now, get the fuck out!"

She could see the vein pulse at his temple as the heat of his angry words stung her face. Her anger was greater than his, though she felt his words hit her in the chest. The only thing which held her back was the knowledge she was playing with a full deck, whereas he was not. Twisted pleasure filled her and her lips curled up at the corners as she took half a step toward him. She looked around the room as best she could. Twelve faces watched on warily, bodies poised for action, tension filled the space, she sucked just a little of it in and felt power fill her, giving her strength. Just a smidgen to get her through this.

Jezzie looked back at Roth and Athon and gave them a wan smile as Nithe squeezed her hand and whispered along the link.

They'll understand.

Athon, trust me I wanted to tell you before, but I couldn't, I promise.

She sent the thought to him as quickly as she could and then shut the link down fast, but not before his utter confusion rippled back at her. She stepped forward, giving herself enough room for her revelation.

"My name is Jezebeth Lucinda Poisson, and I should look like her, asshole, since she's my mother." Jezzie's colorful wings unfurled, her shadows escaped her hold to flow about her in a writhing mass, and her eyes burned with the raging fires of a thousand hells.

"What the fuck!" She had no idea who'd exclaimed the words into the silent void, and she didn't care. Her entire focus was centered on the man in front of her, her tattered childhood expectations, his utterly frozen expression, and the confusion twisting the slow-moving cogs behind his eyes. Ah, there you go, maybe.

"Yeah . . . Hi, Dad," she murmured, her eyes locked onto his dark brown, almost black eyes as the room erupted around them. Not that either of them noticed, locked as they were in the moment.

It was the little, old, odd woman from earlier in the hallway who snapped them from their staring contest as she entered the room and bustled about setting up tea and coffee on the sideboard, as if it were an everyday occurrence for the Devil to discover he had a daughter. As far as she knew it could be. Jezzie had never contemplated whether her father had other children before, siblings bound by blood, or what it could mean. Though the way his mouth dropped open, his eyes widened, and his skin paled as he stumbled back was nothing short of utter shock, or maybe terror—she couldn't get a read on his tumultuous emotions when hers were just as chaotic—told her otherwise. She tucked away her wings and tried to settle her unruly shadows, with very little luck.

"Three, two, one," the odd old lady counted and everything slowed down.

The one named Deus jumped forward a second too late as her father hit the ground hard. She'd knocked the devil out cold with two little words. Fuck! Everything was about to change . . . again.

CHAPTER 42

He watched Luc hit the deck, he collapsed as if his bones had turned to jelly. Never had Ramiel seen his friend, the mighty Lucifer, toppled by the words of a female. Not that she was just any female, of course. From all appearances, she was his progeny. One he clearly knew nothing about. Odd, because angels could usually sense their progeny up until adulthood. Something didn't add up. As the head of the Praesidium it was his job to question oddities such as this. Had the Almighty changed the rules on them? It wouldn't be the first time they'd been the victims of some multi-Realm reshuffle or game of whimsy. He looked away from his fallen friend and latched his gaze on the girl. He cleared his throat.

"Come here, daughter of Lucifer, if that is who you really are?" his silky tone, like a spider to a fly, dared her to refuse.

"I don't respond well to orders, mister. Especially not from strange men I don't know, and whose emotions and intentions are locked away so tightly within the Almighty's golden cage that is . . . well . . . you. Praesidium, I assume? I mean, you practically scream it," the sassy chit responded. Though the look in her eyes screamed both concern and forced calm. He had a feeling the concern was not for herself. One of his brows rose in response.

Ramiel noted the movement of her hands as she reached out to both of the males, Nithe and Athon. They quickly stepped to either side of her and took one each. Athon looked back over his shoulder at Roth, but the male looked stunned, oddly defeated, angry, as if his blood were turned to ice as he stepped up to cover her back, almost reluctantly. Jezzie didn't turn to look at him, but Ramiel noted her visible shudder, the goosebumps on her skin, and the hitch in her breath. Interesting, not all was well in their little lover's paradise.

"Ramiel, at your service. There, you know who I am, now walk your ass front and center, missy, before I have to do this the hard way," he ended with a growl.

A low growl built in the room until the roar of a dragon filled the space and shook the paintings on the walls. Several bottles and glasses behind the bar rattled and crashed to the floor, sending shards of glass and splatters of alcohol flying. Jezzie's eyes darted to Nithe and in an instant she was face to face with her lover, she stared into his eyes and caressed his jaw. The male whimpered softly and pulled her into a tight embrace as he glared daggers at Ramiel. What the actual fuck was happening?

The girl spun around in the male's arms and looked him in the eye. "Seriously? Knowing who you are just makes me trust you less. But since Ballzy said to give you a chance, I suppose I must. Though it doesn't get you off the hook for everything, and if you even think of doing anything hinky toward me, or my men, I'll suck out your soul and swallow it down like a fine whiskey," she said with a catlike smile.

He snorted in response, but Athon shook his head. "She's not joking, Ram. Don't piss her off or you won't be around to know she was being literal."

His eyes widened slightly of their own accord and his brain spun in circles because nothing made sense.

"Who the fuck is Ballzy?" He was so fucking confused.

"Ah, Balthazar, duh." She looked at him as if he were stupid, and maybe he was.

"How do you know Ballzy, I mean Balthazar? And why in all of the Almighty's realms do you call him Ballzy?" He had the feeling he both did and didn't want to know the answer to the last one.

"How about we get into all of that after Daddy dearest wakes up. If you drop your shield . . . I'll show you mine if you show me yours. Or you can just verify with Leraie. Otherwise I'm assuming you want to have your little vamp friend take a sample and compare it to the unconscious and non-consenting male at your feet?"

"What little vamp friend?" Marcus asked brusquely.

"The one standing by the picture of, oh would you look at that, Madame de Pompadour, how fitting." Jezzie smiled as if she knew something they didn't. "Don't worry, sweetie, I won't let them hurt you. Us suckers need to stick together. Plus, I already know more than enough about you to know you're not going to hurt me and mine."

Every set of eyes, except his and hers swiveled to look at the spot against the wall. The spot he knew hid his bodyguard. He'd protested the need, but the Almighty and Leraie had both insisted, more like ordered, and who was he to win that fight? No one but a servant, that's who.

"Come on out, Liana," he said with a sigh. He was going to cop so much shit for this, he just knew it.

A shimmer preceded her unveiling, like a fucking invisibility cloak, of all things. How original. Liana was tall, slender, toned, with curves that were subtle yet alluring in a way that screamed athleticism and softness at the same time. The fact she was utterly deadly was somehow hidden by a gentleness he didn't trust.

"I can explain—" Ramiel started, but was cut off as Malphas and Fynn pinned Liana to the wall, and Deus overrode his attempt to speak.

"How did you get in here? And for how long?" he practically bellowed.

"Each and every time Ramiel has been here in the last few months. In fact, I was surprised no one noticed, I expected more from the renowned Devil's 13, to be honest. That it took Jezzie over there to point out my presence is just utterly delightful," she replied with a smug smile, her voice full of sugar and tangy lime.

Ramiel looked at the ceiling, mentally asking what he'd done to deserve this torture, as voices started to merge and the aggression in the room started to spike once more.

"Cut it out," came a whispered command that stopped them all. "Let her go. She's here with my permission and knowledge."

At Luc's words, Liana's feet made contact with the floor, and she shook herself loose from the barely there hold Malphas and Fynn still had on her arms. All eyes pivoted to Luc, who was lifting himself to his feet and swearing under his breath.

"What the fuck, dude," he directed at Deus. "You just let me go down like that?" He chuckled as he shook his head.

As Luc found his bearings, Ramiel focused on Jezzie instead. She watched Luc with trepidation. The same way a child fearing rejection approaches a parent for a puppy. She huddled back into the heat of her men. He felt calm radiate through the room, as Nithe rubbed her shoulders and Athon nuzzled the top of her head with his cheek. His eyes narrowed. Was it coming from her? Was she manipulating them all?

Luc pushed through the crowd, blocking Ram from the guy's "daughter", and took a tentative step toward her. He needed to see how this played out, but Nithe's next words, delivered straight at him with a steely edge and an acid-filled gaze, caused his brain to cease working. The male's bitterness and anger hit him in the chest harder than any physical fist could.

"It's okay, *a stór*, talk to your father. We've got your back. We'll sort out you and yours, and focus on me and mine later . . ."

THE BEAST within him roared for freedom, beating on the internal flesh of its cage. Nithe knew he couldn't let the dragon out, not there, not then. Faced with his father, he tried to make sense of the rage which swirled in his head, the pain slashing his heart, and the tiny spark of hope hidden deep within the soul of the child he'd once been. Balthazar's words trickled into his mind. . .

"DON'T BELIEVE a word that piece of shit said about your father . . . Would not act with such dishonor . . . Open mind . . ."

Yeah, right. The male, his 'father', looked as if he'd snap the head off a baby turtle for daring to glance his way. He could, from the look of him, imagine the guy sending his unwanted halfling of a son to a known torturer just to hide his dirty little secret. Anything was possible, and he wasn't about to jump up and throw a party for the guy just because Balthazar had given him a decent review. Though the shock on his face meant he was either surprised to see him, or didn't know who the hell he was, at all.

Jezzie half turned toward him, her hand slipped free of his and came to rest over his heart.

"*Mo shíorghrá?*"

"I'm okay, *a stór*. Now is not the time. Though I could use your help to calm him down, please?" His Jezzie, always thinking of him.

"Of course, Ni, you shouldn't even need to ask. I should've already done so." Jezzie shook her head as if to clear it.

"Not at all. It's not every day you knock the Devil on his ass." His arm slipped around her waist and ushered her closer.

"I'm just glad I was here to see it," Dante piped up, sliding over to stand next to Athon.

"A front row seat, even." Jezzie giggled and Athon gave the doofus a high-five.

He pushed Raum from his thoughts and focused on Jezzie and Lucifer.

Lucifer stood shakily a few feet from them, incredulity clear on his face. Thoughts must be whirling around in his head because hope warred with disbelief in his eyes, sadness mixed with joy. Jezzie shared them all with him, the others too, maybe. Suspicion flashed across his features, his jaw tensed.

"Maybe we should come back later," Jezzie mumbled hastily as she turned toward the door and rested her forehead on Roth's chest. His arms stayed at his sides, fists clenched hard until his knuckles turned white. Nithe and his dragon both felt a pulse of rage slither through them at Roth's behavior. What the fuck was up with him? Sadness filled Jezzie's heart, he could feel its crushing weight, but anger sparked the fire in her eyes as she looked up at Roth. She shook her head, stepped around him, and made her way to the door. He and Athon both followed after her. It was no surprise to him they were on the same page when they both pushed past Roth simultaneously, deliberately bumping him with their shoulders.

"Stay, please?" Lucifer's whispered plea stopped her in her tracks, hand mid-turn on the doorknob.

Nithe looked back at one of the most famous of all angels and felt a pang of sympathy. He was on his knees, head down, tears falling to the carpet. When he looked up, his gaze, while still bewildered, held an amazement and hope which both squeezed Nithe's heart almost painfully and lightened it at the same time. It'd be nice to see Jezzie and Lucifer build a happy bond. He glanced at Ramiel, who still looked like a fish out of water, and felt the pang in his heart strike again.

Jezzie shifted on her feet. He could sense her conflicted emotions. Her hope, hesitancy, and fear. He pulled her to his side and whispered in her ear.

"He's not going to bite you, a stór, and if he does, I'm pretty sure you can take him. Or we will. Go, offer him comfort. From what you told me, it wasn't his fault and this must be hard for him to understand." He nudged her forward a step.

Jezzie paused, took a large, deep breath and slowly walked toward her father. Tentatively, she reached out and placed a hand lightly on his shoulder. His eyes snapped to hers. Nithe looked at Athon and Roth, both men wore similar looks of shock. The sizzle and snap of a familiar bond clicked into place between Jezzie and Lucifer. The bond between them as mates allowed them to feel the connection between father and daughter, and the different bonds rolled against each other to ascertain the other's intentions. Jezzie lowered herself to the floor and held his hands in hers.

"How old are you, daughter of mine? Where have you been? Why did I not know of you?" Lucifer whispered with reverence, "Tell me everything. Tell me about your mother. How does she live? Does she still? Where is my sweet Decaria? Can you forgive me for my absence in your life?"

To hear the Devil have a bout of word vomit was an entirely odd experience for Nithe, and he tried not to snort in amusement. Jezzie looked over her shoulder at him and raised her brows before poking her tongue out at him. Athon, though, apparently had no such qualms about letting loose his amusement.

Jezzie turned back to Lucifer and bowed her head, her deep breath echoed in the eerie silence that had fallen about the room, before she looked up and said, "Father, some things are not mine to explain, nor mine to share. There is still a lot I don't know myself, and I would hate to give misinformation.

"Mother wasn't around much as I grew up. Not her fault, so don't blame her, she needed to keep us hidden and the chances were better if we were apart. Aunt Rai Rai raised me, mostly. And no, she isn't my real aunt, at least not by birth, and neither has ever disclosed in much detail the circumstances leading up to my birth or why we must remain hidden, except that there is a traitor to the Almighty hidden in plain sight and what he looks like. The better to protect me and keep me safe, I suppose. My aunt can probably tell you more, but she may choose not to. She has no love for Angel kind, except for me, of course, and Leraie.

"What I can tell you is everything you wish to know of me. It just might take some time as we get to know each other. For now, know that I am 74 years old. Yes, Decaria is my mother, as I said before. Shit! They're probably worried sick. I've been missing for over a decade. What must they think?" Jezzie's panic floods the bond and even Roth takes a step forward.

"Jezzie, your aunt, she wouldn't happen to be a witch, by any chance? One with a penchant for de-nutting her male foes?" Deus questioned.

"You've met?" Jezzie smiled. "Is she okay?"

"She seemed to be fine, other than being utterly unhinged. We had an encounter before we visited you in Nestradia. She's been sending gifts ever since. Looks like we need to have a little chat with your aunt." Deus smiled, almost gleefully.

"Good luck finding her if she doesn't want to be found. Plus, if anyone even thinks about hurting my aunt they'll find themselves on the receiving end of a pretty epic suckfest . . ." Jezzie's protective streak arched its back.

"Pretty sure she'll come if you call, don't you think?"

"Maybe, maybe not. Witches are notoriously careful and

unpredictable, and I should know." Jezzie wiggled the end of her nose and giggled.

"What do you mean?" Lucifer asked.

"Well, Aunt Rai Rai taught me many things growing up, including basic magic. According to Leraie, I'm not a born witch but have been granted the blessing of being a learned and gifted one. Essentially, I'm a witch, angel, and psychic vamp all mixed into one. A one of a kind hybrid with unique powers the universe has never seen before. Whatever that means." Jezzie shook her head in bemusement.

Lucifer looked shocked and Ramiel seemed ready to pounce at the unknown element in the room, even more than before.

"What exactly can you do?" her father asked.

"You've seen my wings. The fire that fills my gaze. The blood-red shadows which swirl around me and keep me safe. They act on my command, but also independently. They have a voice, are one entity, ancient and gifted. Attached to my soul through darkness. They are learning to speak after a silence spanning our known existence," she trailed off to the sounds of in drawn breaths.

Roth's voice cut through the air, "Is that what the voice in my head is? Since I met you it's driven me mad." His anger bristled the hair on Nithe's nape, and he reached out as if to restrain him, but Roth turned toward the door in disgust.

"I think so, though, she's always spoken to me in one way or another. Just not with words. If you listen carefully and pay attention, they've probably been talking to you too." She shook her head. "Anyway, back on track. My powers . . . well, Shadow Hounds collect souls and deliver them to perdition, the Well, whatever, yeah?" Lucifer nodded. "Me? I don't do that. The vamp part of me allows me to taste, feel, see the emotions of others and feed on them. Something I need to survive. I can feed you your fantasies or drown you in your worst nightmares. Take but a sip and leave you unaltered, or take too much and leave you devoid of all emotion, take the sane and leave behind insanity. Fairly common in my kind. The difference is I don't just need emotions to sustain me. Your sword takes the soul into its core and stores it until delivery, where it relinquishes its captive. Me, I take the soul into myself and devour its energy to sustain my immortality."

Everyone gasped. Ramiel drew his golden sword. Even Roth moved to stand as a protective wall between their girl and the head of the Praesidium.

"Oh, no," Jezzie hurried to add. "I only take from the irredeemably corrupted. I test them first. I feed their darkest fantasies and give them what they want. If they take the bait I offer and their souls are as black as tar, then they are lost, and I cannot allow them freedom. The stronger the evil is in their soul when I consume them, the longer they keep me in existence. Funnily enough, I came pretty close to drying out the night I first met Roth. It's what led to me meeting Balthazar, actually."

"Hmm, We'll come back to your 'gifts' later, but I'm very interested in hearing in more detail how you met Balthazar, aren't you, Lucifer?" Ramiel said, pointedly. "Since no one other than us, Leraie, and the Almighty themselves knows his current situation. Maybe once the room is a little more empty you can fill us in?"

A chorus of, 'We're not leaving,' filled the room and Lucifer chuckled as he shook his head.

"No point in them leaving, everyone here's already been vetted, except my daughter and her mate. Both of whom I trust are well aware of more than we ourselves are in some areas, right?"

Jezzie and Nithe nodded.

"They're her mates too, don't forget. That's gotta be hella weird, by the way," Dante gleefully pointed out, gesturing to Athon and Roth. Both of whom looked at their General awkwardly.

"Okay, where do you want me to start?" Jezzie knew it was a loaded question, but wanted to see how impatient Ramiel really was.

"At the beginning," came his brusque response.

"I was born at one minute past midnight on January 1st, 1946, bare assed and beautiful . . ."

"Not what I meant, though I'm sure Luc would love to hear all about that some other time. Skip to Balthazar and how you met the Archangel of Vengeance."

Once they were all seated around the giant table with food and refreshments, Jezzie did just that. Roth clenched his fists and gritted his teeth when she recalled sleeping with him. Lucifer vowed to slice off his dick and Athon and Nithe shared a glance of understanding. Everyone has a past, not all of it is pretty. When it came to Raum, Jezzie cast a glance his way and paused. It was his choice how much he shared. He chose to gloss over the more vile details and was vague about his past before Raum, still, the tension in the room rose to fever pitch and Ramiel looked fit to kill. If the motherfucker had looked scary before, it'd been nothing compared to this.

They wrapped it all up with their escape and the Princes, but their tongues ceased to work at the mere thought of Michael.

By the time they were done, Jezzie looked visibly wilted and fatigued. It was late and all he wanted to do was wrap her in his arms and watch her sleep. If staying awake kept the demons from his own dreams far away, he'd take it as a bonus.

CHAPTER 43

Nithe took note of Roth's silence as he practically seethed all the way back to their rooms. Nithe vibrated with tension at the thought of what the big buffoon might come out with once they were behind closed doors. He had the feeling his bondmate would've already made a run for it if not for the arm Athon had placed around his shoulders as they'd exited the meeting room. That, and Jezzie's resolve to ignore him completely kept him striding forward.

The moment the door clicked shut behind them Jezzie padded her way slowly across the living room toward the bedrooms. Roth clearly had other plans and halted abruptly and flung Athon's arm away before he spoke.

"Did you sleep with Balthazar, *the* Balthazar?"

His words froze Nithe and Athon to the spot.

"Come on, Roth, not tonight. Can't you see she's been through enough of an emotional wringer. This can wait. She's ours now," Athon chided.

"No. Answer the question, Jezzie!"

Jezzie's dragging steps came to a halt on the thick, plush carpet, her head down.

"You really want to get into this now, Roth? Why does it matter? I already told you anyway." Weariness clung to her words.

She sounded tired and already half asleep. He just wanted to bundle her up in bed, all of them together, and be her big spoon. But there was a bug up Roth's ass, and if his bondmate wasn't careful he'd find himself with a face full of fist.

"Just answer the damn question, Jezzie," Roth practically snarled.

Their girl straightened her spine and spun on her heels. The last of her strength fuelled her movements as she stalked up to the hulking mass of seriously dumbass male who was intent on being a major prick.

Nithe took a step forward protectively as Athon inched toward Roth, but Jezzie stopped them both with a glare. She came to a halt a bare inch from the idiot's chest and invaded his personal space; in much the same way he was invading her privacy.

"Fine, have it your way. Yes! Yes, I fucked Balthazar Morrigan. He was charming, attractive, and he gave off a daddy vibe which my seriously fucked up issues immediately latched onto. He also saved my fucking life. So, yes, thirteen years ago on the backend of a drugged and hungover shitfest of a week I slept with him. One time. Are you happy now, Roth? Does knowing make you feel better? Or do you want all the dirty little details? The way his hands felt on my body? What he said to get into my pants? Whether I climaxed? How many times I let him take me? No?

"Maybe if you came at this conversation with compassion, reason, and understanding instead of anger and accusation we'd both feel a heck of a lot better right now. You don't hear me questioning your past sexual exploits and interactions by throwing around angry accusations, do you? No, because it's none of my fucking business unless you want to share it. It's your past, not mine. You can sleep in your old room, or your new one while you think about if you truly even wanna be with me. I'm too tired to deal with this shit right now. Ni, Ath, sleep wherever you need, I just don't want to see that jackass until morning.

"Oh, and just so you know, if I'd been able to feed on that scumbag in the alley when you interrupted me none of it would have happened in the first place, and yet I, quite frankly, have no regrets. I'd go back in time and fuck him all over again if it meant I'd still end up here with all of you. Despite your shitty attitude right now, dumbass!"

Nithe watched her march into the bathroom and slam the door shut behind her as Roth muttered something about needing some time alone. He'd been acting weird the whole morning, ever since they'd returned really. No, ever since he'd returned from his and Athon's old room and whatever errands he'd run. Something must've happened. When he'd returned he hadn't joined them in the shower, instead he'd been waiting for them in their new, bigger, probably very temporary living room where they'd eaten before being summoned to the meeting room.

Nithe shared a worried look with Athon, who followed Roth out into the hallway and wherever he was headed. He knew Athon would keep an eye on him, just in case the guy did something totally, irreversibly, heartbreakingly stupid.

He took a deep ragged breath in and let it out slowly, his turbulent thoughts and haywire emotions heavy on his already overwhelmed psyche. One more big breath in and he headed into the bathroom to comfort the only being who truly understood him.

He heard her soft whimpers as soon as he pushed through the silent door. They reached into his chest and squeezed his heart. When he rounded the corner to the shower his heart damn near broke. She was huddled on the cold tiles of the shower, the heated spray cascading over her trembling form. Nithe didn't stop to undress, instead he stepped straight in and sat beside her, pulled her onto his lap, and hugged her tight. Together they cried, both happy and sad, angry and confused, as the warmth of the water washed their tears away and calmed his chaotic thoughts. He found comfort in her closeness, something he desperately needed, and felt she did too, after the emotional roller-coaster of meeting their respective fathers, and Roth's dickwad behavior. His dragon pushed close to the surface, but unlike normal, he didn't seek to shift, content to be near Jezzie and her touch.

When Nithe finally spoke, his lips moved like a barely there kiss on the top of her head, "Your dad wasn't exactly ecstatic to realize his newfound, fully grown daughter is in a multi-partner relationship, much less with two of his closest friends, and me, the unknown wildcard."

"Yeah, I noticed," she replied with a chuckle.

"You were amazing, by the way. Not just with how you shut that shit down, and shut it down hard, but also with how you handled everything. You are amazing. I know it wasn't easy, especially with Roth being a prat, but for what it's worth, I'm proud of you." His fingers traced slow patterns over her soft skin lovingly.

"It's worth so much more than you think, mo shíorghrá. You are worth so much more than you think. Ramiel would be the biggest idiot in all the realms if he can't see how wonderful you are." She tilted her head up and her lips captured his in the lightest of kisses, her tongue tasted the seam of his lips like a ghostly lover.

Her eyes sparkled up at him as she caressed his cheek and huskily murmured, "Aren't you uncomfortable in these sopping wet clothes?"

'Yes! Oh gods yes, take them off,' yelled his dragon along the link, causing Jezzie's lilting laugh to fill the echoing room. Nithe, too, couldn't help but chuckle at his dragon's impatience.

"It's been a big day, *a stór*, are you sure? 'Cos I cannae guarantee I can hold back if you strip me naked and put your pretty little hands all over me." The lust in his voice caused his accent to thicken and in response Jezzie bit her bottom lip as he felt her squirm on his thigh, seeking friction.

"I need you, Ni. I want your big, thick, hard cock to fill me, to stoke the fire of desire which rages through my blood and sate it with the bliss and ecstasy of your cock exploding in rapture." Her brows rose up and down quickly as her words came to a halt, and a mischievous smirk graced her water-kissed lips.

Such kissable lips, which begged to be claimed. A claim his desperately aching soul needed to reassert. His lips crashed down on hers with forceful passion as she ripped his shirt free from his body and tore his pants off . . . Wait, what? How could she do that when he was seated on the ground with her firmly in his lap? He broke the kiss to look down at their bodies. Jezzie's swirling red shadows twisted around them, ripping every scrap of material from his body. Including his shoes and socks, he realized as he wiggled his suddenly bare toes.

"She wants you too," Jezzie stated with a grin.

"She?" He was confused, she'd never assigned her shadows a gender before.

"Yes, angel-dragon boy. I is a she, I has decided. You don'ts have a shadow, but no worry, your dragon is mine now too. And yes, I is one shadow, nots shadows, as they all thinks, same for the others. Not thats we minds being shadows. Though I is special. But they will learn in times. I even has a name . . . I think," whispered a voice from within the writhing wisps. "Come out and play with me, my bigs, hunky dragon."

His vision shifted and he felt his dragon's eyes take over. His shock was pushed back as Jezzie moved to straddle him and both his and his dragon's lust burst free. Before she had time to blink, Nithe grabbed her waist and lifted her up as he stood, carefully so they wouldn't slip, and exited the shower. She slid down his body slowly, taking her time to rub her wet body over his, before she turned away.

One hand whipped out to grab her wrist and spin her back as he pointed to the floor. His cock ached to take her, and take her he would. Right there, right then. Her shadows reached out to grab a fluffy towel, as if reading his mind, and she probably was, and lay it on the ground.

Jezzie looked up at him, waiting, a question in her wide eyes as she the right side of her lower lip.

"On your hands and knees, my treasure. I want you head down, ass up, and ready to take every last bit of my cock into your dripping wet pussy. Understand? Oh, and be a good girl, and lube me up nice and wet with that pretty little mouth of yours first," he commanded.

"Yes, Ni. As you wish, my lord," Jezzie simpered eagerly as she dropped to her knees on the towel. Her hands and mouth moving voraciously over his cock.

"I think that's enough. Into position. Yes, that's it. Knees apart a little further. So pretty. I can see all of you, *a stór*. Your pretty pink lips spread and glistening just for me, such a good girl you are," he praised as she did as she was told. His words caused her pussy to clench and the glisten turned into a drip.

He pressed his cock slowly into her and became lost to all thought. The slow glide became one hard thrust after another, almost brutal in the search for satisfaction, the need to claim what was his. Vague voices whispered dirty, sexy words in his head and he registered on some level his dragon and the shadows engaged in the link version of phone sex, link sex, but he was too far gone to care.

Pulling free he flipped her over and slammed back into her. Her pleasured moans and his name filled his ears as he leaned forward and bit into the mark he'd placed on her when they'd unwittingly claimed each other. The bond crackled, popped, and zinged, flaring brighter as it was reaffirmed, sparking their orgasms to overtake them as they came together on one final thrust.

<hr>

"WHAT THE FUCK ARE YOU DOING?" Ath demanded, his voice angry and a little scared.

Roth shook his head, he didn't want to deal with this right now. His heart was breaking, fuelled by anger and a fear he never thought he'd feel again. He couldn't confide in Athon, couldn't let him see his internal battle, the hesitation he felt at what he needed to do.

"Look at me, *Corazón*!" His lover's voice cut through to his very soul and anger burned through his veins. At himself, at existence, at Athon and the course their path had taken, then and now, he didn't know, didn't care.

He welcomed it, embraced its blinding warmth and turned it on the one person he'd sworn never to hurt again. The one person he hoped could take it. The one person he hoped would one day understand. It just wouldn't, couldn't, be this day.

As Athon touched his shoulder Roth pushed him away. "Back off, Leviathon. Just leave me the fuck alone!" he yelled, angrily.

"What the hell happened?" Ath asked him, confused. "Why are you doing this? Why are you acting like a giant asshole today? Talk to me, *Corazón*!" His hand reached out again, but Roth flinched away.

"Don't call me that. I can't be yours right now. I can't belong to anyone right now. Maybe not ever," he snapped.

"What? Why? Because she slept with the Angel of Vengeance before we all got together? You're joking, right?" Athon asked, incredulously.

"So what if that is the reason? Huh?" he snarked back.

"Would you expect her to abandon you when she finds out about Mara? Or anyone else we fucked in the past? And she will find out one day, we can't hide it from her forever if we want this to work." Athon tried to reason with him.

"It's not just that, Ath. She's our boss's, our oldest friend's, daughter, and here we are are fucking her. How fucked up is that? I can't do that to him. You saw his face once he realized what we'd done. He was pissed, and he has every right to be. I don't need that shit in my life. Maybe I don't want this to work, after all. Maybe I don't want to deal with Balthazar, or her freaky eating of souls and siphoning off of feelings, or dealing with Nithe's protective ass, and whatever else we don't know yet," he paused to take a breath and brace himself as he gestured between them, "Maybe I don't want this either, not anymore."

Athon's face fell briefly, before steel filled his gaze and anger tensed his muscles. "You know what? Fuck you, Azaroth. It's more than fucking, for all of us, and you should know that. You don't love me anymore? Prove it!" he growled, as he shoved Roth as hard as he could.

Good. His anger is what he wanted, what he needed, as he shoved him back and pressed Athon to the back of the door as he slammed his mouth to his. He wasn't gentle, nor simply dominant, rather he was brutal, callous, and cold. His teeth bit and he felt the tinny tang of Athon's blood on his tongue.

Anger rode him, desperation drove him, and Athon took it all. Clothing flew as they stripped each other bare and punished each other with their bodies. Darkness filled the room as someone or something hit the light switch, and Roth welcomed its reflection of their angry lust.

Somehow Athon ended up on the floor on his hands and knees, his bare ass pressed against Roth's hard cock. Athon's low whimper caused him to pause.

"You love me. I know you do," Athon whispered on a breath. Desperation filled him and Roth's anger at everything raced back as he spit on his palm, coated his cock with it, and thrust into his soon to be ex-lover's ass, over and over again.

Athon's grunt of pain soon turned to gasps and moans as Roth pressed one hand between his shoulders and forced his head to the carpet. His other one reached around to grasp Athon's cock and stroke it until they both were spent.

He pulled out and felt his way to the bathroom, grabbed two towels and cleaned himself up with one, before he grabbed some clothes and got dressed quickly. As he grabbed his bags and walked past Athon, he tossed the towel at him. His eyes had adjusted to the darkness, but he couldn't bring himself to look at him.

"See," Athon whispered, "I knew you loved me. Stay."

The last word hit Roth in the chest like a poisoned arrow. No matter what his heart wanted, his mouth knew what to do.

"I did. But now? There's a realm of distance between love and lust, Leviathon. Sorry," he uttered, and as the door slammed behind him he was on his way to inform Deus of his plans, even as his shadows screamed at him to stay.

<hr>

No, not again. This can't be happening. Jezzie's nothing like that bitch Mara. Why would Roth do this? Sure it was a lot and finding out Luc's her dad was huge, but Roth couldn't do this. He can't leave him like this, not again.

He could still feel the roughness of Roth's hands on his skin, the nip of his teeth and the pleasant, burning ache in his used and cum-filled ass.

Roth's barely audible apology as he'd left him laying on the floor in the dark bounced off the walls of his skull and reverberated through his entire being.

He didn't know how long he stayed there, naked, alone, his used and sated body rapidly cooling as tears slipped from his eyes as he curled up on his side on the floor. Only when he saw light shimmer through his eyelids and felt the telltale warmth of Jezzie and Nithe's bodies pressed against him did he drift off into a fitful slumber.

CHAPTER 44

J ezzie shifted restlessly in her slumber. Something niggled at her subconscious mind. The niggle became a nudge, which turned into a hammer that tore through her and wrenched her awake. Sweat coated her skin, sticking the cool sheets to her overheated body and the wet sheen of salty tears stung her cheeks.

Nithe moved beside her, as if he sensed her distress, reaching over she smoothed a hand over his creased brow until he settled and his soft snores returned.

Still, something pressed in on her mind, seeking entry. All of a sudden she remembered how she'd blocked the link to her mates. She'd needed the solitude of her own thoughts and feelings. Time to process the massive emotions of the day, she also hadn't wanted to deal with whatever bug had crawled up Roth's ass and turned him into Mr Mega-Prick. But the feelings barreling into her had her regretting that decision in a heartbeat. Panic, fear, hurt, shame, desperation, and pain swirled together in a tornado of despair. It knocked the wind from Jezzie's lungs and left her wheezing as her chest constricted and torment flooded her system.

Athon! Her mind screamed out to him, the link returned nothing but a torrent of tortured whimpers.

Jezzie tried to reach Roth, but the link met a dead end. Nothing but a wall she couldn't push through.

She slid from the bed, hastily shoving the twisted covers from her legs as she reached for her robe.

"Jezzie?" Nithe queried sleepily.

"Athon needs us. Something's very wrong. Roth's not responding. So much pain . . ." Her tears felt like acid burning down her cheeks.

Nithe moved into action and in what seemed like an instant he was out of bed and shoving his long legs into a pair of loose pants. Jezzie barely noticed as she raced out the door leaving Nithe to follow.

Did she know where she was going? No. Did she care? No. The link was like a ribbon she could follow, tugging her in the direction she needed to go. So Jezzie let it lead her to a large black door, she paused and gently turned the knob, took one deep breath, and then another. Until she saw her beloved laying naked and broken on the floor.

Her knees buckled as she reached his side. She curled her body around his instinctively. Her hands rubbed at his chill-pebbled skin, her lips whispered useless words of comfort into his colorful, mussed hair. Jezzie felt Nithe join them rather than heard him. She looked up as he gently hovered a hand above Athon's shoulder.

Athon's sobs grew louder and Nithe started to move his hand away, afraid of hurting the male Jezzie knew he respected and had started to care about.

"No, don't," Athon's croaky voice whimpered. "Please don't leave me too. I'm so sorry. So, so sorry. He's gone. Please don't hate me, Jez," he begged, before his tears overtook him and his voice failed him.

Nithe stood, lifting Athon into his arms and carried him to the bed before carefully laying him down. Jezzie quickly wrapped herself around him again. Nithe curled his body around Athon's, mirroring Jezzie, but from behind, and together they held him until his sobs faded into the deeper breathing of a restless sleep.

Nithe caught her eye as she looked up from Athon's head tucked against her chest, and with a lift of his brow across the link he asked, *Where is he?*

Roth's absence and Athon's distress struck like a knife to Jezzie's heart. Athon was their priority at that moment. Roth's behavior would be something to figure out later. Still, Jezzie felt anger rise over her concern for the male's whereabouts.

Apparently, when the going gets tough, Roth tucks tail and runs the fuck away.

It could be something else, a stór. Let's talk about it when Athon wakes and has showered. Maybe we can figure this out and talk some sense into Roth. Nithe's eyes were full of worry and sympathy as he pulled the covers up to cover them all and her eyes drifted shut on a final desperate plea through the link to Roth.

Where are you? You hurt me, that's fine. But Athon? Fix this. We love you. Only to be met with a wall of black similar to a dreamless sleep.

———

BLOCKING them out was one of the hardest things Roth ever had to do, but he had no choice. Not right now. He could only pray they'd understand once it was all over and done. Once the bitch was banished from existence, and he didn't have to worry about her ever again.

Deus hadn't really understood. In fact, he'd argued until he was blue in the face and threatened to call Lucifer in to stop him from leaving. Warned him he might even end up Fallen. Still, Roth had no choice but to take the chance. Only Leraie's arrival had kept Deus from following through on his threat to call the boss in. Roth could see the anger and confusion in his friend's eyes as Leraie had sighed wearily and told Deus to let him go. She'd then rounded on him and told him she thought him a fool, they were stronger together than apart, and while she'd help him, his reprieve wouldn't last long so he better figure his shit out fast.

Mrs Briars had handed him a bag with food and clothing as she glared at him disapprovingly. She tut-tutted even as he went through the portal to his hidden location.

All he needed to do was find and destroy his greatest nightmare, then he'd find the traitor who'd allowed her into the fortress.

He'd do anything to get his new family back. Jezzie's confusion and Athon's agony tore strips from his skin and left gouges in his heart. He hated himself for doing it. He hated himself for bringing this evil to their door. He hated her.

Mara was on borrowed time, she just didn't know it yet.

ATHON'S DREAMS were a swirling mass of torment, confusion, pain, and anger. Images of Roth laughing at his broken heart, Nithe's smirk at Roth leaving, Jezzie's angry glare as she laid the blame of Roth's choices at his feet.

In his slumber he felt sweat coat his chilled skin, his toes curled, and silent tears slid down his cheeks. His exhausted mind wondered if the tears would ever stop. He knew the answer though. As long as Roth was gone the ones falling on his cheeks might halt their salty tracks, but the ones pouring from his heart would continue their silent, unseen journey.

Warm bodies bracketed him at his back and front as he swam closer to wakefulness. Scents drifted to him and he inhaled deeply. Jezzie. Only Jez could smell so sweet. His tender ass shifted back to rub against the body at his back, but the arm that wrapped around him didn't feel like Roth. Disappointment began to fill him. Nithe gave him a light squeeze and withdrew his arm, though he didn't move away.

"I know you're awake, Athon, and I know you're not okay, but we are here for you. We are family and we will figure this out."

Nithe's warm breath and soothing whisper eased the tension from Athon's shoulders as it glided over his neck. Emotion swelled in his throat and all he could do was croak out a soft 'thank you.'

"Jezzie was awake most of the night. She refused to sleep, wanting to watch over you herself until Morpheus would not take no for an answer. I think she'll sleep for a while still. Do you feel up to a shower? Food?" Nithe rolled out of bed carefully, and stood.

His concerned look caused guilt to swell in Athon's chest. Not about Roth. Roth made his own choices, he knew that, even as he wondered if he'd made it worse. No, his guilt was for the shadows he saw under Nithe's eyes as he rolled over, careful not to disturb a slumbering Jezzie. Had the male slept at all? It was doubtful by the look of him. Nithe stretched and yawned, the muscles in his defined chest and arms stretching and bunching with the effort, as if to prove Athon right. If he yawned any wider his jaw was liable to dislocate and the tendons in his neck to snap.

As if in answer to Nithe's question, his stomach chose that moment to let loose an almighty rumble to rival a lion's roar.

Nithe chuckled and reached out his hand.

"Come on, you go shower and relax, and I'll hunt down some food. Do you need a hand with anything?"

Athon looked Nithe's large hand, then down at his own nakedness and felt heat travel up his chest to his cheeks . . . the ones on his face obviously. Though this other ones did clench slightly, reminding him of what he and Roth had done before he left.

"I'm fine, I think I can handle it." He knew he sounded gruff, but tears threatened to spill, and he refused to let them fall again. Not right now. Right now he had to face the day and the questions he knew were coming.

"Alright, So . . . um . . . how does one get food around here?" Nithe asked, kinda sheepishly as his own stomach grumbled its hunger.

It was Athon's turn to chuckle, and it felt so good. Weird, but good. Fuck, he was so fucking conflicted. It was all too much, so he pointed at the phone by the bed, held up two fingers between almost maniacal laughs, and bolted for the bathroom. He locked the door behind him, and the instant water hit the black tiles he stepped in. Head under the spray he let the water wash away his tears and muffle the uncontrollable giggle-sobs that wracked his body. With it went the remnants of Roth's body against his. His heart wouldn't be so easy to wash clean. By the time he turned the taps off only one word echoed in his brain.

Why?

Jezzie had roused from her sleep at the smell of fresh cooked bacon and maple syrup covered pancakes. Nithe and Athon had both laughed as she'd zombie-walked her way over to the coffee table and plopped down in one of two armchairs, immediately grabbed a strip of crispy bacon and moaned loudly as she shoved it in her mouth. She'd glared at them, but Nithe saw the smile she barely hid and the happiness she felt at making Athon laugh. It did funny things to his insides, so he too stuffed his mouth full of the delicious breakfast and contemplated what they were going to do in silence, save for the occasional crunch of bacon and sensual, food-induced moan.

When Jezzie let out a sigh of full stomached contentment, he and Athon both put aside their plates. Noting her gaze shifting to the pile of clothing he'd placed on the floor beside the couch earlier, he reached down and gathered it up before passing it to her.

"Your clothes, milady."

It was then she seemed to notice both males were already fully dressed, showered, and ready for the day.

"How? When?" she asked incredulously. "I barely closed my eyes."

"Sorry, *a stór*, but it's closer to brunch than breakfast. That Mrs Briars lady is one amazing cook. She was a sweet lass to make us food between the allotted times, too. Said we deserved a lovely home cooked meal, before she tutted under her breath about faithless idiots."

"Okay, I'm just going to jump in the shower real quick and then we need to come up with a game plan to get that idiot mate of ours back." She winked at Athon before adding, "and we will get him back, my love. I promise you that. Even if I have to drag him kicking and screaming. We will get answers, at the very least."

She emerged twenty minutes later from a cloud of steam backlit by dim lighting, the very image of the warrior he knew her to be. Albeit one dressed for comfort instead of war.

She grabbed Athon's hand as she passed his armchair and dragged him over to the couch. Nithe shifted over as far as the armrest would allow, knowing it would still be a tight squeeze. She guided him to a seated position, looked at the small gap between them, shrugged her shoulders, and lay herself down across their legs. Her head on one low armrest, her legs hanging over the other as she looked up at the jewel toned ceiling with its intricate plaster work. She took a deep breath and looked first at Nithe, then directly into Athon's mesmerizing, unique eyes.

"We might not know each other very well yet, Athon, but I want us to. I want you to know everything about me, about my life, my past, everything. I want you, all three of you, to be my future. Even Roth. I can't reveal everything right now, but I can share my truths with you. We have forever to learn the rest, because I want to learn everything about each of one you, too."

"As do I," Nithe added, his gaze locking with Athon's as the male turned his head to look at him. "I offer you the same honesty and trust I hope to earn from you. This is not an easy thing. In fact, it can be bloody brutal. I might fuck up. I'm prone to PTSD reactions on occasion. But I promise I'll always try my best."

Athon reached out and put his arm behind Nithe's neck and pulled him in for a quick side-hug before retracting it and wiping at an imaginary tear.

"Aw, Nithe, I didn't know you felt that way," he simpered, batting his lashes with comedic exaggeration.

"Idiot." Nithe laughed as he ruffled Athon's hair roughly. "Good to see that grin back though." Before said grin had a chance to drop from Athon's face Jezzie sat up and shifted onto the male's lap.

"So, first thing first. Balthazar. Yes I did have sex with him. No, I did not have sex with him more than once. Do I like him like that? No. Did he try to have sex with me again? Absolutely. Did he put me in, and see me in compromising situations after we had sex? Yes. I was a restricted visitor who was unable to leave after all. After a while I think he just wanted to get a rise out of me. He wanted to know who and what I was, but I couldn't have told him then, even if I'd wanted to. By the time Nithe arrived it felt more like we teetered closer to friends than enemies. Especially when we found out his true mission, and that's he was undercover or something." Jezzie spoke quickly as if she feared interruption. It was good they both had exceptional hearing, or they might have missed it all.

She filled Athon in on the backstory about the alley, Roth, Demon's Den, her bargain with Balthazar, and all the juicy bits she hadn't mentioned in front of her father. All things Nithe already knew. Still, he watched Athon's face intently, gauging his reaction to each new piece of information.

"Wait, do you mean *the* Balthazar. As in the Angel of fucking Vengeance, that Balthazar is 'The Tzar' of Demon's Den? Really? How did I not catch that earlier?" Athon uttered incredulously.

"So I've been told." Jezzie shifted uncomfortably on Athon's lap and shrugged her shoulders.

"Holy shit!"

"Do you know him?" she queried, obviously curious.

"Most angels do. By title if not name. Very early on in our creation it was decided it would be better for humans, angels, and every other species if they didn't have a name or face to match to the righteous avenger should he come to call. Thus, only a few of us know who he really is. Lucifer, Michael, Ramiel, and Leraie, of course, were all created before or at the same time as him, so they are all friends. Were all friends, anyway. By extension, every one of The Devil's 13, and probably the higher up in Ram and Mike's hierarchy as well, but don't quote me. We all took vows to keep his identity secret. He wasn't much of a people person, so most angels never saw him to question his designation. Preferred to spend most of his time away from the Heavenly Planes. The Earth Realm was a particular fave of his. Until one day he resigned his position and left forever. No one could find him, and we were ordered to stop looking. Everyone was surprised the Almighty just let him go, we all thought for certain he'd end up Fallen, or worse . . . mortal. But nope. Don't get me wrong, there is beauty in mortality, but none of us could imagine Balthazar growing old and dying. It was unfathomable." Athon hurried to halt his runaway mouth.

"Yeah, well he's definitely not a wrinkly old man. And Ramiel definitely knows what he's been up to at Demon's Den, I think," Nithe pointed out.

"He really owns that place?" Athon asked.

"Yeah, suits him though." Jezzie chuckled.

"Damn." He seemed to be having trouble processing that little tidbit.

Nithe took a deep breath and centered himself. Jezzie noticed and reached out to take hold of his hand. Athon tensed as if awaiting a blow.

"So, um, just to put it out there . . . I know we talked about how I grew up thinking my dad was someone he wasn't. That I'm a hybrid, like Jezzie but different. I know you noticed the color of my wings and their appearance. After I left the dragon realm I was secretly recruited for what I now know was nothing short of a suicide torture mission. The

Praesidium was going to track me as I put myself out there for Raum to find." At Athon's gasp Nithe paused and nodded.

"I see you've heard of the fallen asshole and his sadistic tendencies. Well they insisted they'd find us before anything happened to me. I had nothing to lose, or so I thought. Long story short, they didn't. Raum took me to Demon's Den to try to break Jezzie for his boss. Not Balthazar by the way. But before Jezzie incapacitated him, and we left Demon's Den, he couldn't resist adding fuel to my misery. See. . . apparently he knew everything about me before he found me, even the things buried deep down inside me, things I didn't even know. Like who my father is. Mindfuck central right there. The guy who signed off on my mission is apparently my sperm donor. The head of the Praesidium himself . . . Ramiel."

"Oh for love of fucking ducks!" Jezzie snorted and burst into giggles at Athon's exclamation. "Not literally, of course. Jezzie's mind meet gutter." He playfully swatted her firm, round butt.

"Yeah, not the reaction I was expecting." Nithe laughed.

"Want me to beat the shit out of him for you? Not that I think you'd need my help, but over the years I've watched and learned quite a few of his weaknesses. My code name isn't Snake for no reason. Always know your allies just as well as you do your enemies." Athon's offer was touching. Nithe felt the bond strengthen as he pondered his response.

"So you're not going to tell me to hear the guy out? That he wouldn't do something like this?" he finally replied.

"No. Why would I?"

"Balthazar did." Athon snorted at Nithe's reasoning.

"Balthazar knows the guy, I'll give him that. But, Ram can be a right prick when he wants to be, and if he made this big of a fuck up, knowingly or not, then he deserves to have to work his ass off and have his ass handed to him. We'll let you have first run at him, but I'm sure we're all going to want a piece of him, even Roth."

It took about two seconds from the time Roth's name left Athon's lips for it to hit them in the chest. The bond stretched as if searching but when it found nothing it sizzled and crackled like oil in a fryer around their hearts. Jezzie sighed and leaned her head against Athon's shoulder.

"Speaking of Roth, what the fuck is up with him at the moment?" Nithe found himself uttering.

"I don't know," Athon murmured, eyes downcast. "He's never been so intentionally cruel to me before. He was fine earlier. Happy, excited. Then he left us in the room, and when he came back it was like a switch had flipped. He's only ever withdrawn like that once bef—" Athon halted suddenly, his face turned ashen.

"This has happened before? When? Why?" Jezzie peppered him with questions. He could tell she didn't mean to be abrupt, she just needed a clue, any clue as to why Roth had changed.

Athon bit his lip. "The same way there is information that is not yours to share, that is Roth's story. I can only share my part of it. This was a very, very long time ago. Please understand that, Jezzie. In hindsight I was an idiot and Roth knew it, but he loved me enough to try. We always knew we were meant to be together, but something was missing. We are both bisexual, obviously, and our lady eluded us. One day, I met someone and I thought she was perfect, but her perfection housed an evil, corrupted ugliness that I'll never forgive myself for exposing him to. Roth, for his part, disliked her on sight, but for me, he gave her a chance . . . It didn't end well. After it was all said and done, our relationship was nothing but dust. Until you, Jezzie." Athon took a deep breath in at the curve of Jezzie's neck, but she stiffened in his arms.

"Wait, so he either realized he doesn't like me, he thinks I'm just like her—whatever her name is—or something happened to trigger his trauma? I'm assuming whatever the bitch did was traumatic, right?" she pressed.

"You'd be right about that, my love," Athon agreed.

"Shit!" Nithe offered, in an attempt to fill the silence that followed.

"We seem to be saying that a lot lately," Athon noted, mildly amused even in the heaviness of the moment.

"We will find him and get answers, Athon. We deserve at least that. Did he say anything else before he left?" Nithe couldn't stand to see either of them doubt their awesomeness as they were.

"Just that he didn't love me anymore. Although, there's no way he would leave without speaking with Deus and your dad, Jez. Fuck! That's such a weird thing to think about." He chuckled awkwardly.

"Luc tracks everyone. He's linked to all of us to give orders and monitor our location in emergencies, though he respects our privacy . . . mostly."

"Right then, Deus and Dad it is. I say it's time we see what they know about our stubborn jackass of a mate's whereabouts, don't you? Wait . . . Deus is the twatty one who called my aunt unhinged, isn't he?" Her smile took on the calculated cattiness one would expect in a devious minx of a witch. Nithe couldn't help the pride blooming in his chest as he followed her and Athon from the room.

CHAPTER 45

"Where is he?" Jezzie's question rang through the room as the black, heavy, wooden door she'd just thrown open thudded back against the wall beside it. The crack and crumble of broken plaster from the door knob embedding into the masonry caused her to wince momentarily before her resolve returned. She was there for answers, and answers she'd get.

Her eyes zeroed in on her father. He was seated behind the polished, black desk on what appeared to be a throne of the same Victorian era style, except as he pushed back and stood she realized peripherally it'd been upgraded with wheels. When her eyes met his, she saw sadness in them and worry. Her powers reached out to feel his emotions, learning their taste and texture as she familiarized herself with the biological link they shared. His emotions were real, not feigned. She felt his questions and his anger. They grew to match hers, and she quickly pulled back, aware her own feelings had started to feed his.

"Where is he?" she repeated. Her tone was more even and less aggressive, but by no means any less assertive.

"I don't know, Jezzie. What happened?" Lucifer, her dad—Athon was right, it was still a bit weird—asked gently.

"Yeah, Jezzie, why don't you tell us why he left? It sure as shit wasn't anything we did. But you come here with him and Athon and in less than twelve hours he disappears," Deus, the twatty prick, arrogantly accused.

His tone irked her already agitated nerves and her shadows slipped free of their housing. They flicked out in Deus's direction, pinned the asinine male to the wall and covered his mouth. Jezzie hadn't noted his presence until he'd spoken, but she sure as shit noticed him now. She took a deep breath, reigning in her rage.

"He was fine until we came here, asshole. So whatever is going on with him has something to do with being back here. You already have a strike against you for calling my aunt unhinged. You don't want a second, trust me. Just tell me where he went so we can go retrieve him and figure this out, because I neither have the time, nor the patience, to deal with your stupidity right now." She sighed as she asked the shadows to retreat, thankful when they did. She didn't want to make enemies here, and harming one of her father's closest friends wouldn't be the smartest move she'd ever made.

"I can't tell you, sorry." He didn't sound sorry in the least. "Even if I did, I wouldn't tell you, though. My loyalty is to Lucifer and my fellow Hounds, not you, sweetheart."

"Hmm, I'm not going to play the daddy card here," she murmured as she got all up in his face, noting how his eyes darted Lucifer's way and reading the shimmer of cynicism radiating from him. "I don't need to. I have ways of getting what I want that you can't even fathom. My aunt is a master at sending messages and extracting information, and I was a most studious and diligent student." For a brief second the scent and taste of fear hit her senses and a flash akin to intrigue glinted in Deus's eyes. "And don't ever call me sweetheart again."

"Deus, back off. Don't be a prick, leave my daughter alone." Lucifer drew Deus's gaze, but Jezzie refused to look away. Internally she cursed his interference as she felt Deus's amusement rise.

"See, Daddy to the rescue." His barely audible words slithered into her ears. One part of her cringed while another rejoiced at Lucifer's parental concern.

Lucifer heaved a frustrated sigh, "Dude, I can still hear you."

"Dumbass," Athon snickered from behind Jezzie.

Reaching out with her psychic energy she pried at the bars surrounding Deus's strongest emotions and inhaled. She forced his fear of losing control to the forefront of his mind and watched his face turn white. Only for a second, mind. She didn't want to hurt him . . . much, he just needed a little lesson.

Lucifer watched, confusion followed by stunned realization dawning in his expression.

"Tell her, Deus." Her father directed his words at his friend, but his eyes didn't leave her face.

"Fine! We don't know where he is. It's true; I can see your disbelief. Yes, he came to see me. He was intent on leaving. He was angry, but more than that he looked defeated. Nothing I said swayed him and in the end Leraie intervened. She called him an idiot, said he deserved to know what he was willing to put you all through and that some time to come to his senses was his punishment for his stupidity. She sent him through a portal with some supplies. And that's that. We can't track him. Luc can't link with him. Nothing. Sorry." Deus bit the side of his bottom lip and shrugged his shoulders.

"That wasn't so hard was it, buddy?" Luc mimicked Deus's taunting tone from earlier with genuine amusement and affection. Movement caught her eye before she could respond.

From a high backed chair in front of the large desk Ramiel rose. He moved around it and turned to face them, his feet soundless on the thick, luxurious carpet. Carpet which matched the color of her hair. It also matched her mother's hair and was probably the reason it'd been chosen in the first place.

Jezzie felt the fine, barely visible hairs on the nape of her neck stand on end. Nithe's inner turmoil and agitation radiated through the link and slowly leaked into the room. She felt Athon shift closer to him as she herself stepped away from Deus and back to his side.

Thank you, Athon. The words flowed through their bonded link in tandem and Jezzie wasn't sure who sent them first, her or Nithe. Athon's small smile, and the way he shifted quickly onto the balls of his feet and back down again told her he'd received the message loud and clear and was pleased they'd noticed his support. What surprised her most, though, was Nithe's ability to send the message to Athon at all. They weren't mates, and hadn't bonded, as far as she knew. She supposed it could happen. Hell, it was possible. Angels weren't supposed to have mates at all, so who was she to claim to know how any of it worked. It was a thought for further pondering. Later. Once they got Roth back. Once whatever new drama was about to hit the fan had settled.

When she turned her head back toward Ramiel his eyes weren't on her, or Athon. Instead, he'd focused his piercing gaze on Nithe. Studying him in a way that reminded her of how her aunt looked at her grimoire when the result of a spell didn't match what was written.

Before he could voice whatever questions she could clearly see hovering behind his tightly sealed lips, a knock on the door frame had her and the guys shifting to the side.

"Marco, what's up?" her dad asked the angel who looked directly at him, his eyes shifting to Ramiel with a nod before he strode over and handed him a sheet of paper.

"Shamsiel said to give you this. No news is good news, right, Ram?" Marco's voice reminded her of scones and brandy. Undisputed, refined elegance.

Jezzie could almost picture him at home in the palace ballrooms of centuries past. He looked the part too. Perfect posture, lean frame, and broad shoulders, not too broad as to be burly, mind. Okay, maybe not the reality of what men from that time actually looked like, but definitely the cover models from the many historical romance novels she'd devoured over the years. Yet, compared to her mates, he did nothing for her, not even a slight catch in her breath.

"Shut it, smart-ass. Not in either of these cases, it isn't." Ramiel sighed heavily.

"Well, while you ponder whatever is going on, Ram, how about we clear the air here about Roth's recent idiocy. There's also a few things Jezzie, my daughter . . . damn I like saying that . . ." He smiled at her, and she felt her heart expand in her chest. "Might be able to help us out with information wise. I'd also like a chance to get to know Nithe. Especially since it seems he's essentially my new son-in-law. Which begs the question of a wedding in our future, once Roth comes to his senses. Please, take a seat." Lucifer gestured to the black, three-seater Chesterfield sofa which sat up against the wall beside his desk. "Marco, you can stay if you wish, but it'll be standing room only. Deus, Ramiel, if you don't mind." He nodded toward the two armchairs in front of him.

"Does he always ramble like that?" Nithe whispered across Jezzie to Athon once they'd seated themselves. Her two men bracketed her on either side, a strong yet gentle hand resting on each of her thighs.

From his perch across the room Deus chortled, "Dude, he can hear you, we all can."

"Yeah, I know. Wasn't trying to hide it. I heard somewhere that nothing gets past the Devil, except maybe a drunken dare and the promise of a kiss. And the latter is not something I want to do with my father-in-law." Nithe threw said father-in-law a cheeky wink. Lucifer barked out a laugh as he slapped his thigh, but Jezzie caught the light of recognition that brightened his eyes at the joke as he watched Nithe with more interest. He'd recognized the words as being Uncle Micah's, now he just needed to figure out how Nithe knew them. Nithe was such a clever guy, and he was all hers, she thought as pride filled her.

Before her father could voice his questions or suspicions, Ramiel's deep voice filled the wood paneled room, echoing straight through her, and from the way Nithe stiffened against her, through him as well.

"Jezebeth, are you aware your mother is currently wanted for murder?"

"Excuse me?" Jezzie's brows felt as if they touched her hairline, they'd risen so much. Her back straightened as she went on alert, ready for a fight.

"Breathe, daughter-mine. I'm sure there is an explanation. Unfortunately she was caught on camera turning a mage into a puddle of goo. On the upside, the mage in question was not who he purported himself to be and seems to have had affiliations with someone who is actively working against the Hounds and the Praesidium, amongst others." Lucifer sent a pointed glare in Ramiel's direction, but the big guy just shrugged his shoulders.

"Still, until we can locate and question her the case remains open, and she's a wanted fugitive."

"Good luck with that. No one finds my mother if she doesn't want to be found." Internally she added, except Rai Rai, herself, and possibly Leraie . . . but they didn't need to know that.

"Hmm, but, Jezzie, not even your aunt can find her. She's been searching too. We met her at the site of the mage's death. It's where she lost her ability to track her." Lucifer sounded worried to the point Jezzie felt her heart skip a beat before tripping into a run.

"What proof do you have of this murder?" she asked in a hushed voice.

Her mind mulled over the possibilities as she tried to focus on the thread of her mother's heartbeat. It was something she'd always been able to do, something Leraie and Aunt Rai Rai had taught her to focus on as a child whenever she'd been scared, missed her mother, or felt lonely. It was there, but faint. Disconnected, as if she were too far away to follow and surrounded by a tunnel of darkness which felt neither malevolent nor good, instead it oozed neutrality. As if it just existed for the purpose of existing, both out of time and space, neither here nor there. Lost.

"Shit!" she exclaimed, before relaying what she felt to the group.

Everyone looked at her expectantly with varying expressions. Curiosity led the charge, but hope, disappointment, and confusion played across everyone's features at least once.

Lucifer shifted to the side closest to her and a large screen appeared as two doors retracted on the wall behind his desk. Looking at the images she recognized her mother the instant she appeared. Nithe grunted beside her. She caught his recognition of the city of Thisavrós, and he shared with her his conflicted feelings.

The mage himself carried an aura of deceit she knew the others couldn't see, it was a preview of the taste of his emotions and blackened soul only her and her mother's kind could see . . . Unless you were a witch as uniquely powerful as her aunt. Fainter than the senses of even angelkind could detect. A familiar taint surrounded him, similar to Raum's. A connection to their master? Normally she would have to be near the person to catch these details, but she hadn't yet released her connection to her mother's heartbeat, and it was possible her impressions of the mage were flowing back to Jezzie along the fragile link. It was a plausible deduction, if flimsy, but she had no other explanations.

Giving voice to these impressions and thoughts elicited a variety of reactions and responses, the majority of which she ignored. Her beloved males stayed silent, though they did shift closer to her. Lucifer paused the video, Ramiel looked at her with a calculated curiosity.

"Please, show me the rest." Jezzie looked pointedly at the screen, ignoring him. Questions were for later, right now her mother was missing, and she needed to know why.

"It gets rather gory, Jezzie," Lucifer warned.

"Aw, that's sweet, Dad. I do like this overprotective side of you, but honestly, I've seen, and probably done worse." Jezzie laughed at his look of surprise. "I get it. I'm your daughter, you just discovered me, so it's all new. But I'm not a baby, not a little kid, not some rebellious or innocent, naïve teenager. It's a lot to take in, and it's going to take time for us both to adjust. I've never had a dad either, you know. Now, on with the show." She gave him her best 'I'm super fine' smile and flicked her fingers toward the screen.

"You heard the girl, Luc. She's up for the show." Deus raised his brows comically. If the dipshit thought she'd crack at a little gore he was going to be sorely disappointed.

The footage resumed and Jezzie wasn't surprised at what she saw. At all. In fact she cheered loudly as the mage dropped into the gooey abyss of his death, causing her mates to chuckle amid the incredulous looks the others threw her way. Even her father seemed shocked at her reaction.

"I'm the daughter of the Devil himself. Seriously, what did you expect?" she blurted out.

When her mother fell into the dark vortex of a portal which opened at her feet, Jezzie's amusement ceased on a dime.

"As soon as I saw this I went there, and, well, I may have been consumed by my anger . . ." Her dad looked a little sheepish. Damn, he'd Deviled out on their asses, hadn't he?

"No shit!" whispered Deus.

"Shut it, Duke," Lucifer snapped. "Anyway, your aunt saved the day, and brought me back to myself and to reason. She felt your mother disappear and came to investigate herself. Though, neither she nor we have had any luck locating her."

"Nor can we find your aunt, which is also an oddity that sets my teeth on edge," Ramiel interjected, his annoyance as clear as the grinding of his back teeth.

"Yep, I'd just love to meet that little witch again myself." Deus sounded almost maniacally gleeful. To the point Jezzie was almost worried for her aunt, until she remembered her aunt's favorite pastime and her worry turned into amusement. Deus had no idea what he'd be getting into.

Her smile seemed to disturb the arrogant idiot, she just hoped it was enough of a warning to leave her aunt alone. Unfortunately she had a feeling it only urged him on in his folly.

"It's definitely my mom, but you knew that already. The death was justified, at least to me and her. He knew something . . . had been a part of something bad." Jezzie turned the conversation back to her mother.

"Your aunt said as much, but we still need to find your mother." Ramiel leaned back in his chair and stretched his arms over his head.

It was only then she noticed the scars his flesh bore, as the light glinted off of the pale lines etched into his tanned arms. Their existence confused her. The questions were how many of the scars were salted wounds and how many pacts held Ramiel bound?

Ramiel caught her staring and winked. "Pretty, aren't they?" Pride ran through his words, and she felt she had her answer. He seemed to cherish every one of them as if they were a reward he'd earned and yearned to display.

Looking back at Lucifer, she asked, "Can I call my aunt? I'm sure she's beside herself with worry."

"Please, feel free." He practically flew from his seat and ushered her to take his place.

His seat felt warm and smelled of him, which gave her a comfort she never thought she'd have, a fatherly hug without arms even touching her.

"Oh, do you want some privacy?" Deus asked when she paused. "Too bad, I'm not missing this."

Probably a good thing, she thought, at least this way he might get the hint. Jezzie dialed her aunt's private number and immediately her face appeared on the screen.

"Jezzie, my dear girl, where have you been? I've been worried sick, you silly, wonderful girl. Leraie said you'd be calling, but not when. So

I've been sitting on tenterhooks all week. What took you so long. Where are you? Why is that arrogant asshat there, and why is he smirking at me? Is that Lucifer? Oh shit, well, I guess that cat's out of the bag then. It is, isn't it? Are you okay? Are you hurt? Do you need me to come get you? Oh, who's that handsome one next to Mr Rainbow? Is that Ramiel? Oh shit, are you in trouble? Am I? What—"

"Rai Rai, take a breather." Jezzie laughed. "I'm okay, I promise. Yes, he knows he's my dad. I'm not sure why Ramiel is here actually. Deus is an asshat, I agree." Both Jezzie and her aunt smirked at said asshat, who had the gall to look offended.

"As for the two handsome men on the couch, they are my mates. Well, two of them. Azaroth did a runner, but we're going to get him back. Aunt, meet Leviathon and Nitierien. Guys, this is my Aunt Rai Rai."

"Oh my gosh. That's wonderful, Jezzie, my girl. Do you need me to castrate the other one? Did he hurt you? I can help you track him if you want? Where are you? I feel like I asked you that already." She laughed at her aunt's rapid fire words. She always talked like this when she was excited, worried, or in a hurry. More so when it was all three, like now.

"I'm fine. I'm at dad's fortress. I'll call you later to talk about mom and catch up. You have something to get back to, yes?"

"You never miss a thing, my sweet girl. Call me in a few hours, I should be done by then." Her aunt turned her head toward a muted groan. "Oh shush down, drama queen, it'll be over soon. Damn fertility spells," she muttered as Jezzie cut the feed.

"Care to share what that was about?" Deus asked.

"Or where she is? I have a few questions," Ramiel tacked on.

"Nope, to both questions. Now, moving on. Ramiel, what can we do for you? I can practically feel the curiosity and questions bubbling away under your skin."

"Yeah, Ramiel. Why don't you ask what you so desperately want you know," Nithe practically spat as Jezzie moved to retake her place between him and Athon. She felt Athon shift his arm behind her to Nithe's shoulder, whether for comfort or caution, she wasn't sure. Either way, she had a feeling things were about to get messy.

CHAPTER 46

Nithe took a deep breath, centered himself as much as he could, and shackled the inner rage of his dragon as he focussed his attention on Jezzie. He needed to remain calm, to not allow Ramiel to see how much his betrayal still hurt.

It was obvious to him Ramiel was floundering with a lack of knowledge as to his identity. Maybe he'd been an insignificant blip on the angel's radar. Maybe he was so used to betraying 'family' that they all blurred together. Maybe, just maybe, on the wing and prayer of a childlike, innocent hope, he truly was as dumbfounded and unaware as Balthazar believed. Nithe wouldn't hold his breath though.

"You are obviously a very intelligent and observant young lady. I am not here by chance, nor was my visit on a whim. I have many questions, but I'll start with the easier ones first. I'd like for both you and Nithe to, for the record this time, tell me about your interactions with Balthazar, and by extension Raum. As you may or may not be aware, Raum is currently in the custody of the Praesidium and our interrogation division has met a roadblock in uncovering more information. From what I gathered from your previous revelations I need to confirm and gather more intel about how Raum came to be incapacitated before Balthazar called me in to retrieve him."

"What exactly do you want to know?" Jezzie hesitantly asked, while giving Nithe's thigh a gentle caress.

"Everything. Start from the beginning. Leave nothing out." Ramiel stared at him as if trying to see into the truth of him. Something he was suddenly aware the Angel of Justice might just be able to do. Corrupted or not.

He immediately felt Jezzie reach out to him as Athon's hand shifted on his shoulder.

It's okay, a stór. It's time. I'm okay. Athon, hold on to your britches though. Things might get a bit wild, but I've got this. He sent the words along the link, hopeful they'd make it to both of them. He felt connected to Athon, despite the lack of an official bond. Their slight nods reassured him they'd heard him loud and clear.

He stayed silent as Jezzie told her story, including as much detail as she could remember . . . which was a lot more than Athon or the others had heard last time. He allowed his mind to focus on his own thoughts and the details he knew he was going to have to relive. Jezzie going first was both a blessing and a curse. They'd shared all of it before, so he wasn't missing anything, but sometimes time to order and plan your thoughts made it harder to get them out, not easier. Still, he didn't want to just blurt out word vomit either, which was the likely outcome if Jezzie hadn't taken the lead.

It took a lot longer than he'd thought it would, since Ramiel kept interrupting to ask questions and try to poke non-existent holes in Jezzie's truth. But when they reached the point of Nithe's arrival to Demon's Den Jezzie paused and looked up into his eyes.

Tears lined her lower lids, ready to spill. Not in pity, but in sadness, pride, and a pain that matched his own. A pain she felt because he felt it. A pain that would always live within him, just as it would live within her. A pain he needed to unleash, even as he wanted to bury it further within the graveyard of his brutalized past.

He knew he shouldn't start his story where Jezzie left off. Too many questions would come from that. But he couldn't start at the beginning, not yet. He needed Ramiel to feel his pain, to know his truth, see his scars, bear the burden of his agony before he revealed his beginnings. He needed to see his father's truth as it was revealed, to see the heart of the man who'd chosen his fate, who'd sent his son into the lair of the foulest of Fallen to be the plaything of the beast.

"It might be best to keep Jezzie's parentage under wraps a little longer. It's an ace up our sleeve and with at least one traitor here, somewhere in your ranks, maybe we could use the information later, yes?" Ramiel asked with a lift of his brow.

"Agreed, though I want to shout it to all and throw a party I'll wait until we have everything lined up. That okay, Jezzie?"

"Sure, I guess," she agreed.

"Nithe? Your turn? Before you start you should know I had my people look into you and it seems you're a ghost. Nothing came up. I'm very interested to find out why that is." Ramiel waited expectantly, suspicion clear in his gaze.

Sure, Nithe thought, let's do this. But first. "I don't know. Maybe because you or one of your 'people' cleaned up the mess, but forgot about the elephant in the room? Probably because no one expected me to make it out alive? Though put me and my lady in a room with Esidriel and I'm sure you'll get your answers once we make her squeal."

"What are you implying, boy?" Ramiel gritted out, anger replacing suspicion, but Nithe just shrugged and started his story at a point where the bitter tang of bile and self-loathing were most manageable.

"Raum heard about Jezzie from a demon informant. He bragged about it, thinking I'd never have anyone to tell. I wouldn't have, if not for Jezzie and Balthazar. We walked through the woods that hide his home and used a portal to travel to the field outside Demon's Den."

"Why'd he take you with him? And why . . . how were you with him?" Deus knew by the expression on his face he'd fucked up when both Nithe and Ramiel turned twin glares in his direction.

"Normally he wouldn't. Raum has what can only be termed an unnatural hatred for the female gender. Infant, child, adult, or geriatric, it matters not. He hates them all. Considers them weak and inferior. Thus, he felt I may be a useful tool in breaking Balthazar's 'captive'. As to the how, it wasn't because we were besties, but I'll get to that." Nithe heard his voice as if he were disconnected from it. His emotions hidden behind the wall of facts. This part was easy. Soon enough he knew it wouldn't be.

His words flowed like heated venom through the room. The details of his journey from Raum's hidey-hole of a home, up to and including Jezzie and him leaving Demon's Den. He left out the part about Ramiel being his father, but not for long.

"So you think I sent you there?" Ramiel asked, looking offended.

"Is it so hard to fathom?" Nithe's eyes bore into him, trying to discern his truth.

"It is a tactic we tried before, yes. But only with trained operatives who volunteered. Not civilians or other species. And not for a long time."

"Well, I was there for a long time. And I'm not just a dragon. Plus, that was the whole spiel. He kept detecting them so why not send someone who wasn't so easy to figure out. They'd get me out before he even got me alone. You signed off on it once the bitch put my paperwork in and off to Hell I went. No offense, sir." He directed the last part at Lucifer with a look.

"No probs. My place is pretty sweet, and I don't want to imagine what you went through."

"What do you mean, you're not just a dragon? Who did you meet with and how?"

"You might want to have a chat with Esidriel on that one. If she wasn't acting for you then she was acting against you."

"Against me how?"

"Nithe, would it be easier to show him than tell him? I can help." Jezzie looked up at him, her sadness easing as he looked into her eyes and a soft smile replaced the drawn lines of her mouth.

"Are you sure, *a stór*?"

"Absolutely, Just tell me who you want to see and who you don't."

"Might as well let the cat out of the bag all at once. I'm sure Deus can tell the others. I don't want to do this again if I don't have to." Nithe's shoulders slumped, the weight of a thousand nightmares returned with the power of a locomotive to the chest.

"Okay, fair warning. This isn't going to be pretty, so anyone who wants to step out now needs to do so. Everyone within these walls is about to see what Nithe wants you to."

Athon stood and held Nithe's other hand. He hadn't fully registered he'd stood, not until Jezzie was beside him and took his other hand in hers. He felt comfort and peace as the dragon in him settled with an angrily whispered, "Make him see it all."

No one moved to leave. Though everyone stood. Those already standing stood a little straighter, expectation on their faces. Deus looked unfazed. Ramiel, concerned. And so he should be.

Jezzie rolled her shoulders, and he heard the cracks in her neck as she loosened her body up.

"So I need you all to come and hold hands in a circle. I'm going to use a memory spell Aunt Rai Rai taught me and feed it with Nithe's memories and emotions. This isn't going to be easy. You might feel what he felt and see what he saw. In essence, for the short time we do this, you may think you are him. I'll speed it up a bit, so it shouldn't take long, but this is your last chance to back out." Jezzie looked around. Again, no one moved.

One by one they joined the circle, palm met palm and Jezzie jolted slightly beside him as if a current had zipped through her body. He himself felt a fissure of fear leach into his blood. He looked up and found his eyes locked with an older set of identical ones. Huh, his eyes, without his dragon present, came from his father . . . Ironic that his father was about to see through his.

"One more thing, once we start, you can't opt out. You're in til it's over, got it?" Everyone nodded at Jezzie, giving their consent.

Before he could take another breath his heart jolted and tears filled his eyes.

THE GREEN AND red hills of his birthplace spread out before him. White, snow-capped mountains towered in the distance and the cries of a child rang through the fresh, flower scented air. Warm arms held him close and a mother's love filled his little body. He looked up and her face peered down at him.

Memories sped by, his childhood a rollicking riot of laughter and adventure . . . And then it stopped. Frozen on the image of horrified faces as they stared at his wings. Where was his dragon? Why didn't he come out first? What was he? His mother turned from him. His "father" banished him. His first glance in a mirror and his shiny, golden, dragon wings were covered in leathery feathers. They all turned their backs on him. His family, his friends.

Fleeing. The bar, drinking 'til he was near to blind. And then . . . Esidriel. The deal. His duty due to his hybrid status. Wasn't like he had shit to lose, so why not? Whoever this Raum guy was, he couldn't be that bad, right?

They curbed his dragon so he would be unknown, but it left him powerless. They said they'd come for him, but they never did. Years, decades, what could be centuries. Trapped, tormented, tortured. Vivid impalings, slice and dices, depravities too sick to name. They each replayed like scenes from a horror film no one would ever dare make. His dragon silenced, no one to talk to, then the walk to freedom, to Jezzie. He showed them it all. What she saw, what Raum said. His father revealed. Jezzie's manifestation, and Balthazar's words.

EVERY THOUGHT, every feeling of pain, confusion, despair, anger was poured into every memory, saturating through to everyone.

Jezzie shut the link and released them from the hold the memories had taken. Nithe's eyes stayed locked on Ramiel's. Someone, more than one maybe, retched and vomited, the acid scent filled the room. Apropos to the situation, Nithe thought.

"Congratulations, or condolences, whichever fits, seeing as how I'm here now and not in some makeshift grave somewhere." Yeah, Nithe could admit he had some, from his perspective, justifiable anger issues toward the old man who stood opposite him. Though in looks they could be brothers, his eyes gave away his age as they swirled in what appeared to be confusion, revulsion, and anger.

He didn't speak at first. Still and solid like a statue. Lucifer tried to speak to no avail, words stuck in his throat. Ramiel drew a blade from beneath his coat and through his shirt he sliced a line of sparkling ruby across his chest above his heart. One word fell from his lips, his eyes still locked on Nithe, as the fiery light of rage of injustice filled his gaze. "Sorry." He rushed forward with all the ungainly grace of an oafish troll and pulled Nithe into a fierce, bone breaking hug that lasted half a second. He stepped back into a small portal and disappeared, leaving behind a shocked Nithe who stood frozen in a shirt now stained with his father's blood.

Jezzie and Athon held him tight, their warmth and strength kept him upright when all he wanted was to sink into the floor.

Lucifer was before him in an instant, hands on his shoulders, like a brand, but he didn't flinch, he didn't show his weakness. He didn't dare. For if he folded now, would he ever be repaired?

"Whatever happens next, son, we've got you. You are one of ours. And for ours, we'll gladly go to war. Old friends or not. Welcome to the family."

"Fae dumplings and Elven mead, anyone?" Mrs Briars's sweet elderly voice from the doorway broke through the silent tenseness of the room and Lucifer stepped back. Everyone took a deep breath as Mrs Briars basically thrust a bowl and tankard into everyone's hands, pushed them either into a seat or onto the ground and told them to eat. "Eat, drink, you need it. Here's some extra for you three," she said as she looked at Athon, Jezzie, and him. "I added a little Dragon Ale to yours, love, you could use it." The little old lady winked at him, and he found himself smiling even though his brain was spinning in circles and vivid nightmares performed circus tricks behind his eyes.

CHAPTER 47
SHADOW HOUND FORTRESS

THREE WEEKS LATER . . .

A hole resided in his chest. Larger than it ever was before. His missing piece was out of reach. From touch, from sight, from sense. The why of it haunted him. It didn't make sense. The longer he was gone the harder it was to pretend. Athon knew the pain of losing him, but not like this. Before, he could see him, he could have his back, be his friend, find comfort in knowing he was safe. Now, he knew nothing. Jezzie knew nothing, which worried him even more because with her abilities, her connection to them all, she should.

His shadows writhed under his skin, breaking out in wispy slivers, uneasy and in pain themselves, as if trying to taste the air, to find him on their own.

Nithe had found distraction by gaming with Dante in his den. Jezzie had returned to her secret room, intent on finding a way to locate their missing mate. Every day she went, one week turned into two, and still her search turned into nothing as hope began to fade.

The door to his old room clicked open and his eyes strained against the intrusive harshness of light. Here, in the dark, surrounded by the scent of Roth he could almost convince himself the male had never left him. But the lie he told himself turned to ashes on his tongue as he was brought back to reality by the light airy scent of Jezzie invading his nose.

"Leave me be, please, Jezzie. Every day it gets harder."

"I know, Ath, I feel it too. The shadows within me want him back as much as we do. The pain gets deeper every minute he's gone. But should we suffer for his choices? I've found no way to find him in my search. Leraie's powers are stronger than mine, and until she chooses to aid us, we must play the waiting game. Come with me? Be with me?" Jezzie held out her hand, with its delicate, long fingers, and smiled at him softly.

"Why?" he asked, almost suspiciously.

"We haven't spent time together alone much, and frankly, you need to get the fuck out of this room before it completely does your head in."

He sighed heavily, he knew she was right. Every minute he was in here he felt he was slipping away and when he found his way back out it was like lashes struck his heart anew.

"Okay, let me just grab a few things, yeah?"

"Sure, need a hand?" Jezzie looked around as she turned on the overhead lights. He watched as he squinted even more. Her eyes took everything in, as if she were soaking in the parts of him and Roth she'd never gotten to know.

Grabbing a bag he placed it on the bed and tossed in one of Roth's old shirts, then another, and another. He figured Jezzie and Nithe could use one too. Or maybe it was just him and Jezzie. Nithe seemed pretty pissed at Roth right now, so who knew?

His eyes skipped over an ornate, black, wooden box and doubled back. Venice. It had been a gift Roth had given him in Venice. He'd known how much Athon loved puzzle boxes.

He picked it up reverently, the carvings of gondolas and masked beauties paled in comparison to the warmth Roth's eyes had held when he'd handed it to him all those years ago.

"It's beautiful, Athon, like you," Jezzie whispered. " Bring it, too." And so he did.

With a heavy sigh they turned off the lights, shut the door, and walked hand in hand to Athon's new room.

Jezzie helped him unpack the bag, he placed the box on his bedside table and turned back to Jezzie who took his face between her palms. Goodness, she was beautiful.

"This is his choice, Ath, for however long, but we do not have to stop living because of it. I want you, need you, crave you. Do you want me too?" Her hands slid down over his chest, teasingly.

They'd spent every night wrapped up in a tangle of limbs. The three of them in the large communal bed. Afraid to be apart, drawing comfort from each other. They'd kissed, they'd touched, they'd loved. But always together. Ever since Roth left Athon's feelings of not being enough had stopped him from seeking her on his own. She'd been so busy trying to find a way to bring Roth back he'd felt guilty at the thought of distracting her. Silly, he knew, but his reality all the same.

"No guilt, no shame. Roth didn't leave because of you, if anything he left because of me. Do you blame me?" she asked.

"Of course not. You hold no blame here, Jezzie. You are right. His actions are his own. I only wish I knew why he chose this." His sigh echoed through the room, ragged to his own ears.

"Do you love me? Do you want me? Would you like to kiss me all over and have my lips wrapped around you, before you take me to the blissful place and make me scream your name as you thrust your cock into me over and over again?" Her sultry eyes glittered as they dipped to look at the rising evidence of his arousal. Her pretty pink tongue slipped out to wet her lower lip, narrowly missing the bite of her teeth that followed.

"Heavens yes, I love you, I want you more than you know. Desire for you courses through my body every time I breathe in the scent of you, every time I hear or think your name. Your smile brings me to my knees, and I am laid bare with want of you," his whispered words brushed over her lips, and her breath caught between them in a silent tug-o-war.

"Then take me. Take me with every pent-up emotion. Take me with all of your love, all of your pain, all of your anger. Love me like you hate me, like you want to break me. Love me like you own me. Because you do. As I own you."

Desire burned through his blood like wildfire at her words. He'd always been the submissive to Roth's Dominant. The slave to his Master. It was what he liked, it was their dynamic, and he loved it. But with

Jezzie it could be different. It didn't have to be the same. What would it be like to bend her over, pin her down, force his hard cock between her legs and take her? Watch her gag around his cock, not because Roth told them to do it, but because he, Athon, made her, because she wanted it too, because her submission to him was her choice. It was always about choice. If she chose this, how far could he . . . would he go?

"Wherever it takes you, my lord." Her lust-filled gaze defied the demure, innocent look upon her face as she peered up at him through thick lashes and dropped into a slight curtsy.

"Such a good little wench, aren't you? Hmm. Take your clothes off, slowly." His groan filled the room as she took him at his words and with agonizingly slow movements slipped each button on her blouse free. She left it gaping open, and she lifted her foot to the bed beside him and undid her boot and removed it, only to repeat the process for the other one. The whole while his gaze was riveted to the flashes of bared breast each time she moved. He growled his warning milliseconds before the hidden darkness within him snapped to the fore, and he pulled her up for a punishing kiss, teeth scraped, lips bled, tongues dueled with a fierceness and urgency that would not be denied.

"Forget the clothes, bend over. Now!" The command left his lips, alien and wild as he pushed her face down onto the raised bed.

He bunched up her skirt in his fists, chuckling deeply when he found no impediment to be bare skin.

"Such a naughty wench, aren't you? You want this so bad, don't you? You want my big, hard, hot cock to stretch you wide and deep, thrusting into you until you scream? But will you scream in ecstasy, or pain?"

"Why not both?" came her sassy response. "Give me your best shot, my lord." Her words turned to moans at the first gentle slap of his palm on her backside. Each one a little firmer than the last, until her pale skin turned a vibrant pink.

His fingers slid between her aroused folds, tauntingly close to her clit, before he pulled back and without warning thrust his long length balls deep into her welcoming warmth. Her shout of surprise blended with his guttural groan and was music to his ears.

The harder he thrust, his hands gripping her hips and pulling her back into him, the louder she moaned. His name became a mantra on her lips, and he felt his release nearing its peak. Reaching forward he grabbed a fistful of her loose hair and pulled her back up, his cock still buried deep inside her. His free hand made its way to her throat, stroking light lines up and down the elegant column.

"Say my name," he demanded in a lust-roughed voice.

"Athon," she murmured back.

He lightly squeezed her throat. "Try again, wench."

"Yes, Master. As you wish." Athon lifted her knees onto the bed and pressed impossibly closer.

"Better. Now, scream it." He plowed into her in a punishing rhythm, his palm over her throat, not to hurt but enough that his Jezzie knew who she belonged to. Just as he was about to spill his load deep inside her, he tugged her head back, gave her throat a little extra squeeze, and bit down hard on her neck.

Her body rippled around his, her release meeting the heights of his, and before he could process it he was flipped onto his back and Jezzie's teeth were buried in the skin above his heart. Another release ripped through him as she slammed herself back down onto his still hard cock.

SNUGGLING WITH A SMILING Athon was just what she'd needed. The orgasms and bond affirmation were amazing too, but this was what they both needed to reset after the craziness they were going through. Jezzie loved sliding her fingers through his rainbow hair, and her palms over the tattoos which decorated his skin. Her tongue itched to lick and nibble at his multiple piercings. Soon. In the moment she was content.

Her eyes caught sight of the beautiful, obviously old box Athon had collected from his and Roth's old room. It looked similar to one she'd seen before in Aunt Rai Rai's house.

"What do you keep in there?" she asked Athon, pointing at the box.

"Nothing, it's the strangest thing. I love puzzle boxes, but I absolutely suck at solving their puzzles and getting them open. So it's never been opened by me." His self-deprecating chuckle filled the room and made her smile.

"Mind if I try?" She didn't want to be nosy or overstep, but she was utterly curious as to what secrets such an old, unopened box might hold within it.

"Sure, go nuts. Just don't break it, please. It was a gift from Roth." Athon loved the box, she felt it through the link as much as she heard it in his words. She would have handled it with kid gloves regardless, but she'd do so even more knowing what it meant to him.

Jezzie gently picked it up and turned it over. She studied every carving intently. From the clothing the ladies wore to the expressions on their faces. The ripples in the water and the lines of every gondola. For such a small box that fit in so easily in her hands, the intricate details were divinely carved. A masterpiece of artistic talent as well as very cleverly put together. It wasn't something you'd normally come across twice in one lifetime, but Jezzie noted the slightly lower dip in one lady's décolletage and the way the water twisted against the current. The join at the base of the gondola on which she was carried called to Jezzie as did the slightly more ornate *fero da prora* on its prow.

With a slight adjustment so the box was upside down between her and Athon. He watched her avidly as she pressed the tip of one fingernail between the lady's breasts and another into the circular design of the *fero da prora*. A soft click filled the silent room and Jezzie felt Athon flinch beside her as if startled. The base popped open on its hidden hinge and they both released a pent-up breath.

"You did it, Jez," Athon exclaimed in breathless excitement. "How did you know? I've been studying it for hundreds of years and never figured it out." He looked at her like an eager puppy and caved into the urge to join him in his joyful celebration.

She popped the box onto the bedside table, and they jumped around in each other's arms. Their naked bobbly bits bounced in the breeze as she told him of her Aunt's box until curiosity had them both pausing to glance back at the open treasure chest.

"Shall we discover its secrets?" Athon pondered aloud.

"You do the honors, Ath, you've waited long enough." With a gentle nudge she urged him toward it.

"But you opened it, Jez. I want to do this together." He glanced back at her, his hand reached for hers.

"Are you sure?" She didn't want to intrude on such a special moment.

"Of course, I am. You are part of my special moments now, missy. Best get used to it." She smiled up at him, her heart flip-flopped at his words.

Together they sat back on the bed, him cross-legged, her on her knees, and he placed the box on the mattress between them. His eyes stayed glued to hers and hers to his.

"On the count of three?" She nodded in response. "One, two." He took a big, deep breath in, "Three." They looked down and stared in disbelief at what they saw.

There, resting on a bed of pristine white parchment lay four small black velvet bags, each tied with a matching satin bow holding a crisp white tag. A name was beautifully penned on each one.

"Azaroth," Athon read each one as he lifted it out, opened it, and revealed the finely crafted band within. He placed it down atop the bag and opened each remaining one. "Leviathon, Nitierien, and Jezebeth."

Jezzie stared at the three masculine bands and one more delicate, feminine one. Clearly they were made from a metal not of earthly origins. They glittered up at her with a magic and ethereal beauty she'd never in her life seen before. Almost tauntingly they stared back at her, reminding her Roth wasn't here.

"So, Roth knew the whole time how to open it, huh?" Jezzie looked at Athon, who shook his head as if to clear it of sand.

"It would seem so," he muttered, as he reached in to pull free the ribbon wrapped letter which upon which the rings had sat, and read it aloud:

> *Athon, Jezzie, Nithe,*
>
> *My beloved mates and bondmate. This is something I never thought I'd find myself experiencing, never something I thought myself worthy of attaining. It is with a heart full of love, acceptance, grace, and faith in our bonds that I pledge to love each one of you in a way that is unique to you alone. I promise to always put each of your needs before my own. As the humans would say, I promise to love, honor, protect, and support you in all that you do. My heart belongs*

with you all, and it shall never fade. No matter time, nor distance our love, our bond, shall never be forsaken. From now until eternity, or until the darkness once more devours all known things.

Ever Yours,
Azaroth

"WELL, shit. I wasn't expecting that." Nithe's voice broke the strained silence. They looked over to find him standing in the doorways, hands in his pockets with the look of dumbfounded confusion painted on his very handsome face.

"He even had a ring for you, Nithe. Why would he leave after doing that, after writing such things. Did I truly do something so wrong? Would he toy with us like this? Is that it? Is it a game?"

"It's not a game, Jez. He wouldn't do that." Athon defended Roth, and it made Jezzie even angrier as her heart broke over their missing mate all over again.

"How do you know, Athon? Look what he did to you. You never thought he'd do that either, did you?" The look on Athon's face stopped her anger in her tracks and shame filled her at his kicked puppy expression. She'd lashed out in her anger and pain and hurt him without thought. "I'm so sorry, Ath."

"It's okay, Jezzie. You are right. I never thought he would do that, but I should have had more faith in him. Dug deeper to find the truth. I know him, better than anyone else. He'd never do what he did if he wasn't protecting one, or all, of us. This proves it."

Athon held up a cream, recycled looking piece of handmade paper. By the folded creases marring its surface it had clearly been folded to fit in the box. Jezzie hadn't noticed Athon remove it but he stared at it with an intense hatred that sent prickles along her spine. Great, who was she going to have to kill now?

"Mara."

"What or who is Mara?" Nithe asked, as he sauntered over with his easy, long-legged gait and picked up his ring to spin it with his fingers. He liked it here, Jezzie knew. She loved seeing him make friends and find a sense of peace outside their bonds.

"Mara was someone we, Roth and I, once knew. She was my greatest mistake and my one regret. She cost me literal centuries with Roth, and was the cause of his most painful memories. Is why you struggle to see past the blackness of the void he created to hide those memories, even from himself."

"Okay, but she's in the past, right? What could she have done to make Roth leave us now?" Jezzie looked at him, dreading the answer. Instead, Athon handed her the letter, so she could read it for herself. Nithe propped himself behind her so he could see it too.

Azaroth,

Oh how the mighty have fallen. Look at you all loved up. Back with Leviathon, and with two new mates to boot? You've surprised me. I thought you'd learned your lesson the last time.

You are unworthy of love, you are the barren wasteland where hope goes to die. The crusher of innocent dreams.

How do I know? Oh, I know all, idiot. And if you don't sever your ties to your beloved mates, I'll sever them for you. Starting with the pretty redhead and ending with Leviathon. I'm sure I could comfort him as he writhes in the tortured agony of losing them. I may not be able to kill him but some things, some places, are worse than death itself.

If you want them to live . . . Run!
And never look back.

Your Biggest Hater,
Mara
Kiss kiss, sweetie

"I HATE THE BITCH ALREADY. Where can I find her and what are her weaknesses?" Fiery shadows filled the room and Athon's black shadows merged with hers. Nithe's dragon roared his displeasure and projected his image into the whirlwind of their chaotic fury.

"Tell us about her," the dragon intoned at the same time her shadows said the same words. Athon's though, remained silent, petulantly so, and with great reluctance from what Jezzie's shadows whispered in her ear.

"I can tell you what I know of her." Athon sighed. "But some things only Roth can share. His story is his own, the same way Nithe's story belongs only to him. Once a very long time ago, there was an idiot who tried to rush love. Who blindly sought a missing piece when said piece wasn't even born. That idiot was me . . ."

CHAPTER 48

They sat in silence as Athon's words met their end. Jezzie held his hand, her thumb stroked over his fingers softly.

"You're not an idiot, you know. It's a long time to be missing a piece of yourself, you got impatient, that's all. No one could have predicted what she'd do." Nithe was the one to voice what she herself was thinking.

Athon looked up at him with devastatingly soulful eyes, sad and hopeful. Jezzie watched them, her mind returning to the note from that psychotic bitch and the implications of it returned full blast.

"When do you think he got the letter? And how? I mean, it had to be after we got here but before we met with everyone, right? But how would she have known so fast, and did she get in here herself or does she have a spy? Who knew we were coming or that we were here before the meeting?" Jezzie barely paused to take a breath, her words tumbled out in rapid fire succession. Both males looked at her with lowered brows, clearly pondering her questions.

"Get dressed, you two, we need to go speak with your father, Jezzie. He needs to know about this, and it's time we contacted Leraie and have a little chat. I'm beyond ready to end this mystery shit and get Roth back home, here, with us." Nithe's gruff voice sent flutters directly to the horny bitch at her core. She refrained from jumping him as best she could because she wanted the same things he did and getting Roth back was more important. Still, she couldn't resist swatting at his sexy ass as she fled Athon's room for her own.

She dressed as fast as she was able, though she nearly fell while pulling on a skater dress, lacy underwear, and hiking boots. She wanted boots because if they found Roth she was sorely tempted to kick his ass for leaving in the first place and the dress because she wanted to look cute and sexy doing it.

Once done she headed back to Athon's room, only to stop and watch them together. A small smile played on her lips as Athon and Nithe embraced each other. It wasn't one of those bro hugs, one full of macho bravado and 'it's not a hug' hugs. It was a hug of comfort, support, and genuine care. With a final, gentle pat on the back they pulled apart. Athon grasped the letter from Mara in his hand tightly.

"I put the rings and Roth's letter back. No one but us needs to see those yet." Athon took a deep breath and continued, "Let's do this. Let's get our idiot back." They all chuckled and headed out the door.

Lucifer's door opened as they approached and Jezzie was met with a glare. Doe-like lavender eyes shot sparks at her from a lightly tanned face framed by collarbone length blue-black hair.

"Lily," Lucifer's voice called out, and the woman half turned back. "Just remember, nothing's actually changed between us, sweetheart, deep down you know that." Lily shut the door behind her and turned back to them, her chin in the air as she shouldered Jezzie out of her way.

"You okay, Lil?" Athon asked, concern in his voice.

"Yeah, I'm fine. Why wouldn't I be? Not like everything's changing or anything, right?" Lily threw one more glare at Jezzie over her shoulder before she stormed away. Jezzie caught the faint taint of jealousy and unease wafting her way beneath the anger Lily used to mask them, and shook her head.

Jezzie knew she was going to have to figure out what was up with this Lily chick at some point. If Lucifer was involved with her. Jezzie wasn't sure how her mom would react to the news. Right now, though, she needed to focus on the bigger problem they seemed to have.

Athon knocked on the door, shaking his head as he did so. Jezzie watched as the long strands swayed around and realized that since Roth left Athon hadn't bothered to style his hair, not that she minded, it was still sexy as fuck.

Lucifer was happy to see them, his arms wrapped around her in an unexpected hug, and it felt like she was a little girl getting a daddy hug at the end of the day. At least that was what she thought it would have felt like, since she'd never received one before.

"What can I do for you today?" Her father looked at her, a cheeky spark in his eyes.

She hated to be the one to put it out. Luckily for her, Athon spoke up first.

"We have a problem. A big one. There may be a traitor in our midst."

"We know, we are working on it already, but you knew that, so what's going on?" The spark left her father's eyes and her smile faltered in response.

"Well, either the spy is working with more than one person, or we have two spies working for two different people." Athon cut Lucifer off before he could open his mouth to respond. "Somehow, Mara either left this herself for Roth, or had someone else leave it for him to find. We believe it's the reason he left." He handed over the crumpled paper. "You know what happened last time she got her claws into him. She fucked him up in the head for centuries. I can't believe no one has caught her yet."

"Oh, I'll catch her," Jezzie vowed. "And I'll have fun with her before I hand her over too."

"Calm down, dearest," Nithe soothed. "We'll get her together." He winked with a smirk. "Can't let you have all the fun."

"Shit!" Lucifer exclaimed, his eyes locked to the paper. "It definitely was hand delivered and not through our mail system. Her name would have been flagged in the scanning process. It doesn't match the handwriting samples we have on file for her either." He moved to flick through a cabinet until he pulled out a thick folder, dropped it on his desk and leafed through it.

"Yeah, nah, not a match. The words are right, they follow along the lines of what she'd probably say, but she didn't personally write this. Not unless she's taken handwriting and calligraphy classes in the last ten years. Possible but not likely. Looks like someone here wrote this for her, using Mara's words, and following her directions. Which means someone here is in active communication with the most wanted female angel criminal in all of our history. Like things couldn't get any worse . . ."

"Could Mara be working with Raum?" The question popped out of Jezzie's mouth as soon as it entered her head.

"Maybe, but he hates females, remember? So I don't think it's likely," Nithe interjected. "But they might have the same connections, the same boss. Do we know what Mara's motivation is? Why does she hate Roth so much?"

"Good points. No, we don't. And it's not just Azaroth she's gone after, or angels either. She's done similar things before to multiple individuals and lots of species. Sometimes to bad people, sometimes to good ones. Lots of death, destruction, and disappearances." Lucifer turned the file around and spread the loose-leaf papers out.

Scenes the like Jezzie was all too familiar with littered the table along with witness recounts, notes, and photographic evidence. Her eyes snagged on one photograph in particular, a couple posed next to a wooden staircase. A sense of dread filled her mind, fear swept like acrid smoke into her lungs and her eyes stung with unshed tears and terror.

Nithe and Athon touched her shoulders, pulling her back to reality. What the fuck was that? The feeling faded before she could grasp the reason for her reaction and she snuggled back into the waiting warmth of her mates bodies.

"So, what are we going to do?" Nithe's hand rubbed up and down her back soothingly.

"I think it's time we called Leraie back in. We need Roth back. If we have someone doing Mara's dirty work they aren't going to make another move without him here." Lucifer sighed deeply.

A dramatic pop sounded from behind their backs and Jezzie caught Lucifer rolling his eyes.

"You rang, my boy?" Leraie's distinctive voice rang out in her best impersonation of a TV witch of a mother-in-law.

"Drama Queen," he tossed back.

"Of course. It's boring to be anything else. Let me guess . . . you want me to bring Roth back? No can do."

"But—" Jezzie started but Leraie cut her off.

"I know, I know . . . Mara. You found the letter, my clever girl. Yes, he is an idiot. That's why I let him go. A few weeks isn't the few months I was planning on, but it'll do. You're just going to have to go get him, is all. He's safe where he is, and you will be too. Take some time to sort it all out. The four of you. We can come up with a plan for the other stuff later. Well, you can since I can't 'interfere' according to our blessed leader." Leraie's lip curled and sarcasm dripped like venom from her words. Her frustration with her limitations clear as day to the naked eye, and ear.

"What are you waiting for? Go!" Her words halted milliseconds before a portal swept sideways at them and swallowed them whole, Jezzie's last sight was of Lucifer appearing annoyed and Leraie looking as pleased as punch before the portal took effect and zipped them away.

UTTER MISERY ENCOMPASSED Roth as rage beat at the cage of his chest. Impotent and unrelenting. He felt small, useless, afraid, and angry. The feelings felt foreign but real. A strange paradox of his and not his. Memories of his time with Mara moved like a carousel through his brain and he longed to switch off the ride. His shadows lashed at his body, cursing his stupidity. His choice to run and protect than to stay and defend.

"But was it stupid to protect his family, his loved ones from the horrors Mara could unleash on them? Wasn't that a major part of his purpose, his design? Or was it his flaw?" he whimpered, the four walls closing in a little more with every day that passed.

"And to loves and cherish thems, that's part of our purposes too, idiots," his shadows yelled back. "To kiss thems, and licks them, and fucks them, too."

The thought of being intimate with his mates again tore through him and filled him with equal parts desire and shame. He didn't deserve them after how he'd treated them. How he'd pushed them aside and berated them, how he'd shamed and denigrated them.

"I love more than just my mates," he defended. "My whole family, including the Hounds, are at risk. If she can get to me, she can get to them. And I definitely don't want to fuck anyone other than my mates."

"Goods, justss our mates, always our mates. All threes of thems."

Roth shook his head. What? Three? Nithe was Jezzie's mate, his bondmate, his family.

"That'sss what you thinks. You can see how sexy he is, I knows you can. Thinks abouts it."

"No more thinking, no more pain. It hurts too much in here. We need more firewood." He wasn't sure if he was referring to the pain in his chest, within the cocoon of his shadows, the cabin walls, or his never-ceasing existence.

Roth straightened his back, pulled the unruly shadows in before he lost his sanity, and pushed the memories from his mind.

Heading out the door he tore off his shirt and tossed it on a chair on the porch and grabbed the ax from its place near the steps.

Some good, old-fashioned hard work until he could neither see nor stand should help numb the agony. Please let if fucking help.

Jezzie was fucking tired of being shoved through fething portals. It was getting to be a bad habit at this point. And seriously, why the hell couldn't Leraie just open a portal and step out right in front of his damn door? Oh, that's right, some dumb fuck decided you can't just appear inside someone else's illusion bubble. No, instead you had to walk up to, and through the stupid thing.

Why'd Roth have to go and make this one so frickin' huge, anyway? Anyone would think he didn't want our awesome company. It was enough to hurt a girl's feelings really.

Well, he better not be stupid enough to think he could just up and leave us behind so easily. He owed her an explanation, and he was going to sing like a bird. More importantly, he owed Athon a massive, huge, ass kissing apology. They were both hurting so bad.

That's the thing with bonded mates, apparently, no distance was too far, the bond was always there. Roth's turmoil and torment pulsed through, however faintly, and while the line of telepathic communication was closed on his end, his feelings slipped through the closer they traveled.

Yes, she was pissed. He'd been gone too long already. She'd been so upset when he left she'd locked down her emotional response and focussed on searching for a way to get him back. At one point she'd raged, said good riddance, and given up. If he hadn't wanted her badly enough then he was free to walk, which he did, but it hadn't made it hurt any less.

Now they knew about Mara's note and were on their way to his hideout thanks to Leraie finally helping them. They'd set off happy and ready to kiss him senseless and drag his hot ass home. The longer they walked, the more angry she got though.

As they traversed the rocky terrain of the Australian wilderness, the bush as they called it there. The dry sticks on the ground flicked up to randomly scratch at Jezzie's legs. The twigs on the almost bare branches which crowded their way forward snagged at her clothing and hair. Why in the name of the Devil's daughter had she worn a freaking dress again? Yeah, the old 'turn up looking cute and sexy, so he can't resist you' thing was turning into more of a 'lost in the woods for three weeks' kinda look. Bleeding scratches and cuts, torn clothing, tangled and knotted hair. Yep, she looked totally badass and not pathetic at all. Cue sarcasm so strong her eyes nearly rolled into the back of her head at her own internal monologue.

Seriously though, she could fight monsters in Nestradia, taunt and lure evil psychopaths to their deaths, and endure torture all while looking flawless, but the bloody Australian outback had her looking like an angry, deranged mess in less than an hour. Go figure.

They'd been walking for about forty minutes already and despite those irritations she had to admit the air was so clean and pure, the sun was bright in the sky, despite the evident chill carried on the winter breeze. Even the sounds of the birds and other wildlife made the place feel almost magical . . . If you could forget about the deadly creatures the place was known for and avoid the damned sticks and prickles. The cat-head bindis were the worst. She could feel them embedding themselves into the bottom of her boots while other spiky things were tall enough to scratch her legs. Fuckers were going to be a pain in the ass to remove.

Her lips tilted up into a wicked smirk. Athon had been so serious of late. Too serious, really, and he hated earth snakes . . . Ironic really, given he'd told her his code name in the Hounds was 'Snake' because Leviathon meant serpent in the old language. He'd been named such for his unique eyes.

"Hey guys, did you know Australia is home to a huge number of some of the most deadly and dangerous animals on earth? You might want to be careful, those sticks and branches might just be snakes in disguise, boys," Jezzie trilled, smiling.

In an awesome show of great timing a branch lashed out to bite at Athon's arm. "Argh," he practically squealed as he leaped sideways, straight into Nithe's unprepared arms. Nithe hadn't yet gotten comfortable with uncontrolled and unexpected contact with others, only Jezzie, but progress was being made with Athon. Nithe quickly set Athon back on his feet after calming his frayed nerves. Good thing too, because Jezzie was too busy laughing her ass off.

"Fuck! Jez, was that really necessary, a stór?" Nithe chided.

"Yeah, what the fuck, babe? I just about had a heart attack. I mean, if an angel ever could have one of those I'd have been roast on toast," Athon added, before he gasped and silence reigned. Not that she noticed at first.

"Umm, Jez, sweets," Athon loudly whispered. "Stand very still. There's a huuuge fucking spider in your hair." Nithe stood beside him nodding along frantically.

"Uh-huh, sure there is." She winked. They were obviously trying to get back at her. They knew she hated spiders more than any other creature. All those legs and eyes. She wasn't going to fall for it. There was no spi— The feel of something as it moved out of her hair onto her forehead froze her in shock. Outwardly she was a statue, but inside she was freaking the fuck out in a major way. The memory of Tim Dennison's pet tarantula crawling up her six-year-old arm from where he'd hidden it in her backpack made black spots dance through her vision.

Athon picked up a large stick and slowly made his way toward her.

"Wh-what are you going to do with that thing?" Jezzie stammered out, her voice quivering.

"Well, after that little scare you gave me I could very well just try to squash the creepy thing into a gooey, bloody mess on your face . . . But since I love you so damn much, and doing so would probably cause a head injury we don't have time to deal with, I'm just going to try to flick it off," replied Athon, sarcasm thick in his suddenly gruff voice.

The look on Ath's face brought her back to herself, hard and fast. The instant the spider was gone and Athon stepped back she threw herself into his arms and tried to calm her racing thoughts.

"Oh my gosh, I'm so sorry, Ath. I don't know what's happening to me at the moment. My brain's all over the place and I'm just so fucking scared. I didn't mean to turn into such a bitch. Are you okay?"

"Don't stress, Jez. If I know Roth, and I do, he weaved a light layer of confusion into his illusion. In fact, I wouldn't be surprised if the Almighty's own power didn't infuse this thing. On humans and civilians it just makes them walk away, on our kind it can have varied effects. Apparently it brings out your inner bitch." Athon's hand glided over her hair and down to the base of her spine, the repetitive movement soothing her immensely.

They walked another twenty minutes in silence before a flash of vibrant blue feathers caught Jezzie's eye, and she paused to observe the small black, white, and blue bird as it perched delicately on a thicket of brambles. It didn't stay still long and was soon joined by a small brown-hued bird of a similar, if not the same, subspecies. They started to flit and flutter about, as if engaging in an intricate dance mid-flight, not a care in the world. Playful, that's what they were. Jezzie couldn't help but smile at the simple joy of watching them, a giggle escaped her at their antics. They seemed so in tune with each other and their surroundings. Something Jezzie was not familiar with these days. Athon and Nithe were amazing, but without Roth it was like a limb had been severed, and they hadn't learned to live without it yet. She wasn't sure she ever could.

Athon felt it as strongly as she did, Nithe too, to a lesser extent. They'd had long conversations, even longer snuggle times, devising ways to get him back, to convince him to stay. All to no avail. Until now. This was their chance. Suddenly she found each of her hands clasped in a gentle grip. One on each side, both cradling her close.

When Jezzie and the guys finally continued on down the unused path to pass by the cheeky birds that had alighted onto a thin branch, side by side they cocked their tiny heads curiously at the interlopers in their home, before swooping down into the underbrush together, and out of sight.

They eventually came to a small clearing, a wooden cabin stood blocking their path. A sweaty and fed up Jezzie paused, hand raised to knock on the door.

She wanted, no, needed her mates to feel joy in their love, in the bond they had. Not just with her but with each other as well. To feel whole and complete. All of them. Roth was hers as much as she was his, and it was about time the stubborn assed doofus realized their bond, their love, was forever. And there wasn't a damn thing he or that bitch Mara could do about it!

Well, apparently there was something he could do about it. He could refuse to open the fucking door, or he'd already abandoned his little hideaway and Leraie was wrong as to his whereabouts. Where the hell was he? Not like he couldn't just pop away to anywhere he wanted to on a whim . . .

Oh, wait. Yes he could. Why hadn't they planned for this?

CHAPTER 49

Where the fuck was he? He should be here. Surely Leraie would've known if he'd left. What if he'd known when they crossed the barrier? What if he'd fled their impending arrival? Where would he have gone? Should they have stayed away? Thoughts and questions flew through Athon's mind so fast he felt as if he'd lost his mind. He became blind to the door before them, a vortex of soundless negativity flooded his being until he thought he'd be sick from the void left by his shrinking, shriveling heart.

A sharp tug pulled at his arm. His vision cleared, his heartbeat resumed in his chest as he gulped in some much-needed air. Not that he couldn't survive without it, but it would be an unpleasant experience to say the least. His chest expanded and the weight lifted as his ears rejoined reality and he heard what Jezzie had already noticed.

From deep in the wooded area behind the cabin came the rhythmic thunk of something being struck. He listened closer, after the thunk came a crack and a softer thunk.

Jezzie tugged at his arm again, and they followed the noises from the porch, around the cabin, and into the trees. Light struggled to break through the canopy of branches and leaves, sound from the outside world became muffles, and the musty, earthy smell of damp soil and rotting leaves and moss filled their noses.

Athon's feet stopped moving, his eyes transfixed on a shirtless Roth. Sweat glistened on his exposed torso, the muscles of his back and arms bulged and rippled with every swing of the ax as it lifted above his head and came down with a thunk and a crack on the timber blocks. As they hit the ground, Roth picked them up and tossed them onto one of the many piles of firewood littered around him. He'd clearly been out there a while, judging by how many trees he'd felled.

Athon felt fingers under his chin. He looked at Nithe as the male lifted his and Jezzie's chins from their slack-jawed positions, amusement dancing in his eyes as he indicated Athon should wipe the drool from the corner of his mouth. Jezzie gulped in some air and leaned against him as if weak in the knees, and he knew just how she felt. Roth was and always would be a devastatingly handsome male, but naked and sweaty he was the epitome of a fantasy come to life.

Roth straightened his back, lifted the ax above his head, then stopped. Frozen for a second as he seemed to register the shift in the atmosphere and was pulled out of his hyper-focused state. He turned, ax lowering, his eyes alighting on them. Athon swore he could see the longing in Roth's gaze, his body shifting closer to them. The four of them were locked in a state of mesmerized want. A need so strong Jezzie shifted forward on unsteady feet. He saw her lick her lips, her nostrils flared as if taking in the flavor and smell of him, and she probably was. He felt a ripple along the bond they shared.

His longing smells so sweet, like nectar bursting on my tongue. Jezzie's silent words came just before the scent and taste of Roth's feelings flowed into his senses. A split second later they turned to ashes and bitterness as Roth's eyes filled with hostility.

"What are you doing here? I thought I made my feelings perfectly clear already." He spat his annoyance their way, his eyes locked on Athon's.

Despite the anger and the venom dripping from his words, Athon recognized the fear behind them.

Anger rose and pulsed through the bond with Jezzie. Athon snapped his gaze away from Roth and looked down at her watching as heat flushed her cheeks as her inner fire was stoked. The wrath of the Devil's daughter smoldered in her eyes.

"Yours aren't the only feelings which matter, Roth. You should have trusted us. At the very least you should have trusted Athon. I'd have understood not trusting Nithe and I, but him? Come on, you fucked up there. Big time," Jezzie bit out.

"Leave. Get the fuck away from me. You have no idea of what you speak, and I don't want you here." His eyes searched the trees, as if looking for spies among the branches and underbrush.

"Oh, for goodness' sake, we're safe here. No one can see us. No one even knows we've left the fortress other than Leraie and Lucifer, and not even my father knows where the heck we are."

Roth looked at them in stunned surprise, as if he hadn't even considered that Leraie would offer him such protection. Athon remained silent, he wasn't sure he could talk yet, even if he knew what he wanted to say. Nithe was just staring down Roth, waiting for him to get the memo that they weren't going anywhere anytime soon.

"Now, let's go inside. You need to put a shirt on or something. We need to talk, and neither I nor Athon can do so while you look like that." Jezzie waved her hand, gesturing toward Roth's naked chest and tight, fitted jeans.

She spun on her heels, grabbed his hand and Nithe's, and headed for the front porch without looking back. Once they were out of Roth's sight the tight muscles of her stick straight posture relaxed, her shoulders momentarily slumped, and she released a pent up breath. Athon placed his wrist flat to hers and felt their speeding pulses start to slow.

"This isn't going to be easy, you know," he whispered.

"I know, but we can and will get through this. The bond is strong, and we are stronger together than apart." Jezzie squeezed his hand.

"And if he puts up too much of a fight, I'm happy to kick his ass and my dragon can carry him kicking and screaming back home." Nithe's jovial tone and the smirk on his half serious face conjured up the image of him doing just that.

ROTH STEPPED onto the porch and pushed through the front door, not bothering to invite them in. If they considered him rude, they could always leave sooner. By the time they stepped into the cabin behind him, he'd already toweled off and donned a fresh shirt. He stood at the kitchen sink and stared out of the window above it, bracing himself to resist the temptation to pull them close and never let them go again.

"Since you all seem to have something you want to say, you better spit it out already and leave. I have shit to do so this better not take long." Roth forced annoyed boredom into the words.

"For the love of the Almighty, you're a stubborn jackass sometimes, aren't you? Out here in the middle of nowhere with a fully stocked, magical cabin, and you've got things to do? That's pure bullshit. You sure as shit don't need any more firewood, unless you're planning to take down every tree out there for absolutely no reason? It's not even cold out, idiot." Nithe chuckled as Roth leveled a glare at him.

"You need to come home and stop this nonsense, Roth. We're all hurting and there's no reason for it," Jezzie asserted.

"What nonsense? Seriously, a guy can't just be done with this thing we have—had? You all think so highly of yourselves, huh?" Roth hated the words even as he spoke them.

"Cut the crap, Roth," Nithe spat. "They may not want to hurt your fragile little feel feels, but I'm not afraid of doing so. See, if you can hurt them as much as you have, in my mind you kinda deserve it. But these two love you, so you need to face the truth, we aren't leaving without answers, and we aren't leaving without you. We found Mara's note. We know why you left."

Roth felt the color drain from his face at the implication. He turned to Athon, hurt and betrayal stung his already broken heart. Athon shook his head.

"It's a bullshit threat, Roth. A means of control and manipulation, and you chose to leave us instead of fight to keep us. You let her win, again. Don't you know how strong we are? How much stronger we are together? We have the entirety of Hell on our side, and you're just going to roll over and let some bitch with a boner for hurting you keep us apart?" Nithe ended with a sneer. The dragon peeked out through his eyes.

"It's not that simple. You don't know what you're fucking talking about." Roth felt shame and anger go to war in his belly.

"Maybe not, but that's only because instead of talking to us, you shut us out and ran like a little bitch." Roth saw Jezzie flinch at Nithe's words, and he couldn't stop the protectiveness he felt for her spill out.

"Watch the language, Nithe." He nodded toward Jezzie.

"Why? What do you care? She's heard worse, said worse, you know," he shot back.

"I care, more than you know. Mara is dangerous. She got to me in my own home. How the fuck could she do that? You don't know what she did to me. What she made me suffer. What she made me do. And no matter how strong you think you are . . . How strong I thought I was . . . You can't fight it . . . You can't fight her."

Roth felt his strength crumble like stone walls to dust. The torment of his time with Mara flooded out of him in a rush. Every torrid act of depravity he endured, every time he was forced to commit those foul atrocities. The pain, the shame, the smells, the tastes, the hands upon his person that made him want to vomit. He felt powerless to stop it. As powerless as he'd been back then. He threw the words at them, one last shield to keep them away. But as his words slowed, then halted, he breathed, and with his breath came a weird new sense of calm, love, and catharsis. A weight lifted, a burden shared, and when he looked into Athon's bloodshot eyes he saw strength and hope.

His gaze shifted to Jezzie's tear stained face, love and barely leashed retribution shimmered from her in an almost tangible way. Her hands were clenched at her sides, as if struggling to hold herself back. He somehow knew the anger wasn't directed at him, but rather for him, and it filled his deflated heart a little more with hope.

He hesitated to look at Nithe. The dragon's energy pulled at the room like a vacuum.

"Look at me," Nithe demanded softly.

Roth slowly turned his gaze and locked onto Nithe's golden-green eyes. In them he saw pride, strength, camaraderie, and understanding.

"You are not to blame for the sins of others. A very wise lady once told me that." Nithe looked at Jezzie, pulled her close, and placed a kiss atop her head.

"Plus, I could read your thoughts and feelings just now, Roth. Something wasn't right with them. They seemed kind of artificial, too sweet, like an additive of some kind. I've never come across it before. I don't think you did those things, but until we look into it more I can't be sure." Jezzie's soft words had his brain recoiling as if struck and confused.

"Got anything stronger than water in this place?" Nithe queried. "I think we need to lay all the cards on the table and figure this out. You've missed a lot since you left, and while it might feel like an info dump, you need to know some shit. I'd rather be drinking my way to drunk if I'm going to rehash the shitshow of my past again, thanks."

Without a word Roth retrieved four shot glasses and a bottle of tequila from the cupboard and placed them on the round table before he sat in one of the six chairs and braced himself for whatever the fuck was about to hit him next. He watched as Jezzie grabbed a knife, some limes, and a shaker of salt before she sat and set to work prepping them. He threw back a double shot of the fiery liquid before one for each of them and another for himself.

It was a good thing he did because by the time Jezzie and Athon were done informing him of the possible traitors in their home and Nithe had revealed the full extent of his past trauma, Roth felt like he'd taken a hit to the brain from a train. It definitely wasn't the copious amount of angel tequila. Ramiel being his father was just the cherry on the weird ass cake.

He looked down and saw that Jezzie and Athon each held the hand of a man he viewed with newfound respect and understanding. What he'd been through with Raum caused the fire of hatred to burn bright in his chest, urged toward higher flames by the fact Jezzie had witnessed some of that monster's depraved acts both in person and in Nithe's memories.

Nithe had told them how Jezzie had saved him, saved his dragon. How she'd helped heal his invisible wounds enough that he could function. That while he may never be how he was, while he may never be free of the scars, he was free of blame and guilt. He was free of shame. And so Roth's hope grew wings ten seconds before his face hit the table and the lights went out

WHEN HE CAME TO, he found himself on a pile of blankets in front of the lit fireplace. Two bodies were pressed up against his and as he shifted they snuggled closer. Jezzie's long red hair was spread out over his chest in a tangle and Athon's unique scent filled his nose. Contentment settled over him, until he realized something . . . someone was missing and looked around.

"It's all good, enjoy the peace. Today is a new day, or night as it were, and all that jazz. It got cold so I lit the fire, hope you don't mind." Nithe was seated on the couch. The tequila bottle in one fist rested on his knee. Roth could see the memories swirling, the PTSD that had been triggered by speaking his truth.

"You okay?" Such a cliché thing to ask someone who clearly wasn't okay, and as such he expected the look of sarcastic amusement Nithe sent him.

Then the male winked and with a small smile said, "I will be. She helps." He nodded at Jezzie. "So does Athon. You do too, you know, and if you come to your senses we'll help you too. Raum fucked me up in more ways than one. The situation with Ramiel isn't helping, and now Mara, but our girl can whoop anyone's ass and so can we, together."

"I doubt it's going to be that easy, dude." Roth sighed.

"Nothing worth having ever is. Dreams don't come true just because you wish upon a star and want them to. Reality is a fuck ton messier than that. You and I know that better than most. Plus, you've been around since creation, so I'm sure you've seen some shit, grandpa." Nithe laughed and Roth chuckled, he pulled the pillow from under his head and tossed it at the lug with the smart mouth.

Jezzie snort-snored and Athon turned over.

"How long have you been awake?" Roth asked as the others slowly roused. He untangled himself and stood on unsteady feet, his eyes glued to the bottle gripped tight in Nithe's hand..

"This stuff is lolly water," Nithe responded, acknowledging the direction of his gaze with a sad smile. "Does jack shit for my dragon side. A nice little buzz though. You've only been out about two hours. I couldn't sleep, so I made you all comfy and sat here pondering existence, life, the universe, all that existential shit."

"I'm sorry for being an asshole to you. I'm sorry for what you went through with Raum." Roth's apology was met with a flinch at his monster's name.

"No need for that. The only one who can apologize for Raum, is Raum, and he never will. Even if he did, it would be worthless. Early breakfast?" Nithe shook off his melancholy mood and jumped up.

In the kitchen area of the room he quickly set about frying bacon and eggs, preparing buttered toast and brewing some extra strength coffee. Roth watched on, giving the male his space and reflecting on their similarities and their differences. He felt unworthy in a lot of respects. He'd hurt them all, and he knew he couldn't take it back. Could he even go back? Leave this place and put them in danger? Face his family? Would Luc even let him come back?

"You're projecting, you know?" Jezzie wrapped her arms around him from behind and kissed his back through his shirt. "Everyone wants you back, Azi. We can and will fix this. Mara, the bitch, will meet her retribution. We'll make her pay together. We love you."

"How? How can you love me after everything I said to you all, did to you all?" Shame and guilt threatened to swallow him whole.

Athon stepped in front of him and took his face in his hands. He drew him closer and gazed into Roth's tormented eyes as Jezzie stepped back and let him go.

"Azaroth, my love, you are safe in my heart. You need never hide from me, not your pain, nor your torment, or your scars." Athon reached down, removed the leather cuffs at Roth's wrists, and gently caressed the exposed scar-roughened skin beneath. "Not your fear, your rage, or your jealousy, your joy nor your indecision. And most definitely not you love or your desires, for me or our girl, or anyone else. Rest assured you are secure in my love, in my heart, as you have always been, as is Jezebeth, and even Nithe. Nothing, and no one, can break us apart." Athon stared deep into Roth eyes, into his soul and something in him started to shatter, to soften.

Athon stepped back and Jezzie slipped into his place. He looked at her, not sure what was happening or what to say. She pulled him down by the collar of his shirt and placed her lips close to his.

"Just listen. I may be Lucifer's daughter, Azi," she murmured, her lips brushed against his with every syllable. Her tongue darted out to wet the plump flesh and licked at his, as if she couldn't resist sneaking a taste of them. "But I'm a woman fully grown, and I am completely capable of choosing who to spend my existence with. That our shadows agree is a decided bonus, but the choice is ours and no one else's. I choose you, Azi, if you'll have me. I choose you. I choose all three of you. My heart belongs to you all, eternally. Even when you make dumbass decisions, and we need to track you down and drag you back . . . No one will ever tear us apart. They can die trying though." Roth leaned back, his lips parting, preparing to speak, but Jezzie placed a single finger against them, and shivered as if his warm breath sent tingles over her skin, before she continued.

"And if you don't want to come back? Then we go where you go. You will never be alone, my love, never again. Don't worry about Dad either. Who do you think called Leraie in and convinced her to send us here?" Her smile lit the room and Roth couldn't help but respond in kind.

A flicker of movement behind Jezzie had Roth's wary mask slip cautiously back into place. Looking over her shoulder he knew Jezzie caught sight of Nithe pushing his lean body away from the kitchen bench when she stepped to the side and slightly away. He'd almost forgotten the male was there at all, but of course where else would he be? He'd been making breakfast after all.

Resisting them and walking, more like running away, had been one of the hardest moments of his life, and denying the temptation to race back to her arms and take back his harsh words had been torturous in the extreme. So he was loath to let her go now. Especially without knowing what Nithe was planning to do. He felt like a bit of a coward at the thought.

Nithe stepped toward Roth, eyes deadly serious. They softened as he came chest to chest with him. He tilted his head, almost as a lover would, his gaze pinned Roth to the spot. What the fuck was the guy up to? Nithe was the one major wildcard in this whole scenario, besides whatever Mara had planned.

Nobody had been expecting the half dragon, half angel to firmly wedge himself into what he and Athon had always assumed would be their own little triad. Nithe had more power to destroy them than anyone else, because Jezzie would be destroyed if he ever forced her to choose between them, whereas Roth and Athon had always known they were a package deal. What did they really know about the guy anyway in terms of how he really felt about them? Roth knew hardly anything until a few hours ago because he'd fled pretty fast upon finding Mara's note using the realization Lucifer was Jezzie's dad and her link to Balthazar as an excuse to leave. That little note from Mara had fucked with his head a lot, he could admit that. It had ignited his fight or flight instincts.

He didn't get a bad vibe from Nithe, but he hated unknowns. Unknowns usually led to trouble. A warm hand slid behind his neck, cupping Roth's nape in the warmth of his palm, bringing his face a hair's breadth away. Nithe drew in a deep breath, and slowly released it, his lashes fluttering closed before they suddenly snapped open, and a light shone in them the likes of which Roth had never witnessed before.

"Be still, Azaroth, I will nae ever hurt our girl like that, you have my word. I love her so much it hurts, in the best of ways. She is like the sun giving life to the world, the moon to the tides, and the stars that bring magic to the mundane. I may not yet be ready for certain things, like you and Athon. But know this, I will never shame you for it. I find your love for each other so beautiful, and I am nae averse to watching, as you know, with or without Jezzie." He chuckled with a wink. Roth's eyes widened with every word Nithe spoke, his breath shuddering through him as desire hit his groin.

"I do love you, Azaroth, be clear on that. I love you, just as I love Leviathon. Not as I love Jezzie, that'd be fucking weird for me right now, too much, too soon, thanks to Raum. But I love you more than I love my own brothers, my own blood. I love you second only to Jezebeth. I love you more than I love myself, more than my next breath. I would lay down my existence for our girl without a second thought, and I would do the same for you. I'll be there for all of you, together and separately. If you and Athon need time together you can be secure in the knowledge that Jezzie is being showered with affection too. She will never be lonely with the three of us loving her. You *are* my fucking family now, and that will nae ever change. I will spend my entire existence making sure you know it. No one gets to fuck with my family and get away with it." Leaning back, Nithe tilted Roth's face up with a gentle finger and placed a chaste kiss of promise to his soft lips. Sealing the bond he'd just declared before them all.

"More than one someone already has, though. Which means we have some work to do to bring down their 'already dead, they just don't know it yet' asses," he added.

Roth's arms moved so fast Nithe was likely unprepared for the intensity of the hug bestowed upon him, or for the thumps to his back as emotion spilled forth and the two males embraced. It didn't take long for another set of arms to join the huddle, and a few moments later they felt the unmistakable pulse of energy that was Jezzie zap their skin, it very quickly became a Jezebeth burrito situation. Yep, she was definitely the meat in this scenario, and she seemed totally fine with judging by her murmured moans of contentment.

CHAPTER 50

The hum of desire hit Nithe like an anvil as his lips pressed softly against Roth's. He hadn't expected it, had been struggling with the newly surfacing feelings for Athon already. When Roth embraced him he took a moment to hide his surprise, closed his eyes and processed the idea that he found the male in his arms more than just aesthetically pleasing to the eye.

Questions haunted him, memories plagued his heightened mind. After Raum, could he ever bring himself to trust anyone other than Jezzie with his body? Was he willing to try? Maybe. He inhaled a deep breath and reminded himself to take one moment at a time.

His skin tingled as Jezzie squeezed herself into their hug, and he felt Athon join them. She wiggled and squirmed. Her beautiful butt rubbed against his growing erection, teasing him. He pressed closer, pushing her harder into Roth's body and eliciting a groan from the male as her hips and chest connected more firmly with his. Hands reached around and grabbed a hold of his hips, fingers digging in and pulling him forward, but not painfully so, not unpleasantly. Roth's arms were still around Nithe's shoulders, Jezzie's were around Roth's waist. Athon looked into his eyes over Roth's shoulder and bit his lip, and desire burned through the blood in his veins, directly to the beating pulse of his cock.

Jezzie pushed back, her head near his collarbone as she looked up at Roth, placed a finger at the top of his shirt, and slowly released her shadows. As her finger trailed down to his belted waist the fabric tore open with a gentle savageness which mirrored the lust in Roth's eyes. She raised her hand to his shoulders and pushed the ruined fabric off and to the floor, but her shadows had other plans and wrapped around Roth's cock and balls. Roth gasped and groaned and Nithe smiled, he was familiar with the shadows joining in intimately, but it was clear Roth hadn't been expecting it.

Athon gasped from behind Roth. He exclaimed, "Holy fuck." It filled the cabin, causing Nithe to bite his lip in amusement. That was until he himself felt Jezzie's shadows wrap around him and dance over his sensitive flesh. As they all groaned and thrust their hips forward into the mystical energy Nithe felt his pants and boxers pool around his ankles. He'd removed his shoes hours ago, so he kicked them free from his feet. Roth and Athon did the same.

"*A stór*, you want this? Yes?" Jezzie nodded at his question. "All three of us, at once?" Another nod. "Strip, my treasure. Fast." His dragon roughened his voice, having slipped past his defenses. Their shared desire pulsed along the link and Jezzie urged his dragon to come out and play. Her shadows pressed to his chest and pulled at the energy of his dragon, almost begging. It was fucking hot.

Jezzie extracted herself and spun to face them, her hips swayed with every step. Her movements slowed to a seductive rhythm, as if a song played in her head as she slowly reached for the hem of her dress and in one tortuously long lift she pulled it up and over her head. Her boyleg underwear and matching black bra stood out starkly against her pale skin.

"All of it. Every last stitch," Roth demanded, his dominant side coming to the fore. Jezzie's eyebrows rose, her lips quirked up in one corner and amusement lit her eyes alongside desire as she sauntered up to the male.

"Uh, Uh. Oh, Azi, you may dominate Ath, but you don't dominate me. That's not fair, you see? You and I have a different dynamic. You're not my bitch, but I'm not yours either." She turned her head to Athon. "What is your wish, my lord?" she simpered.

"Take off your panties, Jez. Slowly, so slowly. As you slip them down over your hips, over your damp pussy, I want you to run your fingers through your folds and coat them in your desire. Both hands. Good girl," he praised as she did as instructed. "Now place one set against Roth's lips and the other at Nithe's and let them taste you."

Nithe flicked out his tongue and drew it up the seam between her two fingers. He took hold of her wrist and maneuvered her glistening digits into his mouth, licking and sucking them clean. Her scent filled his senses and pre-cum leaked out of him. His eyes fixed on Athon, who smiled as he stroked himself as he watched his orders being played out.

Roth groaned deep in his throat as he pulled her fingers free of his lips. "Fucking hell, that's so fucking hot. Make her do something else, Ath."

"We're going to take you, Jezzie. All of us. Three cocks to fill all of you. Three cocks to love you. Do you want us to do that?" Athon looked Jezzie in the eyes and waited for the implication to set in.

"With all my slutty little heart, but I want something else too, my lord. If I may?" Her teeth nibbled her lower lips as she looked up at each of them through her thick lashes.

Nithe chuckled, he knew that cheeky, faux demure look.

"Speak," Athon commanded.

"After you all fill me up with your cocks, I want Nithe and Roth inside me while you fuck Roth. I want you to control his thrusts into me by thrusting into him, and I want us all to come together."

"That's a lot of wants, wench." He considered her with raging desire evident in his eyes and his silky voice. "Such a dirty, sexy, utterly filthy mind she has. Lucky us." He smiled at Roth and Nithe. "What do you think?"

Nithe reached out and unclipped Jezzie's bra, pushed it off her shoulders and let it slip to the floor before he scooped her up from behind and carried her to the makeshift bed he'd made them earlier.

Jezzie slid to her knees as he lowered her to her feet, her tongue flicked out, scooping up the evidence of his desire. Roth and Athon followed them over and stood around her. Her eyes lit up as three cocks surrounded her. One at her lips and one at each cheek. Her hands wrapped around the cocks beside her and her mouth found the tip of

Nithe's, teasing him. Warm lips parted and a soft tongue swirled around the head before engulfing him in fire and flames. Desire licked at his balls and he could have cum on the spot but Athon grabbed her hair and pulled her back, forcing his cock into her mouth. The greedy fucker.

Roth reached down and cupped one generous breast, the rosy tip peaked and hardened under his ministrations as if begging for more. Moans slipped out of Jezzie's stuffed throat as Nithe gave his attention to her neglected breast. Got to make things fair and not leave it out. Her breasts were perfect for her, they balanced out her curves and were so responsive. Hard and darkened nipples when aroused, soft and pink circles when she wasn't. He could look at and taste them for eternity. And he sure as shit intended to.

Athon removed her mouth from his cock and turned her to Roth. His cock kissed her lips as they opened and Athon pressed her head forward. No words were needed. Instinct kicked in to guide them, and they watched her worship them. They in turn worshiped her.

They lowered her to the blankets. Lips kissed her all over. Love filled the cabin as they took turns tasting every part of her. Her lips were reddened from their hungry attention and her pussy dripped with desire. Whenever she was ready, on the edge of climax, they retreated and switched positions. Never letting her fall. Her moans turned to cries of frustration, and they were oh, so sweet. Soon. Soon she would fall over that edge into painfully sweet rapture, and they would all be there to fall with her.

Athon moved to her head and his cock rested at her lips. Jezzie propped herself up and turned toward him, taking him into the sweet haven of her mouth. Nithe moved between her legs, spreading them wide over his thighs. His hard cock slid against her labia and the sight almost undid him. He thrust gently, reveling in the feeling before entering her slowing and thrusting home. Her orgasm rocketed through her, her inner muscles spasmed and milked him, but he held back and praised her as she came back down.

He pulled out, her desire coating him and lay beside her, turning her body to the side toward Athon. He lifted her top leg up and forward as Roth used two fingers to spread lube over her anus to prepare her for his entry. Roth looked him in the eye and hesitated, but Nithe nodded and took a deep breath as Roth warmed up some more lube and gently coated Nithe's cock with his fisted hand. If he took extra time and was a little more thorough than he needed to be, Nithe didn't notice as his cock pulsed and twitched from the attention. A moan escaped his pinched lips, and he almost begged him to keep going when he stopped.

Athon and Jezzie had stopped what they were doing to look at them. Athon bit down on his lower lip then licked it. Jezzie couldn't see much but her parted lips, heavy breathing, and the intensity of her eyes said she liked it.

He leaned forward and brushed the hair back from her shoulder. Tender kisses trailed along her neck, and as he lined himself up and pressed into her tight hole he took her earlobe between his teeth and whispered, "Relax, a stór. We've got you. Good girl, that's it. Take it all, every last inch. Feel my balls against your pussy. Soon you will be so full of cock and cum you'll be dripping with it. Just think. Athon and Roth are going to take turns stuffing your tight little pussy with their big, hard cocks, and I'm going to be able to feel them moving against mine as I fuck your ass. Would you like that?"

Between moaning and panting, Jezzie nodded frantically as Roth and Athon looked on. They looked at each other, as if seeking affirmation, and nodded as if agreeing they were alright with what was happening. Good, Nithe never wanted to come between them or their bond.

Once he was fully seated within her and he felt her body relax as she pressed herself further onto him, he thrust in and out a few times before rolling to his back and taking her with him. Her legs fell on either side of his. He moved his legs apart and bent his knees, spreading her wide and exposed her pussy and the sight of his cock buried deep in her ass.

Athon moved to press his cock into her dripping opening. She nodded as he checked she was ready, before he plunged in and took her hard and fast. Nithe was still, as still as he could be, teeth gritted and body tense as he fought the urge to thrust and parry with Athon's cock. He could feel the hard, hot length moving through the thin barrier separating them, the piercing rolled and rubbed over him, and it felt so fucking good.

Jezzie's internal muscles clamped down on them both as another orgasm ripped through her. She cried out their names and her moans faded into satisfied, incoherent mumbles. Athon went still, fighting the need to spend himself inside her. Not yet. Nithe smiled a wicked smile and lifted Jezzie's hips slightly. He moved his cock in and out of her just a little bit, enough to elicit a strangled groan from Athon and for Jezzie to slam her ass back down on his length.

Nithe lifted Jezzie off him and moved them both to the couch. He sat down and pulled her back onto his lap as he entered her ass again. Legs spread to the side Roth took Athon's place at her pussy, and Nithe almost came undone, again. They moved together, finding a rhythm that worked for them. Nithe reached around and played with Jezzie's perfect clit, and breathy moans escaped her as she came again and again. His fingers brushed Roth's cock as he slid in and out of her and their eyes locked momentarily. Until Jezzie pulled Roth down for a hungry kiss, bending him over herself and allowing Athon to position his already lubed cock at Roth's opening.

Athon pushed into him and Roth tensed. Jezzie kissed him again and Athon ran his palms over his shoulders until he relaxed and widened his knees on the floor. Nithe held Jezzie up as he thrust his hips into her, Roth's thrusts were driven by Athon, his cock slid with perfect friction against Nithe's. Their moans, groans, and exclamations of ecstasy drove them on, fed their desire as much as the friction of their bodies, and filled the air.

Nithe felt his dragon break through his skin, scales covered his arms and his vision shifted, and his tongue became forked. He felt a sensation ripple through him, and he looked up. Energy shimmered out of him and above them all a swirling mass of green and gold performed a seductive and intimate dance with the red and black shadows coming from Jezzie and the guys. Without thought Nithe bit Jezzie's shoulder, Roth leaned forward, over Jezzie and bit Nithe as Jezzie bit his arm, and Athon latched onto wherever he could on Roth.

As if struck by lightning a stronger link snapped into place, opening up thoughts, feelings, sensations. Jezzie's pleasure became his, as did Roth and Athon's, and his became theirs. An overload of sensation turned moans into almost animalistic sounds of passion and pleasure as the veil of individuality was ripped from them, and they fell into the abyss of ultimate satisfaction amid clawing hands, and biting teeth.

Sometime later they pulled apart and snuggled on the blanketed floor. Nithe couldn't help but wonder if Roth had a washing machine, because they definitely needed cleaning later. As the air dried their sweat slicked skin and crusted their cum covered parts Nithe pulled some scrap of energy from deep within and rose to go start the shower.

Under the hot spray he stretched his sated muscles and worked out some kinks he hadn't known he had. Jezzie wandered in, and he held her close as he gently washed her tender flesh, taking extra care to make sure she was okay. Athon and Roth entered the shower as he and Jezzie toweled off and headed out to reheat the long since cold breakfast. Thank fuck he'd had the foresight to turn everything off before all that started, or they'd have burned the fucking cabin down around them and probably not even have noticed.

Once dressed they cleared the sullied blankets and aired out the room from the smell of sex. Nithe decided to remake breakfast since the previous one was beyond repair and no longer edible. Except the bacon, which Jezzie wolfed down.

They ate in content silence. No one wanted reality to intrude on the moment. Eventually, they pulled the cushions off the armchairs and settled back in front of the fireplace to snuggle. Jezzie rested her head on Athon's shoulder while wrapped in Nithe's arms. Athon was similarly positioned in Roth's embrace.

"So, what do we do now? Do we go home? Stay here? We can't let her win." Athon breathed into Jezzie's hair as he spoke.

"We go back. I'm not going to hide from her or let her ruin my happiness any longer." Roth sighed deeply. "So you finally figured out how to open the box, huh?"

"Actually, Jezzie did it," Athon chuckled.

Roth blushed. "So, uh, um . . ." He went silent.

"Yeah, we found her letter . . . and yours." Jezzie looked up at Roth with big doe eyes.

"And the rings," Nithe added, his eyebrows wiggling as he looked over at Roth.

Roth looked away sheepishly.

"Did you mean it?" Nithe prompted.

"Every word." This time Roth looked straight at him, then at Jezzie and Athon.

"Athon, I've wanted to marry you since marriage was created. Back then it wasn't really done, but when it was, I knew you wouldn't until we found our missing piece, pieces as it turned out. Jezzie, Nithe, I want you in my existence forever. So yes, I meant every word, and if I had the rings here with us now I'd ask you in a heartbeat to be mine. All of you."

There was a knock at the door. They all jumped to their feet, weapons appeared as they moved into defensive positions. No one knew where they were. Was it Mara? As if she'd knock on the fucking door. Athon looked out the window and slowly opened the door.

"There's no one there." Jezzie looked out.

Nithe looked down at the door mat and bent to scoop up the carved wooden box which sat there. He turned to Roth and laughed as he tossed it to him.

"Looks like Leraie had something delivered to you."

Without hesitation Roth dropped to one knee and opened the box. Four little bags fell into his palm and he asked the question they were never going to say no to . . .

"Will you all marry me?"

CHAPTER 51

She was engaged. How the fuck had that happened? She knew
how it happened, of course, but she'd never thought it'd happen
to her. Jezzie had steeled herself against the hope of it for so long.
Her mother and aunt's past relationships hadn't boded well for a happily
ever after, and she'd figured from the evidence of her own failed forays
into the dating world that she would be no exception.

As soon as they were back at the fortress, Jezzie had called Aunt Rai
Rai and told her the happy news. Her aunt was excited, but cautious
about Roth's sudden change of heart, but caution swiftly shifted to anger
when she found out the cause of his desertion. At Mara, not at Roth. If
there was one thing her aunt hated with a passion, other than unfaithful
men, it was women like Mara. Those who destroyed relationships out of
jealousy and for petty, psycho joy.

Jezzie's heart had landed with a thud in her chest when the reality of
what her mother's disappearance meant. She couldn't call her to tell her
the news, feel her arms around her in celebration, or introduce her to the
wonderful men who would be her sons-in-law. They didn't even know
when she would be back and since they wanted to perform the
ceremony as soon as possible, it was unlikely she'd get to witness it. Rai
Rai had promised come hell or high water, she'd be there. Nothing was

keeping her away, not even the demons of her own past, whatever that meant.

"Hey, guys, I'm going to nip into my spell room for a bit. I need to tell Tana the exciting news. Nithe, you wanna come with, and we can tell the princes too?" She couldn't wait to see Tana's face when she told her. Would Leraie let her come to the wedding she wondered?

"Absolutely. I wish you could come too," Nithe directed at Roth and Athon.

"Leraie said soon, should we try again and see if it works this time?" Athon piped up.

"I don't see why not. Fingers crossed." Jezzie held up both hands with her fingers crossed, and they walked to what looked like an ornately carved wall decoration. It was exactly the same as the one in her uncle's home in Nestradia and as Jezzie lay her hand on the curve of the woman's cheek she came alive, winked and opened to reveal Jezzie's spell room.

Nithe stepped through first and Jezzie followed. Athon and Roth lined up next, and from the look on Ath's face he was prepared to hit an invisible barrier . . . it didn't happen. Both of them stepped into her sacred space, filling it with their big, hunky bodies and making it feel extra cozy.

Jezzie showed them around with a big smile and led them to the door at the opposite side of the circular room. Opening it up she stepped through and out into the stone corridor of her uncle's home. Nithe was next.

"Fuck!" Roth exclaimed, as his face smooshed up against the invisible barrier that wouldn't budge and let them through.

"It's progress at least, right?" Nithe laughed. Jezzie whacked his arms with a smile.

"Wait here, and we'll go get Tana, so we can tell her the news together, okay?" She was so excited she couldn't stop bouncing on the balls of her feet.

"Sure thing, Jez. Don't be long though, we might get bored and decide to get busy. Tana doesn't need to see that," Athon joked.

With a laugh, Jezzie grabbed Nithe's hand and ran off down the corridor, careful not to trip over her own feet.

"Tana! Tana! Where the fuck are you, Tana!" Her voice echoed off the walls, floor, and ceiling as she bellowed, laughed, gasped for air, and bellowed again.

"Holy shit, Coz. What wicked bitch died for you to be cackling like that and bursting my eardrums?" Tana appeared from around the corner as they skidded to a halt.

"Language, girls. Remember you are ladies descended from the highest order of angels, act like it." Uncle Micah grinned as Jezzie squealed and threw herself into his arms like a child for a bear hug.

"What are you doing back so soon? You only just left a few hours ago. Did you forget something? Is everything okay?" Panic filled her uncle's eyes slowly.

"No, no, nothing like that. We got Roth back, and we have some news we want to share. Come with us!" Jezzie reassured as she pulled him along after her. "You too, T."

They hurried back the way they came, and she let go of Uncle Micah's hand before stepping into the room and turning back around. Tana and her uncle knew the rules so didn't try to enter. Just as Roth and Athon came to join them her uncle's features blurred leaving only a vague set of features. A tear slipped from her eye, unbidden.

"Hey, Tana. Who's that with you? And why can't we see them?" Athon asked.

"Oh, this is my dad. Say hi, Dad."

"Hi, Dad." His joke caused Jezzie and Tana to groan dramatically, but the guys just laughed.

She shared a look with Tana and Nithe at the distorted sound of her uncle's voice. Obviously the Almighty's game was still afoot.

"So, what's the important news?" Tana prompted.

The guys all looked at Jezzie, waiting for her to answer. "Well . . . we're engaged. I'm getting married!" Jezzie squealed as she jumped back through the doorway and into her equally as excited cousin's arms. They jumped around, cried and laughed.

When they finally calmed down, they turned around to see the guys staring at them like they were crazy. Her uncle shrugged his blurry shoulders at them and said, "Girls, gotta love 'em." With a laugh.

"Congratulations, J Bear!" Tana was beaming from ear to ear.

"When's the wedding? I better be invited and Leraie better let me come."

"Soon, we were thinking New Years, and yeah, she damn well better let you. I can't get married without my Maid of Honor now, can I?"

"Seriously? Oh my gosh, yes! A thousand times yes!" Tana exclaimed.

"Huh, that's exactly what Jezzie said when Roth asked us to marry him." Nithe laughed.

"So wait, you are all marrying Roth? Why aren't you all marrying Jezzie?" Tana's eyebrows furrowed in confusion.

"Oh, they are, T. We are all marrying each other, right, guys?" Jezzie jumped in.

"Absolutely. We are a package deal," Roth added.

"Have you told your father about this yet, Jezzie?" Uncle Micah smirked through the haze around him.

"Not yet. Should I have told him first? This having a dad thing is so weird and new." Jezzie felt anxiety bubble inside her. She didn't want to hurt her dad's feelings, but they were also not as close as she was with Tana and her uncle. At least not yet.

"He'll be fine, Jezebeth. Don't stress. But you might find he becomes a bit of a bridezilla, even though it's not his wedding, and he's not the bride." Uncle Micah laughed. "You should have seen him at Adam and Eve's wedding and every one of Henry the VIII's. Diva nightmares with him prancing about." He proceeded to prance and flap his hands about performing an exaggerated sniffle for effect.

"Oh, dear lord, don't remind us. That was so embarrassing." Athon facepalmed. "Hey, do we know you?" Suspicion laced his voice.

Jezzie pushed Nithe back through the door and yelled over her shoulder, "Tana, can you tell the princes the news please? Thanks, bye, gotta go." Just before the woman in the willow slammed the door shut.

Athon peered at her curiously until she sighed, shrugged her shoulders and said, "This whole 'the Almighty's Plan' shit is getting old fast."

"Right, got it." Athon nodded. "We'll know when we need to, I'm sure. Are you okay, Jez? I know you want to tell us whatever it is, but I'm assuming you can't?"

"Yep, I just hope nobody's pissed at me when it comes out." She sighed leaning into his strength.

"I'm sure they'll understand." Roth ruffled her hair and she glared at him playfully.

"Let's go share our good news with Lucifer and the rest of the gang, and then I feel like I could use a workout." Roth stretched his shoulders.

Athon wiggled his eyebrows and sent him a lascivious look.

"Not that kind of workout . . . okay maybe that kind, but only after we hit the gym," he responded as they walked back into their living room and he looked at the clock on the wall. "Yep everyone should be training about now so we can kill two birds with one feather."

"It's a stone, dude. Not a feather." Nithe snickered.

"Ah, but you can kill with a feather too, bro. It just takes more skill and finesse and a lot less brute strength." Roth cocked his head to the side and smiled.

"Ah, yes, Claudius, I remember that one." Athon sighed. "Historians are still debating it to this day."

Nithe went to look up Claudius while they all got changed into gym gear. Jezzie couldn't wait to stretch her aching muscles and run through some training exercises. It had been a while since she'd practiced her skills. Uncle Micah would be disappointed she'd neglected her training. He wanted her to be fully in control of her powers and fit enough to defend herself if the need arose.

The gymnasium was magnificent. Not as beautiful or idyllic as Paradise but impressive nonetheless. It was a huge underground structure with mats, weights, a boxing ring, and a free use area. There were also several hand-to-hand weapons training areas and a gun range. Everything was fully stocked, clean, and best of all, it didn't smell like dirty jockstraps.

"Where do we fly?" Nithe asked.

"Outside, we take the tunnel out to the fields and mountains." The sound of Dante's voice behind them made them all jump.

"Sneaky little shit," Roth cussed.

"Says he who ran away," Dante retorted, slapping Roth on the back of the head. "Don't do something that stupid again. My little sis deserves better."

"I swear upon the Almighty themself," Roth promised.

As they made their way toward one of the hand-to-hand areas other members of her dad's team came up and gave her a smile and Roth a slap on the back. They didn't speak, but they didn't have to. They were all clearly pleased to have him back.

Only Lily kept her distance, a scowl darkened her expression more than any storm cloud could. Seriously, what was her problem?

Jezzie stretched her neck, and limbered up her muscles before she slowly called forth her wings and let them unfurl. Freedom coursed through her body and she relished the rush that came with it. Her weapons manifested into her hands and she drew the blades from their sheaths, the gentle hiss of the steel sang through her veins. She felt the illusion slip over her as she concentrated on the image of Leraie, amid gasps and exclamations from those present.

"Anyone up to putting me through my paces?" she asked in her best Leraie impersonation as she looked around, her eyes locking on Lily's lavender ones. Lily snorted and turned away.

"I am," a lightly husky voice came from her right.

"Sorry, I'm shit with names. You are?" He was shorter than the others, but not by much, lean and muscular with an almost feral gleam in his moss green eyes. Like a monster hid beneath the surface of his refined demeanor.

"Fenris, but you can call me Fynn. Swords, yes? Whenever you're ready." Without another word he turned and strode into the arena, pulled two katanas from behind his back, and assumed his position on the mat.

He was brutal and he didn't hold back, but Jezzie held her own. She parried every thrust and got a slice in here and there. Blood dripped from her arm where he'd managed to nick her flesh. From the corner of her eye she saw Nithe holding Roth back as Athon stared on. She tracked every move Fynn made, watching him, not his blades. His left hand twitched. Was it his weak one or was he trying to fool her? Was he going to attack with it? He wasn't tiring and neither was she. Nithe fed her energy, as did Roth and Athon.

Dante cheered from the sidelines when she caught Fynn behind the knee with the flat of her blade and took him down with a rolling knee to the chest as she moved it between his legs. Her other blade rested lightly at his throat.

"Bravo, Jezzie. Not everyday Fynn gets his ass handed to him. You must have had an excellent teacher." When her dad had arrived she didn't know, but the pride in his eyes sure felt nice.

"I did, two, actually."

"Of course she fucking did." Venom practically seared her as Lily spoke.

"What's your problem? If you're fucking my dad or some shit and this is some fucked up jealousy thing—"

"Ew, no, that's disgusting . . . Sorry, Luc—"

"Nope. I agree. Jezzie, it's not like that. Lily is like a daughter to me and I think this whole me having a blood related daughter has stirred up some old insecurities . . ." Her dad paused as if he'd said more than he'd intended.

Jezzie released Fynn and the image of Leraie as she pushed herself up. Her blades disappeared, and she walked right up to Lily and looked her up and down slowly. The female angel flinched ever so slightly so Jezzie took a step back.

"There doesn't need to be a problem here, Lily. I can respect your relationship with my father, but I need you to respect mine. They may not look the same, and they shouldn't. I'm not here to push you away but rather to be a part of your family, his family. Sure, some things will change, but change doesn't have to be bad. I came here and gained a father. I gained a brother." She nodded at Dante. "And I'd be honored to gain a sister if you ever decide you want one. It's up to you. I mean, he's definitely old enough to have two daughters, and it might be fun seeing how many gray hairs we can give the old man."

Lily looked stunned at Jezzie's playful demeanor and a welling of tears threatened to break the banks of her lower eyelids, but she held them back masterfully.

"I'll think about it." she eventually said with her head high and a shrug of her shoulders before she walked away.

"Could have gone worse," Luc muttered. "Thank you, Jezzie. She'll come around. I hope."

"No probs, Dad. Got any other kids I need to watch out for?" Jezzie winked comically.

Luc stepped into the gym for the first time in what felt like years. He didn't know why but the urge had taken over and he'd dragged his ass down to the lowest level of the fortress as if drawn by some compulsion.

The moment he'd cleared the threshold he'd heard Dante loudly cheering and seen him jumping around like a crazed banana loving chimpanzee. The fucking child. Must be a great fight, he'd thought as he wandered over to see what all the fuss was about.

As he'd neared the arena the spectators had made room for him. To his utter shock Leraie had swords drawn and was circling one of his best swordsmen. Fynn had blood running from a cut on his cheek, and a gash in his side. But what caused his heart to stutter in his chest and fatherly panic to blossom in his bloodstream was the blood coating Jezzie's arm and upper thigh. Wait, it was Leraie, wasn't it? The hazy image of Leraie superimposed over Jezzie was confusing as fuck.

He knew better than to rush in and interrupt the fight. He was more likely to cause greater injury if he did so, as both opponents looked equally as blood thirsty and deadly. Before he could blink Jezzie/Leraie had taken Fynn to the mat and the battle was over. Fynn yielded. She was magnificent.

The moment she released Fynn the illusion dropped and her injuries vanished as if they'd never been.

Her words to Lily warmed his heart and he made a note to spend some extra time with Lil.

It was good to have Azaroth back again. Jezzie, Athon, and Nithe were certainly happy to have him home too. He led them out of the gym, through the common areas and up toward his office. He needed to catch up on what was going on and discuss the plans for the Christmas season with his daughter. It would be Jezzie's first Christmas with him, and he wanted her to have everything she wanted. He had so many holidays to make up for.

As they went to round the last bend he ushered them ahead of him, but before they reached his door he almost crashed into a wall of male muscle. Everyone had come to a screeching halt.

An agitated and startled Abbie stood shocked in their path.

"Are you okay, Abaddon? Is there something you need from me?" Luc asked, curious she should be so near his personal office.

"Um, yeah, I'm fine," she said with a small shaky smile. But as her gaze turned to Roth tears burst from her eyes and shaky sobs hiccuped out of her. "I'm so sorry. So very sorry. I didn't mean to. I didn't want to. I didn't know what else to do. I owe her so much, you don't understand. Please, Roth, forgive me. Mara said it was a joke, that you'd understand. I'm so sorry for the letter and all the pain I caused. You are my brothers, my family. I'll do anything to make it right." Her shaky sobs turned to full-blown snot bubbles as she begged for forgiveness and apologized profusely.

It took a moment for reality and deduction to set in before Luc realized what Abbie was talking about. It was her. She'd planted Mara's note in Roth and Athon's room. He'd known the writing was familiar, just not whose. Abbie was in contact with Mara. Abbie was a traitor.

Feelings of wrath surged to the surface as he demanded Mara's location, but Abbie refused to give her up. His shadows lashed at her, pinning her arms to the side, but Jezzie's cool touch on his arm reined them back in.

"Chill, Dad. You catch more bees with honey. What's going on, Abbie? What do you owe her? What hold does she have on you? You know she's hurt so many. She hurt Roth so bad. Athon too. Your brothers in arms. Why would you protect someone like that?" Anger and confusion threaded through Jezzie's voice.

Abbie stayed silent.

"I can taste your fear, your anger, and your pain. I can taste the betrayal and the love, and I can see the light and dark swirling inside you like a giant tornado about to rip you apart. Save yourself, Abbie. Before it's too late."

Abbie spoke.

"My life. I owe her my life and my sanity. And I owe her nothing less."

Luc could see the anger radiating off of Roth, he was beyond pissed.

He struggled to believe it, it was a betrayal worse than a knife to the heart that one of his own would help someone like that.

"You were one of us. We . . . I trusted you. How could you betray us thus?" he growled, shaking with pure rage.

Deus, get your ass here. We have a problem. Abbie's been working with Mara. Get her out of my sight. Put her in the cells and call Ramiel. She can wait there for the arrival of the Praesidium and face their judgment, he called over the link. He was getting too old for this shit.

As Deus led Abbie away, Jezzie looked up and sighed. "So, I guess now's not the best time to tell you we're getting married, huh?"

From highs to lows and back again. What a fucking day.

Anxiety gripped her chest, heart beating like a drum.

Louder, louder.

Shut up! Her brain screamed, silently and unheard.

Her breaths came quickly and harshly. Her stomach in knots as her chest heaved. The taste of acid-like vomit on the back of her tongue.

How? How had it come to this? Censored thoughts and bottled emotions. All she'd wanted was an ear to listen, empathy, and understanding. Arms to hold her, lips to reassure her.

Why must frustration, anger, and guilt be the cage in which her mind was trapped? Why must she remain so broken? So alone when she had no more reason to be lonely?

But deep inside she knew the answer. The how and the why. Trapped again. How was she to know she'd traded one prison for another all those years ago? When for her savior she'd turned her friends to foes. At least before Mara she hadn't known what a friend was, if only that were still so.

Abbie slumped her head and resigned herself to whatever fate awaited her. She certainly deserved it, she thought.

CHAPTER 52

December passed in a whirlwind of activity. The fortress was abuzz with the news of a wedding and Jezzie and Nithe were introduced as Roth and Athon's mates. Excitement had taken on a life of its own at the news that angels could have fated and bonded mates.

Christmas came and went, and as the decorations started to come down the wedding preparations began in earnest. The morning of New Year's Eve dawned with a beautiful glow and Jezzie almost felt sick to her stomach. In fact she was, several times. She wasn't scared, more like too excited. The butterflies in her stomach were running out of room for all their fluttering.

Ramiel had arrived a week ago to spend Christmas with them, and while his relationship with Nithe was still formal, and occasionally frosty, the two had made peace with the fact they had both been manipulated, lied to, and betrayed. Esidriel now sat in the cell furthest from Raum, but equally as unpleasant. He was staying for the wedding having said there was not a snowball's chance in Nestradia he'd miss his only child's bonding ceremony. Especially since he'd missed everything else.

The fallout from Abbie's betrayal still rippled through the fortress like an atom bomb, lingering long after the initial explosion. Angels looked at each other with suspicion where before there had been none. It was disconcerting and Jezzie felt the unease crawling under her skin. Probably another reason she felt so sick lately. The side effects of twitchy, negative emotions coupled with the deception of Abbie tasted like pickles in wine. Really bad wine. Ramiel was set to escort the traitor to Praesidium HQ after the wedding festivities were completed. It didn't help that Ramiel, Deus, and Marco had confided that another traitor still lurked in their midst.

Ramiel had mentioned multiple times he'd like Jezzie to use her gifts on Raum, in a controlled setting of course. Her mates and father had protested, but her palms and shadows literally itched to get into his head and pull the answers from him in a gooey, mushy, messy way. So she had let him know she was open to it . . . after the wedding.

On a happier note Lily had slowly come around and the two of them were now quite friendly. It could have been the old man socks and the 'father of two' photo frame she'd gifted Lucifer for Christmas that'd done the trick, but Jezzie preferred to think it was her winning personality.

Dante had been acting all twitchy and on edge since he'd opened his gift from her father for Christmas. All that was in it was a note which said 'Retribution will be as sweet as blue cotton candy' and a voucher for The Sweet Place Candy Shop. Athon and Roth had joyfully explained the Hades hair incident and Deus had retold a few more of Dante's past escapades, all of which led to a rollicking good time filled with laughter and joy.

Jezzie slowly started to feel at home. Still, she couldn't wait to wrap her arms around her aunt and have Tana by her side. She wished her whole family could share this day with her. She still had her mirror, so she hoped that if she set it up just right her uncle might just be able to watch from afar. He had handed her a gorgeous veil when she'd visited the day before. He and Tana had both wanted her to wear it as her something borrowed. It had been worn by Tana's mother at her binding ceremony to Uncle Micah. Leraie had saved it and brought it to him not long after he'd first arrived in Nestradia.

"Up and at 'em, missy," Mrs B chimed as she swept into the room with a trolley piled high with food and a long gown trailing behind her from the hanger in her hand.

Jezzie laughed. "Mrs B, if you expect me to eat all that you're going to need a bigger dress for me to wear."

"I've already let it out, you sassy witch." Mrs B grinned. "I thought you'd like to eat with your cousin and aunt while you get ready."

Tana ran into the room and leaped onto Jezzie's bed.

"Your uncle couldn't make it, and trust me, he's kicking up a stink about it, I can promise you that, but Leraie said he'll be watching. You just won't see him." Mrs B set about hanging up the beautiful emerald green satin gown then set out the food.

"Where are the guys?" Jezzie tried to look out the door hoping they hadn't seen the dress yet, but Mrs B blocked her view.

"They're in Roth and Athon's old room getting ready. You'll see them later. At the ceremony. Lucifer was especially clear on that . . . and so many other things. He's worse than any bride I've ever encountered," she muttered as she turned back to the door. "What are you waiting for, woman? Get your witchy ass in here already. You've made her wait long enough."

"Alright, alright, keep your bonnet on, you crotchety old bat." Aunt Rai Rai swept into the room with a flourish.

"Yet I'm still younger than you, you old sow." Mrs B laughed. "Even if I don't look it." The two women embraced like old friends.

"You came!" Jezzie and her aunt flew into each other's arms, and breathed each other in.

"Of course I did, silly child. I wouldn't miss this for the world, and no man could ever change that." Whatever her aunt meant by that was lost on her as she was released. Mrs B stacked boxes and bags by the bed. Some for now, some for later.

They ate and caught up on missed events and she introduced Tana. Her aunt brought her lingerie and earrings, and a special medallion she placed inside Jezzie's bodice, above her heart, before she was laced into her gown with strict instructions that she'd need it back later and no one, under any circumstances, was to see it or know about it. It was very, very old and important but the feelings behind it were pure and held the ability to tether loved ones through the ages.

"I'm so happy for you, my special little witchling." Pride shone from her aunt's eyes as she held Jezzie's face in her hands.

Her hair was arranged in a cascade of curls, pinned into place with a jeweled headpiece secured on the side of her head. The gown was utterly gorgeous as she swayed and watched the skirt swish in the mirror. It complemented her red hair and made her gray eyes sparkle. She'd opted for minimal makeup and comfortable, sparkly, green ballet-style shoes.

When Mrs B came back and told her it was time to go, she was shocked to find so much time had passed, it certainly hadn't felt like it. Tana picked up both bouquets and handed the larger one over. Her Maid of Honor looked beautiful in her dress and her smile had Jezzie getting all giddy again as they left the room and headed downstairs.

Lucifer stood waiting in the hall outside the communal dining room. He'd gone to great lengths to turn the space into the perfect ceremony and reception venue. It was large enough to fit all the angels who lived in the fortress, plus more. Which was a very good thing, since they were all invited. Jezzie had been banned from seeing what he'd had set up behind those big oak double doors, but she didn't care. As long as three very handsome and specific males were waiting at the end of the aisle that's all she cared about.

"You look like an angel, daughter mine," her father gushed.

"Aw, thanks, Dad. I kinda am one." She winked back.

"Oh you know what I meant. I just wish your mother was here with us." He sighed deeply, sadness pinched his expression, but he focussed on her again and it dissipated.

"I do too." A tear slipped down the end of her nose and dripped onto the hem of her skirt.

"None of that. Deca wouldn't want either of you moping." Aunt Rai Rai appeared behind them in a swirl of magical energy and Luc looked at her curiously.

"I know you." He cocked his head to the side.

"Of course you do, I saved your ass in Thisavrós, and you might recall I was with Decaria the night you met, but I doubt it. The two of you only had eyes for each other." Rai Rai rolled her eyes with sass.

"No. I knew you in your earliest form. A word, in private, if you please?" The look on his face was inscrutable. It could be good, or it could be bad. Jezzie just had to trust her father wouldn't ruin the wedding with whatever he had to say.

They spoke in a side room for several minutes before emerging, and when they did her aunt looked slightly perturbed, while her father looked rather pleased. Rai Rai seemed to give herself a good shake before rejoining them, her smile back in place, even if a little forced.

"So, Niece, if you have me and Tana standing up for you, who do the guys have with them?" Rai Rai asked, with what seemed a twinkle in her eye.

"Sorry, Tana," Jezzie replied, giving her cousin a small smile. "Nithe chose Thad and the Almighty granted his request for leave from Nestradia until the festivities are over. Athon chose Dante, and Roth chose Caine."

Her aunt's breath seemed to lose itself to the vortex of her quick inhale, she coughed repeatedly, as if it was choking her.

"Aunt, are you okay? Is something wrong?" Jezzie patted her on the back as Tana handed her a flute of champagne from the sideboard near the door.

"No, no, everything's fine," she mumbled, taking a few deep breaths and large swallows of the bubbly drink.

"This should be fun." Her father beamed, looking as proud as punch. "A toast, yes?" He picked up and handed a flute to each of them, and replaced Aunt Rai Rai's empty one. "To new beginnings, fated love, and my daughter's eternal happiness."

"Cheers." All but Jezzie downed their drinks in one go. Jezzie only got to take a small sip before her aunt snatched it out of her hand and downed that one too.

"Sorry." She laughed nervously. "Not every day I get to help give my niece away. It's a lot more nerve wracking than I'd ever imagined."

The faint hint of music made its way through the thick oak doors to Jezzie's ears and stomach flipped, her hands trembled and her cheeks almost hurt from how large her smile became.

"Are you ready, my dear?" her father asked as he held out his arm to her. Her aunt stepped up to her other side and did the same. Tana took her position in front as the doors slowly opened to reveal a sea of onlookers.

"Let's do this." She watched Tana walk down the aisle before her, mentally begging her cousin to hurry the fuck up.

CAINE FROZE. For a split second the woman who walked beside Jezzie appeared as someone else, before her features morphed and shifted into something else. She was beautiful either way, but the image he saw first was like a dagger to heart and searing pain blazed its way through his mind so fiercely he had to look away.

He caught sight of Deus and saw desire and intrigue stamped on his face as he also watched her. Irrational jealousy and rage set fire to his veins and flooded through him. Not again. No, please, not again. Memories triggered from deep in his subconscious. He'd buried them as best he could, though they tormented him and plagued him still. The onslaught almost brought him to his knees. Pain, but not his. Terror, but not his. The choices of his past pointed fingers of blame. Blood filled his vision and his body shook from the inside out.

He hadn't realized he'd taken a step until Roth placed a hand on his shoulder and Deus stepped in front of him.

"Breathe, Brother. When was the last time you worked out your demons?" Deus looked him in the eyes, concern mixed with caution.

Caine understood why. His demons had the ability to incapacitate him, and they all feared one day he'd never come back. The idea of it wasn't something which particularly scared Caine. Fuck! The peace would be nice, right? What he did fear was letting his brothers and sisters down. Failing them would be as if he'd failed her all over again, as if he'd failed his brother again, and he'd failed them both so many times already.

He looked over Deus's shoulder as the trio reached the altar. Athon and Roth were very lucky males. Jezzie looked radiant as she smiled at them, love filled the air and he felt so very alone. The mysterious woman raised her brows at him, a quirk to her lips. When she looked at Deus, scorn flashed bright in her eyes. Damn, what had Deus done this time? Deus squeezed his arm as he chuckled softly and returned to his seat. Caine shook off the feelings which plagued him. This was a time for joy and celebration, he could have a mental breakdown later, when no one was around.

"I HEREBY PRONOUNCE YOU, with the blessing of the Almighty themself, husbands and wife. You may all kiss . . . well, each other, I guess," Leraie loudly declared as cheers filled the room and echoed off the high ceiling.

Jezzie's heart rate skyrocketed as she kissed each of her husbands and by the time they pulled apart her face was flushed and her breathing unsteady. Her whole being felt full and complete and tears of happiness filled her eyes. Nithe wrapped his arms around her and Roth and Athon smooshed up close.

Do we walk out now? she asked only them.

Not yet, mi amor. Athon smiled at her, his eyes alight.

Her father's loud whistle rang through the rafters, catching everyone off guard. He raised and lowered his hands in a gesture for people to once again take their seats, and they did.

"I have an announcement to make. An important one, not just for myself, but for what it means for the angel species as a whole." Her father's tone was confusing, she felt his joy and his nervousness, but he sounded so serious at the same time. "As you are aware, Jezebeth and Nitierien are Azaroth and Leviathon's fated mates. What only a select few already knew until now is that Jezebeth is my biological daughter." The masses gasped and all seemed to stop breathing at once. "What does this mean, you might ask? Especially since angels can already have children with other angels and humans? Well, see, both of their mothers are neither angels, nor human. Those rules too seem to be changing."

The room exploded with conversations, whispered words and

shouted questions. Jezzie watched Marcos and Fynn slip out into the hallway as shadowed figures swirled around every exit.

"Enough!" bellowed her father. "You can discuss this later. Any questions can be asked another day. This day we celebrate this joyous union and all it represents. For Hell's sake, it's not every day one witnesses the Devil's daughter get married. Let's celebrate!!"

A flash of light momentarily blinded Jezzie. A powerful feminine voice commanded her attention even before she caught sight of the goddess standing beside her father. And she was nothing short of a goddess, both in power and in beauty. She held such a raw brutality about her, her face lit with frustration and anger as it was. But there was a softness there too, like a mother with her children as she brushed their hair and loved them.

"Not yet you don't," the goddess boomed, halting any who would dare take her father's cue to leave. "My son, come." She held out her hand, palm up to Nithe and beckoned him closer.

Jezzie watched, curious, but not worried. A sense of rightness and peace wafted from the female, despite the anger she sensed in her.

"I cannot believe they kept me from you, my boy. You are born of my land, my rivers run through your veins and the soul of one of my dragons beats in time with your heart. By rights, you are mine to protect, mine to bless, and I have failed you. I promise, had I known what they did to you I would have halted it in an instant. Trust me when I say I will be having words with those fickle bitches of fate and the Almighty who still supports them."

Nithe's face reflected his awe and shock at the one who spoke so passionately about him. Was this his mother? Jezzie pondered, but quickly discarded the notion. She'd seen the image of his mother in his memories and this beauty before them was not her. Who then? Though it was quickly answered as she held aloft a masterpiece of forged steel and leather hilted lethality and placed it in Nithe's outstretched palms.

"It is with long overdue pride and honor that I, Tiamat, Goddess of Dragons, Watcher of the Realm, and Bearer of Blessings, bestow upon you, Nitierien Kenacdrath, blooded kin to the rightful king of Thisavros, Thaddeus Drakenos, your dragon sword. Forged in the blessed waters, deep beneath the mountain by my hand. May it keep you and your loved ones safe and mete out the justice you are bound to seek. Congratulations, my son. Both on your vows here today and for your coming of age here today. The latter was long overdue. Now, I'm off to give the ones responsible an earful. They will regret it." With that she nodded to Lucifer and disappeared in the same manner in which she'd arrived.

"Um, so, I guess we can now celebrate?" It was somewhere between a question and a command, but as Nithe turned and grinned a cacophony of cheers filled the hall.

Jezzie and the guys threw their arms around Nithe, careful of the sword he placed at his side as food filled tables and drinks flowed. Music played and angels danced. Her aunt, she noticed, avoided both Deus and Caine, but not the others. Deus she could understand. Caine had her raise an eyebrow. Soon she was too immersed in her males to worry about who her aunt interacted with as the party whirled around her.

Holy fuck! He was not expecting that. Shock rippled through the crowd around him, and he took the moment to let his shadows slip out and swirl around the exits. Leaving the dining hall was easy. He'd gotten used to slinking around. It was imperative he not get caught as he doubted Lucifer would be very lenient in his punishment for his betrayal. He knew it was risky, but this was news Gabriel needed to know, and he needed to know it from him. How he hadn't known before now was a question which burned in his belly. He'd have to find out why Sthenno hadn't told him later.

He made the call. Expletives filled his ears that made even him blush. Damn, Gabe was pissed. As he hit the end call button he didn't see the two shadows converging on him until it was too late. His muffled screams turned to whimpers, and then to silence as they swept him away and down to the buried depths of the dungeons.

THEY DANCED, they ate, they kissed, and they enjoyed the spectacle that was an angel hosted wedding reception. Halfway through the guys ushered Jezzie sneakily out of the room and up to the meeting room. They entered to a loud chorus of, "Surprise!" Tears flowed as she saw her father, Aunt, Tana, Thad, Leraie, Ramiel, and the Devil's 13 packed into the otherwise bare room. How they'd gotten the big assed table out she had no idea but it had to be some kind of magic.

Leraie winked at her. "Clever girl."

What surprised her most though were the decorations. Balloons, streamers, a 'Happy Birthday' banner, and a massive purple birthday cake, from behind which stepped a delighted Mrs Briars.

"What is all this?" she asked.

"Well, it's your birthday, right? Well, it will be in like, twelve minutes, anyway." Athon squeezed her hand.

"So we wanted to celebrate. The wedding was perfect, but your birthday is just as important." Roth kissed the top of her head.

"And there was no way in a snowball's chance your dad was going to pass up the opportunity to finally throw his baby girl a birthday party for the first time." Nithe grinned over at her father who looked at her proudly.

"I hope you—" He didn't even get to finish before she threw herself into his arms and kissed his cheek.

"Thanks, Daddy. It's amazing!" Jezzie hid her face in his shoulder and held on in a way one can only do to a parental figure.

"Okay, enough of the sappy stuff. You can have all the daddy-daughter hugs later. It's present time!" Her aunt grabbed her arms and led her over to some artfully arranged cushions on the floor and plonked her down. The guys sat around her as a present was thrust into her hands.

Some were wedding gifts, some were just for her. Jezzie had never had a birthday party before. Not one where anyone other than her mother, Aunt Rai Rai, and Leraie had come anyway. She felt so very overwhelmed. The gifts were all so thoughtful and unique, none more so than Lily's. Matching sister pendants sat in a dark blue velvet box and as they placed one around each other's necks they both made a promise to share the bond of sisterhood forever.

"I also have a gift for you," Leraie spoke up. "The cabin in South Eastern Australia is yours, eternally protected by divine intervention. You may use it any time you wish."

"Thank you, Grandma Raie. How did you know I was going to ask?" Jezzie queried. To which Leraie gave her a 'don't turn into a dumbass now' look. "Right, silly me." Jezzie laughed.

Dante approached her aunt, a swagger entered his step. Jezzie wondered just how much he'd had to drink as he opened his mouth and this purler came out, "So, wanna go back to my place, pretty lady?"

Her aunt looked down her nose as Deus snorted and the rest of the room groaned. She placed her finger on the tip of his nose and smiled.

"Oh, so tempting. Especially since we are already here, but I don't think you'd like the consequences should you disappoint me." She trailed her finger down over the slight bulge in his pants. "And since Jezzie's taken you on as a brother it'd be a shame to hurt you, not to mention it'd feel a little incestuous on my end, even if it technically isn't."

"Go play with a different toy, Dante. You really don't want to lose your nuts today." Deus cackled as he sidled up to her aunt. Hm, this should be interesting, Jezzie thought, but her attention was soon diverted as a large unmarked box was placed on the floor before her.

"Who is this one from? I thought we already opened them all?" Tana looked around and gasped.

"Special delivery," intoned an ethereal voice.

"Seriously? Now you make an entrance?" Leraie rolled her eyes.

"Oh, shush, you big baby. Why shouldn't the Almighty deign to offer the blessings in person and in private."

All eyes turned to the newcomer. She was stunning. Her shimmering robes floated on a non-existent breeze, as did her wavy black hair. Her dark skin held a golden glow, as if metallic makeup had been dusted over it to give it a heavenly luster.

"Go on, Jezebeth, open it. He was very insistent you do so, and I'd hate to disappoint one of my chosen." The Almighty pointed at the box, but her eyes were locked on Mrs B with an intensity that was unnerving.

Jezzie lifted the lid on the box slowly and peered inside. Fucking Ballzy! The fucking curtains, as a birthday and wedding present.

Seriously? Jezzie laughed delightedly, and uncontrollably. Looking over her shoulder she saw her mates' eyes almost touch their hairlines.

"Balthazar," she squeaked out. The name was met with grumbles and groans. When they saw the figures on the fabric move and heard the sounds they made their eyes widened and their mouths hung open.

Jezzie gently lifted the curtains out of the box and unfolded them. The cheeky rascals she encountered in her cell winked at her, and she laughed again, showing the others what Balthazar sent.

Over in the corner Jezzie spotted Mrs Briars, frozen to the spot, her eyes fixed on the figures making love on the fabric. For a second nothing happened, then magic swirled around her and lifted her into the air. When her feet touched down on the floor again, her hair looked a little blonder with pastel pink streaks and her face about fifteen human years younger. The same expression graced all their faces as they looked at Mrs Briars like guppies out of water, but her gaze was focussed on the image on the curtain still.

On a single breath out she exclaimed, *"Tuo narttu, suolistan hänet kuin vitun galhild kun saan hänet käsiini."*

Jezzie blinked at the use of the Finnish language. The accent was way off, strangely captivating and mildly terrifying, and Athon whispered the word Fae on a breath filled with awe. Jezzie looked from Mrs B to the curtains. The figures on the curtain froze and the woman shrieked as she scampered behind the men who shielded her protectively with confused looks on their faces as they searched around for threats in the crowd around them. Mrs B fell through the floor and vanished an instant after.

"Now that that's out of the way, back to me. The Diva's in the house, and I've got some things to say." All eyes focused back on the Almighty. "As you've all finally figured out, yes, you do now have the ability to find your soul mate, or mates as it sometimes is, and form the bonds most other supernatural beings already could. This is my gift to you. You will know when you have found them by your ability to dream, and to dream in color. Astral dreaming is rare, and due to Jezebeth's particular hybrid genetics it came very easily." She paused for effect but no one dared speak.

"Along with your mated bond your once passive shadows, mist, etc . . . may find the bond will likely form for them as well and through doing so their full sentience may be attained. As is the case with Jezzie's shadows and Roth and Athon's too. Nithe's dragon has even bonded with Jezzie's shadows."

"What does that mean?" Malphas piped up.

"It means we are here. We are not just weapons you wield." Jezzie's shadows spoke up, manifesting into a ghostly shape in front of her. "We are all, together, shadows. I am but one shadow of the collective darkness. We are whole and we are individuals. We are the darkness, the mist is the light. One side of the coin, the never ceasing sway of the eternal pendulum. But make no mistake, we came first. For darkness ruled long before light entered existence. We are what was, before time existed. We are the darkness to the light. The everlasting evidence of what came before creation. Without us your 'Almighty' would not be. Without the darkness, the light cannot see."

"Yeah, yeah, you done now? Drama queens." The Almighty waved her manicured hand and Jezzie's shadows retreated sullenly. She added, "Sorry it took so long, but even I have to follow the plan. All things will come to pass, but free will sure can be a fucking nuisance."

"What about Cara?" Luc's voice projected a question but Jezzie felt the demand of it hit the room with a thud.

"All in good time, my son, if you are patient enough," came her answer.

Her father looked pissed off and on the verge of outright demanding a better explanation.

"Don't take that tone with me, child, not even in your mind," she admonished.

"Surely you could have just told us about this 'gift' and the fucking side effects, instead of just letting us bumble our way through thinking some of us were going nuts. Sorry, Luc. Why screw with us?" Dante let loose.

"You will watch your tone, too, young man! I brought you into this existence, and you can bet your ass I have the power to take you out of it! You should be grateful I'm so fond of you all. I don't expect a thank you just yet. In fact, you may hate me and the journey you need to take, but one day you may just understand the twisted logic of the way things need to happen. It is very confusing, even for me. Sometimes, you have to break shit to make shit, or it just doesn't turn out right. So, this time, I'll give you a pass, Dante," she said, as she looked at him over the rim of her glasses, her finger pointing at him sternly.

"You forget, my children, I make the rules. Forget the past and fulfill the destinies laid out before you. In good time you will find her again, Luc. As of now, she has other tasks she must complete before she can be returned to you. I am sorry she missed this, Jezebeth," she apologized, indicating the wedding decorations and the newlyweds. "Believe me, if she could be here she would. But sometimes to win a war one must make sacrifices. Both big and small. Oh, and Luc, don't be too hard on Abbie, there are things you do not know. That you don't want to know. Not yet. But you will. Right now she has my protection, and I'll be keeping her with me for a while, as we have some work to do as well, her and I."

Abbie suddenly appeared at the Almighty's side looking lost, weary, and slightly baffled. Then just as the Almighty had appeared they both disappeared. Leaving behind her disembodied voice with one final message, "Oh, and Dante, to answer your question . . . You may be waiting a while. He finds far too much joy in your torment. Be afraid. Be very afraid." The Almighty's voice faded away on a laugh, leaving everyone utterly confused.

"So, moving on from her highness's theatrics, I have one more gift for you." Aunt Rai Rai handed each of the newlyweds a small blue box. "Open them together."

Jezzie furrowed her brow as she took out the white cotton baby onesie, the words 'Part Witch, Pure Badass' were emblazoned on the front. She looked over to see the guys held matching onesies all with different wording. Nithe's said, 'Part Dragon, Pure Heartbreaker.' Athon's said, 'Part Vampire, Pure Cutie.' Finally, Roth's said, Part Angel, Pure Hellion."

"Rai Rai, what is this?" Jezzie asked hesitantly.

"That wasn't nervousness the last few days, Jez. Congratulations, you four! I'm so excited to be a Great Aunt. And just so you know, yes, the little one is made up of the DNA of all of you, not just two."

"How do you—" Athon started to say.

"Second sight, dear boy." Jezzie looked at her aunt, knowing her second sight was never wrong.

For the second time since she'd arrived at the fortress, the Devil himself hit the deck. Apparently realizing you were going to be a Grandpa was a bit of a shock to the system. Ramiel stood in utter shock at the news too but he didn't tumble over.

A few minutes later her father was up and hugging everyone while Jezzie checked in with a very excited soon to be Aunt Lily. Tana burst into tears and Thad tried to hug her, but she shoved him away and Leraie ushered them out of the room after they said their goodbyes. Imprisonment in Nestradia waited for no one.

The viewscreen light flickered on the glass wall of windows and the screen automatically dropped down. Ramiel and her father looked at each other knowingly before accepting the call.

A face appeared on the screen and Jezzie recognized it immediately from the sketches her mother and aunt had forced her to memorize. Gabriel.

"Congratulations, Lucifer. I hear you are both a father and a father-in-law now. Such happy circumstances." He seriously sounded like a sniveling snake to Jezzie's ears.

"Thanks, Gabe. I'm so blessed to be able to lay claim to both of those honors. Let me introduce to you my daughter, Jezebeth Lucinda Poisson."

Jezzie moved to her father's side and into Gabriel's view, girding herself for a war of words.

"No! It can't be. I . . ." Gabriel gasped out, before seeming to remember himself and swallowing hard, his Adam's apple bobbed as fear entered his eyes.

"You what? Killed me yourself, Gabriel? Yeah, no, you didn't. Not really. Psychic vamps can cast illusions around their bodies, or didn't you know that? She told me about you, you know. You tried to hide your identity from her like the coward you truly are. Right up until you thought you'd won. After that you were ever so happy to show your face and spill the poison of your hatred, your so-called justifiable reasons, weren't you?" Jezzie enjoyed the look of stricken panic that washed over Gabriel's features. Even his lips lost their color.

"She knew you were coming. Friends in high places, and all. You killed nothing but an illusion, but she felt it all, every slice, every perverted lick on the illusion's flesh. There was no soul to collect. Not that you hung around long enough to realize it, or even collect it yourself. So quick were you to flee the scene. No angel came for her. You were content to let her soul walk the earth for eternity, growing bitter and angry with every passing year, without respite. All because of whom she loved."

Gabriel's mouth opened and shut, but no sound came out, fear held him mute.

"Nothing to say, Gabriel? Hmm, not surprising. My mother made sure I knew your face in case I ever crossed your stinking path. Now, knowing who exactly you are, and from what I've pieced together from where I've been for almost two decades, I'm sure I know more of your secrets than I'm sure you'd like. You can bet your ass I'll spill them as soon as I can, and then, when you think you're safe, or the worst has been done to you, I'll feast on your slimy, putrid soul, bit by itty bitty bit."

Jezzie's fangs descended slowly, her tongue toyed with the sharp points and blood welled to the surface of the pink flesh, coating her teeth ruby red.

Gabriel's face lost even more color, his ghostly pallor matched by the panic and fear which filled his eyes and caused the vein at his throat to pulse and twitch at a satisfyingly rapid rate.

"Bye bye now." Jezzie ended the call with a wave of her hand.

Before she could look around and take in everyone's reaction, another message light came on. She thought about ignoring it, but something in her heart told her not to. This time there was no video.

"Congratulations, my dear. I truly wish I could have been there in person. It was a beautiful ceremony from what I did get to see. You looked beautiful. Now, Nithe, Roth, Athon, take care of my niece, there are forces at play here, unpredictable ones. Not everyone is who they seem to be, enemies may be allies and trusted friends play nasty games. Also, tell my brother he still owes me a drink for saving his ass in Florence. Peace out, from your amazing Uncle Micah." The message ended and Jezzie turned to look at everyone behind her to find everyone looking at her.

"Yeah, about that . . ."

THE END . . .

But is it really?
Or is it just the beginning?

ONE MONTH LATER . . .

Jezzie stared at the heavy iron door to the cell. It was inlaid with silver, wolfsbane, and enough enchantments to keep even the Almighty locked up inside, should anyone actually survive trying to put them in there. Raum didn't stand a chance of ever leaving his new home . . . not like she intended to give him the rest of eternity to find that out though. The dark gray stone beneath her feet grounded her, the matching walls with their archaic torches and flickering flames added to the ambience of the place. A dungeon straight out of a medieval tale. Except she wasn't the princess, this time she was the executioner. Her father-in-law stood beside her, a worried look on his face as he glanced down at her still flat belly.

"Are you sure about this? Maybe it's not such a good idea." Concern laced his words.

"Are you kidding? I've been hungering for this opportunity ever since our encounter at Demon's Den. He'll give us answers, and he'll pay for what he's done. Plus, I've been extra hungry lately thanks in no small part to your son." She gave Ramiel a cheeky wink. "Open up and let's do this."

Ramiel hesitated, but eventually relented. The big, fat, magical key entered the lock and turned. The door swung inward, Jezzie crossed the threshold, and felt the stones beneath her feet turn to ice.

The monster of her husband's nightmares knelt chained like an animal to the floor, his arms stretched outward above his head. Still, the fucker had the gall to look at her with mocking amusement.

"Hi there, asshole. Enjoying your new digs?" Jezzie goaded with a sneer. She felt his nervous energy sizzle, followed by his arrogant pride as it burned through her nose with an acrid tang.

"Ah, Balthazar's little whore. So nice of you to pop in for a visit. How's my pet doing these days? Does he miss me? I sure do miss him."

The lascivious glint in his eyes fired the hatred in Jezzie's blood even higher, and she was ever so glad she'd only agreed to do this if Ramiel stayed out of the room. It was hard enough to control her own hatred, without having to control Nithe's father's as well.

Her smile was full of hate, she could feel it fester. She pulled in a breath and tasted his unease, his pride, his envy. Oh, yes, his envy . . .

"My husband is doing just fine, thanks for asking," she replied, keeping her tone to a bored disinterest. "The wedding was lovely and the four of us are so very happy. Thanks for introducing us, by the way."

Raum's eyes flashed, disdain and fury flooded the room. She'd taken away his toy and the little boy in him was hella mad.

Thank fuck they'd gotten Nithe away from him. Balthazar deserved a freaking huge hug next time she saw him.

"Did you come here to flaunt that, or was there something you wanted?" Raum sneered. If a look could burn her to a crisp, she'd be overcooked bacon already.

"Actually, there is. See, I'm here to extract all of your itty bitty little secrets from that soon to be ooey gooey mind of yours. We already suspect Gabriel is your unrequited love . . . Whoops, sorry . . . your boss, we just need to confirm the extent of his treachery and what you've done, both under his orders and at your own behest."

"And you think you can do that? When everyone here has tried and failed? Little girl, you don't stand a chance." Raum cackled, and what once would have been an elegant, if not creepy, sound, was now roughened by a dryness and the start of a maniacal spiral into insanity.

"You see, Raum, I'm part psychic vamp, but I'm also my Daddy's little girl. So, once I finish feeding off of your emotions and memories, I'm going to suck your putrid soul out and devour it whole. Lucifer would be so proud of his daughter for taking out the trash, don't you think?"

Fear bloomed, and disbelief followed. He thought she was bluffing, but soon enough he'd realize she wasn't. She watched him build up his mental defenses, brick by brick, already knowing how she was going to tear them down.

Her shadow filled the room and swirled around him angrily, lashing at his pathetic flesh. He filled his mind with images of Nithe and all the things he'd done to him, and Jezzie sucked at the poison that was his soul. The more he tried to fight the harder she pulled. Her control started to slip when he pushed the memory of his first time with Nithe into his mind and thus into hers. She pulled harder, and she didn't want to stop. She could end this now, she could devour him whole, and he'd be gone from existence forever.

Images of a past far before Nithe flickered like a vintage movie, little frames of things he'd done. And then, a snippet of memory which froze her blood in her veins and halted her feeding frenzy. Jezzie released him from her hold and his head slumped to his chest.

While she felt like crying at the pain and destruction this being had caused she smiled with knowledge of the end he would receive. Most fitting in her opinion. Jezzie took a deep breath and pulled herself together as she crouched down and drew Raum's gaze back to her, a chilling smile lifted her lips and lit a taunting fire in her gaze.

"The hammer's going to hit. The ax is going to fall. Soon you'll wish you were still stuck here on your knees. Nothing can save you now from the wrath of Vengeance when he comes to call. Goodbye, Raum. Thanks for the memories."

The door slammed shut behind her as she exited, and she looked up at Ramiel. "Gabriel is confirmed, even more than he was before." She shook her head. "I swore I'd be the one to end that sack of shit, but I was wrong. That honor belongs to another, not I. It's time to call in Balthazar. Just make sure you bring the photograph he keeps in his desk drawer when you go to get him. Whatever you do, don't let him know you have it, and don't use it before you have to. Only do so if you're prepared to get no further answers. For your safety, I recommend you exit stage left immediately and leave him to it. If he needs me, you know where I am."

Balthazar's story will be continued in *Book Two of the Realms of Magic and Mayhem Series.*
When Vengeance Vows

Coming Soon . . .

Acknowledgments

To my readers,

If you made it this far . . . Thank you so much for giving my book a try. I can only hope you enjoyed it and wish to stick around for more. If you didn't, that's okay. Not every book is for every person. In a world filled with strong emotions please let love win. I'd love your feedback either way, but please be conscious and respectful of others, including me.

As with any endeavor there are so many cogs in the wheel, so many people to thank and acknowledge. This being my debut novel it's hard to know exactly where to start. From the first time I picked up a romance novel at fourteen years old I've been an avid reader, and when I wasn't reading I was making up spinoff stories in my head. So I want to start off there, I suppose.

I'd like to say a massive thank you to some of my favorite authors: Gena, J.R, Sherrilyn, and Kresley. Even though you probably don't know it, you have inspired me to take the leap into the world of writing and pushed me to achieve my dreams. I hope I did okay.

To Naomi: thank you for encouraging everyone you interact with. You don't know it, but because of you I have an editor and a friend for life and discovered some of the best people and authors in the indie author community.

To Grace, Jade, Lexie, Kerry, and so many more: Thank fuck I found you ladies! You are all so amazing at what you do and I adore your work, but beyond that you are so supportive of everyone, especially newbies like me. Your whole darn personalities are fucking gorgeous!

To my Bitchin' Betas: Mary, Cindy, Leigh, Joy, Brittney, Jessica, and Ashley, you are all amazing. Thank you for your honesty and advice. Sorry it took so long to get it written. I hope it was worth it in the end.

To my super special Alpha Queens: Lin, Maria, Erin, Theresa, and Natasha, thank you for putting up with me and sticking with me through this very long process and all of my self-doubt. You supported me, encouraged me and helped me find the confidence to realize I can do this. I couldn't have done this without you amazing ladies.

To Tash from DAZED Designs: I couldn't have asked for a more perfect cover. You are such an amazingly talented artist and an absolute gem of a human being. The formatting is fucking perfect too. I'll be your Trash Panda Groupie any day!

And last, but definitely not least, to Lin Lasky, on top of being on my alpha team, being an amazing cheerleader and fantastic person, you deigned to bless me with your editing prowess and your friendship. You are one of the main reasons this book is a thing. Without you poking and prodding for every new chapter I may have given up. Ride or die, my coffee fuelled dragon warrior woman!! P.S. she claimed Nithe already lol.

Love,
xx Wren xx

About the Author

Wren Smythe is a debut author from South Australia, Australia. She is married with three wonderful children and two fur babies. Wren first started reading romance at an early age with sweet romances and picked up her first steamy read at the age of fourteen. After that she was hooked and never put them down. Sometimes spending every waking moment when not at school or work reading as much as she could and going through a bag of books in less than a week or weekend. It has long been her dream to write her own novels and poems, the only thing holding her back was herself. Thanks to some fantastic author groups and an encouraging indie community this dream is becoming a reality.

If you want to share your thoughts or your love of her books feel free to email her at wrensmytheauthor@gmail.com. Alternatively, you can follow her on Instagram and Facebook, join her Facebook reader group: *Wren Smythe's Reader Realm*, or feel free to recommend this book to others to help make it a success.

www.ingramcontent.com/pod-product-compliance
Lightning Source LLC
Chambersburg PA
CBHW050058120726
47904CB00004B/1130